CHINUA ACHEBE

THE
AFRICAN TRILOGY

Things Fall Apart
No Longer at Ease
Arrow of God

PICADOR
published by Pan Books
in association with Heinemann

Things Fall Apart first published 1958 by William Heinemann Ltd
No Longer at Ease first published 1960 by William Heinemann Ltd
Arrow of God first published 1964 by William Heinemann Ltd
This Picador collection first published 1988 by Pan Books Ltd,
Cavaye Place, London SW10 9PG
in association with William Heinemann Ltd
9 8 7 6 5 4

Things Fall Apart © Chinua Achebe 1958
No Longer at Ease © Chinua Achebe 1960
Arrow of God © Chinua Achebe 1964, 1974

ISBN 0 330 30331 7

Printed and bound in Great Britain by
Richard Clay Ltd, Bungay, Suffolk

Chinua Achebe was born in 1930 in the village of Ogidi in Eastern Nigeria. After studying medicine and literature at the University of Ibadan, he went to work for the Nigerian broadcasting company in Lagos. *Things Fall Apart*, his first novel, was published in 1958. It has sold over two million copies, and has been translated into 30 languages. It was followed by *No Longer at Ease*, then *Arrow of God* (which won the first New Statesman Jock Campbell Prize), then *A Man of the People* (a novel dealing with post-independence Nigeria). Achebe has also written short stories and children's books, and *Beware Soul Brother*, a book of his poetry, won the Commonwealth Poetry Prize in 1972.

Achebe has been at the Universities of Nigeria, Massachusetts and Connecticut, and among the many honours he has received are the award of a Fellowship of the Modern Language Association of America, and doctorates from the Universities of Stirling, Southampton and Kent. He has followed Heinrich Böll, the Nobel prizewinner, as the second recipient of the Scottish Art's Council Neil Gunn Fellowship.

Turning and turning in the widening gyre
The falcon cannot hear the falconer;
Things fall apart; the centre cannot hold;
Mere anarchy is loosed upon the world.
  W. B. Yeats: 'The Second Coming'

CONTENTS

PREFACE

I take the decision by Picador to issue my first three novels in one impressive volume thirty years after the publication of *Things Fall Apart* as a mark of confidence in the continuing interest and relevance of my early fiction for which I can only express the most profound satisfaction.

Things Fall Apart and its sequel, *No Longer At Ease*, came originally as one piece of work to my unpractised hand. I saw a family saga encompassing three Igbo generations which would correspond roughly to the times of my own grandfather, my father and myself. But no sooner had I completed the first draft of the work than even my apprentice eyes recognized a story lacking sufficient body, standing too thin on the ground. Two options seemed open to me then: either to blow the thing out into the kind of hefty novel that I rarely read myself, or else to revise my plan altogether and aim for three separate books of moderate proportions. I took the second choice, started again and slowly filled out the first generation of the saga, the story of Okonkwo, into *Things Fall Apart*. And the rest, as we say, is history. Now Picador has stepped in to offer those of my readers who may love big novels a fine opportunity to sample what I might have achieved in 1958 had I been able to find the requisite energy! With one hefty hell of a qualification, though; to which I shall come anon.

The first novel on its way, helped along by generous words from such eminent practitioners as Angus Wilson and V. S. Pritchett, I settled down to tackle the middle story, only to discover to my utter dismay that the fabulous energy which had propelled the tale of my grandfather's times had deserted me in the throes of the succeeding episode.

One of the reviewers of *Things Fall Apart* (Pritchett, I believe) had entered a caveat: that my second novel might prove more difficult to write. I don't know how people get to know these things, but the second novel did not prove merely more difficult; it proved quite impossible to write.

The major problem was this: my father's generation were the very people after all who, no matter how sympathetically one wished to look upon their predicament, did open the door to the white man. But could I, even in the faintest, most indirect, most delicate allusiveness, dare to suggest that my father may have been something . . . of a . . . traitor? *Tufia!* And I don't mean this in a sentimental, soft-headed, filial-duty sense at all, but in relation to concrete things I knew about the man. So the only permissible interpretation of my difficulty had to be that I was perhaps not old enough, or simply did not know as much as I should about what happened.

It was not for nothing that the Igbo people made the strong saying that if a child began asking questions about what happened to his father before he was old enough to avenge him, what happened to the man would, in all likelihood, happen to the child as well. So with the folk wisdom which enjoins us to tread warily that narrowest of paths between the forbidden homesteads of rashness and cowardice I postponed the story of my father, and moved on to write about my own generation.

The novel which emerged proved totally different from *Things Fall Apart*, the tragedy of its protagonist issuing not in the dramatic starkness of clear and momentous confrontations but in a succession of messy, debilitating ambushes. Although not the second book I had originally planned, *No Longer At Ease* was the second I wrote and it managed, by that fact perhaps, to inherit all the difficulty the critic had prophesied. I personally consider it as good of its kind, as I am capable of fabricating, but I don't think it has been very well understood. Perhaps it will have better luck now.

Arrow of God does go back to an earlier time than *No Longer*

At Ease, but it is not the missing story of my father's generation. Rather it is an enrichment of the old story of Africa in its initial struggle for its land and mind against the ruthless invaders from the West. Those readers who were inclined to fault Okonkwo for his extreme inflexibility in opposing the white man's presence now had a chance in *Arrow of God* to observe the fate of a different kind of man altogether, a priest of high intellect, who is even ready to welcome the ideas of change albeit on the only basis possible for a man of honour – that his human dignity and initiative must not be taken away from him. And look what happens to him too!

Meanwhile the story of my father waits. I know a lot more now than I did when I put it aside more than twenty-five years ago. His sensational masquerade dancing, for instance, before he renounced the devil and all his works, was something he, a devout evangelist, never divulged to me before he passed on. There is a great story in that generation that navigated the perilous cross-roads. But why rush into it and perhaps get things (if not yourself) tangled up? Another folk wisdom wants to ask the man who, after eating the sauce, is in such a hurry to finish licking his fingers if he plans perchance to put them away, like utensils, on the bamboo ledge.

One final point. This distinguished one-volume edition of my novels is another indication that African writing is becoming, at least for the moderately knowledgeable, a normal part of world literature today. Thirty years ago things were rather different. Legend has it that on receiving the manuscript of *Things Fall Apart*, William Heinemann was at a loss how to proceed, having never seen an African novel before. Fortunately someone turned up who knew of a certain lecturer at the London School of Economics just back from a teaching spell at the University of Ghana. To his eternal credit Dr Donald Macrae wrote what they say was the shortest recommendation any reader had ever written for Heinemann: *The best first novel since the war.*

In retrospect I am truly astonished at my indebtedness to Scotsmen who, beginning with that intrepid reader, Macrae, and Angus Wilson, singled me out for special promotion. Only God knows what might have happened to me had I fallen into other hands. For even in the face of my escort of heavy guns (like Angus Wilson in *The Observer*) the journey was not entirely plain sailing. One irate reviewer, borrowing cleverly from the same Yeatsian source that had provided my title captioned her review: THREE CHEERS FOR MERE ANARCHY! And went straight ahead to put a pointed question: How would novelist Achebe like to go back to wearing raffia skirts or to the mindless times of his grandfather instead of holding the modern job he has in Lagos?

Perhaps the Scottish affair is a mere coincidence. Or perhaps there may be an instinctive response there to my underdog colonial experience and all its painful aftermath. Or, who knows, there may indeed exist between us a shared disposition which enabled me when the Scottish Arts Council brought me to Edinburgh as its 1974 Neil Gunn Fellow to tell my audience that I felt so completely at home in the world of the peasants and fishermen of Neil Gunn's fiction that I suspected he and I must be at heart pre-industrial men.

Chinua Achebe

Amherst, Massachusetts
January 1, 1988

THINGS
FALL APART

PART ONE

CHAPTER ONE

Okonkwo was well known throughout the nine villages and even
beyond. His fame rested on solid personal achievements. As a
young man of eighteen he had brought honour to his village by
throwing Amalinze the Cat. Amalinze was the great wrestler who
for seven years was unbeaten, from Umuofia to Mbaino. He was
called the Cat because his back would never touch the earth. It
was this man that Okonkwo threw in a fight which the old men
agreed was one of the fiercest since the founder of their town
engaged a spirit of the wild for seven days and seven nights.

The drums beat and the flutes sang and the spectators held their
breath. Amalinze was a wily craftsman, but Okonkwo was as
slippery as a fish in water. Every nerve and every muscle stood
out on their arms, on their backs and their thighs, and one almost
heard them stretching to breaking point. In the end Okonkwo
threw the Cat.

That was many years ago, twenty years or more, and during this
time Okonkwo's fame had grown like a bushfire in the harmattan.
He was tall and huge, and his bushy eyebrows and wide nose gave
him a very severe look. He breathed heavily, and it was said that,
when he slept, his wives and children in their outhouses could hear
him breathe. When he walked, his heels hardly touched the ground
and he seemed to walk on springs, as if he was going to pounce
on somebody. And he did pounce on people quite often. He had
a slight stammer and whenever he was angry and could not get
his words out quickly enough, he would use his fists. He had no

patience with unsuccessful men. He had had no patience with his father.

Unoka, for that was his father's name, had died ten years ago. In his day he was lazy and improvident and was quite incapable of thinking about tomorrow. If any money came his way, and it seldom did, he immediately bought gourds of palm wine, called round his neighbours and made merry. He always said that whenever he saw a dead man's mouth he saw the folly of not eating what one had in one's lifetime. Unoka was, of course, a debtor, and he owed every neighbour some money, from a few cowries to quite substantial amounts.

He was tall but very thin and had a slight stoop. He wore a haggard and mournful look except when he was drinking or playing on his flute. He was very good on his flute, and his happiest moments were the two or three moons after the harvest when the village musicians brought down their instruments, hung above the fireplace. Unoka would play with them, his face beaming with blessedness and peace. Sometimes another village would ask Unoka's band and their dancing *egwugwu* to come and stay with them and teach them their tunes. They would go to such hosts for as long as three or four markets, making music and feasting. Unoka loved the good fare and the good fellowship, and he loved this season of the year, when the rains had stopped and the sun rose every morning with dazzling beauty. And it was not too hot either, because the cold and dry harmattan wind was blowing down from the north. Some years the harmattan was very severe and a dense haze hung on the atmosphere. Old men and children would then sit round log fires, warming their bodies. Unoka loved it all, and he loved the first kites that returned with the dry season, and the children who sang songs of welcome to them. He would remember his own childhood, how he had often wandered around looking for a kite sailing leisurely against the blue sky. As soon as he found one he would sing with his whole being, welcoming it back from its long, long journey, and asking it if it had brought home any lengths of cloth.

That was years ago, when he was young. Unoka, the grown-up, was a failure. He was poor and his wife and children had barely enough to eat. People laughed at him because he was a loafer, and they swore never to lend him any more money because he never paid back. But Unoka was such a man that he always succeeded in borrowing more, and piling up his debts.

One day a neighbour called Okoye came in to see him. He was reclining on a mud bed in his hut playing on the flute. He immediately rose and shook hands with Okoye, who then unrolled the goatskin which he carried under his arm, and sat down. Unoka went into an inner room and soon returned with a small wooden disc containing a kola nut, some alligator pepper and a lump of white chalk.

'I have kola,' he announced when he sat down, and passed the disc over to his guest.

'Thank you. He who brings kola brings life. But I think you ought to break it,' replied Okoye passing back the disc.

'No, it is for you, I think,' and they argued like this for a few moments before Unoka accepted the honour of breaking the kola. Okoye, meanwhile, took the lump of chalk, drew some lines on the floor, and then painted his big toe. As he broke the kola, Unoka prayed to their ancestors for life and health, and for protection against their enemies. When they had eaten they talked about many things: about the heavy rains which were drowning the yams, about the next ancestral feast and about the impending war with the village of Mbaino. Unoka was never happy when it came to wars. He was, in fact, a coward and could not bear the sight of blood. And so he changed the subject and talked about music, and his face beamed. He could hear in his mind's ear the blood-stirring and intricate rhythms of the *ekwe* and the *udu* and the *ogene*, and he could hear his own flute weaving in and out of them, decorating them with a colourful and plaintive tune. The total effect was gay and brisk, but if one picked out the flute as it went up and down and then broke up into short snatches, one saw that there was sorrow and grief there.

Okoye was also a musician. He played on the *ogene*. But he was not a failure like Unoka. He had a large barn full of yams and he had three wives. And now he was going to take the Idemili title, the third highest in the land. It was a very expensive ceremony and he was gathering all his resources together. That was in fact the reason why he had come to see Unoka. He cleared his throat and began:

'Thank you for the kola. You may have heard of the title I intend to take shortly.'

Having spoken plainly so far, Okoye said the next half a dozen sentences in proverbs. Among the Ibo the art of conversation is regarded very highly, and proverbs are the palm oil with which words are eaten. Okoye was a great talker and he spoke for a long time, skirting round the subject and then hitting it finally. In short, he was asking Unoka to return the two hundred cowries he had borrowed from him more than two years before. As soon as Unoka understood what his friend was driving at, he burst out laughing. He laughed loud and long and his voice rang out clear as the *ogene*, and tears stood in his eyes. His visitor was amazed, and sat speechless. At the end, Unoka was able to give an answer between fresh outbursts of mirth.

'Look at that wall,' he said, pointing at the far wall of his hut, which was rubbed with red earth so that it shone. 'Look at those lines of chalk'; and Okoye saw groups of short perpendicular lines drawn in chalk. There were five groups, and the smallest group had ten lines. Unoka had a sense of the dramatic and so he allowed a pause, in which he took a pinch of snuff and sneezed noisily, and then he continued: 'Each group there represents a debt to someone, and each stroke is one hundred cowries. You see, I owe that man a thousand cowries. But he has not come to wake me up in the morning for it. I shall pay you, but not today. Our elders say that the sun will shine on those who stand before it shines on those who kneel under them. I shall pay my big debts first.' And he took another pinch of snuff, as if that was paying the big debts first. Okoye rolled his goatskin and departed.

When Unoka died he had taken no title at all and he was heavily in debt. Any wonder then that his son Okonkwo was ashamed of him? Fortunately, among these people a man was judged according to his worth and not according to the worth of his father. Okonkwo was clearly cut out for great things. He was still young but he had won fame as the greatest wrestler in the nine villages. He was a wealthy farmer and had two barns full of yams, and had just married his third wife. To crown it all he had taken two titles and had shown incredible prowess in two inter-tribal wars. And so although Okonkwo was still young, he was already one of the greatest men of his time. Age was respected among his people, but achievement was revered. As the elders said, if a child washed his hands he could eat with kings. Okonkwo had clearly washed his hands and so he ate with kings and elders. And that was how he came to look after the doomed lad who was sacrificed to the village of Umuofia by their neighbours to avoid war and bloodshed. The ill-fated lad was called Ikemefuna.

CHAPTER TWO

Okonkwo had just blown out the palm oil lamp and stretched himself on his bamboo bed when he heard the *ogene* of the town-crier piercing the still night air. *Gome, gome, gome, gome*, boomed the hollow metal. Then the crier gave his message, and at the end of it beat his instrument again. And this was the message. Every man of Umuofia was asked to gather at the market-place tomorrow morning. Okonkwo wondered what was amiss, for he knew certainly that something was amiss. He had discerned a clear overtone of tragedy in the crier's voice, and even now he could still hear it as it grew dimmer and dimmer in the distance.

The night was very quiet. It was always quiet except on moonlight nights. Darkness held a vague terror for these people, even the bravest among them. Children were warned not to whistle at night for fear of evil spirits. Dangerous animals became even more sinister and uncanny in the dark. A snake was never called by its name at night, because it would hear. It was called a string. And so on this particular night as the crier's voice was gradually swallowed up in the distance, silence returned to the world, a vibrant silence made more intense by the universal trill of a million million forest insects.

On a moonlight night it would be different. The happy voices of children playing in open fields would then be heard. And perhaps those not so young would be playing in pairs in less open places, and old men and women would remember their youth. As the Ibo say: 'When the moon is shining the cripple becomes hungry for a walk.'

But this particular night was dark and silent. And in all the nine villages of Umuofia a town-crier with his *ogene* asked every man to be present tomorrow morning. Okonkwo on his bamboo bed tried to figure out the nature of the emergency — war with a neighbouring clan? That seemed the most likely reason, and he was not afraid of war. He was a man of action, a man of war. Unlike his father he could stand the look of blood. In Umuofia's latest war he was the first to bring home a human head. That was his fifth head; and he was not an old man yet. On great occasions such as the funeral of a village celebrity he drank his palm wine from his first human head.

In the morning the market-place was full. There must have been about ten thousand men there, all talking in low voices. At last Ogbuefi Ezeugo stood up in the midst of them and bellowed four times, '*Umuofia kwenu*', and on each occasion he faced a different direction and seemed to push the air with a clenched fist. And ten thousand answered '*Yaa!*' each time. Then there was perfect silence. Ogbuefi Ezeugo was a powerful orator and was always chosen to speak on such occasions. He moved his hand over his white head and stroked his white beard. He then adjusted his cloth, which was passed under his right arm-pit and tied above his left shoulder.

'*Umuofia kwenu*,' he bellowed a fifth time, and the crowd yelled in answer. And then suddenly like one possessed he shot out his left hand and pointed in the direction of Mbaino, and said through gleaming white teeth firmly clenched: 'Those sons of wild animals have dared to murder a daughter of Umuofia.' He threw his head down and gnashed his teeth, and allowed a murmur of suppressed anger to sweep the crowd. When he began again, the anger on his face was gone and in its place a sort of smile hovered, more terrible and more sinister than the anger. And in a clear, unemotional voice he told Umuofia how their daughter had gone to market at Mbaino and had been killed. That woman, said Ezeugo, was the wife of Ogbuefi Udo, and he pointed to a man who sat near him with a bowed head. The crowd then shouted with anger and thirst for blood.

Many others spoke, and at the end it was decided to follow the normal course of action. An ultimatum was immediately dis-patched to Mbaino asking them to choose between war on the one hand, and on the other the offer of a young man and a virgin as compensation.

Umuofia was feared by all its neighbours. It was powerful in war and in magic, and its priests and medicine-men were feared in all the surrounding country. Its most potent war-medicine was as old as the clan itself. Nobody knew how old. But on one point there was general agreement – the active principle in that medicine had been an old woman with one leg. In fact, the medicine itself was called *agadi-nwayi*, or old woman. It had its shrine in the centre of Umuofia, in a cleared spot. And if anybody was so foolhardy as to pass by the shrine after dusk he was sure to see the old woman hopping about.

And so the neighbouring clans who naturally knew of these things feared Umuofia, and would not go to war against it without first trying a peaceful settlement. And in fairness to Umuofia it should be recorded that it never went to war unless its case was clear and just and was accepted as such by its Oracle – the Oracle of the Hills and the Caves. And there were indeed occasions when the Oracle had forbidden Umuofia to wage a war. If the clan had disobeyed the Oracle they would surely have been beaten, because their dreaded *agadi-nwayi* would never fight what the Ibo call *a fight of blame*.

But the war that now threatened was a just war. Even the enemy clan knew that. And so when Okonkwo of Umuofia arrived at Mbaino as the proud and imperious emissary of war, he was treated with great honour and respect, and two days later he was returned home with a lad of fifteen and a young virgin. The lad's name was Ikemefuna, whose sad story is still told in Umuofia unto this day.

The elders, or *ndichie*, met to hear a report of Okonkwo's mission. At the end they decided, as everybody knew they would, that the girl should go to Ogbuefi Udo to replace his murdered wife. As for the boy, he belonged to the clan as a whole, and there was no hurry to decide his fate. Okonkwo was, therefore, asked on behalf of the clan to look after him in the interim. And so for three years Ikemefuna lived in Okonkwo's household.

Okonkwo ruled his household with a heavy hand. His wives, especially the youngest, lived in perpetual fear of his fiery temper, and so did his little children. Perhaps down in his heart Okonkwo was not a cruel man. But his whole life was dominated by fear, the fear of failure and of weakness. It was deeper and more intimate than the fear of evil and capricious gods and of magic, the fear of the forest, and the forces of nature, malevolent, red in tooth and claw. Okonkwo's fear was greater than these. It was not external but lay deep within himself. It was the fear of himself, lest he should be found to resemble his father. Even as a little boy he had resented his father's failure and weakness, and even now he still remembered how he had suffered when a playmate had told him that his father was *agbala*. That was how Okonkwo first came to know that *agbala* was not only another name for a woman, it could also mean a man who had taken no title. And so Okonkwo was ruled by one passion – to hate everything that his father Unoka had loved. One of those things was gentleness and another was idleness.

During the planting season Okonkwo worked daily on his farms from cock-crow until the chickens went to roost. He was a very strong man and rarely felt fatigue. But his wives and young children were not as strong, and so they suffered. But they dared not complain openly. Okonkwo's first son, Nwoye, was then twelve years old but was already causing his father great anxiety for his incipient laziness. At any rate, that was how it looked to his father, and he sought to correct him by constant nagging and beating. And so Nwoye was developing into a sad-faced youth.

Okonkwo's prosperity was visible in his household. He had a large compound enclosed by a thick wall of red earth. His own hut, or *obi*, stood immediately behind the only gate in the red walls. Each of his three wives had her own hut, which together formed a half moon behind the *obi*. The barn was built against one end of the red walls, and long stacks of yam stood out prosperously in it. At the opposite end of the compound was a shed for the goats, and each wife built a small attachment to her hut for the hens. Near

the barn was a small house, the 'medicine house' or shrine where
Okonkwo kept the wooden symbols of his personal god and of his
ancestral spirits. He worshipped them with sacrifices of kola nut,
food and palm wine, and offered prayers to them on behalf of
himself, his three wives and eight children.

So when the daughter of Umuofia was killed in Mbaino, Ikemefuna
came into Okonkwo's household. When Okonkwo brought him
home that day he called his most senior wife and handed him
over to her.

'He belongs to the clan,' he told her. 'So look after him.'

'Is he staying long with us?' she asked.

'Do what you are told, woman,' Okonkwo thundered, and
stammered. 'When did you become one of the *ndichie* of Umuofia?'

And so Nwoye's mother took Ikemefuna to her hut and asked
no more questions.

As for the boy himself, he was terribly afraid. He could not
understand what was happening to him or what he had done. How
could he know that his father had taken a hand in killing a daughter
of Umuofia? All he knew was that a few men had arrived at their
house, conversing with his father in low tones, and at the end he
had been taken out and handed over to a stranger. His mother had
wept bitterly, but he had been too surprised to weep. And so the
stranger had brought him, and a girl, a long, long way from home,
through lonely forest paths. He did not know who the girl was,
and he never saw her again.

CHAPTER THREE

Okonkwo did not have the start in life which many young men usually had. He did not inherit a barn from his father. There was no barn to inherit. The story was told in Umuofia of how his father, Unoka, had gone to consult the Oracle of the Hills and the Caves to find out why he always had a miserable harvest.

The Oracle was called Agbala, and people came from far and near to consult it. They came when misfortune dogged their steps or when they had a dispute with their neighbours. They came to discover what the future held for them or to consult the spirits of their departed fathers.

The way into the shrine was a round hole at the side of a hill, just a little bit bigger than the round opening into a henhouse. Worshippers and those who came to seek knowledge from the god crawled on their belly through the hole and found themselves in a dark, endless space in the presence of Agbala. No one had ever beheld Agbala, except his priestess. But no one who had ever crawled into his awful shrine had come out without the fear of his power. His priestess stood by the sacred fire which she built in the heart of the cave and proclaimed the will of the god. The fire did not burn with a flame. The glowing logs only served to light up vaguely the dark figure of the priestess.

Sometimes a man came to consult the spirit of his dead father or relative. It was said that when such a spirit appeared, the man saw it vaguely in the darkness, but never heard its voice. Some people even said that they had heard the spirits flying and flapping their wings against the roof of the cave.

Many years ago when Okonkwo was still a boy his father, Unoka, had gone to consult Agbala. The priestess in those days was a woman called Chika. She was full of the power of her god, and she was greatly feared. Unoka stood before her and began his story.

'Every year,' he said sadly, 'before I put any crop in the earth, I sacrifice a cock to Ani, the owner of all land. It is the law of our fathers. I also kill a cock at the shrine of Ifejioku, the god of yams. I clear the bush and set fire to it when it is dry. I sow the yams when the first rain has fallen, and stake them when the young tendrils appear. I weed—'

'Hold your peace!' screamed the priestess, her voice terrible as it echoed through the dark void. 'You have offended neither the gods nor your fathers. And when a man is at peace with his gods and his ancestors, his harvest will be good or bad according to the strength of his arm. You, Unoka, are known in all the clan for the weakness of your matchet and your hoe. When your neighbours go out with their axe to cut down virgin forests, you sow your yams on exhausted farms that take no labour to clear. They cross seven rivers to make their farms; you stay at home and offer sacrifices to a reluctant soil. Go home and work like a man.'

Unoka was an ill-fated man. He had a bad *chi* or personal god, and evil fortune followed him to the grave, or rather to his death, for he had no grave. He died of the swelling which was an abomination to the earth goddess. When a man was afflicted with swelling in the stomach and the limbs he was not allowed to die in the house. He was carried to the Evil Forest and left there to die. There was the story of a very stubborn man who staggered back to his house and had to be carried again to the forest and tied to a tree. The sickness was an abomination to the earth, and so the victim could not be buried in her bowels. He died and rotted away above the earth, and was not given the first or the second burial. Such was Unoka's fate. When they carried him away, he took with him his flute.

With a father like Unoka, Okonkwo did not have the start in

life which many young men had. He neither inherited a barn nor a title, nor even a young wife. But in spite of these disadvantages, he had begun even in his father's lifetime to lay the foundations of a prosperous future. It was slow and painful. But he threw himself into it like one possessed. And indeed he was possessed by the fear of his father's contemptible life and shameful death.

There was a wealthy man in Okonkwo's village who had three huge barns, nine wives and thirty children. His name was Nwakibie and he had taken the highest but one title which a man could take in the clan. It was for this man that Okonkwo worked to earn his first seed yams.

He took a pot of palm wine and a cock to Nwakibie. Two elderly neighbours were sent for, and Nwakibie's two grown-up sons were also present in his *obi*. He presented a kola nut and an alligator pepper, which was passed round for all to see and then returned to him. He broke it, saying: 'We shall all live. We pray for life, children, a good harvest and happiness. You will have what is good for you and I will have what is good for me. Let the kite perch and let the eagle perch too. If one says no to the other, let his wing break.'

After the kola nut had been eaten Okonkwo brought his palm wine from the corner of the hut where it had been placed and stood it in the centre of the group. He addressed Nwakibie, calling him 'Our father'.

'*Nna ayi*,' he said. 'I have brought you this little kola. As our people say, a man who pays respect to the great paves the way for his own greatness. I have come to pay you my respects and also to ask a favour. But let us drink the wine first.'

Everybody thanked Okonkwo and the neighbours brought out their drinking horns from the goatskin bags they carried. Nwakibie brought down his own horn, which was fastened to the rafters. The younger of his sons, who was also the youngest man in the group, moved to the centre, raised the pot on his left knee and began to pour out the wine. The first cup went to Okonkwo, who must taste his wine before anyone else. Then the group drank, beginning with the eldest man. When everyone had drunk two or three horns, Nwakibie sent for his wives. Some of them were not at home and only four came in.

'Is Anasi not in?' he asked them. They said she was coming. Anasi was the first wife and the others could not drink before her, and so they stood waiting.

Anasi was a middle-aged woman, tall and strongly built. There was authority in her bearing and she looked every inch the ruler of the womenfolk in a large and prosperous family. She wore the anklet of her husband's titles, which the first wife alone could wear.

She walked up to her husband and accepted the horn from him. She then went down on one knee, drank a little and handed back the horn. She rose, called him by his name and went back to her hut. The other wives drank in the same way, in their proper order, and went away.

The men then continued their drinking and talking. Ogbuefi Idigo was talking about the palm wine tapper, Obiako, who suddenly gave up his trade.

'There must be something behind it,' he said, wiping the foam of wine from his moustache with the back of his left hand. 'There must be a reason for it. A toad does not run in the daytime for nothing.'

'Some people say the Oracle warned him that he would fall off a palm tree and kill himself,' said Akukalia.

'Obiako has always been a strange one,' said Nwakibie. 'I have heard that many years ago, when his father had not been dead very long, he had gone to consult the Oracle. The Oracle said to him, "Your dead father wants you to sacrifice a goat to him". Do you know what he told the Oracle? He said, "Ask my dead father if he ever had a fowl when he was alive".' Everybody laughed heartily except Okonkwo, who laughed uneasily because, as the saying goes, an old woman is always uneasy when dry bones are mentioned in a proverb. Okonkwo remembered his own father.

At last the young man who was pouring out the wine held up half a horn of the thick, white dregs and said, 'What we are eating is finished'. 'We have seen it,' the others replied. 'Who will drink the dregs?' he asked. 'Whoever has a job in hand,' said Idigo, looking at Nwakibie's elder son, Igwelo, with a mischievous twinkle in his eye.

Everybody agreed that Igwelo should drink the dregs. He accepted the half-full horn from his brother and drank it. As Idigo had said, Igwelo had a job in hand because he had married his first wife a month or two before. The thick dregs of palm wine were supposed to be good for men who were going in to their wives.

After the wine had been drunk Okonkwo laid his difficulties before Nwakibie.

'I have come to you for help,' he said. 'Perhaps you can already guess what it is. I have cleared a farm but have no yams to sow. I know what it is to ask a man to trust another with his yams, especially these days when young men are afraid of hard work. I am not afraid of work. The lizard that jumped from the high iroko tree to the ground said he would praise himself if no one else did. I began to fend for myself at an age when most people still suck at their mothers' breasts. If you give me some yam seeds I shall not fail you.'

Nwakibie cleared his throat. 'It pleases me to see a young man like you these days when our youth have gone so soft. Many young men have come to me to ask for yams but I have refused because I knew they would just dump them in the earth and leave them to be choked by weeds. When I say no to them they think I am hardhearted. But it is not so. Eneke the bird says that since men have learnt to shoot without missing, he has learnt to fly without perching. I have learnt to be stingy with my yams. But I can trust you. I know it as I look at you. As our fathers said, you can tell a ripe corn by its look. I shall give you twice four hundred yams. Go ahead and prepare your farm.'

Okonkwo thanked him again and again and went home feeling happy. He knew that Nwakibie would not refuse him, but he had not expected he would be so generous. He had not hoped to get more than four hundred seeds. He would now have to make a bigger farm. He hoped to get another four hundred yams from one of his father's friends at Isiuzo.

Share-cropping was a very slow way of building up a barn of one's own. After all the toil one only got a third of the harvest. But for a young man whose father had no yams, there was no other way. And what made it worse in Okonkwo's case was that he had to support his mother and two sisters from his meagre harvest. And supporting his mother also meant supporting his father. She could not be expected to cook and eat while her husband starved. And so at a very early age when he was striving desperately to build a barn through share-cropping Okonkwo was also fending for his father's house. It was like pouring grains of corn into a bag full of holes. His mother and sisters worked hard enough, but they grew women's crops, like coco-yams, beans and cassava. Yam, the king of crops, was a man's crop.

The year that Okonkwo took eight hundred seed-yams from Nwakibie was the worst year in living memory. Nothing happened at its proper time; it was either too early or too late. It seemed as if the world had gone mad. The first rains were late, and, when they came, lasted only a brief moment. The blazing sun returned, more fierce than it had ever been known, and scorched all the green that had appeared with the rains. The earth burned like hot coals and roasted all the yams that had been sown. Like all good farmers, Okonkwo had begun to sow with the first rains. He had sown four hundred seeds when the rains dried up and the heat returned. He watched the sky all day for signs of rain-clouds and lay awake all night. In the morning he went back to his farm and saw the withering tendrils. He had tried to protect them from the smouldering earth by making rings of thick sisal leaves around them. But by the end of the day the sisal rings were burnt dry and grey. He changed them every day, and prayed that the rain might fall in the night. But the drought continued for eight market weeks and the yams were killed.

Some farmers had not planted their yams yet. They were the lazy easy-going ones who always put off clearing their farms as long as they could. This year they were the wise ones. They sympathized with their neighbours with much shaking of the head, but inwardly they were happy for what they took to be their own foresight.

Okonkwo planted what was left of his seed-yams when the rains finally returned. He had one consolation. The yams he had sown before the drought were his own, the harvest of the previous year. He still had the eight hundred from Nwakibie and the four hundred from his father's friend. So he would make a fresh start.

But the year had gone mad. Rain fell as it had never fallen before. For days and nights together it poured down in violent torrents, and washed away the yam heaps. Trees were uprooted and deep gorges appeared everywhere. Then the rain became less violent. But it went on from day to day without a pause. The spell of sunshine which always came in the middle of the wet season did not appear. The yams put on luxuriant green leaves, but every farmer knew that without sunshine the tubers would not grow.

That year the harvest was sad, like a funeral, and many farmers wept as they dug up the miserable and rotting yams. One man tied his cloth to a tree branch and hanged himself.

Okonkwo remembered that tragic year with a cold shiver throughout the rest of his life. It always surprised him when he thought of it later that he did not sink under the load of despair. He knew he was a fierce fighter, but that year had been enough to break the heart of a lion.

'Since I survived that year,' he always said, 'I shall survive anything.' He put it down to his inflexible will.

His father, Unoka, who was then an ailing man, had said to him during that terrible harvest month: 'Do not despair. I know you will not despair. You have a manly and a proud heart. A proud heart can survive a general failure because such a failure does not prick its pride. It is more difficult and more bitter when a man fails *alone*.'

Unoka was like that in his last days. His love of talk had grown with age and sickness. It tried Okonkwo's patience beyond words.

CHAPTER FOUR

'Looking at a king's mouth,' said an old man, 'one would think he never sucked at his mother's breast.' He was talking about Okonkwo, who had risen so suddenly from great poverty and misfortune to be one of the lords of the clan. The old man bore no ill-will towards Okonkwo. Indeed he respected him for his industry and success. But he was struck, as most people were, by Okonkwo's brusqueness in dealing with less successful men. Only a week ago a man had contradicted him at a kindred meeting which they held to discuss the next ancestral feast. Without looking at the man Okonkwo had said: 'This meeting is for men'. The man who had contradicted him had no titles. That was why he had called him a woman. Okonkwo knew how to kill a man's spirit.

Everybody at the kindred meeting took sides with Osugo when Okonkwo called him a woman. The oldest man present said sternly that those whose palm-kernels were cracked for them by a benevolent spirit should not forget to be humble. Okonkwo said he was sorry for what he had said, and the meeting continued.

But it was really not true that Okonkwo's palm-kernels had been cracked for him by a benevolent spirit. He had cracked them himself. Anyone who knew his grim struggle against poverty and misfortune could not say he had been lucky. If ever a man deserved his success, that man was Okonkwo. At an early age he had achieved fame as the greatest wrestler in all the land. That was not luck. At the most one could say that his *chi* or personal god was good. But the Ibo people have a proverb that when a man says yes his *chi* says yes also. Okonkwo said yes very strongly; so his *chi* agreed. And not only his *chi* but his clan too, because it judged a man by the work of his hands. That was why Okonkwo had been chosen by the nine villages to carry a message of war to their enemies unless they agreed to give up a young man and a virgin to atone for the murder of Udo's wife. And such was the deep fear that their enemies had for Umuofia that they treated Okonkwo like a king and brought him a virgin who was given to Udo as a wife, and the lad Ikemefuna.

The elders of the clan had decided that Ikemefuna should be in Okonkwo's care for a while. But no one thought it would be as long as three years. They seemed to forget all about him as soon as they had taken the decision.

At first Ikemefuna was very much afraid. Once or twice he tried to run away, but he did not know where to begin. He thought of his mother and his three-year-old sister and wept bitterly. Nwoye's mother was very kind to him and treated him as one of her own children. But all he said was: 'When shall I go home?' When Okonkwo heard that he would not eat any food he came into the hut with a big stick in his hand and stood over him while he swallowed his yams, trembling. A few moments later he went behind the hut and began to vomit painfully. Nwoye's mother went to him and placed her hands on his chest and on his back. He was ill for three market weeks, and when he recovered he seemed to have overcome his great fear and sadness.

He was by nature a very lively boy and he gradually became popular in Okonkwo's household, especially with the children. Okonkwo's son, Nwoye, who was two years younger, became quite inseparable from him because he seemed to know everything. He could fashion out flutes from bamboo stems and even from the elephant grass. He knew the names of all the birds and could set clever traps for the little bush rodents. And he knew which trees made the strongest bows.

Even Okonkwo himself became very fond of the boy — inwardly, of course. Okonkwo never showed any emotion openly, unless it be the emotion of anger. To show affection was a sign of weakness;

the only thing worth demonstrating was strength. He therefore treated Ikemefuna as he treated everybody else – with a heavy hand. But there was no doubt that he liked the boy. Sometimes when he went to big village meetings or communal ancestral feasts he allowed Ikemefuna to accompany him, like a son, carrying his stool and his goatskin bag. And, indeed, Ikemefuna called him father.

Ikemefuna came to Umuofia at the end of the carefree season between harvest and planting. In fact he recovered from his illness only a few days before the Week of Peace began. And that was also the year Okonkwo broke the peace, and was punished, as was the custom, by Ezeani, the priest of the earth goddess.

Okonkwo was provoked to justifiable anger by his youngest wife, who went to plait her hair at her friend's house and did not return early enough to cook the afternoon meal. Okonkwo did not know at first that she was not at home. After waiting in vain for the dish he went to her hut to see what she was doing. There was nobody in the hut and the fireplace was cold.

'Where is Ojiugo?' he asked his second wife, who came out of her hut to draw water from a gigantic pot in the shade of a small tree in the middle of the compound.

'She has gone to plait her hair.'

Okonkwo bit his lips as anger welled up within him.

'Where are her children? Did she take them?' he asked with unusual coolness and restraint.

'They are here,' answered his first wife, Nwoye's mother. Okonkwo bent down and looked into her hut. Ojiugo's children were eating with the children of his first wife.

'Did she ask you to feed them before she went?'

'Yes,' lied Nwoye's mother, trying to minimize Ojiugo's thoughtlessness.

Okonkwo knew she was not speaking the truth. He walked back to his *obi* to wait Ojiugo's return. And when she returned he beat her very heavily. In his anger he had forgotten that it was the Week of Peace. His first two wives ran out in great alarm pleading with him that it was the sacred week. But Okonkwo was not the man to stop beating somebody half-way through, not even for fear of a goddess.

Okonkwo's neighbours heard his wife crying and sent their voices over the compound walls to ask what was the matter. Some of them came over to see for themselves. It was unheard of to beat somebody during the sacred week.

Before it was dusk Ezeani, who was the priest of the earth goddess, Ani, called on Okonkwo in his *obi*. Okonkwo brought out kola nut and placed it before the priest.

'Take away your kola nut. I shall not eat in the house of a man who has no respect for our gods and ancestors.'

Okonkwo tried to explain to him what his wife had done, but Ezeani seemed to pay no attention. He held a short staff in his hand which he brought down on the floor to emphasize his points.

'Listen to me,' he said when Okonkwo had spoken. 'You are not a stranger in Umuofia. You know as well as I do that our forefathers ordained that before we plant any crops in the earth we should observe a week in which a man does not say a harsh word to his neighbour. We live in peace with our fellows to honour our great goddess of the earth without whose blessing our crops will not grow. You have committed a great evil.' He brought down his staff heavily on the floor. 'Your wife was at fault, but even if you came into your *obi* and found her lover on top of her, you would still have committed a great evil to beat her.' His staff came down again. 'The evil you have done can ruin the whole clan. The earth goddess whom you have insulted may refuse to give us her increase, and we shall all perish.' His tone now changed from anger to command. 'You will bring to the shrine of Ani tomorrow one she-goat, one hen, a length of cloth and a hundred cowries.' He rose and left the hut.

Okonkwo did as the priest said. He also took with him a pot of palm wine. Inwardly, he was repentant. But he was not the man to go about telling his neighbours that he was in error. And so people said he had no respect for the gods of the clan. His enemies said his good fortune had gone to his head. They called him the little bird *nza* who so far forgot himself after a heavy meal that he challenged his *chi*.

No work was done during the Week of Peace. People called on their neighbours and drank palm wine. This year they talked of nothing else but the *nso-ani* which Okonkwo had committed. It was the first time for many years that a man had broken the sacred peace. Even the oldest men could only remember one or two other occasions somewhere in the dim past.

Ogbuefi Ezeudu, who was the oldest man in the village, was telling two other men who came to visit him that the punishment for breaking the Peace of Ani had become very mild in their clan.

'It has not always been so,' he said. 'My father told me that he had been told that in the past a man who broke the peace was dragged on the ground through the village until he died. But after a while this custom was stopped because it spoilt the peace which it was meant to preserve.'

'Somebody told me yesterday,' said one of the younger men, 'that in some clans it is an abomination for a man to die during the Week of Peace.'

'It is indeed true,' said Ogbuefi Ezeudu. 'They have that custom in Obodoani. If a man dies at this time he is not buried but cast into the Evil Forest. It is a bad custom which these people observe because they lack understanding. They throw away large numbers of men and women without burial. And what is the result? Their clan is full of the evil spirits of these unburied dead, hungry to do harm to the living.'

After the Week of Peace every man and his family began to clear the bush to make new farms. The cut bush was left to dry and fire was then set to it. As the smoke rose into the sky kites appeared from different directions and hovered over the burning field in silent valediction. The rainy season was approaching when they would go away until the dry season returned.

Okonkwo spent the next few days preparing his seed-yams. He looked at each yam carefully to see whether it was good for sowing. Sometimes he decided that a yam was too big to be sown as one seed and he split it deftly along its length with his sharp knife. His eldest son, Nwoye, and Ikemefuna helped him by fetching the yams in long baskets from the barn and in counting the prepared seeds in groups of four hundred. Sometimes Okonkwo gave them a few yams each to prepare. But he always found fault with their effort, and he said so with much threatening.

'Do you think you are cutting up yams for cooking?' he asked Nwoye. 'If you split another yam of this size, I shall break your jaw. You think you are still a child. I began to own a farm at your age. And you,' he said to Ikemefuna, 'do you not grow yams where you come from?'

Inwardly Okonkwo knew that the boys were still too young to understand fully the difficult art of preparing seed-yams. But he thought that one could not begin too early. Yam stood for manliness, and he who could feed his family on yams from one harvest to another was a very great man indeed. Okonkwo wanted his son to be a great farmer and a great man. He would stamp out the disquieting signs of laziness which he thought he already saw in him.

'I will not have a son who cannot hold up his head in the gathering of the clan. I would sooner strangle him with my own hands. And if you stand there staring at me like that,' he swore, 'Amadiora will break your head for you!'

Some days later, when the land had been moistened by two or three heavy rains, Okonkwo and his family went to the farm with baskets of seed-yams, their hoes and matchets, and the planting began. They made single mounds of earth in straight lines all over the field and sowed the yams in them.

Yam, the king of crops, was a very exacting king. For three or four moons it demanded hard work and constant attention from cock-crow till the chickens went back to roost. The young tendrils were protected from earth-heat with rings of sisal leaves. As the rains became heavier the women planted maize, melons and beans between the yam mounds. The yams were then staked, first with little sticks and later with tall and big tree branches. The women weeded the farm three times at definite periods in the life of the yams, neither early nor late.

And now the rains had really come, so heavy and persistent that even the village rain-maker no longer claimed to be able to intervene. He could not stop the rain now, just as he would not attempt to start it in the heart of the dry season, without serious danger to his own health. The personal dynamism required to counter the forces of these extremes of weather would be far too great for the human frame.

And so nature was not interfered with in the middle of the rainy season. Sometimes it poured down in such thick sheets of water that earth and sky seemed merged in one grey wetness. It was then uncertain whether the low rumbling of Amadiora's thunder came from above or below. At such times, in each of the countless thatched huts of Umuofia, children sat around their mother's cooking fire telling stories, or with their father in his *obi* warming themselves from a log fire, roasting and eating maize. It was a brief resting period between the exacting and arduous planting season and the equally exacting but light-hearted month of harvests.

Ikemefuna had begun to feel like a member of Okonkwo's family. He still thought about his mother and his three-year-old sister, and he had moments of sadness and depression. But he and Nwoye had become so deeply attached to each other that such moments became less frequent and less poignant. Ikemefuna had an endless stock of folk tales. Even those which Nwoye knew already were told with a new freshness and the local flavour of a different clan. Nwoye remembered this period very vividly till the end of his life. He even remembered how he had laughed when Ikemefuna told him that the proper name for a corn-cob with only a few scattered grains was *eze-agadi-nwayi*, or the teeth of an old woman. Nwoye's mind had gone immediately to Nwayieke, who lived near the udala tree. She had about three teeth and was always smoking her pipe.

Gradually the rains became lighter and less frequent, and earth and sky once again became separate. The rain fell in thin, slanting showers through sunshine and quiet breeze. Children no longer stayed indoors but ran about singing:

> The rain is falling, the sun is shining,
> Alone Nnadi is cooking and eating.

Nwoye always wondered who Nnadi was and why he should live all by himself, cooking and eating. In the end he decided that Nnadi must live in that land of Ikemefuna's favourite story where the ant holds his court in splendour and the sands dance for ever.

CHAPTER FIVE

The Feast of the New Yam was approaching and Umuofia was in
a festival mood. It was an occasion for giving thanks to Ani, the
earth goddess and the source of all fertility. Ani played a greater
part in the life of the people than any other deity. She was the
ultimate judge of morality and conduct. And what was more, she
was in close communion with the departed fathers of the clan whose
bodies had been committed to earth.

The Feast of the New Yam was held every year before the harvest
began, to honour the earth goddess and the ancestral spirits of the
clan. New yams could not be eaten until some had first been offered
to these powers. Men and women, young and old, looked forward
to the New Yam Festival because it began the season of plenty —
the new year. On the last night before the festival, yams of the
old year were all disposed of by those who still had them. The new
year must begin with tasty, fresh yams and not the shrivelled and
fibrous crop of the previous year. All cooking-pots, calabashes and
wooden bowls were thoroughly washed, especially the wooden
mortar in which yam was pounded. Yam foo-foo and vegetable soup
was the chief food in the celebration. So much of it was cooked
that, no matter how heavily the family ate or how many friends
and relations they invited from neighbouring villages, there was
always a huge quantity of food left over at the end of the day. The
story was always told of a wealthy man who set before his guests
a mound of foo-foo so high that those who sat on one side could
not see what was happening on the other, and it was not until late

in the evening that one of them saw for the first time his in-law who had arrived during the course of the meal and had fallen to on the opposite side. It was only then that they exchanged greetings and shook hands over what was left of the food.

The New Yam Festival was thus an occasion for joy throughout Umuofia. And every man whose arm was strong, as the Ibo people say, was expected to invite large numbers of guests from far and wide. Okonkwo always asked his wives' relations, and since he now had three wives his guests would make a fairly big crowd.

But somehow Okonkwo could never become as enthusiastic over feasts as most people. He was a good eater and he could drink one or two fairly big gourds of palm wine. But he was always uncomfortable sitting around for days waiting for a feast or getting over it. He would be very much happier working on his farm.

The festival was now only three days away. Okonkwo's wives had scrubbed the walls and the huts with red earth until they reflected light. They had then drawn patterns on them in white, yellow and dark green. They then set about painting themselves with cam wood and drawing beautiful black patterns on their stomachs and on their backs. The children were also decorated, especially their hair, which was shaved in beautiful patterns. The three women talked excitedly about the relations who had been invited, and the children revelled in the thought of being spoilt by these visitors from motherland. Ikemefuna was equally excited. The New Yam Festival seemed to him to be a much bigger event here than in his own village, a place which was already becoming remote and vague in his imagination.

And then the storm burst. Okonkwo, who had been walking about aimlessly in his compound in suppressed anger, suddenly found an outlet.

'Who killed this banana tree?' he asked.

A hush fell on the compound immediately.

'Who killed this tree? Or are you all deaf and dumb?'

As a matter of fact the tree was very much alive. Okonkwo's second wife had merely cut a few leaves off it to wrap some food, and she said so. Without further argument Okonkwo gave her a sound beating and left her and her only daughter weeping. Neither of the other wives dared to interfere beyond an occasional and tentative, 'It is enough, Okonkwo,' pleaded from a reasonable distance.

His anger thus satisfied, Okonkwo decided to go out hunting. He had an old rusty gun made by a clever blacksmith who had come to live in Umuofia long ago. But although Okonkwo was a great man whose prowess was universally acknowledged, he was not a hunter. In fact he had not killed a rat with his gun. And so when he called Ikemefuna to fetch his gun, the wife who had just been beaten murmured something about guns that never shot. Unfortunately for her, Okonkwo heard it and ran madly into his room for the loaded gun, ran out again and aimed at her as she clambered over the dwarf wall of the barn. He pressed the trigger and there was a loud report accompanied by the wail of his wives and children. He threw down the gun and jumped into the barn, and there lay the woman, very much shaken and frightened but quite unhurt. He heaved a heavy sigh and went away with the gun.

In spite of this incident the New Yam Festival was celebrated with great joy in Okonkwo's household. Early that morning as he offered a sacrifice of new yam and palm oil to his ancestors he asked them to protect him, his children and their mothers in the new year.

As the day wore on his in-laws arrived from three surrounding villages, and each party brought with them a huge pot of palm wine. And there was eating and drinking till night, when Okonkwo's in-laws began to leave for their homes.

The second day of the new year was the day of the great wrestling match between Okonkwo's village and their neighbours. It was difficult to say which the people enjoyed more – the feasting and fellowship of the first day or the wrestling contest of the second. But there was one woman who had no doubt whatever in her mind. She was Okonkwo's second wife, Ekwefi, whom he nearly shot. There was no festival in all the seasons of the year which gave her as much pleasure as the wrestling match. Many years ago when she was the village beauty Okonkwo had won her heart by throwing the Cat in the greatest contest within living memory. She did not marry him because he was too poor to pay her bride-price. But a few years later she ran away from her husband and came to live with Okonkwo. All this happened many years ago. Now Ekwefi was a woman of forty-five who had suffered a great deal in her time. But her love of wrestling contests was still as strong as it was thirty years ago.

It was not yet noon on the second day of the New Yam Festival. Ekwefi and her only daughter, Ezinma, sat near the fireplace waiting for the water in the pot to boil. The fowl Ekwefi had just killed was in the wooden mortar. The water began to boil, and in one deft movement she lifted the pot from the fire and poured the boiling water on to the fowl. She put back the empty pot on the circular pad in the corner, and looked at her palms, which were black with soot. Ezinma was always surprised that her mother could lift a pot from the fire with her bare hands.

'Ekwefi,' she said, 'is it true that when people are grown up, fire does not burn them?' Ezinma, unlike most children, called her mother by her name.

'Yes,' replied Ekwefi, too busy to argue. Her daughter was only ten years old but she was wiser than her years.

'But Nwoye's mother dropped her pot of hot soup the other day and it broke on the floor.'

Ekwefi turned the hen over in the mortar and began to pluck the feathers.

'Ekwefi,' said Ezinma, who had joined in plucking the feathers, 'my eyelid is twitching.'

'It means you are going to cry,' said her mother.

'No,' Ezinma said, 'it is this eyelid, the top one.'

'That means you will see something.'

'What will I see?' she asked.

'How can I know?' Ekwefi wanted her to work it out herself.

'Oho,' said Ezinma at last. 'I know what it is – the wrestling match.'

At last the hen was plucked clean. Ekwefi tried to pull out the horny beak but it was too hard. She turned round on her low stool and put the beak in the fire for a few moments. She pulled again and it came off.

'Ekwefi!' a voice called from one of the other huts. It was Nwoye's mother, Okonkwo's first wife.

'Is that me?' Ekwefi called back. That was the way people answered calls from outside. They never answered yes for fear it might be an evil spirit calling.

'Will you give Ezinma some fire to bring to me?' Her own children and Ikemefuna had gone to the stream.

Ekwefi put a few live coals into a piece of broken pot and Ezinma carried it across the clean-swept compound to Nwoye's mother.

'Thank you, Nma,' she said. She was peeling new yams, and in a basket beside her were green vegetables and beans.

'Let me make the fire for you,' Ezinma offered.

'Thank you, Ezigbo,' she said. She often called her Ezigbo, which means 'the good one'.

Ezinma went outside and brought some sticks from a huge bundle of firewood. She broke them into little pieces across the sole of her foot and began to build a fire, blowing it with her breath.

'You will blow your eyes out,' said Nwoye's mother, looking up from the yams she was peeling. 'Use the fan.' She stood up and pulled out the fan which was fastened into one of the rafters. As soon as she got up, the troublesome nanny-goat, which had been dutifully eating yam peelings, dug her teeth into the real thing, scooped out two mouthfuls and fled from the hut to chew the cud in the goats' shed. Nwoye's mother swore at her and settled down again to her peeling. Ezinma's fire was now sending up thick clouds of smoke. She went on fanning it until it burst into flames. Nwoye's mother thanked her and she went back to her mother's hut.

Just then the distant beating of drums began to reach them. It came from the direction of the *ilo*, the village playground. Every village had its own *ilo* which was as old as the village itself and where all the great ceremonies and dances took place. The drums beat the unmistakable wrestling dance – quick, light and gay, and it came floating on the wind.

Okonkwo cleared his throat and moved his feet to the beat of the drums. It filled him with fire as it had always done from his youth. He trembled with the desire to conquer and subdue. It was like the desire for woman.

'We shall be late for the wrestling,' said Ezinma to her mother.

'They will not begin until the sun goes down.'

'But they are beating the drums.'

'Yes. The drums begin at noon but the wrestling waits until the sun begins to sink. Go and see if your father has brought out yams for the afternoon.'

'He has. Nwoye's mother is already cooking.'

'Go and bring our own, then. We must cook quickly or we shall be late for the wrestling.'

Ezinma ran in the direction of the barn and brought back two yams from the dwarf wall.

Ekwefi peeled the yams quickly. The troublesome nanny-goat sniffed about, eating the peelings. She cut the yams into small pieces and began to prepare a pottage, using some of the chicken.

At that moment they heard someone crying just outside their compound. It was very much like Obiageli, Nwoye's sister.

'Is that not Obiageli weeping?' Ekwefi called across the yard to Nwoye's mother.

'Yes,' she replied. 'She must have broken her water-pot.'

The weeping was now quite close and soon the children filed in, carrying on their heads various sizes of pots suitable for their years. Ikemefuna came first with the biggest pot, closely followed by Nwoye and his two younger brothers. Obiageli brought up the rear, her face streaming with tears. In her hand was the cloth pad on which the pot should have rested on her head.

'What happened?' her mother asked, and Obiageli told her mournful story. Her mother consoled her and promised to buy her another pot.

Nwoye's younger brothers were about to tell their mother the true story of the accident when Ikemefuna looked at them sternly and they held their peace. The fact was that Obiageli had been making *inyanga* with her pot. She had balanced it on her head, folded her arms in front of her and began to sway her waist like a grown-up young lady. When the pot fell down and broke she burst out laughing. She only began to weep when they got near the iroko tree outside their compound.

The drums were still beating, persistent and unchanging. Their sound was no longer a separate thing from the living village. It was like the pulsation of its heart. It throbbed in the air, in the sunshine, and even in the trees, and filled the village with excitement.

Ekwefi ladled her husband's share of the pottage into a bowl and covered it. Ezinma took it to him in his *obi*.

Okonkwo was sitting on a goatskin already eating his first wife's meal. Obiageli, who had brought it from her mother's hut, sat on the floor waiting for him to finish. Ezinma placed her mother's dish before him and sat with Obiageli.

'Sit like a woman!' Okonkwo shouted at her. Ezinma brought her two legs together and stretched them in front of her.

'Father, will you go to see the wrestling?' Ezinma asked after a suitable interval.

'Yes,' he answered. 'Will you go?'

'Yes.' And after a pause she said: 'Can I bring your chair for you?'

'No, that is a boy's job.' Okonkwo was specially fond of Ezinma. She looked very much like her mother, who was once the village beauty. But his fondness only showed on very rare occasions.

'Obiageli broke her pot today,' Ezinma said.

'Yes, she has told me about it,' Okonkwo said between mouthfuls.

'Father,' said Obiageli, 'people should not talk when they are eating or pepper may go down the wrong way.'

'That is very true. Do you hear that, Ezinma? You are older than Obiageli but she has more sense.'

He uncovered his second wife's dish and began to eat from it. Obiageli took the first dish and returned to her mother's hut. And then Nkechi came in, bringing the third dish. Nkechi was the daughter of Okonkwo's third wife.

In the distance the drums continued to beat.

CHAPTER SIX

The whole village turned out on the *ilo*, men, women and children. They stood round in a huge circle leaving the centre of the playground free. The elders and grandees of the village sat on their own stools brought there by their young sons or slaves. Okonkwo was among them. All others stood except those who came early enough to secure places on the few stands which had been built by placing smooth logs on forked pillars.

The wrestlers were not there yet and the drummers held the field. They too sat just in front of the huge circle of spectators, facing the elders. Behind them was the big and ancient silk-cotton tree which was sacred. Spirits of good children lived in that tree waiting to be born. On ordinary days young women who desired children came to sit under its shade.

There were seven drums and they were arranged according to their sizes in a long wooden basket. Three men beat them with sticks, working feverishly from one drum to another. They were possessed by the spirit of the drums.

The young men who kept order on these occasions dashed about, consulting among themselves and with the leaders of the two wrestling teams, who were still outside the circle, behind the crowd. Once in a while two young men carrying palm fronds ran round the circle and kept the crowd back by beating the ground in front of them or, if they were stubborn, their legs and feet.

At last the two teams danced into the circle and the crowd roared and clapped. The drums rose to a frenzy. The people surged forwards. The young men who kept order flew around, waving their palm fronds. Old men nodded to the beat of the drums and remembered the days when they wrestled to its intoxicating rhythm.

The contest began with boys of fifteen or sixteen. There were only three such boys in each team. They were not the real wrestlers; they merely set the scene. Within a short time the first two bouts were over. But the third created a big sensation even among the elders who did not usually show their excitement so openly. It was as quick as the other two, perhaps even quicker. But very few people had ever seen that kind of wrestling before. As soon as the two boys closed in, one of them did something which no one could describe because it had been as quick as a flash. And the other boy was flat on his back. The crowd roared and clapped and for a while drowned the frenzied drums. Okonkwo sprang to his feet and quickly sat down again. Three young men from the victorious boy's team ran forward, carried him shoulder-high and danced through the cheering crowd. Everybody soon knew who the boy was. His name was Maduka, the son of Obierika.

The drummers stopped for a brief rest before the real matches. Their bodies shone with sweat, and they took up fans and began to fan themselves. They also drank water from small pots and ate kola nuts. They became ordinary human beings again, talking and laughing among themselves and with others who stood near them. The air, which had been stretched taut with excitement, relaxed again. It was as if water had been poured on the tightened skin of a drum. Many people looked around, perhaps for the first time, and saw those who stood or sat next to them.

'I did not know it was you,' Ekwefi said to the woman who had stood shoulder to shoulder with her since the beginning of the matches.

'I do not blame you,' said the woman. 'I have never seen such a large crowd of people. Is it true that Okonkwo nearly killed you with his gun?'

'It is true indeed, my dear friend. I cannot yet find a mouth with which to tell the story.'

'Your *chi* is very much awake, my friend. And how is my daughter, Ezinma?'

'She has been very well for some time now. Perhaps she has come to stay.'

'I think she has. How old is she now?'

'She is about ten years old.'

'I think she will stay. They usually stay if they do not die before the age of six.'

'I pray she stays,' said Ekwefi with a heavy sigh.

The woman with whom she talked was called Chielo. She was the priestess of Agbala, the Oracle of the Hills and the Caves. In ordinary life Chielo was a widow with two children. She was very friendly with Ekwefi and they shared a common shed in the market. She was particularly fond of Ekwefi's only daughter, Ezinma, whom she called 'my daughter'. Quite often she bought bean-cakes and gave Ekwefi some to take home to Ezinma. Anyone seeing Chielo in ordinary life would hardly believe she was the same person who prophesied when the spirit of Agbala was upon her.

The drummers took up their sticks again and the air shivered and grew tense like a tightened bow.

The two teams were ranged facing each other across the clear space. A young man from one team danced across the centre to the other side and pointed at whomever he wanted to fight. They danced back to the centre together and then closed in.

There were twelve men on each side and the challenge went from one side to the other. Two judges walked around the wrestlers and when they thought they were equally matched, stopped them. Five matches ended in this way. But the really exciting moments were when a man was thrown. The huge voice of the crowd then rose to the sky and in every direction. It was even heard in the surrounding villages.

The last match was between the leaders of the teams. They were among the best wrestlers in all the nine villages. The crowd wondered who would throw the other this year. Some said Okafo was the better man; others said he was not the equal of Ikezue. Last year neither of them had thrown the other even though the judges had allowed the contest to go on longer than was the custom. They had the same style and one saw the other's plans beforehand. It might happen again this year.

Dusk was already approaching when their contest began. The drums went mad and the crowds also. They surged forward as the two young men danced into the circle. The palm fronds were helpless in keeping them back.

Ikezue held out his right hand. Okafo seized it, and they closed in. It was a fierce contest. Ikezue strove to dig in his right heel behind Okafo so as to pitch him backwards in the clever *ege* style. But the one knew what the other was thinking. The crowd had surrounded and swallowed up the drummers, whose frantic rhythm was no longer a mere disembodied sound but the very heartbeat of the people.

The wrestlers were now almost still in each other's grip. The muscles on their arms and their thighs and on their backs stood out and twitched. It looked like an equal match. The two judges were already moving forward to separate them when Ikezue, now desperate, went down quickly on one knee in an attempt to fling his man backwards over his head. It was a sad miscalculation. Quick as the lightning of Amadiora, Okafo raised his right leg and swung it over his rival's head. The crowd burst into a thunderous roar. Okafo was swept off his feet by his supporters and carried home shoulder-high. They sang his praise and the young women clapped their hands:

> Who will wrestle for our village?
>   Okafo will wrestle for our village.
> Has he thrown a hundred men?
>   He has thrown four hundred men.
> Has he thrown a hundred Cats?
>   He has thrown four hundred Cats.
> Then send him word to fight for us.

CHAPTER SEVEN

For three years Ikemefuna lived in Okonkwo's household and the elders of Umuofia seemed to have forgotten about him. He grew rapidly like a yam tendril in the rainy season, and was full of the sap of life. He had become wholly absorbed into his new family. He was like an elder brother to Nwoye, and from the very first seemed to have kindled a new fire in the younger boy. He made him feel grown-up; and they no longer spent the evenings in mother's hut while she cooked, but now sat with Okonkwo in his *obi*, or watched him as he tapped his palm tree for the evening wine. Nothing pleased Nwoye now more than to be sent for by his mother or another of his father's wives to do one of those difficult and masculine tasks in the home, like splitting wood, or pounding food. On receiving such a message through a younger brother or sister, Nwoye would feign annoyance and grumble aloud about women and their troubles.

Okonkwo was inwardly pleased at his son's development, and he knew it was due to Ikemefuna. He wanted Nwoye to grow into a tough young man capable of ruling his father's household when he was dead and gone to join the ancestors. He wanted him to be a prosperous man, having enough in his barn to feed the ancestors with regular sacrifices. And so he was always happy when he heard him grumbling about women. That showed that in time he would be able to control his women-folk. No matter how prosperous a man was, if he was unable to rule his women and his children (and especially his women) he was not really a man. He was like the man in the song who had ten and one wives and not enough soup for his foo-foo.

So Okonkwo encouraged the boys to sit with him in his *obi*, and he told them stories of the land – masculine stories of violence and bloodshed. Nwoye knew that it was right to be masculine and to be violent, but somehow he still preferred the stories that his mother used to tell, and which she no doubt still told to her younger children – stories of the tortoise and his wily ways, and of the bird eneke-nti-oba who challenged the whole world to a wrestling contest and was finally thrown by the cat. He remembered the story she often told of the quarrel between Earth and Sky long ago, and how Sky withheld rain for seven years, until crops withered and the dead could not be buried because the hoes broke on the stony Earth. At last Vulture was sent to plead with Sky, and to soften his heart with a song of the suffering of the sons of men. Whenever Nwoye's mother sang this song he felt carried away to the distant scene in the sky where Vulture, Earth's emissary, sang for mercy. At last Sky was moved to pity, and he gave to Vulture rain wrapped in leaves of coco-yam. But as he flew home his long talon pierced the leaves and the rain fell as it had never fallen before. And so heavily did it rain on Vulture that he did not return to deliver his message but flew to a distant land, from where he had espied a fire. And when he got there he found it was a man making a sacrifice. He warmed himself in the fire and ate the entrails.

That was the kind of story that Nwoye loved. But he now knew that they were for foolish women and children, and he knew that his father wanted him to be a man. And so he feigned that he no longer cared for women's stories. And when he did this he saw that his father was pleased, and no longer rebuked him or beat him. So Nwoye and Ikemefuna would listen to Okonkwo's stories about tribal wars or how, years ago, he had stalked his victim, overpowered him and obtained his first human head. And as he told them of the past they sat in darkness or the dim glow of logs, waiting for the women to finish their cooking. When they finished, each brought her bowl of foo-foo and bowl of soup to her husband. An oil lamp was lit and Okonkwo tasted from each bowl, and then passed two shares to Nwoye and Ikemefuna.

In this way the moons and the seasons passed. And then the locusts came. It had not happened for many a long year. The elders said locusts came once in a generation, reappeared every year for seven years and then disappeared for another lifetime. They went back to their caves in a distant land, where they were guarded by a race of stunted men. And then after another lifetime these men opened the caves again and the locusts came to Umuofia.

They came in the cold harmattan season after the harvests had been gathered, and ate up all the wild grass in the fields.

Okonkwo and the two boys were working on the red outer walls of the compound. This was one of the lighter tasks of the after-harvest season. A new cover of thick palm branches and palm leaves was set on the walls to protect them from the next rainy season. Okonkwo worked on the outside of the wall and the boys worked from within. There were little holes from one side to the other in the upper levels of the wall, and through these Okonkwo passed the rope, or *tie-tie*, to the boys and they passed it round the wooden stays and then back to him; and in this way the cover was strengthened on the wall.

The women had gone to the bush to collect firewood, and the little children to visit their playmates in the neighbouring compounds. The harmattan was in the air and seemed to distil a hazy feeling of sleep on the world. Okonkwo and the boys worked in complete silence, which was only broken when a new palm frond was lifted on to the wall or when a busy hen moved dry leaves about in her ceaseless search for food.

And then quite suddenly a shadow fell on the world, and the sun seemed hidden behind a thick cloud. Okonkwo looked up from his work and wondered if it was going to rain at such an unlikely time of the year. But almost immediately a shout of joy broke out in all directions, and Umuofia, which had dozed in the noonday haze, broke into life and activity.

'Locusts are descending,' was joyfully chanted everywhere, and men, women and children left their work or their play and ran into the open to see the unfamiliar sight. The locusts had not come for many, many years, and only the old people had seen them before.

At first, a fairly small swarm came. They were the harbingers sent to survey the land. And then appeared on the horizon a slowly-moving mass like a boundless sheet of black cloud drifting towards Umuofia. Soon it covered half the sky, and the solid mass was now broken by tiny eyes of light like shining stardust. It was a tremendous sight, full of power and beauty.

Everyone was now about, talking excitedly and praying that the locusts should camp in Umuofia for the night. For although locusts had not visited Umuofia for many years, everybody knew by instinct that they were very good to eat. And at last the locusts did descend. They settled on every tree and on every blade of grass; they settled on the roofs and covered the bare ground. Mighty tree branches broke away under them, and the whole country became the brown-earth colour of the vast, hungry swarm.

Many people went out with baskets to try to catch them, but the elders counselled patience till nightfall. And they were right. The locusts settled in the bushes for the night and their wings became wet with dew. Then all Umuofia turned out in spite of the cold harmattan, and everyone filled his bags and pots with locusts. The next morning they were roasted in clay pots and then spread in the sun until they became dry and brittle. And for many days this rare food was eaten with solid palm oil.

Okonkwo sat in his *obi* crunching happily with Ikemefuna and Nwoye, and drinking palm wine copiously, when Ogbuefi Ezeudu came in. Ezeudu was the oldest man in this quarter of Umuofia. He had been a great and fearless warrior in his time, and was now accorded great respect in all the clan. He refused to join in the meal, and asked Okonkwo to have a word with him outside. And so they walked out together, the old man supporting himself with his stick. When they were out of earshot, he said to Okonkwo:

'That boy calls you father. Do not bear a hand in his death.' Okonkwo was surprised, and was about to say something when the old man continued:

'Yes, Umuofia has decided to kill him. The Oracle of the Hills and the Caves has pronounced it. They will take him outside Umuofia as is the custom, and kill him there. But I want you to have nothing to do with it. He calls you his father.'

The next day a group of elders from all the nine villages of

Umuofia came to Okonkwo's house early in the morning, and before they began to speak in low tones Nwoye and Ikemefuna were sent out. They did not stay very long, but when they went away Okonkwo sat still for a very long time supporting his chin in his palms. Later in the day he called Ikemefuna and told him that he was to be taken home the next day. Nwoye overheard it and burst into tears, whereupon his father beat him heavily. As for Ikemefuna, he was at a loss. His own home had gradually become very faint and distant. He still missed his mother and sister and would be very glad to see them. But somehow he knew he was not going to see them. He remembered once when men had talked in low tones with his father; and it seemed now as if it was happening all over again.

Later, Nwoye went to his mother's hut and told her that Ikemefuna was going home. She immediately dropped the pestle with which she was grinding pepper, folded her arms across her breast and sighed, 'Poor child'.

The next day, the men returned with a pot of wine. They were all fully dressed as if they were going to a big clan meeting or to pay a visit to a neighbouring village. They passed their cloths under the right armpit, and hung their goatskin bags and sheathed matchets over their left shoulders. Okonkwo got ready quickly and the party set out with Ikemefuna carrying the pot of wine. A deathly silence descended on Okonkwo's compound. Even the very little children seemed to know. Throughout that day Nwoye sat in his mother's hut and tears stood in his eyes.

At the beginning of their journey the men of Umuofia talked and laughed about the locusts, about their women, and about some effeminate men who had refused to come with them. But as they drew near to the outskirts of Umuofia silence fell upon them too.

The sun rose slowly to the centre of the sky, and the dry, sandy footway began to throw up the heat that lay buried in it. Some birds chirruped in the forests around. The men trod dry leaves on the sand. All else was silent. Then from the distance came the faint beating of the *ekwe*. It rose and faded with the wind – a peaceful dance from a distant clan.

'It is an *ozo* dance,' the men said among themselves. But no one was sure where it was coming from. Some said Ezimili, others Abame or Aninta. They argued for a short while and fell into silence again, and the elusive dance rose and fell with the wind. Somewhere a man was taking one of the titles of his clan, with music and dancing and a great feast.

The footway had now become a narrow line in the heart of the forest. The short trees and sparse undergrowth which surrounded the men's village began to give way to giant trees and climbers which perhaps had stood from the beginning of things, untouched by the axe and the bushfire. The sun breaking through their leaves and branches threw a pattern of light and shade on the sandy footway.

Ikemefuna heard a whisper close behind him and turned round sharply. The man who had whispered now called out aloud, urging the others to hurry up.

'We still have a long way to go,' he said. Then he and another man went before Ikemefuna and set a faster pace.

Thus the men of Umuofia pursued their way, armed with sheathed matchets, and Ikemefuna, carrying a pot of palm wine on his head, walked in their midst. Although he had felt uneasy at first, he was not afraid now. Okonkwo walked behind him. He could hardly imagine that Okonkwo was not his real father. He had never been fond of his real father, and at the end of three years he had become very distant indeed. But his mother and his three-year-old sister . . . of course she would not be three now, but six. Would he recognize her now? She must have grown quite big. How his mother would weep for joy, and thank Okonkwo for having looked after him so well and for bringing him back. She would want to hear everything that had happened to him in all these years. Could he remember them all? He would tell her about Nwoye and his mother, and about the locusts . . . Then quite suddenly a thought came upon him. His mother might be dead. He tried in vain to force the thought out of his mind. Then he tried to settle the matter the way he used to settle such matters when he was a little boy. He still remembered the song:

Eze elina, elina!
  Sala
Eze ilikwa ya
Ikwaba akwa oligholi
Ebe Danda nechi eze
Ebe Uzuzu nete egwu
  Sala

He sang it in his mind, and walked to its beat. If the song ended on his right foot, his mother was alive. If it ended on his left, she was dead. No, not dead, but ill. It ended on the right. She was alive and well. He sang the song again, and it ended on the left. But the second time did not count. The first voice gets to Chukwu, or God's house. That was a favourite saying of children. Ikemefuna felt like a child once more. It must be the thought of going home to his mother.

One of the men behind him cleared his throat. Ikemefuna looked back, and the man growled at him to go on and not stand looking back. The way he said it sent cold fear down Ikemefuna's back. His hands trembled vaguely on the black pot he carried. Why had Okonkwo withdrawn to the rear? Ikemefuna felt his legs melting under him. And he was afraid to look back.

As the man who had cleared his throat drew up and raised his matchet, Okonkwo looked away. He heard the blow. The pot fell and broke in the sand. He heard Ikemefuna cry, 'My father, they have killed me!' as he ran towards him. Dazed with fear, Okonkwo drew his matchet and cut him down. He was afraid of being thought weak.

As soon as his father walked in, that night, Nwoye knew that Ikemefuna had been killed, and something seemed to give way inside him, like the snapping of a tightened bow. He did not cry. He just hung limp. He had had the same kind of feeling not long ago, during the last harvest season. Every child loved the harvest season. Those who were big enough to carry even a few yams in a tiny basket went with grown-ups to the farm. And if they could not help in digging up the yams, they could gather firewood together for roasting the ones that would be eaten there on the farm.

This roasted yam soaked in red palm oil and eaten in the open farm was sweeter than any meal at home. It was after such a day at the farm during the last harvest that Nwoye had felt for the first time a snapping inside him like the one he now felt. They were returning home with baskets of yams from a distant farm across the stream when they had heard the voice of an infant crying in the thick forest. A sudden hush had fallen on the women, who had been talking, and they had quickened their steps. Nwoye had heard that twins were put in earthenware pots and thrown away in the forest, but he had never yet come across them. A vague chill had descended on him and his head had seemed to swell, like a solitary walker at night who passes an evil spirit on the way. Then something had given way inside him. It descended on him again, this feeling, when his father walked in, that night after killing Ikemefuna.

CHAPTER EIGHT

Okonkwo did not taste any food for two days after the death of Ikemefuna. He drank palm wine from morning till night, and his eyes were red and fierce like the eyes of a rat when it was caught by the tail and dashed against the floor. He called his son, Nwoye, to sit with him in his *obi*. But the boy was afraid of him and slipped out of the hut as soon as he noticed him dozing.

He did not sleep at night. He tried not to think about Ikemefuna, but the more he tried the more he thought about him. Once he got up from bed and walked about his compound. But he was so weak that his legs could hardly carry him. He felt like a drunken giant walking with the limbs of a mosquito. Now and then a cold shiver descended on his head and spread down his body.

On the third day he asked his second wife, Ekwefi, to roast plantains for him. She prepared it the way he liked – with slices of oil-bean and fish.

'You have not eaten for two days,' said his daughter Ezinma when she brought the food to him. 'So you must finish this.' She sat down and stretched her legs in front of her. Okonkwo ate the food absent-mindedly. 'She should have been a boy,' he thought as he looked at his ten-year-old daughter. He passed her a piece of fish.

'Go and bring me some cold water,' he said. Ezinma rushed out of the hut, chewing the fish, and soon returned with a bowl of cool water from the earthen pot in her mother's hut.

Okonkwo took the bowl from her and gulped the water down.

He ate a few more pieces of plantain and pushed the dish aside.

'Bring me my bag,' he asked, and Ezinma brought his goatskin bag from the far end of the hut. He searched in it for his snuff-bottle. It was a deep bag and took almost the whole length of his arm. It contained other things apart from his snuff-bottle. There was a drinking horn in it, and also a drinking gourd, and they knocked against each other as he searched. When he brought out the snuff-bottle he tapped it a few times against his kneecap before taking out some snuff on the palm of his left hand. Then he remembered that he had not taken out his snuff-spoon. He searched his bag again and brought out a small, flat, ivory spoon, with which he carried the brown snuff to his nostrils.

Ezinma took the dish in one hand and the empty water bowl in the other and went back to her mother's hut. 'She should have been a boy,' Okonkwo said to himself again. His mind went back to Ikemefuna and he shivered. If only he could find some work to do he would be able to forget. But it was the season of rest between the harvest and the next planting season. The only work that men did at this time was covering the walls of their compound with new palm fronds. And Okonkwo had already done that. He had finished it on the very day the locusts came, when he had worked on one side of the wall and Ikemefuna and Nwoye on the other.

'When did you become a shivering old woman?' Okonkwo asked himself. 'You are known in all the nine villages for your valour in war. How can a man who has killed five men in battle fall to pieces because he has added a boy to their number? Okonkwo, you have become a woman indeed.'

He sprang to his feet, hung his goatskin bag on his shoulder and went to visit his friend, Obierika.

Obierika was sitting outside under the shade of an orange tree making thatches from leaves of the raffia palm. He exchanged greetings with Okonkwo and led the way into his *obi*.

'I was coming over to see you as soon as I finished that thatch,' he said, rubbing off the grains of sand that clung to his thighs.

'Is it well?' Okonkwo asked.

'Yes,' replied Obierika. 'My daughter's suitor is coming today and I hope we will clinch the matter of the bride-price. I want you to be there.'

Just then Obierika's son's, Maduka, came into the *obi* from outside, greeted Okonkwo and turned towards the compound.

'Come and shake hands with me,' Okonkwo said to the lad. 'Your wrestling the other day gave me much happiness.' The boy smiled, shook hands with Okonkwo and went into the compound.

'He will do great things,' Okonkwo said. 'If I had a son like him I should be happy. I am worried about Nwoye. A bowl of pounded yams can throw him in a wrestling match. His two younger brothers are more promising. But I can tell you, Obierika, that my children do not resemble me. Where are the young suckers that will grow when the old banana tree dies? If Ezinma had been a boy I would have been happier. She has the right spirit.'

'You worry yourself for nothing,' said Obierika. 'The children are still very young.'

'Nwoye is old enough to impregnate a woman. At his age I was already fending for myself. No, my friend, he is not too young. A chick that will grow into a cock can be spotted the very day it hatches. I have done my best to make Nwoye grow into a man, but there is too much of his mother in him.'

'Too much of his grandfather,' Obeirika thought, but he did not say it. The same thought also came to Okonkwo's mind. But he had long learnt how to lay that ghost. Whenever the thought of his father's weakness and failure troubled him he expelled it by thinking about his own strength and success. And so he did now. His mind went to his latest show of manliness.

'I cannot understand why you refused to come with us to kill that boy,' he asked Obierika.

'Because I did not want to,' Obierika replied sharply. 'I had something better to do.'

'You sound as if you question the authority and the decision of the Oracle, who said he should die.'

'I do not. Why should I? But the Oracle did not ask me to carry out its decision.'

'But someone had to do it. If we were all afraid of blood, it would not be done. And what do you think the Oracle would do then?'

'You know very well, Okonkwo, that I am not afraid of blood; and if anyone tells you that I am, he is telling a lie. And let me tell you one thing, my friend. If I were you I would have stayed at home. What you have done will not please the Earth. It is the kind of action for which the goddess wipes out whole families.'

'The Earth cannot punish me for obeying her messenger,' Okonkwo said. 'A child's fingers are not scalded by a piece of hot yam which its mother puts into its palm.'

'That is true,' Obierika agreed. 'But if the Oracle said that my son should be killed I would neither dispute it nor be the one to do it.'

They would have gone on arguing had Ofoedu not come in just then. It was clear from his twinkling eyes that he had important news. But it would be impolite to rush him. Obierika offered him a lobe of the kola nut he had broken with Okonkwo. Ofoedu ate slowly and talked about the locusts. When he finished his kola nut he said:

'The things that happen these days are very strange.'

'What has happened?' asked Okonkwo.

'Do you know Ogbuefi Ndulue?' Ofoedu asked.

'Ogbuefi Ndulue of Ire village,' Okonkwo and Obierika said together.

'He died this morning,' said Ofoedu.

'That is not strange. He was the oldest man in Ire,' said Obierika.

'You are right,' Ofoedu agreed. 'But you ought to ask why the drum has not been beaten to tell Umuofia of his death.'

'Why?' asked Obierika and Okonkwo together.

'That is the strange part of it. You know his first wife who walks with a stick?'

'Yes. She is called Ozoemena.'

'That is so,' said Ofoedu. 'Ozoemena was, as you know, too old to attend Ndulue during his illness. His younger wives did that. When he died this morning, one of these women went to Ozoemena's hut and told her. She rose from her mat, took her stick and walked over to the *obi*. She knelt on her knees and hands at the threshold and called her husband, who was laid on a mat. "Ogbuefi Ndulue," she called, three times, and went back to her

63

hut. When the youngest wife went to call her again to be present at the washing of the body, she found her lying on the mat, dead.'

'That is very strange indeed,' said Okonkwo. 'They will put off Ndulue's funeral until his wife has been buried.'

'That is why the drum has not been beaten to tell Umuofia.'

'It was always said that Ndulue and Ozoemena had one mind,' said Obierika. 'I remember when I was a young boy there was a song about them. He could not do anything without telling her.'

'I did not know that,' said Okonkwo. 'I thought he was a strong man in his youth.'

'He was indeed,' said Ofoedu.

Okonkwo shook his head doubtfully.

'He led Umuofia to war in those days,' said Obierika.

Okonkwo was beginning to feel like his old self again. All that he required was something to occupy his mind. If he had killed Ikemefuna during the busy planting season or harvesting it would not have been so bad; his mind would have been centred on his work. Okonkwo was not a man of thought but of action. But in the absence of work, talking was the next best.

Soon after Ofoedu left, Okonkwo took up his goatskin bag to go.

'I must go home to tap my palm trees for the afternoon,' he said.

'Who taps your tall trees for you?' asked Obierika.

'Umezulike,' replied Okonkwo.

'Sometimes I wish I had not taken the *ozo* title,' said Obierika. 'It wounds my heart to see these young men killing palm trees in the name of tapping.'

'It is so indeed,' Okonkwo agreed. 'But the law of the land must be obeyed.'

'I don't know how we got that law,' said Obierika. 'In many other clans a man of title is not forbidden to climb the palm tree. Here we say we cannot climb the tall tree but he can tap the short ones standing on the ground. It is like Dimaragana, who would not lend his knife for cutting up dog-meat because the dog was taboo to him, but offered to use his teeth.'

'I think it is good that our clan holds the *ozo* title in high esteem,' said Okonkwo. 'In those other clans you speak of, *ozo* is so low that every beggar takes it.'

'I was only speaking in jest,' said Obierika. 'In Abame and Aninta the title is worth less than two cowries. Every man wears the thread of title on his ankle, and does not lose it even if he steals.'

'They have indeed soiled the name of *ozo*,' said Okonkwo as he rose to go.

'It will not be very long now before my in-laws come,' said Obierika.

'I shall return very soon,' said Okonkwo, looking at the position of the sun.

There were seven men in Obierika's hut when Okonkwo returned. The suitor was a young man of about twenty-five, and with him were his father and uncle. On Obierika's side were his two elder brothers and Maduka, his sixteen-year-old son.

'Ask Akueke's mother to send us some kola nuts,' said Obierika to his son. Maduka vanished into the compound like lightning. The conversation at once centred on him, and everybody agreed that he was as sharp as a razor.

'I sometimes think he is too sharp,' said Obierika, somewhat indulgently. 'He hardly ever walks. He is always in a hurry. If you are sending him on an errand he flies away before he has heard half of the message.'

'You were very much like that yourself,' said his eldest brother. 'As our people say, "When mother-cow is chewing grass its young ones watch its mouth". Maduka has been watching your mouth.'

As he was speaking the boy returned, followed by Akueke, his half-sister, carrying a wooden dish with three kola nuts and alligator pepper. She gave the dish to her father's eldest brother and then shook hands, very shyly, with her suitor and his relatives. She was about sixteen and just ripe for marriage. Her suitor and his relatives surveyed her young body with expert eyes as if to assure themselves that she was beautiful and ripe.

She wore a coiffure which was done up into a crest in the middle of the head. Cam wood was rubbed lightly into her skin, and all over her body were black patterns drawn with *uli*. She wore a black necklace which hung down in three coils just above her full, succulent breasts. On her arms were red and yellow bangles, and on her waist were four or five rows of *jigida*, or waist-beads.

When she had shaken hands, or rather held out her hand to be shaken, she returned to her mother's hut to help with the cooking.

'Remove your *jigida* first,' her mother warned as she moved near the fireplace to bring the pestle resting against the wall. 'Every day I tell you that *jigida* and fire are not friends. But you will never hear. You grew your ears for decoration, not for hearing. One of these days your *jigida* will catch fire on your waist, and then you will know.'

Akueke moved to the other end of the hut and began to remove the waist-beads. It had to be done slowly and carefully, taking each string separately, else it would break and the thousand tiny rings would have to be strung together again. She rubbed each string downwards with her palms until it passed the buttocks and slipped down to the floor around her feet.

The men in the *obi* had already begun to drink the palm wine which Akueke's suitor had brought. It was a very good wine and powerful, for in spite of the palm fruit hung across the mouth of the pot to restrain the lively liquor, white foam rose and spilled over.

'That wine is the work of a good tapper,' said Okonkwo.

The young suitor, whose name was Ibe, smiled broadly and said to his father: 'Do you hear that?' He then said to the others: 'He will never admit that I am a good tapper.'

'He tapped three of my best palm trees to death,' said his father, Ukegbu.

'That was about five years ago,' said Ibe, who had begun to pour out the wine, 'before I learnt how to tap.' He filled the first horn and gave to his father. Then he poured out for the others. Okonkwo brought out his big horn from the goatskin bag, blew into it to remove any dust that might be there, and gave it to Ibe to fill.

As the men drank, they talked about everything except the thing for which they had gathered. It was only after the pot had been emptied that the suitor's father cleared his voice and announced the object of their visit.

Obierika then presented to him a small bundle of short broom-sticks. Ukegbu counted them.

'They are thirty?' he asked.

Obierika nodded in agreement.

'We are at last getting somewhere,' Ukegbu said, and then turning to his brother and his son he said: 'Let us go out and whisper together.' The three rose and went outside. When they returned Ukegbu handed the bundle of sticks back to Obierika. He counted them; instead of thirty there were now only fifteen. He passed them over to his eldest brother, Machi, who also counted them and said:

'We had not thought to go below thirty. But as the dog said, "If I fall down for you and you fall down for me, it is play". Marriage should be a play and not a fight; so we are falling down again.' He then added ten sticks to the fifteen and gave the bundle to Ukegbu.

In this way Akueke's bride-price was finally settled at twenty bags of cowries. It was already dusk when the two parties came to this agreement.

'Go and tell Akueke's mother that we have finished,' Obierika said to his son, Maduka. Almost immediately the woman came in with a big bowl of foo-foo. Obierika's second wife followed with a pot of soup, and Maduka brought in a pot of palm wine.

As the men ate and drank palm wine they talked about the customs of their neighbours.

'It was only this morning,' said Obierika, 'that Okonkwo and I were talking about Abame and Aninta, where titled men climb trees and pound foo-foo for their wives.'

'All their customs are upside-down. They do not decide bride-price as we do, with sticks. They haggle and bargain as if they were buying a goat or a cow in the market.'

'That is very bad,' said Obierika's eldest brother. 'But what is good in one place is bad in another place. In Umunso they do not bargain at all, not even with broomsticks. The suitor just goes on bringing bags of cowries until his in-laws tell him to stop. It is a bad custom because it always leads to a quarrel.'

'The world is large,' said Okonkwo. 'I have even heard that in some tribes a man's children belong to his wife and her family.'

'That cannot be,' said Machi. 'You might as well say that the woman lies on top of the man when they are making the children.'

'It is like the story of white men who, they say, are white like this piece of chalk,' said Obierika. He held up a piece of chalk, which every man kept in his *obi* and with which his guests drew lines on the floor before they ate kola nuts. 'And these white men, they say, have no toes.'

'And have you never seen them?' asked Machi.

'Have you?' asked Obierika.

'One of them passes here frequently,' said Machi. 'His name is Amadi.'

Those who knew Amadi laughed. He was a leper, and the polite name for leprosy was 'the white skin'.

CHAPTER NINE

For the first time in three nights, Okonkwo slept. He woke up once in the middle of the night and his mind went back to the past three days without making him feel uneasy. He began to wonder why he had felt uneasy at all. It was like a man wondering in broad daylight why a dream had appeared so terrible to him at night. He stretched himself and scratched his thigh where a mosquito had bitten him as he slept. Another one was wailing near his right ear. He slapped the ear and hoped he had killed it. Why do they always go for one's ears? When he was a child his mother had told him a story about it. But it was as silly as all women's stories. Mosquito, she had said, had asked Ear to marry him, whereupon Ear fell on the floor in uncontrollable laughter. 'How much longer do you think you will live?' she asked. 'You are already a skeleton.' Mosquito went away humiliated, and any time he passed her way he told Ear that he was still alive.

Okonkwo turned on his side and went back to sleep. He was roused in the morning by someone banging on his door.

'Who is that?' he growled. He knew it must be Ekwefi. Of his three wives Ekwefi was the only one who would have the audacity to bang on his door.

'Ezinma is dying,' came her voice, and all the tragedy and sorrow of her life were packed in those words.

Okonkwo sprang from his bed, pushed back the bolt on his door and ran into Ekwefi's hut.

Ezinma lay shivering on a mat beside a huge fire that her mother had kept burning all night.

'It is *iba*,' said Okonkwo as he took his matchet and went into the bush to collect the leaves and grasses and barks of trees that went into making the medicine for *iba*.

Ekwefi knelt beside the sick child, occasionally feeling with her palm the wet, burning forehead.

Ezinma was an only child and the centre of her mother's world. Very often it was Ezimna who had decided what food her mother should prepare. Ekwefi even gave her such delicacies as eggs, which children were rarely allowed to eat because such food tempted them to steal. One day as Ezimna was eating an egg Okonkwo had come in unexpectedly from his hut. He was greatly shocked and swore to beat Ekwefi if she dared to give the child eggs again. But it was impossible to refuse Ezinma anything. After her father's rebuke she developed an even keener appetite for eggs. And she enjoyed above all the secrecy in which she now ate them. Her mother always took her into their bedroom and shut the door.

Ezinma did not call her mother *Nne* like all children. She called her by her name, Ekwefi, as her father and other grown-up people did. The relationship between them was not only that of mother and child. There was something in it like the companionship of equals, which was strengthened by such little conspiracies as eating eggs in the bedroom.

Ekwefi had suffered a good deal in her life. She had borne ten children and nine of them had died in infancy, usually before the age of three. As she buried one child after another her sorrow gave way to despair and then to grim resignation. The birth of her children, which should be a woman's crowning glory, became for Ekwefi mere physical agony devoid of promise. The naming ceremony after seven market weeks became an empty ritual. Her deepening despair found expression in the names she gave her children. One of them was a pathetic cry, Onwumbiko – 'Death, I implore you'. But Death took no notice; Onwumbiko died in his fifteenth month. The next child was a girl, Ozoemena – 'May it not happen again'. She died in her eleventh month, and two others after her. Ekwefi then became defiant and called her next child Onwuma – 'Death may please himself'. And he did.

After the death of Ekwefi's second child, Okonkwo had gone to a medicine-man, who was also a diviner of the Afa Oracle, to inquire what was amiss. This man told him that the child was an *ogbanje*, one of those wicked children who, when they died, entered their mothers' wombs to be born again.

'When your wife becomes pregnant again,' he said, 'let her not sleep in her hut. Let her go and stay with her people. In that way she will elude her wicked tormentor and break its evil cycle of birth and death.'

Ekwefi did as she was asked. As soon as she became pregnant she went to live with her old mother in another village. It was there that her third child was born and circumcised on the eighth day. She did not return to Okonkwo's compound until three days before the naming ceremony. The child was called Onwumbiko.

Onwumbiko was not given proper burial when he died. Okonkwo had called in another medicine-man who was famous in the clan for his great knowledge about *ogbanje* children. His name was Okagbue Uyanwa. Okagbue was a very striking figure, tall, with a full beard and a bald head. He was light in complexion and his eyes were red and fiery. He always gnashed his teeth as he listened to those who came to consult him. He asked Okonkwo a few questions about the dead child. All the neighbours and relations who had come to mourn gathered round them.

'On what market-day was it born?' he asked

'*Oye*,' replied Okonkwo.

'And it died this morning?'

Okonkwo said yes, and only then realized for the first time that the child had died on the same market-day as it had been born. The neighbours and relations also saw the coincidence and said among themselves that it was very significant.

'Where do you sleep with your wife, in your *obi* or in her own hut?' asked the medicine-man.

'In her hut.'

'In future call her into your *obi*.'

The medicine-man then ordered that there should be no mourning for the dead child. He brought out a sharp razor from the goatskin bag slung from his left shoulder and began to mutilate the child. Then he took it away to bury in the Evil Forest, holding it by the ankle and dragging it on the ground behind him. After such treatment it would think twice before coming again, unless it was one of the stubborn ones who returned, carrying the stamp of their mutilation – a missing finger or perhaps a dark line where the medicine-man's razor had cut them.

By the time Onwumbiko died Ekwefi had become a very bitter woman. Her husband's first wife had already had three sons, all strong and healthy. When she had borne her third son in succession, Okonkwo had slaughtered a goat for her, as was the custom. Ekwefi had nothing but good wishes for her. But she had grown so bitter about her own *chi* that she could not rejoice with others over their good fortune. And so, on the day that Nwoye's mother celebrated the birth of her three sons with feasting and music, Ekwefi was the only person in the happy company who went about with a cloud on her brow. Her husband's wife took this for malevolence, as husbands' wives were wont to. How could she know that Ekwefi's bitterness did not flow outwards to others but inwards into her own soul; that she did not blame others for their good fortune but her own evil *chi* who denied her any?

At last Ezinma was born, and although ailing she seemed determined to live. At last Ekwefi accepted her, as she had accepted others – with listless resignation. But when she lived on to her fourth, fifth and sixth years, love returned once more to her mother, and, with love, anxiety. She determined to nurse her child to health, and she put all her being into it. She was rewarded by occasional spells of health during which Ezinma bubbled with energy like fresh palm wine. At such times she seemed beyond danger. But all of a sudden she would go down again. Everybody knew she was an *ogbanje*. These sudden bouts of sickness and health were typical of her kind. But she had lived so long that perhaps she had decided to stay. Some of them did become tired of their evil rounds of birth and death, or took pity on their mothers, and stayed. Ekwefi believed deep inside her that Ezinma had come to stay. She believed because it was that faith alone that gave her own life any kind of meaning. And this faith had been strengthened when a year or so ago a medicine-man had dug up Ezinma's *iyi-uwa*. Everyone knew then that she would live because her bond with the world of *ogbanje* had been broken. Ekwefi was reassured. But such was her anxiety for her daughter that she could not rid herself completely of her fear. And although she believed that the *iyi-uwa* which had been dug up was genuine, she could not ignore the fact that some really evil children sometimes misled people into digging up a specious one.

But Ezinma's *iyi-uwa* had looked real enough. It was a smooth pebble wrapped in a dirty rag. The man who dug it up was the same Okagbue who was famous in all the clan for his knowledge in these matters. Ezinma had not wanted to co-operate with him at first. But that was only to be expected. No *ogbanje* would yield her secrets easily, and most of them never did because they died too young – before they could be asked questions.

'Where did you bury your *iyi-uwa*?' she asked in return.

'You know what it is. You buried it in the ground somewhere so that you can die and return again to torment your mother.'

Ezinma looked at her mother, whose eyes, sad and pleading, were fixed on her.

'Answer the question at once,' roared Okonkwo, who stood beside her. All the family were there and some of the neighbours too.

'Leave her to me,' the medicine-man told Okonkwo in a cool, confident voice. He turned again to Ezinma. 'Where did you bury your *iyi-uwa*?'

'Where they bury children,' she replied, and the quiet spectators murmured to themselves.

'Come along then and show me the spot,' said the medicine-man.

The crowd set out with Ezinma leading the way and Okagbue following closely behind her. Okonkwo came next and Ekwefi followed him. When she came to the main road, Ezinma turned left as if she was going to the stream.

'But you said it was where they bury children?' asked the medicine-man.

'No,' said Ezinma, whose feeling of importance was manifest in her sprightly walk. She sometimes broke into a run and stopped again suddenly. The crowd followed her silently. Women and children returning from the stream with pots of water on their heads wondered what was happening until they saw Okagbue and guessed that it must be something to do with *ogbanje*. And they all knew Ekwefi and her daughter very well.

When she got to the big udala tree Ezinma turned left into the bush, and the crowd followed her. Because of her size she made her way through trees and creepers more quickly than her followers. The bush was alive with the tread of feet on dry leaves and sticks and the moving aside of tree branches. Ezinma went deeper and deeper and the crowd went with her. Then she suddenly turned round and began to walk back to the road. Everybody stood to let her pass and then filed after her.

'If you bring us all this way for nothing I shall beat sense into you,' Okonkwo threatened.

'I have told you to let her alone. I know how to deal with them,' said Okagbue.

Ezinma led the way back to the road, looked left and right and turned right. And so they arrived home again.

'Where did you bury your *iyi-uwa*?' asked Okagbue when Ezinma finally stopped outside her father's *obi*. Okagbue's voice was unchanged. It was quiet and confident.

'It is near that orange tree,' Ezinma said.

'And why did you not say so, you wicked daughter of Akalogoli?' Okonkwo swore furiously. The medicine-man ignored him.

'Come and show me the exact spot,' he said quietly to Ezinma.

'It is here,' she said when they got to the tree.

'Point at the spot with your finger,' said Okagbue.

'It is here,' said Ezinma touching the ground with her finger. Okonkwo stood by, rumbling like thunder in the rainy season.

'Bring me a hoe,' said Okagbue.

When Ekwefi brought the hoe, he had already put aside his goatskin bag and his big cloth and was in his underwear, a long and thin strip of cloth wound round the waist like a belt and then passed between the legs to be fastened to the belt behind. He immediately set to work digging a pit where Ezinma had indicated. The neighbours sat around watching the pit becoming deeper and deeper. The dark top-soil soon gave way to the bright-red earth with which women scrubbed the floor and walls of huts. Okagbue worked tirelessly and in silence, his back shining with perspiration. Okonkwo stood by the pit. He asked Okagbue to come up and rest while he took a hand. But Okagbue said he was not tired yet.

Ekwefi went into her hut to cook yams. Her husband had brought out more yams than usual because the medicine-man had to be fed. Ezinma went with her and helped in preparing the vegetables.

'There is too much green vegetable,' she said.

'Don't you see the pot is full of yams?' Ekwefi asked. 'And you know how leaves become smaller after cooking.'

'Yes,' said Ezinma, 'that was why the snake-lizard killed his mother.'

'Very true,' said Ekwefi.

'He gave his mother seven baskets of vegetables to cook and in the end there were only three. And so he killed her,' said Ezinma.

'That is not the end of the story.'

'Oho,' said Ezinma, 'I remember now. He brought another seven baskets and cooked them himself. And there were again only three. So he killed himself too.'

Outside the *obi* Okagbue and Okonkwo were digging the pit to find where Ezinma had buried her *iyi-uwa*. Neighbours sat around, watching. The pit was now so deep that they no longer saw the digger. They only saw the red earth he threw up mounting higher and higher. Okonkwo's son, Nwoye, stood near the edge of the pit because he wanted to take in all that happened.

Okagbue had again taken over the digging from Okonkwo. He worked, as usual, in silence. The neighbours and Okonkwo's wives were now talking. The children had lost interest and were playing.

Suddenly Okagbue sprang to the surface with the agility of a leopard.

'It is very near now,' he said. 'I have felt it.'

There was immediate excitement and those who were sitting jumped to their feet.

'Call your wife and child,' he said to Okonkwo. But Ekwefi and Ezinma had heard the noise and run out to see what it was.

Okagbue went back into the pit, which was now surrounded by

spectators. After a few more hoe-fuls of earth he struck the *iyi-uwa*. He raised it carefully with the hoe and threw it to the surface Some women ran away in fear when it was thrown. But they soon returned and everyone was gazing at the rag from a reasonable distance. Okagbue emerged and without saying a word or even looking at the spectators he went to his goatskin bag, took out two leaves and began to chew them. When he had swallowed them, he took up the rag with his left hand and began to untie it. And then the smooth, shiny pebble fell out. He picked it up.

'Is this yours?' he asked Ezinma.

'Yes,' she replied. All the women shouted with joy because Ekwefi's troubles were at last ended.

All this had happened more than a year ago and Ezinma had not been ill since. And then suddenly she had begun to shiver in the night. Ekwefi brought her to the fireplace, spread her mat on the floor and built a fire. But she had got worse and worse. As she knelt by her, feeling with her palm the wet, burning forehead, she prayed a thousand times. Although her husband's wives were saying that it was nothing more than *iba*, she did not hear them.

Okonkwo returned from the bush carrying on his left shoulder a large bundle of grasses and leaves, roots and barks of medicinal trees and shrubs. He went into Ekwefi's hut, put down his load and sat down.

'Get me a pot,' he said, 'and leave the child alone.'

Ekwefi went to bring the pot and Okonkwo selected the best from his bundle, in their due proportions, and cut them up. He put them in the pot and Ekwefi poured in some water.

'Is that enough?' she asked when she had poured in about half of the water in the bowl.

'A little more . . . I said a *little*. Are you deaf?' Okonkwo roared at her.

She set the pot on the fire and Okonkwo took up his matchet to return to his *obi*.

'You must watch the pot carefully,' he said as he went, 'and don't allow it to boil over. If it does its power will be gone.' He went away to his hut and Ekwefi began to tend the medicine pot almost as if it was itself a sick child. Her eyes went constantly from Ezinma to the boiling pot and back to Ezinma.

Okonkwo returned when he felt the medicine had cooked long enough. He looked it over and said it was done.

'Bring a low stool for Ezinma,' he said, 'and a thick mat.'

He took down the pot from the fire and placed it in front of the stool. He then roused Ezinma and placed her on the stool, astride the steaming pot. The thick mat was thrown over both. Ezinma struggled to escape from the choking overpowering steam, but she was held down. She started to cry.

When the mat was at last removed she was drenched in perspiration. Ekwefi mopped her with a piece of cloth and she lay down on a dry mat and was soon asleep.

CHAPTER TEN

Large crowds began to gather on the village *ilo* as soon as the edge had worn off the sun's heat and it was no longer painful on the body. Most communal ceremonies took place at that time of the day, so that even when it was said that a ceremony would begin 'after the midday meal' everyone understood that it would begin a long time later, when the sun's heat had softened.

It was clear from the way the crowd stood or sat that the ceremony was for men. There were many women, but they looked on from the fringe like outsiders. The titled men and elders sat on their stools waiting for the trials to begin. In front of them was a row of stools on which nobody sat. There were nine of them. Two little groups of people stood at a respectable distance beyond the stools. They faced the elders. There were three men in one group and three men and one woman in the other. The woman was Mgbafo and the three men with her were her brothers. In the other group were her husband, Uzowulu, and his relatives. Mgbafo and her brothers were as still as statues into whose faces the artist has moulded defiance. Uzowulu and his relative, on the other hand, were whispering together. It looked like whispering, but they were really talking at the top of their voices. Everybody in the crowd was talking. It was like the market. From a distance the noise was a deep rumble carried by the wind.

An iron gong sounded, setting up a wave of expectation in the crowd. Everyone looked in the direction of the *egwugwu* house. *Gome, gome, gome, gome* went the gong, and a powerful flute blew a high-pitched blast. Then came the voices of the *egwugwu*, guttural and awesome. The wave struck the women and children and there was a backward stampede. But it was momentary. They were already far enough where they stood and there was room for running away if any of the *egwugwu* should go towards them.

The drum sounded again and the flute blew. The *egwugwu* house was now a pandemonium of quavering voices: *Aru oyim de de de de dei!* filled the air as the spirits of the ancestors, just emerged from the earth, greeted themselves in their esoteric language. The *egwugwu* house into which they emerged faced the forest, away from the crowd, who saw only its back with the many-coloured patterns and drawings done by specially chosen women at regular intervals. These women never saw the inside of the hut. No woman ever did. They scrubbed and painted the outside walls under the supervision of men. If they imagined what was inside, they kept their imagination to themselves. No woman ever asked questions about the most powerful and the most secret cult in the clan.

Aru oyim de de de dei! flew around the dark, closed hut like tongues of fire. The ancestral spirits of the clan were abroad. The metal gong beat continuously now and the flute, shrill and powerful, floated on the chaos.

And then the *egwugwu* appeared. The women and children sent up a great shout and took to their heels. It was instinctive. A woman fled as soon as an *egwugwu* came in sight. And when, as on that day, nine of the greatest masked spirits in the clan came out together it was a terrifying spectacle. Even Mgbafo took to her heels and had to be restrained by her brothers.

Each of the nine *egwugwu* represented a village of the clan. Their leader was called Evil Forest. Smoke poured out of his head.

The nine villages of Umuofia had grown out of the nine sons of the first father of the clan. Evil Forest represented the village of Umeru, or the children of Eru, who was the eldest of the nine sons.

'*Umuofia kwenu!*' shouted the leading *egwugwu*, pushing the air with his raffia arms. The elders of the clan replied, '*Yaa!*'

'*Umuofia kwenu!*'

'*Yaa!*'

'*Umuofia kwenu!*'

'*Yaa!*'

Evil Forest then thrust the pointed end of his rattling staff into the earth. And it began to shake and rattle, like something agitating with a metallic life. He took the first of the empty stools and the eight other *egwugwu* began to sit in order of seniority after him.

Okonkwo's wives, and perhaps other women as well, might have noticed that the second *egwugwu* had the springy walk of Okonkwo. And they might also have noticed that Okonkwo was not among the titled men and elders who sat behind the row of *egwugwu*. But if they thought these things they kept them within themselves. The *egwugwu* with the springy walk was one of the dead fathers of the clan. He looked terrible with the smoked raffia body, a huge wooden face painted white except for the round hollow eyes and the charred teeth that were as big as a man's fingers. On his head were two powerful horns.

When all the *egwugwu* had sat down and the sound of the many tiny bells and rattles on their bodies had subsided, Evil Forest addressed the two groups of people facing them.

'Uzowulu's body, I salute you,' he said. Spirits always addressed humans as 'bodies'. Uzowulu bent down and touched the earth with his right hand as a sign of submission.

'Our father, my hand has touched the ground,' he said.

'Uzowulu's body, do you know me?' asked the spirit.

'How can I know you, father? You are beyond our knowledge.'

Evil Forest then turned to the other group and addressed the eldest of the three brothers.

'The body of Odukwe, I greet you,' he said, and Odukwe bent down and touched the earth. The hearing then began.

Uzowulu stepped forward and presented his case.

'That woman standing there is my wife, Mgbafo. I married her with my money and my yams. I do not owe my in-laws anything. I owe them no yams. I owe them no coco-yams. One morning three of them came to my house, beat me up and took my wife and children away. This happened in the rainy season. I have waited in vain for my wife to return. At last I went to my in-laws and said to them, "You have taken back your sister. I did not send her away. You yourselves took her. The law of the clan is that you should return her bride-price.'' But my wife's brothers said they had nothing to tell me. So I have brought the matter to the fathers of the clan. My case is finished. I salute you.'

'Your words are good,' said the leader of the *egwugwu*. 'Let us hear Odukwe. His words may also be good.'

Odukwe was short and thick-set. He stepped forward, saluted the spirits and began his story.

'My in-law has told you that we went to his house, beat him up and took our sister and her children away. All that is true. He told you that he came to take back her bride-price and we refused to give it him. That also is true. My in-law, Uzowulu, is a beast. My sister lived with him for nine years. During those years no single day passed in the sky without his beating the woman. We have tried to settle their quarrels time without number and on each occasion Uzowulu was guilty—'

'It is a lie!' Uzowulu shouted.

'Two years ago,' continued Odukwe, 'when she was pregnant, he beat her until she miscarried.'

'It is a lie. She miscarried after she had gone to sleep with her lover.'

'Uzowulu's body, I salute you,' said Evil Forest, silencing him. 'What kind of lover sleeps with a pregnant woman?' There was a loud murmur of approbation from the crowd. Odukwe continued:

'Last year when my sister was recovering from an illness, he beat her again so that if the neighbours had not gone in to save her she would have been killed. We heard of it, and did as you have been told. The law of Umuofia is that if a woman runs away from her husband her bride-price is returned. But in this case she ran away to save her life. Her two children belong to Uzowulu. We do not dispute it, but they are too young to leave their mother. If, on the other hand, Uzowulu should recover from his madness and come in the proper way to beg his wife to return she will do so on the understanding that if he ever beats her again we shall cut off his genitals for him.'

The crowd roared with laughter. Evil Forest rose to his feet and order was immediately restored. A steady cloud of smoke rose from his head. He sat down again and called two witnesses. They were both Uzowulu's neighbours, and they agreed about the beating. Evil Forest then stood up, pulled out his staff and thrust it into the earth again. He ran a few steps in the direction of the women; they all fled in terror, only to return to their places almost immediately. The nine *egwugwu* then went away to consult together in their house. They were silent for a long time. Then the metal gong sounded and the flute was blown. The *egwugwu* had emerged once again from their underground home. They saluted one another and then reappeared on the *ilo*.

'*Umuofia kwenu!*' roared Evil Forest, facing the elders and grandees of the clan.

'*Yaa!*' replied the thunderous crowd, then silence descended from the sky and swallowed the noise.

Evil Forest began to speak and all the while he spoke everyone was silent. The eight other *egwugwu* were as still as statues.

'We have heard both sides of the case,' said Evil Forest. 'Our duty is not to blame this man or to praise that, but to settle the dispute.' He turned to Uzowulu's ground and allowed a short pause.

'Uzowulu's body, do you know me?'

'How can I know you, father? You are beyond our knowledge,' Uzowulu replied.

'I am Evil Forest. I kill a man on the day that his life is sweetest to him.'

'That is true,' replied Uzowulu.

'Go to your in-laws with a pot of wine and beg your wife to return to you. It is not bravery when a man fights with a woman.' He turned to Odukwe, and allowed a brief pause.

'Odukwe's body, I greet you,' he said.

'My hand is on the ground,' replied Odukwe.

'Do you know me?'

'No man can know you,' replied Odukwe.

'I am Evil Forest, I am Dry-meat-that-fills-the-mouth, I am Fire-that-burns-without-faggots. If your in-law brings wine to you, let your sister go with him. I salute you.' He pulled his staff from the hard earth and thrust it back.

'*Umuofia kwenu!*' he roared, and the crowd answered.

'I don't know why such a trifle should come before the *egwugwu*,' said one elder to another.

'Don't you know what kind of man Uzowulu is? He will not listen to any other decision,' replied the other.

As they spoke two other groups of people had replaced the first before the *egwugwu*, and a great land case began.

CHAPTER ELEVEN

The night was impenetrably dark. The moon had been rising later and later every night until now it was seen only at dawn. And whenever the moon forsook evening and rose at cock-crow the nights were as black as charcoal.

Ezinma and her mother sat on a mat on the floor after their supper of yam foo-foo and bitter leaf soup. A palm-oil lamp gave out yellowish light. Without it, it would have been impossible to eat; one could not have known where one's mouth was in the darkness of that night. There was an oil lamp in all the four huts on Okonkwo's compound, and each hut seen from the others looked like a soft eye of yellow half-light set in the solid massiveness of night.

The world was silent except for the shrill cry of insects, which was part of the night, and the sound of wooden mortar and pestle as Nwayieke pounded her foo-foo. Nwayieke lived four compounds away, and she was notorious for her late cooking. Every woman in the neighbourhood knew the sound of Nwayieke's mortar and pestle. It was also part of the night.

Okonkwo had eaten from his wives' dishes and was now reclining with his back against the wall. He searched his bag and brought out his snuff-bottle. He turned it on to his left palm, but nothing came out. He hit the bottle against his knee to shake up the tobacco. That was always the trouble with Okeke's snuff. It very quickly went damp, and there was too much saltpetre in it. Okonkwo had not bought snuff from him for a long time. Idigo was the man who knew how to grind good snuff. But he had recently fallen ill.

Low voices, broken now and again by singing, reached Okonkwo from his wives' huts as each woman and her children told folk stories. Ekwefi and her daughter, Ezinma, sat on a mat on the floor. It was Ekwefi's turn to tell a story.

'Once upon a time,' she began, 'all the birds were invited to a feast in the sky. They were very happy and began to prepare themselves for the great day. They painted their bodies with red cam wood and drew beautiful patterns on them with *uli*.

'Tortoise saw all these preparations and soon discovered what it all meant. Nothing that happened in the world of the animals ever escaped his notice; he was full of cunning. As soon as he heard of the great feast in the sky his throat began to itch at the very thought. There was a famine in those days and Tortoise had not eaten a good meal for two moons. His body rattled like a piece of dry stick in his empty shell. So he began to plan how he would go to the sky.'

'But he had no wings,' said Ezinma.

'Be patient,' replied her mother. 'That is the story. Tortoise had no wings, but he went to the birds and asked to be allowed to go with them.'

' "We know you too well," said the birds when they had heard him. "You are full of cunning and you are ungrateful. If we allow you to come with us you will soon begin your mischief."

' "You do not know me," said Tortoise. "I am a changed man. I have learnt that a man who makes trouble for others is also making it for himself."

'Tortoise had a sweet tongue, and within a short time all the birds agreed that he was a changed man, and they each gave him a feather, with which he made two wings.

'At last the great day came and Tortoise was the first to arrive at the meeting-place. When all the birds had gathered together, they set off in a body. Tortoise was very happy and voluble as he flew among the birds, and he was soon chosen as the man to speak for the party because he was a great orator.

' "There is one important thing which we must not forget," he said as they flew on their way. "When people are invited to a great feast like this, they take new names for the occasion. Our hosts in the sky will expect us to honour this age-old custom."

'None of the birds had heard of this custom but they knew that Tortoise, in spite of his failings in other directions, was a widely-travelled man who knew the customs of different peoples. And so they each took a new name. When they had all taken, Tortoise also took one. He was to be called *All of you.*

'At last the party arrived in the sky and their hosts were very happy to see them. Tortoise stood up in his many-coloured plumage and thanked them for their invitation. His speech was so eloquent that all the birds were glad they had brought him, and nodded their heads in approval of all he said. Their hosts took him as the king of the birds, especially as he looked somewhat different from the others.

'After kola nuts had been presented and eaten, the people of the sky set before their guests the most delectable dishes Tortoise had ever seen or dreamt of. The soup was brought out hot from the fire and in the very pot in which it had been cooked. It was full of meat and fish. Tortoise began to sniff aloud. There was pounded yam and also yam pottage cooked with palm oil and fresh fish. There were also pots of palm wine. When everything had been set before the guests, one of the people of the sky came forward and tasted a little from each pot. He then invited the birds to eat. But Tortoise jumped to his feet and asked: "For whom have you prepared this feast?"

' "For all of you," replied the man.

'Tortoise turned to the birds and said: "You remember that my name is *All of you.* The custom here is to serve the spokesman first and the others later. They will serve you when I have eaten."

'He began to eat and the birds grumbled angrily. The people of the sky thought it must be their custom to leave all the food for their king. And so Tortoise ate the best part of the food and then drank two pots of palm wine, so that he was full of food and drink and his body filled out in his shell.

'The birds gathered round to eat what was left and to peck at the bones he had thrown all about the floor. Some of them were too angry to eat. They chose to fly home on an empty stomach.

But before they left each took back the feather he had lent to Tortoise. And there he stood in his hard shell full of food and wine but without any wings to fly home. He asked the birds to take a message for his wife, but they all refused. In the end Parrot, who had felt more angry than the others, suddenly changed his mind and agreed to take the message.

' "Tell my wife," said Tortoise, "to bring out all the soft things in my house and cover the compound with them so that I can jump down from the sky without very great danger." '

'Parrot promised to deliver the message, and then flew away. But when he reached Tortoise's house he told his wife to bring out all the hard things in the house. And so she brought out her husband's hoes, matchets, spears, guns and even his cannon. Tortoise looked down from the sky and saw his wife bringing things out, but it was too far to see what they were. When all seemed ready he let himself go. He fell and fell and fell until he began to fear that he would never stop falling. And then like the sound of his cannon he crashed on the compound.'

'Did he die?' asked Ezinma.

'No,' replied Ekwefi. 'His shell broke into pieces. But there was a great medicine-man in the neighbourhood. Tortoise's wife sent for him and he gathered all the bits of shell and stuck them together. That is why Tortoise's shell is not smooth.'

'There is no song in the story,' Ezinma pointed out.

'No,' said Ekwefi. 'I shall think of another one with a song. But it is your turn now.'

'Once upon a time,' Ezinma began, 'Tortoise and Cat went to wrestle against Yams – no, that is not the beginning. Once upon a time there was a great famine in the land of animals. Everybody was lean except Cat, who was fat and whose body shone as if oil was rubbed on it . . .'

She broke off because at that very moment a loud and high-pitched voice broke the outer silence of the night. It was Chielo, the priestess of Agbala, prophesying. There was nothing new in that. Once in a while Chielo was possessed by the spirit of her god and she began to prophesy. But tonight she was addressing her prophecy and greetings to Okonkwo, and so everyone in his family listened. The folk stories stopped.

'*Agbala do-o-o-o! Agbala ekeneo-o-o-o-o,*' came the voice like a sharp knife cutting through the night. '*Okonkwo! Agbala ekene gio-o-o-o! Agbala cholu ifu ada ya Ezinmao-o-o-o!*'

At the mention of Ezinma's name Ekwefi jerked her head sharply like an animal that had sniffed death in the air. Her heart jumped painfully within her.

The priestess had now reached Okonkwo's compound and was talking with him outside his hut. She was saying again and again that Agbala wanted to see his daughter, Ezinma. Okonkwo pleaded with her to come back in the morning because Ezinma was now asleep. But Chielo ignored what he was trying to say and went on shouting that Agbala wanted to see his daughter. Her voice was as clear as metal, and Okonkwo's women and children heard from their huts all that she said. Okonkwo was still pleading that the girl had been ill of late and was asleep. Ekwefi quickly took her to their bedroom and placed her on their high bamboo bed.

The priestess suddenly screamed. 'Beware, Okonkwo!' she warned. 'Beware of exchanging words with Agbala. Does a man speak when a god speaks? Beware!'

She walked through Okonkwo's hut into the circular compound and went straight towards Ekwefi's hut. Okonkwo came after her.

'Ekwefi,' she called, 'Agbala greets you. Where is my daughter, Ezinma? Agbala wants to see her.'

Ekwefi came out from her hut carrying her oil lamp in her left hand. There was a light wind blowing, so she cupped her right hand to shelter the flame. Nwoye's mother, also carrying an oil lamp, emerged from her hut. Her children stood in the darkness outside their hut watching the strange event. Okonkwo's youngest wife also came out and joined the others.

'Where does Agbala want to see her?' Ekwefi asked.

'Where else but in his house in the hills and the caves?' replied the priestess.

'I will come with you, too,' Ekwefi said firmly.

'*Tufia-a!*' the priestess cursed, her voice crackling like the angry bark of thunder in the dry season. 'How dare you, woman, to go before the mighty Agbala of your own accord? Beware, woman, lest he strike you in his anger. Bring me my daughter.'

Ekwefi went into her hut and came out again with Ezinma.

'Come, my daughter,' said the priestess. 'I shall carry you on my back. A baby on its mother's back does not know that the way is long.'

Ezinma began to cry. She was used to Chielo calling her 'my daughter'. But it was a different Chielo she now saw in the yellow half-light.

'Don't cry, my daughter,' said the priestess, 'lest Agbala be angry with you.'

'Don't cry,' said Ekwefi, 'she will bring you back very soon. I shall give you some fish to eat.' She went into the hut again and brought down the smoke-black basket in which she kept her dried fish and other ingredients for cooking soup. She broke a piece in two and gave it to Ezinma, who clung to her.

'Don't be afraid,' said Ekwefi, stroking her head, which was shaved in places, leaving a regular pattern of hair. They went outside again. The priestess bent down on one knee and Ezinma climbed on her back, her left palm closed on her fish and her eyes gleaming with tears.

'*Agbala do-o-o-o! Agbala ekeneo-o-o-o!* . . .' Chielo began once again to chant greetings to her god. She turned round sharply and walked through Okonkwo's hut, bending very low at the eaves. Ezinma was crying loudly now, calling on her mother. The two voices disappeared into the thick darkness.

A strange and sudden weakness descended on Ekwefi as she stood gazing in the direction of the voice like a hen whose only chick has been carried away by a kite. Ezinma's voice soon faded away and only Chielo was heard moving farther and farther into the distance.

'Why do you stand there as though she had been kidnapped?' asked Okonkwo as he went back to his hut.

'She will bring her back soon,' Nwoye's mother said.

But Ekwefi did not hear these consolations. She stood for a while, and then, all of a sudden, made up her mind. She hurried through Okonkwo's hut and went outside.

'Where are you going?' he asked.

'I am following Chielo,' she replied and disappeared in the darkness. Okonkwo cleared his throat, and brought out his snuff-bottle from the goatskin bag by his side.

The priestess's voice was already growing faint in the distance. Ekwefi hurried to the main footpath and turned left in the direction of the voice. Her eyes were useless to her in the darkness. But she picked her way easily on the sandy footpath hedged on either side by branches and damp leaves. She began to run, holding her breasts with her hands to stop them flapping noisily against her body. She hit her left foot against an outcropped root, and terror seized her. It was an ill omen. She ran faster. But Chielo's voice was still a long way away. Had she been running too? How could she go so fast with Ezinma on her back? Although the night was cool, Ekwefi was beginning to feel hot from her running. She continually ran into the luxuriant weeds and creepers that walled in the path. Once she tripped up and fell. Only then did she realize with a start, that Chielo had stopped her chanting. Her heart beat violently and she stood still. Then Chielo's renewed outburst came from only a few paces ahead. But Ekwefi could not see her. She shut her eyes for a while and opened them again in an effort to see. But it was useless. She could not see beyond her nose.

There were no stars in the sky because there was a rain-cloud. Fireflies went about with their tiny green lamps, which only made the darkness more profound. Between Chielo's outbursts the night was alive with the shrill tremor of forest insects woven into the darkness.

'*Agbala do-o-o-o!* . . . *Agbala ekeneo-o-o-o!* . . .' Ekwefi trudged behind, neither getting too near nor keeping too far back. She thought they must be going towards the sacred cave. Now that she walked slowly she had time to think. What would she do when they got to the cave? She would not dare to enter. She would wait at the mouth, all alone in that fearful place. She thought of all the terrors of the night. She remembered the night, long ago, when she had seen *Ogbu-agali-odu*, one of those evil essences loosed upon the world by the potent 'medicines' which the tribe had made in the distant past against its enemies but had now forgotten how to control. Ekwefi had been returning from the stream with her mother on a dark night like this when they saw its glow as it flew in their direction. They had thrown their water-pots and lain by the roadside expecting the sinister light to descend on them and kill them. That was the only time Ekwefi ever saw *Ogbu-agali-odu*. But although it had happened so long ago, her blood still ran cold whenever she remembered that night.

The priestess's voice came at longer intervals now, but its vigour was undiminished. The air was cool and damp with dew. Ezinma sneezed. Ekwefi muttered, 'Life to you'. At the same time the priestess also said, 'Life to you, my daughter'. Ezinma's voice from the darkness warmed her mother's heart. She trudged slowly along.

And then the priestess screamed. 'Somebody is walking behind me!' she said. 'Whether you are spirit or man, may Agbala shave your head with a blunt razor! May he twist your neck until you see your heels!'

Ekwefi stood rooted to the spot. One mind said to her: 'Woman, go home before Agbala does you harm.' But she could not. She stood until Chielo had increased the distance between them and she began to follow again. She had already walked so long that she began to feel a slight numbness in the limbs and in the head. Then it occurred to her that they could not have been heading for the cave. They must have bypassed it long ago; they must be going towards Umuachi, the farthest village in the clan. Chielo's voice now came after long intervals.

It seemed to Ekwefi that the night had become a little lighter. The cloud had lifted and a few stars were out. The moon must be preparing to rise, its sullenness over. When the moon rose late in the night, people said it was refusing food, as a sullen husband refuses his wife's food when they have quarrelled.

'*Agbala do-o-o-o! Umuachi! Agbala ekene unuo-o-o-o!*' It was just as Ekwefi had thought. The priestess was now saluting the village of Umuachi. It was unbelievable, the distance they had covered. As they emerged into the open village from the narrow forest track the darkness was softened and it became possible to see the vague shape of trees. Ekwefi screwed her eyes up in an effort to see her daughter and the priestess, but whenever she thought she saw their shape it immediately dissolved like a melting lump of darkness. She walked numbly along.

Chielo's voice was now rising continuously, as when she first set out. Ekwefi had a feeling of spacious openness, and she guessed they must be on the village *ilo*, or playground. And she realized too with something of a jerk that Chielo was no longer moving forward. She was, in fact, returning. Ekwefi quickly moved away from her line of retreat. Chielo passed by, and they began to go back the way they had come.

It was a long and weary journey and Ekwefi felt like a sleepwalker most of the way. The moon was definitely rising, and although it had not yet appeared on the sky its light had already melted down the darkness. Ekwefi could now discern the figure of the priestess and her burden. She slowed down her pace so as to increase the distance between them. She was afraid of what might happen if Chielo suddenly turned round and saw her.

She had prayed for the moon to rise. But now she found the half-light of the incipient moon more terrifying than darkness. The world was now peopled with vague, fantastic figures that dissolved under her steady gaze and then formed again in new shapes. At one stage Ekwefi was so afraid that she nearly called out to Chielo for companionship and human sympathy. What she had seen was the shape of a man climbing a palm tree, his head pointing to the earth and his legs skywards. But at that very moment Chielo's voice rose again in her possessed chanting, and Ekwefi recoiled, because there was no humanity there. It was not the same Chielo who sat with her in the market and sometimes bought bean-cakes for Ezinma, whom she called her daughter. It was a different woman – the priestess of Agbala, the Oracle of the Hills and Caves. Ekwefi trudged along between two fears. The sound of her benumbed steps seemed to come from some other person walking behind her. Her arms were folded across her bare breasts. Dew fell heavily and the air was cold. She could no longer think, not even about the terrors of night. She just jogged along in a half-sleep, only waking to full life when Chielo sang.

At last they took a turning and began to head for the caves. From then on, Chielo never ceased in her chanting. She greeted her god in a multitude of names – the owner of the future, the messenger of earth, the god who cut a man down when his life was sweetest to.him. Ekwefi was also awakened and benumbed fears revived.

The moon was now up and she could see Chielo and Ezinma clearly. How a woman could carry a child of that size so easily and for so long was a miracle. But Ekwefi was not thinking about that. Chielo was not a woman that night.

'*Agbala do-o-o-o! Agbala ekeneo-o-o! Chi negbu madu ubosi ndu ya nato ya uto daluo-o-o! . . .*'

Ekwefi could already see the hills looming in the moonlight. They formed a circular ring with a break at one point through which the foot-track led to the centre of the circle.

As soon as the priestess stepped into this ring of hills her voice was not only doubled in strength but was thrown back on all sides. It was indeed the shrine of a great god. Ekwefi picked her way carefully and quietly. She was already beginning to doubt the wisdom of her coming. Nothing would happen to Ezinma, she thought. And if anything happened to her could she stop it? She would not dare to enter the underground caves. Her coming was quite useless, she thought.

As these things went through her mind she did not realize how close they were to the cave mouth. And so when the priestess with Ezinma on her back disappeared through a hole hardly big enough to pass a hen, Ekwefi broke into a run as though to stop them. As she stood gazing at the circular darkness which had swallowed them, tears gushed from her eyes, and she swore within her that if she heard Ezinma cry she would rush into the cave to defend her against all the gods in the world. She would die with her.

Having sworn that oath, she sat down on a stony ledge and waited. Her fear had vanished. She could hear the priestess's voice, all its metal taken out of it by the vast emptiness of the cave. She buried her face in her lap and waited.

She did not know how long she waited. It must have been a very long time. Her back was turned on the footpath that led out of the hills. She must have heard a voice behind her and turned round sharply. A man stood there with a matchet in his hand. Ekwefi uttered a scream and sprang to her feet.

'Don't be foolish,' said Okonkwo's voice. 'I thought you were going into the shrine with Chielo,' he mocked.

Ekwefi did not answer. Tears of gratitude filled her eyes. She knew her daughter was safe.

'Go home and sleep,' said Okonkwo. 'I shall wait here.'

'I shall wait too. It is almost dawn. The first cock has crowed.'

As they stood there together, Ekwefi's mind went back to the days when they were young. She had married Anene because Okonkwo was too poor then to marry. Two years after her marriage to Anene she could bear it no longer and she ran away to Okonkwo. It had been early in the morning. The moon was shining. She was going to the stream to fetch water. Okonkwo's house was on the way to the stream. She went in and knocked at his door and he came out. Even in those days he was not a man of many words. He just carried her into his bed and in the darkness began to feel around her waist for the loose end of her cloth.

CHAPTER TWELVE

On the following morning the entire neighbourhood wore a festive air because Okonkwo's friend, Obierika, was celebrating his daughter's *uri*. It was the day on which her suitor (having already paid the greater part of her bride-price) would bring palm wine not only to her parents and immediate relatives but to the wide and extensive group of kinsmen called *umunna*. Everybody had been invited – men, women and children. But it was really a woman's ceremony and the central figures were the bride and her mother.

As soon as day broke, breakfast was hastily eaten and women and children began to gather at Obierika's compound to help the bride's mother in her difficult but happy task of cooking for a whole village.

Okonkwo's family was astir like any other family in the neighbourhood. Nwoye's mother and Okonkwo's youngest wife were ready to set out for Obierika's compound with all their children. Nwoye's mother carried a basket of coco-yams, a cake of salt and smoked fish which she would present to Obierika's wife. Okonkwo's youngest wife, Ojiugo, also had a basket of plantains and coco-yams and a small pot of palm oil. Their children carried pots of water.

Ekwefi was tired and sleepy from the exhausting experiences of the previous night. It was not very long since they had returned. The priestess, with Ezinma sleeping on her back, had crawled out of the shrine on her belly like a snake. She had not as much as

looked at Okonkwo and Ekwefi or shown any surprise at finding
them at the mouth of the cave. She looked straight ahead of her
and walked back to the village. Okonkwo and his wife followed
at a respectful distance. They thought the priestess might be going
to her house, but she went to Okonkwo's compound, passed
through his *obi* and into Ekwefi's hut and walked into her bedroom.
She placed Ezinma carefully on the bed and went away without
saying a word to anybody.

Ezinma was still sleeping when everyone else was astir, and
Ekwefi asked Nwoye's mother and Ojiugo to explain to Obeirika's
wife that she would be late. She had got ready her basket of coco-
yams and fish, but she must wait for Ezinma to wake.

'You need some sleep yourself,' said Nwoye's mother. 'You look
very tired.'

As they spoke Ezinma emerged from the hut, rubbing her eyes
and stretching her spare frame. She saw the other children with
their water-pots and remembered that they were going to fetch
water for Obierika's wife. She went back to the hut and brought
her pot.

'Have you slept enough?' asked her mother.

'Yes,' she replied. 'Let us go.'

'Not before you have had your breakfast,' said Ekwefi. And she
went into her hut to warm the vegetable soup she had cooked
last night.

'We shall be going,' said Nwoye's mother. 'I will tell Obierika's
wife that you are coming later.' And so they all went to help
Obierika's wife – Nwoye's mother with her four children and
Ojiugo with her two.

As they trooped through Okonkwo's *obi* he asked: 'Who will
prepare my afternoon meal?'

'I shall return to do it,' said Ojiugo.

Okonkwo was also feeling tired and sleepy, for although nobody
else knew it, he had not slept at all last night. He had felt very
anxious but did not show it. When Ekwefi had followed the
priestess, he had allowed what he regarded as a reasonable and
manly interval to pass and then gone with his matchet to the shrine,
where he thought they must be. It was only when he had got there

that it had occurred to him that the priestess might have chosen to go round the villages first. Okonkwo had returned home and sat waiting. When he thought he had waited long enough he again returned to the shrine. But the Hills and the Caves were as silent as death. It was only on his fourth trip that he had found Ekwefi, and by then he had become gravely worried.

Obierika's compound was as busy as an ant hill. Temporary cooking tripods were erected on every available space by bringing together three blocks of sun-dried earth and making a fire in their midst. Cooking pots went up and down the tripods, and foo-foo was pounded in a hundred wooden mortars. Some of the women cooked the yams and the cassava, and others prepared vegetable soup. Young men pounded the foo-foo or split firewood. The children made endless trips to the stream.

Three young men helped Obierika to slaughter the two goats with which the soup was made. They were very fat goats, but the fattest of all was tethered to a peg near the wall of the compound. It was as big as a small cow. Obierika had sent one of his relatives all the way to Umuike to buy that goat. It was the one he would present alive to his in-laws.

'The market of Umuike is a wonderful place,' said the young man who had been sent by Obeirika to buy the giant goat. 'There are so many people on it that if you threw up a grain of sand it would not find a way to fall to earth again.'

'It is the result of a great medicine,' said Obierika. 'The people of Umuike wanted their market to grow and swallow up the markets of their neighbours. So they made a powerful medicine. Every market-day, before the first cock-crow, this medicine stands on the market-ground in the shape of an old woman with a fan. With this magic fan she beckons to the market all the neighbouring clans. She beckons in front of her and behind her, to her right and to her left.'

'And so everybody comes,' said another man, 'honest men and thieves. They can steal your cloth from off your waist in that market.'

'Yes,' said Obeirika. 'I warned Nwankwo to keep a sharp eye

and a sharp ear. There was once a man who went to sell a goat.
He led it on a thick rope which he tied round his wrist. But as
he walked through the market he realized that people were pointing
at him as they do to a madman. He could not understand it until
he looked back and saw that what he led at the end of the tether
was not a goat but a heavy log of wood.'

'Do you think a thief can do that kind of thing single-handed?'
asked Nwankwo.

'No,' said Obierika. 'They use medicine.'

When they had cut the goats' throats and collected the blood
in a bowl, they held them over an open fire to burn off the hair,
and the smell of burning hair blended with the smell of cooking.
Then they washed them and cut them up for the women to prepare
the soup.

All this ant-hill activity was going smoothly when a sudden
interruption came. It was a cry in the distance: *Oji odu achu iiiji-o-
o! (The one that uses its tail to drive flies away!)* Every woman
immediately abandoned whatever she was doing and rushed out
in the direction of the cry.

'We cannot all rush out like that, leaving what we are cooking
to burn in the fire,' shouted Chielo, the priestess. 'Three or four
of us should stay behind.'

'It is true,' said another woman. 'We will allow three or four
women to stay behind.'

Five women stayed behind to look after the cooking-pots, and
all the rest rushed away to see the cow that had been let loose. When
they saw it they drove it back to its owner, who at once paid the
heavy fine which the village imposed on anyone whose cow was
let loose on his neighbours' crops. When the women had exacted
the penalty they checked among themselves to see if any woman
had failed to come out when the cry had been raised.

'Where is Mgbogo?' asked one of them.

'She is ill in bed,' said Mgbogo's next-door neighbour. 'She has
iba.'

'The only other person is Udenkwo,' said another woman, 'and
her child is not twenty-eight days yet.'

Those women whom Obeirika's wife had not asked to help her

with the cooking returned to their homes, and the rest went back, in a body, to Obierika's compound.

'Whose cow is it?' asked the women who had been allowed to stay behind.

'It was my husband's,' said Ezelagbo. 'One of the young children had opened the gate of the cow-shed.'

Early in the afternoon the first two pots of palm wine arrived from Obierika's in-laws. They were duly presented to the women, who drank a cup or two each, to help them in their cooking. Some of it also went to the bride and her attendant maidens, who were putting the last delicate touches of razor to her coiffure and cam wood on her smooth skin.

When the heat of the sun began to soften, Obierika's son, Maduka, took a long broom and swept the ground in front of his father's *obi*. And as if they had been waiting for that, Obierika's relatives and friends began to arrive, every man with his goatskin bag hung on one shoulder and a rolled goatskin mat under his arm. Some of them were accompanied by their sons bearing carved wooden stools. Okonkwo was one of them. They sat in a half circle and began to talk of many things. It would not be long before the suitors came.

Okonkwo brought out his snuff-bottle and offered it to Ogbuefi Ezenwa, who sat next to him. Ezenwa took it, tapped it on his kneecap, rubbed his left palm on his body to dry it before tipping a little snuff into it. His actions were deliberate, and he spoke as he performed them:

'I hope our in-laws will bring many pots of wine. Although they come from a village that is known for being close-fisted, they ought to know that Akueke is the bride for a king.'

'They dare not bring fewer than thirty pots,' said Okonkwo. 'I shall tell them my mind if they do.'

At that moment Obierika's son, Maduka, led out the giant goat from the inner compound, for his father's relatives to see. They all admired it and said that that was the way things should be done. The goat was then led back to the inner compound.

Very soon after, the in-laws began to arrive. Young men and boys in single file, each carrying a pot of wine, came first. Obierika's relatives counted the pots as they came in. Twenty, twenty-five. There was a long break, and the hosts looked at each other as if to say, 'I told you.' Then more pots came. Thirty, thirty-five, forty, forty-five. The hosts nodded in approval and seemed to say, 'Now they are behaving like men'. Altogether there were fifty pots of wine. After the pot-bearers came Ibe, the suitor, and the elders of his family. They sat in a half-moon, thus completing a circle with their hosts. The pots of wine stood in their midst. Then the bride, her mother and half a dozen other women and girls emerged from the inner compound, and went round the circle shaking hands with all. The bride's mother led the way, followed by the bride and the other women. The married women wore their best cloths and the girls wore red and black waist-beads and anklets of brass.

When the women retired, Obierika presented kola nuts to his in-laws. His eldest brother broke the first one. 'Life to all of us,' he said as he broke it. 'And let there be friendship between your family and ours.'

The crowd answered: '*Ee-e-e!*'

'We are giving you our daughter today. She will be a good wife to you. She will bear you nine sons like the mother of our town.'

'*Ee-e-e!*'

The oldest man in the camp of the visitors replied: 'It will be good for you and it will be good for us.'

'*Ee-e-e!*'

'This is not the first time my people have come to marry your daughter. My mother was one of you.'

'*Ee-e-e!*'

'And this will not be the last, because you understand us and we understand you. You are a great family.'

'*Ee-e-e!*'

'Prosperous men and great warriors.' He looked in the direction of Okonkwo. 'Your daughter will bear us sons like you.'

'*Ee-e-e!*'

The kola was eaten and the drinking of palm wine began. Groups of four or five men sat round with a pot in their midst. As the evening wore on, food was presented to the guests. There were huge bowls of foo-foo and steaming pots of soup. There were also pots of yam pottage. It was a great feast.

As night fell, burning torches were set on wooden tripods and the young men raised a song. The elders sat in a big circle and the singers went round singing each man's praise as they came before him. They had something to say for every man. Some were great farmers, some were orators who spoke for the clan; Okonkwo was the greatest wrestler and warrior alive. When they had gone round the circle they settled down in the centre, and girls came from the inner compound to dance. At first the bride was not among them. But when she finally appeared holding a cock in her right hand, a loud cheer rose from the crowd. All the other dancers made way for her. She presented the cock to the musicians and began to dance. Her brass anklets rattled as she danced and her body gleamed with cam wood in the soft yellow light. The musicians with their wood, clay and metal instruments went from song to song. And they were all gay. They sang the latest song in the village:

> If I hold her hand
>   She says, 'Don't touch!'
> If I hold her foot
>   She says, 'Don't touch!'
> But when I hold her waist-beads
>   She pretends not to know.

The night was already far spent when the guests rose to go, taking their bride home to spend seven market weeks with her suitor's family. They sang songs as they went, and on their way they paid short courtesy visits to prominent men like Okonkwo, before they finally left for their village. Okonkwo made a present of two cocks to them.

CHAPTER THIRTEEN

Go-di-di-go-go-di-go. Di-go-go-di-go. It was the *ekwe* talking to the clan. One of the things every man learned was the language of the hollowed-out instrument. *Diim! Diim! Diim!* boomed the cannon at intervals.

The first cock had not crowed, and Umuofia was still swallowed up in sleep and silence when the *ekwe* began to talk, and the cannon shattered the silence. Men stirred on their bamboo beds and listened anxiously. Somebody was dead. The cannon seemed to rend the sky. *Di-go-go-di-go-di-di-go-go* floated in the message-laden night air. The faint and distant wailing of women settled like a sediment of sorrow on the earth. Now and again a full-chested lamentation rose above the wailing whenever a man came into the place of death. He raised his voice once or twice in manly sorrow and then sat down with the other men listening to the endless wailing of the women and the esoteric language of the *ekwe*. Now and again the cannon boomed. The wailing of the women would not be heard beyond the village, but the *ekwe* carried the news to all the nine villages and even beyond. It began by naming the clan: *Umuofia obodo dike*, 'the land of the brave'. *Umuofia obodo dike! Umuofia obodo dike!* It said this over and over again, and as it dwelt on it, anxiety mounted in every heart that heaved on a bamboo bed that night. Then it went nearer and named the village: *Iguedo of the yellow grinding-stone!* It was Okonkwo's village. Again and again Iguedo was called and men waited breathlessly in all the nine villages. At last the man was named and people sighed 'E-u-u, Ezeudu is dead'. A cold shiver ran down Okonkwo's back as he remembered the last time the old man had visited him 'That boy calls you father,' he had said. 'Bear no hand in his death.'

Ezeudu was a great man, and so all the clan was at his funeral. The ancient drums of death beat, guns and cannon were fired, and men dashed about in frenzy, cutting down every tree or animal they saw, jumping over walls and dancing on the roof. It was a warrior's funeral, and from morning till night warriors came and went in their age-groups. They all wore smoked raffia skirts and their bodies were painted with chalk and charcoal. Now and again an ancestral spirit or *egwugwu* appeared from the underworld, speaking in a tremulous, unearthly voice and completely covered in raffia. Some of them were very violent, and there had been a mad rush for shelter earlier in the day when one appeared with a sharp matchet and was only prevented from doing serious harm by two men who restrained him with the help of a strong rope tied round his waist. Sometimes he turned round and chased those men, and they ran for their lives. But they always returned to the long rope he trailed behind. He sang, in a terrifying voice, that Ekwensu, or Evil Spirit, had entered his eye.

But the most dreaded of all was yet to come. He was always alone and was shaped like a coffin. A sickly odour hung in the air wherever he went, and flies went with him. Even the greatest medicine-men took shelter when he was near. Many years ago another *egwugwu* had dared to stand his ground before him and had been transfixed to the spot for two days. This one had only one hand and with it carried a basket full of water.

But some of the *egwugwu* were quite harmless. One of them was so old and infirm that he leaned heavily on a stick. He walked unsteadily to the place where the corpse was laid, gazed at it a while and went away again – to the underworld.

The land of the living was not far removed from the domain of the ancestors. There was coming and going between them, especially at festivals and also when an old man died, because an old man was very close to the ancestors. A man's life from birth to death was a series of transition rites which brought him nearer and nearer to his ancestors.

Ezeudu had been the oldest man in the village, and at his death there were only three men in the whole clan who were older, and four or five others in his own age-group. Whenever one of these ancient men appeared in the crowd to dance unsteadily the funeral steps of the tribe, younger men gave way and the tumult subsided.

It was a great funeral, such as befitted a noble warrior. As the evening drew near, the shouting and the firing of guns, the beating of drums and the brandishing and clanging of matchets increased.

Ezeudu had taken three titles in his life. It was a rare achievement. There were only four titles in the clan, and only one or two men in any generation ever achieved the fourth and highest. When they did, they became the lords of the land. Because he had taken titles, Ezeudu was to be buried after dark with only a glowing brand to light the sacred ceremony.

But before this quiet and final rite, the tumult increased tenfold. Drums beat violently and men leaped up and down in frenzy. Guns were fired on all sides and sparks flew out as matchets clanged together in warriors' salutes. The air was full of dust and the smell of gunpowder. It was then that the one-handed spirit came, carrying a basket full of water. People made way for him on all sides and the noise subsided. Even the smell of gunpowder was swallowed in the sickly smell that now filled the air. He danced a few steps to the funeral drums and then went to see the corpse.

'Ezeudu!' he called in his guttural voice. 'If you had been poor in your last life I would have asked you to be rich when you come again. But you were rich. If you had been a coward, I would have asked you to bring courage. But you were a fearless warrior. If you had died young, I would have asked you to get life. But you lived long. So I shall ask you to come again the way you came before. If your death was the death of nature, go in peace. But if a man caused it, do not allow him a moment's rest.' He danced a few more steps and went away.

The drums and the dancing began again and reached fever-heat. Darkness was around the corner, and the burial was near. Guns fired the last salute and the cannon rent the sky. And then from the centre of the delirious fury came a cry of agony and shouts of horror. It was as if a spell had been cast. All was silent. In the centre of the crowd a boy lay in a pool of blood. It was the dead man's sixteen-year-old son, who with his brothers and half-brothers had been dancing the traditional farewell to their father. Okonkwo's gun had exploded and a piece of iron had pierced the boy's heart.

The confusion that followed was without parallel in the tradition of Umuofia. Violent deaths were frequent, but nothing like this had ever happened.

The only course open to Okonkwo was to flee from the clan. It was a crime against the earth goddess to kill a clansman, and a man who committed it must flee from the land. The crime was of two kinds, male and female. Okonkwo had committed the female, because it had been inadvertent. He could return to the clan after seven years.

That night he collected his most valuable belongings into head-loads. His wives wept bitterly and their children wept with them without knowing why. Obierika and half a dozen other friends came to help and to console him. They each made nine or ten trips carrying Okonkwo's yams to store in Obierika's barn. And before the cock crowed Okonkwo and his family were fleeing to his motherland. It was a little village called Mbanta, just beyond the borders of Mbaino.

As soon as the day broke, a large crowd of men from Ezeudu's quarter stormed Okonkwo's compound, dressed in garbs of war. They set fire to his houses, demolished his red walls, killed his animals and destroyed his barn. It was the justice of the earth goddess, and they were merely her messengers. They had no hatred in their hearts against Okonkwo. His greatest friend, Obierika, was among them. They were merely cleansing the land which Okonkwo had polluted with the blood of a clansman.

Obeirika was a man who thought about things. When the will of the goddess had been done, he sat down in his *obi* and mourned his friend's calamity. Why should a man suffer so grievously for an offence he had committed inadvertently? But although he thought for a long time he found no answer. He was merely led into greater complexities. He remembered his wife's twin children, whom he had thrown away. What crime had they committed? The Earth had decreed that they were an offence on the land and must be destroyed. And if the clan did not exact punishment for an offence against the great goddess, her wrath was loosed on all the land and not just on the offender. As the elders said, if one finger brought oil it soiled the others.

PART TWO

CHAPTER FOURTEEN

Okonkwo was well received by his mother's kinsmen in Mbanta. The old man who received him was his mother's youngest brother, who was now the eldest surviving member of that family. His name was Uchendu, and it was he who had received Okonkwo's mother twenty and ten years before when she had been brought home from Umuofia to be buried with her people. Okonkwo was only a boy then and Uchendu still remembered him crying the traditional farewell: 'Mother, mother, mother is going'.

That was many years ago. Today Okonkwo was not bringing his mother home to be buried with her people. He was taking his family of three wives and eleven children to seek refuge in his motherland. As soon as Uchendu saw him with his sad and weary company he guessed what had happened, and asked no questions. It was not until the following day that Okonkwo told him the full story. The old man listened silently to the end and then said with some relief: 'It is a female *ochu*'. And he arranged the requisite rites and sacrifices.

Okonkwo was given a plot of ground on which to build his compound, and two or three pieces of land on which to farm during the coming planting season. With the help of his mother's kinsmen he built himself an *obi* and three huts for his wives. He then installed his personal god and the symbols of his departed fathers. Each of Uchendu's five sons contributed three hundred seed-yams to enable their cousin to plant a farm, for as soon as the first rain came farming would begin.

At last the rain came. It was sudden and tremendous. For two or three moons the sun had been gathering strength till it seemed to breathe a breath of fire on the earth. All the grass had long been scorched brown, and the sand felt like live coals to the feet. Evergreen trees wore a dusty coat of brown. The birds were silenced in the forests, and the world lay panting under the live, vibrating heat. And then came the clap of thunder. It was an angry, metallic and thirsty clap, unlike the deep and liquid rumbling of the rainy season. A mighty wind arose and filled the air with dust. Palm trees swayed as the wind combed their leaves into flying crests like strange and fantastic coiffures.

When the rain finally came, it was in large, solid drops of frozen water which the people called 'the nuts of the water of heaven'. They were hard and painful on the body as they fell, yet young people ran about happily picking up the cold nuts and throwing them into their mouths to melt.

The earth quickly came to life and the birds in the forests fluttered around and chirped merrily. A vague scent of life and green vegetation was diffused in the air. As the rain began to fall more soberly and in smaller liquid drops, children sought for shelter, and all were happy, refreshed and thankful.

Okonkwo and his family worked very hard to plant a new farm. But it was like beginning life anew without the vigour and enthusiasm of youth, like learning to become left-handed in old age. Work no longer had for him the pleasure it used to have, and when there was no work to do he sat in a silent half-sleep.

His life had been ruled by a great passion – to become one of the lords of the clan. That had been his life-spring. And he had all but achieved it. Then everything had been broken. He had been cast out of his clan like a fish on to a dry, sandy beach, panting. Clearly his personal god or *chi* was not made for great things. A man could not rise beyond the destiny of his *chi*. The saying of the elders was not true – that if a man said yea his *chi* also affirmed. Here was a man whose *chi* said nay despite his own affirmation.

The old man, Uchendu, saw clearly that Okonkwo had yielded to despair and he was greatly troubled. He would speak to him after the *isa-ifi* ceremony.

The youngest of Uchendu's five sons, Amikwu, was marrying a new wife. The bride-price had been paid and all but the last ceremony had been performed. Amikwu and his people had taken palm wine to the bride's kinsmen about two moons before Okonkwo's arrival in Mbanta. And so it was time for the final ceremony of confession.

The daughters of the family were all there, some of them having come a long way from their homes in distant villages. Uchendu's eldest daughter had come from Obodo, nearly half a day's journey away. The daughters of Uchendu's brothers were also there. It was a full gathering of *umuada*, in the same way as they would meet if a death occurred in the family. There were twenty-two of them.

They sat in a big circle on the ground and the bride sat in the centre with a hen in her right hand. Uchendu sat by her, holding the ancestral staff of the family. All the other men stood outside the circle, watching. Their wives watched also. It was evening and the sun was setting.

Uchendu's eldest daughter, Njide, asked the questions.

'Remember that if you do not answer truthfully you will suffer or even die at childbirth,' she began. 'How many men have lain with you since my brother first expressed the desire to marry you?'

'None,' she replied simply.

'Answer truthfully,' urged the other women.

'None?' asked Njide.

'None,' she answered.

'Swear on this staff of my fathers,' said Uchendu.

'I swear,' said the bride.

Uchendu took the hen from her, slit its throat with a sharp knife and allowed some of the blood to fall on his ancestral staff.

From that day Amikwu took the young bride to his hut and she became his wife. The daughters of the family did not return

111

to their homes immediately but spent two or three days with their kinsmen.

On the second day Uchendu called together his sons and daughters and his nephew, Okonkwo. The men brought their goatskin mats, with which they sat on the floor, and the women sat on a sisal mat spread on a raised bank of earth. Uchendu pulled gently at his grey beard and gnashed his teeth. Then he began to speak, quietly and deliberately, picking his words with great care:

'It is Okonkwo that I primarily wish to speak to,' he began. 'But I want all of you to note what I am going to say. I am an old man and you are all children. I know more about the world than any of you. If there is any one among you who thinks he knows more let him speak up.' He paused, but no one spoke.

'Why is Okonkwo with us today? This is not his clan. We are only his mother's kinsmen. He does not belong here. He is an exile, condemned for seven years to live in a strange land. And so he is bowed with grief. But there is just one question I would like to ask him. Can you tell me, Okonkwo, why it is that one of the commonest names we give our children is Nneka, or "Mother is Supreme"? We all know that a man is the head of the family and his wives do his bidding. A child belongs to its father and his family and not to its mother and her family. A man belongs to his fatherland and not to his motherland. And yet we say Nneka – "Mother is Supreme". Why is that?'

There was silence. 'I want Okonkwo to answer me,' said Uchendu.

'I do not know the answer,' Okonkwo replied.

'You do not know the answer? So you see that you are a child. You have many wives and many children – more children than I have. You are a great man in your clan. But you are still a child, *my* child. Listen to me and I shall tell you. But there is one more question I shall ask you. Why is it that when a woman dies she is taken home to be buried with her own kinsmen? She is not buried with her husband's kinsmen. Why is that? Your mother was brought home to me and buried with my people. Why was that?'

Okonkwo shook his head.

'He does not know that either,' said Uchendu, 'and yet he is full of sorrow because he has come to live in his motherland for a few years.' He laughed a mirthless laughter, and turned to his sons and daughters. 'What about you? Can you answer my question?'

They all shook their heads.

'Then listen to me,' he said and cleared his throat. 'It's true that a child belongs to its father. But when a father beats his child, it seeks sympathy in its mother's hut. A man belongs to his fatherland when things are good and life is sweet. But when there is sorrow and bitterness he finds refuge in his motherland. Your mother is there to protect you. She is buried there. And that is why we say that mother is supreme. Is it right that you, Okonkwo, should bring your mother a heavy face and refuse to be comforted? Be careful or you may displease the dead. Your duty is to comfort your wives and children and take them back to your fatherland after seven years. But if you allow sorrow to weigh you down and kill you, they will all die in exile.' He paused for a long while. 'These are now your kinsmen.' He waved at his sons and daughters. 'You think you are the greatest sufferer in the world. Do you know that men are sometimes banished for life? Do you know that men sometimes lose all their yams and even their children? I had six wives once. I have none now except that young girl who knows not her right from her left. Do you know how many children I have buried – children I begot in my youth and strength? Twenty-two. I did not hang myself, and I am still alive. If you think you are the greatest sufferer in the world ask my daughter, Akueni, how many twins she has borne and thrown away. Have you not heard the song they sing when a woman dies?

> For whom is it well, for whom is it well?
> There is no one for whom it is well.

'I have no more to say to you.'

CHAPTER FIFTEEN

It was in the second year of Okonkwo's exile that his friend, Obierika, came to visit him. He brought with him two young men, each of them carrying a heavy bag on his head. Okonkwo helped them put down their loads. It was clear that the bags were full of cowries.

Okonkwo was very happy to receive his friend. His wives and children were very happy too, and so were his cousins and their wives when he sent for them and told them who his guest was.

'You must take him to salute our father,' said one of the cousins.

'Yes,' replied Okonkwo. 'We are going directly.' But before they went he whispered something to his first wife. She nodded, and soon the children were chasing one of their cocks.

Uchendu had been told by one of his grandchildren that three strangers had come to Okonkwo's house. He was therefore waiting to receive them. He held out his hands to them when they came into his *obi*, and after they had shaken hands he asked Okonkwo who they were.

'This is Obierika, my great friend. I have already spoken to you about him.'

'Yes,' said the old man, turning to Obierika. 'My son has told me about you, and I am happy you have come to see us. I knew your father, Iweka. He was a great man. He had many friends here and came to see them quite often. Those were good days when a man had friends in distant clans. Your generation does not know that. You stay at home, afraid of your next-door neighbour. Even

114

a man's motherland is strange to him nowadays.' He looked at Okonkwo. 'I am an old man and I like to talk. That is all I am good for now.' He got up painfully, went into an inner room and came back with a kola nut.

'Who are the young men with you?' he asked as he sat down again on his goatskin. Okonkwo told him.

'Ah,' he said. 'Welcome, my sons.' He presented the kola nut to them, and when they had seen it and thanked him, he broke it and they ate.

'Go into that room,' he said to Okonkwo, pointing with his finger. 'You will find a pot of wine there.'

Okonkwo brought the wine and they began to drink. It was a day old, and very strong.

'Yes,' said Uchendu after a long silence. 'People travelled more in those days. There is not a single clan in these parts that I do not know very well. Aninta, Umuazu, Ikeocha, Elumelu, Abame – I know them all.'

'Have you heard,' said Obierika, 'that Abame is no more?'

'How is that?' asked Uchendu and Okonkwo together.

'Abame has been wiped out,' said Obierika. 'It is a strange and terrible story. If I had not seen the few survivors with my own eyes and heard their story with my own ears, I would not have believed. Was it not on an Eke day that they fled into Umuofia?' he asked his two companions, and they nodded their heads.

'Three moons ago,' said Obierika, 'on an Eke market-day a little band of fugitives came into our town. Most of them were sons of our land whose mothers had been buried with us. But there were some too who came because they had friends in our town, and others who could think of nowhere else open to escape. And so they fled into Umuofia with a woeful story.' He drank his palm wine, and Okonkwo filled his horn again. He continued:

'During the last planting season a white man appeared in their clan.'

'An albino,' suggested Okonkwo.

'He was not an albino. He was quite different.' He sipped his wine. 'And he was riding an iron horse. The first people who saw him ran away, but he stood beckoning to them. In the end

115

the fearless ones were near and even touched him. The elders consulted their Oracle and it told them that the strange man would break their clan and spread destruction among them.' Obierika again drank a little of his wine. 'And so they killed the white man and tied his iron horse to their sacred tree because it looked as if it would run away to call the man's friends. I forgot to tell you another thing which the Oracle said. It said that other white men were on their way. They were locusts, it said, and that first man was their harbinger sent to explore the terrain. And so they killed him.'

'What did the white man say before they killed him?' asked Uchendu.

'He said nothing,' answered one of Obierika's companions.

'He said something, only they did not understand him,' said Obierika. 'He seemed to speak through his nose.'

'One of the men told me,' said Obierika's other companion, 'that he repeated over and over again a word that resembled Mbaino. Perhaps he had been going to Mbaino and had lost his way.'

'Anyway,' resumed Obierika, 'they killed him and tied up his iron horse. This was before the planting season began. For a long time nothing happened. The rains had come and yams had been sown. The iron horse was still tied to the sacred silk-cotton tree. And then one morning three white men led by a band of ordinary men like us came to the clan. They saw the iron horse and went away again. Most of the men and women of Abame had gone to their farms. Only a few of them saw these white men and their followers. For many market weeks nothing else happened. They have a big market in Abame on every other Afo day and, as you know, the whole clan gathers there. That was the day it happened. The three white men and a very large number of other men surrounded the market. They must have used a powerful medicine to make themselves invisible until the market was full. And they began to shoot. Everybody was killed, except the old and the sick who were at home and a handful of men and women whose *chi* were wide awake and brought them out of that market.' He paused.

'Their clan is now completely empty. Even the sacred fish in their mysterious lake have fled and the lake has turned the colour of blood. A great evil has come upon their land as the Oracle had warned.'

There was a long silence. Uchendu ground his teeth together audibly. Then he burst out:

'Never kill a man who says nothing. Those men of Abame were fools. What did they know about the man?' He ground his teeth again and told a story to illustrate his point. 'Mother Kite once sent her daughter to bring food. She went, and brought back a duckling. "You have done very well," said Mother Kite to her daughter, "but tell me, what did the mother of this duckling say when you swooped and carried its child away?" "It said nothing," replied the young kite. "It just walked away." "You must return the duckling," said Mother Kite. "There is something ominous behind the silence." And so Daughter Kite returned the duckling and took a chick instead. "What did the mother of the chick do?" asked the old kite. "It cried and raved and cursed me," said the young kite. "Then we can eat the chick," said her mother. "There is nothing to fear from someone who shouts." Those men of Abame were fools.'

'They were fools,' said Okonkwo after a pause. 'They had been warned that danger was ahead. They should have armed themselves with their guns and their matchets even when they went to market.'

'They have paid for their foolishness,' said Obierika. 'But I am greatly afraid. We have heard stories about white men who made the powerful guns and the strong drinks and took slaves away across the seas, but no one thought the stories were true.'

'There is no story that is not true,' said Uchendu. 'The world has no end, and what is good among one people is an abomination with others. We have albinos among us. Do you not think that they came to our clan by mistake, that they have strayed from their ways to a land where everybody is like them?'

Okonkwo's first wife soon finished her cooking and set before their guests a big meal of pounded yams and bitter-leaf soup. Okonkwo's son, Nwoye, brought in a pot of sweet wine tapped from the raffia palm.

'You are a big man now,' Obierika said to Nwoye. 'Your friend Anene asked me to greet you.'

'Is he well?' asked Nwoye.

'We are all well,' said Obierika.

Ezinma brought them a bowl of water with which to wash their hands. After that they began to eat and to drink the wine.

'When did you set out from home?' asked Okonkwo.

'We had meant to set out from my house before cock-crow,' said Obierika. 'But Nweke did not appear until it was quite light. Never make an early morning appointment with a man who has just married a new wife.' They all laughed.

'Has Nweke married a wife?' asked Okonkwo.

'He has married Okadigbo's second daughter,' said Obierika.

'That is very good,' said Okonkwo. 'I do not blame you for not hearing the cock crow.'

When they had eaten, Obierika pointed at the two heavy bags.

'That is the money for your yams,' he said. 'I sold the big ones as soon as you left. Later on I sold some of the seed-yams and gave out others to sharecroppers. I shall do that every year until you return. But I thought you would need the money now and so I brought it. Who knows what may happen tomorrow? Perhaps green men will come to our clan and shoot us.'

'God will not permit it,' said Okonkwo. 'I do not know how to thank you.'

'I can tell you,' said Obierika. 'Kill one of your sons for me.'

'That will not be enough,' said Okonkwo.

'Then kill yourself,' said Obierika.

'Forgive me,' said Okonkwo, smiling. 'I shall not talk about thanking you any more.'

CHAPTER SIXTEEN

When nearly two years later Obierika paid another visit to his friend in exile the circumstances were less happy. The missionaries had come to Umuofia. They had built their church there, won a handful of converts and were already sending evangelists to the surrounding towns and villages. That was a source of great sorrow to the leaders of the clan; but many of them believed that the strange faith and the white man's god would not last. None of his converts was a man whose word was heeded in the assembly of the people. None of them was a man of title. They were mostly the kind of people that were called *efulefu*, worthless, empty men. The imagery of an *efulefu* in the language of the clan was a man who sold his matchet and wore the sheath to battle. Chielo, the priestess of Agbala, called the converts the excrement of the clan, and the new faith was a mad dog that had come to eat it up.

What moved Obierika to visit Okonkwo was the sudden appearance of the latter's son, Nwoye, among the missionaries in Umuofia.

'What are you doing here?' Obierika had asked when after many difficulties the missionaries had allowed him to speak to the boy.

'I am one of them,' replied Nwoye.

'How is your father?' Obierika asked, not knowing what else to say.

'I don't know. He is not my father,' said Nwoye, unhappily. And so Obierika went to Mbanta to see his friend. And he found that Okonkwo did not wish to speak about Nwoye. It was only from Nwoye's mother that he heard scraps of the story.

The arrival of the missionaries had caused a considerable stir in the village of Mbanta. There were six of them and one was a white man. Every man and woman came out to see the white man. Stories about these strange men had grown since one of them had been killed in Abame and his iron horse tied to the sacred silk-cotton tree. And so everybody came to see the white man. It was the time of the year when everybody was at home. The harvest was over.

When they had all gathered, the white man began to speak to them. He spoke through an interpreter who was an Ibo man, though his dialect was different and harsh to the ears of Mbanta. Many people laughed at his dialect and the way he used words strangely. Instead of saying 'myself' he always said 'my buttocks'. But he was a man of commanding presence and the clansmen listened to him. He said he was one of them, as they could see from his colour and his language. The other four black men were also their brothers, although one of them did not speak Ibo. The white man was also their brother because they were all sons of God. And he told them about this new God, the Creator of all the world and all the men and women. He told them that they worshipped false gods, gods of wood and stone. A deep murmur went through the crowd when he said this. He told them that the true God lived on high and that all men when they died went before Him for judgment. Evil men and all the heathen who in their blindness bowed to wood and stone were thrown into a fire that burned like palm-oil. But good men who worshipped the true God lived for ever in His happy kingdom. 'We have been sent by this great God to ask you to leave your wicked ways and false gods and turn to Him so that you may be saved when you die,' he said.

'Your buttocks understand our language,' said someone light-heartedly and the crowd laughed.

'What did he say?' the white man asked his interpreter. But before he could answer, another man asked a question: 'Where is the white man's horse?' he asked. The Ibo evangelists consulted amongst themselves and decided that the man probably meant bicycle. They told the white man and he smiled benevolently.

'Tell them,' he said, 'that I shall bring many iron horses when we have settled down among them. Some of them will even ride the iron horse themselves.' This was interpreted to them but very few of them heard. They were talking excitedly among themselves because the white man had said he was going to live among them. They had not thought about that.

At this point an old man said he had a question. 'Which is this god of yours,' he asked, 'the goddess of earth, the god of the sky, Amadiora of the thunderbolt, or what?'

The interpreter spoke to the white man and he immediately gave his answer. 'All the gods you have named are not gods at all. They are gods of deceit who tell you to kill your fellows and destroy innocent children. There is only one true God and He has the earth, the sky, you and me and all of us.'

'If we leave our gods and follow your god,' asked another man, 'who will protect us from the anger of our neglected gods and ancestors?'

'Your gods are not alive and cannot do you any harm,' replied the white man. 'They are pieces of wood and stone.'

When this was interpreted to the men of Mbanta they broke into derisive laughter. These men must be mad, they said to themselves. How else could they say that Ani and Amadiora were harmless? And Idemili and Ogwugwu too? And some of them began to go away.

Then the missionaries burst into song. It was one of those gay and rollicking tunes of evangelism which had the power of plucking at silent and dusty chords in the heart of an Ibo man. The interpreter explained each verse to the audience, some of whom now stood enthralled. It was a story of brothers who lived in darkness and in fear, ignorant of the love of God. It told of one sheep out on the hills, away from the gates of God and from the tender shepherd's care.

After the singing the interpreter spoke about the Son of God whose name was Jesu Kristi. Okonkwo, who only stayed in the hope that it might come to chasing the men out of the village or whipping them, now said:

'You told us with your own mouth that there was only one god. Now you talk about his son. He must have a wife, then.' The crowd agreed.

'I did not say He had a wife,' said the interpreter, somewhat lamely.

'Your buttocks said he had a son,' said the joker. 'So he must have a wife and all of them must have buttocks.'

The missionary ignored him and went on to talk about the Holy Trinity. At the end of it Okwonkwo was fully convinced that the man was mad. He shrugged his shoulders and went away to tap his afternoon palm wine.

But there was a young lad who had been captivated. His name was Nwoye, Okonkwo's first son. It was not the mad logic of the Trinity that captivated him. He did not understand it. It was the poetry of the religion, something felt in the marrow. The hymn about brothers in darkness and in fear seemed to answer a vague but persistent question that haunted his young soul – the question of the twins crying in the bush and the question of Ikemefuna who was killed. He felt a relief within as the hymn poured into his parched soul. The words of the hymn were like the drops of frozen rain melting on the dry plate of the panting earth. Nwoye's callow mind was greatly puzzled.

CHAPTER SEVENTEEN

The missionaries spent their first four or five nights in the market-place, and went into the village in the morning to preach the gospel. They asked who the king of the village was, but the villagers told them there was no king. 'We have men of high title and the chief priests and the elders,' they said.

It was not very easy getting the men of high title and the elders together after the excitement of the first day. But the missionaries persevered, and in the end they were received by the rulers of Mbanta. They asked for a plot of land to build their church.

Every clan and village had its 'evil forest'. In it were buried all those who died of the really evil diseases, like leprosy and smallpox. It was also the dumping ground for the potent fetishes of great medicine-men when they died. An 'evil forest' was, therefore, alive with sinister forces and powers of darkness. It was such a forest that the rulers of Mbanta gave to the missionaries. They did not really want them in their clan, and so they made them that offer which nobody in his right senses would accept.

'They want a piece of land to build their shrine,' said Uchendu to his peers when they consulted among themselves. 'We shall give them a piece of land.' He paused, and there was a murmur of surprise and disagreement. 'Let us give them a portion of the Evil Forest. They boast about victory over death. Let us give them a real battlefield in which to show their victory.' They laughed and agreed, and sent for the missionaries, whom they had asked to leave them for a while so that they might 'whisper together'. They offered them as much of the Evil Forest as they cared to take. And to their greatest amazement the missionaries thanked them and burst into song.

'They do not understand,' said some of the elders. 'But they will understand when they go to their plot of land tomorrow morning.' And they dispersed.

The next morning the crazy men actually began to clear a part of the forest and to build their house. The inhabitants of Mbanta expected them all to be dead within four days. The first day passed and the second and third and fourth, and none of them died. Everyone was puzzled. And then it became known that the white man's fetish had unbelievable power. It was said that he wore glasses on his eyes so that he could see and talk to evil spirits. Not long after, he won his first three converts.

Although Nwoye had been attracted to the new faith from the very first day, he kept it secret. He dared not go too near the missionaries for fear of his father. But whenever they came to preach in the open market-place or the village playground, Nwoye was there. And he was already beginning to know some of the simple stories they told.

'We have now built a church,' said Mr Kiaga, the interpreter, who was now in charge of the infant congregation. The white man had gone back to Umuofia, where he built his headquarters and from where he paid regular visits to Mr Kiaga's congregation at Mbanta.

'We have now built a church,' said Mr Kiaga, 'and we want you all to come in every seventh day to worship the true God.'

On the following Sunday, Nwoye passed and re-passed the little red-earth and thatch building without summoning enough courage to enter. He heard the voice of singing and although it came from a handful of men it was loud and confident. Their church stood on a circular clearing that looked like the open mouth of the Evil Forest. Was it waiting to snap its teeth together? After passing and re-passing the church, Nwoye returned home.

It was well known among the people of Mbanta that their gods and ancestors were sometimes long-suffering and would deliberately allow a man to go on defying them. But even in such cases they set their limit at seven market weeks or twenty-eight days. Beyond that limit no man was suffered to go. And so excitement mounted in the village as the seventh week approached since the impudent missionaries built their church in the Evil Forest. The villagers were so certain about the doom that awaited these men that one or two converts thought it wise to suspend their allegiance to the new faith.

At last the day came by which all the missionaries should have died. But they were still alive, building a new red-earth and thatch house for their teacher, Mr Kiaga. That week they won a handful more converts. And for the first time they had a woman. Her name was Nneka, the wife of Amadi, who was a prosperous farmer. She was very heavy with child.

Nneka had had four previous pregnancies and childbirths. But each time she had borne twins, and they had been immediately thrown away. Her husband and his family were already becoming highly critical of such a woman and were not unduly perturbed when they found she had fled to join the Christians. It was a good riddance.

One morning Okonkwo's cousin, Amikwu, was passing by the church on his way from the neighbouring village, when he saw Nwoye among the Christians. He was greatly surprised, and when he got home he went straight to Okonkwo's hut and told him what he had seen. The women began to talk excitedly, but Okonkwo sat unmoved.

It was late afternoon before Nwoye returned. He went into the *obi* and saluted his father, but he did not answer. Nwoye turned round to walk into the inner compound when his father, suddenly overcome with fury, sprang to his feet and gripped him by the neck.

'Where have you been?' he stammered.

Nwoye struggled to free himself from the choking grip.

'Answer me,' roared Okonkwo, 'before I kill you!' He seized a heavy stick that lay on the dwarf wall and hit him two or three savage blows.

'Answer me!' he roared again. Nwoye stood looking at him and did not say a word. The women were screaming outside, afraid to go in.

'Leave that boy at once!' said a voice in the outer compound. It was Okonkwo's uncle Uchendu. 'Are you mad?'

Okonkwo did not answer. But he left hold of Nwoye, who walked away and never returned.

He went back to the church and told Mr Kiaga that he had decided to go to Umuofia, where the white missionary had set up a school to teach young Christians to read and write.

Mr Kiaga's joy was very great. 'Blessed is he who forsakes his father and his mother for my sake,' he intoned. 'Those that hear my words are my father and my mother.'

Nwoye did not fully understand. But he was happy to leave his father. He would return later to his mother and his brothers and sisters and convert them to the new faith.

As Okonkwo sat in his hut that night, gazing into a log fire, he thought over the matter. A sudden fury rose within him and he felt a strong desire to take up his matchet, go to the church and wipe out the entire vile and miscreant gang. But on further thought he told himself that Nowye was not worth fighting for. Why, he cried in his heart, should he, Okonkwo, of all people, be cursed with such a son? He saw clearly in it the finger of his personal god or *chi*. For how else could he explain his great misfortune and exile and now his despicable son's behaviour? Now that he had time to think of it, his son's crime stood out in its stark enormity. To abandon the gods of one's father and go about with a lot of effeminate men clucking like old hens was the very depth of abomination. Suppose when he died all his male children decided to follow Nwoye's steps and abandon their ancestors? Okonkwo felt a cold shudder run through him at the terrible prospect, like the prospect of annihilation. He saw himself and his father crowding round their ancestral shrine waiting in vain for worship and sacrifice and finding nothing but ashes of bygone days, and his children the while praying to the white man's god. If such a thing were ever to happen, he, Okonkwo, would wipe them off the face of the earth.

Okonkwo was popularly called the 'Roaring Flame'. As he looked into the log fire he recalled the name. He was a flaming fire. How then could he have begotten a son like Nwoye, degenerate and effeminate? Perhaps he was not his son. No! he could not be. His wife had played him false. He would teach her! But Nwoye resembled his grandfather, Unoka, who was Okonkwo's father. He pushed the thought out of his mind. He, Okonkwo, was called a flaming fire. How could he have begotten a woman for a son? At Nwoye's age Okonkwo had already become famous throughout Umuofia for his wrestling and fearlessness.

He sighed heavily, and as if in sympathy the smouldering log also sighed. And immediately Okonkwo's eyes were opened and he saw the whole matter clearly. Living fire begets cold, impotent ash. He sighed again, deeply.

CHAPTER EIGHTEEN

The young church in Mbanta had a few crises early in its life. At first the clan had assumed that it would not survive. But it had gone on living and gradually becoming stronger. The clan was worried, but not overmuch. If a gang of *efulefu* decided to live in the Evil Forest it was their own affair. When one came to think of it, the Evil Forest was a fit home for such undesirable people. It was true they were rescuing twins from the bush, but they never brought them into the village. As far as the villagers were concerned, the twins still remained where they had been thrown away. Surely the earth goddess would not visit the sins of the missionaries on the innocent villagers?

But on one occasion the missionaries had tried to overstep the bounds. Three converts had gone into the village and boasted openly that all the gods were dead and impotent and that they were prepared to defy them by burning all their shrines.

'Go and burn your mothers' genitals,' said one of the priests. The men were seized and beaten until they streamed with blood. After that nothing happened for a long time between the church and the clan.

But stories were already gaining ground that the white man had not only brought a religion but also a government. It was said that they had built a place of judgement in Umuofia to protect the followers of their religion. It was even said that they had hanged one man who killed a missionary.

Although such stories were now often told they looked like fairytales in Mbanta and did not as yet affect the relationship between the new church and the clan. There was no question of killing a missionary here, for Mr Kiaga, despite his madness, was quite harmless. As for his converts, no one could kill them without having to flee from the clan, for in spite of their worthlessness they still belonged to the clan. And so nobody gave serious thought to the stories about the white man's government or the consequences of killing the Christians. If they became more troublesome than they already were they would simply be driven out of the clan.

And the little church was at that moment too deeply absorbed in its own troubles to annoy the clan. It all began over the question of admitting outcasts.

These outcasts, or *osu*, seeing that the new religion welcomed twins and such abominations, thought that it was possible that they would also be received. And so one Sunday two of them went into the church. There was an immediate stir; but so great was the work the new religion had done among the converts that they did not immediately leave the church when the outcasts came in. Those who found themselves nearest to them merely moved to another seat. It was a miracle. But it only lasted till the end of the service. The whole church raised a protest and were about to drive these people out, when Mr Kiaga stopped them and began to explain.

'Before God,' he said, 'there is no slave or free. We are all children of God and we must receive these our brothers.'

'You do not understand,' said one of the converts. 'What will the heathen say to us when they hear that we receive *osu* into our midst? They will laugh.'

'Let them laugh,' said Mr Kiaga. 'God will laugh at them on the judgement day. Why do the nations rage and the peoples imagine a vain thing? He that sitteth in the heavens shall laugh. The Lord shall have them in derision.'

'You do not understand,' the convert maintained. 'You are our teacher, and you can teach us the things of the new faith. But this is a matter which we know.' And he told him what an *osu* was.

He was a person dedicated to a god, a thing set apart – a taboo for ever, and his children after him. He could neither marry nor be married by the free-born. He was in fact an outcast, living in a special area of the village, close to the Great Shrine. Wherever he went he carried with him the mark of his forbidden caste – long, tangled and dirty hair. A razor was taboo to him. An *osu* could not attend an assembly of the free-born, and they, in turn, could not shelter under his roof. He could not take any of the four titles of the clan, and when he died he was buried by his kind in the Evil Forest. How could such a man be a follower of Christ?

'He needs Christ more than you and I,' said Mr Kiaga.

'Then I shall go back to the clan,' said the convert. And he went. Mr Kiaga stood firm, and it was his firmness that saved the young church. The wavering converts drew inspiration and confidence from his unshakable faith. He ordered the outcasts to shave off their long, tangled hair. At first they were afraid they might die.

'Unless you shave off the mark of your heathen belief I will not admit you into the church,' said Mr Kiaga. 'You fear that you will die. Why should that be? How are you different from other men who shave their hair? The same God created you and them. But they have cast you out like lepers. It is against the will of God, who has promised everlasting life to all who believe in His holy name. The heathen say you will die if you do this or that, and you are afraid. They also said I would die if I built my church on this ground. Am I dead? They said I would die if I took care of twins. I am still alive. The heathen speak nothing but falsehood. Only the word of our God is true.'

The two outcasts shaved off their hair, and soon they were among the strongest adherents of the new faith. And what was more, nearly all the *osu* in Mbanta followed their example. It was in fact one of them who in his zeal brought the church into serious conflict with the clan a year later by killing the sacred python, the emanation of the god of water.

The royal python was the most revered animal in Mbanta and all the surrounding clans. It was addressed as 'Our Father', and was allowed to go wherever it chose, even into people's beds. It ate rats in the house and sometimes swallowed hens' eggs. If a clansman killed a royal python accidentally, he made sacrifices of atonement and performed an expensive burial ceremony such as was done for a man. No punishment was prescribed for a man who killed the python knowingly. Nobody thought that such a thing could ever happen.

Perhaps it never did happen. That was the way the clan at first looked at it. No one had actually seen the man do it. The story had arisen among the Christians themselves.

But, all the same, the rulers and elders of Mbanta assembled to decide on their action. Many of them spoke at great length and in fury. The spirit of war was upon them. Okonkwo, who had begun to play a part in the affairs of his motherland, said that until the abominable gang was chased out of the village with whips there would be no peace.

But there were many others who saw the situation differently, and it was their counsel that prevailed in the end.

'It is not our custom to fight for our gods,' said one of them. 'Let us not presume to do so now. If a man kills the sacred python in the secrecy of his hut, the matter lies between him and the god. We did not see it. If we put ourselves between the god and his victim we may receive blows intended for the offender. When a man blasphemes, what do we do? Do we go and stop his mouth? No. We put our fingers into our ears to stop us hearing. That is a wise action.'

'Let us not reason like cowards,' said Okonkwo. 'If a man comes into my hut and defaecates on the floor, what do I do? Do I shut my eyes? No! I take a stick and break his head. That is what a man does. These people are daily pouring filth over us, and Okeke says we should pretend not to see.' Okonkwo made a sound full of disgust. This was a womanly clan, he thought. Such a thing could never happen in his fatherland, Umuofia.

'Okonkwo has spoken the truth,' said another man. 'We should do something. But let us ostracize these men. We would then not be held accountable for their abominations.'

Everybody in the assembly spoke, and in the end it was decided to ostracize the Christians. Okonkwo ground his teeth in disgust.

That night a bell-man went through the length and breadth of Mbanta proclaiming that the adherents of the new faith were thenceforth excluded from the life and privileges of the clan.

The Christians had grown in number and were now a small community of men, women and children, self-assured and confident. Mr Brown, the white missionary, paid regular visits to them. 'When I think that it is only eighteen months since the Seed was first sown among you,' he said, 'I marvel at what the Lord hath wrought.'

It was Wednesday in Holy Week and Mr Kiaga had asked the women to bring red earth and white chalk and water to scrub the church for Easter; and the women had formed themselves into three groups for this purpose. They set out early that morning, some of them with their water-pots to the stream, another group with hoes and baskets to the village red-earth pit, and the others to the chalk quarry.

Mr Kiaga was praying in the church when he heard the women talking excitedly. He rounded off his prayer and went to see what it was all about. The women had come to the church with empty water pots. They said that some young men had chased them away from the stream with whips. Soon after, the women who had gone for red earth returned with empty baskets. Some of them had been heavily whipped. The chalk women also returned to tell a similar story.

'What does it all mean?' asked Mr Kiaga, who was greatly perplexed.

'The village has outlawed us,' said one of the women. 'The bell-man announced it last night. But it is not our custom to debar anyone from the stream or the quarry.'

Another woman said. 'They want to ruin us. They will not allow us into the markets. They have said so.'

Mr Kiaga was going to send into the village for his men-converts when he saw them coming on their own. Of course they had all heard the bell-man, but they had never in all their lives heard of women being debarred from the stream.

'Come along,' they said to the women. 'We will go with you to meet those cowards.' Some of them had big sticks and some even matchets.

But Mr Kiaga restrained them. He wanted first to know why they had been outlawed.

'They say that Okoli killed the sacred python,' said one man. 'It is false,' said another. 'Okoli told me himself that it was false.' Okoli was not there to answer. He had fallen ill on the previous night. Before the day was over he was dead. His death showed that the gods were still able to fight their own battles. The clan saw no reason then for molesting the Christians.

CHAPTER NINETEEN

The last big rains of the year were falling. It was the time for treading red earth with which to build walls. It was not done earlier because the rains were too heavy and would have washed away the heap of trodden earth, and it could not be done later because harvesting would soon set in, and after that the dry season.

It was going to be Okonkwo's last harvest in Mbanta. The seven wasted and weary years were at last dragging to a close. Although he had prospered in his motherland Okonkwo knew that he would have prospered even more in Umuofia, in the land of his fathers where men were bold and warlike. In these seven years he would have climbed to the utmost heights. And so he regretted every day of his exile. His mother's kinsmen had been very kind to him, and he was grateful. But that did not alter the facts. He had called the first child born to him in exile Nneka – 'Mother is Supreme' – out of politeness to his mother's kinsmen. But two years later when a son was born he called him Nwofia – 'Begotten in the Wilderness'.

As soon as he entered his last year in exile Okonkwo sent money to Obierika to build him two huts in his old compound where he and his family would live until he built more huts and the outside wall of his compound. He could not ask another man to build his own *obi* for him, nor the walls of his compound. Those things a man built for himself or inherited from his father.

As the last heavy rains of the year began to fall, Obierika sent word that the two huts had been built and Okonkwo began to prepare for his return, after the rains. He would have liked to return earlier and build his compound that year before the rains stopped, but in doing so he would have taken something from the full penalty of seven years. And that could not be. So he waited impatiently for the dry season to come.

It came slowly. The rain became lighter and lighter until it fell in slanting showers. Sometimes the sun shone through the rain and a light breeze blew. It was a gay and airy kind of rain. The rainbow began to appear, and sometimes two rainbows, like a mother and her daughter, the one young and beautiful, and the other an old and faint shadow. The rainbow was called the python of the sky.

Okonkwo called his three wives and told them to get things together for a great feast. 'I must thank my mother's kinsmen before I go,' he said.

Ekwefi had some cassava left on her farm from the previous year. Neither of the other wives had. It was not that they had been lazy, but that they had many children to feed. It was therefore understood that Ekwefi would provide cassava for the feast. Nwoye's mother and Ojiugo would provide the other things like smoked fish, palm oil and pepper for the soup. Okonkwo would take care of meat and yams.

Ekwefi rose early on the following morning and went to her farm with her daughter, Ezinma, and Ojiugo's daughter, Obiageli, to harvest cassava tubers. Each of them carried a long cane basket, a matchet for cutting down the soft cassava stem, and a little hoe for digging out the tuber. Fortunately, a light rain had fallen during the night and the soil would not be very hard.

'It will not take us long to harvest as much as we like,' said Ekwefi.

'But the leaves will be wet,' said Ezinma. Her basket was balanced on her head, and her arms folded across her breasts. She felt cold. 'I dislike cold water dropping on my back. We should have waited for the sun to rise and dry the leaves.'

Obiageli called her 'Salt' because she said that she disliked water. 'Are you afraid you may dissolve?'

The harvesting was easy, as Ekwefi had said. Ezinma shook every tree violently with a long stick before she bent down to cut the stem and dig out the tuber. Sometimes it was not necessary to dig. They just pulled the stump and the earth rose, roots snapped below, and the tuber was pulled out.

When they had harvested a sizeable heap they carried it down in two trips to the stream, where every women had a shallow well for fermenting her cassava.

'It should be ready in four days or even three,' said Obiageli. 'They are young tubers.'

'They are not all that young,' said Ekwefi. 'I planted the farm nearly two years ago. It is a poor soil and that is why the tubers are so small.'

Okonkwo never did things by halves. When his wife Ekwefi protested that two goats were sufficient for the feast he told her that it was not her affair.

'I am calling a feast because I have the wherewithal. I cannot live on the bank of a river and wash my hands with spittle. My mother's people have been good to me and I must show my gratitude.'

And so three goats were slaughtered and a number of fowls. It was like a wedding feast. There was foo-foo and yam pottage, egusi soup and bitter-leaf soup and pots and pots of palm wine.

All the *umunna* were invited to the feast, all the descendants of Okolo, who had lived about two hundred years before. The oldest member of this extensive family was Okonkwo's uncle, Uchendu. The kola nut was given to him to break, and he prayed to the ancestors. He asked them for health and children. 'We do not ask for wealth because he that has health and children will also have wealth. We do not pray to have more money but to have more kinsmen. We are better than animals because we have kinsmen. An animal rubs its aching flank against a tree, a man asks his kinsman to scratch him.' He prayed especially for Okonkwo and his family. He then broke the kola nut and threw one of the lobes on the ground for the ancestors.

As the broken kola nuts were passed round, Okonkwo's wives and children and those who came to help them with the cooking began to bring out the food. His sons brought out the pots of palm wine. There was so much food and drink that many kinsmen whistled in surprise. When all was laid out, Okonkwo rose to speak.

'I beg you to accept this little kola,' he said. 'It is not to pay you back for all you did for me in these seven years. A child cannot pay for its mother's milk. I have only called you together because it is good for kinsmen to meet.'

Yam pottage was served first because it was lighter than foo-foo and because yams always came first. Then the foo-foo was served. Some kinsmen ate it with egusi soup and others with bitter-leaf soup. The meat was then shared so that every member of the *umunna* had a portion. Every man rose in order of years and took a share. Even the few kinsmen who had not been able to come had their shares taken out for them in due turn.

As the palm wine was drunk one of the oldest members of the *umunna* rose to thank Okonkwo:

'If I say that we did not expect such a big feast I will be suggesting that we did not know how open-handed our son, Okonkwo is. We all know him, and we expected a big feast. But it turned out to be even bigger than we expected. Thank you. May all you took out return again tenfold. It is good in these days when the younger generation consider themselves wiser than their sires to see a man doing things in the grand, old way. A man who calls his kinsmen to a feast does not do so to save them from starving. They all have food in their own homes. When we gather together in the moonlit village ground it is not because of the moon. Every man can see it in his own compound. We come together because it is good for kinsmen to do so. You may ask why I am saying all this. I say it because I fear for the younger generation, for you people.' He waved his arm where most of the young men sat. 'As for me, I have only a short while to live, and so have Uchendu and Unachukwu and Emefo. But I fear for you young people because you do not understand how strong is the bond of kinship. You do not know what it is to speak with one voice. And what is the result? An abominable religion has settled among you. A man can now leave his father and his brothers. He can curse the gods of his fathers and his ancestors, like a hunter's dog that suddenly goes mad and turns on his master. I fear for you; I fear for the clan.' He turned again to Okonkwo and said, 'Thank you for calling us together'.

PART THREE

CHAPTER TWENTY

Seven years was a long time to be away from one's clan. A man's place was not always there, waiting for him. As soon as he left, someone else rose and filled it. The clan was like a lizard; if it lost its tail it soon grew another.

Okonkwo knew these things. He knew that he had lost his place among the nine masked spirits who administered justice in the clan. He had lost the chance to lead his warlike clan against the new religion, which, he was told, had gained ground. He had lost the years in which he might have taken the highest titles in the clan. But some of these losses were not irreparable. He was determined that his return should be marked by his people. He would return with a flourish, and regain the seven wasted years.

Even in his first year in exile he had begun to plan for his return. The first thing he would do would be to rebuild his compound on a more magnificent scale. He would build a bigger barn than he had before and he would build huts for two new wives. Then he would show his wealth by initiating his sons in the *ozo* society. Only the really great men in the clan were able to do this. Okonkwo saw clearly the high esteem in which he would be held, and he saw himself taking the highest title in the land.

As the years of exile passed one by one it seemed to him that his *chi* might now be making amends for the past disaster. His yams grew abundantly, not only in his motherland but also in Umuofia, where his friend gave them out year by year to sharecroppers.

Then the tragedy of his first son had occurred. At first it appeared as if it might prove too great for his spirit. But it was a resilient spirit, and in the end Okonkwo overcame his sorrow. He had five other sons and he would bring them up in the way of the clan.

He sent for the five sons and they came and sat in his *obi*. The youngest of them was four years old.

'You have all seen the great abomination of your brother. Now he is no longer my son or your brother. I will only have a son who is a man, who will hold his head up among my people. If any one of you prefers to be a woman, let him follow Nwoye now while I am alive so that I can curse him. If you turn against me when I am dead I will visit you and break your neck.'

Okonkwo was very lucky in his daughters. He never stopped regretting that Ezinma was a girl. Of all his children she alone understood his every mood. A bond of sympathy had grown between them as the years had passed.

Ezinma grew up in her father's exile and became one of the most beautiful girls in Mbanta. She was called Crystal of Beauty, as her mother had been called in her youth. The young ailing girl who had caused her mother so much heartache had been transformed, almost overnight, to a healthy, buoyant maiden. She had, it was true, her moments of depression when she would snap at everybody like an angry dog. These moods descended on her suddenly and for no apparent reason. But they were very rare and short-lived. As long as they lasted, she could bear no other person but her father.

Many young men and prosperous middle-aged men of Mbanta came to marry her. But she refused them all, because her father had called her one evening and said to her: 'There are many good and prosperous people here, but I shall be happy if you marry in Umuofia when we return home.'

That was all he had said. But Ezinma had seen clearly all the thought and hidden meaning behind the few words. And she had agreed.

'Your half-sister, Obiageli, will not understand me,' Okonkwo said. 'But you can explain to her.'

Although they were almost the same age, Ezinma wielded a strong influence over her half-sister. She explained to her why they should not marry yet, and she agreed also. And so the two of them refused every offer of marriage in Mbanta.

'I wish she were a boy,' Okonkwo thought within himself. She understood things so perfectly. Who else among his children could have read his thought so well? With two beautiful grown-up daughters his return to Umuofia would attract considerable attention. His future sons-in-law would be men of authority in the clan. The poor and unknown would not dare to come forth.

Umuofia had indeed changed during the seven years Okonkwo had been in exile. The church had come and led many astray. Not only the low-born and the outcast but sometimes a worthy man had joined it. Such a man was Ogbuefi Ugonna, who had taken two titles, and who like a madman had cut the anklet of his titles and cast it away to join the Christians. The white missionary was very proud of him and he was one of the first men in Umuofia to receive the sacrament of Holy Communion, or Holy Feast as it was called in Ibo. Ogbuefi Ugonna had thought of the Feast in terms of eating and drinking, only more holy than the village variety. He had therefore put his drinking-horn into his goatskin bag for the occasion.

But apart from the church, the white men had also brought a government. They had built a court where the District Commissioner judged cases in ignorance. He had court messengers who brought men to him for trial. Many of these messengers came from Umuru on the bank of the Great River, where the white men first came many years before and where they had built the centre of their religion and trade and government. These court messengers were greatly hated in Umuofia because they were foreigners and also arrogant and high-handed. They were called *kotma*, and because of their ash-coloured shorts they earned the additional name of Ashy-Buttocks. They guarded the prison, which was full of men who had offended against the white man's law. Some of these prisoners had thrown away their twins and some had molested the Christians. They were beaten in the prison by the *kotma* and made to work every morning clearing the government compound and fetching wood for the white Commissioner and the court messengers. Some of these prisoners were men of title who should be above such mean occupation. They were grieved by the indignity and mourned for their neglected farms. As they cut grass in the morning the younger men sang in time with the strokes of their matchets:

> *Kotma* of the ash buttocks,
> He is fit to be a slave
> The white man has no sense,
> He is fit to be a slave

The court messengers did not like to be called Ashy-Buttocks, and they beat the men. But the song spread in Umuofia.

Okonkwo's head was bowed in sadness as Obierika told him these things.

'Perhaps I have been away too long,' Okonkwo said, almost to himself. 'But I cannot understand these things you tell me. What is it that has happened to our people? Why have they lost the power to fight?'

'Have you not heard how the white man wiped out Abame?' asked Obierika.

'I have heard,' said Okonkwo. 'But I have also heard that Abame people were weak and foolish. Why did they not fight back? Had they no guns and matchets? We would be cowards to compare ourselves with the men of Abame. Their fathers had never dared to stand before our ancestors. We must fight these men and drive them from the land.'

'It is already too late,' said Obierika sadly. 'Our own men and our sons have joined the ranks of the stranger. They have joined his religion and they help to uphold his government. If we should try to drive out the white men in Umuofia we should find it easy. There are only two of them. But what of our own people who are following their way and have been given power? They would go to Umuru and bring the soldiers, and we would be like Abame.' He paused for a long time and then said: 'I told you on my last visit to Mbanta how they hanged Aneto.'

'What has happened to that piece of land in dispute?' asked Okonkwo.

'The white man's court has decided that it should belong to

Nnama's family, who had given much money to the white man's messengers and interpreter.'

'Does the white man understand our customs about land?'

'How can he when he does not even speak our tongue? But he says that our customs are bad; and our own brothers who have taken up his religion also say that our customs are bad. How do you think we can fight when our own brothers have turned against us? The white man is very clever. He came quietly and peaceably with his religion. We were amused at his foolishness and allowed him to stay. Now he has won our brothers, and our clan can no longer act like one. He has put a knife on the things that held us together and we have fallen apart.'

'How did they get hold of Aneto to hang him?' asked Okonkwo.

'When he killed Oduche in the fight over the land, he fled to Aninta to escape the wrath of the earth. This was about eight days after the fight, because Oduche had not died immediately from his wounds. It was on the seventh day that he died. But everybody knew that he was going to die and Aneto got his belongings together in readiness to flee. But the Christians had told the white man about the accident, and he sent his *kotma* to catch Aneto. He was imprisoned with all the leaders of his family. In the end Oduche died and Aneto was taken to Umuru and hanged. The other people were released, but even now they have not found the mouth with which to tell of their suffering.'

The two men sat in silence for a long while afterwards.

CHAPTER TWENTY-ONE

There were many men and women in Umuofia who did not feel as strongly as Okonkwo about the new dispensation. The white man had indeed brought a lunatic religion, but he had also built a trading store and for the first time palm oil and kernel became things of great price, and much money flowed into Umuofia.

And even in the matter of religion there was a growing feeling that there might be something in it after all, something vaguely akin to method in the overwhelming madness.

This growing feeling was due to Mr Brown, the white missionary, who was very firm in restraining his flock from provoking the wrath of the clan. One member in particular was very difficult to restrain. His name was Enoch and his father was the priest of the snake cult. The story went around that Enoch had killed and eaten the sacred python, and that his father had cursed him.

Mr Brown preached against such excess of zeal. Everything was possible, he told his energetic flock, but everything was not expedient. And so Mr Brown came to be respected even by the clan, because he trod softly on its faith. He made friends with some of the great men of the clan and on one of his frequent visits to the neighbouring villages he had been presented with a carved elephant tusk, which was a sign of dignity and rank. One of the great men in that village was called Akunna and he had given one of his sons to be taught the white man's knowledge in Mr Brown's school.

Whenever Mr Brown went to that village he spent long hours

with Akunna in his *obi* talking through an interpreter about religion. Neither of them succeeded in converting the other but they learnt more about their different beliefs.

'You say that there is one supreme God who made heaven and earth,' said Akunna on one of Mr Brown's visits. 'We also believe in Him and call Him Chukwu. He made all the world and the other gods.'

'There are no other gods,' said Mr Brown. 'Chukwu is the only God and all others are false. You carve a piece of wood – like that one' (he pointed at the rafters from which Akunna's carved *Ikenga* hung), 'and you call it a god. But it is still a piece of wood.'

'Yes,' said Akunna. 'It is indeed a piece of wood. The tree from which it came was made by Chukwu, as indeed all minor gods were. But He made them for His messengers so that we could approach Him through them. It is like yourself. You are the head of your church.'

'No,' protested Mr Brown. 'The head of my church is God Himself.'

'I know,' said Akunna, 'but there must be a head in this world among men. Somebody like yourself must be the head here.'

'The head of my church in that sense is in England.'

'That is exactly what I am saying. The head of your church is in your country. He has sent you here as his messenger. And you have also appointed your own messengers and servants. Or let me take another example, the District Commissioner. He is sent by your king.'

'They have a queen,' said the interpreter on his own account.

'Your queen sends her messenger, the District Commissioner. He finds that he cannot do the work alone and so he appoints *kotma* to help him. It is the same with God, or Chukwu. He appoints the small gods to help Him because His work is too great for one person.'

'You should not think of him as a person,' said Mr Brown, 'It is because you do so that you imagine He must need helpers. And the worst thing about it is that you give all the worship to the false gods you have created.'

'That is not so. We made sacrifices to the little gods, but when they fail and there is no one else to turn to we go to Chukwu. It is right to do so. We approach a great man through his servants. But when his servants fail to help us, then we go to the last source of hope. We appear to pay greater attention to the little gods but that is not so. We worry them more because we are afraid to worry their Master. Our fathers knew that Chukwu was the Overlord and that is why many of them gave their children the name Chukwuka – "Chukwu is Supreme".'

'You said one interesting thing,' said Mr Brown. 'You are afraid of Chukwu. In my religion Chukwu is a loving Father and need not be feared by those who do His will.'

'But we must fear Him when we are not doing His will,' said Akunna. 'And who is to tell His will? It is too great to be known.'

In this way Mr Brown learnt a great deal about the religion of the clan and he came to the conclusion that a frontal attack on it would not succeed. And so he built a school and a little hospital in Umuofia. He went from family to family begging people to send their children to his school. But at first they only sent their slaves or sometimes their lazy children. Mr Brown begged and argued and prophesied. He said that the leaders of the land in the future would be men and women who had learnt to read and write. If Umuofia failed to send her children to the school, strangers would come from other places to rule them. They could already see that happening in the Native Court, where the D.C. was surrounded by strangers who spoke his tongue. Most of these strangers came from the distant town of Umuru on the bank of the Great River where the white man first went.

In the end Mr Brown's arguments began to have an effect. More people came to learn in his school, and he encouraged them with gifts of singlets and towels. They were not all young, these people who came to learn. Some of them were thirty years old or more. They worked on their farms in the morning and went to school in the afternoon. And it was not long before the people began to say that the white man's medicine was quick in working. Mr Brown's school produced quick results. A few months in it were enough to make one a court messenger or even a court clerk. Those who stayed longer became teachers; and from Umuofia labourers went forth into the Lord's vineyard. New churches were established in the surrounding villages and a few schools with them. From the very beginning religion and education went hand in hand.

Mr Brown's mission grew from strength to strength, and because of its link with the new administration it earned a new social prestige. But Mr Brown himself was breaking down in health. At first he ignored the warning signs. But in the end he had to leave his flock, sad and broken.

It was in the first rainy season after Okonkwo's return to Umuofia that Mr Brown left for home. As soon as he had learnt of Okonkwo's return five months earlier, the missionary had immediately paid him a visit. He had just sent Okonkwo's son, Nwoye, who was now called Isaac, to the new training college for teachers in Umuru. And he had hoped that Okonkwo would be happy to hear of it. But Okonkwo had driven him away with the threat that if he came into his compound again, he would be carried out of it.

Okonkwo's return to his native land was not as memorable as he had wished. It was true his two beautiful daughters aroused great interest among suitors and marriage negotiations were soon in progress, but, beyond that, Umuofia did not appear to have taken any special notice of the warrior's return. The clan had undergone such profound change during his exile that it was barely recognizable. The new religion and government and the trading stores were very much in the people's eyes and minds. There were still many who saw these new institutions as evil, but even they talked and thought about little else, and certainly not about Okonkwo's return.

And it was the wrong year too. If Okonkwo had immediately initiated his two sons into the *ozo* society as he had planned he would have caused a stir. But the initiation rite was performed once in three years in Umuofia, and he had to wait for nearly two years for the next round of ceremonies.

Okonkwo was deeply grieved. And it was not just a personal grief. He mourned for the clan, which he saw breaking up and falling apart, and he mourned for the warlike men of Umuofia, who had so unaccountably become soft like women.

CHAPTER TWENTY-TWO

Mr Brown's successor was the Reverend James Smith, and he was a different kind of man. He condemned openly Mr Brown's policy of compromise and accommodation. He saw things as black and white. And black was evil. He saw the world as a battlefield in which the children of light were locked in mortal conflict with the sons of darkness. He spoke in his sermons about sheep and goats and about wheat and tares. He believed in slaying the prophets of Baal.

Mr Smith was greatly distressed by the ignorance which many of his flock showed even in such things as the Trinity and the Sacraments. It only showed that they were seeds sown on a rocky soil. Mr Brown had thought of nothing but numbers. He should have known that the kingdom of God did not depend on large crowds. Our Lord Himself stressed the importance of fewness. Narrow is the way and few the number. To fill the Lord's holy temple with an idolatrous crowd clamouring for signs was a folly of everlasting consequence. Our Lord used the whip only once in His life – to drive the crowd away from His church.

Within a few weeks of his arrival in Umuofia Mr Smith suspended a young woman from the church for pouring new wine into old bottles. This woman had allowed her heathen husband to mutilate her dead child. The child had been declared an *ogbanje*, plaguing its mother by dying and entering her womb to be born again. Four times this child had run its evil round. As so it was mutilated to discourage it from returning.

Mr Smith was filled with wrath when he heard of this. He disbelieved the story which even some of the most faithful confirmed, the story of really evil children who were not deterred by mutilation, but came back with all the scars. He replied that such stories were spread in the world by the Devil to lead men astray. Those who believed such stories were unworthy of the Lord's table.

There was a saying in Umuofia that as a man danced so the drums were beaten for him. Mr Smith danced a furious step and so the drums went mad. The over-zealous converts who had smarted under Mr Brown's restraining hand now flourished in full favour. One of them was Enoch, the son of the snake-priest who was believed to have killed and eaten the sacred python. Enoch's devotion to the new faith had seemed so much greater than Mr Brown's that the villagers called him The Outsider who wept louder than the bereaved.

Enoch was short and slight of build, and always seemed in great haste. His feet were short and broad, and when he stood or walked his heels came together and his feet opened outwards as if they had quarrelled and meant to go in different directions. Such was the excessive energy bottled up in Enoch's small body that it was always erupting in quarrels and fights. On Sundays he always imagined that the sermon was preached for the benefit of his enemies. And if he happened to sit near one of them he would occasionally turn to give him a meaningful look, as if to say, 'I told you so'. It was Enoch who touched off the great conflict between church and clan in Umuofia which had been gathering since Mr Brown left.

It happened during the annual ceremony which was held in honour of the earth deity. At such times the ancestors of the clan who had been committed to Mother Earth at their death emerged again as *egwugwu* through tiny ant holes.

One of the greatest crimes a man could commit was to unmask an *egwugwu* in public, or to say or do anything which might reduce its immortal prestige in the eyes of the uninitiated. And this was what Enoch did.

The annual worship of the earth goddess fell on a Sunday, and

the masked spirits were abroad. The Christian women who had
been to church could not therefore go home. Some of their men
had gone out to beg the *egwugwu* to retire for a short while for
the women to pass. They agreed and were already retiring, when
Enoch boasted aloud that they would not dare to touch a Christian.
Whereupon they all came back and one of them gave Enoch a good
stroke of the cane, which was always carried. Enoch fell on him
and tore off his mask. The other *egwugwu* immediately surrounded
their desecrated companion, to shield him from the profane gaze
of women and children, and led him away. Enoch had killed an
ancestral spirit, and Umuofia was thrown into confusion.

That night the Mother of the Spirits walked the length and
breadth of the clan, weeping for her murdered son. It was a terrible
night. Not even the oldest man in Umuofia had ever heard such
a strange and fearful sound, and it was never to be heard again.
It seemed as if the very soul of the tribe wept for a great evil that
was coming – its own death.

On the next day all the masked *egwugwu* of Umuofia assembled
in the market-place. They came from all the quarters of the clan
and even from the neighbouring villages. The dreaded Otakagu
came from Imo, and Ekwensu, dangling a white cock, arrived from
Uli. It was a terrible gathering. The eerie voices of countless spirits,
the bells that clattered behind some of them, and the clash of
matchets as they ran forwards and backwards and saluted one
another, sent tremors of fear into every heart. For the first time
in living memory the sacred bull-roarer was heard in broad daylight.

From the market-place the furious band made for Enoch's
compound. Some of the elders of the clan went with them, wearing
heavy protections of charms and amulets. These were men whose
arms were strong in *ogwu*, or medicine. As for the ordinary men
and women, they listened from the safety of their huts.

The leaders of the Christians had met together at Mr Smith's
parsonage on the previous night. As they deliberated they could
hear the Mother of Spirits wailing for her son. The chilling sound
affected Mr Smith, and for the first time he seemed to be afraid.

'What are they planning to do?' he asked. No one knew, because
such a thing had never happened before. Mr Smith would have

sent for the District Commissioner and his court messengers, but they had gone on tour on the previous day.

'One thing is clear,' said Mr Smith. 'We cannot offer physical resistance to them. Our strength lies in the Lord.' They knelt down together and prayed to God for delivery.

'O Lord save Thy people,' cried Mr Smith.

'And bless Thine inheritance,' replied the men.

They decided that Enoch should be hidden in the parsonage for a day or two. Enoch himself was greatly disappointed when he heard this, for he had hoped that a holy war was imminent; and there were a few other Christians who thought like him. But wisdom prevailed in the camp of the faithful and many lives were thus saved.

The band of *egwugwu* moved like a furious whirlwind to Enoch's compound and with matchet and fire reduced it to a desolate heap. And from there they made for the church, intoxicated with destruction.

Mr Smith was in his church when he heard the masked spirits coming. He walked quietly to the door which commanded the approach to the church compound, and stood there. But when the first three or four *egwugwu* appeared on the church compound he nearly bolted. He overcame this impulse and instead of running away he went down the two steps that led up to the church and walked towards the approaching spirits.

They surged forward, and a long stretch of bamboo fence with which the church compound was surrounded gave way before them. Discordant bells clanged, matchets clashed and the air was full of dust and weird sounds. Mr Smith heard a sound of footsteps behind him. He turned round and saw Okeke, his interpreter. Okeke had not been on the best of terms with his master since he had strongly condemned Enoch's behaviour at the meeting of the leaders of the church during the night. Okeke had gone as far as to say that Enoch should not be hidden in the parsonage, because he would only draw the wrath of the clan on the pastor. Mr Smith had rebuked him in very strong language, and had not sought his advice that morning. But now, as he came up and stood by him confronting the angry spirits, Mr Smith looked at him and smiled. It was a wan smile, but there was deep gratitude there.

For a brief moment the onrush of the *egwugwu* was checked by the unexpected composure of the two men. But it was only a momentary check, like the tense silence between blasts of thunder. The second onrush was greater than the first. It swallowed up the two men. Then an unmistakable voice rose above the tumult and there was immediate silence. Space was made around the two men, and Ajofia began to speak.

Ajofia was the leading *egwugwu* of Umuofia. He was the head and spokesman of the nine ancestors who administered justice in the clan. His voice was unmistakable and so he was able to bring immediate peace to the agitated spirits. He then addressed Mr Smith, and as he spoke clouds of smoke rose from his head.

'The body of the white man, I salute you,' he said, using the language in which immortals spoke to men.

'The body of the white man, do you know me?' he asked.

Mr Smith looked at his interpreter, but Okeke, who was a native of distant Umuru, was also at a loss.

Ajofia laughed in his guttural voice. It was like the laugh of rusty metal. 'They are strangers,' he said, 'and they are ignorant. But let that pass.' He turned round to his comrades and saluted them, calling them the fathers of Umuofia. He dug his rattling spear into the ground and it shook with metallic life. Then he turned once more to the missionary and his interpreter.

'Tell the white man that we will not do him any harm,' he said to the interpreter. 'Tell him to go back to his house and leave us alone. We liked his brother who was with us before. He was foolish, but we liked him, and for his sake we shall not harm his brother. But this shrine which he built must be destroyed. We shall no longer allow it in our midst. It has bred untold abominations and we have come to put an end to it.' He turned to his comrades, 'Fathers of Umuofia, I salute you'; and they replied with one gutteral voice. He turned again to the missionary. 'You can stay with us if you like our ways. You can worship your own god. It is good that a man should worship the gods and the spirits of his fathers. Go back to your house so that you may not be hurt. Our anger is great but we have held it down so that we can talk to you.'

Mr Smith said to his interpreter: 'Tell them to go away from here. This is the house of God and I will not live to see it desecrated.'

Okeke interpreted wisely to the spirits and leaders of Umuofia: 'The white man says he is happy you have come to him with your grievances, like friends. He will be happy if you leave the matter in his hands.'

'We cannot leave the matter in his hands because he does not understand our customs, just as we do not understand his. We say he is foolish because he does not know our ways, and perhaps he says we are foolish because we do not know his. Let him go away.'

Mr Smith stood his ground. But he could not save his church. When the *egwugwu* went away the red-earth church which Mr Brown had built was a pile of earth and ashes. And for the moment the spirit of the clan was pacified.

CHAPTER TWENTY-THREE

For the first time in many years Okonkwo had a feeling that was akin to happiness. The times which had altered so unaccountably during his exile seemed to be coming round again. The clan which had turned false on him appeared to be making amends.

He had spoken violently to his clansmen when they had met in the market-place to decide on their action. And they had listened to him with respect. It was like the good old days again, when a warrior was a warrior. Although they had not agreed to kill the missionary or drive away the Christians, they had agreed to do something substantial. And they had done it. Okonkwo was almost happy again.

For two days after the destruction of the church, nothing happened. Every man in Umuofia went about armed with a gun or a matchet. They would not be caught unawares, like the men of Abame.

Then the District Commissioner returned from his tour. Mr Smith went immediately to him and they had a long discussion. The men of Umuofia did not take any notice of this, and if they did, they thought it was not important. The missionary often went to see his brother white man. There was nothing strange in that.

Three days later the District Commissioner sent his sweet-tongued messenger to the leaders of Umuofia asking them to meet him in his headquarters. That also was not strange. He often asked them to hold such palavers, as he called them. Okonkwo was among the six leaders he invited.

Okonkwo warned the others to be fully armed. 'An Umuofia man does not refuse a call,' he said. 'He may refuse to do what he is asked; he does not refuse to be asked. But the times have changed, and we must be fully prepared.'

And so the six men went to see the District Commissioner armed with their matchets. They did not carry guns, for that would be unseemly. They were led into the courthouse where the District Commissioner sat. He received them politely. They unslung their goatskin bags and their sheathed matchets, put them on the floor, and sat down.

'I have asked you to come,' began the Commissioner, 'because of what happened during my absence. I have been told a few things but I cannot believe them until I have heard your own side. Let us talk about it like friends and find a way of ensuring that it does not happen again.'

Ogbuefi Ekwueme rose to his feet and began to tell the story.

'Wait a minute,' said the Commissioner. 'I want to bring in my men so that they too can hear your grievances and take warning. Many of them come from distant places and although they speak your tongue they are ignorant of your customs. James! Go and bring in the men.' His interpreter left the courtroom and soon returned with twelve men. They sat together with the men of Umuofia, and Ogbuefi Ekwueme began again to tell the story of how Enoch murdered an *egwugwu*.

It happened so quickly that the six men did not see it coming. There was only a brief scuffle, too brief even to allow the drawing of a sheathed matchet. The six men were handcuffed and led into the guardroom.

'We shall not do you any harm,' said the District Commissioner to them later, 'if only you agree to co-operate with us. We have brought a peaceful administration to you and your people so that you may be happy. If any man ill-treats you we shall come to your rescue. But we will not allow you to ill-treat others. We have a court of law where we judge cases and administer justice just as it is done in my own country under a great queen. I have brought you here because you joined together to molest others, to burn people's houses and their place of worship. That must not happen in the dominion of our queen, the most powerful ruler in the world. I have decided that you will pay a fine of two hundred bags of cowries. You will be released as soon as you agree to this and undertake to collect that fine from your people. What do you say to that?'

The six men remained sullen and silent and the Commissioner left them for a while. He told the court messengers, when he left the guardroom, to treat the men with respect because they were the leaders of Umuofia. They said, 'Yes, sir,' and saluted.

As soon as the District Commissioner left, the head messenger, who was also the prisoners' barber, took down his razor and shaved off all the hair on the men's heads. They were still handcuffed, and they just sat and moped.

'Who is the chief among you?' the court messengers asked in jest. 'We see that every pauper wears the anklet of title in Umuofia. Does it cost as much as ten cowries?'

The six men ate nothing throughout that day and the next. They were not even given any water to drink, and they could not go out to urinate or go into the bush when they were pressed. At night the messengers came in to taunt them and to knock their shaven heads together.

Even when the men were left alone they found no words to speak to one another. It was only on the third day, when they could no longer bear the hunger and the insults, that they began to talk about giving in.

'We should have killed the white man if you had listened to me,' Okonkwo snarled.

'We could have been in Umuru now waiting to be hanged,' someone said to him.

'Who wants to kill the white man?' asked a messenger who had just rushed in. Nobody spoke.

'You are not satisfied with your crime, but you must kill the white man on top of it.' He carried a strong stick, and he hit each man a few blows on the head and back. Okonkwo was choked with hate.

As soon as the six men were locked up, court messengers went into Umuofia to tell the people that their leaders would not be released unless they paid a fine of two hundred and fifty bags of cowries.

'Unless you pay the fine immediately,' said their headman, 'we will take your leaders to Umuru before the big white man, and hang them.'

This story spread quickly through the villages, and was added to as it went. Some said that the men had already been taken to Umuru and would be hanged on the following day. Some said that their families would also be hanged. Others said that soldiers were already on their way to shoot the people of Umuofia as they had done in Abame.

It was the time of the full moon. But that night the voice of children was not heard. The village *ilo* where they always gathered for a moon-play was empty. The women of Iguedo did not meet in their secret enclosure to learn a new dance to be displayed later to the village. Young men who were always abroad in the moonlight kept their huts that night. Their manly voices were not heard on the village paths as they went to visit their friends and lovers. Umuofia was like a startled animal with ears erect, sniffing the silent, ominous air and not knowing which way to turn.

The silence was broken by the village crier beating his sonorous *ogene*. He called every man in Umuofia, from the Akakanma age-group upwards, to a meeting in the market-place after the morning meal. He went from one end of the village to the other and walked all its breadth. He did not leave out any of the main footpaths.

Okonkwo's compound was like a deserted homestead. It was as if cold water had been poured on it. His family was all there, but everyone spoke in whispers. His daughter Ezinma had broken her twenty-eight-day visit to the family of her future husband, and returned home when she heard that her father had been imprisoned, and was going to be hanged. As soon as she got home she went to Obierika to ask what the men of Umuofia were going to do about it. But Obierika had not been home since morning. His wives thought he had gone to a secret meeting. Ezinma was satisfied that something was being done.

On the morning after the village crier's appeal the men of Umuofia met in the market-place and decided to collect without delay two hundred and fifty bags of cowries to appease the white man. They did not know that fifty bags would go to the court messengers, who had increased the fine for that purpose.

CHAPTER TWENTY-FOUR

Okonkwo and his fellow prisoners were set free as soon as the fine was paid. The District Commissioner spoke to them again about the great queen, and about peace and good government. But the men did not listen. They just sat and looked at him and at his interpreter. In the end they were given back their bags and sheathed matchets and told to go home. They rose and left the courthouse. They neither spoke to anyone nor among themselves.

The courthouse, like the church, was built a little way outside the village. The footpath that linked them was a very busy one because it also led to the stream, beyond the court. It was open and sandy. Footpaths were open and sandy in the dry season. But when the rains came the bush grew thick on either side and closed in on the path. It was now dry season.

As they made their way to the village the six men met women and children going to the stream with their waterpots. But the men wore such heavy and fearsome looks that the women and children did not say 'nno' or 'welcome' to them, but edged out of the way to let them pass. In the village little groups of men joined them until they became a sizeable company. They walked silently. As each of the six men got to his compound, he turned in, taking some of the crowd with him. The village was astir in a silent, suppressed way.

Ezinma had prepared some food for her father as soon as news spread that the six men would be released. She took it to him in his *obi*. He ate absent-mindedly. He had no appetite; he only ate to please her. His male relations and friends gathered in his *obi*, and Obierika was urging him to eat. Nobody else spoke, but they noticed the long stripes on Okonkwo's back where the warder's whip had cut into his flesh.

The village crier was abroad again in the night. He beat his iron gong and announced that another meeting would be held in the morning. Everyone knew that Umuofia was at last going to speak its mind about the things that were happening.

Okonkwo slept very little that night. The bitterness in his heart was now mixed with a kind of childlike excitement. Before he had gone to bed he had brought down his war dress, which he had not touched since his return from exile. He had shaken out his smoked raffia skirt and examined the tall feather headgear and his shield. They were all satisfactory, he had thought.

As he lay on his bamboo bed he thought about the treatment he had received in the white man's court, and he swore vengeance. If Umuofia decided on war, all would be well. But if they chose to be cowards he would go out and avenge himself. He thought about wars in the past. The noblest, he thought, was the war against Isike. In those days Okudo was still alive. Okudo sang a war song in a way that no other man could. He was not a fighter, but his voice turned every man into a lion.

'Worthy men are no more,' Okonkwo sighed as he remembered those days. 'Isike will never forget how we slaughtered them in that war. We killed twelve of their men and they killed only two of ours. Before the end of the fourth market week they were suing for peace. Those were days when men were men.'

As he thought of these things he heard the sound of the iron gong in the distance. He listened carefully, and could just hear the crier's voice. But it was very faint. He turned on his bed and his back hurt him. He ground his teeth. The crier was drawing nearer and nearer until he passed by Okonkwo's compound.

'The greatest obstacle in Umuofia,' Okonkwo thought bitterly, 'is that coward, Egonwanne. His sweet tongue can change fire into cold ash. When he speaks he moves our men to impotence. If they had ignored his womanish wisdom five years ago, we would not have come to this.' He ground his teeth. 'Tomorrow he will tell them that our fathers never fought a "war of blame". If they listen to him I shall leave them and plan my own revenge.'

The crier's voice had once more become faint, and the distance had taken the harsh edge off his iron gong. Okonkwo turned from one side to the other and derived a kind of pleasure from the pain his back gave him. 'Let Egonwanne talk about a "war of blame" tomorrow and I shall show him my back and head.' He ground his teeth.

The market-place began to fill as soon as the sun rose. Obierika was waiting in his *obi* when Okonkwo came along and called him. He hung his goatskin bag and his sheathed matchet on his shoulder and went out to join him. Obierika's hut was close to the road and he saw every man who passed to the market-place. He had exchanged greetings with many who had already passed that morning.

When Okonkwo and Obierika got to the meeting-place there were already so many people that if one threw up a grain of sand it would not find its way to the earth again. And many more people were coming from every quarter of the nine villages. It warmed Okonkwo's heart to see such strength of numbers. But he was looking for one man in particular, the man whose tongue he dreaded and despised so much.

'Can you see him?' he asked Obierika.

'Who?'

'Egonwanne,' he said, his eyes roving from one corner of the huge market-place to the other. Most of the men were seated on goatskins on the ground. A few of them sat on wooden stools they had brought with them.

'No,' said Obierika, casting his eyes over the crowd. 'Yes, there he is, under the silk-cotton tree. Are you afraid he would convince us not to fight?'

'Afraid? I do not care what he does to *you*. I despise him and those who listen to him. I shall fight alone if I choose.'

They spoke at the top of their voices because everyone was talking, and it was like the sound of a great market.

'I shall wait till he has spoken,' Okonkwo thought. 'Then I shall speak.'

'But how do you know he will speak against war?' Obierika asked after a while.

'Because I know he is a coward,' said Okonkwo. Obierika did not hear the rest of what he said because at that moment somebody touched his shoulder from behind and he turned round to shake hands and exchange greetings with five or six friends. Okonkwo did not turn around even though he knew the voices. He was in no mood to exchange greetings. But one of the men touched him and asked about the people of his compound.

'They are well,' he replied without interest.

The first man to speak to Umuofia that morning was Okika, one of the six who had been imprisoned. Okika was a great man and an orator. But he did not have the booming voice which a first speaker must use to establish silence in the assembly of the clan. Onyeka had such a voice; and so he was asked to salute Umuofia before Okika began to speak.

'*Umuofia kwenu!*' he bellowed, raising his left arm and pushing the air with his open hand.

'*Yaa!*' roared Umuofia.

'*Umuofia kwenu!*' he bellowed again, and again and again, facing a new direction each time. And the crowd answered, '*Yaa!*'

There was immediate silence as though cold water had been poured on a roaring flame.

Okika sprang to his feet and also saluted his clansmen four times. Then he began to speak:

'You all know why we are here, when we ought to be building our barns or mending our huts, when we should be putting our compounds in order. My father used to say to me: "Whenever you see a toad jumping in broad daylight, then know that something is after its life." When I saw you all pouring into this meeting from the quarters of our clan so early in the morning, I knew that something was after our life.' He paused for a brief moment and then began again:

'All our gods are weeping. Idemili is weeping. Ogwugwu is weeping, Agbala is weeping, and all the others. Our dead fathers

are weeping because of the shameful sacrilege they are suffering
and the abomination we have all seen with our eyes.' He stopped
again to steady his trembling voice.

'This is a great gathering. No clan can boast of greater numbers
or greater valour. But are we all here? I ask you: Are all the
sons of Umuofia with us here?' A deep murmur swept through
the crowd.

'They are not,' he said. 'They have broken the clan and gone
their several ways. We who are here this morning have remained
true to our fathers, but our brothers have deserted us and joined
a stranger to soil their fatherland. If we fight the stranger we shall
hit our brothers and perhaps shed the blood of a clansman. But
we must do it. Our fathers never dreamt of such a thing, they never
killed their brothers. But a white man never came to them. So we
must do what our fathers would never have done. Eneke the bird
was asked why he was always on the wing and he replied: "Men
have learnt to shoot without missing their mark and I have learnt
to fly without perching on a twig." We must root out this evil.
And if our brothers take the side of evil we must root them out
too. And we must do it *now*. We must bale this water now that
it is only ankle-deep . . .'

At this point there was a sudden stir in the crowd and every eye
was turned in one direction. There was a sharp bend in the road
that led from the market-place to the white man's court, and to
the stream beyond it. And so no one had seen the approach of the
five court messengers until they had come round the bend, a few
paces from the edge of the crowd. Okonkwo was sitting at the edge.

He sprang to his feet as soon as he saw who it was. He confronted
the head messenger, trembling with hate, unable to utter a word.
The man was fearless and stood his ground, his four men lined
up behind him.

In that brief moment the world seemed to stand still, waiting.
There was utter silence. The men of Umuofia were merged into
the mute backcloth of trees and giant creepers, waiting.

The spell was broken by the head messenger. 'Let me pass!' he
ordered.

'What do you want here?'

'The white man whose power you know too well has ordered this meeting to stop.'

In a flash Okonkwo drew his matchet. The messenger crouched to avoid the blow. It was useless. Okonkwo's matchet descended twice and the man's head lay beside his uniformed body.

The waiting backcloth jumped into tumultuous life and the meeting was stopped. Okonkwo stood looking at the dead man. He knew that Umuofia would not go to war. He knew because they had let the other messengers escape. They had broken into tumult instead of action. He discerned fright in that tumult. He heard voices asking: 'Why did he do it?'

He wiped his matchet on the sand and went away.

CHAPTER TWENTY-FIVE

When the District Commissioner arrived at Okonkwo's compound at the head of an armed band of soldiers and court messengers he found a small crowd of men sitting wearily in the *obi*. He commanded them to come outside, and they obeyed without a murmur.

'Which among you is called Okonkwo?' he asked through his interpreter.

'He is not here,' replied Obierika.

'Where is he?'

'He is not here!'

The Commissioner became angry and red in the face. He warned the men that unless they produced Okonkwo forthwith he would lock them all up. The men murmured among themselves, and Obierika spoke again.

'We can take you where he is, and perhaps your men will help us.'

The Commissioner did not understand what Obierika meant when he said, 'Perhaps your men will help us'. One of the most infuriating habits of these people was their love of superfluous words, he thought.

Obierika with five or six others led the way. The Commissioner and his men followed, their firearms held at the ready. He had warned Obierika that if he and his men played any monkey tricks they would be shot. And so they went.

There was a small bush behind Okonkwo's compound. The only opening into this bush from the compound was a little round hole in the red-earth wall through which fowls went in and out in their endless search for food. The hole would not let a man through. It was to this bush that Obierika led the Commissioner and his men. They skirted round the compound, keeping close to the wall. The only sound they made was with their feet as they crushed dry leaves.

Then they came to the tree from which Okonkwo's body was dangling, and they stopped dead.

'Perhaps your men can help us bring him down and bury him,' said Obierika. 'We have sent for strangers from another village to do it for us, but they may be a long time coming.'

The District Commissioner changed instantaneously. The resolute administrator in him gave way to the student of primitive customs.

'Why can't you take him down yourselves?' he asked.

'It is against our custom,' said one of the men. 'It is an abomination for a man to take his own life. It is an offence against the Earth, and a man who commits it will not be buried by his clansmen. His body is evil, and only strangers may touch it. That is why we ask your people to bring him down, because you are strangers.'

'Will you bury him like any other man?' asked the Commissioner.

'We cannot bury him. Only strangers can. We shall pay your men to do it. When he has been buried we will then do our duty by him. We shall make sacrifices to cleanse the desecrated land.'

Obierika, who had been gazing steadily at his friend's dangling body, turned suddenly to the District Commissioner and said ferociously: 'That man was one of the greatest men in Umuofia. You drove him to kill himself; and now he will be buried like a dog . . .' He could not say any more. His voice trembled and choked his words.

'Shut up!' shouted one of the messengers, quite unnecessarily.

'Take down the body,' the Commissioner ordered his chief messenger, 'and bring it and all these people to the court.'

'Yes, sah,' the messenger said, saluting.

The Commissioner went away, taking three or four of the soldiers with him. In the many years in which he had toiled to bring civilization to different parts of Africa he had learnt a number of things. One of them was that a District Commissioner must never attend to such undignified details as cutting down a hanged man from the tree. Such attention would give the natives a poor opinion of him. In the book which he planned to write he would stress that point. As he walked back to the court he thought about that book. Every day brought him some new material. The story of this man who had killed a messenger and hanged himself would make interesting reading. One could almost write a whole chapter on him. Perhaps not a whole chapter but a reasonable paragraph, at any rate. There was so much else to include, and one must be firm in cutting out details. He had already chosen the title of the book, after much thought: *The Pacification of the Primitive Tribes of the Lower Niger.*

NO LONGER
AT EASE

For Christie

We returned to our places, these Kingdoms,
But no longer at ease here, in the old dispensation,
With an alien people clutching their gods.
I should be glad of another death.
  T. S. Eliot: 'The Journey of the Magi'

CHAPTER ONE

For three or four weeks Obi Okonkwo had been steeling himself against this moment. And when he walked into the dock that morning he thought he was fully prepared. He wore a smart palm-beach suit and appeared unruffled and indifferent. The proceeding seemed to be of little interest to him. Except for one brief moment at the very beginning when one of the counsel had got into trouble with the judge.

'This court begins at nine o'clock. Why are you late?'

Whenever Mr Justice William Galloway, Judge of the High Court of Lagos and the Southern Cameroons, looked at a victim he fixed him with his gaze as a collector fixes his insect with formalin. He lowered his head like a charging ram and looked over his gold-rimmed spectacles at the lawyer.

'I am sorry, Your Honour,' the man stammered. 'My car broke down on the way.'

The judge continued to look at him for a long time. Then he said very abruptly:

'All right, Mr Adeyemi. I accept your excuse. But I must say I'm getting sick and tired of these constant excuses about the problem of locomotion.'

There was suppressed laughter at the bar. Obi Okonkwo smiled a wan and ashy smile and lost interest again.

Every available space in the courtroom was taken up. There were almost as many people standing as sitting. The case had been the talk of Lagos for a number of weeks and on this last day anyone who could possibly leave his job was there to hear the judgement. Some Civil Servants paid as much as ten shillings and sixpence to obtain a doctor's certificate of illness for the day.

Obi's listlessness did not show any signs of decreasing even when the judge began to sum up. It was only when he said: 'I cannot comprehend how a young man of your education and brilliant promise could have done this' that a sudden and marked change occurred. Treacherous tears came into Obi's eyes. He brought out a white handkerchief and rubbed his face. But he did it as people do when they wipe sweat. He even tried to smile and belie the tears. A smile would have been quite logical. All that stuff about education and promise and betrayal had not taken him unawares. He had expected it and rehearsed this very scene a hundred times until it had become as familiar as a friend.

In fact, some weeks ago when the trial first began, Mr Green, his boss, who was one of the Crown witnesses, had also said something about a young man of great promise. And Obi had remained completely unmoved. Mercifully he had recently lost his mother, and Clara had gone out of his life. The two events following closely on each other had dulled his sensibility and left him a different man, able to look words like 'education' and 'promise' squarely in the face. But now when the supreme moment came he was betrayed by treacherous tears.

Mr Green had been playing tennis since five o'clock. It was most unusual. As a rule his work took up so much of his time that he rarely played. His normal exercise was a short walk in the evenings. But today he had played with a friend who worked for the British Council. After the game they retired to the club bar. Mr Green had a light-yellow sweater over his white shirt, and a white towel hung from his neck. There were many other Europeans in the bar, some half-sitting on the high stools and some standing in groups of twos and threes drinking cold beer, orange squash or gin-and-tonic.

'I cannot understand why he did it,' said the British Council man thoughtfully. He was drawing lines of water with his finger on the back of his mist-covered glass of ice-cold beer.

'I can,' said Mr Green simply. 'What I can't understand is why people like you refuse to face facts.' Mr Green was famous for speaking his mind. He wiped his red face with the white towel on his neck. 'The African is corrupt through and through.' The British Council man looked about him furtively, more from instinct than necessity, for although the club was now open to them technically, few Africans went to it. On this particular occasion there was none, except of course the stewards who served unobtrusively. It was quite possible to go in, drink, sign a cheque, talk to friends and leave again without noticing these stewards in their white uniforms. If everything went right you did not see them.

'They are all corrupt,' repeated Mr Green. 'I'm all for equality and all that. I for one would hate to live in South Africa. But equality won't alter facts.'

'What facts?' asked the British Council man, who was relatively new to the country. There was a lull in the general conversation, as many people were now listening to Mr Green without appearing to do so.

'The fact that over countless centuries the African has been the victim of the worst climate in the world and of every imaginable disease. Hardly his fault. But he has been sapped mentally and physically. We have brought him Western education. But what use is it to him? He is . . .' He was interrupted by the arrival of another friend.

'Hello, Peter. Hello, Bill.'

'Hello.'

'Hello.'

'May I join you?'

'Certainly.'

'Most certainly. What are you drinking? Beer? Right. Steward. One beer for this master.'

'What kind, sir?'

'Heineken.'

'Yes, sir.'

'We were talking about this young man who took a bribe.'
'Oh yes.'

Somewhere on the Lagos mainland the Umuofia Progressive Union was holding an emergency meeting. Umuofia is an Ibo village in Eastern Nigeria and the home town of Obi Okonkwo. It is not a particularly big village but its inhabitants call it a town. They are very proud of its past when it was the terror of their neighbours, before the white man came and levelled everybody down. Those Umuofians (that is the name they call themselves) who leave their home town to find work in towns all over Nigeria regard themselves as sojourners. They return to Umuofia every two years or so to spend their leave. When they have saved up enough money they ask their relations at home to find them a wife, or they build a 'zinc' house on their family land. No matter where they are in Nigeria, they start a local branch of the Umuofia Progressive Union.

In recent weeks the Union had met several times over Obi Okonkwo's case. At the first meeting, a handful of people had expressed the view that there was no reason why the Union should worry itself over the troubles of a prodigal son who had shown great disrespect to it only a little while ago.

'We paid eight hundred pounds to train him in England,' said one of them. 'But instead of being grateful he insults us because of a useless girl. And now we are being called together again to find more money for him. What does he do with his big salary? My own opinion is that we have already done too much for him.'

This view, although accepted as largely true, was not taken very seriously. For, as the President pointed out, a kinsman in trouble had to be saved, not blamed; anger against a brother was felt in the flesh, not in the bone. And so the Union decided to pay for the services of a lawyer from their funds.

But this morning the case was lost. That was why another emergency meeting had been convened. Many people had already arrived at the house of the President on Moloney Street, and were talking excitedly about the judgement.

'I knew it was a bad case,' said the man who had opposed the Union's intervention from the start. 'We are just throwing money away. What do our people say? He that fights for a ne'er-do-well has nothing to show for it except a head covered in earth and grime.'

But this man had no following. The men of Umuofia were prepared to fight to the last. They had no illusions about Obi. He was, without doubt, a very foolish and self-willed young man. But this was not the time to go into that. The fox must be chased away first; after that the hen might be warned against wandering into the bush.

When the time for warning came the men of Umuofia could be trusted to give it in full measure, pressed down and flowing over. The President said it was a thing of shame for a man in the senior service to go to prison for twenty pounds. He repeated twenty pounds, spitting it out. 'I am against people reaping where they have not sown. But we have a saying that if you want to eat a toad you should look for a fat and juicy one.'

'It is all lack of experience,' said another man. 'He should not have accepted the money himself. What others do is tell you to go and hand it to their houseboy. Obi tried to do what everyone does without finding out how it was done.' He told the proverb of the house rat who went swimming with his friend the lizard and died from cold, for while the lizard's scales kept him dry the rat's hairy body remained wet.

The President, in due course, looked at his pocket-watch and announced that it was time to declare the meeting open. Everybody stood up and he said a short prayer. Then he presented three kola nuts to the meeting. The oldest man present broke one of them, saying another kind of prayer while he did it. 'He that brings kola nuts brings life,' he said. 'We do not seek to hurt any man, but if any man seeks to hurt us may he break his neck.' The congregation answered *Amen*. 'We are strangers in this land. If good comes to it may we have our share.' *Amen*. 'But if bad comes let it go to the owners of the land who know what gods should be appeased.' *Amen*. 'Many towns have four or five or even ten of their sons in European posts in this city. Umuofia has only one. And now our enemies say that even that one is too many for us. But our ancestors will not agree to such a thing.' *Amen*. 'An only palm fruit does not get lost in the fire.' *Amen*.

Obi Okonkwo was indeed an only palm fruit. His full name was Obiajulu – 'the mind at last is at rest'; the mind being his father's of course, who, his wife having borne him four daughters before Obi, was naturally becoming a little anxious. Being a Christian convert – in fact a catechist – he could not marry a second wife. But he was not the kind of man who carried his sorrow on his face. In particular, he would not let the heathen know that he was unhappy. He had called his fourth daughter Nwanyidinma – 'a girl is also good'. But his voice did not carry conviction.

The old man who broke the kola nuts in Lagos and called Obi Okonkwo an only palm fruit was not, however, thinking of Okonkwo's family. He was thinking of the ancient and war-like village of Umuofia. Six or seven years ago Umuofians abroad had formed their Union with the aim of collecting money to send some of their brighter young men to study in England. They taxed themselves mercilessly. The first scholarship under this scheme was awarded to Obi Okonkwo five years ago, almost to the day. Although they called it a scholarship it was to be repaid. In Obi's case it was worth eight hundred pounds, to be repaid within four years of his return. They wanted him to read law so that when he returned he would handle all their land cases against their neighbours. But when he got to England he read English; his self-will was not new. The Union was angry but in the end they left him alone. Although he would not be a lawyer, he would get a 'European post' in the Civil Service.

The selection of the first candidate had not presented any difficulty to the Union. Obi was an obvious choice. At the age of twelve or thirteen he had passed his Standard Six examination at the top of the whole province. Then he had won a scholarship to one of the best secondary schools in Eastern Nigeria. At the end of five years he passed the Cambridge School Certificate with distinction in all eight subjects. He was in fact a village celebrity, and his name was regularly invoked at the mission school where he had once been a pupil. (No one mentioned nowadays that he once brought shame to the school by writing a letter to Adolf Hitler during the war. The headmaster at the time had pointed out, almost in tears, that he was a disgrace to the British Empire, and that if he had been older he would surely have been sent to jail for the rest of his miserable life. He was only eleven then, and so got off with six strokes of the cane on his buttocks.)

Obi's going to England caused a big stir in Umuofia. A few days before his departure to Lagos his parents called a prayer meeting at their home. The Reverend Samuel Ikedi of St Mark's Anglican Church, Umuofia, was chairman. He said the occasion was the fulfilment of the prophecy:

> The people which sat in darkness
> Saw a great light,
> And to them which sat in the region
>   and shadow of death
> To them did light spring up.

He spoke for over half an hour. Then he asked that someone should lead them in prayer. Mary at once took up the challenge before most people had had time to stand up, let alone shut their eyes. Mary was one of the most zealous Christians in Umuofia and a good friend of Obi's mother. Hannah Okonkwo. Although Mary lived a long way from the church – three miles or more – she never missed the early morning prayer which the pastor conducted at cock-crow. In the heart of the wet season or the cold harmattan, Mary was sure to be there. Sometimes she came as much as an hour before time. She would blow out her hurricane lamp to save kerosene and go to sleep on the long mud seats.

'Oh God of Abraham, God of Isaac and God of Jacob,' she burst forth, 'the Beginning and the End. Without you we can do nothing. The great river is not big enough for you to wash your hands in. You have the yam and you have the knife, we cannot eat unless you cut us a piece. We are like ants in your sight. We are like little children who only wash their stomach when they bath, leaving their back dry . . .' She went on and on reeling off proverb after proverb and painting picture after picture. Finally, she got round to the subject of the gathering and dealt with it as fully as it deserved, giving among other things, the life history of her friend's son who was about to go to the place where learning finally came to an end.

When she was done, people blinked and rubbed their eyes to get used to the evening light once more.

They sat on long wooden forms which had been borrowed from the school. The chairman had a little table before him. On one side sat Obi in his school blazer and white trousers.

Two stalwarts emerged from the kitchen area, half bent with the gigantic iron pot of rice which they carried between them. Another pot followed. Two young women then brought in a simmering pot of stew hot from the fire. Kegs of palm wine followed, and a pile of plates and spoons which the church stocked for the use of its members at marriages, births, deaths and other occasions such as this.

Mr Isaac Okonkwo made a short speech placing 'this small kola' before his guests. By Umuofia standards he was well-to-do. He had been a catechist of the Church Missionary Society for twenty-five years and then retired on a pension of twenty-five pounds a year. He had been the very first man to build a 'zinc' house in Umuofia. It was therefore not unexpected that he would prepare a feast. But no one had imagined anything on this scale, not even from Okonkwo who was famous for his open-handedness which sometimes bordered on improvidence. Whenever his wife remonstrated against his thriftlessness he replied that a man who lived on the banks of the Niger should not wash his hands with spittle – a favourite saying of his father's. It was odd that he should have rejected everything about his father except this one proverb. Perhaps he had long forgotten that his father often used it.

At the end of the feast the pastor made another long speech. He thanked Okonkwo for giving them a feast greater than many a wedding feast these days.

Mr Ikedi had come to Umuofia from a township, and was able to tell the gathering how wedding feasts had been steadily declining in the towns since the invention of invitation cards. Many of his hearers whistled in disbelief when he told them that a man could not go to his neighbour's wedding unless he was given one of these papers on which they wrote RSVP – Rice and Stew Very Plenty – which was invariably an over-statement.

Then he turned to the young man on his right. 'In times past,' he told him, 'Umuofia would have required of you to fight in her wars and bring home human heads. But these were days of darkness from which we have been delivered by the blood of the Lamb of God. Today we send you to bring knowledge. Remember that the fear of the Lord is the beginning of wisdom. I have heard of young men from other towns who went to the white man's country, but instead of facing their studies they went after the sweet things of the flesh. Some of them even married white women.' The crowd murmured its strong disapproval of such behaviour. 'A man who does that is lost to his people. He is like rain wasted in the forest. I would have suggested getting you a wife before you leave. But the time is too short now. Anyway, I know that we have no fear where you are concerned. We are sending you to learn book. Enjoyment can wait. Do not be in a hurry to rush into the pleasures of the world like the young antelope who danced herself lame when the main dance was yet to come.'

He thanked Okonkwo again, and the guests for answering his call. 'If you had not answered his call, our brother would have become like the king in the Holy Book who called a wedding feast.'

As soon as he had finished speaking, Mary raised a song which the women had learnt at their prayer meeting.

> Leave me not behind Jesus, wait for me
> When I am going to the farm.
> Leave me not behind Jesus, wait for me
> When I am going to the market.
> Leave me not behind Jesus, wait for me
> When I am eating my food.
> Leave me not behind Jesus, wait for me
> When I am having my bath.
> Leave me not behind Jesus, wait for me
> When he is going to the White Man's Country.
> Leave him not behind Jesus, wait for him.

The gathering ended with the singing of 'Praise God from whom all blessings flow'. The guests then said their farewells to Obi, many of them repeating all the advice that he had already been given.

They shook hands with him and as they did so they pressed their presents into his palm, to buy a pencil with, or an exercise book or a loaf of bread for the journey, a shilling there and a penny there – substantial presents in a village where money was so rare, where men and women toiled from year to year to wrest a meagre living from an unwilling and exhausted soil.

CHAPTER TWO

Obi was away in England for a little under four years. He sometimes found it difficult to believe that it was as short as that. It seemed more like a decade than four years, what with the miseries of winter then his longing to return home, taking on the sharpness of physical pain. It was in England that Nigeria first became more than just a name to him. That was the first great thing that England did for him.

But the Nigeria he returned to was in many ways different from the picture he had carried in his mind during those four years. There were many things he could no longer recognize, and others – like the slums of Lagos – which he was seeing for the first time.

As a boy in the village of Umuofia he had heard his first stories about Lagos from a soldier home on leave from the war. Those soldiers were heroes who had seen the great world. They spoke of Abyssinia, Egypt, Palestine, Burma and so on. Some of them had been village ne'er-do-wells, but now they were heroes. They had bags and bags of money, and the villagers sat at their feet to listen to their stories. One of them went regularly to a market in the neighbouring village and helped himself to whatever he liked. He went in full uniform, breaking the earth with his boots, and no one dared touch him. It was said that if you touched a soldier, Government would deal with you. Besides, soldiers were as strong as lions because of the injections they were given in the army. It was from one of these soldiers that Obi had his first picture of Lagos.

'There is no darkness there,' he told his admiring listeners, 'because at night the electric shines like the sun, and people are always walking about, that is, those who want to walk. If you don't want to walk you only have to wave your hand and a pleasure car stops for you.' His audience made sounds of wonderment. Then by way of digression he said: 'If you see a white man, take off your hat for him. The only thing he cannot do is mould a human being.'

For many years afterwards, Lagos was always associated with electric lights and motor cars in Obi's mind. Even after he had at last visited the city and spent a few days there before flying to the United Kingdom his views did not change very much. Of course, he did not really see much of Lagos then. His mind was, as it were, on higher things. He spent the few days with his 'countryman', Joseph Okeke, a clerk in the Survey Department. Obi and Joseph had been classmates at the Umuofia CMS Central School. But Joseph had not gone on to a secondary school because he was too old and his parents were poor. He had joined the Education Corps of the 82nd Division and, when the war ended, the clerical service of the Nigerian Government.

Joseph was at Lagos Motor Park to meet his lucky friend who was passing through Lagos to the United Kingdom. He took him to his lodgings in Obalende. It was only one room. A curtain of light-blue cloth ran the full breadth of the room separating the Holy of Holies (as he called his double spring bed) from the sitting area. His cooking utensils, boxes and other personal effects were hidden away under the Holy of Holies. The sitting area was taken up with two armchairs, a settee (otherwise called 'me and my girl') and a round table on which he displayed his photo album. At night, his houseboy moved away the round table and spread his mat on the floor.

Joseph had so much to tell Obi on his first night in Lagos that it was past three when they slept. He told him about the cinema and the dance halls and about political meetings.

'Dancing is very important nowadays. No girl will look at you if you can't dance. I first met Joy at the dancing school.' 'Who is Joy?' asked Obi who was fascinated by what he was learning of this strange and sinful new world. 'She was my girlfriend for

– let's see . . .' he counted off his fingers '. . . March, April, May, June, July – for five months. She made these pillowcases for me.'

Obi raised himself instinctively to look at the pillow he was lying on. He had taken particular notice of it earlier in the day. It had the strange word OSCULATE sewn on it, each letter a different colour.

'She was a nice girl but sometimes very foolish. Sometimes, though, I wish we hadn't broken up. She was simply mad about me, and she was a virgin when I met her, which is very rare here.'

Joseph talked and talked and finally became less and less coherent. Then without any pause at all his talk was transformed into a deep snore which continued until the morning.

The very next day Obi found himself taking a compulsory walk down Lewis Street. Joseph had brought a woman home and it was quite clear that Obi's presence in the room was not desirable; so he went out to have a look round. The girl was one of Joseph's new finds, as he told him later. She was dark and tall with an enormous pneumatic bosom under a tight-fitting red and yellow dress. Her lips and long fingernails were a brilliant red, and her eyebrows were fine black lines. She looked not unlike those wooden masks made in Ikot Ekpene. Altogether she left a nasty taste in Obi's mouth, like the multi-coloured word OSCULATE on the pillowcase.

Some years later as Obi, newly returned from England, stood beside his car at night in one of the less formidable of Lagos slum areas waiting for Clara to take yards of material to her seamstress, his mind went over his earlier impressions of the city. He had not thought places like this stood side by side with the cars, electric lights and brightly dressed girls.

His car was parked close to a wide-open storm drain from which came a very strong smell of rotting flesh. It was the remains of a dog which had no doubt been run over by a taxi. Obi used to wonder why so many dogs were killed by cars in Lagos, until one day the driver he had engaged to teach him driving went out of his way to run over one. In shocked amazement Obi asked why he had done it. 'Na good luck,' said the man. 'Dog bring good luck for new car. But duck be different. If you kill duck you go get accident or kill man.'

Beyond the storm drain there was a meat stall. It was quite empty of meat or meat-sellers. But a man was working a little machine on one of the tables. It looked like a sewing machine except that it ground maize. A woman stood by watching the man turn the machine to grind her maize.

On the other side of the road a little boy wrapped in a cloth was selling bean cakes or *akara* under a lamp-post. His bowl of *akara* was lying in the dust and he seemed half asleep. But he really wasn't, for as soon as the night-soilman passed swinging his broom and hurricane lamp and trailing clouds of putrefaction the boy quickly sprang to his feet and began calling him names. The man made for him with his broom but the boy was already in flight, his bowl of *akara* on his head. The man grinding maize burst into laughter, and the woman joined in. The night-soilman smiled and went his way, having said something very rude about the boy's mother.

Here was Lagos, thought Obi, the real Lagos he hadn't imagined existed until now. During his first winter in England he had written a callow, nostalgic poem about Nigeria. It wasn't about Lagos in particular, but Lagos was part of the Nigeria he had in mind.

> How sweet it is to lie beneath a tree
> At eventime and share the ecstasy
> Of jocund birds and flimsy butterflies;
> How sweet to leave our earthbound body in its mud,
> And rise towards the music of the spheres,
> Descending soft with wind,
> And the tender glow of the fading sun.

He recalled this poem and then turned and looked at the rotting dog in the storm drain and smiled. 'I have tasted putrid flesh in the spoon,' he said through clenched teeth. 'Far more apt.' At last Clara emerged from the side street and they drove away.

They drove for a while in silence through narrow overcrowded streets. 'I can't understand why you should choose your dressmaker from the slums.' Clara did not reply. Instead she started humming *'Che sarà sarà'*.

The streets were now quite noisy and crowded, which was to be expected on a Saturday night at nine o'clock. Every few yards one met bands of dancers often wearing identical dress or *'aso ebi'*. Gay temporary sheds were erected in front of derelict houses and lit with brilliant fluorescent tubes for the celebration of an engagement or marriage or birth or promotion or success in business or the death of an old relative.

Obi slowed down as he approached three drummers and a large group of young women in damask and velvet swivelling their waists as effortlessly as oiled ball-bearings. A taxi driver hooted impatiently and overtook him, leaning out at the same time to shout: *'Ori oda*, your head no correct!' *'Ori oda* – bloody fool!' replied Obi. Almost immediately a cyclist crossed the road without looking back or giving any signal. Obi jammed on his brakes and his tyres screamed on the tarmac. Clara let out a little scream and gripped his left arm. The cyclist looked back once and rode away, his ambition written for all to see on his black bicycle-bag – FUTURE MINISTER.

Going from the Lagos mainland to Ikoyi on a Saturday night was like going from a bazaar to a funeral. And the vast Lagos cemetery which separated the two places helped to deepen this feeling. For all its luxurious bungalows and flats and its extensive greenery, Ikoyi was like a graveyard. It had no corporate life – at any rate for those Africans who lived there. They had not always lived there, of course. It was once a European reserve. But things had changed, and some Africans in 'European posts' had been given houses in Ikoyi. Obi Okonkwo, for example, lived there, and as he drove from Lagos to his flat he was struck again by these two cities in one. It always reminded him of twin kernels separated by a thin wall in a palm-nut shell. Sometimes one kernel was shiny-black and alive, the other powdery-white and dead.

'What is making you so moody?' He looked sideways at Clara who was ostentatiously sitting as far away from him as she could, pressed against the left door. She did not answer. 'Tell me, darling,' he said, holding her hand in one of his while he drove with the other. 'Leave me, *ojare*,' she said, snatching her hand away.

Obi knew very well why she was moody. She had suggested in her tentative way that they should go to the films. At this stage in their relationship, Clara never said: 'Let us go to films.' She said instead: 'There is a good film at the Capitol.' Obi, who did not care for films, especially those that Clara called good, had said after a long silence: 'Well, if you insist, but I'm not keen.' Clara did not insist, but she felt very much hurt. All evening she had been nursing her feelings. 'It's not too late to go to your film,' said Obi capitulating, or appearing to do so. 'You may go if you want to, I'm not coming,' she said. Only three days before they had gone to see 'a very good film' which infuriated Obi so much that he stopped looking at the screen altogether, except when Clara whispered one explanation or another for his benefit. 'That man is going to be killed,' she would prophesy, and sure as death, the doomed man would be shot almost immediately. From downstairs the shilling-ticket audience participated noisily in the action.

It never ceased to amaze Obi that Clara should take so much delight in these orgies of killing on the screen. Actually it rather amused him when he thought of it outside the cinema. But while he was there he could feel nothing but annoyance. Clara was well aware of this, and tried her best to ease the tedium for him by squeezing his arm or biting his ear after whispering something into it. 'And after all,' she would say sometimes, 'I don't quarrel with you when you start reading your poems to me.' Which was quite true. Only that very morning he had rung her up at the hospital and asked her to come to lunch to meet one of his friends who had recently come to Lagos on transfer from Enugu. Actually Clara had seen the fellow before and didn't like him. So she had said over the telephone that she wasn't keen on meeting him again. But Obi was insistent, and Clara had said: 'I don't know why you should want me to meet people that I don't want to meet.' 'You know, you are a poet, Clara,' said Obi. 'To meet people you don't want to meet, that's pure T. S. Eliot.'

Clara had no idea what he was talking about but she went to lunch and met Obi's friend, Christopher. So the least that Obi could do in return was to sit through her 'very good film', just as she had sat through a very dull lunch while Obi and Christopher theorized about bribery in Nigeria's public life. Whenever Obi and Christopher met they were bound to argue very heatedly about Nigeria's future. Whichever line Obi took, Christopher had to take the opposite. Christopher was an economist from the London School of Economics and he always pointed out that Obi's arguments were not based on factual or scientific analysis, which was not surprising since he had taken a degree in English.

'The Civil Service is corrupt because of these so-called experienced men at the top,' said Obi.

'You don't believe in experience? You think that a chap straight from university should be made a permanent secretary?'

'I didn't say *straight* from the university, but even that would be better than filling our top posts with old men who have no intellectual foundations to support their experience.'

'What about the Land Officer jailed last year? *He* is straight from the university.'

'He is an exception,' said Obi, 'But take one of these old men. He probably left school thirty years ago in Standard Six. He has worked steadily to the top through bribery – an ordeal by bribery. To him the bribe is natural. He gave it and he expects it. Our people say that if you pay homage to the man on top, others will pay homage to you when it is your turn to be on top. Well, that is what the old men say.'

'What do the young men say, if I may ask?'

'To most of them bribery is no problem. They come straight to the top without bribing anyone. It's not that they're necessarily better than others, it's simply that they can afford to be virtuous. But even that kind of virtue can become a habit.'

'Very well put,' conceded Christopher as he took a large piece of meat from the *egusi* soup. They were eating pounded yams and *egusi* soup with their fingers. The second generation of educated Nigerians had gone back to eating pounded yams or *garri* with their fingers for the good reason that it tasted better that way. Also for the even better reason that they were not as scared as the first generation of being called uncivilized.

'Zacchaeus!' called Clara.

'Yes, madam,' answered a voice from the pantry.

'Bring us more soup.'

Zacchaeus had half a mind not to reply, but he thought better of it and said grudgingly: 'Yes, madam.' Zacchaeus had made up his mind to resign as soon as Master married Madam. 'I like Master too much, but this Madam no good,' was his verdict.

CHAPTER THREE

The affair between Obi and Clara could not strictly be called love at first sight. They met at a dance organized by the London branch of the National Council of Nigeria and the Cameroons at the St Pancras Town Hall. Clara had come with a student who was fairly well known to Obi and who introduced them. Obi was immediately struck by her beauty and followed her with his eyes round the hall. In the end he succeeded in getting a dance with her. But he was so flustered that the only thing he could find to say was: 'Have you been dancing very long?' 'No. Why?' was the curt reply. Obi was never a very good dancer, but that night he was simply appalling. He stepped on her toes about four times in the first half-minute. Thereafter she concentrated all her attention on moving her foot sideways just in time. As soon as the dance ended she fled. Obi pursued her to her seat to say: 'Thank you very much.' She nodded without looking.

They did not meet again until almost eighteen months later at the Harrington Dock in Liverpool. For it happened that they were returning to Nigeria the same day on the same boat.

It was a small cargo boat carrying twelve passengers and a crew of fifty. When Obi arrived at the dock the other passengers had all embarked and completed their customs formalities. The short bald-headed customs officer was very friendly. He began by asking Obi whether he had had a happy stay in England. Did he go to a university in England? He must have found the weather very cold.

'I didn't mind the weather very much in the end,' said Obi,

who had learnt that an Englishman might grumble about his weather but did not expect a foreigner to join in.

When he went into the lounge Obi nearly fell over himself at the sight of Clara. She was talking to an elderly woman and a young Englishman. Obi sat with them and introduced himself. The elderly woman, whose name was Mrs Wright, was returning to Freetown. The young man was called Macmillan, an administrative officer in Northern Nigeria. Clara introduced herself as Miss Okeke. 'I think we have met before,' said Obi. Clara looked surprised and somewhat hostile. 'At the NCNC dance in London.' 'I see,' she said, with as much interest as if she had just been told that they were on a boat in the Liverpool Docks, and resumed her conversation with Mrs Wright.

The boat left the docks at 11 a.m. For the rest of the day Obi kept to himself, watching the sea or reading in his cabin. It was his first sea voyage, and he had already decided that it was infinitely better than flying.

He woke up the following morning without any sign of the much talked about seasickness. He had a warm bath before any of the other passengers were up, and went to the rails to look at the sea. Last evening it had been so placid. Now it had become an endless waste of restless, jaggy hillocks topped with white. Obi stood at the rails for nearly an hour drinking in the unspoilt air. 'They that go down to the sea in ships . . .' he remembered. He had very little religion nowadays, but he was nevertheless deeply moved.

When the gong sounded for breakfast his appetite was as keen as the morning air. The seating arrangement had been fixed on the previous day. There was a big central table which seated ten, and six little two-seaters ranged round the room. Eight of the twelve passengers sat on the middle table with the captain at the head and the chief engineer at the other end. Obi sat between Macmillan and a Nigerian Civil Servant called Stephen Udom. Directly in front of him was Mr Jones who was something or other in the United Africa Company. Mr Jones always worked solidly through four of the five heavy courses and then announced to the steward with self-righteous continence: 'Just coffee,' with the emphasis on the 'just'.

In contrast to Mr Jones, the chief engineer hardly touched his food. Watching his face one would think they had served him portions of Epsom Salts, rhubarb and *mist. alba*. He held his shoulders up, his arms pressed against his sides as though he was in constant fear of evacuating.

Clara sat on Mr Jones' left, but Obi studiously refused to look in her direction. She was talking with an Education Officer from Ibadan who was explaining to her the difference between language and dialect.

At first the Bay of Biscay was very calm and collected. The boat was now heading towards a horizon where the sky was light, seeming to hold out a vague promise of sunshine. The sea's circumference was no longer merged with the sky, but stood out in deep clear contrast like a giant tarmac from which God's aeroplane might take off. Then as evening approached, the peace and smoothness vanished quite suddenly. The sea's face was contorted with anger. Obi felt slightly dizzy and top-heavy. When he went down for supper he merely looked at his food. One or two passengers were not there at all. The others ate almost in silence.

Obi returned to his cabin and was going straight to bed when someone tapped at his door. He opened it and it was Clara.

'I noticed you were not looking very well,' she said in Ibo, 'so I brought you some tablets of Avomine.' She gave him an envelope with half a dozen white tablets in it. 'Take two before you go to bed.'

'Thank you *very* much. It's so kind of you.' Obi was completely overwhelmed and all the coldness and indifference he had rehearsed deserted him. 'But,' he stammered, 'am I not depriving you of er . . .'

'Oh no. I've got enough for all the passengers, that's the advantage of having a nurse on board.' She smiled faintly. 'I've just given some to Mrs Wright and Mr Macmillan. Good night, you'll feel better in the morning.'

All night Obi rolled from one edge of the bed to the other in sympathy with the fitful progress of the little ship groaning and creaking in the darkness. He could neither sleep nor keep awake. But somehow he was able to think about Clara most of the night, a few seconds at a time. He had taken a firm decision not to show any interest in her. And yet when he had opened the door and seen her, his joy and confusion must have been very plain. And she had treated him just like another patient. 'I have enough for all the passengers,' she had said. 'I gave some to Mr Macmillan and Mrs Wright.' But then she had spoken in Ibo, for the first time, as if to say. 'We belong together: we speak the same language.' And she had appeared to show some concern.

He was up very early next morning feeling a little better but not yet really well. The crew had already washed the deck and he almost slipped on the wet wood. He took up his favourite position at the rails. Then he heard a woman's light footsteps, turning round and saw it was Clara.

'Good morning,' he said, smiling broadly.

'Good morning,' she said, and made to pass.

'Thank you for the tablets,' he said in Ibo.

'Did they make you feel better?' she asked in English.

'Yes, very much.'

'I am glad,' she said, and passed.

Obi leaned again on the rail to watch the restless sea, which now looked like a wilderness, rock-sharp, angular and mobile. For the first time since they had left Liverpool, the sea became really blue; a plumbless blue set off by the gleaming white tops of countless wavelets clashing and breaking against each other. He heard someone treading heavily and briskly and then fall. It was Macmillan.

'I'm sorry,' he said.

'Oh, it's nothing,' the other said, laughing foolishly and dusting the wet seat of his trousers.

'I very nearly fell myself,' said Obi.

'Look out, Miss Okeke,' said Macmillan as Clara came round again. 'The deck is very treacherous and I've just fallen.' He was still dusting his wet seat.

'The captain said we will reach an island tomorrow,' said Clara.

'Yes, the Madeiras,' said Macmillan. 'Tomorrow evening, I think.'

'And about time, too,' said Obi.

'Don't you like the sea?'

'Yes, but after five days I want a change.'

Obi Okonkwo and John Macmillan suddenly became friends –
from the minute Macmillan fell on the wet deck. They were soon
playing ping-pong together and standing each other drinks.

'What will you have, Mr Okonkwo?' asked Macmillan.

'Beer, please. It's getting rather warm.' He drew his thumb
across his face and flicked the sweat away.

'Isn't it?' said Macmillan, blowing into his chest. 'What's your
first name, by the way? Mine's John.'

'Obi is mine.'

'Obi, that's a fine name. What does it mean? I'm told that all
African names mean something.'

'Well, I don't know about *African* names – Ibo names, yes. They
are often long sentences. Like that prophet in the Bible who called
his son The Remnant Shall Return.'

'What did you read in London?'

'English. Why?'

'Oh, I just wondered. And how old are you? Excuse my being
so inquisitive.'

'Twenty-five,' said Obi. 'And you?'

'Now that's strange, because I'm twenty-five. How old do you
think Miss Okeke is?'

'Women and music should not be dated,' Obi said, smiling. 'I
should say about twenty-three.'

'She is very beautiful, don't you think?'

'Oh yes, she is indeed.'

The Madeiras were now quite close; two hours or so, someone said.
Everyone was at the rails standing one another drinks. Mr Jones
suddenly became poetic. 'Water, water everywhere but not a drop
to drink,' he intoned. Then he became prosaic. 'What a waste of
water!' he said.

It struck Obi suddenly that it was true. What a waste of water.
A microscopic fraction of the Atlantic would turn the Sahara into
a flourishing grassland. So much for the best of all possible worlds.
Excess here and nothing at all there.

The ship anchored at Funchal at sunset. A tiny boat came alongside with a young man at the oars and two boys in it. The younger could not have been more than ten; the other was perhaps two years older. They wanted to dive for money. Immediately the coins were flying into the sea from the high deck. The boys picked up every one of them. Stephen Udom threw a penny. They did not move; they did not dive for pennies, they said. Everyone laughed.

As the sun set, the rugged hills of Funchal and the green trees and the houses with their white walls and red tiles looked like an enchanted isle. As soon as dinner was over Macmillan, Obi and Clara went ashore together. They walked on cobbled streets, past quaint cars in the taxi-rank. They passed two oxen pulling a cart which was just a flat board on wheels with a man and a sack of something in it. They went into little gardens and parks.

'It's a garden city!' said Clara.

After about an hour they came round to the waterfront again. They sat under a huge red and green umbrella and ordered coffee and wine. A man came round and sold them postcards and then sat down to tell them about Madeira wine. He had very few English words, but he left no one in doubt as to what he meant.

'Las Palmas wine and Italian wine pure water. Madeira wine, two eyes, four eyes.' They laughed and he laughed. Then he sold Macmillan tawdry trinkets which everyone knew would tarnish before they got back to their ship.

'Your girlfriend won't like it, Mr Macmillan,' said Clara.

'It's for my steward's wife,' he explained. And then he added: 'I hate to be called Mr Macmillan. It makes me feel so old.'

'I'm sorry,' she said. 'It's John, isn't it? And you are Obi. I am Clara.'

At ten they rose to go because their ship would sail at eleven, or so the captain said. Macmillan discovered he still had some Portuguese coins and ordered another glass of wine, which he shared with Obi. Then they went back to the ship, Macmillan holding Clara's right hand and Obi her left.

The other passengers had not returned and the ship looked deserted. They leaned on the rail and spoke about Funchal. Then

Macmillan said he had an important letter to write home. 'See you in the morning,' he said.

'I think I should write letters, too,' said Clara.

'To England?' asked Obi.

'No, to Nigeria.'

'There's no hurry,' he said, 'you can't post Nigerian letters until you get to Freetown. That's what they said.'

They heard Macmillan bang his cabin door. Their eyes met for a second, and without another word Obi took her in his arms. She was trembling as he kissed her over and over again.

'Leave me,' she whispered.

'I love you.'

She was silent for a while, seeming to melt in his arms.

'You don't,' she said suddenly. 'We're only being silly. You'll forget it in the morning.' She looked at him and then kissed him violently. 'I know I'll hate myself in the morning. You don't— Leave me, there's someone coming.'

It was Mrs Wright, the African lady from Freetown.

'Have you come back?' she asked. 'Where are the others? I have not been able to sleep.' She had indigestion, she said.

CHAPTER FOUR

Unlike mail boats, which docked at the Lagos wharf on fixed days of the week, cargo boats were most unpredictable. So when the MV *Sasa* arrived, there were no friends waiting at the Atlantic Terminal for her passengers. On mail boat days the beautiful and airy waiting-room would be full of gaily dressed friends and relations waiting for the arrival of a boat and drinking iced beer and Coca-Cola or eating buns. Sometimes you found a little group waiting sadly and silently. In such cases you could bet that their son had married a white woman in England.

There was no such crowd for the MV *Sasa*, and it was quite clear that Mr Stephen Udom was deeply disappointed. As soon as Lagos had been sighted he had returned to his cabin to emerge half an hour later in a black suit, bowler hat and rolled umbrella, even though it was a hot October day.

Customs formalities here took thrice as long as at Liverpool and five times as many officials. A young man, almost a boy in fact, was dealing with Obi's cabin. He told him that the duty on his radiogram would be five pounds.

'Right,' said Obi, feeling his hip-pockets. 'Write a receipt for me.' The boy did not write. He looked at Obi for a few seconds, and then said: 'I can reduce it to two pounds for you.'

'How?' asked Obi.

'I fit do it, but you no go get Government receipt.'

For a few seconds Obi was speechless. Then he merely said: 'Don't be silly. If there was a policeman here I would hand you over to him.' The boy fled from his cabin without another word. Obi found him later attending other passengers.

'Dear old Nigeria,' he said to himself as he waited for another official to come to his cabin. In the end one came when all the other passengers had been attended to.

If Obi had returned by mail-boat, the Umuofia Progressive Union (Lagos Branch) would have given him a royal welcome at the harbour. Anyhow, it was decided at their meeting that a big reception should be arranged to which press reporters and photographers should be invited. An invitation was also sent to the Nigerian Broadcasting Service to cover the occasion and to record the Umuofia Ladies' Vocal Orchestra which had been learning a number of new songs.

The reception took place on Saturday afternoon at 4 p.m. on Moloney Street, where the President had two rooms.

Everybody was properly dressed in *agbada* or European suit except the guest of honour, who appeared in his shirtsleeves because of the heat. That was Obi's mistake Number One. Everybody expected a young man from England to be impressively turned out.

After prayers the Secretary of the Union read the Welcome Address. He rose, cleared his throat and began to intone from an enormous sheet of paper.

'Welcome Address presented to Michael Obi Okonkwo, BA (Hons), London, by the officers and members of the Umuofia Progressive Union on the occasion of his return from the United Kingdom in quest of the Golden Fleece.

'Sir, we the officers and members of the above-named Union present with humility and gratitude this token of our appreciation of your unprecedented academic brilliance . . .'

He spoke of the great honour Obi had brought to the ancient town of Umuofia which could now join the comity of other towns in their march towards political irredentism, social equality and economic emancipation.

'The importance of having one of our sons in the vanguard of this march of progress is nothing short of axiomatic. Our people have a saying "Ours is ours, but mine is mine". Every town and village struggles at this momentous epoch in our political evolution to possess that of which it can say: "This is mine". We are happy that today we have such an invaluable possession in the person of our illustrious son and guest of honour.'

He traced the history of the Umuofia Scholarship Scheme which had made it possible for Obi to study overseas, and called it an investment which must yield heavy dividends. He then referred (quite obliquely, of course) to the arrangement whereby the beneficiary from this scheme was expected to repay his debt over four years so that 'an endless stream of students will be enabled to drink deep at the Pierian Spring of knowledge'.

Needless to say, this address was repeatedly interrupted by cheers and the clapping of hands. What a sharp young man their secretary was, all said. He deserved to go to England himself. He wrote the kind of English they admired if not understood: the kind that filled the mouth, like the proverbial dry meat.

Obi's English, on the other hand, was most unimpressive. He spoke 'is' and 'was'. He told them about the value of education. 'Education for service, not for white-collar jobs and comfortable salaries. With our great country on the threshold of independence, we need men who are prepared to serve her well and truly.'

When he sat down the audience clapped from politeness. Mistake Number Two.

Cold beer, minerals, palm wine and biscuits were then served, and the women began to sing about Umuofia and about Obi Okonkwo *nwa jelu oyibo* – Obi who had been to the land of the whites. The refrain said over and over again that the power of the leopard resided in its claws.

'Have they given you a job yet?' the clansmen asked Obi over the music. In Nigeria the government was 'they'. It had nothing to do with you or me. It was an alien institution and people's business was to get as much from it as they could without getting into trouble.

'Not yet. I'm attending an interview on Monday.'

'Of course those of you who know book will not have any difficulty,' said the Vice-President on Obi's left. 'Otherwise I would have suggested *seeing* some of the men before hand.'

'It would not be necessary,' said the President, 'since they would be mostly white men.'

'You think white men don't eat bribe? Come to our department. They eat more than black men nowadays.'

After the reception Joseph took Obi to have dinner at the 'Palm Grove'. It was a neat little place not very popular on Saturday nights when Lagosians wanted a more robust kind of enjoyment. There were a handful of people in the lounge – a dozen or so Europeans and three Africans.

'Who owns this place?'

'I think a Syrian. They own everything in Lagos,' said Joseph.

They sat at one of the empty tables at the corner and then noticed that they were directly under a ceiling fan and moved to another table. Soft light came from large globes around which insects danced furiously. Perhaps they did not notice that each globe carried a large number of bodies which, like themselves, had danced once upon a time. Or if they noticed, they did not care.

'Service!' called Joseph importantly, and a steward appeared in white tunic and trousers, a red cummerbund and red fez. 'What will you have?' he asked Obi. The steward bent forward waiting.

'Really I don't think I want to drink anything more.'

'Nonsense. The day is still young. Have a cold beer.'

He turned to the steward. 'Two Heinekens.'

'Oh no. One will do. Let's share one.'

'Two Heinekens,' repeated Joseph, and the steward went to the bar and soon returned with two bottles on a tray.

'Do they serve Nigerian food here?'

Joseph was surprised at the question. No decent restaurant served Nigerian food. 'Do you want Nigerian food?'

'Of course. I had been dying to eat pounded yams and bitter-leaf soup. In England we made do with semolina, but it isn't the same thing.'

'I must ask my boy to prepare you pounded yams tomorrow afternoon.'

'Good man!' said Obi, brightening up considerably. Then he added in English for the benefit of the European group that sat at the next table: 'I am sick of boiled potatoes.' By calling them boiled he hoped he had put into it all the disgust he felt.

A white hand gripped his chair behind. He turned quickly and saw it was the old manageress holding on to chairs to support her unsteady progress. She must have been well over seventy, if not eighty. She toddled across the lounge and behind the counter. Then she came out again holding a shivering glass of milk.

'Who left that duster there?' she said, pointing a shaking left-hand finger at a yellow rag on the floor.

'I no know,' said the steward who had been addressed.

'Take it away,' she croaked. In the effort to give orders she forgot about the glass of milk. It tilted in her unsteady grip and spilt on her neat floral dress. She went to a seat in the corner and sank in, groaning and creaking like old machinery gone rusty from standing in the rain. It must have been her favourite corner, because her parrot's cage was directly overhead. As soon as she sat down the parrot emerged from its cage on to a projecting rod, lowered its tail and passed ordure, which missed the old lady by a tenth of an inch. Obi raised himself slightly on his seat to see the mess on the floor. But there was no mess. Everything was beautifully organized. There was a tray by the old lady's chair nearly full of wet excrement.

'I don't think the place is owned by a Syrian,' said Obi. 'She is English.'

They had mixed grill, which Obi admitted wasn't too bad. But he was still puzzling in his mind why Joseph had not put him up as he had asked before he left England. Instead, the Umuofia Progressive Union had arranged at their own expense for him to stay at a not particularly good hotel owned by a Nigerian on the outskirts of Yaba.

'Did you get my last letter from England?'

Joseph said yes. As soon as he had got it he had discussed it with the executive of the UPU, and it was agreed that he should be put up in proper fashion at a hotel. As if he read Obi's thoughts, he said: 'You know I have only one room.'

'Nonsense,' said Obi. 'I'm moving out of this filthy hotel tomorrow morning and coming into your place.'

Joseph was amazed, but also very pleased. He tried to raise another objection, but it was clear that his heart was not in it.

'What will the people of other towns say when they hear that a son of Umuofia returned from England and shared a room in Obalende?'

'Let them say what they like.'

They ate in silence for a short while and then Obi said: 'Our people have a long way to go.' At the same time as he was saying it Joseph was also beginning to say something, but he stopped.

'Yes, you were saying something.'

'I said that I believe in destiny.'

'Do you? Why?'

'You remember Mr Anene, our class teacher, used to say that you would go to England. You were so small then with a running nose, and yet at the end of every term you were at the top of the class. You remember we used to call you "Dictionary"?'

Obi was very much embarrassed because Joseph was talking at the top of his voice.

'As a matter of fact, my nose still runs. They say it's hay fever '

'And then,' said Joseph, 'you wrote that letter to Hitler.'

Obi laughed one of his rare loud laughs. 'I wonder what came over me. I still think about it sometimes. What was Hitler to me or I to Hitler? I suppose I felt sorry for him. And I didn't like going into the bush every day to pick palm-kernels as our "Win the War Effort".' He suddenly became serious. 'And when you come to think of it, it was quite immoral of the headmaster to tell little children every morning that for every palm-kernel they picked they were buying a nail for Hitler's coffin.'

They went back to the lounge from the dining-room. Joseph was about to order more beer, but Obi stoutly refused.

From where he sat Obi could see cars passing on Broad Street. A long De Soto pulled up exactly at the entrance and a young handsome man walked into the lounge. Everyone turned to look at him and faint sibilant sounds filled the room as each told his neighbour that it was the Minister of State.

'That's Hon. Sam Okoli,' whispered Joseph. But Obi had

suddenly become like one thunderstruck gazing at the De Soto in the half darkness.

The Honourable Sam Okoli was one of the most popular politicians in Lagos and in Eastern Nigeria where his constituency was. The newspapers called him the best-dressed gentleman in Lagos and the most eligible bachelor. Although he was definitely over thirty, he always looked like a boy just out of school. He was tall and athletic with a flashing smile for all. He walked across to the bar and paid for a tin of Churchman's. All the while Obi's gaze was fixed on the road outside where Clara lounged in the De Soto. He had only caught a lightning glimpse of her. Perhaps it wasn't her at all. The Minister went back to the car, and as he opened the door the pale interior light again bathed the plush cushions. There was no doubt about it now. It was Clara.

'What's the matter?'

'Nothing. I know that girl, that's all.'

'In England?'

Obi nodded.

'Good old Sam! He doesn't spare them.'

CHAPTER FIVE

Obi's theory that the public service of Nigeria would remain corrupt until the old Africans at the top were replaced by young men from the universities was first formulated in a paper read to the Nigerian Students' Union in London. But unlike most theories formed by students in London, this one survived the first impact of home-coming. In fact, within a month of his return Obi came across two classic examples of his old African.

He met the first one at the Public Service Commission where he was boarded for a job. Fortunately for Obi, he had already created a favourable impression on the board before this man made him lose his temper.

It happened that the Chairman of the Commission, a fat jolly Englishman, was very keen on modern poetry and the modern novel, and enjoyed talking about them. The other four members – one European and three Africans – not knowing anything about that side of life, were duly impressed. Or perhaps we should say in strict accuracy that three of them were duly impressed because the fourth was asleep throughout the interview; which on the surface might appear to be quite unimportant had not this gentle-man been the sole representative of one of the three regions of Nigeria. (In the interests of Nigerian unity the region shall remain nameless.)

The chairman's conversation with Obi ranged from Graham Greene to Tutuola and took the greater part of half an hour. Obi said afterwards that he talked a lot of nonsense, but it was a learned and impressive kind of nonsense. He surprised even himself when he began to flow.

'You say you're a great admirer of Graham Greene. What do you think of *The Heart of the Matter*?'

'The only sensible novel any European has written on West Africa and one of the best novels I have read.' Obi paused, and then added almost as an afterthought: 'Only it was nearly ruined by the happy ending.'

The Chairman sat up in his chair.

'Happy ending? Are you sure it's *The Heart of the Matter* you're thinking about? The European police officer commits suicide.'

'Perhaps happy ending is too strong, but there is no other way I can put it. The police officer is torn between his love of a woman and his love of God, and he commits suicide. It's much too simple. Tragedy isn't like that at all. I remember an old man in my village, a Christian convert, who suffered one calamity after another. He said life was like a bowl of wormwood which one sips a little at a time world without end. He understood the nature of tragedy.'

'You think that suicide ruins a tragedy,' said the Chairman.

'Yes. Real tragedy is never resolved. It goes on hopelessly for ever. Conventional tragedy is too easy. The hero dies and we feel a purging of the emotions. A real tragedy takes place in a corner, in an untidy spot, to quote W. H. Auden. The rest of the world is unaware of it. Like that man in *A Handful of Dust* who reads Dickens to Mr Todd. There is no release for him. When the story ends he is still reading. There is no purging of the emotions for us because we are not there.'

'That's most interesting,' said the Chairman. Then he looked round the table and asked the other members if they had any questions for Mr Okonkwo. They all said no, except the man who had been sleeping.

'Why do you want a job in the Civil Service? So that you can take bribes?' he asked.

Obi hesitated. His first impulse was to say it was an idiotic question. He said instead: 'I don't know how you expect me to answer that question. Even if my reason is to take bribes, you don't expect me to admit it before this board. So I don't think it's a very useful question.'

'It's not for you to decide what questions are useful, Mr Okonkwo,' said the Chairman, trying unsuccessfully to look severe. 'Anyhow, you'll be hearing from us in due course. Good morning.'

Joseph was not very happy when Obi told him the story of the interview. His opinion was that a man in need of a job could not afford to be angry.

'Nonsense!' said Obi. 'That's what I call colonial mentality.'

'Call it what you like,' said Joseph in Ibo. 'You know more book than I, but I am older and wiser. And I can tell you that a man does not challenge his *chi* to a wrestling match.'

Joseph's house-boy Mark brought in rice and stew and they immediately fell to. He then went across the street to a shop where iced water was sold at a penny a bottle and brought them two bottles, carrying all the way and back a smudge of soot at the tip of his nose. His eyes were a little red and watery from blowing the fire with his breath.

'You know you have changed a good deal in four years,' Obi remarked after they had been eating for a while in silence. 'Then you had two interests – politics and women.'

Joseph smiled. 'You don't do politics on an empty stomach.'

'Agreed,' said Obi jovially. 'What about women? I have been two days here now and I haven't seen one yet.'

'Didn't I tell you I was getting married?'

'So what?'

'When you have paid a hundred and thirty pounds bride-price and you are only a second-class clerk, you find you haven't got any more to spare on other women.'

'You mean you paid a hundred and thirty? What about the bride-price law?'

'It pushed up the price, that's all.'

'It's a pity my three elder sisters got married too early for us to make money on them. We'll try and make up on the others.'

'It's no laughing matter,' said Joseph. 'Wait until you want to marry. They will probably ask you to pay five hundred, seeing that you are in the senior service.'

'I'm not in the senior service. You have just been telling me that I won't get the job because I told that idiot what I thought of him. Anyway, senior service or no senior service, I'm not paying five hundred pounds for a wife. I shall not even pay one hundred, not even fifty.'

'You are not serious,' said Joseph. 'Unless you are going to be a Reverend Father.'

While he waited for the result of his interview, Obi paid a short visit to Umuofia, his home town, five hundred miles away in the Eastern Region. The journey itself was not very exciting. He boarded a mammy wagon called *God's Case No Appeal* and travelled first class; which meant that he shared the front seat with the driver and a young woman with her baby. The back seats were taken up by traders who travelled regularly between Lagos and the famous Onitsha market on the bank of the Niger. The lorry was so heavily laden that the traders had no room to hang their legs down. They sat with the feet on the same level as their buttocks, their knees drawn up to their chins like roast chickens. But they did not seem to mind. They beguiled themselves with gay and bawdy songs addressed mostly to young women who had become nurses or teachers instead of mothers.

The driver of the lorry was a very quiet man. He was either eating kola nuts or smoking cigarettes. The kola was to keep him awake at night because the journey began in the late afternoon, took all night and ended in the early morning. From time to time he asked Obi to strike a match and light his cigarette for him. Actually it was Obi who offered to do it in the first instance. He had been alarmed to see the man controlling the wheel with his elbows while he fumbled for a match.

Some forty miles or so beyond Ibadan the driver suddenly said: 'Dees b— f— police!' Obi noticed two policemen by the side of the road about three hundred yards away, signalling the lorry to a stop.

'Your particulars?' said one of them to the driver. It was at this point that Obi noticed that the seat they sat on was also a kind of safe for keeping money and valuable documents. The driver asked his passengers to get up. He unlocked the box and brought out a sheaf of papers. The policeman looked at them critically. 'Where your roadwordiness?' The driver showed him his certificate of roadworthiness.

Meanwhile the driver's mate was approaching the other policeman. But just as he was about to hand something over to him Obi looked in their direction. The policeman was not prepared to take a risk; for all he knew Obi might be a CID man. So he drove the driver's mate away with great moral indignation. 'What you want here? Go way!' Meanwhile the other policeman had found fault with the driver's papers and was taking down his particulars, the driver pleading and begging in vain. Finally he drove away, or so it appeared. About a quarter of a mile farther up the road he stopped.

'Why you look the man for face when we want give um him two shillings?' he asked Obi.

'Because he has no right to take two shillings from you,' Obi answered.

'Na him make I no de want carry you book people,' he complained. 'Too too know na him de worry una. Why you put your nose for matter way no concern you? Now that policeman go charge me like ten shillings.'

It was only some minutes later that Obi realized why they had stopped. The driver's mate had run back to the policeman, knowing that they would be more amenable when there were no embarrassing strangers gazing at them. The man soon returned panting from much running.

'How much they take?' asked the driver.

'Ten shillings,' gasped his assistant.

'You see now,' he said to Obi, who was already beginning to feel a little guilty, especially as all the traders behind, having learnt what was happening, had switched their attacks from career girls to 'too know' young men. For the rest of the journey the driver said not a word more to him.

'What an Augean stable!' he muttered to himself. 'Where does one begin? With the masses? Educate the masses?' He shook his head. 'Not a chance there. It would take centuries. A handful of men at the top. Or even one man with vision – an enlightened dictator. People are scared of the word nowadays. But what kind of democracy can exist side by side with so much corruption and ignorance? Perhaps a half-way house – a sort of compromise.' When Obi's reasoning reached this point he reminded himself that England had been as corrupt not so very long ago. He was not really in the mood for consecutive reasoning. His mind was impatient to roam in a more pleasant landscape.

The young woman sitting on his left was now asleep, clasping her baby tightly to her breast. She was going to Benin. That was all he knew about her. She hardly spoke a word of English and he did not speak Bini. He shut his eyes and imagined her to be Clara; their knees were touching. It did not work.

Why did Clara insist that he must not tell his people about her yet? Could it be that she had not quite made up her mind to marry him? That could hardly be. She was as anxious as himself to be formally engaged, only she said he should not go to the expense of buying a ring until he had got a job. Perhaps she wanted to tell her people first. But if so, why all the mystery? Why had she not simply said that she was going to consult her people? Or maybe she was not as guileless as he had assumed and was using this suspense to bind him more strongly to her. Obi examined each possibility in turn and rejected it.

As the night advanced the rushing air became at first cool and refreshing and then chilly. The driver pulled out a dirty brown cloth cap from the mass of rags on which he sat and covered his head with it. The young Benin woman retied her head-cloth to cover her ears. Obi had an old sports jacket which he had bought in his first year in England. He had used it until now to soften the wooden back-rest. He threw it over his back and shoulders. But his feet and legs were now the only really comfortable parts of him. The heat of the engine, which had been a little uncomfortable before, had now been mellowed down by the chilly air until it gently caressed the feet and legs.

Obi was beginning to feel sleepy and his thoughts turned more and more on the erotic. He said words in his mind that he could not say out aloud even when he was alone. Strangely enough, all the words were in his mother tongue. He could say any English word, no matter how dirty, but some Ibo words simply would not proceed from his mouth. It was no doubt his early training that operated this censorship, English words filtering through because they were learnt later in life.

Obi continued in his state of half-sleep until the driver suddenly pulled up by the side of the road, rubbed his eyes and announced that he had caught himself sleeping once or twice. Everyone was naturally concerned about it and tried to be helpful.

'You no get kola nut for eat?' asked one of the traders from the back.

'Weting I been de eat all afternoon?' asked the driver. 'I no fit understand this kind sleep. Na true say I no sleep last night, but that no be first time I been do um.' Everyone agreed that sleep was a most unreasonable phenomenon.

After two or three minutes of general conversation on this subject the driver once more proceeded on his way with the promise and determination to try his best. As for Obi, sleep had fled from his eyes as soon as the driver had pulled up. His mind cleared immediately as if the sun had risen and dried the dew that had settled on it.

The traders burst into song again, this time there was nothing bawdy about it. Obi knew the refrain, he tried to translate it into English, and for the first time its real meaning dawned on him.

> An in-law went to see his in-law
> Oyiemu—o
> His in-law seized him and killed him
> Oyiemu—o
> Bring a canoe, bring a paddle
> Oyiemu—o
> The paddle speaks English
> Oyiemu—o.

On the face of it there was no kind of logic or meaning in the song. But as Obi turned it round and round in his mind, he was struck by the wealth of association that even such a mediocre song could have. First of all it was unheard of for a man to seize his in-law and kill him. To the Ibo mind it was the height of treachery. Did not the elders say that a man's in-law was his *chi*, his personal god? Set against this was another great betrayal; a paddle that begins suddenly to talk in a language which its master, the fisherman, does not understand. In short then, thought Obi, the burden of the song was 'the world turned upside down'. He was pleased with his exegesis and began to search in his mind for other songs that could be given the same treatment. But the song of the traders was now so loud and spicy that he could not concentrate on his thinking.

Nowadays going to England has become as commonplace as going down to the village stream. But five years ago it was different. Obi's return to his village was almost a festival. A 'pleasure' car was waiting at Onitsha to convey him in proper state to Umuofia, some fifty miles away. But before they set out he had a few minutes to look round the great Onitsha market.

The first thing that claimed his attention was an open jeep which blared out local music from a set of loudspeakers. Two men in the car swayed to the music as did many others in the crowd that had gathered round it. Obi was wondering what it was all about when the music suddenly stopped. One of the men held up a bottle for all to see. It contained Long Life Mixture, he said, and began to tell the crowd all about it. Or rather he told them a few things about it, for it was impossible to enumerate all its wonderful virtues. The other man brought out a sheaf of hand-bills and distributed them to the crowd, most of whom appeared to be illiterate. 'This paper will speak to you about Long Life Mixture,' he announced. It was quite clear that if there was something on paper about it, then it must be true. Obi secured one of the bills and read the list of diseases. The first three were: 'Rheumatism, Yellow feaver, dog-bight'.

On the other side of the road, close to the waterfront, a row of women sat selling *garri* from big white enamel bowls. A beggar appeared. He must have been well known because many people called him by name. Perhaps he was a little mad too. His name was One Way. He had an enamel basin and began a tour of the row. The women beat out a rhythm with empty cigarette cups and One Way danced along the row, receiving a handful of *garri* in his basin from each of them in turn. When he got to the end of the row he had received enough *garri* for two heavy meals.

Bands of music-makers went out two miles on the Umuofia-Onitsha road to await Obi's arrival. There were at least five different groups, if one excludes the brass band of the CMS School Umuofia. It looked as if the entire village was celebrating a feast. Those who were not waiting along the road, elderly people especially, were already arriving in large numbers at Mr Okonkwo's compound.

The only trouble was that it might rain. In fact, many people half wished it would rain heavily so as to show Isaac Okonkwo that Christianity had made him blind. He was the only man who failed to see that on an occasion such as this he should take palm wine, a cock and a little money to the chief rain-maker in Umuofia.

'He is not the only Christian we have seen,' said one of the men. 'But it is like the palm wine we drink. Some people can drink it and remain wise. Others lose all their senses.'

'Very true, very true,' said another. 'When a new saying gets to the land of empty men they lose their heads over it.'

At that very moment Isaac Okonkwo was having an argument about rain-making with one of the old men who had come to rejoice with him.

'Perhaps you will also tell me that some men cannot send thunder to their enemies?' asked the old man.

Mr Okonkwo told him that to believe such a thing was to chew the cud of foolishness. It was putting one's head into a cooking-pot.

'What Satan has accomplished in this world of ours is indeed great,' he said. 'For it is he alone that can put such abominable thought into men's stomachs.'

The old man waited patiently for him to finish and said:

'You are not a stranger in Umuofia. You have heard our elders say that thunder cannot kill a son or daughter of Umuofia. Do you know anyone either now or in the past who was so killed?'

Okonkwo had to admit that he knew of no such person. 'But that is the work of God,' he said.

'It is the work of our forefathers,' said the old man. 'They built a powerful medicine to protect themselves from thunder, and not only themselves, but all their descendants for ever.'

'Very true,' said another man. 'Anyone who denies it does so in vain. Let him go and ask Nwokeke how he was hit by thunder last year. All his skin peeled off like snake slough, but he was not killed.'

'Why was he hit at all?' asked Okonkwo. 'He should not have been hit at all.'

'That is a matter between him and his *chi*. But you must know that he was hit in Mbaino and not at home. Perhaps the thunder, seeing him at Mbiano, called him an Mbaino man at first.'

Four years in England had filled Obi with a longing to be back in Umuofia. This feeling was sometimes so strong that he found himself feeling ashamed of studying English for his degree. He spoke Ibo whenever he had the least opportunity of doing so. Nothing gave him greater pleasure than to find another Ibo-speaking student in a London bus. But when he had to speak in English with a Nigerian student from another tribe he lowered his voice. It was humiliating to have to speak to one's countryman in a foreign language, especially in the presence of the proud owners of that language. They would naturally assume that one had no language of one's own. He wished they were here today to see. Let them come to Umuofia now and listen to the talk of men who made a great art of conversation. Let them come and see men and women and children who knew how to live, whose joy of life had not yet been killed by those who claimed to teach other nations how to live.

There were hundreds of people at Obi's reception. For one thing, the entire staff and pupils of the CMS Central School Umuofia were there and their brass band had just finished playing 'Old Calabar'. They had also played an old evangelical tune which in Obi's schooldays Protestant schoolchildren had sung to anti-Catholic words, especially on Empire Day, when Protestants and Catholics competed in athletics.

Otasili osukwu Onyenkuzi Fada
E misisi ya oli awo-o.

214

Which translated into English is as follows:

> Palm-fruit eater, Roman Catholic teacher,
> His missus a devourer of toads.

After the first four hundred handshakes and hundred embraces, Obi was able to sit down for a while with his father's older kinsmen in the big parlour. There were not enough chairs for all of them to sit on, so that many sat on their goatskins spread on the floor. It did not make much difference whether one sat on a chair or on the floor because even those who sat on chairs spread their goatskins on them first.

'The white man's country must be very distant indeed,' suggested one of the men. Everyone knew it was very distant, but they wanted to hear it again from the mouth of their young kinsman.

'It is not something that can be told,' said Obi. 'It took the white man's ship sixteen days – four market weeks – to do the journey.'

'Think of that,' said one of the men to the others. 'Four market weeks. And not in a canoe, but a white man's ship that runs on water as a snake runs on grass.'

'Sometimes for a whole market week there is no land to be seen,' said Obi. 'No land in front, behind, to the right and to the left. Only water.'

'Think of that,' said the man to the others. 'No land for one whole market week. In our folk stories a man gets to the land of spirits when he has passed seven rivers, seven forests and seven hills. Without doubt you have visited the land of spirits.'

'Indeed you have, my child,' said another old man. 'Azik,' he called, meaning Isaac, 'bring us a kola nut to break for this child's return.'

'This is a Christain house,' replied Obi's father.

'A Christian house where kola nut is not eaten?' sneered the man.

'Kola nut is eaten here,' replied Mr Okonkwo, 'but not sacrificed to idols.'

'Who talked about sacrifice? Here is a little child returned from wrestling in the spirit world and you sit there blabbing about Christian house and idols, talking like a man whose palm wine has gone into his nose.' He hissed in disgust, took up his goatskin and went to sit outside.

'This is not a day for quarrels,' said another old man. 'I shall bring a kola nut.' He took his goatskin bag which he had hung from his chair and began to search its depths. As he searched things knocked against one another in it – his drinking-horn, his snuff-bottle and a spoon. 'And we shall break it in the Christian way,' he said as he fished out a kola nut.

'Do not trouble yourself, Ogbuefi Odogwu,' said Okonkwo to him. 'I am not refusing to place a kola nut before you. What I say is that it will not be used as a heathen sacrifice in my house.' He went into an inner room and soon returned with three kola nuts in a saucer. Ogbuefi Odogwu insisted on adding his kola nut to the number.

'Obi, show the kola nut round,' said his father. Obi had already stood up to do so, being the youngest man in the room. When everyone had seen he placed the saucer before Ogbuefi Odogwu, who was the eldest. He was not a Christian, but he knew one or two things about Christianity. Like many others in Umuofia, he went to church once a year at harvest. His only criticism of the Christian service was that the congregation was denied the right to reply to the sermon. One of the things he liked particularly and understood was: 'As it was in the beginning, is now and ever shall be, world without end.'

'As a man comes into this world,' he often said, 'so will he go out of it. When a titled man dies, his anklets of title are cut so that he will return as he came. The Christians are right when they say that as it was in the beginning it will be in the end.'

He took the saucer, drew up his knees together to form a table and placed the saucer there. He raised his two hands, palms facing upwards, and said, 'Bless this kola nut so that when we eat it it will be good in our body in the name of Jesu Kristi. As it was in the beginning it will be at the end. Amen.' Everyone replied Amen and cheered old Odogwu on his performance. Even Okonkwo could not help joining in the cheers.

'You should become a Christian,' he suggested.

'Yes, if you will agree to make me a pastor,' said Odogwu.

Everyone laughed again. Then the conversation veered round again to Obi. Matthew Ogbonna, who had been a carpenter in Onitsha and was consequently a man of the world, said they should all thank God that Obi had not brought home a white wife.

'White wife?' asked one of the men. To him it was rather far-fetched.

'Yes. I have seen it with my two eyes,' said Matthew.

'Yes,' said Obi. 'Many black men who go to the white man's country marry their women.'

'You hear?' asked Matthew. 'I tell you I have seen it with my own two eyes in Onitsha. The woman even had two children. But what happened in the end? She left those children and went back to her country. That is why I say a black man who marries a white woman wastes his time. Her stay with him is like the stay of the moon in the sky. When the time comes she will go.'

'Very true,' said another man who had also travelled. 'It is not her going away that matters. It is her turning the man's face away from his kinsmen while she stays.'

'I am happy that you returned home safe,' said Matthew to Obi.

'He is a son of Iguedo,' said old Odogwu. 'There are nine villages in Umuofia, but Iguedo is Iguedo. We have our faults, but we are not empty men who become white when they see white, and black when they see black.'

Obi's heart glowed with pride within him.

'He is the grandson of Ogbuefi Okonkwo who faced the white man single-handed and died in the fight. Stand up!'

Obi stood up obediently.

'Remark him,' said Odogwu. 'He is Ogbuefi Okonkwo come back. He is Okonkwo *kpom-kwem*, exact, perfect.'

Obi's father cleared his throat in embarrassment. 'Dead men do not come back,' he said.

'I tell you this is Okonkwo. As it was in the beginning so it will be in the end. That is what your religion tells us.'

'It does not tell you that dead men return.'

'Iguedo breeds great men,' said Odogwu changing the subject. 'When I was young I knew of them – Okonkwo, Ezeudu, Obierika, Okolo, Nwosu.' He counted them off with his right

fingers against the left. 'And many others, as many as grains or
sand. Among their fathers we hear of Ndu, Nwosisi, Ikedi, Obika
and his brother Iweka – all giants. These men were great in their
day. Today greatness has changed its tune. Titles are no longer
great, neither are barns or large numbers of wives and children.
Greatness is now in the things of the white man. And so we too
have changed our tune. We are the first in all the nine villages to
send our son to the white man's land. Greatness has belonged to
Iguedo from ancient times. It is not made by man. You cannot
plant greatness as you plant yams or maize. Who ever planted an
iroko tree – the greatest tree in the forest? You may collect all
the iroko seeds in the world, open the soil and put them there.
It will be in vain. The great tree chooses where to grow and we
find it there, so it is with the greatness in men.'

CHAPTER SIX

Obi's homecoming was not in the end the happy event he had dreamt of. The reason was his mother. She had grown so old and frail in four years that he could hardly believe it. He had heard of her long periods of illness, but he had not thought of it quite this way. Now that all the visitors had gone away and she came and hugged him and put her arms round his neck, for the second time tears rose in his eyes. Henceforth he wore her sadness round his neck like a necklace of stone.

His father too was all bones, although he did not look nearly as bad as his mother. It was clear to Obi that they did not have enough good food to eat. It was scandalous, he thought, that after nearly thirty years' service in the church his father should retire on a salary of two pounds a month, a good slice of which went back to the same church by way of class fees and other contributions. And he had his two last children at school, each paying school fees and church fees.

Obi and his father sat up for a long time after the others had gone to bed, in the oblong room which gave on to the outside through a large central door and two windows. This room was called *pieze* in Christian houses. The door and windows were shut to discourage neighbours who would have continued to stream in to see Obi – some of them for the fourth time that day.

There was a hurricane lamp beside the chair on which Obi's father sat. It was his lamp. He washed the globe himself; he would not trust anybody to do it. The lamp itself was older than Obi.

219

The walls of the *pieze* had recently been given a new coat of chalk. Obi had not had a moment until now to look round for such loving tributes. The floor had also been rubbed; but what with the countless feet that had trod on it that day it was already needing another rubbing with red earth and water.

His father broke the silence at length.

'Lord, now lettest thou thy servant depart in peace according to thy word.'

'What is that, Father?' asked Obi.

'Sometimes fear came upon me that I might not be spared to see your return.'

'Why? You seem as strong as ever.'

Obi's father ignored the false compliment, pursuing his own train of thought. 'Tomorrow we shall all worship at church. The pastor has agreed to make it a special service for you.'

'But is it necessary, Father? Is it not enough that we pray together here as we prayed this night?'

'It is necessary,' said his father. 'It is good to pray at home but better to pray in God's house.'

Obi thought: 'What would happen if I stood up and said to him: "Father, I no longer believe in your God"?' He knew it was impossible for him to do it, but he just wondered what would happen if he did. He often wondered like that. A few weeks ago in London he had wondered what would have happened if he had stood up and shouted to the smooth MP lecturing to African students on the Central African Federation: 'Go away, you are all bloody hypocrites!' It was not quite the same thing, though. His father believed fervently in God; the smooth MP was just a bloody hypocrite.

'Did you have time to read your Bible while you were there?'

There was nothing for it but to tell a lie. Sometimes a lie was kinder than the truth. Obi knew why the question had been asked. He had read his verses so badly at prayers that evening.

'Sometimes,' he replied, 'but it was the Bible written in the English language.'

'Yes,' said his father. 'I see.'

There was a long pause in which Obi remembered with shame

how he had stumbled through his portions as a child. In the first verse he had pronounced *ugwu* as mountain when it should be *circumcision*. Four or five voices had promptly corrected him, the first to register being his youngest sister, Eunice, who was eleven and in Standard Four.

The whole family sat round the enormous parlour table with the ancient hurricane lamp in the centre. There were nine people in all – father, brother, six sisters and Obi. When his father called out the portion for the day from the Scripture Union Card, Obi had impressed himself by finding it without difficulty in the Bible which he shared with Eunice. Prayers were then said for the opening of the eyes, and the reading began, each person reading one verse in turn.

Obi's mother sat in the background on a low stool. The four little children of her married daughters lay on the mat by her stool. She could read, but she never took part in the family reading. She merely listened to her husband and children. It had always been like that as far as the children could remember. She was a very devout woman, but Obi used to wonder whether, left to herself, she would not have preferred telling her children the folk-stories that her mother had told her. In fact, she used to tell her eldest daughter stories. But that was before Obi was born. She stopped because her husband forbade her to do so.

'We are not heathens,' he had said. 'Stories like that are not for the people of the Church.'

And Hannah had stopped telling her children folk-stories. She was loyal to her husband and to her new faith. Her mother had joined the Church with her children after her husband's death. Hannah had already grown up when they ceased to be 'people of nothing' and joined the 'people of the Church'. Such was the confidence of the early Christians that they called the others 'the people of nothing' or sometimes, when they felt more charitable, 'the people of the world'.

Isaac Okonkwo was not merely a Christian; he was a catechist. In their first years of married life he made Hannah see the grave responsibility she carried as a catechist's wife. And as soon as she knew what was expected of her she did it, sometimes showing more zeal than even her husband. She taught her children not to accept food in neighbours' houses because she said they offered their food to idols. That fact alone set her children apart from all others for, among the Ibo, children were free to eat where they liked. One day a neighbour offered a piece of yam to Obi who was then four years old. He shook he head like his older and wiser sisters, and then said: 'We don't eat heathen food'. His sister Janet tried too late to cover his mouth with her hand.

But there were occasional set-backs in this crusade. A year or two later when Obi had begun to go to school, such a set-back did take place. There was one lesson which he loved and feared. It was called 'Oral'. During this period the teacher called on any pupil to tell the class a folk-story. Obi loved these stories but he knew none which he could tell. One day the teacher called on him to face the class and tell them a story. As he came out and stood before them he trembled.

'*Olulu ofu oge,*' he began in the tradition of folk-tales, but that was all he knew. His lips quivered but no other sounds came out. The class burst into derisive laughter, and tears filled his eyes and rolled down his cheeks as he went back to his place.

As soon as he got home he told his mother about it. She told him to be patient until his father went to the evening prayer meeting.

Some weeks later Obi was called up again. He faced the class boldly and told one of the new stories his mother had told him. He even added a little touch to the end which made everyone laugh. It was the story of the wicked leopardess who wanted to eat the young lambs of his old friend the sheep. She went to the sheep's hut when she knew she had gone to market and began to search for the young lambs. She did not know that their mother had hidden them inside some of the palm-kernels lying around. At last she gave up the search and brought two stones to crack some of the kernels and eat before going, because she was very, very hungry. As soon as she cracked the first, the nut flew into the bush. She was amazed. The second also flew into the bush. And the third and eldest not only flew into the bush but, in Obi's version, slapped the leopardess in the eyes before doing so.

'You say you have only four days to stay with us?'

'Yes,' said Obi. 'But I will do my best to come again within a year. I must be in Lagos to see about getting a job.'

'Yes,' said his father slowly. 'A job is the first thing. A person who has not secured a place on the floor should not begin to look for a mat.' After a pause he said: 'There are many things to talk about, but not tonight. You are tired and need sleep.'

'I am not very tired, Father. But perhaps it is better to talk tomorrow. There is one thing, however, about which you should have a restful mind. There will be no question of John not finishing his course at the Grammar School.'

'Good night, my son, and God bless you.'

'Good night, Father.'

He borrowed the ancient hurricane lamp to see his way to his room and bed. There was a brand-new white sheet on the old wooden bed with its hard grass-filled mattress. The pillowslips with their delicate floral designs were no doubt Esther's work. 'Good old Esther!' Obi thought. He remembered when he was a little boy and Esther had just become a teacher. Everyone said that she should no longer be called Esther because it was disrespectful, but Miss. So she was called Miss. Sometimes Obi forgot and called her Esther, whereupon Charity told him how rude he was.

In those days Obi got on very well with his three eldest sisters, Esther, Janet and Agnes, but not with Charity, who was his immediate elder. Charity's Ibo name was 'A girl is also good', but whenever they quarrelled Obi called her 'A girl is not good'. Then she would beat him until he cried unless their mother happened to be around, in which case Charity would postpone the beating. She was as strong as iron and was feared by other children in the neighbourhood, even the boys.

Obi did not sleep for a long time after he had lain down. He thought about his responsibilities. It was clear that his parents could no longer stand on their own. They had never relied on his father's meagre pension. He planted yams and his wife planted cassava and coco-yams. She also made soap from leachings of palm ash and oil and sold it to the villagers for a little profit. But now they were too old for these things.

'I must give them a monthly allowance from my salary.' How much? Could he afford ten pounds? If only he did not have to pay back twenty pounds a month to the Umuofia Progressive Union. Then there were John's school fees.

'We'll manage somehow,' he said aloud to himself. 'One cannot have it both ways. There are many young men in this country today who would sacrifice themselves to get the opportunity I have had.'

Outside a strong wind had suddenly arisen and the disturbed trees became noisy. Flashes of lightning showed through the jalousie. It was going to rain. Obi liked rain at night. He forgot his responsibilities and thought about Clara, how heavenly it would be on such a night to feel her cool body against his – the shapely thighs and the succulent breasts.

Why had she said he should not tell his parents about her yet? Could it be that her mind was still not made up? He would have liked to tell his mother at least. He knew she would be overjoyed. She once said she would be ready to depart when she had seen his first child. That was before he went to England; it must have been when Esther's first child was born. She now had three, Janet two, Agnes one. Agnes would have had two if her first child had lived. It must be dreadful to lose one's first child, especially for a little girl like Agnes; she was no more than a little girl really at the time she got married – in her behaviour at least. Even now, she still had not quite grown up. Her mother always told her so. Obi smiled in the darkness as he remembered the little incident after prayers an hour or two ago.

Agnes had been asked to carry the little children, who were already asleep on the floor, to their beds.

'Wake them up to urinate first or they will do it in their beds,' said Esther.

Agnes grabbed the first child by the wrist and pulled him up.

'Agnes! Agnes!' screamed their mother, who was sitting on a low stool beside the sleeping children, 'I have always said that your head is not correct. How often must I tell you to call a child by name before waking him up?'

'Don't you know,' Obi took up, pretending great anger, 'that if you pull him up suddenly his soul may not be able to get back to his body before he wakes?'

The girls laughed. Obi had not changed a bit. He enjoyed teasing them, their mother not excepted. She smiled.

'You may laugh if laughter catches you,' she said indulgently. 'It does not catch me.'

'That is why Father calls them the foolish virgins,' said Obi.

It was now beginning to rain with thunder and lightning. At first large raindrops drummed on the iron roof. It was as though thousands of pebbles, each wrapped separately in a piece of cloth to break its fall, had been let loose from the sky. Obi wished that it was daytime so that he could see a tropical rain once more. It was now gathering strength. The drumming of large single drops gave way to a steady downpour.

'I had forgotten it could rain so heavily in November,' he thought as he rearranged his loincloth to cover his whole body. Actually such rain was unusual. It was as though the deity presiding over the waters in the sky found, on checking his stock and counting off the months on his fingers, that there was too much rain left and that he had to do something drastic about it before the impending dry season.

Obi composed himself and went off to sleep.

CHAPTER SEVEN

Obi's first day in the Civil Service was memorable, almost as memorable as his first day at the bush mission school in Umuofia nearly twenty years before. In those days white men were very rare. In fact, Mr Jones had been the second white man Obi had set eyes on, and he had been nearly seven then. The first white man had been the Bishop of the Niger.

Mr Jones was the Inspector of Schools and was feared throughout the province. It was said that he had fought during the Kaiser's war and that it had gone to his head. He was a huge man, over six feet tall. He rode a motor cycle, which he always left about half a mile away so that he could enter a school unannounced. Then he was sure to catch somebody committing an offence. He visited a school about once in two years and he always did something which was remembered until his next visit. Two years before, he had thrown a boy out of a window. Now it was the headmaster who got into trouble. Obi never discovered what the trouble was because it had all been done in English. Mr Jones was red with fury as he paced up and down, taking such ample strides that at one point Obi thought he was making straight for him. The headmaster, Mr Nduka, was all the while trying to explain something.

'Shut up!' roared Mr Jones, and followed it up with a slap. Simeon Nduka was one of those people who had taken to the ways of the white man rather late in life. And one of the things he had learnt in his youth was the great art of wrestling. In the twinkling of an eye Mr Jones was flat on the floor and the school was thrown into confusion. Without knowing why, teachers and pupils all took to their heels. To throw a white man was like unmasking an ancestral spirit.

That was twenty years ago. Today few white men would dream of slapping a headmaster in his school and none at all would actually do it. Which is the tragedy of men like William Green, Obi's boss.

Obi had already met Mr Green that morning. As soon as he had arrived he had been taken in to be introduced to him. Without rising from his seat or offering his hand Mr Green muttered something to the effect that Obi would enjoy his work; one, if he wasn't bone-lazy, and two, if he was prepared to use his loaf. 'I'm assuming you have one to use,' he concluded.

A few hours later he appeared in Mr Omo's office where Obi had been posted for the day. Mr Omo was the Administrative Assistant. He had put nearly thirty years' service into thousands of files, and would retire, or so he said, when his son had completed his legal studies in England. Obi was spending his first day in Mr Omo's office to learn a few things about office administration.

Mr Omo jumped to his feet as soon as Mr Green came in. Simultaneously he pocketed the other half of the kola nut he was eating.

'Why hasn't the Study Leave file been passed to me?' Mr Green asked.

'I thought . . .'

'You are not paid to think, Mr Omo, but to do what you are told. Is that clear? Now send the file to me immediately.'

'Yes, sir.'

Mr Green slammed the door behind him and Mr Omo carried the file personally to him. When he returned he began to rebuke a junior clerk who, it seemed, had caused all the trouble.

Obi had now firmly decided that he did not like Mr Green and that Mr Omo was one of his old Africans. As if to confirm his opinion the telephone rang. Mr Omo hesitated as he always did when the telephone rang, and then took it up as if it was liable to bite.

'Hello. Yes, sir.' He handed it over to Obi with obvious relief. 'Mr Okonkwo, for you.'

Obi took the telephone. Mr Green wanted to know whether he had received a formal offer of appointment. Obi said, no, he hadn't.

'You say *sir* to your superior officers, Mr Okonkwo,' and the telephone was dropped with a deafening bang.

Obi bought a Morris Oxford a week after he received his letter of appointment. Mr Green gave him a letter to the dealers saying that he was a Senior Civil Servant entitled to a car advance. Nothing more was required. He walked into the shop and got a brand-new car.

Earlier on the same day Mr Omo had sent for him to sign certain documents.

'Where is your stamp?' he asked as soon as Obi arrived.

'What stamp?' asked Obi perplexed.

'You get BA but you no know say you have to affix stamp to agreement?' Mr Omo laughed a laugh of derision. He had very bad teeth blackened by cigarettes and kola nuts. One was missing in front, and when he laughed the gap looked like a vacant plot in a slum. His junior clerks laughed with him out of loyalty.

'You think Government give you sixty pounds without signing agreement?'

It was only then that Obi understood what it was all about. He was to receive sixty pounds outfit allowance.

'This is a wonderful day,' he told Clara on the telephone. 'I have sixty pounds in my pocket, and I'm getting my car at two o'clock.'

Clara screamed with delight. 'Shall I ring Sam and tell him not to bother to send his car this evening?'

The Hon. Sam Okoli, Minister of State, had asked them to drinks and had offered to send his driver to fetch them. Clara lived in Yaba with her first cousin. She had been offered a job as Assistant Nursing Sister, and she would start work in a week or so. Then she would find more suitable lodgings. Obi still shared Joseph's room in Obalende but would move to a senior service flat in Ikoyi at the end of the week.

Obi was disposed to like the Hon. Sam Okoli from the moment he learnt that he had no designs on Clara. In fact he was getting married shortly to Clara's best friend and Clara had been asked to be chief bridesmaid.

'Come in, Clara. Come in, Obi,' he said as if he had known both of them all his life. 'That is a lovely car. How is it behaving? Come right in. You are looking very sweet, Clara. We haven't met, Obi, but I know all about you. I'm happy you are getting married to Clara. Sit down. Anywhere. And tell me what you will drink. Lady first; that is what the white man has brought. I respect the white man although we want them to go. Squash? God forbid! Nobody drinks squash in my house. Samson, bring sherry for Miss.'

'Yes, sah,' said Samson in immaculate white and brass buttons.

'Beer? Why not try a little whisky?'

'I don't touch spirits,' said Obi.

'Many young people from overseas start that way,' said Sam Okoli. 'OK, Samson, one beer, whisky and soda for me.'

Obi looked round the luxurious sitting-room. He had read the controversy in the Press when the Government had decided to build these ministers' houses at a cost of thirty-five thousand each.

'A very good house this,' he said.

'It's not too bad,' said the Minister.

'What an enormous radiogram!' Obi rose from his seat to go and have a closer look.

'It has a recording machine as well,' explained the owner. As if he knew what Obi was thinking, he added: 'It was not part of the house. I paid two-seventy-five pounds for it.' He walked across the room and switched on the tape-recorder.

'How do you like your work on the Scholarship Board? If you press this thing down, it begins to record. If you want to stop, you press this one. This is for playing records and this one is the radio. If I had a vacancy in my Ministry, I would have liked you to come and work there.' He stopped the tape-recorder, wound back and then pressed the play-back knob. 'You will hear all our conversation, everything.' He smiled with satisfaction as he listened to his own voice, adding an occasional commentary in pidgin.

'White man don go far. We just de shout for nothing,' he said.

229

Then he seemed to realize his position. 'All the same they must go. This no be them country.' He helped himself to another whisky, switched on the radio and sat down.

'Do you have just one Assistant Secretary in your Ministry?' asked Obi.

'Yes, at present. I hope to get another one in April. I used to have a Nigerian as my AS but he was an idiot. His head was swollen like a soldier ant because he went to Ibadan University. Now I have a white man who went to Oxford and he says "sir" to me. Our people have a long way to go.'

Obi sat with Clara in the back while the driver he had engaged that morning at four pounds ten a month drove them to Ikeja, twelve miles away, to have a special dinner in honour of the new car. But neither the drive nor the dinner was a great success. It was quite clear that Clara was not happy. Obi tried in vain to make her talk or relax.

'What's the matter?'

'Nothing. I'm just depressed, that's all.'

It had been dark in the car. He put an arm round her and pulled her towards him.

'Not here, please.'

Obi was hurt, especially as he knew his driver had heard.

'I'm sorry, dear,' said Clara putting her hand in his. 'I will explain later.'

'When?' Obi was alarmed by her tone.

'Today. After you have eaten.'

'What do you mean? Aren't you eating?'

She said she did not feel like eating. Obi said in that case he too wouldn't eat. So they decided to eat. But when the food came they merely looked at it, even Obi who had set out with a roaring appetite.

There was a film show which Clara suggested they should see. Obi said no, he wanted to find out what was on her mind. They went for a walk in the direction of the swimming pool.

Until Obi met Clara on board the cargo boat *Sasa* he had thought of love as another grossly over-rated European invention. It was not that he was indifferent to women. On the contrary, he had been quite intimate with a few in England – a Nigerian, a West Indian, English girls, and so on. But these intimacies which Obi regarded as love were neither deep nor sincere. There was always a part of him, the thinking part, which seemed to stand outside it all watching the passionate embrace with cynical disdain. The result was that one half of Obi might kiss a girl and murmur: 'I love you', but the other half would say: 'Don't be silly'. And it was always this second half that triumphed in the end when the glamour had evaporated with the heat, leaving a ridiculous anti-climax.

With Clara it was different. It had been from the very first. There was never a superior half at Obi's elbow wearing a patronizing smile.

'I can't marry you,' she said suddenly as Obi tried to kiss her under the tall mango tree at the edge of the swimming pool, and exploded into tears.

'I don't understand you, Clara.' And he really didn't. Was this the woman's game to bind him more firmly? But Clara was not like that; she had no coyness in her. Not much, anyway. That was one of the things Obi liked best about her. She had seemed so sure of herself that, unlike other women, she did not consider how quickly or cheaply she was captured.

'Why can't you marry me?' He succeeded in sounding unruffled. For answer she threw herself at him and began to weep violently on his shoulder.

'What's the matter, Clara? Tell me.' He was no longer unruffled. There was a hint of tears in his voice.

'I am an *osu*,' she wept. Silence. She stopped weeping and quietly disengaged herself from him. Still he said nothing.

'So you see we cannot get married,' she said, quite firmly, almost gaily – a terrible kind of gaiety. Only the tears showed she had wept.

'Nonsense!' said Obi. He shouted it almost, as if by shouting it now he could wipe away those seconds of silence, when everything had seemed to stop, waiting in vain for him to speak.

Joseph was asleep when he got back. It was past midnight. The door was shut but not locked, and he walked in quietly. But the slight whining of the door was enough to wake Joseph. Without waiting to undress, Obi told him the story.

'The very thing I was thinking to ask you. I was thinking how such a good and beautiful girl could remain unmarried until now.' Obi was undressing absent-mindedly. 'Anyhow, you are lucky to know at the beginning. No harm is done yet. The eye is not harmed by sleep,' Joseph said somewhat pointlessly. He noticed that Obi was not paying any attention.

'I am going to marry her,' Obi said.

'What!' Joseph sat up in bed.

'I am going to marry her.'

'Look at me,' said Joseph, getting up and tying his coverlet as a loincloth. He now spoke in English. 'You know book, but this is no matter for book. Do you know what an *osu* is? But how can you know?' In that short question he said in effect that Obi's mission-house upbringing and European education had made him a stranger in his country – the most painful thing one could say to Obi.

'I know more about it than yourself,' he said, 'and I'm going to marry the girl. I wasn't actually seeking your approval.'

Joseph thought the best thing was to drop the matter for the present. He went back to bed and was soon snoring.

Obi felt better and more confident in his decision now that there was an opponent, the first of hundreds to come no doubt. Perhaps it was not a decision really; for him there could be only one choice. It was scandalous that in the middle of the twentieth century a man could be barred from marrying a girl simply because her great-great-great-great-grandfather had been dedicated to serve a god, thereby setting himself apart and turning his descendants into a forbidden caste to the end of Time. Quite unbelievable. And here was an educated man telling Obi he did not understand. 'Not even my mother can stop me,' he said as he lay down beside Joseph.

At half-past two on the following day he called for Clara and told her they were going to Kingsway to buy an engagement ring.

'When?' was all she could ask.

'Now, now.'

'But I haven't said I . . .'

'Oh don't waste my time. I have other things to do. I haven't got my steward yet, and I haven't bought my pots and pans.'

'Yes, of course, it is tomorrow you are moving into your flat. I'm almost forgetting.'

They went in the car and made for the jeweller's shop in Kingsway and bought a twenty-pound ring. Obi's heavy wad of sixty pounds was now very much reduced. Thirty something pounds. Nearly forty.

'What about a Bible?' Clara asked.

'What Bible?'

'To go with the ring. Don't you know that?'

Obi didn't know that. They went over to the CMS Bookshop and paid for a handsome little Bible with a zip.

'Everything has a zip these days,' said Obi looking instinctively at his trouser front to make sure he had not forgotten to do the zip up, as had happened on one or two occasions.

They spent the whole afternoon shopping. At first Obi was as interested as Clara in the different utensils she was buying for him. But after an hour in which only one little saucepan had been bagged he lost any semblance of interest in the proceedings and simply trudged behind Clara like an obedient dog. She would reject an aluminium pot in one shop, and walk the whole length of Broad Street to another to buy the very same thing at the very same price.

'What is the difference between this one and the one we saw at UTC?'

'Men are blind,' she said.

When Obi got back to Joseph's room it was nearly eleven o'clock. Joseph was still up. In fact he had been waiting all the afternoon to complete the discussion they had suspended last night.

'How is Clara?' he asked. He succeeded in making it sound casual and unrehearsed. Obi was not prepared to plunge headlong into it. He wanted to begin at the fringes as he used to do many years ago when he was confronted with a morning bath in the cold harmattan season. Of all the parts of his body, his back liked cold water the least. He would stand before the bucket of water thinking how best to tackle it. His mother would call: 'Obi, haven't you finished? You will be late for school and they will flog you.' He would then stir the water with one finger. After that he would wash his feet, then his legs up to the knees, then the arm up to the elbow, then the rest of his arms and legs, the face and head, the belly, and finally, accompanied by a leap into the air, his back. He wanted to adopt the same method now.

'She is fine,' he said. 'Your Nigerian police are very cheeky, you know.'

'They are useless,' said Joseph, not wanting to discuss the police.

'I asked the driver to take us to the Victoria Beach Road. When we got there it was so cold that Clara refused to leave her seat. So we stayed at the back of the car, talking.'

'Where was the driver?' asked Joseph.

'He walked a little distance away to gaze at the lighthouse. Anyway, we were not there ten minutes before a police car drew up beside us and one of them flashed his torch. He said: "Good evening, sir." I said: "Good evening." Then he said: "Is she your wife?" I remained very cool and said: "No." Then he said: "Where you pick am?" I couldn't stand that, so I blew up. Clara told me in Ibo to call the driver and go away. The policeman immediately changed. He was Ibo, you see. He said he didn't know we were Ibos. He said many people these days were fond of taking other men's wives to the beach. Just think of that. *"Where you pick am?"* '

'What did you do after that?'

'We came away. We couldn't possibly stay after that. By the way, we are now engaged. I gave her a ring this afternoon.'

'Very good,' said Joseph bitterly. He thought for a while and then asked: 'Are you going to marry the English way or are you going to ask your people to approach her people according to custom?'

'I don't know yet. It depends on what my father says.'

'Did you tell him about it during your visit?'

'No, because I hadn't decided then.'

'He will not agree to it,' said Joseph. 'Tell anyone that I said so.'

'I can handle them,' said Obi, 'especially my mother.'

'Look at me, Obi.' Joseph invariably asked people to look at him. 'What you are going to do concerns not only yourself but your whole family and future generations. If one finger brings oil it soils the others. In future, when we are all civilized, anybody may marry anybody. But that time has not come. We of this generation are only pioneers.'

'What is a pioneer? Someone who shows the way. That is what I am doing. Anyway, it is too late to change now.'

'It is not,' said Joseph. 'What is an engagement ring? Our fathers did not marry with rings. It is not too late to change. Remember you are the one and only Umuofia son to be educated overseas. We do not want to be like the unfortunate child who grows his first tooth and grows a decayed one. What sort of encouragement will your action give to the poor men and women who collected the money?'

Obi was getting a little angry. 'It was a loan, remember. I shall pay it all back to the last anini.'

Obi knew better than anyone else that his family would violently oppose the idea of marrying an *osu*. Who wouldn't? But for him it was either Clara or nobody. Family ties were all very well as long as they did not interfere with Clara. 'If I could convince my mother,' he thought, 'all would be well.'

There was a special bond between Obi and his mother. Of all her eight children Obi was nearest her heart. Her neighbours used to call her 'Janet's mother' until Obi was born, and then she immediately became 'Obi's mother'. Neighbours have an unfailing instinct in such matters. As a child Obi took this special relationship very much for granted. But when he was about ten something happened which gave it concrete form in his young mind. He had a rusty razor-blade with which he sharpened his pencil or sometimes cut up a grasshopper. One day he forgot this implement in his pocket and it cut his mother's hand very badly when she was washing his clothes on a stone in the stream. She returned with the clothes unwashed and her hand dripping with blood. For some reason or other, whenever Obi thought affectionately of his mother, his mind went back to that shedding of her blood. It bound him very firmly to her.

When he said to himself: 'If I could convince my mother,' he was almost certain that he could.

CHAPTER EIGHT

The Umuofia Progressive Union, Lagos Branch, held its meetings on the first Saturday of every month. Obi did not attend the November meeting because he was visiting Umuofia at the time. His friend Joseph made his excuses.

The next meeting took place on 1 December 1956. Obi remembered that date because it was important in his life. Joseph had telephoned him in the office to remind him that the meeting began at 4.30 p.m. 'You will not forget to call for me?' he asked.

'Of course not,' said Obi. 'Expect me at four.'

'Good! See you later.' Joseph always put on an impressive manner when speaking on the telephone. He never spoke Ibo or pidgin English at such moments. When he hung up he told his colleagues: 'That na my brother. Just return from overseas. BA (Honours) Classics.' He always preferred the fiction of Classics to the truth of English. It sounded more impressive.

'What department he de work?'

'Secretary to the Scholarship Board.'

' 'E go make plenty money there. Every student who wan' go England go do see am for house.'

' 'E no be like dat,' said Joseph. 'Him na gentlemen. No fit take bribe.'

'Na so,' said the other in unbelief.

At 4.15 p.m. Obi arrived at Joseph's in his new Morris Oxford. That was one reason why Joseph had looked forward to this particular meeting. He was going to share in the glory of the car.

It was going to be a great occasion for the Umuofia Progressive Union when one of their sons arrived at their meeting in a pleasure-car. Joseph as a very close friend of Obi would reflect some of the glory. He was impeccably turned out for the occasion: grey flannel trousers, white nylon shirt, spotted dark tie and black shoes. Although he did not say it, he was disappointed at Obi's casual appearance. It was true he wanted to share in the glory of the car, but he did not care to be called the outsider who wept louder than the bereaved. It was not beyond Umuofia men to make such embarrassing comments.

The reaction of the meeting was better than even Joseph expected. Although Obi had arrived at his place at 4.15 p.m. Joseph had delayed their departure until 5 p.m. when he knew the meeting would be full. The fine for lateness was one penny, but what was that beside the glory of stepping out of a pleasure-car in the full gaze of Umuofia? As it turned out, nobody thought of the fine. They clapped and cheered and danced when they saw the car pull up.

'*Umuofia kwenu!*' shouted one old man.

'Ya!' replied everyone in unison.

'*Umuofia kwenu!*'

'Ya!'

'*Kwenu!*'

'Ya!'

'*Ife awolu Ogoli azua n'afia,*' he said.

Obi was given a seat beside the President and had to answer innumerable questions about his job and about his car before the meeting settled down again to business.

Joshua Udo, a messenger in the Post Office, had been sacked for sleeping while on duty. According to him, he had not been sleeping but thinking. But the Chief Clerk had been looking for a way to deal with him since he had not completed the payment of ten pounds' bribe which he had promised when he was employed. Joshua was now asking his countrymen to 'borrow' him ten pounds to look for another job.

The meeting had practically agreed to this when it was disturbed by Obi's arrival. The President was just giving Joshua a piece of

his mind on the subject of sleeping in the office, as a preliminary
to lending him public funds.

'You did not leave Umuofia four hundred miles away to come
and sleep in Lagos,' he told him. 'There are enough beds in
Umuofia. If you don't want to work, you should return there. You
messengers are all like that. I have one in my office who is always
getting permission to go to the latrine. Anyway, I move that we
approve of a loan of ten pounds to Mr Joshua Udo for the . . .
er . . . er the explicit purpose of seeking re-engagement.' The last
sentence was said in English because of its legal nature. The loan
was approved. Then by way of light relief someone took up the
President on his statement that it was work that brought them four
hundred miles to Lagos.

'It is money, not work,' said the man. 'We left plenty of work
at home . . . Anyone who likes work can return home, take up
his matchet and go into that bad bush between Umuofia and
Mbaino. It will keep him occupied to his last days.' The meeting
agreed that it was money, not work, that brought them to Lagos.

'Let joking pass,' said the old man who had earlier on greeted
Umuofia in war-like salute. 'Joshua is now without a job. We have
given him ten pounds. But ten pounds does not talk. If you stand
a hundred pounds here where I stand now, it will not talk. That
is why we say that he who has people is richer than he who has
money. Everyone of us here should look out for openings in his
department and put in a word for Joshua.' This was greeted with
approval.

'Thanks to the Man Above,' he continued, 'we now have one
of our sons in the senior service. We are not going to ask him to
bring his salary to share among us. It is in little things like this
that he can help us. It is our fault if we do not approach him. Shall
we kill a snake and carry it in our hand when we have a bag for
putting long things in?' He took his seat.

'Your words are very good,' said the President. 'We have the
same thought in our minds. But we must give the young man time
to look round first and know what is what.'

The meeting supported the President by their murmurs. 'Give
the young man time.' 'Let him settle down.' Obi felt very uneasy.

But he knew they meant well. Perhaps it would not be too difficult to manage them.

The next item on the agenda was a motion of censure on the President and executive for mishandling Obi's reception. Obi was amazed. He had thought that his reception went very well. But not so the three young men who sponsored the motion. Nor, as it turned out, a dozen or so other young people. Their complaint was that they were not given any of the two dozen bottles of beer which had been bought. The top people and elders had monopolized it, leaving the young people with two kegs of sour palm wine. As everyone knew, Lagos palm wine was really no palm wine at all but water – an infinite dilution.

This accusation caused a lively exchange of hard words for the better part of an hour. The President called the young men 'ungrateful' ingrates whose stock-in-trade was 'character-assassination'. One of the young people suggested that it was immoral to use public funds to buy beer for one's private thirst. The words were hard, but Obi felt somehow that they lacked bitterness; especially since they were English words taken straight from today's newspaper. When it was all over the President announced that their honoured son Obi Okonkwo had a few words to say to them. This announcement was received with great joy.

Obi rose to his feet and thanked them for having such a useful meeting, for did not the Psalmist say that it was good for brethren to meet together in harmony? 'Our fathers also have a saying about the danger of living apart. They say it is the curse of the snake. If all snakes lived together in one place, who would approach them? But they live every one unto himself and so fall easy prey to man.' Obi knew he was making a good impression. His listeners nodded their heads and made suitable rejoinders. Of course it was all a prepared speech, but it did not sound over-rehearsed.

He spoke about the wonderful welcome they had given him on his return. 'If a man returns from a long journey and no one says *nno* to him he feels like one who has not arrived.' He tried to improvise a joke about beer and palm wine, but it did not come off, and he hurried to the next point. He thanked them for the sacrifices they had made to send him to England. He would try his best to justify their confidence. The speech which had started off one hundred percent in Ibo was now fifty-fifty. But his audience still seemed highly impressed. They liked good Ibo, but they also admired English. At last he got round to his main subject. 'I have one little request to place before you. As you all know, it takes a little time to settle down again after an absence of four years. I have many little private matters to settle. My request is this, that you give me four months before I start to pay back my loan.'

'That is a small matter,' said someone. 'Four months is a short time. A debt may get mouldy, but it never decays.'

Yes, it was a small matter. But it was clear that not everyone thought so. Obi even heard someone ask what he was going to do with the big money which Government would give him.

'Your words are very good,' said the President at length. 'I do not think anyone here will say no to your request. We will give you four months. Do I speak for Umuofia?'

'Ya!' they replied.

'But there are two words I should like to drop before you. You are very young, a child of yesterday. You know book. But book stands by itself and experience stands by itself. So I am not afraid to talk to you.'

Obi's heart began to pound heavily.

'You are one of us, so we must bare our minds to you. I have lived in this Lagos for fifteen years. I came here on August the sixth, nineteen hundred and forty-one. Lagos is a bad place for a young man. If you follow its sweetness, you will perish. Perhaps you will ask why I am saying all this. I know what Government pays senior service people. What you get in one month is what some of your brothers here get in one year. I have already said that we will give you four months. We can even give you one year. But are we doing you any good?'

A big lump caught in Obi's throat.

'What the Government pays you is more than enough unless you go into bad ways.' Many of the people said: 'God forbid!' 'We cannot afford bad ways,' went on the President. 'We are pioneers building up our families and our town. And those who build must deny ourselves many pleasures. We must not drink because we see our neighbours drink or run after women because our thing stands up. You may ask why I am saying all this. I have heard that you are moving around with a girl of doubtful ancestry, and even thinking of marrying her . . .'

Obi leapt to his feet trembling with rage. At such times words always deserted him.

'Please sit down, Mr Okonkwo,' said the President calmly.

'Sit down, my foot!' Obi shouted in English. 'This is pre-posterous! I could take you to court for that . . . for that . . . for that . . .'

'You may take me to court when I have finished.'

'I am not going to listen to you any more. I take back my request. I shall start paying you back at the end of this month. Now, this minute! But don't you dare interfere in my affairs again. And if this is what you meet about,' he said in Ibo, 'you may cut off my two legs if you ever find them here again.' He made for the door. A number of people tried to intercept him. 'Please sit down.' 'Cool down.' 'There is no quarrel.' Everybody was talking at once. Obi pushed his way through and made blindly for his car with half a dozen people at his heels pleading that he return.

'Drive off!' he screamed at the driver as soon as he got into the car.

'Obi, please,' said Joseph, miserably leaning on the window.

'Get out!'

The car drove off. Half-way to Ikoyi he ordered the driver to stop and go back to Lagos, to Clara's lodgings.

CHAPTER NINE

The prospect of working with Mr Green and Mr Omo did not particularly appeal to Obi, but he soon found that it was not as bad as he had thought. For one thing he was given a separate office, which he shared with Mr Green's attractive English secretary. He saw very little of Mr Omo and only saw Mr Green when he rushed in to bark orders at him or at Miss Marie Tomlinson.

'Isn't he odd?' said Miss Tomlinson on one occasion. 'But he's really not a bad man.'

'Of course not,' replied Obi. He knew that many of these secretaries were planted to spy on Africans. One of their tactics was to pretend to be very friendly and broadminded. One had to watch what one said. Not that he cared whether or not Mr Green knew what he thought of his type. In fact, he ought to know. But he was not going to get it through an *agent provocateur*.

As the weeks passed, however, Obi's guard began to come down 'small small', as they say. It started with Clara's visit to his office one morning to tell him something or other. Miss Tomlinson had heard her voice on the telephone a few times and had commented on its attractiveness. Obi introduced them, and was a little surprised at the English woman's genuine delight. When Clara left she talked about nothing else for the rest of the day. 'Isn't she beautiful? Aren't you lucky? When are you getting married? I shouldn't wait if I were you,' and so on and so forth.

Obi felt like a clumsy schoolboy earning his first praise for doing something extraordinarily clever. He began to see Miss

Tomlinson in a different light. If it was part of her tactics, it was really a very clever one for which she deserved credit. But it did not look clever or forced. It seemed to have come straight from her heart.

The telephone rang and Miss Tomlinson answered it.

'Mr Okonkwo? Right. Hold on for him. For you, Mr Okonkwo.'

Obi's telephone was in parallel with hers. He thought it was Clara, but it was only the receptionist downstairs.

'A gentleman? Send him up, please. He want speak to me there? All right, I de come down. Now now.'

The gentleman was in a three-piece suit and carried a rolled umbrella. Obviously a new arrival from England.

'Good morning. My name is Okonkwo.'

'Mark is mine. How do you do?'

They shook hands.

'I've come to consult you about something – semi-official and semi-private.'

'Let's go up to my office, shall we?'

'Thank you very much.'

Obi led the way.

'You have just come back to Nigeria?' he asked as they mounted the stairs.

'I've been back now six months.'

'I see.' He opened the door. 'After you.'

Mr Mark stepped in, and then pulled up suddenly as if he had seen a snake across his path. But he recovered quickly enough and walked in.

'Good morning,' he said to Miss Tomlinson, all smiles. Obi dragged another chair to his table and Mr Mark sat down.

'And what can I do for you?'

To his amazement Mr Mark replied in Ibo:

'If you don't mind, shall we talk in Ibo? I didn't know you had a European here.'

'Just as you like. Actually I didn't think you were Ibo. What is your problem?' He tried to sound casual.

'Well, it is like this. I have a sister who has just passed her

School Certificate in Grade One. She wants to apply for a Federal Scholarship to study in England.'

Although he spoke in Ibo, there were some words that he had to say in English. Words like 'School Certificate' and 'scholarship'. He lowered his voice to a whisper when he came to them.

'You want application forms?' asked Obi.

'No, no, no. I have got those. But it is like this. I was told that you are the secretary of the Scholarship Commission and I thought that I should see you. We are both Ibos and I cannot hide anything from you. It is all very well sending in forms, but you know what our country is. Unless you see people . . .'

'In this case it is not necessary to see anybody. The only . . .'

'I was actually thinking of coming round to your house, but the man who told me about you did not know where you lived.'

'I'm sorry, Mr Mark, but I really don't understand what you are driving at.' He said this in English, much to Mr Mark's consternation. Miss Tomlinson pricked up her ears like a dog that is not quite sure whether someone has mentioned bones.

'I'm sorry – er – Mr Okonkwo. But don't get me wrong. I know this is the wrong place to – er . . .'

'I don't think there is any point in continuing this discussion,' Obi said in English. 'If you don't mind, I'm rather busy.' He rose to his feet. Mr Mark also rose, muttered a few apologies and made for the door.

'He's forgotten his umbrella,' remarked Miss Tomlinson as Obi returned to his seat.

'Oh dear!' He took the umbrella and rushed out.

Miss Tomlinson was eagerly waiting to hear what he would say when he came back, but he simply sat down as if nothing had happened and opened a file. He knew she was watching him, and he wrinkled his forehead in pretended concentration.

'That was short and sweet,' she said.

'Oh yes. He is a nuisance.' He did not look up and the conversation lapsed.

Throughout that morning Obi felt strangely elated. It was not unlike the feeling he had some years ago in England after his first woman. She had said almost in so many words what she was coming

for when she agreed to visit Obi in his lodgings. 'I'll teach you
how to dance the high life when you come,' he had said. 'That
would be grand,' she replied eagerly, 'and perhaps a little low life
too.' And she had smiled mischievously. When the day arrived Obi
was scared. He had heard that it was possible to disappoint a
woman. But he did not disappoint her, and when it was over he
felt strangely elated. She said she thought she had been attacked
by a tiger.

After his encounter with Mr Mark he did feel like a tiger. He
had won his first battle hands-down. Everyone said it was
impossible to win. They said a man expects you to accept 'kola'
from him for services rendered, and until you do, his mind is never
at rest. He feels like an inexperienced kite that carried away a
duckling and was ordered by its mother to return it because the
duck had said nothing, made no noise, just walked away. 'There
is some grave danger in that kind of silence. Go and get a chick.
We know the hen. She shouts and curses, and the matter ends
there.' A man to whom you do a favour will not understand if you
say nothing, make no noise, just walk away. You may cause more
trouble by refusing a bribe than by accepting it. Had not a Minister
of State said, albeit in an unguarded, alcoholic moment, that the
trouble was not in receiving bribes, but in failing to do the thing
for which the bribe was given? And if you refuse, how do you know
that a 'brother' or a 'friend' is not receiving on your behalf, having
told everyone that he is your agent? Stuff and nonsense! It was
easy to keep one's hands clean. It required no more than the ability
to say: 'I'm sorry, Mr So-and-So, but I cannot continue this
discussion. Good morning.' One could not, of course, be unduly
arrogant. After all, the temptation was not really overwhelming.
But in all modesty one could not say it had been non-existent. Obi
was finding it more and more impossible to live on what was left
of his forty-seven pounds ten after he had paid twenty to the
Umuofia Progressive Union and sent ten to his parents. Even now
he had no idea where John's school fees for next term would come
from. No, one could not say he had no need for money.

He had just finished his lunch of pounded yams and egusi soup
and was sprawling on the sofa. The soup had been particularly

well prepared – with meat and fresh fish – and he had over-eaten. Whenever he ate too much pounded yam he felt like a boa that had swallowed a goat. He sprawled helplessly, waiting for some of it to digest, to give him room to breathe.

A car pulled up outside. He thought it was one of the five other occupants of the block of six flats. He knew none of them by name, and only some by sight. They were all Europeans. He spoke about once a month with one of them, the tall PWD man who lived on the other side of the same floor. But his speaking to him had nothing to do with sharing the same floor. This man was in charge of the common garden and collected ten and sixpence every month from each occupant to pay the garden boy. So Obi knew him well by sight. He also knew one of those upstairs who regularly brought an African prostitute home on Saturday nights.

The car started again. It was clearly a taxi, for only taxi-drivers could rev up their engines that way. There was a timid knock on Obi's door. Who could it be? Clara was on duty that afternoon. Joseph, perhaps. For months now he had been trying to regain the blissful seat in Obi's affections which he had lost at that ill-fated meeting of the Umuofia Progressive Union. His crime was that he had told the President in confidence of Obi's engagement to an outcast girl. He had pleaded for forgiveness: he had only told the President in confidence in the hope that he might use his position as the father of Umuofia people in Lagos to reason privately with Obi.

'Never mind,' Obi had told him. 'Let us forget about it.' But he had not forgotten. He had stopped visiting Joseph in his lodgings. As for Clara, she did not want to set eyes on Joseph again. Obi was sometimes amazed and terrified at the intensity of her hate, knowing how much she had liked him before. Now he was slippery, he was envious, he was even capable of poisoning Obi. The incident, like a bath of palm wine on incipient measles, had brought all the ugly rashes to the surface.

Obi opened the door with a very dark frown on his face. Instead of Joseph, there was a girl at the door.

'Good afternoon,' he said, completely transformed.

'I am looking for Mr Okonkwo,' she said.

'Speaking. Come right in.' He was surprised at his own sudden gaiety; the girl was, after all, a complete stranger, albeit a most attractive one. So he pulled in his horns.

'Please sit down. By the way, I don't think we've met before.'

'No. I am Elsie Mark.'

'Please to meet you, Miss Mark.' She smiled a most delicious smile, showing a faultless set of immaculate teeth. There was a little gap between the two front ones, rather like Clara's. Someone had said that girls with that kind of teeth are very warm-blooded. He sat down. He wasn't shy as he usually was with girls, and yet he didn't know what to say next.

'You must be surprised at my visit.' She was now speaking in Ibo.

'I didn't know you were Ibo.' As soon as he said it light broke through. What was left of his gaiety vanished. The girl must have noticed a change in his expression or perhaps a movement of the hands. She avoided his eyes and her words came hesitantly. She was testing the slippery ground with one wary foot after another before committing her whole body.

'I'm sorry my brother came to your office. I told him not to.'

'It's perfectly all right,' Obi found himself saying. 'I told him that – er – that with your Grade One certificate you stood a very good chance. It all depends on you really, how much you impress members of the Board at the interview.'

'The most important thing,' she said, 'is to be sure that I am selected to appear before the Board.'

'Yes. But as I said, you stand as good a chance as anybody else.'

'But people with Grade One are sometimes left out in favour of those with Grade Two or even Three.'

'I've no doubt that may happen sometimes. But all other things being equal . . . I'm sorry I haven't offered you anything. I'm a very bad host. Can I bring you a Coca-Cola?' She smiled shyly with her eyes. 'Yes?' He rushed off to his refrigerator and brought out a bottle. He took a long time opening it and pouring it into a glass. He was thinking furiously.

She accepted the glass and smiled her thanks. She must be

about seventeen or eighteen. A mere girl, Obi thought. And already so wise in the ways of the world. They sat in silence for a long time.

'Last year,' she said suddenly, 'none of the girls in our school who got Grade One was given a scholarship.'

'Perhaps they did not impress the Board.'

'It wasn't that. It was because they did not see the members at home.'

'So you intend to see the members?'

'Yes.'

'Is a scholarship as important as all that? Why doesn't a relation of yours pay for you to go to a university?'

'Our father spent all his money on our brother. He went to read Medicine but failed his exams. He switched over to Engineering and failed again. He was in England for twelve years.'

'Was that the man who came to see me today?' She nodded. 'What does he do for a living?'

'He is teaching in a Community Secondary School.' She was now looking very sad. 'He returned at the end of the last year because our father died and we had no more money.'

Obi felt very sorry for her. She was obviously an intelligent girl who had set her mind, like so many other young Nigerians on university education. And who could blame them? Certainly not Obi. It was rather sheer hypocrisy to ask if a scholarship was as important as all that or if university education was worth it. Every Nigerian knew the answer. It was yes.

A university degree was the philosopher's stone. It transmuted a third-class clerk on one hundred and fifty a year into a senior Civil Servant on five hundred and seventy, with car and luxuriously furnished quarters at nominal rent. And the disparity in salary and amenities did not tell even half the story. To occupy a 'European post' was second only to actually being a European. It raised a man from the masses to the élite whose small talk at cocktail parties was: 'How's the car behaving?'

'Please, Mr Okonkwo, you must help me. I'll do whatever you ask.' She avoided his eyes. Her voice was a little unsteady, and Obi thought he saw a hint of tears in her eyes.

'I'm sorry, terribly sorry, but I don't see that I can make any promises.'

Another car drew up outside with a screech of brakes, and Clara rushed in, as was her fashion, humming a popular song. She stopped abruptly on seeing the girl.

'Hello, Clara. This is Miss Mark.'

'How do you do?' she said stiffly, with a slight nod of the head. She did not offer her hand. 'How did you like the soup?' she asked Obi. 'I'm afraid I prepared it in a hurry.' In those two short sentences she sought to establish one or two facts for the benefit of the strange girl. First, by her sophisticated un-Nigerian accent she showed that she was a been-to. You could tell a been-to not only by her phonetics, but by her walk – quick, short steps instead of the normal leisurely gait. In company of her less fortunate sisters she always found an excuse for saying: 'When I was in England . . .' Secondly, her proprietary air seemed to tell the girl: 'You had better try elsewhere.'

'I thought you were on this afternoon.'

'It was a mistake. I'm off today.'

'Why did you have to go away then, after making the soup?'

'Oh, I had such a lot of washing to do. Aren't you offering me anything to drink? OK, I'll serve myself.'

'I'm terribly sorry, dear. Sit down. I'll get it for you.'

'No. Too late.' She went to the fridge and took out a bottle of ginger-beer. 'What's happened to the other ginger-beer?' she asked. 'There were two.'

'I think you had one yesterday.'

'Did I? Oh yes, I remember.' She came back and sank heavily into the sofa beside Obi. 'Gosh, it's hot!'

'I think I must be going,' said Miss Mark.

'I'm sorry I can't promise anything definite,' said Obi, getting up. She did not answer, only smiled sadly.

'How are you getting back to town?'

'Perhaps I will see a taxi.'

'I'll run you down to Tinubu Square. Taxis are very rare here. Come along, Clara, let's take her down to Tinubu.'

'I'm sorry I came at such an awkward time,' said Clara as they drove back to Ikoyi from Tinubu Square.

'Don't be ridiculous. What do you mean awkward time?'

'You thought I was on duty.' She laughed. 'I'm sorry about that. Who is she, anyway? I must say she is very good-looking. And I went and poured sand into your *garri*. I'm sorry, my dear.'

Obi told her not to behave like a silly little girl. 'I won't say another word to you if you don't shut up,' he said.

'You needn't say anything if you don't want to. Shall we call and say hello to Sam?'

The Minister was not in when they got to his house. It appeared there was a Cabinet meeting.

'Wetin Master and Madam go drink?' asked his steward.

'Make you no worry, Samson. Just tell Minister say we call.'

'You go return again?' asked Samson.

'Not today.'

'You say you no go drink small sometin?'

'No, thank you. We go drink when we come again. Bye-bye.'

When they got back to Obi's flat he said: 'I had a very interesting experience today.' And he told her of Mr Mark's visit to his office and gave her a detailed account of all that transpired between Miss Mark and himself before her arrival.

When he finished, Clara said nothing for a little while.

'Are you satisfied?' asked Obi.

'I think you were too severe on the man,' she said.

'You think I should have encouraged him to talk about bribing me?'

'After all, offering money is not as bad as offering one's body. And yet you gave her a drink and a lift back to town.' She laughed. 'Na so this world be.'

Obi wondered.

CHAPTER TEN

For one brief moment a year ago Mr Green had taken an interest in Obi's personal affairs – if one could call it taking an interest. Obi had just taken delivery of his new car.

'You will do well to remember,' said Mr Green, 'that at this time every year you will be called upon to cough up forty pounds for your insurance.' It was like the voice of Joel the son of Pethuel. 'It is, of course, none of my business really. But in a country where even the educated have not reached the level of thinking about tomorrow, one has a clear duty.' He made the word 'educated' taste like vomit. Obi thanked him for his advice.

And now at last the day of the Lord had come. He spread the insurance renewal letter before him on the table. Forty-two pounds! He had just a little over thirteen pounds in the bank. He folded the letter and put it into one of his drawers where he had his personal bits and pieces like postage stamps, receipts and quarterly statement from the bank. A letter in a semi-literate hand caught his eye. He brought it out and read again.

Dear Sir,

    It is absolutely deplorable to me hence I have to beg you respectfully to render me with help. At one side of it looks shameful of my asking you for this help, but if only I am sincere to myself, having the truth that I am wanting because of the need, I wish you pardon me. My request from you is 30/– (thirty shillings), assuring you of every truth to do the refund prompt, on the pay-day, 26 November 1957.

I wish the best of your consideration.

Yours obedient servant,
Charles Ibe.

Obi had forgotten all about it. No wonder Charles flitted in and out of his office nowadays without stopping to exchange greetings in Ibo. Charles was one of the messengers in the department. Obi had asked him what the great need was, and he said his wife had just given birth to their fifth child. Obi, who happened to be carrying about four pounds in his pocket, had lent him thirty shillings straight away and forgotten all about it – until now. He sent for Charles and asked him in Ibo (so that Miss Tomlinson would not understand) why he had not fulfilled his promise. Charles scratched his head and renewed his promise, this time for the end of December.

'I shall find it difficult to trust you in future,' Obi said in English.

'Ah no, *Oga*, Master. E no be like dat I beg. I go pay end of mont prompt.' He then reverted to Ibo. 'Our people have a saying that a debt may become mouldy but it never rots. There are many people in this department, but I did not go to them. I came to you.'

'That was very kind of you,' said Obi, knowing full well that the point would be missed. It was.

'Yes, there are many people here, but I did not go to them. I take you as my special master. Our people have a saying that when there is a big tree small ones climb on its back to reach the sun. You are a small boy in years, but . . .'

'O.K., Charles. End of December. If you fail I shall report the matter to Mr Green.'

'Ah! I no go fail at all. If I fail my *Oga*, who I go go meet next time?'

And on that rhetorical note the matter rested for the moment. Obi looked at Charles's letter again and saw with wry amusement that in the original manuscript he had written: 'My request from you is only 30/– (thirty shillings)'; he had then crossed out 'only', no doubt after mature deliberation.

He shoved the letter back in the drawer to spend the night with the insurance notice. There was nothing for it but to go to the bank manager tomorrow morning and ask for an overdraft of fifty pounds. He had been told that it was fairly easy for a senior Civil Servant, whose salary was paid into the bank, to obtain an overdraft of that order. Meanwhile there was little point in thinking about it any more. Charles's attitude was undoubtedly the healthiest in these circumstances. If one didn't laugh, one would have to cry. It seemed that was the way Nigeria was built.

But no amount of philosophy could take his mind right off that notice. 'No one can say I have been extravagant. If I had not sent thirty-five pounds at the end of last month to pay for mother's treatment in a private hospital, I would have been all right – or if not exactly all right, at least above water. Anyway, I'll pull through,' he assured himself. 'The beginning was bound to be a little difficult. What do our people say? The start of weeping is always hard. Not a particularly happy proverb, but none the less true.'

If the Umuofia Progressive Union had granted him four month's grace things might have turned out differently. But all that was now past history. He had made up his quarrel with the Union. It was quite clear they had meant no harm. And even if they had, was it not true, as the President had said at the reconciliation meeting, that anger against a kinsman was felt in the flesh, not in the marrow? The Union had pleaded with him to accept the four months' grace from that moment. But he had refused with the lie that his circumstances were now happier.

And if one thought objectively of the matter – as though it related to Mr B. and not to one's self – could one blame those poor men for being critical of a senior service man who appeared reluctant to pay twenty pounds a month? They had taxed themselves mercilessly to raise eight hundred pounds to send him to England. Some of them earned no more than five pounds a month. He earned nearly fifty. They had wives and school-going children; he had none. After paying the twenty pounds he would have thirty left. And very soon he would have an increment which alone was as big as some people's salary.

Obi admitted that his people had a sizeable point. What they did not know was that, having laboured in sweat and tears to enrol their kinsman among the shining élite, they had to keep him there. Having made him a member of an exclusive club whose members greet one another with 'How's the car behaving?' did they expect him to turn round and answer: 'I'm sorry, but my car is off the road. You see I couldn't pay my insurance premium'? That would be letting the side down in a way that was quite unthinkable. Almost as unthinkable as a masked spirit in the old Ibo society answering another's esoteric salutation: 'I'm sorry, my friend, but I don't understand your strange language. I'm but a human being wearing a mask.' No, these things could not be.

Ibo people, in their fair-mindedness, have devised a proverb which says that it is not right to ask a man with elephantiasis of the scrotum to take on smallpox as well, when thousands of other people had not had even their share of small diseases. No doubt it is not right. But it happens. 'Na so dis world be,' they say.

Having negotiated a loan of fifty pounds from the bank and gone straight to hand it over to the insurance company, Obi returned to his office to find his electricity bill for November. When he opened it he came very close to crying. Five pounds seven and three.

'Anything the matter?' asked Miss Tomlinson.

'Oh no. Not at all.' He pulled himself together. 'It's only my electricity bill.'

'How much do you find it comes to a month?'

'This one is five-seven and three.'

'It's sheer robbery what they charge for electricity here. In England you would pay less than that for a whole quarter.'

Obi was not in the mood for comparisons. The sudden impact of the insurance notice had woken him up to the real nature of his financial position. He had surveyed the prospects for the next few months and found them pretty alarming. At the end of the month he would have to renew his vehicle licence. A whole year was out of the question, but even a quarter alone was four pounds. And then the tyres. He could possibly postpone renewing them for another month or so, but they were already as smooth as the tube. Everyone said that it was surprising that his first set of tyres did not give him two years or even eighteen months. He could not contemplate four new tyres at thirty pounds. So he would have to retread his present set, one at a time beginning with the spare in his boot. That would cut the price down by half. They would probably last only six months as Miss Tomlinson told him. But six months might be long enough for things to improve a little. No one told him about income tax. That was to come, but not for another two months.

As soon as he finished his lunch he immediately set about introducing sweeping economy measures in his flat. His new steward boy, Sebastian, stood by, no doubt wondering what had possessed his master. He had started off his lunch by complaining that there was too much meat in the soup.

'I am not a millionaire, you know,' he had said. God knows, Clara used twice as much meat when she made the soup herself! thought Sebastian.

'And in future,' Obi continued, 'I shall only give you money to go to the market once a week.'

Every switch in the flat lit two bulbs. Obi set about pruning them down. The rule in future was to be one switch, one bulb. He had often wondered why there should be two lamps in the bathroom and lavatory. It was typical Government planning. There was no single light on the flight of concrete stairs running through the middle of the block, with the result that people often collided with one another there or slipped one step. And yet there were two lamps in the lavatory where no one wanted to look closely at what one was doing.

Having dealt with the lamps, he turned to Sebastian again. 'In future the water-heater must not be turned on. I will have cold baths. The fridge must be switched off at seven o'clock in the evening and on again at twelve noon. Do you understand?'

'Yes, sir. But meat no go spoil so?'

'No need to buy plenty meat at once.'

'Yes, sir.'

'Buy small today; when he finish buy small again.'

'Yes, sir. Only I tink you say I go de go market once every week.'

'I said nothing of the sort. I said I would only give you money once.'

Sebastian now understood. 'Na de same ting. Instead to give me money two times. You go give me now one time.'

Obi knew he would not get very far pursuing the matter in the abstract.

That evening he had a serious disagreement with Clara. He had not wanted to tell her about the overdraft, but as soon as she saw him she asked what the matter was. He tried to fob her off with some excuse. But he had not planned it, so it didn't hold together. Clara's way of getting anything from him was not to argue but to refuse to talk. And as she usually did three-quarters of the talking when they were together, the silence soon became too heavy to bear. Obi would then ask her what the matter was, which was usually the prelude to doing whatever she wanted.

'Why didn't you tell me?' she asked when he had told her about the overdraft.

'Well, there was no need. I'll pay it easily in five monthly instalments.'

'That's not the point. You don't think I should be told when you're in difficulty.'

'I wasn't in difficulty. I wouldn't have mentioned it if you hadn't pressed me.'

'I see,' was all she said. She went across the room and picked up a woman's magazine lying on the floor and began to read.

After a couple of minutes, Obi said with synthetic light-heartedness: 'It's very rude to be reading when you have a visitor.'

'You should have known I was very badly brought up.' Any reflection on her family was a very risky subject and often ended in tears. Even now her eyes were beginning to look glazed.

'Clara,' he said putting his arm around her. She was all tensed up. 'Clara.' She did not answer. She was turning the pages of the magazine mechanically. 'I don't understand why you want to quarrel.' Not a sound. 'I think I had better be going.'

'I think so, too.'

'Clara, I'm very sorry.'

'About what? Leave me, *ojare*.' She pushed his arm off.

Obi sat for another couple of minutes gazing at the floor.

'All right.' He sprang to his feet. Clara remained where she was, turning the pages.

'Bye-bye.'

'Good-bye.'

When he got back to the flat he told Sebastian not to cook any supper.

'I don start already.'

'Then you can stop,' he shouted, and went into his bedroom. He stopped for a brief moment to look at Clara's photograph on the dressing-table. He turned it on its face and went to undress. He threw his cloth over his shoulder, toga-wise, and returned to his sitting-room to get a book. He looked along the shelves a number of times without deciding what to read. Then his eye rested on A. E. Housman's *Collected Poems*. He took it down and returned to his bedroom. He picked up Clara's photograph and stood it on its feet again. Then he went and lay down.

He opened the book where a piece of paper was showing, its top frayed and browned from exposure to dust. On it was written a poem called 'Nigeria'.

> God bless our noble fatherland,
> Great land of sunshine bright,
> Where brave men chose the way of peace,
> To win their freedom fight.
> May we preserve our purity,
> Our zest for life and jollity.
>
> God bless our noble countrymen
> And women everywhere.
> Teach them to walk in unity
> To build our nation dear;
> Forgetting region, tribe or speech,
> But caring always each for each.

At the bottom was written 'London, July 1955'. He smiled, put the piece of paper back where he found it and began to read his favourite poem 'Easter Hymn'.

CHAPTER ELEVEN

Obi was now on the best of terms with Miss Tomlinson. He had begun to lower his guard 'small small' from the day she went into raptures over Clara. She was now Marie to him and he was Obi to her.

'Miss Tomlinson is rather a mouthful,' she had said one day. 'Why not plain Marie?'

'I was going to suggest that myself. But you're not *plain* Marie. You are the exact opposite of plain.'

'Oh,' she said with a delightful jerk of the head. 'Thank you.' She stood up and executed a mock curtsy.

They talked, frankly, of many things. Whenever there was nothing urgent to do, Marie had the habit of folding her arms and resting them on her typewriter. She would wait in that posture until Obi raised his eyes from what he was doing. Mr Green was usually the subject of discussion, or at least the occasion for starting it. Once started, it took whatever direction it pleased.

'I had tea with the Greens yesterday,' she might say. 'They are a most delightful couple, you know. He is quite different at home. Do you know he pays school fees for his steward's son? But he says the most outrageous things about educated Africans.'

'I know,' said Obi. 'He will make a very interesting case for a psychologist. Charles – you know the messenger – told me that some time ago the AA wanted to sack him for sleeping in the office. But when the matter went up to Mr Green, he tore out the query from Charles's personal file. He said the poor man must be suffering from malaria, and the next day he bought him a tube of quinacrine.'

Marie was about to place yet another brick in position in their reconstruction of a strange character when Mr Green sent for her to take some dictation. She was just saying that he was a very devout Christian, a sidesman at the Colonial Church.

Obi had long come to admit to himself that, no matter how much he disliked Mr Green, he nevertheless had some admirable qualities. Take, for instance, his devotion to duty. Rain or shine, he was in his office half an hour before the official time and quite often worked long after two, or returned again in the evening. Obi could not understand it. Here was a man who did not believe in a country, and yet worked so hard for it. Did he simply believe in duty as a logical necessity? He continually put off going to see his dentist because, as he always said, he had some urgent work to do. He was like a man who had some great and supreme task that must be completed before a final catastrophe intervened. It reminded Obi of what he had once read about Mohammed Ali of Egypt, who in his old age worked in frenzy to modernize his country before his death.

In the case of Green it was difficult to see what his deadline was, unless it was Nigeria's independence. They said he had put in his resignation when it was thought that Nigeria might become independent in 1956. In the event it did not happen and Mr Green was persuaded to withdraw his resignation.

A most intriguing character, Obi thought, drawing profiles on his blotting-pad. One thing he could never draw properly was a shirt collar. Yes, a very interesting character. It was clear he loved Africa, but only Africa of a kind: the Africa of Charles, the messenger, the Africa of his garden-boy and steward-boy. He must have come originally with an ideal – to bring light to the heart of darkness, to tribal head-hunters performing weird ceremonies and unspeakable rites. But when he arrived, Africa played him false. Where was his beloved bush full of human sacrifice? There was St George horsed and caparisoned, but where was the dragon? In 1900 Mr Green might have ranked among the great missionaries; in 1935 he would have made do with slapping headmasters in the presence of their pupils; but in 1957 he could only curse and swear.

With a flash of insight Obi remembered his Conrad which he had read for his degree. 'By the simple exercise of our will we can exert a power for good practically unbounded.' That was Mr Kurtz before the heart of darkness got him. Afterwards he had written: 'Exterminate all the brutes.' It was not a close analogy, of course. Kurtz had succumbed to the darkness, Green to the incipient dawn. But their beginning and their end were alike. 'I must write a novel on the tragedy of the Greens of this century,' he thought, pleased with his analysis.

Later that morning a ward attendant from the General Hospital brought a little parcel to him. It was from Clara. One of the most wonderful things about her was her writing. It was so feminine. But Obi was not thinking about writing just now. His heart was pounding heavily.

'You may go,' he told the ward servant who was waiting to take a message. He started opening the parcel, but stopped again, his hands trembling. Marie was not there at the moment, but she might come in at any time. He thought of taking the parcel to the lavatory. Then a better idea occurred to him. He pulled out one of the drawers and began to untie the parcel inside it. For some reason he knew, despite the size of the parcel, that it contained his ring. And some money too! Yes, five-pound notes. But he didn't see any ring. He sighed with relief and then read the little note enclosed.

Darling,
    I'm sorry about yesterday. Go to the bank straight away and cancel that overdraft. See you in the evening.

Love, Clara.

His eyes misted. When he looked up, he saw that Marie was watching him. He hadn't even noticed when she returned to the office.

'What's the matter, Obi?'

'Nothing,' he said, improvising a smile. 'I was lost in thought.'

Obi wrapped up the fifty pounds carefully and put it in his pocket. How had Clara come by so much money? he wondered.

But of course she was reasonably well paid and she had not studied nursing on any progressive union's scholarship. It was true that she sent money to her parents, but that was all. Even so, fifty pounds was a lot of money.

All the way from Ikoyi to Yaba he was thinking how best he could make her take the money back. He knew it was going to be difficult, if not impossible. But it was quite out of the question for him to take fifty pounds from her. The question was how to make her take it back without hurting her. He might say that he would look silly taking an overdraft today and paying it off tomorrow, that the manager might think he had stolen the money. Or he might ask her to keep it until the end of the month, when he would really need it. She might ask: 'Why not keep it yourself?' He would answer: 'I might spend it before then.'

Whenever Obi had a difficult discussion with Clara he planned all the dialogue beforehand. But when the time came it always took a completely different course. And so it did on this occasion. Clara was ironing when he arrived.

'I'll finish in a second,' she said. 'What did the bank manager say?'

'He was very pleased.'

'In future don't be a silly little boy. You know the proverb about digging a new pit to fill up an old one?'

'Why did you trust so much money to that sly-looking man?'

'You mean Joe? He's a great friend of mine. He's a ward servant.'

'I didn't like his looks. What is the proverb about digging a new pit to fill up an old one?'

'I have always said you should go and study Ibo. It means borrowing from the bank to pay the insurance.'

'I see. You prefer digging two pits to fill up one. Borrowing from Clara to pay the bank to pay the insurance.'

Clara made no answer.

'I did not go to the bank. I didn't see how I could. How could I take so much money from you?'

'Please, Obi, stop behaving like a small boy. It is only a loan. If you don't want it you can return it. Actually I have been thinking all afternoon about the whole thing. It seems I have been interfering in your affairs. All I can say is, I'm very sorry. Have you got the money here?' She held out her hand.

Obi took her hand and pulled her towards him. 'Don't misunderstand me, darling.'

That evening they called on Christopher, Obi's economist friend. Clara had gradually come round to liking him. Perhaps he was a little too lively, which was not a serious fault. But she feared he might influence Obi for the worse in the matter of women. He seemed to enjoy going around with four or five at once. He even said there was nothing like love, at any rate in Nigeria. But he was very likeable really, quite unlike Joseph who was a bush-man.

As was to be expected, Christopher had a girl with him when Clara and Obi arrived. Clara had not met this one before, although apparently Obi had.

'Clara, meet Bisi,' said Christopher. The two girls shook hands and said: 'Pleased to meet you.' 'Clara is Obi's—'

'Shut up,' Clara completed for him. But it was like trying to complete a sentence for a stammerer. You might as well save your breath.

'Obi's *you know*,' completed Christopher.

'Have you been buying new records?' asked Clara going through a little pile of records on one of the chairs.

'Me? At this time of the month? They are Bisi's. What can I offer you?'

'Champagne.'

'Ah? Na Obi go buy you that-o. Me I never reach that grade yet. Na squash me get-o.' They laughed.

'Obi, what about some beer?'

'If you'll split a bottle with me.'

'Fine. What are you people doing this evening? Make we go dance somewhere?'

Obi tried to make excuses, but Clara cut him short. They would go, she said.

'Na film I wan' go,' said Bisi.

'Look here, Bisi, we are not interested in what you want to do. It's for Obi and me to decide. This na Africa, you know.'

Whether Christopher spoke good or 'broken' English depended

on what he was saying, where he was saying it, to whom and how he wanted to say it. Of course that was to some extent true of most educated people, especially on Saturday nights. But Christopher was rather outstanding in thus coming to terms with a double heritage.

Obi borrowed a tie from him. Not that it mattered at the Imperial, where they had chosen to go. But one didn't want to look like a boma-boy.

'Shall we all come into your car, Obi? It's a long time since I had a chauffeur.'

'Yes, let's all go together. Although it's going to be difficult after the dance to take Bisi home, then Clara, then you. But it doesn't matter.'

'No. I had better bring my car,' said Christopher. Then he whispered something into Obi's ear to the effect that he wasn't actually thinking of taking Bisi back that night, which was rather obvious.

'What are you whispering to him?' asked Clara.

'For men only,' said Christopher.

There was very little parking space at the Imperial and many cars were already there. After a little to-ing and fro-ing Obi finally squeezed in between two other cars, directed by half a dozen half-clad little urchins who were standing around.

'Na me go look your car for you,' chorused three of them at once.

'OK, make you look am well,' said Obi to none in particular. 'Lock up your side,' he said quietly to Clara.

'I go look am well, sir,' said one of the boys stepping across Obi's path so that he would remark him well as the right person to receive a threepence 'dash' at the end of the dance. In principle Obi never gave anything to these juvenile delinquents. But it would be bad policy to tell them so now and then leave your car at their mercy.

Christopher and Bisi were already waiting for them at the gate. The place was not as crowded as they thought it might be. In fact the dance floor was practically empty, but that was because the band was playing a waltz. Christopher found a table and two chairs and the two girls sat.

'You are not going to stand all night,' said Clara. 'Tell one of the stewards to get you chairs.'

'Never mind,' said Christopher. 'We'll soon get chairs.'

He had hardly completed this sentence when the band struck up a high-life. In under thirty seconds the dance floor was invaded. Those who were caught with a glass of beer in mid-air either put it down again or quickly swallowed its contents. Unfinished cigarettes were, according to status of the smoker, either thrown on the floor and stepped on or carefully put out, to be continued later.

Christopher moved past three or four tables in front and grabbed two chairs that had just been vacated.

'Mean old thing!' said Obi as he took one. Bisi was wriggling in her chair and singing with the soloist.

> Nylon dress is a lovely dress,
> Nylon dress is a country dress.
> If you want to make your baby happy
> Nylon is good for her.

'We are wasting a good dance,' said Obi.

'Why not go and dance with Bisi? Clara and I can watch the chairs.'

'Shall we?' Obi said, standing. Bisi was already up with a faraway look in her eyes.

> If you want to make your baby happy
> Go to the shop and get a doz'n of nylon.
> She will know nobody but you alone
> Nylon is good for her.

The next dance was again a high-life. If fact most of the dances were high-lifes. Occasionally a waltz or a blues was played so that the dancers could relax and drink their beer, or smoke. Christopher and Clara danced next while Obi and Bisi kept an eye on their chairs. But soon it was only Obi; someone had asked Bisi to dance.

There were as many ways of dancing the high-life as there were people on the floor. But, broadly speaking, three main patterns could be discerned. There were four or five Europeans whose dancing reminded one of the early motion pictures. They moved like triangles in an alien dance that was ordained for circles. There were others who made very little real movement. They held their women close, breast to breast and groin to groin, so that the dance could flow uninterrupted from one to the other and back again. The last group were the ecstatic ones. They danced apart, spinning, swaying or doing intricate syncopations with their feet and waist. They were the good servants who had found perfect freedom. The vocalist drew the microphone up to his lips to sing 'Gentleman Bobby'.

> I was playing moi guitar *jeje*,
> A lady gave me a kiss.
> Her husband didn't like it,
> He had to drag him wife away.
> Gentlemen, please hold your wife.
> Father and mum, please hold your girls.
> The calypso is so nice,
> If they follow, don't blame Bobby.

The applause and cries of 'Anchor! Anchor!' that followed this number seemed to suggest that no one blamed Gentleman Bobby. And why should they? He was playing his guitar *jeje* – quietly, soberly, unobtrusively, altogether in a law-abiding fashion, when a woman took it upon herself to plant a kiss on him. No matter how one looked at it, no blame could possibly attach to the innocent musician.

The next number was a quickstep. In other words, it was time to drink and smoke and generally cool down. Obi ordered soft drinks. He was relieved that no one wanted anything more expensive.

The group on their right – three men and two women – interested him very much. One of the women was quiet, but the other talked all the time at the top of her voice. Her nylon blouse was practically transparent, revealing a new brassière. She had not danced the last number. She had said to the man who asked her: 'No petrol, no fire,' which clearly meant no beer, no dance. The man had then come to Obi's table and asked Bisi. But that could not be anything like a permanent settlement. Now that no one was dancing, the woman was saying for all to hear: 'The table is dry'.

At two o'clock Obi and his party rose to go, despite Bisi's reluctance. Christopher reminded her that she had originally elected to go to the films which ended at eleven. She replied that that was no reason why they should leave the dance when it was just beginning to warm up. Anyway, they went. Christopher's car was parked a long way away, so they said good night outside the gate and parted.

Obi opened the driver's door with the key, got in, and leaned sideways to open for Clara. But her door was unlocked.

'I thought you locked this door?'

'Yes, I did,' she said.

Panic seized Obi. 'Good Lord!' he cried.

'What is it?' She was alarmed.

'Your money.'

'Where is it? Where did you leave it?'

He pointed at the now empty glove-box. They stared at it in silence. He opened his door quietly, went out, looked vacantly on the ground and then leaned against the car. The street was completely deserted. Clara opened her door and went out too. She went round to his side of the car, took his hand in hers and said: 'Let's go.' He was trembling. 'Let's go, Obi,' she said again, and opened his door for him.

CHAPTER TWELVE

After Christmas Obi got a letter from his father to say that his mother was again ill in hospital and to ask when he was coming home on local leave as he had promised. He hoped it would be very soon because there was an urgent matter he must discuss with him.

It was obvious that news had reached them about Clara. Obi had written some months ago to say there was a girl he was interested in and that he would tell them more about her when he got home on two weeks' local leave. He had not told them that she was an *osu*. One didn't write about such things. That would have to be broken very gently in conversation. But now it appeared that someone else had told them.

He folded the letter carefully and put it in his shirt pocket and tried not to think about it, especially about his mother's illness. He tried to concentrate on the file he was reading, but he read every line five times, and even then he did not understand what he read. He took up the telephone to ring Clara at the hospital, but when the operator said 'Number, please', he put it down again. Marie was typing steadily. She had plenty of work to do before the next week's board meeting. She was a very good typist; the keys did not strike separately when she typed.

Sometimes Mr Green sent for Marie to take dictation, sometimes he came out himself to give it. It all depended on how he was feeling at the time. He came out now.

'Please take down a quick answer to this. ''Dear sir, with

reference to your letter of – whatever the date was – I beg to inform you that Government pays a dependant's allowance to *bona fide* wives of Government scholars and not to their girlfriends . . ." Will you read that over to me?' Marie did, while he paced up and down. 'Change that second *Government* to *its*,' he said. Marie made the alteration and then looked up.

'That's all. "I am your obedient servant, Me".' Mr Green always ended his letters that way, saying the words *obedient servant* with a contemptuous tongue in the cheek. He turned to Obi and said: 'You know, Okonkwo, I have lived in your country for fifteen years and yet I cannot begin to understand the mentality of the so-called educated Nigerian. Like this young man at the University College, for instance, who expects the Government not only to pay his fees and fantastic allowances and find him an easy, comfortable job at the end of his course, but also to pay his intended. It's absolutely incredible. I think Government is making a terrible mistake in making it so easy for people like that to have so-called university education. Education for what? To get as much as they can for themselves and their family. Not the least bit interested in the millions of their countrymen who die every day from hunger and disease.'

Obi made some vague noises.

'I don't expect you to agree with me, of course,' said Mr Green, and disappeared.

Obi rang Christopher and they arranged to go and play tennis that afternoon with two newly arrived teachers at a Roman Catholic convent in Apapa. He had never really found out how Christopher discovered them. All he knew was that about two weeks ago he had been asked to come round to Christopher's flat and meet two Irish girls who were very interested in Nigeria. When Obi had got there at about six Christopher was already teaching them in turns how to dance the high-life. He was obviously relieved when Obi arrived; he immediately appropriated the better-looking of the two girls and left the other to Obi. She was all right when she wasn't trying to smile. Unfortunately she tried to smile rather frequently. But otherwise she wasn't too bad, and very soon it was too dark to see, anyway.

The girls were really interested in Nigeria. They already knew a few words of Yoruba, although they had only been in the country three weeks or so. They were rather more anti-English than Obi, which made him somewhat uneasy. But as the evening wore on he like them more and more, especially the one assigned to him.

They had fried plantains with vegetable and meat for dinner. The girls said they enjoyed it very much, although it was clear from the running of their eyes and noses that there was too much pepper in it.

They resumed their dancing soon afterwards, in semi-darkness and in silence except when they occasionally teased one another. 'Why are you so silent, you two?' or: 'Keep moving; don't stand on one spot.'

After a few opening skirmishes Obi won a couple of tentative kisses. But when he tried something more ambitious, Nora whispered sharply: 'No! Catholics are not allowed to kiss like that.'

'Why not?'

'It's a sin.'

'How odd.'

They continued dancing and occasionally kissing with their lips alone.

Before they finally took them home at eleven Obi and Christopher had promised to go and play tennis with them on some evenings. They had gone twice in quick succession; then other things had claimed their interest. Obi had thought of them again because he wanted something, like a game of tennis, to occupy his mind in the afternoon and perhaps tire him out so that he could sleep at night.

As soon as Christopher's car drew up, a white-clad Mother appeared suddenly at the door of the convent chapel. Obi drew his attention to the fact. She was too far away for them to see the expression on her face, but he felt it was hostile. The girls were having their afternoon prep, and so the convent was very quiet. They went up the stairs that led to Nora and Pat's flat above the classroom, the Mother following them with her eyes until they disappeared into the sitting-room.

The girls were having tea and buns. They looked pleased to see their visitors, but somehow not quite as pleased as usual. They seemed a little embarrassed.

'Have some tea,' they said together, as if they had been rehearsing the phrase, and before their guests had settled down properly in their chairs. They drank their tea almost in silence. Although Obi and Christopher were dressed for tennis and carried rackets, the girls did not say anything about playing. After tea they sat where they were, attempting valiantly to keep what conversation there was going.

'What about a game?' Christopher asked when the conversation finally expired. There was a pause. Then Nora explained quite simply without any false apologies that the Mother had spoken to them seriously about going around with African men. She had warned them that if the Bishop knew of it they might find themselves sent back to Ireland.

Pat said it was all silly and ridiculous. She actually used the word *ridiculosity*, which made Obi smile internally. 'But we don't want to be sent back to Ireland.'

Nora promised that they would occasionally go to visit the boys at Ikoyi. But it would be best if they did not come to the convent because the Mother and the Sisters were watching.

'What are you two, anyway? Daughters?' asked Christopher. But this was not very well received and the visit was soon afterwards brought to a close.

'You see,' said Christopher as soon as they got back into the car. 'And they call themselves missionaries!'

'What do you expect the poor girls to do?'

'I wasn't thinking of them. I mean the Mothers and Sisters and fathers and children.'

Obi found himself in the unusual role of defending Roman Catholics.

On their way home they stopped to say hello to Christopher's newest girlfriend Florence. He was so taken with her that he even mentioned marriage. But that was impossible because the girl was going to England next September to study nursing. She was out when they got to her place, and Christopher left a note for her.

'I have not seen Bisi for a long time,' he said. And they went to see her. But she, too, was out.

'What a day for visits!' said Obi. 'We had better go home.'

Christopher talked about Florence all the way. Should he try and persuade her not to go to England?

'I shouldn't if I were you,' Obi said. He told him of one old catechist in Umuofia many, many years ago when Obi was a little boy. This man's wife was a very good friend of Obi's mother and often visited them. One day he overheard her telling his mother how her education had been cut short at Standard One because the man was impatient to get married. She sounded very bitter about it, although it must have happened at least twenty years before. Obi remembered this particular visit very well because it took place on a Saturday. On the following morning the catechist had been unable to take the service because his wife had broken his head with the wooden pestle used for pounding yams. Obi's father, as a retired catechist, had been asked to conduct the service at very short notice.

'Talking about going to England reminds me of a girl who practically offered herself to me. Have I told you the story?'

'No.'

Obi told him the story of Miss Mark, starting with her brother's visit to his office.

'What happened to her in the end?'

'Oh, she is in England. She got the scholarship all right.'

'You are the biggest ass in Nigeria,' said Christopher, and they began a long argument on the nature of bribery.

'If a girl offers to sleep with you, that is not bribery,' said Christopher.

'Don't be silly,' replied Obi. 'You mean you honestly cannot see anything wrong in taking advantage of a young girl straight from school who wants to go to a university?'

'You are being sentimental. A girl who comes the way she did is not an innocent little girl. It's like the story of the girl who was given a form to fill in. She put down her name and her age. But when she came to sex she wrote: "Twice a week".' Obi could not help laughing.

'Don't imagine that girls are angels.'

'I was not imagining any such thing. But it is scandalous that a man of your education can see nothing wrong in going to bed with a girl before you let her appear before the board.'

'This girl was appearing before the board, anyway. That was all she expected you to do: to see that she did appear. And how do you know she did not go to bed with the board members?'

'She probably did.'

'Well then, what good have you done her?'

'Very little, I admit,' said Obi, trying to put his thoughts in order, 'but perhaps she will remember that there was one man at least who did not take advantage of his position.'

'But she probably thinks you are impotent.'

There was a short pause.

'Now tell me, Christopher. What is *your* definition of bribery?'

'Well, let's see . . . The use of improper influence.'

'Good. I suppose—'

'But the point is, there was no influence at all. The girl was going to be interviewed, anyway. She came voluntarily to have a good time. I cannot see that bribery is involved at all.'

'Of course, I know you're not really serious.'

'I am dead serious.'

'But I'm surprised you cannot see that the same argument can be used for taking money. If the applicant is getting the job, anyway, then there is no harm in accepting money from him.'

'Well—'

'Well, what?'

'You see, the difference is this.' He paused. 'Let's put it this way. No man wants to part with his money. If you accept money from a man you make him poorer. But if you go to bed with a girl who asks for it, I don't see that you have done any harm.'

They argued over dinner and late into the night. But no sooner had Christopher said good night than Obi's thoughts returned to the letter he had received from his father.

CHAPTER THIRTEEN

Obi was granted two weeks' local leave from 10 to 24 February.
He decided to set out for Umuofia very early on the 11th, spend
the night at Benin and conclude the journey the following day. Clara
exchanged duties with another nurse so as to be free to help
with his packing. She spent the whole day – and the night – in
Obi's flat.

When they went to sleep she said she had something to tell him
and began to cry. Obi had not learnt to cope with tears; he was
always alarmed. 'What's the matter, Clara?' But he only got warm
tears on the arm which lay between her head and the pillow. Clara
cried silently, but Obi could feel from the way her body shook that
she was crying violently. He kept asking: 'What's the matter?
What's the matter?' and getting more and more alarmed.

'Excuse me,' she said. She got up and went to the dressing table
where her handbag stood, brought out a handkerchief and blew
her nose. Then she went back to the bed with the handkerchief,
and sat on the edge.

'Come and tell me what is the trouble,' said Obi, gently pulling
her down. He kissed her and it tasted salty. 'What is it?'

Clara said she was very sorry to let him down at this eleventh
hour. But she was sure it would be in everybody's best interest
if they broke off their engagement. Obi was deeply stung, but he
said nothing for a long time. Afterwards Clara repeated that she
was very sorry. There was another long silence.

Then Obi said: 'I can understand . . . It's perfectly all right

. . . I don't blame you in the least.' He wanted to add: 'Why should you throw yourself away on someone who can't make both ends meet?' But he did not want to sound sentimental. He said instead: 'Thank you very much for everything.' He sat up in bed. Then he got up altogether and began to pace the room in his pyjamas. It was too dark for Clara to see him – which heightened the effect. But he soon realized that he would have regarded such action, if somebody else had performed it, as cheaply theatrical, and so he stopped and returned to bed, but not close to Clara. He was, however, soon persuaded to move closer and to talk.

Clara begged him not to misunderstand her. She said she was taking her present step because she did not want to ruin his life. 'I have thought about the whole matter very carefully. There are two reasons why we should not get married.'

'What are they?'

'Well, the first is that your family will be against it. I don't want to come between you and your family.'

'Bunk! Anyway, what is the second reason?' She could not remember what it was. It didn't matter, anyway. The first reason was quite enough.

'I'll tell you what the second reason is,' said Obi.

'What is it?'

'You don't want to marry someone who has to borrow money to pay for his insurance.' He knew it was a grossly unfair and false accusation, but he wanted her to be on the defensive. She nearly started crying again. He pulled her towards him and began to kiss her passionately. She soon responded with equal spirit. 'No, no, no! Don't be a naughty boy . . . You should apologize first for what you said.'

'I'm very sorry, darling.'

'O.K. I forgive you. No! Wait a minute.'

Obi set out just before six in the morning. If Clara had not been there he would not have been able to wake up as early as five-thirty. He felt a little light in the head and heavy in the eyes. He had a cold bath, washing his arms and legs first, then the head, the stomach and the back in that order. He hated cold baths, but he could not afford to switch on the electric heater, and there was no doubt, he thought as he dried himself, that one felt very brisk after a cold bath. As with weeping, it was only the beginning that was difficult.

Although he had two weeks, he proposed to spend only one at home for reasons of money. To home people, leave meant the return of the village boy who had made good in the town, and everyone expected to share in his good fortune. 'After all,' they argued, 'it was our prayers and our libations that did it for him.' They called leave *lifu*, meaning *to squander*.

Obi had exactly thirty-four pounds, nine and threepence when he set out. Twenty-five pounds was his local leave allowance, which was paid to all senior Civil Servants for no other reason than that they went on local leave. The rest was the remains of his January salary. With thirty-four pounds one might possibly last two weeks at home, although a man like Obi, with a car and a 'European post', would normally be expected to do better. But sixteen pounds ten shillings was to go into brother John's school fees for the second term which began in April. Obi knew that unless he paid the fees now that he had a lump sum in his pocket he might not be able to do so when the time came.

Obi seemed to look over the shoulders of everyone who came out to welcome him home.

'Where is Mother?' his eyes kept asking. He did not know whether she was still in hospital or at home, and he was afraid to ask.

'Your mother returned from hospital last week,' said his father as they entered the house.

'Where is she?'

'In her room,' said Eunice, his youngest sister.

Mother's room was the most distinctive in the whole house, except perhaps for Father's. The difficulty in deciding arose from the fact that one could not compare incomparable things. Mr Okonkwo believed utterly and completely in the things of the white man. And the symbol of the white man's power was the written word, or better still, the printed word. Once before he went to

England, Obi heard his father talk with deep feeling about the mystery of the written word to an illiterate kinsman:

'Our women made black patterns on their bodies with the juice of the *uli* tree. It was beautiful, but it soon faded. If it lasted two market weeks it lasted a long time. But sometimes our elders spoke about *uli* that never faded, although no one had ever seen it. We see it today in the writing of the white man. If you go to the native court and look at the books which clerks wrote twenty years ago or more, they are still as they wrote them. They do not say one thing today and another tomorrow, or one thing this year and another next year. Okoye in the book today cannot become Okonkwo tomorrow. In the Bible Pilate said: "What is written is written." It is *uli* that never fades.'

The kinsman had nodded his head in approval and snapped his fingers.

The result of Okonkwo's mystic regard for the written word was that his room was full of old books and papers – from Blackie's *Arithmetic* which he used in 1908 to Obi's Durrell, from obsolete cockroach-eaten translations of the Bible into the Onitsha dialect to yellowed Scripture Union Cards of 1920 and earlier. Okonkwo never destroyed a piece of paper. He had two boxes full of them. The rest were preserved on top of his enormous cupboard, on tables, on boxes and on one corner of the floor.

Mother's room, on the other hand, was full of mundane things. She had her box of clothes on a stool. On the other side of the room were pots of solid palm oil with which she made black soap. The palm oil was separated from the clothes by the whole length of the room, because as she always said, clothes and oil were not kinsmen, and just as it was the duty of clothes to try and avoid oil it was also the duty of the oil to do everything to avoid clothes.

Apart from these two, Mother's room also had such things as last year's coco-yams, kola nuts preserved with banana leaves in empty oil pots, palm-ash preserved in an old cylindrical vessel which, as the older children told Obi, had once contained biscuits. In the second stage of its life it had served as a water vessel until it sprang about five leaks which had to be carefully covered with paper before it got its present job.

As he looked at his mother on her bed, tears stood in Obi's eyes. She held out her hand to him and he took it – all bone and skin like a bat's wing.

'You did not see me when I was ill,' she said. 'Now I am as healthy as a young girl.' She laughed without mirth. 'You should have seen me three weeks ago. How is your work? Are Umuofia people in Lagos all well? How is Joseph? His mother came to see me yesterday and I told her we were expecting you . . .'

Obi answered: 'They are well, yes, yes and yes.' But his heart all the while was bursting with grief.

Later that evening a band of young women who had been making music at a funeral was passing by Okonkwo's house when they heard of Obi's return, and decided to go in and salute him.

Obi's father was up in arms. He wanted to drive them away, but Obi persuaded him that they could do no harm. It was ominous the way he gave in without a fight and went and shut himself up in his room. Obi's mother came out to the *pieze* and sat on a high chair by the window. She liked music even when it was heathen music. Obi stood in the main door, smiling at the singers who had formed themselves on the clean-swept ground outside. As if from a signal the colourful and noisy weaver birds on the tall palm tree flew away in a body, deserting temporarily their scores of brown nests which looked like giant bootees.

Obi knew some of the singers well. But there were others who had been married into the village after he had gone to England. The leader of the song was one of them. She had a strong piercing voice that cut the air with a sharp edge. She sang a long recitative before the others joined in. They called it 'The Song of the Heart'.

> A letter came to me the other day.
> I said to Mosisi: 'Read my letter for me.'
> Mosisi said to me: 'I do not know how to read.'
> I went to Innocenti and asked him to read my letter.
> Innocenti said to me: 'I do not know how to read.'
> I asked Simonu to read for me. Simonu said:
> 'This is what the letter has asked me to tell you:
> *He that has a brother must hold him to his heart,*

For a kinsman cannot be bought in the market,
Neither is a brother bought with money.'

Is everyone here?
(*Hele ee he ee he*)
Are you all here?
(*Hele ee he ee he*)
The letter said
That money cannot buy a kinsman,
(*Hele ee he ee he*)
That he who has brothers
Has more than riches can buy.
(*Hele ee he ee he*)

CHAPTER FOURTEEN

Obi's serious talks with his father began after the family had prayed and all but the two of them had gone to bed. The prayers had taken place in Mother's room because she was again feeling very weak, and whenever she was unable to join the others in the parlour her husband conducted prayers in her room.

The devil and his works featured prominently in that night's prayers. Obi had a shrewd suspicion that his affair with Clara was one of the works. But it was only a suspicion; there was nothing yet to show that his parents had actually heard of it.

Mr Okonkwo's easy capitulation in the afternoon on the matter of heathen singing was quite clearly a tactical move. He let the enemy gain ground in a minor skirmish while he prepared his forces for a great offensive.

He said to Obi after prayers: 'I know you must be tired after the great distance you have travelled. There is something important we must talk about, but it can wait until tomorrow, till you have had time to rest.'

'We can talk now,' said Obi. 'I am not too tired. We get used to driving long distances.'

'Come to my room then,' said his father, leading the way with the ancient hurricane lamp. There was a small table in the middle of the room. Obi remembered when it was bought. Carpenter Moses had built it and offered it to the church at harvest. It was put up for auction after the Harvest Service and sold. He could not now remember how much his father had paid for it, eleven and threepence perhaps.

'I don't think there is kerosene in this lamp,' said his father, shaking the lamp near his ear. It sounded quite empty. He brought half a bottle of kerosene from his cupboard and poured a little into the lamp. His hands were no longer very steady and he spilt some of the kerosene. Obi did not offer to do it for him because he knew his father would never dream of letting children pour kerosene into his lamp; they would not know how to do it properly.

'How were all our people in Lagos when you left them?' he asked. He sat on his wooden bed while Obi sat on a low stool facing him, drawing lines with his finger on the dusty top of the Harvest table.

'Lagos is a very big place. You can travel the distance from here to Abame and still be in Lagos.'

'So they said. But you have a meeting of Umuofia people?' It was half-question, half-statement.

'Yes. We have a meeting. But it is only once a month.' And he added: 'It is not always that one finds time to attend.' The fact was he had not attended since November.

'True,' said his father. 'But in a strange land one should always move near one's kinsmen.' Obi was silent, signing his name in the dust on the table. 'You wrote to me some time ago about a girl you had seen. How does that matter stand now?'

'That is one reason why I came. I want us to go and meet her people and start negotiations. I have no money now, but at least we can begin to talk.' Obi had decided that it would be fatal to sound apologetic or hesitant.

'Yes,' said his father. 'That is the best way.' He thought a little and again said yes, it was the best way. Then a new thought seemed to occur to him. 'Do we know who this girl is and where she comes from?' Obi hesitated just enough for his father to ask the question again in a different way. 'What is her name?'

'She is the daughter of Okeke, a native of Mbaino.'

'Which Okeke? I know about three. One is a retired teacher, but it would not be that one.'

'That is the one,' said Obi.

'Josiah Okeke?'

Obi said, yes, that was his name.

His father laughed. It was the kind of laughter one sometimes heard from a masked ancestral spirit. He would salute you by name and ask you if you knew who he was. You would reply with one hand humbly touching the ground that you did not, that he was beyond human knowledge. Then he might laugh as if through a throat of metal. And the meaning of that laughter was clear: 'I did not really think you would know, you miserable human worm!'

Obi's father's laughter vanished as it had come – without warning, leaving no footprints.

'You cannot marry the girl,' he said quite simply.

'Eh?'

'I said you cannot marry the girl.'

'But why, Father?'

'Why? I shall tell you why. But first tell me this. Did you find out or try to find out anything about this girl?'

'Yes.'

'What did you find out?'

'That they are *osu*.'

'You mean to tell me that you knew, and you ask me why?'

'I don't think it matters. We are Christians.' This had some effect, nothing startling though. Only a little pause and a slightly softer tone.

'We are Christians,' he said. 'But that is no reason to marry an *osu*.'

'The Bible says that in Christ there are no bond or free.'

'My son,' said Okonkwo, 'I understand what you say. But this thing is deeper than you think.'

'What is *this thing*? Our fathers in their darkness and ignorance called an innocent man *osu*, a thing given to idols, and thereafter he became an outcast, and his children, and his children's children for ever. But have we not seen the light of the Gospel?' Obi used the very words that his father might have used in talking to his heathen kinsmen.

There was a long silence. The lamp was now burning too brightly. Obi's father turned down the wick a little and then resumed his silence. After what seemed ages he said: 'I know Josiah Okeke very well.' He was looking steadily in front of him. His voice sounded tired. 'I know him and I know his wife. He is a good man and a great Christian. But he is *osu*. Naaman, captain of the host of Syria, was a great man and honourable, he was also a mighty man of valour, but he was a leper.' He paused so that this great and felicitous analogy might sink in with all its heavy and dreadful weight.

'*Osu* is like leprosy in the minds of our people. I beg of you, my son, not to bring the mark of shame and of leprosy into your family. If you do, your children and your children's children unto the third and fourth generations will curse your memory. It is not for myself I speak; my days are few. You will bring sorrow on your head and on the heads of your children. Who will marry your daughters? Whose daughters will your sons marry? Think of that, my son. We are Christians, but we cannot marry our own daughters.'

'But all that is going to change. In ten years things will be quite different to what they are now.'

The old man shook his head sadly but said no more. Obi repeated his points again. What made an *osu* different from other men and women? Nothing but the ignorance of their forefathers. Why should they, who had seen the light of the Gospel, remain in that ignorance?

He slept very little that night. His father had not appeared as difficult as he had expected. He had not been won over yet, but he had clearly weakened. Obi felt strangely happy and excited. He had not been through anything quite like this before. He was used to speaking to his mother like an equal, even from his childhood, but his father had always been very different. He was not exactly remote from his family, but there was something about him that made one think of the patriarchs, those giants hewn from granite. Obi's strange happiness sprang not only from the little ground he had won in the argument, but from the direct human contact he had made with his father for the first time in his twenty-six years.

As soon as he woke up in the morning he went to see his mother. It was six o'clock by his watch, but still very dark. He groped his way to her room. She was awake, for she asked who it was as soon as he entered the room. He went and sat on her bed and felt her temperature with his palm. She had not slept much on account of the pain in her stomach. She said she had now lost faith in the European medicine and would like to try a native doctor.

At that moment Obi's father rang his little bell to summon the family to morning prayers. He was surprised when he came in with the lamp and saw Obi already there. Eunice came in wrapped up in her loincloth. She was the last of the children and the only one at home. That was what the world had come to. Children left their old parents at home and scattered in all directions in search of money. It was hard on an old woman with eight children. It was like having a river and yet washing one's hands in spittle.

Behind Eunice came Joy and Mercy, distant relations who had been sent by their parents to be trained in housekeeping by Mrs Okonkwo.

Afterwards, when they were alone again, she listened silently and patiently to the end. Then she raised herself up and said: 'I dreamt a bad dream, a very bad dream one night. I was lying on a bed spread with white cloth and I felt something creepy against my skin. I looked down on the bed and found that a swarm of white termites had eaten it up, and the mat and the white cloth. Yes, termites had eaten up the bed right under me.'

A strange feeling like cold dew descended on Obi's head.

'I did not tell anybody about that dream in the morning. I carried it in my heart wondering what it was. I took down my Bible and read the portion for the day. It gave me some strength, but my heart was still not at rest. In the afternoon your father came in with a letter from Joseph to tell us that you were going to marry an *osu*. I saw the meaning of my death in the dream. Then I told your father about it.' She stopped and took a deep breath. 'I have nothing to tell you in this matter except one thing. If you want to marry this girl, you must wait until I am no more. If God hears my prayers, you will not wait long.' She stopped again. Obi was terrified by the change that had come over her. She looked strange as if she had suddenly gone off her head.

'Mother!' he called, as if she was going away. She held up her hand for silence.

'But if you do the thing while I am alive, you will have my blood on your head, because I shall kill myself.' She sank down completely exhausted.

Obi kept to his room throughout that day. Occasionally he fell asleep for a few minutes. Then he would be woken up by the voices of neighbours and acquaintances who came to see him. But he refused to see anybody. He told Eunice to say that he was unwell from long travelling. He knew that it was a particularly bad excuse. If he was unwell, then surely that was all the more reason why he should be seen. Anyway, he refused to be seen, and the neighbours and acquaintances felt wounded. Some of them spoke their mind there and then, others managed to sound as if nothing had happened. One old woman even prescribed a cure for the illness, even though she had not seen the patient. Long journeys, she said, were very troublesome. The thing to do was to take strong purgative medicine to wash out all the odds and ends in the belly.

Obi did not appear for evening prayers. He heard his father's voice as if from a great distance, going on for a very long time. Whenever it appeared to have finished, his voice rose again. At last Obi heard several voices saying the Lord's Prayer. But everything sounded far away, as voices and the cries of insects sound to a man in a fever.

His father came into his room with his hurricane lamp and asked how he felt. Then he sat down on the only chair in the room, took up his lamp again and shook it for kerosene. It sounded satisfactory and he turned the wick down, until the flame was practically swallowed up in the lamp's belly. Obi lay perfectly still on his back, looking up at the bamboo ceiling, the way he had been told as a child not to sleep. For it was said if he slept on his back and a spider crossed the ceiling above him he would have bad dreams.

He was amazed at the irrelevant thoughts that passed through his mind at this the greatest crisis in his life. He waited for his father to speak that he might put up another fight to justify himself. His mind was troubled not only by what had happened but also by the discovery that there was nothing in him with which to challenge it honestly. All day he had striven to rouse his anger and his conviction, but he was honest enough with himself to realize that the response he got, no matter how violent it sometimes appeared, was not genuine. It came from the periphery, and not the centre, like the jerk in the leg of a dead frog when a current is applied to it. But he could not accept the present state of his mind as final, so he searched desperately for something that would trigger off the inevitable reaction. Perhaps another argument with his father, more violent than the first; for it was true what the Ibos say, that when a coward sees a man he can beat he becomes hungry for a fight. He had discovered he could beat his father.

But Obi's father sat in silence, declining to fight. Obi turned on his side and drew a deep breath. But still his father said nothing.

'I shall return to Lagos the day after tomorrow,' Obi said finally.

'Did you not say you had a week to spend with us?'

'Yes, but I think it will be better if I return earlier.'

After this there was another long silence. Then his father spoke, but not about the thing that was on their minds. He began slowly and quietly, so quietly that his words were barely audible. It seemed as if he was not really speaking to Obi. His face was turned sideways so that Obi saw it in vague profile.

'I was no more than a boy when I left my father's house and went with the missionaries. He placed a curse on me. I was not there but my brothers told me it was true. When a man curses his own child it is a terrible thing. And I was his first son.'

Obi had never heard about the curse. In broad daylight and in happier circumstances he would not have attached any importance to it. But that night he felt strangely moved with pity for his father.

'When they brought me word that he had hanged himself I told them that those who live by the sword must perish by the sword. Mr Braddeley, the white man who was our teacher, said it was not the right thing to say and told me to go home for the burial. I refused to go. Mr Braddeley thought I spoke about the white man's messenger whom my father killed. He did not know I spoke about Ikemefuna with whom I grew up in my mother's hut until the day came when my father killed him with his own hands.' He paused to collect his thoughts, turned in his chair and faced the bed on which Obi lay. 'I tell you all this so that you may know what it was in those days to become a Christian. I left my father's house, and he placed a curse on me. I went through fire to become a Christian. Because I suffered I understand Christianity – more than you will ever do.' He stopped rather abruptly. Obi thought it was a pause, but he had finished.

Obi knew the sad story of Ikemefuna who was given to Umuofia by her neighbours in appeasement. Obi's father and Ikemefuna became inseparable. But one day the Oracle of the Hills and the Caves decreed that the boy should be killed. Obi's grandfather loved the boy. But when the moment came it was his matchet that cut him down. Even in those days some elders said it was a great wrong that a man should raise his hands against a child that called him father.

CHAPTER FIFTEEN

Obi did the 500-odd miles between Umuofia and Lagos in a kind
of daze. He had not even stopped for lunch at Akure which was
the normal half-way house for travellers from Eastern Nigeria to
Lagos, but had driven numbly, mile after mile, from morning till
evening. Only once did the journey come alive, just before Ibadan.
He had taken a sharp corner at speed and come face to face with
two mammy-wagons, one attempting to overtake the other. Less
than half a second lay between Obi and a total smash. In that half-
second he swerved his car into the bush on the left.

One of the lorries stopped, but the other went on its way. The
driver and passengers of the good lorry rushed to see what had
happened to him. He himself did not know yet whether anything
had happened to him. They helped him push his car out, much
to the joy of the women passengers who were already crying and
holding their breasts. It was only after Obi had been pushed back
on to the road that he began to tremble.

'You very lucky-o,' said the driver and his passengers, some in
English and others in Yoruba. 'Dese reckless drivers,' he said
shaking his head sadly. '*Olorun!*' He left the matter in the hands
of God. 'But you lucky-o as no big tree de for dis side of road.
When you reach home make you tank your God.'

Obi examined his car and found no damage except one or two
little dents.

'Na Lagos you de go?' asked the driver. Obi nodded, still unable
to talk.

287

'Make you take am *jeje*. Too much devil de for dis road. If you see one accident way we see for Abeokuta side – *Olorun!*' The women talked excitedly, with their arms folded across their breasts, gazing at Obi as if he was a miracle. One of them repeated in broken English that Obi must thank God. A man agreed with her. 'Na only by God of power na him make you still de talk.' Actually Obi wasn't talking, but the point was cogent nonetheless.

'Dese drivers! Na waya for dem.'

'No be all drivers de reckless,' said the good driver. 'Dat one na foolish somebody. I give am signal make him no overtake but he just come *fiam.*' The last word, combined with a certain movement of the arm meant *excessive speed*.

The rest of the journey had passed without incident. It was getting dark when Obi arrived in Lagos. The big signboard which welcomes motorists to the federal territory of Lagos woke in him a feeling of panic. During the last night he spent at home he had worked out how he was going to tell Clara. He would not go to his flat first and then return to tell her. It would be better to stop on his way and take her with him. But when he got to Yaba where she lived he decided that it was better to get home first and then return. So he passed.

He had a wash and changed his clothes. Then he sat down on the sofa and for the first time felt really tired. Another thought occurred to him. Christopher might be able to give him useful advice. He got into the car and drove off, not knowing definitely whether he was going to Chrisopher's or Clara's. But in the end it was to Clara that he went.

On his way he ran into a long procession of men, women and children in white flowing gowns gathered at the waist with red and yellow sashes. The women, who were in the majority, wore white head-ties that descended to their back. They sang and clapped their hands and danced. One of the men kept beat with a hand-bell. They held up all traffic, for which Obi was inwardly grateful. But impatient taxi-drivers serenaded them with long and deafening blasts of their horns as they slowly parted for them to pass. In front two white-clad boys carried a banner which proclaimed the Eternal Sacred Order of Cherubim and Seraphim.

Obi had done his best to make the whole thing sound unimportant. Just a temporary set-back and no more. Everything would work out nicely in the end. His mother's mind had been affected by her long illness but she would soon get over it. As for his father, he was as good as won over. 'All we need do is lie quiet for a little while,' he said.

Clara had listened in silence, rubbing her engagement ring with her right fingers. When he stopped talking, she looked up at him and asked if he had finished. He did not answer.

'Have you finished?' she asked again.

'Finished what?'

'Your story.'

Obi drew a deep breath by way of answer.

'Don't you think . . . Anyway, it doesn't matter. There is only one thing I regret. I should have known better anyway. It doesn't really matter.'

'What are you talking about, Clara? . . . Oh, don't be silly,' he said as she pulled off her ring and held it out to him.

'If you don't take it, I shall throw it out of the window.'

'Please do.'

She didn't throw it away, but went outside to his car and dropped it in the glove-box. She came back and, holding out her hand in mock facetiousness, said: 'Thank you very much for everything.'

'Come and sit down, Clara. Let's not be childish. And please don't make things more difficult for me.'

'You are making things difficult for yourself. How many times did I tell you that we were deceiving ourselves? But I was always told I was being childish. Anyway, it doesn't matter. There is no need for long talk.'

Obi sat down again. Clara went to lean on the window and look outside. Once Obi began to say something, but gave it up after the first three words or so. After another ten minutes of silence Clara asked, hadn't he better be going?

'Yes,' he said, and got up.

'Good night.' She did not turn from her position. She had her back to him.

'Good night,' he said.

'There was something I wanted to tell you, but it doesn't matter. I ought to have been able to take care of myself.'

Obi's heart flew into his mouth. 'What is it?' he asked in great alarm.

'Oh, nothing. Forget about it. I'll find a way out.'

Obi had been shocked by the crudity of Christopher's reaction to his story. He said the most uncharitable things, and he was always interrupting. As soon as Obi mentioned his parents' opposition he took over from him.

'You know, Obi,' he said, 'I had wanted to discuss that matter with you. But I have learnt not to interfere in a matter between a man and a woman, especially with chaps like you who have wonderful ideas about love. A friend came to me last year and asked my advice about a girl he wanted to marry. I knew this girl very very well. She is, you know, very liberal. So I told my friend: "You shouldn't marry this girl." Do you know what this bloody fool did? He went and told the girl what I said. That was why I didn't tell you anything about Clara. You may say that I am not broad-minded, but I don't think we have reached the stage where we can ignore all our customs. You may talk about education and so on, but I am not going to marry an *osu*.'

'We're not talking about your marriage now.'

'I'm sorry. What did your mother actually say?'

'She really frightened me. She said I should wait until she is dead, or else she would kill herself.'

Christopher laughed. 'There was one woman in my place who returned from market one day and found that her two children had fallen into a well and drowned. She wept throughout that day and the next saying that she wanted to go and fall into the well, too. But, of course, her neighbours held her back every time she got up. But after three days her husband got rather fed up and ordered that she should be left alone to do what she liked. She rushed to the well, but when she got there she first had a peep and then she put her right foot in, brought it out and put her left . . .'

'How interesting!' Obi said interrupting him. 'But I can assure

you my mother meant every word she said. Anyway, what I came
to ask you about is quite different. I think she is pregnant.'

'Who?'

'Don't be silly. Clara.'

'Well, well, that is going to be troublesome.'

'Do you know of any . . .'

'Doctor? No. But I know that James went to see one or two of
them when he got into trouble recently. I tell you what. I'll find
out from him tomorrow morning and give you a ring.'

'Not my telephone!'

'Why not? I shall only read out addresses. It's going to cost you
some money. Of course you will say I am callous, but my attitude
to these things is quite different. When I was in the East a girl
came to me and said: "I can't find my period." I said to her: "Go
and look for it." It sounds callous, but . . . I don't know. The
way I look at it is this: how do I know that I am responsible? I
make sure that I take every possible precaution. That's all. I know
that your case is quite different. Clara had no time for any other
person. But even so . . .'

There must have been something about Obi which made the old
doctor uneasy. He had seemed willing enough at the beginning,
and actually asked one or two sympathetic questions. Then he went
into an inner room and when he came out he was a changed man.

'I am sorry, my dear young man,' he said, 'but I cannot help
you. What you are asking me to do is a criminal offence for which
I could go to jail and lose my licence. But apart from that I have
my reputation to safeguard – twenty years' practice without a
single blot. How old are you?'

'Twenty-six.'

'Twenty-six. So you were six years old when I began to practise
medicine. And in all those years I have not had anything to do with
these shady things. Why don't you marry the girl anyway? She
is very good looking.'

'I don't want to marry him,' said Clara sullenly, the first thing
she had said since they came in.

'What's wrong with him? He seems a nice young man to me.'

'I say I won't marry him. Isn't that enough?' she almost screamed, and rushed out of the room. Obi went quietly after her and they drove off. No single word passed between them all the way to the house of the next doctor who had been recommended to Obi.

He was young and very business-like. He said he had no taste for the job they were asking him to do. 'It is not medicine,' he said. 'I did not spend seven years in England to study *that*. However, I shall do it for you if you are prepared to pay my fee. Thirty pounds. To be paid before I do anything. No cheques. Raw cash. What say you?'

Obi asked if he wouldn't take anything less than thirty pounds.

'I'm sorry, but my price is fixed. It is a very minor operation, but it is a crime. We are all criminals, you know. I'm taking a big risk. Go and think about it and come back tomorrow at two, with the money.' He rubbed his hands together in a way that struck Obi as particularly sinister. 'If you are coming,' he said to Clara, 'you must not eat.'

As they were leaving he asked Obi: 'Why don't you marry her?' He received no answer.

CHAPTER SIXTEEN

The most immediate problem was how to raise thirty pounds before two o'clock the next day. There was also Clara's fifty pounds which he must return. But that could wait. The simplest thing would be to go to a money-lender, borrow thirty pounds and sign that he had received sixty. But he would commit suicide before he went to a money-lender.

He had already checked on what was left of the money he took home. He went to his box and checked again. It was twelve pounds in notes plus some loose coins he carried in his pocket. He had given only five pounds for his mother and nothing to his father because he had decided that, as things were, he must find Clara's fifty pounds quite soon.

It would be pointless asking Christopher. His salary never went beyond the tenth of the month. The only thing that saved him from starvation was the brilliant system he had evolved with his cook. At the beginning of every month Christopher gave him all the 'chop money' for the month. 'Until the next pay day,' he would say, 'my life is in your hands.'

Obi once asked him what would happen if the man absconded with the money half-way through the month. Christopher said he knew he wouldn't. It was most unusual for a 'master' to have so much confidence in his 'boy,' even when, as in this case, the boy was almost twice the master's age and treated him as a son.

In his extremity Obi even thought of the President of the Umuofia Progressive Union. But rather than do that he would go to a money-lender. Apart from the fact that the President would want to know why a young man in the senior service should want to borrow money from a man of family on less than half his salary, it would appear as if Obi had accepted the principle that his town-people could tell him whom not to marry. 'I haven't descended so low yet,' he said aloud.

At last a very good idea struck him. Perhaps it wasn't all that good when you came to look at it closely, but it was much better than all the other ideas. He would ask the Hon. Sam Okoli. He would tell him quite frankly what he needed the money for and that he would repay in three months' time. Or perhaps he should not tell him what he needed the money for. It was not fair on Clara to tell even one person more than was absolutely necessary. He had only told Christopher because he thought he might know what doctors to consult. As soon as he had got back to his flat that evening it had occurred to him that he had not stressed the need for secrecy and he had rushed to the telephone. There was only one telephone for the block of six flats but it was just outside the door.

'Hello. Oh yes, Chris. I forgot to mention it. When you are getting the addresses from that chap don't tell him who it's for . . . Not for my sake, but . . . you know.'

Christopher told him, fortunately in Ibo, that pregnancy could not be covered with the hand.

Obi told him not to be a bloody fool. 'Yes, tomorrow morning. Not at the office, no, here. I'm not starting work till next week, Wednesday. Oh yes. Many thanks. Bye-bye.'

The doctor counted his wad of notes carefully, folded it and put it in his pocket. 'Come back at five o'clock,' he told Obi, dismissing him. But when Obi got to his car he could not drive away. All kinds of frightening thoughts kept crowding into his mind. He did not believe in premonition and such stuff, but somehow he felt that he wasn't going to see Clara again.

As he sat in the driver's seat, paralysed by his thoughts, the doctor and Clara came out and entered a car that was parked by the side of the road. The doctor must have said something about him because Clara looked in his direction once and immediately took her eyes away. Obi wanted to rush out of his car and shout: 'Stop. Let's go and get married now,' but he couldn't and didn't. The doctor's car drove away.

It could not have been more than a minute, or at most two. Obi's mind was made up. He reversed his car and chased after the doctor's to stop them. But they were no longer in sight. He tried first one turning and then another. He dashed across a major road and was missed by a huge red bus by a hair's breadth. He backed, went forward, turned right and left like a panicky fly trapped behind the windscreen. Cyclists and pedestrians cursed him. At one stage the whole of Lagos rose in one loud protest: 'ONE WAY! ONE WAY!!' He stopped, backed into a side street, and then went in the opposite direction.

After about half an hour of this mad and aimless exercise Obi pulled up by the side of the road. He felt in his right pocket, then in his left for a handkerchief. Finding none, he rubbed his eyes with the back of his hand. Then he placed his arms on the steering wheel and put his head on them. His face and arms gradually became wet where they came in contact, and dripped with sweat. It was the worst time of the day and the worst time of the year – the last couple of months before the rains broke. The air was dead, heavy and hot. It lay on the earth like a mantle of lead. Inside Obi's car it was worse. He had not wound down the glass at the back and the heat was trapped inside. He did not notice it, but even if he had noticed it he would not have done anything about it.

At five o'clock he returned to the clinic. The doctor's attendant said he was out. Obi asked if she knew where he had gone. The girl answered a curt 'no'.

'There is something very important that I must tell him. Can't you try and find him for me . . . or . . .'

'I don't know where he has gone to,' she said. Her accent was about as gentle as the splitting of hard wood with an axe.

Obi waited for an hour and a half before the doctor returned – without Clara. Sweat rained down his body.

'Oh, are you here?' the doctor asked. 'Come back tomorrow morning.'

'Where is she?'

'Don't worry, she will be all right. But I want to have her under observation tonight in case of complications.'

'Can't I see her?'

'No. Tomorrow morning. That is, if she wants to see you. Women are very funny creatures, you know.'

He told his house-boy Sebastian not to cook supper.

'Master no well?'

'No.'

'Sorry, sir.'

'Thank you. Go away now. I'll be all right in the morning.'

He wanted a book to look at, so he went to his shelf. The pessimism of A. E. Housman once again proved irresistible. He took it down and went to his bedroom. The book opened at the place where he had put the paper on which he had written the poem 'Nigeria' in London about two years ago.

> God bless our noble fatherland
> Great land of sunshine bright,
> Where brave men chose the way of peace,
> To win their freedom fight.
> May we preserve our purity,
> Our zest for life and jollity.
>
> God bless our noble countrymen
> And women everywhere.
> Teach them to work in unity
> To build our nation dear;
> Forgetting region, tribe or speech,
> But caring always each for each.
>
> London, July 1955.

He quietly and calmly crumpled the paper in his left palm until it was a tiny ball, threw it on the floor and began to turn the pages of the book forwards and backwards. In the end he did not read any poem. He put the book down on the little table by his bed.

The doctor was seeing new patients in the morning. They sat on two long forms in the corridor and went in one by one behind the green door blinds of the consulting room. Obi told the attendant that he was not a patient and that he had an urgent appointment with the doctor. It was not the same attendant as he had met on the previous day.

'What kin' appointment you get with doctor when you no be patient?' she asked. Some of the waiting patients laughed and applauded her wit.

'Man way no sick de come see doctor?' she repeated for the benefit of those on whom the subtlety of the original statement might have been lost.

Obi paced up and down the corridor until the doctor's bell rang again. The attendant tried to block his way. He pushed her aside and went in. She rushed in after him to protest that he had jumped the queue. But the doctor paid no attention to her.

'Oh yes,' he said to Obi after a second or two's hesitation as if trying to remember where he had seen that face before. 'She is at a private hospital. You remember I told you some of them develop complications. But there is nothing to worry about. A friend of mine is looking after her in his hospital.' He gave him the name of the hospital.

When Obi came out, one of the patients was waiting to have a word with him.

'You tink because Government give you car you fit do what you like? You see all of we de wait here and you just go in. You tink na play we come play?'

Obi passed on without saying a word.

'Foolish man. He tink say because him get car so derefore he can do as he like. Beast of no nation!'

In the hospital a nurse told Obi that Clara was very ill and that visitors were not allowed to see her.

CHAPTER SEVENTEEN

'Did you have a good leave?' Mr Green asked when he saw Obi. It was so unexpected that for a little while Obi was too confused to answer. But he managed in the end to say that he did, thank you very much.

'It often amazes me how you people can have the effrontery to ask for local leave. The idea of local leave was to give Europeans a break to go to cool places like Jos or Buea. But today it is completely obsolete. But for an African like you, who has too many privileges as it is, to ask for two weeks to go on a swan, it makes me want to cry.'

Obi said he wouldn't be worried if local leave was abolished. But that was for Government to decide.

'It's people like you who ought to make the Government decide. That is what I have always said. There is no single Nigerian who is prepared to forgo a little privilege in the interests of his country. From your ministers down to your most junior clerk. And you tell me you want to govern yourselves.'

The talk was cut short by a telephone call for Mr Green. He returned to his room to take it.

'There's a lot of truth in what he says,' Marie ventured after a suitable interval.

'I'm sure there is.'

'I don't mean about you, or anything of the sort. But quite frankly, there are too many holidays here. Mark you, I don't really mind. But in England I never got more than two weeks' leave in the year. But here, what is it? Four months.' At this point Mr Green returned.

'It is not the fault of Nigerians,' said Obi. 'You devised these soft conditions for yourselves when every European was automatically in the senior service and every African automatically in the junior service. Now that a few of us have been admitted into the senior service, you turn round and blame us.' Mr Green passed on to Mr Omo's office next door.

'I suppose so,' said Marie, 'but surely it's time someone stopped all the Moslem holidays.'

'Nigeria is a Moslem country, you know.'

'No it isn't. You mean the North.'

They argued for a little while longer and Marie suddenly changed the subject.

'You look run down, Obi.'

'I have not been very well.'

'Oh, I'm sorry. What is it? Fever?'

'Yes, a slight touch of malaria.'

'Why don't you take paludrine?'

'I sometimes forget.'

'Tut-tut,' she said. 'You ought to be ashamed of yourself. And what does your fiancée say? She is a nurse, isn't she?'

Obi nodded.

'If I were you, I should go and see a doctor. You do look ill, believe me.'

Later that morning Obi went to consult Mr Omo about a salary advance. Mr Omo was the authority on General Orders and Financial Instructions, and should be able to tell him whether such a thing was possible and under what conditions. He had taken a firm decision about Clara's fifty pounds. He must find it in the next two months and pay it into her bank. Perhaps they would get over the present crisis, perhaps not. But whatever happened he must return the money.

He had at last succeeded in seeing her at the hospital. But as soon as she saw him she had turned on her bed and faced the wall. There were other patients in the ward and most of them saw what had happened. Obi had never felt so embarrassed in his life. He left at once.

Mr Omo said it was possible to give an officer a salary advance under special conditions. The way he said it, it appeared the special conditions were not unconnected with his personal pleasure.

'And by the way,' he said dropping the matter of advance, 'you have to submit statement of expenditure in respect of the twenty-five pounds and refund the balance.'

Obi had not realized that the allowance was not a free gift to be spent as one liked. He now learnt to his horror that, subject to a maximum of twenty-five pounds, he was allowed to claim so much for every mile of the return journey. Mr Omo called it claiming 'on an actuality basis'.

Obi returned to his desk to do a little arithmetic, using the mileage chart. He discovered that the return journey from Lagos to Umuofia amounted to only fifteen pounds. 'That's just too bad,' he thought. Mr Omo should have warned him when he gave him twenty-five. Anyway, it was too late to do anything about it now. He couldn't possibly refund ten pounds. He would have to say that he spent his leave in the Cameroons. Pity, that.

The chief result of the crisis in Obi's life was that it made him examine critically for the first time the mainspring of his actions. And in doing so he uncovered a good deal that he could only regard as sheer humbug. Take this matter of twenty pounds every month to his town union, which in the final analysis was the root cause of all his troubles. Why had he not swallowed his pride and accepted the four months' exemption which he had been allowed, albeit with a bad grace? Could a person in his position afford that kind of pride? Was it not a common saying among his people that a man should not, out of pride and etiquette, swallow his phlegm?

Having seen the situation in its true light, Obi decided to stop payment forthwith until such a time as he could do it conveniently. The question was: Should he go and tell his town union? He decided against that, too. He would not give them another opportunity to pry into his affairs. He would just stop paying and, if they asked him why, he would say he had some family commitments which he must clear first. Everyone understood family commitments and would sympathize. If they didn't it was just too bad. They would not take a kinsman to court, not for that kind of reason anyway.

As he turned these things over in his mind the door opened and a messenger entered. Involuntarily Obi jumped to his feet to accept an envelope. He looked it over and turned it round and saw that it had not been opened. He put it in his shirt pocket and sank to his seat. The messenger had vanished as soon as he delivered the letter.

His decision to write to Clara had been taken last night. Thinking again about the hospital incident, Obi had come to the conclusion that his anger was not justified. Or at any rate, Clara had far more to be angry about than he had. She was no doubt thinking that it was no thanks to him that she was still alive. She could not, of course, know how many anxious days and sleepless nights that he had passed through. But even if she did, would she be impressed? What comfort did a dead man derive from the knowledge that his murderer was in sackcloth and ashes?

Obi who nowadays spent all his time in bed had got himself out and gone to his writing-desk. Writing letters did not come easily to him. He worked out every sentence in his mind first before he set it down on paper. Sometimes he spent as long as ten minutes on the opening sentence. He wanted to say: 'Forgive me for what has happened. It was all my fault . . .' He ruled against it; that kind of self reproach was sheer humbug. In the end he wrote:

'I can understand your not wanting ever to set eyes on me again. I have wronged you terribly. But I cannot believe that it is all over. If you give me another chance, I shall never fail you again.'

He read it over and over again. Then he re-wrote the whole letter, changing *I cannot believe* to *I cannot bring myself to believe*.

He left home very early in the morning so that he could drop the letter at the hospital before reporting for duty at eight o'clock. He dared not go into the ward; he stood outside waiting for a nurse to show up. Large numbers of patients were already queueing up in front of the consulting room. The air smelt of carbolic and strange drugs. Perhaps the hospital wasn't really dirty, although it looked so. A little to the right a pregnant woman was vomiting into an open drain. Obi did not want to see the vomit, but his eyes kept wandering there on their own account.

Two ward servants passed by Obi and he heard one say to the other:

'Wetin de sick dat nursing sister?'

'Me I no know-o,' the other answered as if he had been charged with complicity. 'Dis kind well today sick tomorrow pass me.'

'Dey say dey don givam belle.'

CHAPTER EIGHTEEN

Altogether Clara was in hospital for five weeks. As soon as she was discharged she was granted seventy days' leave and she left Lagos. Obi heard of it from Christopher, who heard of it from his girlfriend who was a nurse in the General Hospital.

After one more failure Obi had been advised not to try to see Clara again in her present frame of mind. 'She will come round,' said Christopher. 'Give her time.' Then he quoted in Ibo the words of encouragement which the bedbug was said to have spoken to her children when hot water was poured on them all. She told them not to lose heart because whatever was hot must in the end turn cold.

Obi's plan to pay fifty pounds into her account had come to nothing for various reasons. One day he had received a registered parcel slip. He wondered who could be sending him a registered parcel. It turned out to have been the Commissioner of Income Tax.

Marie advised him to arrange in future to pay by monthly instalments through his bank. 'That way you don't notice it,' she said.

That was, of course, useful advice for the next tax year. As for the present, he had to find thirty-two pounds pretty soon.

On top of it all came his mother's death. He sent all he could find for her funeral, but it was already being said to his eternal shame that a woman who had borne so many children, one of whom was in a European post, deserved a better funeral than she got. One Umuofia man who had been on leave at home when she died

had brought the news to Lagos to the meeting of the Umuofia
Progressive Union.

'It was a thing of shame,' he said. Someone else wanted to
know, by the way, why that beast (meaning Obi) had not obtained
permission to go home. 'That is what Lagos can do to a young
man. He runs after sweet things, dances breast to breast with
women and forgets his home and his people. Do you know what
medicine that *osu* woman may have put into his soup to turn his
eyes and ears away from his people?'

'Do you ever see him in our meetings these days?' asked another.
'He has found better company.'

At this stage one of the older members of the meeting raised his
voice. He was a very pompous man.

'Everything you have said is true. But there is one thing I want
you to learn. Whatever happens in this world has a meaning. As
our people say: "Wherever something stands, another thing stands
beside it." You see this thing called blood. There is nothing like
it. That is why when you plant a yam it produces another yam,
and if you plant an orange it bears oranges. I have seen many things
in my life, but I have never yet seen a banana tree yield a coco-
yam. Why do I say this? You young men here, I want you to listen
because it is from listening to old men that you learn wisdom. I
know that when I return to Umuofia I cannot claim to be an old
man. But here in this Lagos I am an old man to the rest of you.'
He paused for effect. 'This boy that we are all talking about, what
has he done? He was told that his mother died and he did not care.
It is a strange and surprising thing, but I can tell you that I have
seen it before. His father did it.'

There was some excitement at this. 'Very true,' said another
old man.

'I say that his father did the same thing,' said the first man very
quickly, lest the story be taken from his mouth. 'I am not guessing
and I am not asking you not to mention it outside. When this boy's
father – you all know him, Isaac Okonkwo – when Isaac
Okonkwo heard of the death of his father he said that those who
kill with the matchet must die by the matchet.'

'Very true,' said the other man again. 'It was the talk of Umuofia in those days and for many years. I was a very little boy at the time, but I heard of it.'

'You see that,' said the President. 'A man may go to England, become a lawyer or a doctor, but it does not change his blood. It is like a bird that flies off the earth and lands on an ant hill. It is still on the ground.'

Obi had been utterly prostrated by the shock of his mother's death. As soon as he saw a post office messenger in khaki and steel helmet walking towards his table with the telegram he had known.

His hand trembled violently as he signed the receipt and the result was nothing like his signature.

'Time of receipt,' said the messenger.

'What is the time?'

'You got watch.'

Obi looked at his watch, for, as the messenger had pointed out, he had one.

Everybody was most kind. Mr Green said he could take a week's leave if he wished. Obi took two days. He went straight home and locked himself up in his flat. What was the point in going to Umuofia? She would have been buried by the time he got there, anyway. The thought of going home and not finding her! In the privacy of his bedroom he let tears run down his face like a child.

The effect of his tears was startling. When he finally went to sleep he did not wake up even once in the night. Such a thing had not happened to him for many years. In the last few months he had hardly known any sleep at all.

He woke with a start and saw that it was broad daylight. For a brief moment he wondered what had happened. Then yesterday's thought woke violently. Something caught in his throat. He got out of bed and stood gazing at the light coming in through the louvres. Shame and guilt filled his heart. Yesterday his mother had been put into the ground and covered with red earth and he could not keep as much as one night's vigil for her.

'Terrible!' he said. His thoughts went to his father. Poor man, he would be completely lost without her. For the first month or so it would not be too bad. Obi's married sisters would all return home. Esther could be relied upon to look after him. But in the end they would all have to go away again. That was the time the blow would really fall – when everyone began to go away. Obi wondered whether he had done the right thing in not setting out for Umuofia yesterday. But what could have been the point in going? It was more useful to send all the money he could for the funeral instead of wasting it on petrol to get home.

He washed his head and face and shaved with an old razor. Then he nearly burnt his mouth out by brushing his teeth with shaving cream which he mistook for toothpaste.

As soon as he returned from the bank he went and lay down again. He did not get up until Joseph came at about three in the afternoon. He came in a taxi. Sebastian opened the door for him.

'Put these bottles in the fridge,' he told him.

Obi came out from his bedroom and found bottles of beer at the doorstep. There must have been a dozen. 'What is that, Joseph?' he asked. Joseph did not reply immediately. He was helping Sebastian to put them away first.

'They are mine,' he said at last. 'I will use them for something.'

Before very long a number of Umuofia people began to arrive. Some came in taxis, not singly like Joseph but in teams of three or four, sharing the fare among them. Others came on bicycles. Altogether there were over twenty-five.

The President of the Umuofia Progressive Union asked whether it was permissible to sing hymns in Ikoyi. He asked because Ikoyi was a European reservation. Obi said he would rather they did not sing, but he was touched most deeply that so many of his people had come, in spite of everything, to condole with him. Joseph called him aside and told him in a whisper that he had brought the beer to help him entertain those who would come.

'Thank you,' Obi said, fighting back the mist which threatened to cover his eyes.

'Give them about eight bottles, and keep the rest for those who will come tomorrow.'

Everybody on arrival went to Obi and said '*Ndo*' to him. He answered some with a word and some with a nod of the head. No one dwelt unduly on his sorrow. They simply told him to take heart and were soon talking about the normal affairs of life. The news of the day was about the popular politicians until he took it into his head to challenge the national hero.

'He is a foolish somebody,' said one of the men in English.

'He is like the little bird *nza* who after a big meal so far forgot himself as to challenge his *chi* to single combat,' said another Ibo.

'What he saw in Obodo will teach him sense,' said yet another. 'He went to address his people, but everyone in the crowd covered his nose with a handkerchief because his words stank.'

'Was that not where they beat him?' asked Joseph.

'No, that was in Abame. He went there with lorry-loads of women supporters. But you know Abame people; they don't waste time. They beat him up well and seized his women's head-ties. They said it was not proper to beat women, so they took their head-ties from them.'

In the far corner a little group was having a different conversation. There was a lull in the bigger discussion and the voice of Nathaniel was heard telling a story.

'Tortoise went on a long journey to a distant clan. But before he went he told his people not to send for him unless something new under the sun happened. When he was gone, his mother died. The question was how to make him return to bury his mother. If they told him that his mother had died, he would say it was nothing new. So they told him that his father's palm tree had borne a fruit at the end of its leaf. When tortoise heard this, he said he must return home to see his great monstrosity. And so his bid to escape the burden of his mother's funeral was foiled.'

There was a long and embarrassed silence when Nathaniel finished his story. It was clear that he had not meant it for more than a few ears around him. But he had suddenly found himself talking to the whole room. And he was not the man to stop in mid-story.

Again Obi slept all night and woke up in the morning with a feeling of guilt. But it was not as poignant as yesterday's. And it very soon vanished altogether, leaving a queer feeling of calm. Death was a very odd thing, he thought. His mother was not three days dead and yet she was already so distant. When he tried last night to picture her he found the picture a little blurred at the edges.

'Poor mother!' he said, trying by manipulation to produce the right emotion. But it was no use. The dominant feeling was of peace.

He had a large and unseemly appetite when breakfast came, but he deliberately refused to eat more than a very little. At eleven, however, he could not help drinking a little *garri* soaked in cold water with sugar. As he drank it with a spoon he caught himself humming a dance tune.

'Terrible!' he said.

Then he remembered the story of King David, who refused food when his beloved son was sick, but washed and ate when he died. He, too, must have felt this kind of peace. The peace that passeth all understanding.

CHAPTER NINETEEN

When the period of guilt was over Obi felt like metal that was passed through fire. Or, as he himself put it in one of his spasmodic entries in his diary: 'I wonder why I am feeling like a brand-new snake just emerged from its slough.' The picture of his poor mother returning from the stream, her washing undone and her palm bleeding where his rusty blade had cut into it, vanished. Or rather it took on a secondary place. He now remembered her as the woman who got things done.

His father, although uncompromising in conflicts between church and clan, was not really a man of action but of thought. It was true he sometimes took precipitous and violent decisions, but such occasions were rare. When faced with a problem under normal circumstances, he was apt to weigh it and measure it and look it up and down, postponing action. He relied heavily on his wife at such moments. He always said in jest that it all started on their wedding day. And he would tell how she had cut the cake first.

When the missionaries brought their own kind of marriage, they also brought the wedding cake. But it was soon adapted to suit the people's sense of drama. The bride and the groom were given a knife each. The master of ceremonies counted 'One, two, three, go!' and the first to cut the cake was the senior partner. On Isaac's wedding day his wife had cut the cake first.

But the story that Obi came to cherish even more was that of the sacred he-goat. In his second year of marriage his father was catechist in a place called Aninta. One of the great gods of Aninta

was Udo, who had a he-goat that was dedicated to him. This goat
became a menace at the mission. Apart from resting and leaving
droppings in the church, it destroyed the catechist's yam and maize
crops. Mr Okonkwo complained a number of times to the priest
of Udo, but the priest (no doubt a humorous old man) said that
Udo's he-goat was free to go where it pleased and do what it
pleased. If it chose to rest in Okonkwo's shrine, it probably showed
that their two gods were pals. And there the matter would have
stood had not the he-goat one day entered Mrs Okonkwo's kitchen
and eaten up the yam she was preparing to cook – and that at
a season when yam was as precious as elephant tusks. She took
a sharp matchet and hewed off the beast's head. There were angry
threats from village elders. The women for a time refused to buy
from her or sell to her in the market. But so successful had been
the emasculation of the clan by the white man's religion and
government that the matter soon died down. Fifteen years before
this incident the men of Aninta had gone to war with their neighbours and reduced them to submission. Then the white man's
government had stepped in and ordered the surrender of all
firearms in Aninta. When they had all been collected, they were
publicly broken by soldiers. There is an age grade in Aninta today
called the Age Group of the Breaking of the Guns. They are the
children born in that year.

These thoughts gave Obi a queer kind of pleasure. They seemed
to release his spirit. He no longer felt guilt. He, too, had died.
Beyond death there are no ideals and no humbug, only reality. The
impatient idealist says: 'Give me a place to stand and I shall move
the earth.' But such a place does not exist. We all have to stand
on the earth itself and go with her at her pace. The most horrible
sight in the world cannot put out the eye. The death of a mother
is not like a palm tree bearing fruit at the end of its leaf, no matter
how much we want to make it so. And that is not the only illusion
we have . . .

It was again the season for scholarships. There was so much work
now that Obi had to take some files home every day. He was just
settling down to work when a new model Chevrolet pulled up

outside. He saw it quite clearly from his writing-desk. Who could it be? It looked like one of those prosperous Lagos businessmen. Whom could he want? All the other occupants of the flat were unimportant Europeans on the lower rungs of the Civil Service.

The man knocked on Obi's door, and Obi jumped up to open it for him. He probably wanted to ask him the way to somewhere else. Non-residents of Ikoyi always got lost among its identical flats.

'Good afternoon,' he said.

'Good afternoon. Are you Mr Okonkwo?'

Obi said yes. The man came in and introduced himself. He wore a very expensive *agbada*.

'Please have a seat.'

'Thank you.' He brought out a little towel from somewhere in the folds of his flowing gown and mopped his face. 'I don't want to waste your time,' he said, mopping one forearm and then the other under the wide sleeves of his *agbada*. 'My son is going to England in September. I want him to get scholarship. If you can do it for me here is fifty pounds.' He brought out a wad of notes from the front pocket of his *agbada*.

Obi told him it was not possible. 'In the first place I don't give scholarships. All I do is go through the applications and recommend those who satisfy the requirements to the Scholarship Board.'

'That's all I want,' said the man. 'Just recommend him.'

'But the Board may not select him.'

'Don't worry about that. Just do your own . . .'

Obi was silent. He remembered the boy's name. He was already on the short list. 'Why don't you pay for him? You have money. The scholarship is for poor people.'

The man laughed. 'No man has money in this world.' He rose to his feet, placed the wad of notes on the occasional table before Obi. 'This is just small kola,' he said. 'We will make good friends. Don't forget the name. We will see again. Do you ever go to the club? I have never seen you before.'

'I'm not a member.'

'You must join,' he said. 'Bye-bye.'

The wad of notes lay where he had placed it for the rest of the day and all night. Obi placed a newspaper over it and secured the

311

door. 'This is terrible!' he muttered. 'Terrible!' he said aloud. He woke up with a start in the middle of the night and he did not go to sleep again for a long time afterwards.

'You dance very well,' he whispered as she pressed herself against him breathing very fast and hard. She put her arms round his neck and brought her lips within a centimetre of his. They no longer paid any attention to the beat of the high life. Obi steered her towards his bedroom. She made a half-hearted show of resistance, then followed.

Obviously she was not an innocent schoolgirl. She knew her job. She was on the short list already, anyway. All the same, it was a great let-down. No point in pretending that it wasn't. One should at least be honest. He took her back to Yaba in his car. On his return journey he called on Christopher to tell him about it so that perhaps they might laugh it off. But he left again without having told the story. Some other day, perhaps.

Others came. People would say that Mr So-and-so was a gentleman. He would take money, but he would do his stuff, which was a big advertisement, and others would follow. But Obi stoutly refused to countenance anyone who did not possess the minimum educational and other requirements. On that he was unshakeable.

In due course he paid off his bank overdraft and his debt to the Hon. Sam Okoli, MHR. The worst was now over, and Obi ought to have felt happier. But he didn't.

Then one day someone brought twenty pounds. As the man left, Obi realized that he could stand it no more. People say that one gets used to these things, but he had not found it like that at all. Every incident had been a hundred times worse than the one before it. The money lay on the table. He would have preferred not to look in its direction, but he seemed to have no choice. He just sat looking at it, paralysed by his thoughts.

There was a knock at the door. He sprang to his feet, grabbed the money and ran towards the bedroom. A second knock caught him almost at the door of the bedroom and transfixed him there. Then he saw on the floor for the first time the hat which his visitor had forgotten, and he breathed a sigh of relief. He thrust the money into his pocket and went to the door and opened it. Two people entered – one was his recent visitor, the other a complete stranger.

'Are you Mr Okonkwo?' asked the stranger. Obi said yes in a voice he could hardly have recognized. The room began to swim round and round. The stranger was saying something, but it sounded distant – as things sound to a man in a fever. He then searched Obi and found the marked notes. He began to say some more things, invoking the name of the Queen, like a District Officer in the bush reading the Riot Act to an uncomprehending and delirious mob. Meanwhile the other man used the telephone outside Obi's door to summon a police van.

Everybody wondered why. The learned judge, as we have seen, could not comprehend how an educated young man and so on and so forth. The British Council man, even the men of Umuofia, did not know. And we must presume that, in spite of his certitude, Mr Green did not know either.

ARROW OF GOD

To the memory of my father
Isaiah Okafor Achebe

PREFACE TO SECOND EDITION

Whenever people have asked me which among my novels is my favourite I have always evaded a direct answer, being strongly of the mind that in sheer invidiousness that question is fully comparable to asking a man to list his children in the order in which he loves them. A paterfamilias worth his salt will, if he must, speak about the peculiar attractiveness of each child.

For *Arrow of God* that peculiar quality may lie in the fact that it is the novel which I am most likely to be caught sitting down to read again. On account of that I have also become aware of certain structural weaknesses in it which I now take the opportunity of a new edition to remove.

Arrow of God has ardent admirers as well as ardent detractors. To the latter nothing more need be said. To the others I can only express the hope that the changes I have made will meet with their approval. But in the nature of things there may well be some so steadfast in their original affection that they will see these changes as uncalled for or even unjustified. Perhaps changes are rarely called for or justified, and yet we keep making them. We should be ready at the very least to salute those who stand fast, the spiritual descendants of that magnificent man, Ezeulu, in the hope that they will forgive us. For had he been spared Ezeulu might have come to see his fate as perfectly consistent with his high historic destiny as victim, consecrating by his agony – thus raising to the stature of a ritual passage – the defection of his people. And he would gladly have forgiven them.

Chinua Achebe

CHAPTER ONE

This was the third nightfall since he began to look for signs of the new moon. He knew it would come today but he always began his watch three days early because he must not take a risk. In this season of the year his task was not too difficult; he did not have to peer and search the sky as he might do when the rains came. Then the new moon sometimes hid itself for days behind rain clouds so that when it finally came out it was already half-grown. And while it played its game the Chief Priest sat up every evening waiting.

His *obi* was built differently from other men's huts. There was the usual, long threshold in front but also a shorter one on the right as you entered. The eaves on this additional entrance were cut back so that sitting on the floor Ezeulu could watch that part of the sky where the moon had its door. It was getting darker and he constantly blinked to clear his eyes of the water that formed from gazing so intently.

Ezeulu did not like to think that his sight was no longer as good as it used to be and that some day he would have to rely on someone else's eyes as his grandfather had done when his sight failed. Of course he had lived to such a great age that his blindness became like an ornament on him. If Ezeulu lived to be so old he too would accept such a loss. But for the present he was as good as any young man, or better because young men were no longer what they used to be. There was one game Ezeulu never tired of playing on them. Whenever they shook hands with him he tensed his arm and put all his power into the grip, and being unprepared for it they winced and recoiled with pain.

The moon he saw that day was as thin as an orphan fed grudgingly by a cruel foster-mother. He peered more closely to make sure he was not deceived by a feather of cloud. At the same time he reached nervously for his *ogene*. It was the same at every new moon. He was now an old man but the fear of the new moon which he felt as a little boy still hovered round him. It was true that when he became Chief Priest of Ulu the fear was often overpowered by the joy of his high office; but it was not killed. It lay on the ground in the grip of the joy.

He beat his *ogene*: gome, gome, gome, gome . . . and immediately children's voices took up the news on all sides. *Onwa atuo!* . . . *onwa atuo!* . . . *onwa atuo!* . . . He put the stick back into the iron gong and leaned it on the wall.

The little children in his compound joined the rest in welcoming the moon. Obiageli's tiny voice stood out like a small *ogene* among drums and flutes. He could also make out the voice of his youngest son, Nwafo. The women too were in the open, talking.

'Moon,' said the senior wife, Matefi, 'may your face meeting mine bring good fortune.'

'Where is it?' asked Ugoye, the younger wife. 'I don't see it. Or am I blind?'

'Don't you see beyond the top of the ukwa tree? Not there. Follow my finger.'

'Oho, I see it. Moon, may your face meeting mine bring good fortune. But how is it sitting? I don't like its posture.'

'Why?' asked Matefi.

'I think it sits awkwardly – like an evil moon.'

'No,' said Matefi. 'A bad moon does not leave anyone in doubt. Like the one under which Okuata died. Its legs were up in the air.'

'Does the moon kill people?' asked Obiageli, tugging at her mother's cloth.

'What have I done to this child? Do you want to strip me naked?'

'I said does the moon kill people?'

'It kills little girls,' said Nwafo, her brother.

'I did not ask you, ant-hill nose.'

'You will soon cry, long throat.'
The moon kills little boys
The moon kills ant-hill nose
The moon kills little boys . . . Obiageli turned everything into
a song.

Ezeulu went into his barn and took down one yam from the bamboo
platform built specially for the twelve sacred yams. There were
eight left. He knew there would be eight; nevertheless he counted
them carefully. He had already eaten three and had the fourth in
his hand. He checked the remaining ones again and went back to
his *obi*, shutting the door of the barn carefully after him.

His log fire was smouldering. He reached for a few sticks of
firewood stacked in the corner, set them carefully on the fire and
placed the yam, like a sacrifice, on top.

As he waited for it to roast he planned the coming event in his
mind. It was Oye. Tomorrow would be Afo and the next day
Nkwo, the day of the great market. The festival of the Pumpkin
Leaves would fall on the third Nkwo from that day. Tomorrow
he would send for his assistants and tell them to announce the day
to the six villages of Umuaro.

Whenever Ezeulu considered the immensity of his power over
the year and the crops and, therefore, over the people he wondered
if it was real. It was true he named the day for the feast of the
Pumpkin Leaves and for the New Yam feast; but he did not choose
it. He was merely a watchman. His power was no more than the
power of a child over a goat that was said to be his. As long as
the goat was alive it could be his; he would find it food and take
care of it. But the day it was slaughtered he would know soon
enough who the real owner was. No! the Chief Priest of Ulu was
more than that, must be more than that. If he should refuse to
name the day there would be no festival – no planting and no
reaping. But could he refuse? No Chief Priest had ever refused.
So it could not be done. He would not dare.

Ezeulu was stung to anger by this as though his enemy had
spoken it.

'Take away that word *dare*,' he replied to this enemy. 'Yes, I

say, take it away. No man in all Umuaro can stand up and say that
I dare not. The woman who will bear the man who will say it has
not been born yet.'

But this rebuke brought only momentary satisfaction. His mind
never content with shallow satisfactions crept again to the brinks
of knowing. What kind of power was it if it would never be used?
Better to say that it was not there, that it was no more than the
power in the anus of a proud dog who sought to put out a furnace
with his puny fart . . . He turned the yam with a stick.

His youngest son, Nwafo, now came into the *obi*, saluted Ezeulu
by name and took his favourite position on the mud-bed at the far
end, close to the shorter threshold. Although he was still only a
child it looked as though the deity had already marked him out
as his future Chief Priest. Even before he had learnt to speak more
than a few words he had been strongly drawn to the god's ritual.
It could almost be said that he already knew more about it than
even the eldest. Nevertheless no one would be so rash as to say
openly that Ulu would do this or do that. When the time came
that Ezeulu was no longer found in his place Ulu might choose
the least likely of his sons to succeed him. It had happened before.

Ezeulu attended the yam very closely, rolling it over with the
stick again and again. His eldest son, Edogo, came in from his
own hut.

'Ezeulu!' he saluted.

'*E-e-i!*'

Edogo passed through the hut into the inner compound to his
sister Akueke's temporary home.

'Go and call Edogo,' said Ezeulu to Nwafo.

The two came back and sat down on the mud-bed. Ezeulu turned
his yam once more before he spoke.

'Did I ever tell you anything about carving a deity?'

Edogo did not reply. Ezeulu looked in his direction but did not
see him clearly because that part of the obi was in darkness. Edogo
on his part saw his father's face lit up by the fire on which he was
roasting the sacred yam.

'Is Edogo not there?'

'I am here.'

'I said what did I tell you about carving the image of gods? Perhaps you did not hear my first question; perhaps I spoke with water in my mouth.'

'You told me to avoid it.'

'I told you that, did I? What is this story I hear then – that you are carving an *alusi* for a man of Umuagu?'

'Who told you?'

'Who told me? Is it true or not is what I want to know, not who told me.'

'I want to know who told you because I don't think he can tell the difference between the face of a deity and the face of a Mask.'

'I see. You may go, my son. And if you like you may carve all the gods in Umuaro. If you hear me asking you about it again take my name and give it to a dog.'

'What I am carving for the man of Umuagu is not . . .'

'It is not me you are talking to. I have finished with you.'

Nwafo tried in vain to make sense out of these words. When his father's temper cooled he would ask. Then his sister, Obiageli, came in from the inner compound, saluted Ezeulu and made to sit on the mud-bed.

'Have you finished preparing the bitter-leaf?' asked Nwafo.

'Don't you know how to prepare bitter-leaf? Or are your fingers broken?'

'Keep quiet there, you two.' Ezeulu rolled the yam out of the fire with the stick and quickly felt it between his thumb and first finger, and was satisfied. He brought down a two-edged knife from the rafters and began to scrape off the coat of black on the roast yam. His hands were covered in soot when he had finished, and he clapped them together a few times to get them clean again. His wooden bowl was near at hand and he cut the yam into it and waited for it to cool.

When he began eating Obiageli started to sing quietly to herself. She should have known by now that her father never gave out even the smallest crumbs of the yam he ate without palm oil at every new moon. But she never ceased hoping.

He ate in silence. He had moved away from the fire and now sat with his back against the wall, looking outwards. As was usual with him on these occasions his mind seemed to be fixed on distant thoughts. Now and again he drank from a calabash of cold water which Nwafo had brought for him. As he took the last piece Obiageli returned to her mother's hut. Nwafo put away the wooden bowl and the calabash and stuck the knife again between two rafters.

Ezeulu rose from his goatskin and moved to the household shrine on a flat board behind the central dwarf wall at the entrance. His *ikenga*, about as tall as a man's forearm, its animal horn as long as the rest of its human body jostled with faceless *okposi* of the ancestors black with the blood of sacrifice, and his short personal staff of *ofo*. Nwafo's eyes picked out the special *okposi* which belonged to him. It had been carved for him because of the convulsions he used to have at night. They told him to call it Namesake, and he did. Gradually the convulsions had left him.

Ezeulu took the *ofo* staff from the others and sat in front of the shrine, not astride in a man's fashion but with his legs stretched in front of him to one side of the shrine, like a woman. He held one end of the short staff in his right hand and with the other end hit the earth to punctuate his prayer:

> *Ulu, I thank you for making me see another new moon. May I see it again and again. This household may it be healthy and prosperous. As this is the moon of planting may the six villages plant with profit. May we escape danger in the farm – the bite of a snake or the sting of the scorpion, the mighty one of the scrubland. May we not cut our shinbone with the matchet or the hoe. And let our wives bear male children. May we increase in numbers at the next counting of the villages so that we shall sacrifice to you a cow, not a chicken as we did after the last New Yam feast. May children put their fathers into the earth and not fathers their children. May good meet the face of every man and every woman. Let it come to the land of the riverain folk and to the land of the forest peoples.*

He put the *ofo* back among the *ikenga* and the *okposi*, wiped his mouth with the back of his hand and returned to his place. Every time he prayed for Umuaro bitterness rose into his mouth, a great smouldering anger for the division which had come to the six villages and which his enemies sought to lay on his head. And for what reason? Because he had spoken the truth before the white man. But how could a man who held the holy staff of Ulu know that a thing was a lie and speak it? How could he fail to tell the story as he had heard it from his own father? Even the white man, Wintabota, understood, though he came from a land no one knew. He had called Ezeulu the only witness of truth. That was what riled his enemies – that the white man whose father or mother no one knew should come to tell them the truth they knew but hated to hear. It was an augury of the world's ruin.

The voices of women returning from the stream broke into Ezeulu's thoughts. He could not see them because of the darkness outside. The new moon having shown itself had retired again. But the night bore marks of its visit. The darkness was not impenetrable as it had been lately, but open and airy like a forest from which the undergrowth had been cut. As the women called out 'Ezeulu' one after another he saw their vague forms and returned their greeting. They left the *obi* to their right and went into the inner compound through the only other entrance – a high, carved door in the red, earth walls.

'Are these not the people I saw going to the stream before the sun went down?'

'Yes,' said Nwafo. 'They went to Nwangene.'

'I see.' Ezeulu had forgotten temporarily that the nearer stream, Ota, had been abandoned since the oracle announced yesterday that the enormous boulder resting on two other rocks at its source was about to fall and would take a softer pillow for its head. Until the *alusi* who owned the stream and whose name it bore had been placated no one would go near it.

Still, Ezeulu thought, he would speak his mind to whoever brought him a late supper tonight. If they knew they had to go to Nwangene they should have set out earlier. He was tired of having his meal sent to him when other men had eaten and forgotten.

Obika's great, manly voice rose louder and louder into the night air as he approached home. Even his whistling carried farther than some men's voices. He sang and whistled alternately.

'Obika is returning,' said Nwafo.

'The night bird is early coming home today,' said Ezeulu, at the same time.

'One day soon he will see Eru again,' said Nwafo, referring to the apparition Obika had once seen at night. The story had been told so often that Nwafo imagined he was there.

'This time it will be Idemili or Ogwugwu,' said Ezeulu with a smile, and Nwafo was full of happiness.

About three years ago Obika had rushed into the *obi* one night and flung himself at his father shivering with terror. It was a dark night and rain was preparing to fall. Thunder rumbled with a deep, liquid voice and flash answered flash.

'What is it, my son?' Ezeulu asked again and again, but Obika trembled and said nothing.

'What is it, Obika?' asked his mother, Matefi, who had run into the *obi* and was now shaking worse than her son.

'Keep quiet there,' said Ezeulu. 'What did you see, Obika?'

When he had cooled a little Obika began to tell his father what he had seen at a flash of lightning near the ugili tree between their village, Umuachala, and Umunneora. As soon as he had mentioned the place Ezeulu had known what it was.

'What happened when you saw It?'

'I knew it was a spirit; my head swelled.'

'Did he not turn into the Bush That Ruined Little Birds? On the left?'

His father's confidence revived Obika. He nodded and Ezeulu nodded twice. The other women were now ranged round the door.

'What did he look like?'

'Taller than any man I know.' He swallowed a lump. 'His skin was very light . . .like . . . like . . .'

'Was he dressed like a poor man or was it like a man of great wealth?'

'He was dressed like a wealthy man. He had an eagle's feather in his red cap.'

His teeth began to knock together again.

'Hold yourself together. You are not a woman. Had he an elephant tusk?'

'Yes. He carried a big tusk across his shoulder.'

The rain had now began to fall, at first in big drops that sounded like pebbles on the thatch.

'There is no cause to be afraid, my son. You have seen Eru, the Magnificent, the One that gives wealth to those who find favour with him. People sometimes see him at that place in this kind of weather. Perhaps he was returning home from a visit to Idemili or the other deities. Eru only harms those who swear falsely before his shrine.' Ezeulu was carried away by his praise of the god of wealth. The way he spoke one would have thought he was the proud priest of Eru rather than Ulu who stood above Eru and all the other deities. 'When he likes a man wealth flows like a river into his house; his yams grow as big as human beings, his goats produce threes and his hens hatch nines.'

Matefi's daughter, Ojiugo, brought in a bowl of foo-foo and a bowl of soup, saluted her father and set them before him. Then she turned to Nwafo and said: 'Go to your mother's hut; she has finished cooking.'

'Leave the boy alone,' said Ezeulu who knew that Matefi and her daughter resented his partiality for his other wife's son. 'Go and call your mother for me.' He made no move to start eating and Ojiugo knew there was going to be trouble. She went back to her mother's hut and called her.

'I don't know how many times I have said in this house that I shall not eat my supper when every other man in Umuaro is retiring to sleep,' he said as soon as Matefi came in. 'But you will not listen. To you whatever I say in this house is no more effective than the fart a dog breaks to put out a fire . . .'

'I went all the way to Nwangene to fetch water and . . .'

'If you like you may go to Nkisa. What I am saying is that if you want that madness of yours to be cured, bring my supper at this time another day . . .'

When Ojiugo came to collect the bowls she found Nwafo polishing off the soup. She waited for him to finish, full of anger. Then she gathered the bowls and went to tell her mother about it. This was not the first time or the second or third. It happened every day.

'Do you blame a vulture for perching over a carcass?' said Matefi. 'What do you expect a boy to do when his mother cooks soup with locust beans for fish? She saves her money to buy ivory bracelets. But Ezeulu will never see anything wrong in what she does. If it is me then he knows what to say.'

Ojiugo was looking towards the other woman's hut which was separated from theirs by the whole length of the compound. All she could see was the yellowish glow of the palm-oil lamp between the low eaves and the threshold. There was a third hut which formed a half moon with the other two. It had belonged to Ezeulu's first wife, Okuata, who died many years ago. Ojiugo hardly knew her; she only remembered she used to give a piece of fish and some locust beans to every child who went to her hut when she was making her soup. She was the mother of Adeze, Edogo and Akueke. After her death her children lived in the hut until the girls married. Then Edogo lived there alone until he married two years ago and built a small compound of his own besides his father's. Now Akueke had been living in the hut again since she left her husband's house. They said the man ill-treated her. But Ojiugo's mother said it was a lie and that Akueke was headstrong and proud, the kind of woman who carried her father's compound into the house of her husband.

Just when Ojiugo and her mother were about to begin their meal, Obika came home singing and whistling.

'Bring me his bowl,' said Matefi. 'He is early today.'

Obika stooped at the low eaves and came in hands first. He saluted his mother and she said '*Nno*' without any warmth. He sat down heavily on the mud-bed. Ojiugo had brought his soup bowl of fired clay and was now bringing down his foo-foo from the bamboo ledge. Matefi blew into the soup bowl to remove dust and ash and ladled soup into it. Ojiugo set it before her brother and went outside to bring water in a gourd.

After the first swallow Obika tilted the bowl of soup towards the light and inspected it critically.

'What do you call this, soup or coco-yam porridge?'

The women ignored him and went on with their own interrupted meal. It was clear he had drunk too much palm wine again.

Obika was one of the handsomest young men in Umuaro and all the surrounding districts. His face was very finely cut and his nose stood *gem*, like the note of a gong. His skin was, like his father's, the colour of terracotta. People said of him (as they always did when they saw great comeliness) that he was not born for these parts among the Igbo people of the forests; that in his previous life he must have sojourned among the riverain folk whom the Igbo called Olu.

But two things spoilt Obika. He drank palm wine to excess, and he was given to sudden and fiery anger. And being as strong as rock he was always inflicting injury on others. His father who preferred him to Edogo, his quiet and brooding half-brother, nevertheless said to him often: 'It is praiseworthy to be brave and fearless, my son, but sometimes it is better to be a coward. We often stand in the compound of a coward to point at the ruins where a brave man used to live. The man who has never submitted to anything will soon submit to the burial mat.'

But for all that Ezeulu would rather have a sharp boy who broke utensils in his haste than a slow and careful snail.

Not very long ago Obika had come very close indeed to committing murder. His half-sister, Akueke, often came home to say that her husband had beaten her. One early morning she came again with her face all swollen. Without waiting to hear the rest of the story Obika set out for Umuogwugwu, the village of his brother-in-law. On the way he stopped to call his friend, Ofoedu, who was never absent from the scene of a fight. As they approached Umuogwugwu Obika explained to Ofoedu that he must not help in beating Akueke's husband.

'Why have you called me then?' asked the other, angrily. 'To carry your bag?'

'There may be work for you. If Umuogwugwu people are what I take them to be they will come out in force to defend their brother. Then there will be work for you.'

No one in Ezeulu's compound knew where Obika had gone until he returned a little before noon with Ofoedu. On their heads was Akueke's husband tied to a bed, almost dead. They set him down under the ukwa tree and dared anyone to move him. The women and the neighbours pleaded with Obika and showed him the threatening ripe fruit on the tree, as big as water-pots.

'Yes. I put him there on purpose, to be crushed by the fruit — the beast.'

Eventually the commotion brought Ezeulu, who had gone into the nearby bush, hurrying home. When he saw what was happening he wailed a lament on the destruction Obika would bring to his house and ordered him to release his in-law.

For three markets Ibe could barely rise from his bed. Then one evening his kinsmen came to seek satisfaction from Ezeulu. Most of them had gone out to their farms when it had all happened. For three markets and more they had waited patiently for someone to explain why their kinsman should be beaten up and carried away.

'What is this story we hear about Ibe?' they asked.

Ezeulu tried to placate them without admitting that his son had done anything seriously wrong. He called his daughter, Akueke, to stand before them.

'You should have seen her the day she came home. Is this how you marry women in your place? If it is your way then I say you will not marry my daughter like that.'

The men agreed that Ibe had stretched his arm too far, and so no one could blame Obika for defending his sister.

'Why do we pray to Ulu and to our ancestors to increase our numbers if not for this thing?' said their leader. 'No one eats numbers. But if we are many nobody will dare molest us, and our daughters will hold their heads up in their husbands' houses. So we do not blame Obika too much. Do I speak well?' His companions answered 'yes', and he continued.

'We cannot say that your son did wrong to fight for his sister. What we do not understand, however, is why a man with a penis between his legs should be carried away from his house and village. It is as if to say: You are nothing and your kinsmen can do nothing. This is the part we do not understand. We have not come with wisdom but with foolishness because a man does not go to his in-law with wisdom. We want you to say to us: You are wrong; this is how it is or that is how it is. and we shall be satisfied and go home. If someone says to us afterwards: Your kinsman was beaten up and carried away; we shall know what to reply. Our great in-law, I salute you.'

Ezeulu employed all his skill in speaking to pacify his in-laws. They went home happier than they came. But it was hardly likely that they would press Ibe to carry palm wine to Ezeulu and ask for his wife's return. It looked as if she would live in her father's compound for a long time.

When he finished his meal Obika joined the others in Ezeulu's hut. As usual Edogo spoke for all of them. As well as Obika, Oduche and Nwafo were there also.

'Tomorrow is Afo,' said Edogo, 'and we have come to find out what work you have for us.'

Ezeulu thought for a while as though he was unprepared for the proposal. Then he asked Obika how much of the work on his new homestead was still undone.

'Only the woman's barn,' he replied. 'But that could wait. There will be no coco-yam to put into it until harvest time.'

'Nothing will wait,' said Ezeulu. 'A new wife should not come into an unfinished homestead. I know such a thing does not trouble the present age. But as long as we are there we shall continue to point out the right way . . . Edogo, instead of working for me tomorrow take your brothers and the women to build the barn. If Obika has no shame, the rest of us have.'

'Father, I have a word to say.' It was Oduche.

'I am listening.'

Oduche cleared his throat as if he was afraid to begin.

'Perhaps they are forbidden to help their brothers build a barn,' said Obika thickly.

'You are always talking like a fool,' Edogo snapped at him. 'Has Oduche not worked as hard as yourself on your homestead? I should say harder.'

'It is Oduche I am waiting to hear,' said Ezeulu, 'not you two jealous wives.'

'I am one of those they have chosen to go to Okperi tomorrow and bring the loads of our new teacher.'

'Oduche!'

'Father!'

'Listen to what I shall say now. When a handshake goes beyond the elbow we know it has turned to another thing. It was I who sent you to join those people because of my friendship to the white man, Wintabota. He asked me to send one of my children to learn the ways of his people and I ageed to send you. I did not send you so that you might leave your duty in my household. Do you hear me? Go and tell the people who chose you to go to Okperi that I said no. Tell them that tomorrow is the day on which my sons and my wives and my son's wife work for me. Your people should know the custom of this land; if they don't you must tell them. Do you hear me?'

'I hear you.'

'Go and call your mother for me. I think it is her turn to cook tomorrow.'

CHAPTER TWO

Ezeulu often said that the dead fathers of Umuaro looking at the world from Ani-Mmo must be utterly bewildered by the way of the new age. At no other time but now could Umuaro have taken war to Okperi in the circumstances in which they did. Who would have imagined that Umuaro would go to war so sorely divided? Who would have thought that they would disregard the warning of the priest of Ulu who originally brought the six villages together and made them what they were? But Umuaro had grown wise and strong in its own conceit and had become like the little bird, *nza*, who ate and drank and challenged his personal god to single combat. Umuaro challenged the deity which laid the foundation of their villages. And – what did they expect? – he thrashed them, thrashed them enough for today and for tomorrow!

In the very distant past, when lizards were still few and far between, the six villages – Umuachala, Umunneora, Umuagu, Umuezeani, Umuogwugwu and Umuisiuzo – lived as different peoples, and each worshipped its own deity. Then the hired soldiers of Abam used to strike in the dead of night, set fire to the houses and carry men, women and children into slavery. Things were so bad for the six villages that their leaders came together to save themselves. They hired a strong team of medicine-men to install a common deity for them. This deity, which the fathers of the six villages made, was called Ulu. Half of the medicine was buried at a place which became Nkwo market and the other half thrown into the stream which became Mili Ulu. The six villages then took the name of Umuaro, and the priest of Ulu became their Chief Priest. From that day they were never again beaten by an enemy. How could such a people disregard the god who founded their town and protected it? Ezeulu saw it as the ruin of the world.

On the day, five years ago, when the leaders of Umuaro decided to send an emissary to Okperi with white clay for peace or new palm frond for war, Ezeulu spoke in vain. He told the men of Umuaro that Ulu would not fight an unjust war.

'I know,' he told them, 'my father said this to me that when our village first came here to live the land belonged to Okperi. It was Okperi who gave us a piece of their land to live in. They also gave us their deities – their Udo and their Ogwugwu. But they said to our ancestors – mark my words – the people of Okperi said to our fathers: "We give you our Udo and our Ogwugwu; but you must call the deity we give you not Udo but the son of Udo, and not Ogwugwu but the son of Ogwugwu." This is the story as I heard it from my father. If you choose to fight a man for a piece of farmland that belongs to him I shall have no hand in it.'

But Nwaka had carried the day. He was one of the three people in all the six villages who had taken the highest title in the land, Eru, which was called after the lord of wealth himself. Nwaka came from a long line of prosperous men and from a village which called itself first in Umuaro. They said that when the six villages first came together they offered the priesthood of Ulu to the weakest among them to ensure that none in the alliance became too powerful.

'*Umuaro kwenu!*' Nwaka roared.

'*Hem!*' replied the men of Umuaro.

'*Kwenu!*'

'*Hem!*'

'*Kwezuenu!*'

'*Hem!*'

He began to speak almost softly in the silence he had created with his salutation.

'Wisdom is like a goatskin bag; every man carries his own. Knowledge of the land is also like that. Ezeulu has told us what his father told him about the olden days. We know that a father

334

does not speak falsely to his son. But we also know that the lore of the land is beyond the knowledge of many fathers. If Ezeulu had spoken about the great deity of Umuaro which he carries and which his fathers carried before him I would have paid attention to his voice. But he speaks about events which are older than Umuaro itself. I shall not be afraid to say that neither Ezeulu nor any other in this village can tell us about these events.' There were murmurs of approval and of disapproval but more of approval from the assembly of elders and men of title. Nwaka walked forward and back as he spoke; the eagle feather in his red cap and bronze band on his ankle marked him out as one of the lords of the land – a man favoured by Eru, the god of riches.

'My father told me a different story. He told me that Okperi people were wanderers. He told me three or four different places where they sojourned for a while and moved on again. They were driven away by Umuofia, then by Abame and Aninta. Would they go today and claim all those sites? Would they have laid claim on our farmland in the days before the white man turned us upside down? Elders and Ndichie of Umuaro, let everyone return to his house if we have no heart in the fight. We shall not be the first people who abandoned their farmland or even their homestead to avoid war. But let us not tell ourselves or our children that we did it because the land belonged to other people. Let us rather tell them that their fathers did not choose to fight. Let us tell them also that we marry the daughters of Okperi and their men marry our daughters, and that where there is this mingling men often lose the heart to fight. *Umuaro Kwenu!*'

'*Hem!*'

'*Kwezuenu!*'

'*Hem!*'

'I salute you all.'

The long uproar that followed was largely of approbation. Nwaka had totally destroyed Ezeulu's speech. The last glancing blow which killed it was the hint that the Chief Priest's mother had been a daughter of Okperi. The assembly broke up into numerous little groups of people talking to those who sat nearest to them. One man said that Ezeulu had forgotten whether it was his father or his mother who told him about the farmland. Speaker after speaker rose and spoke to the assembly until it was clear that all the six villages stood behind Nwaka. Ezeulu was not the only man of Umuaro whose mother had come from Okperi. But none of the others dared go to his support. In fact one of them, Akukalia, whose language never wandered far from 'kill and despoil', was so fiery that he was chosen to carry the white clay and the new palm frond to his motherland, Okperi.

The last man to speak that day was the oldest man from Akukalia's village. His voice was now shaky but his salute to the assembly was heard clearly in all corners of the Nkwo market place. The men of Umuaro responded to his great effort with the loudest *Hem*! of the day. He said quietly that he must rest to recover his breath, and those who heard laughed.

'I want to speak to the man we are sending to Okperi. It is now a long time since we fought a war and many of you may not remember the custom. I am not saying that that Akukalia needs to be reminded. But I am an old man, and an old man is there to talk. If the lizard of the homestead should neglect to do the things for which its kind is known, it will be mistaken for the lizard of the farmland.

'From the way Akukalia spoke I saw that he was in great anger. It is right that he should feel like that. But we are sending him to his motherland to fight. We are sending you, Akukalia, to place the choice of war or peace before them. Do I speak for Umuaro?' They gave him power to carry on.

'We do not want Okperi to choose war; nobody eats war. If they choose peace we shall rejoice. But whatever they say you are not to dispute with them. Your duty is to bring word back to us. We all know you are a fearless man but while you are there put your fearlessness in your bag. If the young men who will go with you talk with too loud a voice it shall be your duty to cover their fault. I have in my younger days gone on such errands and know the temptations too well. I salute you.'

Ezeulu who had taken in everything with a sad smile now sprang to his feet like one stung in the buttocks by a black ant.

'*Umuaro Kwenu!*' he cried.

'*Hem!*'

'I salute you all.' It was like the salute of an enraged Mask. 'When an adult is in the house the she-goat is not left to suffer the pains of parturition on its tether. That is what our ancestors have said. But what have we seen here today? We have seen people speak because they are afraid to be called cowards. Others have spoken the way they spoke because they are hungry for war. Let us leave all that aside. If in truth the farmland is ours, Ulu will fight on our side. But if it is not we shall know soon enough. I would not have spoken again today if I had not seen adults in the house neglecting their duty. Ogbuefi Egonwanne, as one of the three oldest men in Umuaro, should have reminded us that our fathers did not fight a war of blame. But instead of that he wants to teach our emissary how to carry fire and water in the same mouth. Have we not heard that a boy sent by his father to steal does not go stealthily but breaks the door with his feet? Why does Egonwanne trouble himself about small things when big ones are overlooked? We want war. How Akukalia speaks to his mother's people is a small thing. He can spit into their face if he likes. When we hear a house has fallen do we ask if the ceiling fell with it? I salute you all.'

Akukalia and his two companions set out for Okperi at cock-crow on the following day. In his goatskin bag he carried a lump of white chalk and a few yellow palm fronds cut from the summit of the tree before they had unfurled to the sun. Each man also carried a sheathed matchet.

The day was Eke, and before long Akukalia and his companions began to pass women from all the neighbouring villages on their way to the famous Eke Okperi market. They were mostly women from Elumelu and Abame who made the best pots in all the surrounding country. Everyone carried a towering load of five or six or even more big water pots held together with a net of ropes on a long basket, and seemed in the half-light like a spirit with a fantastic head.

As the men of Umuaro passed company after company of these

market women they talked about the great Eke market in Okperi to which folk from every part of Igbo and Olu went.

'It is the result of an ancient medicine,' Akukalia explained. 'My mother's people are great medicine-men.' There was pride in his voice. 'At first Eke was a very small market. Other markets in the neighbourhood were drawing it dry. Then one day the men of Okperi made a powerful deity and placed their market in its care. From that day Eke grew and grew until it became the biggest market in these parts. This deity which is called Nwanyieke is an old woman. Every Eke day before cock-crow she appears in the market pl. _ with a broom in her right hand and dances round the vast open space beckoning with her broom in all directions of the earth and drawing folk from every land. That is why people will not come near the market before cock-crow; if they did they would see the ancient lady in her task.'

'They tell the same story of the Nkwo market beside the great river at Umuru,' said one of Akukalia's companions. 'There the medicine has worked so well that the market no longer assembles only on Nkwo days.'

'Umuru is no match for my mother's people in medicine,' said Akukalia. 'Their market has grown because the white man took his merchandise there.'

'Why did he take his merchandise there,' asked the other man, 'if not because of their medicine? The old woman of the market has swept the world with her broom, even the land of the white men where they say the sun never shines.'

'Is it true that one of their woman in Umuru went outside without the white hat and melted like sleeping palm oil in the sun?' asked the other companion.

'I have also heard it,' said Akukalia. 'But many lies are told about the white man. It was once said that he had no toes.'

As the sun rose the men came to the disputed farmland. It had not been cultivated for many years and was thick with browned spear grass.

'I remember coming with my father to this very place to cut grass for our thatches,' said Akukalia. 'It is a thing of surprise to me that my mother's people are claiming it today.'

'It is all due to the white man who says, like an elder to two fighting children: You will not fight while I am around. And so the younger and weaker of the two begins to swell himself up and to boast.'

'You have spoken the truth,' said Akukalia. 'Things like this would never have happened when I was a young man, to say nothing of the days of my father. I remember all this very well,' he waved over the land. 'That ebenebe tree over there was once hit by thunder, and people cutting thatch under it were hurled away in every direction.'

'What you should ask them,' said the other companion who had spoken very little since they set out, 'what they should tell us is why, if the land was indeed theirs, why they let us farm it and cut thatch from it for generation after generation, until the white man came and reminded them.'

'It is not our mission to ask them any question, except the one question which Umuaro wants them to answer,' said Akukalia. 'And I think I should remind you again to hold your tongues in your hand when we get there and leave the talking to me. They are very difficult people; my mother was no exception. But I know what they know. If a man of Okperi says to you come, he means run away with all your strength. If you are not used to their ways you may sit with them from cock-crow until roosting-time and join in their talk and their food, but all the while you will be floating on the surface of the water. So leave them to me because when a man of cunning dies a man of cunning buries him.'

The three emissaries entered Okperi about the time when most people finished their morning meal. They made straight for the compound of Uduezue, the nearest living relation to Akukalia's mother. Perhaps it was the men's unsmiling faces that told Uduezue, or maybe Okperi was not altogether unprepared for the mission from Umuaro. Nevertheless Uduezue asked them about their people at home.

'They are well,' replied Akukalia impatiently. 'We have an urgent mission which we must give to the rulers of Okperi at once.'

'True?' asked Uduezue. 'I was saying to myself: What could

bring my son and his people all this way so early? If my sister, your mother, were still alive, I would have thought that something had happened to her.' He paused for a very little while. 'An important mission; yes. We have a saying that a toad does not run in the day unless something is after it. I do not want to delay your mission, but I must offer you a piece of kola nut.' He made to rise.

'Do not worry yourself. Perhaps we shall return after our mission. It is a big load on our head, and until we put it down we cannot understand anything we are told.'

'I know what it is like. Here is a piece of white clay then. Let me agree with you and leave the kola nut until you return.'

But the men declined even to draw lines on the floor with the clay. After that there was nothing else to say. They had rebuffed the token of goodwill between host and guest, their mission must indeed be grave.

Uduezue went into his inner compound and soon returned with his goatskin bag and sheathed matchet. 'I shall take you to the man who will receive your message,' he said.

He led the way and the others followed silently. They passed an ever-thickening crowd of market people. As the planting season was near many of them carried long baskets of seed-yams. Some of the men carried goats also in long baskets. But now and again there was a man clutching a fowl; such a man never trod the earth firmly, especially when he was a man who had known better times. Many of the women talked boisterously as they went; the silent ones were those who had come from far away and had exhausted themselves. Akukalia thought he recognized some of the towering headloads of water pots they had left behind on their way.

Akukalia had not visited his mother's land for about three years and he now felt strangely tender towards it. When as a little boy he had first come here with his mother he had wondered why the earth and sand looked white instead of red-brown as in Umuaro. His mother had told him the reason was that in Okperi people washed every day and were clean while in Umuaro they never touched water for the whole four days of the week. His mother was very harsh to him and very quarrelsome, but now Akukalia felt tender even towards her.

Uduezue took his three visitors to the house of Otikpo, the town-crier of Okperi. He was in his *obi* preparing seed-yams for the market. He rose to greet his visitors. He called Uduezue by his name and title and called Akukalia *Son of our Daughter*. He merely shook hands with the other two whom he did not know. Otikpo was very tall and of spare frame. He still looked like the great runner he had been in his youth.

He went into an inner room and returned with a rolled mat which he spread on the mud-bed for his visitors. A little girl came in from the inner compound calling, 'Father, father'.

'Go away, Ogbanje,' he said. 'Don't you see I have strangers?'

'Nweke slapped me.'

'I shall whip him later. Go and tell him I shall whip him.'

'Otikpo, let us go outside and whisper together,' said Uduezue.

They did not stay very long. When they came back Otikpo brought a kola nut in a wooden bowl. Akukalia thanked him but said that he and his companions carried such heavy loads on their heads that they could neither eat nor drink until the burden was set down.

'True?' asked Otikpo. 'Can this burden you speak of come down before me and Uduezue, or does it require the elders of Okperi?'

'It requires the elders.'

'Then you have come at a bad time. Everybody in Igboland knows that Okperi people do not have other business on their Eke day. You should have come yesterday or the day before, or tomorrow or the day after. *Son of our Daughter*, you should know our habits.'

'Your habits are not different from the habits of other people,' said Akukalia. 'But our mission could not wait.'

'True?' Otikpo went outside and raising his voice called his neighbour, Ebo, and came in again.

'The mission could not wait. What shall we do now? I think you should sleep in Okperi today and see the elders tomorrow.'

Ebo came in and saluted generally. He was surprised to see so many people, and was temporarily at a loss. Then he began to shake hands all round, but when Akukalia's turn came he refused to take Ebo's hand.

'Sit down, Ebo,' said Otikpo. 'Akukalia has a message for Okperi which forbids him to eat kola nut or shake hands. He wants to see the elders and I have told him it is not possible today.'

'Why did they choose today to bring their message? Have they no market where they come from? If that is all you are calling me for I must go back and prepare for market.'

'Our message cannot wait, I have said that before.'

'I have not yet heard of a message that could not wait. Or have you brought us news that Chukwu, the high god, is about to remove the foot that holds the world? If not then you must know that Eke Okperi does not break up because three men have come to town. If you listen carefully even now you can hear its voice; and it is not even half full yet. When it is full you can hear it from Umuda. Do you think a market like that will stop to hear your message?' He sat down for a while; nobody else spoke.

'You can now see, *Son of our Daughter*, that we cannot get our elders together before tomorrow,' said Otikpo.

'If war came suddenly to your town how do you call your men together, *Father of my mother*? Do you wait till tomorrow? Do you not beat your *ikolo*?'

Ebo and Otikpo burst into laughter. The three men from Umuaro exchanged glances. Akukalia's face began to look dangerous. Uduezue sat as he had done since they first came in, his chin in his left hand.

'Different people have different customs,' said Otikpo after his laugh. 'In Okperi it is not our custom to welcome strangers to our market with the *ikolo*.'

'Are you telling us, *Father of my Mother*, that you regard us as market women? I have borne your insults patiently. Let me remind you that my name is Okeke Akukalia of Umuaro.'

'Ooh, of Umuaro,' said Ebo, still smarting from the rebuffed handshake. 'I am happy you have said of Umuaro. The name of this town is Okperi.'

'Go back to your house,' shouted Akukalia, 'or I will make you eat shit.'

'If you want to shout like a castrated bull you must wait until you return to Umuaro. I have told you this place is called Okperi.'

Perhaps it was deliberate, perhaps accidental. But Ebo had just said the one thing that nobody should ever have told Akukalia who was impotent and whose two wives were secretly given to other men to bear his children.

The ensuing fight was grim. Ebo was no match for Akukalia and soon had a broken head, streaming with blood. Maddened by pain and shame he made for his house to get a matchet. Women and children from all the nearby compounds were now out, some of them screaming with fright. Passers-by also rushed in, making futile motions of intervention.

What happened next was the work of Ekwensu, the bringer of evil. Akukalia rushed after Ebo, went into the *obi*, took the *ikenga* from his shrine, rushed outside again and, while everyone stood aghast, split it in two.

Ebo was last to see the abomination. He had been struggling with Otikpo who wanted to take the matchet from him and so prevent bloodshed. But when the crowd saw what Akukalia had done they called on Otikpo to leave the man alone. The two men came out of the hut together. Ebo rushed towards Akukalia and then seeing what he had done stopped dead. He did not know, for one brief moment, whether he was awake or dreaming. He rubbed his eyes with the back of his left hand. Akukalia stood in front of him. The two pieces of his *ikenga* lay where their violator had kicked them in the dust.

'Move another step if you call yourself a man. Yes, I did it. What can you do?'

So it was true. Still Ebo turned round and went into his *obi*. At his shrine he knelt down to have a close look. Yes, the gap where his *ikenga*, the strength of his right arm, had stood stared back at him – an empty patch, without dust, on the wooden board. '*Nna doh! Nna doh!*' he wept, calling on his dead father to come to his aid. Then he got up and went into his sleeping-room. He was there a little while before Otikpo, thinking he might be doing violence to himself, rushed into the room to see. But it was too late. Ebo pushed him aside and came into the *obi* with his loaded gun. At the threshold he knelt down and aimed. Akukalia, seeing the danger, dashed forward. Although the bullet had caught him in the chest he continued running with his matchet held high until he fell at the threshold, his face hitting the low thatch before he went down.

When the body was brought home to Umuaro everyone was stunned. It had never happened before that an emissary of Umuaro was killed abroad. But after the first shock people began to say that their clansman had done an unforgivable thing.

'Let us put ourselves in the place of the man he made a corpse before his own eyes,' they said. 'Who would bear such a thing? What propitiation or sacrifice would atone for such sacrilege? How would the victim set about putting himself right again with his fathers unless he could say to them: Rest, for the man that did it has paid with his head? Nothing short of that would have been adequate.'

Umuaro might have left the matter there, and perhaps the whole land dispute with it as Ekwensu seemed to have taken a hand in it. But one small thing worried them. It was small but at the same time it was very great. Why had Okperi not deigned to send a message to Umuaro to say this was what happened and that was what happened? Everyone agreed that the man who killed Akukalia had been sorely provoked. It was also true that Akukalia was not only a son of Umuaro; he was also the son of a daughter of Okperi, and what had happened might be likened to he-goat's head dropping into he-goat's bag. Yet when a man was killed something had to be said, some explanation given. That Okperi had not cared to say anything beyond returning the corpse was a mark of the contempt in which they now held Umuaro. And that could not be overlooked. Four days after Akukalia's death criers went through the six villages at nightfall.

The assembly in the morning was very solemn. Almost everyone who spoke said that although it was not right to blame a corpse it must be admitted that their kinsman did a great wrong. Many of them, especially the older men, asked Umuaro to let the matter drop. But there were others who, as the saying was, pulled out their hair and chewed it. They swore that they would not live and see Umuaro spat upon. They were, as before, led by Nwaka. He spoke with his usual eloquence and stirred many hearts.

Ezeulu did not speak until the last. He saluted Umuaro quietly and with great sadness.

'*Umuaro kwenu!*'

'*Hem!*'

'*Umuaro obodonesi kwenu!*'

'*Hem!*'

'*Kwezuenu!*'

'*Hem!*'

'The reed we were blowing is now crushed. When I spoke two markets ago in this very place I used the proverb of the she-goat. I was then talking to Ogbuefi Egonwanne who was the adult in the house. I told him that he should have spoken up against what we were planning, instead of which he put a piece of live coal into the child's palm and ask him to carry it with care. We all have seen with what care he carried it. I was not then talking to Egonwanne alone but to all the elders here who left what they should have done and did another, who were in the house and yet the she-goat suffered in her parturition.

'Once there was a great wrestler whose back had never known the ground. He wrestled from village to village until he had thrown every man in the world. Then he decided that he must go and wrestle in the land of the spirits, and become champion there as well. He went, and beat every spirit that came forward. Some had seven heads, some ten; but he beat them all. His companion who sang his praise on the flute begged him to come away, but he would not, his blood was roused, his ear nailed up. Rather than heed the call to go home he gave a challenge to the spirits to bring out their best and strongest wrestler. So they sent him his personal god, a little wiry spirit who seized him with one hand and smashed him on the stony earth.

'Men of Umuaro, why do you think our fathers told us this story? They told it because they wanted to teach us that no matter how strong or great a man was he should never challenge his *chi*. This is what our kinsman did – he challenged his *chi*. We were his flute player, but we did not plead with him to come away from death. Where is he today? The fly that has no one to advise it follows

345

the corpse into the grave. But let us leave Akukalia aside; he has gone the way his *chi* ordained.

'But let the slave who sees another cast into a shallow grave know that he will be buried in the same way when his day comes. Umuaro is today challenging his *chi*. Is there any man or woman in Umuaro who does not know Ulu, the deity that destroys a man when his life is sweetest to him? Some people are still talking of carrying war to Okperi. Do they think that Ulu will fight in blame? Today the world is spoilt and there is no longer head or tail in anything that is done. But Ulu is not spoilt with it. If you go to war to avenge a man who passed shit on the head of his mother's father, Ulu will not follow you to be soiled in the corruption. Umuaro, I salute you.'

The meeting ended in confusion. Umuaro was divided in two. Many people gathered round Ezeulu and said they stood with him. But there were others who went with Nwaka. That night he held another meeting with them in his compound and they agreed that three or four Okperi heads must fall to settle the matter.

Nwaka ensured that no one came to that night meeting from Ezeulu's village, Umuachala. He held up his palm-oil lamp against the face of any who came to see him clearly. Altogether he sent fifteen people away.

Nwaka began by telling the assembly that Umuaro must not allow itself to be led by the Chief Priest of Ulu. 'My father did not tell me that before Umuaro went to war it took leave from the priest of Ulu,' he said. 'The man who carries a deity is not a king. He his there to perform his god's ritual and to carry sacrifice to him. But I have been watching this Ezeulu for many years. He is a man of ambition; he wants to be king, priest, diviner, all. His father, they said, was like that too. But Umuaro showed him that Igbo people knew no kings. The time has come to tell his son also.

'We have no quarrel with Ulu. He is still our protector, even though we no longer fear Abam warriors at night. But I will not see with these eyes of mine his priest making himself lord over us. My father told me many things, but he did not tell me that Ezeulu was king in Umuaro. Who is he, anyway? Does anybody here enter his compound through the man's gate? If Umuaro decided to have a king we know where he would come from. Since when did

Umuachala become head of the six villages? We all know that it was jealousy among the big villages that made them give the priesthood to the weakest. We shall fight for our farmland and for the contempt Okperi has poured on us. Let us not listen to anyone trying to frighten us with the name of Ulu. If a man says yes, his *chi* also says yes. And we have all heard how the people of Aninta dealt with their deity when he failed them. Did they not carry him to the boundary between them and their neighbours and set fire on him? I salute you.'

The war was waged from one Afo to the next. On the day it began Umuaro killed two men of Okperi. The next day was Nkwo, and so there was no fighting. On the two following days, Eke and Oye, the fighting grew fierce. Umuaro killed four men and Okperi replied with three, one of the three being Akukalia's brother, Okoye. The next day, Afo, saw the war brought to a sudden close. The white man, Wintabota, brought soldiers to Umuaro and stopped it. The story of what these soldiers did in Abame was still told with fear, and so Umuaro made no effort to resist but laid down their arms. Although they were not yet satisfied they could say without shame that Akukalia's death had been avenged, that they had provided him with three men on whom to rest his head. It was also a good thing perhaps that the war was stopped. The death of Akukalia and his brother in one and the same dispute showed that Ekwensu's hand was in it.

The white man, not satisfied that he had stopped the war, had gathered all the guns in Umuaro and asked the soldiers to break them in the face of all, except three or four which he carried away. Afterwards he sat in judgement over Umuaro and Okperi and gave the disputed land to Okperi.

CHAPTER THREE

Captain T. K. Winterbottom stood at the veranda of his bungalow on Government Hill to watch the riot of the year's first rain. For the past month or two the heat had been building up to an unbearable pitch. The grass had long been burnt out, and the leaves of the more hardy trees had taken on the red and brown earth colour of the country. There was only two hours' respite in the morning before the country turned into a furnace and perspiration came down in little streams from the head and neck. The most exasperating was the little stream that always coursed down behind the ear like a fly, walking. There was another moment of temporary relief at sundown when a cool wind blew. But this treacherous beguiling wind was the great danger of Africa. The unwary European who bared himself to it received the death-kiss.

Captain Winterbottom had not known real sleep since the dry, cool harmattan wind stopped abruptly in December; and it was now mid-February. He had grown pale and thin, and in spite of the heat his feet often felt cold. Every morning after the bath which he would have preferred cold but must have hot to stay alive (since Africa never spared those who did what they liked instead of what they had to do), he looked into the mirror and saw his gums getting whiter and whiter. Perhaps another bout of fever was on the way. At night he had to imprison himself inside a mosquito net which shut out whatever air movement there was outside. His bedclothes were sodden and his head formed a waterlogged basin on the pillow. After the first stretch of unrestful sleep he would lie awake, tossing about until he was caught in the distant throb of drums. He would wonder what unspeakable rites went on in the forest at night, or was it the heartbeat of the African darkness? Then one night he was terrified when it suddenly occurred to him that no matter where he lay awake at night in Nigeria the beating of the drums came with the same constancy and from the same elusive distance. Could it be that the throbbing came from his own heat-stricken brain? He attempted to smile it off but the skin on his face felt too tight. This dear old land of waking nightmares!

Fifteen years ago Winterbottom might have been so depressed by the climate and the food as to have doubts about service in Nigeria. But he was now a hardened coaster, and although the climate still made him irritable and limp, he would not now exchange the life for the comfort of Europe. His strong belief in the value of the British mission in Africa was, strangely enough, strengthened during the Cameroon campaign of 1916 when he fought against the Germans. That was how he had got the title of captain but unlike many other colonial administrators who also saw active service in the Cameroon he carried his into peacetime.

Although the first rain was overdue, when it did come it took people by surprise. Throughout the day the sun had breathed fire as usual and the world had lain prostrate with shock. The birds which sang in the morning were silenced. The air stood in one spot, vibrating with the heat; the trees hung limp. Then without any sign a great wind arose and the sky darkened. Dust and flying leaves filled the air. Palm trees and coconut trees swayed from their waists; their tops gave them the look of giants fleeing against the wind, their long hair streaming behind them.

Winterbottom's servant, John, rushed around closing doors and windows and picking up papers and photographs from the floor. Sharp and dry barks of thunder broke into the tumult. The world which had dozed for months was suddenly full of life again, smelling of new leaves to be born. Winterbottom, at the railing of his veranda, was also a changed man. He let the dust blow into his eyes and for once envied the native children running around naked and singing to the coming rain.

'What are they saying?' he asked John, who was now carrying in the deck chairs.

'Dem talk say make rain come quick quick.'

Four other children ran in from the direction of the Boys' quarters to join the rest on Winterbottom's lawn which was the only space big enough for their play.

'Are all these your pickin, John?' There was something like envy in his voice.

'No, sir,' said John, putting down the chair and pointing. 'My pickin na dat two wey de run yonder and dat yellow gal. Di oder two na Cook im pickin. Di oder one yonder na Gardener him brodder pickin.'

They had to shout to be heard. The sky was now covered with restless, black clouds except at the far horizon where a narrow rim of lightness persisted. Long streaks of lightning cracked the clouds angrily and impatiently only to be wiped off again.

When it began the rain fell like large pebbles. The children intensified their singing as the first frozen drops hit them. Sometimes it was quite painful, but it only made them laugh the more. They scrambled to pick up the frozen drops and throw them into their mouths before they melted.

It rained for almost an hour and stopped clean. The trees were washed green and the leaves fluttered happily. Winterbottom looked at his watch and it was almost six. In the excitement of the year's first rain he had forgotten his tea and biscuits which John had brought in just before five; he picked up a biscuit and began to munch. Then he remembered that Clarke was coming to dinner and went to the kitchen to see what Cook was doing.

Okperi was not a very big station. There were only five Europeans living on Government Hill: Captain Winterbottom, Mr Clarke, Roberts, Wade and Wright. Captain Winterbottom was the District Officer. The Union Jack flying in front of his bungalow declared he was the King's representative in the district. He took the salute on Empire Day at the march past of all the schoolchildren in the area – one of the few occasions when he wore his white uniform and sword. Mr Clarke was his Assistant District Officer. He was only four weeks old in the station, and had come to replace poor John Macmillan, who had died from cerebral malaria.

The other Europeans did not belong to the Administration. Roberts was an Assistant Superintendent of Police in charge of the local detachment. Wade was in charge of the prison; he was also called Assistant Superintendent. The other man, Wright, did not really belong to the station. He was a Public Works Department man supervising the new road to Umuaro. Captain Winterbottom had already had cause to talk to him seriously about his behaviour, especially with native women. It was absolutely imperative, he told him, that every European in Nigeria, particularly those in such a lonely outpost as Okperi, should not lower themselves in the eyes of the natives. In such a place the District Officer was something of a school prefect, and Captain Winterbottom was determined to do his duty. He would go as far as barring Wright from the club unless he showed a marked change.

The club was the old Regimental Mess the army left behind when their work of pacification was done in these parts and then moved on. It was a small wooden bungalow containing the mess room, ante-room, and a veranda. At present the mess room was used as bar and lounge, the ante-room as library where members saw the papers of two or three months ago and read Reuter's telegrams – ten words twice a week.

Tony Clarke was dressed for dinner, although he still had more than an hour to go. Dressing for dinner was very irksome in the heat, but he had been told by many experienced coasters that it was quite imperative. They said it was a general tonic which one must take if one was to survive in this demoralizing country. For to neglect it could become the first step on the slippery gradient of ever profounder repudiations. Today was quite pleasant because the rain had brought some coolness. But there had been days when Tony Clarke had foregone a proper dinner to avoid the torment of a starched shirt and tie. He was now reading the final chapter of *The Pacification of the Primitive Tribes of the Lower Niger*, by George Allen, which Captain Winterbottom had lent him. From time to time he glanced at his gold watch, a present from his father when he left home for service in Nigeria or, as George Allen would have said, to answer the call. He had now had the book for over a fortnight and must finish and take it back this evening. One of the ways in which the tropics were affecting him was the speed of his reading, although in its own right the book was also pretty dull; much too smug for his taste. But he was now finding the last few paragraphs quite stirring. The chapter was headed THE CALL.

> For those seeking but a comfortable living and a quiet occupation Nigeria is closed and will be closed until the earth has lost some of its deadly fertility and until the people live under something like sanitary conditions. But for those in search of a strenuous life, for those who can deal with men as others deal with material, who can grasp great situations, coax events, shape destinies and ride on the crest of the wave of time Nigeria is holding out her hands. For the men who in India have made the Briton the law-maker, the organizer, the engineer of the world this new, old land has great rewards and honourable work. I know we can find the men. Our mothers do not draw us with nervous grip back to the fireside of boyhood, back into the home circle, back to the purposeless sports of middle life; it is our greatest pride that they do – albeit tearfully – send us fearless and erect, to lead the backward races into line. 'Surely we are the people!' Shall it be the Little Englander for whom the Norman fought the Saxon on his field? Was it for him the archers bled at Crecy and Poitiers, or Cromwell drilled his men? Is it only for the desk our youngsters read of Drake and Frobisher, of Nelson, Clive and men like Mungo Park? Is it for the counting-house they learn of Carthage, Greece and Rome? No, no; a thousand times no! The British race will take its place, the British blood will tell. Son after son will leave the Mersey, strong in the will of his parents today, stronger in the deed of his fathers in the past, braving the climate, taking the risks, playing his best in the game of life.

'That's rather good,' said Mr Clarke, and glanced at his watch again. Captain Winterbottom's bungalow was only two minutes' walk away, so there was plenty of time. Before he came to Okperi Clarke had spent two months at Headquarters being broken in, and he would never forget the day he was invited to dinner by His Honour the Lieutenant-Governor. For some curious reason he had imagined that the time was eight o'clock and arrived at Government House on the dot. The glittering Reception Hall was empty and Clarke would have gone into the front garden to wait had not one of the stewards come forward and offered him a drink. He sat uneasily on the edge of a chair with a glass of sherry in his hand, wondering whether he should not even now withdraw into the shade of one of the trees in the garden until the other guests arrived. Then it was too late. Someone was descending the stairs at a run, whistling uninhibitedly. Clarke sprang to his feet. His Honour glowered at him for a brief moment before he came forward to shake hands. Clarke introduced himself and was about to apologize. But HH gave him no chance.

'I was under the impression that dinner was at eight-fifteen.' Just then his aide-de-camp came in and, seeing a guest, looked worried, shook his watch and listened for its ticking.

'Don't worry, John. Come and meet Mr Clarke who came a little early.' He left the two together and went upstairs again. Throughout the dinner he never spoke to Clarke again. Very soon other guests began to arrive. But they were all very senior people and took no interest at all in poor Clarke. Two of them had their wives; the rest including HH were either unmarried or had wisely left their wives at home in England.

The worst moment for Clarke came when HH led his guests into the Dining-Room and Clarke could not find his name anywhere. The rest took no notice; as soon as HH was seated they all took their places. After what looked to Clarke like hours the ADC noticed him and sent one of the stewards to get a chair. Then he must have had second thoughts, for he stood up and offered his own place to Clarke.

Captain Winterbottom was drinking brandy and ginger ale when Tony Clarke arrived.

'It's nice and cool today, thank God.'

'Yes, the first rain was pretty much overdue,' said Captain Winterbottom.

'I had no idea what a tropical storm looked like. It will be cooler now, I suppose.'

'Well, not exactly. It will be fairly cool for a couple of days that's all. You see, the rainy season doesn't really begin until May or even June. Do sit down. Did you enjoy that?'

'Yes, thank you very much. I found it most interesting. Perhaps Mr Allen is a trifle too dogmatic. One could even say a little smug.'

Captain Winterbottom's Small Boy, Boniface, came forward with a silver tray.

'What Massa go drink?'

'I wonder.'

'Why not try some Old Coaster?'

'What's that?'

'Right. That's fine.' For the first time he looked at the Small Boy in his starched white uniform and saw that he was remarkably handsome.

Captain Winterbottom seemed to read his thought.

'He's a fine specimen, isn't he? He's been with me four years. He was a little boy of about thirteen – by my own calculation, they've no idea of years – when I took him on. He was absolutely raw.'

'When you say they've no idea of years . . .'

'They understand seasons, I don't mean that. But ask a man how old he is and he doesn't begin to have an idea.'

The Small Boy came back with the drink.

'Thank you very much,' said Mr Clarke as he took it.

'Yessah.'

Thousands of flying ants swarmed around the tilley lamp on a stand at the far corner. They soon lost their wings and crawled on the floor. Clarke watched them with great interest, and then asked if they stung.

'No, they are quite harmless. They are driven out of the ground by the rain.'

The crawling ones were sometimes hooked up in twos at their tails.

'It was rather interesting what you said about Allen. A little smug, I think you said.'

'That was the impression I had – sometimes. He doesn't allow, for instance, for there being anything of value in native institutions. He might really be one of the missionary people.'

'I see you are one of the progressive ones. When you've been here as long as Allen was and understood the native a little more

354

you might begin to see things in a slightly different light. If you saw, as I did, a man buried alive up to his neck with a piece of roast yam on his head to attract vultures you know . . . Well, never mind. We British are a curious bunch, doing everything half-heartedly. Look at the French. They are not ashamed to teach their culture to backward races under their charge. Their attitude to the native ruler is clear. They say to him: "This land has belonged to you because you have been strong enough to hold it. By the same token it now belongs to us. If you are not satisfied come out and fight us." What do we British do? We flounder from one expedient to its opposite. We do not only promise to secure old savage tyrants on their thrones – or more likely filthy animal skins – we not only do that, but we now go out of our way to invent chiefs where there were none before. They make me sick.' He swallowed what was left in his glass and shouted to Boniface for another glass. 'I wouldn't really mind if this dithering was left to old fossils in Lagos, but when young Political Officers get infected I just give up. If someone is positive we call him smug.'

Mr Clarke admitted that whatever judgement he made was made in ignorance and that he was open to correction.

'Boniface!'

'Yessah.'

'Bring another drink for Mr Clarke.'

'No really I think I've had . . .'

'Nonsense. Dinner won't be ready for another hour at least. Try something else if you prefer. Whisky?' Clarke accepted another brandy with great reluctance.

'That's a very interesting collection of firearms.' Mr Clarke had been desperately searching for a new subject. Then luckily he lit on a collection of quaint-looking guns arranged like trophies near the low window of the living-room. 'Are they native guns?' He had stumbled on a redeeming theme.

Captain Winterbottom was transformed.

'Those guns have a long and interesting history. The people of Okperi and their neighbours, Umuaro, are great enemies. Or they were before I came into the story. A big savage war had broken out between them over a piece of land. This feud was made worse by the fact that Okperi welcomed missionaries and government while Umuaro, on the other hand, has remained backward. It was only in the last four or five years that any kind of impression has been made there. I think I can say with all modesty that this change came about after I had gathered and publicly destroyed all firearms in the place except, of course, this collection here. You will be going there frequently on tour. If you hear anyone talking about Otiji-Egbe, you know they are talking about me. Otiji-Egbe means Breaker of Guns. I am even told that all children born in that year belong to a new age-grade of the Breaking of the Guns.'

'That's most interesting. How far is this other village, Umuaro?' Clarke knew instinctively that the more ignorant he seemed the better.

'Oh, about six miles, not more. But to the native that's a foreign country. Unlike some of the more advanced tribes in Northern Nigeria, and to some extent Western Nigeria, the Ibos never developed any kind of central authority. That's what our headquarters people fail to appreciate.'

'Yes. I see.'

'This war between Umuaro and Okperi began in a rather interesting way. I went into it in considerable detail . . . Boniface! How are you doing, Mr Clarke? Fine? You ought to drink more; it's good for malaria . . . As I was saying, this war started because a man from Umuaro went to visit a friend in Okperi one fine morning and after he'd had one or two gallons of palm wine – it's quite incredible how much of that dreadful stuff they can tuck away – anyhow, this man from Umuaro having drunk his friend's palm wine reached for his *ikenga* and split it in two. I may explain that *ikenga* is the most important fetish in the Ibo man's arsenal, so to speak. It represents his ancestors to whom he must make daily sacrifice. When he dies it is split in two; one half is buried with him and the other half is thrown away. So you can see the implication of what our friend from Umuaro did in splitting the host's fetish. This was, of course, the greatest sacrilege. The outraged host reached for his gun and blew the other fellow's head off. And so a regular war developed between the two villages, until I stepped in. I went into the question of the ownership of the piece of land which was the remote cause of all the unrest and found without any shade of doubt that it belonged to Okperi. I should mention that every witness who testified before me – from both sides without exception – perjured themselves. One thing you must remember in dealing with natives is that like children they are great liars. They don't lie simply to get out of trouble. Sometimes they would spoil a good case by a pointless lie. Only one man – a kind of priest-king in Umuaro – witnessed against his own people. I have not found out what it was, but I think he must have had some pretty fierce tabu working on him. But he was a most impressive figure of a man. He was very light in complexion, almost red. One finds people like that now and again among the Ibos. I have a theory that the Ibos in the distant past assimilated a small non-negroid tribe of the same complexion as the Red Indians.'

Winterbottom stood up. 'Now what about some dinner,' he said.

CHAPTER FOUR

In the five years since the white man broke the guns of Umuaro the enmity between Ezeulu and Nwaka of Umunneora grew and grew until they were at the point which Umuaro people called *kill and take the head*. As was to be expected this enmity spread through their two villages and before long there were several stories of poisoning. From then on few people from the one village would touch palm wine or kola nut which had passed through the hands of a man from the other.

Nwaka was known for speaking his mind; he never paused to bite his words. But many people trembled for him that night in his compound when he had all but threatened Ulu by reminding him of the fate of another deity that failed his people. It was true that the people of Aninta burnt one of their deities and drove away the priest. But it did not follow that Ulu would also allow himself to be bullied and disgraced. Perhaps Nwaka counted on the protection of the personal god of his village. But the elders were not foolish when they said that a man might have Ngwu and still be killed by Ojukwu.

But Nwaka survived his rashness. His head did not ache, nor his belly; and he did not groan in the middle of the night. Perhaps this was the meaning of the recitative he sang at the Idemili festival that year. He had a great Mask which he assumed on this and other important occasions. The Mask was called Ogalanya or Man of Riches, and at every Idemili festival crowds of people from all the villages and their neighbours came to the *ilo* of Umunneora to see this great Mask bedecked with mirrors and rich cloths of many colours.

That year the Mask spoke a monologue full of boast. Some of those who knew the language of ancestral spirits said that Nwaka spoke of his challenge to Ulu.

Folk assembled, listen and hear my words. There is a place, Beyond Knowing, where no man or spirit ventures unless he holds in his right hand his kith and his left hand his kin. But I, Ogalanya, Evil Dog that Warms His Body through the Head, I took neither kith nor kin and yet went to this place.

The flute called him Ogalanya Ajo Mmo, and the big drum replied.

When I got there the first friend I made turned out to be a wizard. I made another friend and found he was a poisoner. I made my third friend and he was a leper. I, Ogalanya, who cuts kpom and pulls waa, I made friends with a leper from whom even a poisoner flees.

The flute and the drum spoke again. Ogalanya danced a few steps to the right and then to the left, turned round sharply and saluted empty air with his matchet.

I returned from my sojourn. Afo passed, Nkwo passed, Eke passed, Oye passed. Afo came round again. I listened, but my head did not ache, my belly did not ache; I did not feel dizzy. Tell me, folk assembled, a man who did this, is his arm strong or not?

The crowd replied: 'His arm is indeed very strong.' The flute and all the drums joined in the reply.

In the five years since these things happened people sometimes ask themselves how a man could defy Ulu and live to boast. It was better to say that it was not Ulu the man taunted; he had not called the god's name. But if it was, where did Nwaka get this power? For when we see a little bird dancing in the middle of the pathway we must know that its drummer is in the nearby bush.

Nwaka's drummer and praise-singer was none other than the priest of Idemili, the personal deity of Umunneora. This man, Ezidemili, was Nwaka's great friend and mentor. It was he who fortified Nwaka and sent him forward. For a long time no one knew this. There were few things happening in Umuaro which

Ezeulu did not know. He knew that the priests of Idemili and Ogwugwu and Eru and Udo had never been happy with their secondary role since the villages got together and made Ulu and put him over the older deities. But he would not have thought that one of them would go so far as to set someone to challenge Ulu. It was only the incident of the sacred python that opened Ezeulu's eyes. But that was later.

The friendship between Nwaka and Ezidemili began in their youth. They were often seen together. Their mothers had told them that they were born within three days of each other, Nwaka being the younger. They were good wrestlers. But in other ways they were very different. Nwaka was tall and of a light skin; Ezidemili was very small and black as charcoal; and yet it was he who had the other like a goat on a lead. Later their lives took different paths, but Nwaka still sought the other's advice before he did any important thing. This was strange because Nwaka was a great man and a great orator who was called Owner of Words by his friends.

It was his friendship with Ezidemili which gradually turned him into Ezeulu's mortal enemy. One of the ways Ezidemili accomplished this was to constantly assert that in the days before Ulu the true leaders of each village had been men of high title like Nwaka.

One day as Nwaka sat with Ezidemili in his *obi* drinking palm wine and talking about the affairs of Umuaro their conversation turned, as it often did, on Ezeulu.

'Has anybody ever asked why the head of the priest of Ulu is removed from the body at death and hung up in the shrine?' asked Ezidemili rather abruptly. It was as though the question having waited for generations to be asked had now broken through by itself. Nwaka had no answer to it. He knew that when an Ezeulu or an Ezidemili died their heads were separated from their body and placed in their shrine. But no one had ever told him why this happened.

'In truth I do not know,' he said.

'I can tell you that even Ezeulu does not know.'

Nwaka emptied the wine in his horn and hit it twice on the floor.

He knew that a great story was coming, but did not want to appear too expectant. He poured himself another hornful.

'It is a good story, but I do not think that I have ever told it to anyone before. I heard it from the mouth of the last Ezidemili just before he died.' He paused and drank a little from his horn. 'This palm wine has water in it. Every boy in Umuaro knows that Ulu was made by our fathers long ago. But Idemili was there at the beginning of things. Nobody made it. Do you know the meaning of Idemili?'

Nwaka shook his head slightly because of the horn at his lips.

'Idemili means Pillar of Water. As the pillar of this house holds the roof so does Idemili hold up the Raincloud in the sky so that it does not fall down. Idemili belongs to the sky and that is why I, the priest, cannot sit on bare earth.'

Nwaka nodded his head . . . Every boy in Umuaro knew that Ezidemili did not sit on bare earth.

'And that is why when I die I am not buried in the earth, because the earth and the sky are two different things. But why is the priest of Ulu buried in the same way? Ulu has no quarrel with earth; when our fathers made it they did not say that his priest should not touch the earth. But the first Ezeulu was an envious man like the present one; it was he himself who asked his people to bury him with the ancient and awesome ritual accorded to the priest of Idemili. Another day when the present priest begins to talk about things he does not know, ask him about this.'

Nwaka nodded again in admiration and fillipped his fingers.

The place where the Christians built their place of worship was not far from Ezeulu's compound. As he sat in his *obi* thinking of the Festival of the Pumpkin Leaves, he heard their bell: *gome, gome, gome, gome, gome*. His mind turned from the festival to the new religion. He was not sure what to make of it. At first he had thought that since the white man had come with great power and conquest it was necessary that some people should learn the ways of his deity. That was why he had agreed to send his son, Oduche, to learn the new ritual. He also wanted him to learn the white man's wisdom, for Ezeulu knew from what he saw of

Wintabota and the stories he heard about his people that the white man was very wise.

But now Ezeulu was becoming afraid that the new religion was like a leper. Allow him a handshake and he wants to embrace. Ezeulu had already spoken strongly to his son who was becoming more strange every day. Perhaps the time had come to bring him out again. But what would happen if, as many oracles prophesied, the white man had come to take over the land and rule? In such a case it would be wise to have a man of your family in his band. As he thought about these things Oduche came out from the inner compound wearing a white singlet and a towel which they had given him in the school. Nwafo came out with him, admiring his singlet. Oduche saluted his father and set out for the mission because it was Sunday morning. The bell continued ringing in its sad monotone.

Nwafo came back to the *obi* and asked his father whether he knew what the bell was saying. Ezeulu shook his head.

'It is saying: Leave your yam, leave your coco-yam and come to church. That is what Oduche says.'

'Yes,' said Ezeulu thoughtfully. 'It tells them to leave their yam and their coco-yam, does it? Then it is singing the song of extermination.'

They were interrupted by loud and confused talking inside the compound, and Nwafo ran out to see what it was. The voices were getting louder and Ezeulu who normally took no interest in women's shouting began to strain his ear. But Nwafo soon rushed back.

'Oduche's box is moving,' he said, out of breath with excitement. The tumult in the compound grew louder. As usual the voice of Ezeulu's daughter, Akueke, stood out above all others.

'What is called "Oduche's box is moving"?' he asked, rising with deliberate slowness to belie his curiosity.

'It is moving about the floor.'

'There is nothing that a man will not hear nowadays.' He went into his inner compound through the door at the back of his *obi*. Nwafo ran past him to the group of excited women outside his mother's hut. Akueke and Matefi did most of the talking. Nwafo's mother, Ugoye, was speechless. Now and again she rubbed her palms together and showed them to the sky.

Akueke turned to Ezeulu as soon as she saw him. 'Father, come and see what we are seeing. This new religion . . .'

'Shut your mouth,' said Ezeulu, who did not want anybody, least of all his own daughter, to continue questioning his wisdom in sending one of his sons to join the new religion.

The wooden box had been brought from the room where Oduche and Nwafo slept and placed in the central room of their mother's hut where people sat during the day.

The box, which was the only one of its kind in Ezeulu's compound, had a lock. Only people of the church had such boxes made for them by the mission carpenter and they were highly valued in Umuaro. Oduche's box was not actually moving; but it seemed to have something inside it struggling to be free. Ezeulu stood before it wondering what to do. Whatever was inside the box became more violent and actually moved the box around. Ezeulu waited for it to calm down a little, bent down and carried the box outside. The women and children scattered in all directions.

'Whether it be bad medicine or good one, I shall see it today,' he said as he carried the box at arm's length like a potent sacrifice. He did not pass through his *obi*, but took the door in the red-earth wall of his compound. His second son, Obika, who had just come in followed him. Nwafo came closely behind Obika, and the women and children followed fearfully at a good distance. Ezeulu looked back and asked Obika to bring him a matchet. He took the box right outside his compound and finally put it down by the side of the common footpath. He looked back and saw Nwafo and the women and children.

'Every one of you go back to the house. The inquisitive monkey gets a bullet in the face.'

They moved back not into the compound but in front of the *obi*. Obika took a matchet to his father who thought for a little while and put the matchet aside and sent him for the spear used in digging up yams. The struggling inside the box was as fierce as ever. For a brief moment Ezeulu wondered whether the wisest thing was not to leave the box there until its owner returned. But what would it mean? That he, Ezeulu, was afraid of whatever power his son had imprisoned in a box. Such a story must never be told of the priest of Ulu.

He took the spear from Obika and wedged its thin end between the box and its lid. Obika tried to take the spear from him, but he would not hear it.

'Stand aside,' he told him. 'What do you think is fighting inside? Two cocks?' He clenched his teeth in an effort to lever the top open. It was not easy and the old priest was covered with sweat by the time he succeeded in forcing the box. What they saw was enough to blind a man. Ezeulu stood speechless. The women and the children who had watched from afar came running down. Ezeulu's neighbour, Anosi, who was passing by branched in, and soon a big crowd had gathered. In the broken box lay an exhausted royal python.

'May the Great Deity forbid,' said Anosi.

'An abomination has happened,' said Akueke.

Matefi said: 'If this is medicine, may it lose its potency.'

Ezeulu let the spear fall from his hand. 'Where is Oduche?' he asked. No one answered. 'I said where is Oduche?' His voice was terrible.

Nwafo said he had gone to church. The sacred python now raised its head above the edge of the box and began to move in its dignified and unhurried way.

'Today I shall kill the boy with my own hands,' said Ezeulu as he picked up the matchet which Obika had brought at first.

'May the Great Deity forbid such a thing,' said Anosi.

'I have said it.'

Oduche's mother began to cry, and the other women joined her. Ezeulu walked slowly back to his *obi* with the matchet. The royal python slid away into the bush.

'What is the profit of crying?' Anosi asked Ugoye. 'Won't you find where your son is and tell him not to return home today?'

'He has spoken the truth, Ugoye,' said Matefi. 'Send him away to your kinsmen. We are fortunate the python is not dead.'

'You are indeed fortunate,' said Anosi to himself as he continued on his way to Umunneora to buy seed-yams from his friend. 'I have already said that what this new religion will bring to Umuaro wears a hat on its head.' As he went he stopped and told anyone he met what Ezeulu's son had done. Before midday the story had reached the ears of Ezidemili whose deity, Idemili, owned the royal python.

It was five years since Ezeulu promised the white man that he would send one of his sons to church. But it was only two years ago that he fulfilled the promise. He wanted to satisfy himself that the white man had not come for a short visit but to build a house and live.

At first Oduche did not want to go to church. But Ezeulu called him to his *obi* and spoke to him as a man would speak to his best friend and the boy went forth with pride in his heart. He had never heard his father speak to anyone as an equal.

'The world is changing,' he had told him. 'I do not like it. But I am like the bird Eneke-nti-oba. When his friends asked him why he was always on the wing he replied: "Men of today have learnt to shoot without missing and so I have learnt to fly without perching." I want one of my sons to join these people and be my eye there. If there is nothing in it you will come back. But if there is something there you will bring home my share. The world is like a Mask dancing. If you want to see it well you do not stand in one place. My spirit tells me that those who do not befriend the white man today will be saying *had we known* tomorrow.'

Oduche's mother, Ugoye, was not happy that her son should be chosen for sacrifice to the white man. She tried to reason with her husband, but he was impatient with her.

'How does it concern you what I do with my sons? You say you do not want Oduche to follow strange ways. Do you not know that in a great man's household there must be people who follow all kinds of strange ways? There must be good people and bad people, honest workers and thieves, peacemakers and destroyers; that is the mark of a great *obi*. In such a place, whatever music you beat on your drum there is somebody who can dance to it.'

If Oduche had any reluctance left after his father had talked to him it was removed as soon as he began to go to church. He found that he could learn very quickly and he began to think of the day when he could speak the language of the white man, just as their teacher, Mr Molokwu, had spoken with Mr Holt when he had visited their church. But there was somebody else who had impressed Oduche even more. His name was Blackett, a West Indian missionary. It was said that this man, although black, had more knowledge than white men. Oduche thought that if he could get one-tenth of Blackett's knowledge he would be a great man in Umuaro.

He made very good progress and was popular with his teacher and members of the church. He was younger than most other converts, being only fifteen or sixteen. The teacher, Mr Molokwu, expected great things of him and was preparing him for baptism when he was transferred to Okperi. The new teacher was a man from the Niger Delta. He spoke the white man's language as if it was his own. His name was John Goodcountry.

Mr Goodcountry told the converts of Umuaro about the early Christians of the Niger Delta who fought the bad customs of their people, destroyed shrines and killed the sacred iguana. He told them of Joshua Hart, his kinsman, who suffered martyrdom in Bonny.

'If we are Christians, we must be ready to die for the faith,' he said. 'You must be ready to kill the python as the people of the rivers killed the iguana. You address the python as Father. It is nothing but a snake, the snake that deceived our first mother, Eve. If you are afraid to kill it do not count yourself a Christian.'

The first Umuaro man to kill and eat a python was Josiah Madu of Umuagu. But the story did not spread outside the little group of Christians, most of whom refused, however, to follow Josiah's example. They were led by Moses Unachukwu, the first and the most famous convert in Umuaro.

Unachukwu was a carpenter, the only one in all those parts. He had learnt the trade under the white missionaries who built the Onitsha Industrial Mission. In his youth he had been conscripted to carry the loads of the soldiers who were sent to destroy Abame as a reprisal for the killing of a white man. What Unachukwu saw during that punitive expedition taught him that the white man was not a thing of fun. And so after his release he did not return to Umuaro but made his way to Onitsha, where he became houseboy to the carpenter-missionary, J. P. Hargreaves. After over ten years' sojourn in a strange land, Unachukwu returned to Umuaro with the group of missionaries who succeeded after two previous failures in planting the new faith among his people. Unachukwu regarded the success of this third missionary effort as due largely to himself. He saw his sojourn in Onitsha as a parallel to that of the Moses of the Old Testament in Egypt.

As the only carpenter in the neighbourhood Moses Unachukwu built almost single-handed the new church in Umuaro. Now he was not only a lay reader but a pastor's warden although Umuaro did not have a pastor as yet, only a catechist. But it showed the great esteem in which Moses Unachukwu was held in the young church. The last catechist, Mr Molokwu, consulted him in whatever he did. Mr Goodcountry, on the other hand, attempted from the very first to ignore him. But Moses was not a man to be ignored lightly.

Mr Goodcountry's teaching about the sacred python gave Moses the first opportunity to challenge him openly. To do this he used not only the Bible but, strangely enough for a convert, the myths of Umuaro. He spoke with great power for, coming as he did from the village which carried the priesthood of Idemili, he knew perhaps more than others what the python was. On the other side, his great knowledge of the Bible and his sojourn in Onitsha which was the source of the new religion gave him confidence. He told the new teacher quite bluntly that neither the Bible nor the catechism asked converts to kill the python, a beast full of ill omen.

'Was it for nothing that God put a curse on its head?' he asked, and then turned abruptly into the traditions of Umuaro. 'Today there are six villages in Umuaro; but this has not always been the case. Our fathers tell us that there were seven before, and the seventh was called Umuama.' Some of the converts nodded their support. Mr Goodcountry listened patiently and contemptuously.

'One day six brothers of Umuama killed the python and asked one of their number, Iweka, to cook yam pottage with it. Each of them brought a piece of yam and a bowl of water to Iweka. When he finished cooking the yam pottage the men came one by one and took their pieces of yam. Then they began to fill their bowls to the mark with the yam stew. But this time only four of them took their measure before the stew got finished.'

Moses Unachukwu's listeners smiled, except Mr Goodcountry vho sat like a rock. Oduche smiled because he had heard the story ıs a little boy and forgotten it until now.

'The brothers began to quarrel violently, and then to fight. Very soon the fighting spread throughout Umuama, and so fierce was it that the village was almost wiped out. The few survivors fled their village, across the great river to the land of Olu where they are scattered today. The remaining six villages seeing what had happened to Umuama went to a seer to know the reason, and he told them that the royal python was sacred to Idemili; it was this deity which had punished Umuama. From that day the six villages decreed that henceforth anyone who killed the python would be regarded as having killed his kinsman.' Moses ended by counting on his fingers the villages and clans which also forbade the killing of the snake. Then Mr Goodcountry spoke.

'A story such as you have just told us is not fit to be heard in the house of God. But I allowed you to go on so that all may see the foolishness of it.' There was murmuring from the congregation which might have stood either for agreement or disagreement.

'I shall leave it to your own people to answer you.' Mr Goodcountry looked round the small congregation, but no one spoke. 'Is there no one here who can speak up for the Lord?'

Oduche who had thus far inclined towards Unachukwu's position had a sudden stab of insight. He raised his hand and was about to put it down again. But Mr Goodcountry had seen him.

'Yes?'

'It is not true that the Bible does not ask us to kill the serpent. Did not God tell Adam to crush its head after it had deceived his wife?' Many people clapped for him.

'Do you hear that, Moses?'

Moses made to answer, but Mr Goodcountry was not going to give him another opportunity.

'You say you are the first Christian in Umuaro, you partake of the Holy Meal; and yet whenever you open your mouth nothing but heathen filth pours out. Today a child who sucks his mother's breast has taught you the Scriptures. Is it not as Our Lord himself said that the first shall become last and the last become first. The world will pass away but not one single word of Our Lord will be set aside.' He turned to Oduche. 'When the time comes for your baptism you will be called Peter; on this rock will I build my Church.'

This caused more clapping from a part of the congregation. Moses was now fully aroused.

'Do I look to you like someone you can put in your bag and walk away?' he asked. 'I have been to the fountainhead of this new religion and seen with my own eyes the white people who brought it. So I want to tell you now that I will not be led astray by outsiders who choose to weep louder than the owners of the corpse. You are not the first teacher I have seen; you are not the second; you are not the third. If you are wise you will face the work they sent you to do here and take your hand off the python. You can say that I told you so. Nobody here has complained to you that the python has ever blocked his way as he came to church. If you want to do your work in peace you will heed what I have said, but if you want to be the lizard that ruined his own mother's funeral you may carry on as you are doing.' He turned to Oduche. 'As for you, they may call you Peter or they may call you Paul or Barnabas; it does not pull a hair from me. I have nothing to say to a mere boy who should be picking palm nuts for his mother. But since you have also become our teacher I shall be waiting for the day when you will have the courage to kill a python in this Umuaro. A coward may cover the ground with his words but when the time comes to fight he runs away.'

At that moment Oduche took his decision. There were two pythons – a big one and a small one – which lived almost entirely in his mother's hut, on top of the wall which carried the roof. They did no harm and kept the rats away; only once were they suspected of frightening away a hen and swallowing her eggs. Oduche decided that he would hit one of them on the head with a big stick. He would do it so carefully and secretly that when it finally died people would think it had died of its own accord.

Six days passed before Oduche found a favourable moment, and during this time his heart lost some of its strength. He decided to take the smaller python. He pushed it down from the wall with his stick but could not bring himself to smash its head. Then he thought he heard people coming and had to act quickly. With lightning speed he picked it up as he had seen their neighbour, Anosi, do many times, and carried it into his sleeping-room. A new and exciting thought came to him then. He opened the box which Moses had built for him, took out his singlet and towel and locked the python inside. He felt a great relief within. The python would die for lack of air, and he would be responsible for its death without being guilty of killing it, which seemed to him a very happy compromise.

Ezeulu's first son, Edogo, had left home early that day to finish the mask he was carving for a new ancestral spirit. It was now only five days to the Festival of the Pumpkin Leaves when this spirit was expected to return from the depths of the earth and appear to men as a Mask. Those who would act as his attendants were making great plans for his coming; they had learnt their dance and were now anxious about the mask Edogo was carving for them. There were other carvers in Umuaro besides him; some of them were even better. But Edogo had a reputation for finishing his work on time unlike Obiako, the master carver, who only took up his tools when he saw his customers coming. If it had been any other kind of carving Edogo would have finished it long ago, working at it any moment his hands were free. But a mask was different; he could not do it in the home under the profane gaze of women and children but had to retire to the spirit-house built for such work at a secluded corner of the Nkwo market place where no one who had not been initiated into the secret of Masks would dare to approach.

The hut was dark inside although the eye got used to it after a short while. Edogo put down the white *okwe* wood on which he was going to work and then unslung his goatskin bag in which he carried his tools. Apart from the need for secrecy, Edogo had always found the atmosphere of this hut right for carving masks. All around him were older masks and other regalia of ancestral spirits, some of them older than even his father. They produced a certain ambience which gave power and cunning to his fingers. Most of the masks were for fierce, aggressive spirits with horns and teeth the size of fingers. But four of them belonged to maiden-spirits and were delicately beautiful. Edogo remembered with a smile what Nwanyinma told him when he first married his wife. Nwanyinma was a widow with whom he had made friends in his bachelor days. In her jealousy against the younger rival she had told Edogo that the only woman whose breasts stayed erect year after year was the maiden-spirit.

Edogo sat down on the floor near the entrance where there was the most light and began to work. Now and again he heard people talking as they passed through the market place from one village of Umuaro to another. But when his carving finally got hold of him he heard no more voices.

The mask was beginning to come out of the wood when Edogo suddenly stopped and turned his ear in the direction of the voices which had broken into his work. One of the voices was very familiar; yes, it was their neighbour, Anosi. Edogo listened very hard and then stood up and went to the wall nearest the market centre. He could now hear quite clearly. Anosi seemed to be talking to two or three other men he had just met.

'Yes. I was there and saw it with my own eyes,' he was saying. 'I would not have believed it had somebody else told me. I saw the box opened and a python inside it.'

'Do not repeat it,' said one of the others. 'It cannot be true.'

'That is what everybody says: it cannot be true. But I saw it with my own eyes. Go to Umuachala now and see the whole village in turmoil.'

'What that man Ezeulu will bring to Umuaro is pregnant and nursing a baby at the same time.'

'I have heard many things, but never till today have I heard of an abomination of this kind.'

By the time Edogo reached home his father was still in a very bad temper, only that now his anger was not so much against Oduche as against all the double-faced neighbours and passers-by whose words of sympathy barely concealed the spitefulness in their hearts. And even if they had been sincere Ezeulu would still have resented anybody making him an object of pity. At first his anger smouldered inwardly. But the last group of women who went in to see his wives, looking like visitors to a place of death, inflamed his wrath. He heard them in the inner compound shouting: 'E-u-u! What shall we do to the children of today?' Ezeulu strode into the compound and ordered them to leave.

'If I see any one of you still here when I go and come back she will know that I am an evil man.'

'What harm have we done in coming to console another woman?'

'I say leave this place at once!'

The women hurried out saying: 'Forgive us; we have erred.'

It was therefore a very irate Ezeulu to whom Edogo told his story of what he had heard at the Nkwo market place. When he finished his father asked him curtly:

'And what did you do when you heard that?'

'What should I have done?' Edogo was surprised and a little angry at his father's tone.

'Don't you hear him?' asked Ezeulu of no one. 'My first son, somebody says to your hearing that your father has committed an abomination, and you ask me what you should have done. When I was your age I would have known what to do. I would have come out and broken the man's head instead of hiding in the spirit-house.'

Edogo was now really angry but he controlled his tongue. 'When you were my age your father did not send one of his sons to worship the white man's god.' He walked away to his own hut full of bitterness for having broken off his carving to come and see what was happening at home, only to be insulted.

'I blame Obika for his fiery temper,' thought Ezeulu, 'but how much better is a fiery temper than this cold ash!' He inclined backwards and rested his head on the wall behind him and began to gnash his teeth.

It was a day of annoyance for the Chief Priest – one of those days when it seemed he had woken up on the left side. As if he had not borne enough vexation already he was now visited, at sunset, by a young man from Umunneora. Because of the hostility between Ezeulu's village and Umunneora he did not offer the man kola nut lest he should have a bellyache later and attribute it to Ezeulu's hospitality. The man did not waste much time before he gave his message.

'I am sent by Ezidemili.'

'True? I trust he is well.'

'He is well,' replied the messenger. 'But at the same time he is not.'

'I do not understand you.' Ezeulu was now very alert. 'If you have a message, deliver it because I have no time to listen to a boy learning to speak in riddles.'

The young man ignored the insult. 'Ezidemili wants to know what you are going to do about the abomination which has been committed in your house.'

'That what happened?' asked the Chief Priest, holding his rage firmly with two hands.

'Should I repeat what I have just said?'

'Yes.'

'All right. Ezidemili wants to know how you intend to purify your house of the abomination that your son committed.'

'Go back and tell Ezidemili to eat shit. Do you hear me? Tell Ezidemili that Ezeulu says he should go and fill his mouth with shit. As for you, young man, you may go in peace because the world is no longer what it was. If the world had been what it was I would have given you something to remind you always of the day you put your head into the mouth of a leopard.' The young man wanted to say something but Ezeulu did not allow him.

'If you want to do something with your life, take my advice and say not another word here.' Ezeulu rose threateningly to his full height; the young man decided to heed his advice and rose to go.

CHAPTER FIVE

Captain T. K. Winterbottom stared at the memorandum before him with irritation and a certain amount of contempt. It came from the Lieutenant-Governor through the Resident through the Senior District Officer to him, the last two adding each his own comment before passing the buck down the line. Captain Winterbottom was particularly angry at the tone of the Senior District Officer's minute. It was virtually a reprimand for what he was pleased to describe as Winterbottom's stonewalling on this issue of the appointment of Paramount Chiefs. Perhaps if this minute had been written by any other person Captain Winterbottom would not have minded so much; but Watkinson had been his junior by three years and had been promoted over him.

'Any fool can be promoted,' Winterbottom always told himself and his assistants, 'provided he does nothing but try. Those of us who have a job to do have no time to try.'

He lit his pipe and began to pace his spacious office. He had designed it himself and had made it open and airy. As he walked up and down he noticed for the first time, although it had always been there, the singing of prisoners, as they cut the grass outside. It was amazing how tall it had grown with the two rainfalls which had come so close together. He went to the window and watched the prisoners for a while. One of them supplied the beat with something that looked like a piece of stone on an empty bottle and sang a short solo; the others sang the chorus and swung their blades to the beat. Captain Winterbottom removed his pipe, placed it on

the window-sill, cupped his hands over his mouth and shouted:
'Shut up there!' They all looked up and saw who it was and
stopped their music. Their blades went up and down haphazardly
thereafter. Then their warder who had been standing under the
shade of a mango tree a little distance away thought it was safest
to take his men to another spot where they would not disturb the
DO. So he marched them off in a ragged double file to another
part of Government Hill. They all wore dirty-white jumpers made
from baft and a skull cap to match. Two of them carried headpans
and the soloist clutched his bottle and stone. As soon as they settled
down in their new place he raised a song and blades swung up and
down to the beat:

> When I cut grass and you cut
> What's your right to call me names?

Back at his desk Captain Winterbottom read the Lieutenant-
Governor's memorandum again:

My purpose in these paragraphs is limited to impressing on all
Political officers working among the tribes who lack Natural
Rulers the vital necessity of developing without any further delay
an effective system of 'indirect rule' based on native institutions.

To many colonial nations native administration means government by white men. You are all aware that HMG considers this
policy as mistaken. In place of the alternative of governing
directly through Administrative Officers there is the other
method of trying while we endeavour to purge the native system
of its abuses to build a higher civilization upon the soundly
rooted native stock that had its foundation in the hearts and
minds and thoughts of the people and therefore on which we
can more easily build, moulding it and establishing it into lines
consonant with modern ideas and higher standards, and yet all
the time enlisting the real force of the spirit of the people, instead
of killing all that out and trying to start afresh. We must not
destroy the African atmosphere, the African mind, the whole
foundation of his race . . .

Words, words, words. Civilization, African mind, African

atmosphere. Has His Honour ever rescued a man buried alive up to his neck, with a piece of roast yam on his head to attract vultures? He began to pace up and down again. But why couldn't someone tell the bloody man that the whole damn thing was stupid and futile. He knew why. They were all afraid of losing their promotion or the OBE.

Mr Clarke walked in to say he was off on his first tour of the district. Captain Winterbottom waved him away with 'Have a good trip' which he said almost without looking at him. But as he turned to go he called him back.

'When you are in Umuaro find out as much as you can – very discreetly of course – about Wright and his new road. I've heard all kinds of ugly stories of whippings and that kind of business. Without prejudging the issue I may say that I wouldn't put anything past Wright, from sleeping with native women to birching their men . . . All right, I'll see you in a week's time. Take care of yourself. Remember, no chances with the water. Have a good trip.'

This short interruption made it possible for Captain Winterbottom to return to the Lieutenant-Governor's memorandum with diminished anger. Instead he now felt tired and resigned. The great tragedy of British colonial administration was that the man on the spot who knew his African and knew what he was talking about found himself being constantly overruled by starry-eyed fellows at headquarters.

Three years ago they had put pressure on Captain Winterbottom to appoint a Warrant Chief for Okperi against his better judgement. After a long palaver he had chosen one James Ikedi, an intelligent fellow who had been among the very first people to receive missionary education in these parts. But what had happened? Within three months of this man receiving his warrant Captain Winterbottom began to hear rumours of his high-handedness. He had set up an illegal court and a private prison. He took any woman who caught his fancy without paying the customary bride-price. Captain Winterbottom went into the whole business thoroughly and uncovered many more serious scandals. He decided to suspend the fellow for six months, and accordingly withdrew his warrant. But after three months the Senior Resident who had just come back from leave and had no firsthand knowledge of the matter ruled that the rascal be reinstated. And no sooner was he back in power than he organized a vast system of mass extortion.

There was at that time a big programme of road and drainage construction following a smallpox epidemic. Chief James Ikedi teamed up with a notorious and drunken road overseer who had earned the title of Destroyer of Compounds from the natives. The plans for the roads and drains had long been completed and approved by Captain Winterbottom himself and as far as possible did not interfere with people's homesteads. But this overseer went around intimidating the villagers and telling them that unless they gave him money the new road would pass through the middle of their compound. When some of them reported the matter to their chief he told them there was nothing he could do; that the overseer was carrying out the orders of the white man and anyone who had no money to give should borrow from his neighbour or sell his goats or yams. The overseer took his toll and moved on to another compound, choosing only the wealthy villagers. And to convince them that he meant business he actually demolished the compounds of three people who were slow in paying, although no road or drain was planned within half a mile of their homes. Needless to say, Chief Ikedi took a big slice of this illegal tax.

Thinking of this incident Captain Winterbottom could find some excuse for the overseer. He was a man from another clan; in the eyes of the native, a foreigner. But what excuse could one offer for a man who was their blood brother and chief? Captain Winterbottom could only put it down to cruelty of a kind which Africa alone produced. It was this elemental cruelty in the psychological make-up of the native that the starry-eyed European found so difficult to understand.

Chief Ikedi was of course a very clever man and when Captain Winterbottom began to investigate this second scandal it was quite impossible to incriminate him; he had covered up his tracks so well. So Captain Winterbottom lost his main quarry, at any rate for the present; he had no doubt however that he would catch him one of these days. As for the overseer he sentenced him to eighteen months' penal servitude.

There was no doubt whatever in the mind of Captain Winterbottom that Chief Ikedi was still corrupt and highhanded, only cleverer than ever before. The latest thing he did was to get his people to make him an *obi* or king, so that he was now called His Highness Ikedi the First, Obi of Okperi. This among a people who abominated kings! This was what British administration was doing among the Ibos, making a dozen mushroom kings grow where there was none before.

Captain Winterbottom slept on the Lieutenant-Governor's memorandum and decided that there was little he could do to stop the stupid trend. He had already sacrificed his chances of promotion by too frequently speaking his mind; practically all the officers who joined the Nigerian Service when he did were now Residents and he was not even a Senior District Officer. Not that he cared particularly, but in this matter of Indirect Rule there did not seem to be any point in continuing his objection when fellows who until now had been one with him in opposition had suddenly swung round to blame him for not implementing it. He was now under orders to find a chief and his duty was clear. But he must not repeat the mistake of looking for some mission-educated smart alec. As far as Umuaro was concerned his mind was practically made up. He would go for that impressive-looking fetish priest who alone of all the witnesses who came before him in the Okperi versus Umuaro land case spoke the truth. Provided of course he was still alive. Captain Winterbottom remembered seeing him again once or twice during his routine visits to Umuaro. But that was at least two years ago.

CHAPTER SIX

The outrage which Ezeulu's son committed against the sacred python was a very serious matter; Ezeulu was the first to admit it. But the ill will of neighbours and especially the impudent message sent him by the priest of Idemili left him no alternative but to hurl defiance at them all. He was full of amazement at the calumny which even people he called his friends were said to be spreading against him.

'It is good for a misfortune like this to happen once in a while,' he said, 'so that we can know the thoughts of our friends and neighbours. Unless the wind blows we do not see the fowl's rump.'

He sent for his wife and asked her where her son was. She stood with her arms folded across her breasts and said nothing. For the past two days she had been full of resentment against her husband because it was he who sent Oduche to the church people in spite of her opposition. Why should he now sharpen his matchet to kill him for doing what they taught him in the church?

'Am I talking to a person or a carved *nkwu*?'

'I don't know where he is.'

'You do not know? *He he he he he he,*' he laughed mechanically and then became very serious again. 'You must be telling me in your mind that a man who brings home ant-infested faggots should not complain if he is visited by lizards. You are right. But do not tell me you don't know where your son is . . .'

'Is he my son now?'

He ignored her question.

'Do not tell me you don't know where he is because it is a lie. You may call him out from where you are hiding him. I have not killed anybody before and I will not start with my son.'

'But he will not go to that church again.'

'That is a lie also. I have said that he will go there and he will go. If anybody does not like it he can come and jump on my back.'

That afternoon Oduche returned, looking like a fowl soaked in the rain. He greeted his father fearfully but he ignored him completely. In the inner compound the women welcomed him without enthusiasm. The little children, especially Obiageli, searched him closely as if to see whether he had altered in any way.

Although Ezeulu did not want anybody to think that he was troubled or to make him appear like an object of pity, he did not ignore the religious implications of Oduche's act. He thought about it seriously on the night of the incident. The custom of Umuaro was well known and he did not require the priest of Idemili to instruct him. Every Umuaro child knows that if a man kills the python inadvertently he must placate Idemili by arranging a funeral for the snake almost as elaborate as a man's funeral. But there was nothing in the custom of Umuaro for the man who puts the snake into a box. Ezeulu was not saying that it was not an offence, but it was not serious enough for the priest of Idemili to send him an insulting message. It was the kind of offence which a man put right between himself and his personal god. And what was more the Festival of the New Pumpkin Leaves would take place in a few days. It was he, Ezeulu, who would then cleanse the six villages of this and countless other sins, before the planting season.

Not very long after Oduche's return Ezeulu was visited by one of his in-laws from Umuogwugwu. This man, Onwuzuligbo, was one of those who came to Ezeulu one year this planting season to find out why their kinsman and husband of Ezeulu's daughter had been beaten and carried away from their village.

'It looks as if my death is near,' said Ezeulu.

'Why is that, in-law? Do I look like death?'

'When a man sees an unfamiliar sight, then perhaps his death is coming.'

'You are right, in-law, it is indeed a long time since I came to see you. But we have a saying that the very thing which kills mother rat prevents its little ones from opening their eyes. If all goes well we hope to come and go again as in-laws should.'

Ezeulu sent his son, Nwafo, to bring a kola nut from his mother. Meanwhile he reached for the little wooden bowl which had a lump of white clay in it.

'Here is a piece of *nzu*,' he said as he rolled the chalk towards his guest, who picked it up and drew on the floor between his legs three erect lines and a fourth lying down under them. Then he painted one of his big toes and rolled the chalk back to Ezeulu who put it away again.

After they had eaten a kola nut Onwuzuligbo cleared his throat and thanked Ezeulu, and then asked:

'Is our wife well?'

'Your wife? She is well. Nothing troubles her except hunger. Nwafo, go and call Akueke to salute her husband's kinsman.'

Nwafo soon returned and said she was coming. Akueke came in almost at once. She saluted her father and shook hands with Onwuzuligbo.

'Is your wife, Ezinma, well?' she asked.

'She is well today. Tomorrow is what we do not know.'

'And her children?'

'We have no trouble except hunger.'

'Aaah!' said Akueke, 'that cannot be true. Look how well fed you are.'

When Akueke went back to the inner compound Onwuzuligbo told Ezeulu that his people had sent him to say that they would like to pay a visit to their in-law on the following morning.

'I shall not run away from my house,' said Ezeulu.

'We shall not bring war to you. We are coming to whisper together like in-law and in-law.'

Ezeulu was grateful for the one happy event in a week of trouble and vexation. He sent for his head wife, Matefi, and told her to get ready to cook for his in-laws tomorrow.

'Which in-laws?' she asked.

'Akueke's husband and his people.'

'There is no cassava in my hut, and today is not a market.'

'So what do you want me to do?' asked Ezeulu.

'I don't want you to do anything. But Akueke may have some cassava if you ask her.'

'This madness which they say you have must now begin to know its bounds. You are telling me to go and find cassava for you. What has Akueke to do with it; is she my wife? I have told you many times that you are a wicked woman. I have noticed that you will not do anything happily unless it is for yourself or your children. Don't let me speak my mind to you today.' He paused. 'If you want this compound to contain the two of us, go and do what I told you. If Akueke's mother were alive she would not draw a line between her children and yours and you know it. Go away from here before I rise to my feet.'

Although Ezeulu was very anxious for his daughter, Akueke, to return to her husband nobody expected him to say so openly. A man who admitted that his daughter was not always welcome in his home or that he found her presence irksome was in effect telling her husband to treat her as roughly as he liked. So when Akueke's husband finally came round to announcing his intention to take his wife home, Ezeulu made a show of objecting.

'It is right for a man to take his wife home,' he said. 'But I want to remind you that when we begin to plant crops it will be one year since she began to live in my compound. Did you bring yams or coco-yams or cassava to feed her and her child? Or do you think that they are still carrying the breakfast they ate in your house last year?'

Ibe and his people made some vague, apologetic noises.

'What I want to know,' said Ezeulu, 'is how you will pay me for taking care of your wife for one year.'

'In-law, I understand you very well,' said Onwuzuligbo. 'Leave everything to us. You know that a man's debt to his father-in-law can never be fully discharged. When we buy a goat or a cow we pay for it and it becomes our own. But when we marry a wife we must go on paying until we die. We do not dispute that we owe you. Our debt is even greater than you say. What about all the years from her birth to the day we took her from you? Indeed we owe you a great debt, but we ask you to give us time.'

'Let me agree with you,' said Ezeulu, 'but I am agreeing in cowardice.'

Besides Ezeulu's two grown-up sons, Edogo and Obika, his younger brother was also present. His name was Okeke Onenyi. He had said very little so far; but now it appeared to him that his brother was yielding too readily and he decided to speak.

'My in-laws, I salute you. I have not said anything because the man who has no gift for speaking says his kinsmen have said all there is to say. Since you began to speak I have been listening very hard to hear one thing from your mouth, but I have not heard it. Different people have different reasons for marrying. Apart from children which we all want, some men want a woman to cook their meals, some want a woman to help on the farm, others want someone they can beat. What I want to learn from your mouth is whether our in-law has come because he has no one to beat when he wakes up in the morning nowadays.'

Onwuzuligbo promised on behalf of his kinsman that Akueke would not be beaten in future. Then Ezeulu sent for her to find out whether she wanted to return to her husband. She hesitated and then said she would go if her father was satisfied.

'My in-laws, I salute you,' said Ezeulu. 'Akueke will return but not today. She will need a little time to get ready. Today is Oye; she will come back to you on the Oye after next. When she comes, treat her well. It is not bravery for a man to beat his wife. I know a man and his wife must quarrel; there is no abomination in that. Even brothers and sisters from the same womb do disagree; how much more two strangers. No, you may quarrel, but let it not end in fighting. I shall say no more at present.'

Ezeulu was grateful to Ulu for bringing about so unexpectedly the mending of the quarrel between Akueke and her husband. He was sure that Ulu did it to put him in the right mind for purifying the six villages before they put their crops into the ground. That very evening his six assistants came to him for their orders and he sent them to announce each man in his own village that the Feast of the Pumpkin Leaves would take place on the following Nkwo.

Ugoye was still cooking supper when the crier's *ogene* sounded. Ugoye was notorious for her late cooking. Although Ezeulu often rebuked Matefi for cooking late Ugoye deserved the rebuke even more. But she was wiser than the senior wife; she never cooked late on the days she sent food to her husband. But on all other days her pestle would be heard far into the night. She was particularly slack when, as now, she was forbidden to cook for any grown man on account of her uncleanness.

Her daughter, Obiageli, and Akueke's daughter, Nkechi, were telling each other stories. Nwafo sat on the small mud-seat at the foot of the hut's central pillar watching them with a superior air and pointing out now and again their mistakes.

Ugoye stirred the soup on the fire and tasted it by running her tongue on the back of the ladle. The sound of the *ogene* caught her in the action.

'Keep quiet, you children, and let me hear what they are saying.'

Gome, gome, gome, gome. 'Ora Obodo, listen! Ezeulu has asked me to announce that the Festival of the Pumpkin Leaves will take place on the coming Nkwo.' *Gome, gome, gome, gome.* 'Ora Obodo! Ezeulu has asked me . . .'

Obiageli had broken off her story so that her mother could hear the crier's message. While she waited impatiently her eyes fell on the soup ladle and, to occupy herself, she picked it up from the wooden bowl where it lay and proceeded to lick it dry.

'Glutton,' said Nwafo. 'It is this lick lick lick which prevents woman from growing a beard.'

'And where, big man, is your beard?' asked Obiageli.

Gome, gome, gome, gome. 'Folks of the village. The Chief Priest of Ulu has asked me to tell every man and every woman that the Festival of the First Pumpkin Leaves will be held on the coming Nkwo market day.' *Gome, gome, gome, gome.*

The crier's voice was already becoming faint as he took his message down the main pathway of Umuachala.

'Shall we go back to the beginning?' asked Nkechi.

'Yes,' said Obiageli. 'The big ukwa fruit has fallen on Nwaka Dimkpolo and killed him. I shall sing the story and you reply.'

'But I was replying before,' protested Nkechi, 'it is now my turn to sing.'

'You are going to spoil everything now. You know we did not complete the story before the crier came.'

'Do not agree, Nkechi,' said Nwafo. 'She wants to cheat you because she is bigger than you are.'

'Nobody has called your name in this, ant-hill nose.'

'You are asking for a cry.'

'Don't listen to him, Nkechi. After this it will be your turn to sing and I shall reply.' Nkechi agreed and Obiageli began to sing again:

> And who will punish this Water for me?
> *E-e Nwaka Dimkpolo*
> Earth will dry up this water for me
> *E-e Nwaka Dimkpolo*
> Who will punish this Earth for me? . . .

'No, no, no,' Nkechi broke in.

'What can happen to Earth, silly girl?' asked Nwafo.

'I said it on purpose to test Nkechi,' said Obiageli.

'It is a lie, as old as you are you can't even tell a simple story.'

'If it pains you, come and jump on my back, ant-hill nose.'

'Mother, if Obiageli abuses me again I shall beat her.'

'Touch her if you dare and I shall cure you of your madness this night.'

'Let us change to another story,' said Obiageli. 'This one has no end.' At the same time she reached for the ladle which had just returned from another visit to the soup pot on the fire. But her mother snatched it from her.

CHAPTER SEVEN

The market place was filling up steadily with men and women from every quarter. Because it was specially their day, the women wore their finest cloths and ornaments of ivory and beads according to the wealth of their husbands or, in a few exceptional cases, the strength of their own arms. Most of the men brought palm wine in pots carried on the head or gourds dangling by the side from a loop of rope. The first people to arrive took up positions under the shade of trees and began to drink with their friends, their relations and their in-laws. Those who came after sat in the open which was not hot yet.

A stranger to this year's festival might go away thinking that Umuaro had never been more united in all its history. In the atmosphere of the present gathering the great hostility between Umunneora and Umuachala seemed, momentarily, to lack significance. Yesterday if two men from the two villages had met they would have watched each other's movement with caution and suspicion; tomorrow they would do so again. But today they drank palm wine freely together because no man in his right mind would carry poison to a ceremony of purification; he might as well go out into the rain carrying potent, destructive medicines on his person.

Ezeulu's younger wife examined her hair in a mirror held between her thighs. She could not help feeling that she did a better job of Akueke's hair than Akueke did on hers. But she was very pleased with the black patterns of *uli* and faint yellow lines of *ogalu* on her body. In previous years she would have been among the first to

arrive at the market-place; she would have been carefree and joyful.
But this year her feet seemed to drag because of the load on her
mind. She was going to pray for the cleansing of her hut which
Oduche had defiled. She was no longer one of many, many Umuaro
women taking part in a general and all-embracing rite. Today she
stood in special need. The weight of this feeling all but crushed
the long-awaited pleasure of wearing her new ivory bracelets which
had earned her so much envy and hostility from her husband's other
wife, Matefi.

She was still polishing the ivory when Matefi set out for the Nkwo
market place. Before she went she called out from the middle of
the compound:

'Is Obiageli's mother ready?'

'No. We shall be following. You need not wait.'

When she was fully prepared Ugoye went behind her hut to the
pumpkin which she specially planted after the first rain and cut
four leaves, tied them together with banana string and returned
to her hut. She put the leaves down on a stool and went to the
bamboo shelf to examine the soup pot and the foo-foo which
Obiageli and Nwafo would eat at midday.

Akueke stopped at the threshold and peeped into Ugoye's hut.

'So you are not ready to go yet? What are you fussing about like
a hen in search of a nest?' she asked. 'At this rate we shall find
nowhere to stand at the market-place.' Then she came into the hut
carrying her own bunch of pumpkin leaves. They admired each
other's cloths and Akueke praised Ugoye's ivory once again.

As soon as they set out Akueke asked:

'What do you think was Matefi's annoyance this morning?'

'I should ask you; is she not your father's wife?'

'Her face was as big as a mortar. Did she ask if you were ready
to go?'

'She did; but it went no deeper than the lips.'

'In all the time I have come across bad people,' said Akueke,
'I have not yet met anyone like her. Her own badness whistles.
Since my father asked her to cook for my husband and his people
the day before yesterday her belly has been full of bile.'

On ordinary Nkwo days the voice of the market carried far in all directions like the approach of a great wind. Today it was as though all the bees in the world were passing overhead. And people were still flowing in from all the pathways of Umuaro. As soon as they emerged from their compound Ugoye and Akueke joined one such stream. Every woman of Umuaro had a bunch of pumpkin leaves in her right hand; any woman who had none was a stranger from the neighbouring villages coming to see the spectacle. As they approached Nkwo its voice grew bigger and bigger until it drowned their conversation.

They were just in time to see the arrival of the five wives of Nwaka and the big stir they caused. Each of them wore not anklets but two enormous rollers of ivory reaching from the ankle almost to the knee. Their walk was perforce slow and deliberate, like the walk of an Ijele Mask lifting and lowering each foot with weighty ceremony. On top of all this the women were clad in many coloured velvets. Ivory and velvets were not new in Umuaro but never before had they been seen in such profusion from the house of one man.

Obika and his good friend, Ofoedu, sat with three other young men from Umuagu on the crude mat woven on the ground by exposed roots of an *ogbu* tree. In their midst stood two black pots of palm wine. Just outside their circle one empty pot lay on its side. One of the men was already drunk, but neither Obika nor Ofoedu appeared to have drunk a drop yet.

'Is it true, Obika,' asked one of the men, 'that your new bride has not returned after her first visit?'

'Yes, my friend,' Obika replied light-heartedly. 'My things always turn our differently from other people's. If I drink water it sticks between my teeth.'

'Do not heed him,' said Ofoedu. 'Her mother is ill and her father asked if she could stay back and look after her for a while.'

'Aha, I knew the story I heard could not be true. How could a young bride hesitate over a handsome *ugonachomma* like Obika?'

'Ah, my friend, come out from that,' said the half-drunk man. 'She may not like the size of his penis.'

'But she has never seen it,' said Obika.

'You are talking to small boys of yesterday: She has not seen it!'

Soon after, the great Ikolo sounded. It called the six villages of
Umuaro one by one in their ancient order: Umunneora, Umuagu,
Umuezeani, Umuogwugwu, Umuisiuzo and Umuachala. As it
called each village an enormous shout went up in the market-place.
It went through the number again but this time starting from the
youngest. People began to hurry through their drinking before the
arrival of the Chief Priest.

The Ikolo now beat unceasingly; sometimes it called names of
important people of Umuaro, like Nwaka, Nwsosisi, Igboneme and
Uduezue. But most of the time it called the villages and their deities.
Finally it settled down to saluting Ulu, the deity of all Umuaro.

Obiozo Ezikolo was now an old man, but his mastery of the king
of all drums was still unrivalled. Many years ago when he was still
a young man the six villages had decided to confer the *ozo* title on
him for his great art which stirred the hearts of his kinsmen so
powerfully in times of war. Now in his old age it was a marvel where
he got the strength to work as he did. Even climbing on to the
Ikolo was a great feat for a man half his age. Now those who were
near enough surrounded the drum and looked upwards to admire
the ancient drummer. A man well known to him raised his voice
and saluted him. He shouted back: 'An old woman is never old
when it comes to the dance she knows.' The crowd laughed.

The Ikolo was fashioned in the olden days from a giant iroko
tree at the very spot where it was felled. The Ikolo was as old as
Ulu himself at whose order the tree was cut down and its trunk
hollowed out into a drum. Since those days it had lain on the same
spot in the sun and in the rain. Its body was carved with men and
pythons and little steps were cut on one side; without these the
drummer could not climb to the top to beat it. When the Ikolo
was beaten for war it was decorated with skulls won in past wars.
But now it sang of peace.

A big *ogene* sounded three times from Ulu's shrine. The Ikolo
took it up and sustained an endless flow of praises to the deity.
At the same time Ezeulu's messengers began to clear the centre
of the market-place. Although they were each armed with a whip

of palm frond they had a difficult time. The crowd was excited and it was only after a struggle that the messengers succeeded in clearing a small space in the heart of the market-place, from which they worked furiously with their whips until they had forced all the people back to form a thick ring at the edges. The women with their pumpkin leaves caused the greatest difficulty because they all struggled to secure positions in front. The men had no need to be so near and so they formed the outside of the ring.

The *ogene* sounded again. The Ikolo began to salute the Chief Priest. The women waved their leaves from side to side across their faces, muttering prayers to Ulu, the god that kills and saves.

Ezeulu's appearance was greeted with a loud shout that must have been heard in all the neighbouring villages. He ran forward, halted abruptly and faced the Ikolo. 'Speak on,' he said to it, 'Ezeulu hears what you say.' Then he stooped and danced three or four steps and rose again.

He wore smoked raffia which descended from his waist to the knee. The left half of his body – from forehead to toes – was painted with white chalk. Around his head was a leather band from which an eagle's feather pointed backwards. In his right hand he carried *Nne Ofo*, the mother of all staffs of authority in Umuaro, and in his left he held a long iron staff which kept up a quivering rattle whenever he stuck its pointed end into the earth. He took a few long strides, pausing on each foot. Then he ran forward again as though he had seen a comrade in the vacant air; he stretched his arm and waved his staff to the right and to the left. And those who were near enough heard the knocking together of Ezeulu's staff and another which no one saw. At this many fled in terror before the priest and the unseen presences around him.

As he approached the centre of the market place Ezeulu reenacted the First Coming of Ulu and how each of the four Days put obstacles in his way.

> At that time, when lizards were still in ones and twos, the whole people assembled and chose me to carry their new deity. I said to them:
> 'Who am I to carry this fire on my bare head? A man who knows that his anus is small does not swallow an udala seed.'
> They said to me:

'*Fear not. The man who sends a child to catch a shrew will also give him water to wash his hand.*'

I said: '*So be it.*'

And we set to work. That day was Eke: we worked into Oye and then into Afo. As day broke on Nkwo and the sun carried its sacrifice I carried my Alusi and, with all the people behind me, set out on that journey. A man sang with the flute on my right and another replied on my left. From behind the heavy tread of all the people gave me strength. And then all of a sudden something spread itself across my face. On one side it was raining, on the other side it was dry. I looked again and saw that it was Eke.

I said to him: '*Is it you Eke?*'

He replied: '*It is I, Eke, the One that makes a strong man bite the earth with his teeth.*'

I took a hen's egg and gave him. He took it and ate and gave way to me. We went on, past streams and forests. Then a smoking thicket crossed my path, and two men were wrestling on their heads. My followers looked once and took to their heels. I looked again and saw that it was Oye.

I said to him: '*Is it you Oye across my path?*'

He said: '*It is I, Oye, the One that began cooking before Another and so has more broken pots.*'

I took a white cock and gave him. He took it and made way for me. I went on past farmlands and wilds and then I saw that my head was too heavy for me. I looked steadily and saw that it was Afo.

I said: '*Is it you Afo?*'

He said: '*It is I, Afo, the great river that cannot be salted.*'

I replied: '*I am Ezeulu, the hunchback more terrible than a leper.*'

Afo shrugged and said: '*Pass, your own is worse than mine.*'

I passed and the sun came down and beat me and the rain came down and drenched me. Then I met Nkwo. I looked on his left and saw an old woman, tired, dancing strange steps on the hill. I looked to the right and saw a horse and saw a ram. I slew the horse and with the ram I cleaned my matchet, and so removed that evil.

By now Ezeulu was in the centre of the market-place. He struck the metal staff into the earth and left it quivering while he danced a few more steps to the *Ikolo* which had not paused for breath since the priest emerged. All the women waved their pumpkin leaves in front of them.

Ezeulu looked round again at all the men and women of Umuaro, but saw no one in particular. Then he pulled the staff out of the ground, and with it in his left hand and the *Mother of Ofo* in his right he jumped forward and began to run round the market-place.

All the women set up a long, excited ululation and there was renewed jostling for the front line. As the fleeing Chief Priest reached any section of the crowd the women there waved their leaves round their heads and flung them at him. It was as though thousands and thousands of giant, flying insects swarmed upon him.

Ugoye who had pushed and shoved until she got to the front murmured her prayer over and over again as the Chief Priest approached the part of the circle where she stood:

> *Great Ulu who kills and saves, I implore you to cleanse my household of all defilement. If I have spoken it with my mouth or seen it with my eyes, or if I have heard it with my ears or stepped on it with my foot or if it has come through my children or my friends or kinsfolk let it follow these leaves.*

She waved the small bunch in a circle round her head and flung it with all her power at the Chief Priest as he ran past her position.

The six messengers followed closely behind the priest and, at intervals, one of them bent down quickly and picked up at random one bunch of leaves and continued running. The Ikolo drum worked itself into a frenzy during the Chief Priest's flight especially its final stages when he, having completed the full circle of the market-place, ran on with increasing speed into the sanctuary of his shrine, his messengers at his heels. As soon as they disappeared the Ikolo broke off its beating abruptly with one last *kome*. The mounting tension which had gripped the entire market place and seemed to send its breath going up, up and up exploded with this last beat of the drum and released a vast and deep breathing down. But the moment of relief was very short-lived. The crowd seemed to rouse itself quickly to the knowledge that their Chief Priest was safe in his shrine, triumphant over the sins of Umuaro which he was now burying deep into the earth with the six bunches of leaves.

As if someone had given them a sign, all the women of

Umunneora broke out from the circle and began to run round the market place, stamping their feet heavily. At the beginning it was haphazard but soon everyone was stamping together in unison and a vast cloud of dust rose from their feet. Only those whose feet were weighed down by age or by ivory were out of step. When they had gone round they rejoined the standing crowd. Then the women of Umuagu burst through from every part of the huge circle to begin their own run. The others waited and clapped for them; no one ran out of turn. By the time the women of the sixth village ran their race the pumpkin leaves that had lain so thickly all around were smashed and trodden into the dust.

As soon as the running was over the crowd began to break up once more into little groups of friends and relations. Akueke sought out her elder sister, Adeze, whom she had last seen running with the other women of Umuezeani. She did not search very far because Adeze stood out in any crowd. She was tall and bronze-skinned; if she had been a man she would have resembled her father even more than Obika. 'I thought perhaps you had gone home,' said Adeze. 'I saw Matefi just now but she had not seen you at all.'

'How could she see me? I'm not big enough for her to see.'

'Are you two quarrelling again? I thought I saw it on her face. What have you done to her this time?'

'My sister, leave Matefi and her trouble aside and let us talk about better things.'

At that point Ugoye joined them.

'I have been looking for you two all over the market-place,' she said. She embraced Adeze whom she called *Mother of my Husband*.

'How are the children?' asked Adeze. 'Is it true you have been teaching them to eat python?'

'You think it is something for making people laugh?' Ugoye sounded very hurt. 'No wonder you are the only person in Umuaro who did not care to come and ask what was happening.'

'Was anything happening? Nobody told me. Was it a fire or did someone die?'

'Do not mind Adeze, Ugoye,' said her sister, 'she is worse than her father.'

'Did you expect what the leopard sired to be different from the leopard?'

No one replied.

'Do not be angry with me, Ugoye. I heard everything. But our enemies and those jealous of us were waiting to see us running up and down in confusion. It is not Adeze will give them that satisfaction. That mad woman, Akueni Nwosisi, whose family has committed every abomination in Umuaro came running to me to show her pity. I asked her whether someone who put a python in a box was not to be preferred to her kinsman caught behind the house copulating with a she-goat.'

Ugoke and Akueke laughed. They could clearly visualize their aggressive sister putting this question.

'You are coming with us?' asked Akueke.

'Yes, I must see the children. And perhaps I shall exact a fine or two from Ugoye and Matefi; I fear they look after my father half-heartedly.'

'Please, husband, I implore you,' cried Ugoye in mock fear. 'I do my best. It is your father who ill-treats me. And when you talk to him,' she added seriously, 'ask him why at his age he must run like an antelope. Last year he could not get up for days after the ceremony.'

'Don't you know,' asked Akueke looking furtively back to see if a man was near; there was no one; even so she lowered her voice, 'Don't you know that in his younger days he used to run as Ogbazulobodo? As Obika does now.

'It is you people, especially the two of you, who lead him astray. He likes to think that he is stronger than any young man of today and you people encourage him. If he were my father I would let him know the truth.'

'Is he not your husband?' asked Adeze. 'If he dies tomorrow are you not the one to sit in ashes in the cooking-place for seven markets? Is it you or me will wear sackcloth for one year?'

'What am I telling you?' asked Akueke, changing the subject. 'My husband and his people came the other day.'

'What did they come for?'

'What else would they come for?'

'So they are tired of waiting, small beasts of the bush. I thought they were waiting for you to take palm wine to beg them.'

'Don't abuse my husband's people, or we shall fight,' said Akueke pretending anger.

'Please forgive me. I did not know that you and he had suddenly become palm oil and salt again. When are you going back to him?'

'One market come next Oye.'

CHAPTER EIGHT

The new road which Mr Wright was building to connect Okperi with its enemy, Umuaro, had now reached its final stages. Even so it would not be finished before the onset of the rainy season if it was left to the paid gang he was using. He had thought of increasing the size of this gang but Captain Winterbottom had told him that far from authorizing any increase he was at that very moment considering a retrenchment as the Vote for Capital Works for the financial year was already largely overspent. Mr Wright had then toyed with the idea of reducing the labourers' pay from threepence a day to something like twopence. But this would not have increased the labour force substantially; not even halving their pay would have achieved the desired results, even if Mr Wright could have found it in his heart to treat the men so meanly. In fact he had got very much attached to this gang and knew their leaders by name now. Many of them were, of course, bone lazy and could only respond to severe handling. But once you got used to them they could be quite amusing. They were as loyal as pet dogs and their ability to improvise songs was incredible. As soon as they were signed on the first day and told how much they would be paid they devised a work song. Their leader sang: '*Lebula toro toro*' and all the others replied: '*A day*', at the same time swinging their matchets or wielding their hoes. It was a most effective work-song and they sang it for many days:

Lebula toro toro
A day
Lebula toro toro
A day

And they sang it in English too!

Anyhow there was only one alternative left to Mr Wright if he was to complete the road before June and get away from this hole of a place. He had to use unpaid labour. He asked for permission to do this, and after due consideration Captain Winterbottom gave his approval. In the letter conveying it he pointed out that it was the policy of the Administration to resort to this method only in the most exceptional circumstances . . . 'The natives cannot be an exception to the aphorism that the labourer is worthy of his hire.'

Mr Wright who had come to Government Hill from his PWD Road Camp about five miles away to get this reply, glanced through it, crumpled it and put it in the pocket of his khaki shorts. Like all practical types he had little respect for administrative red tape.

When the leaders of Umuaro were told to provide the necessary labour for the white man's new, wide road they held a meeting and decided to offer the services of the two latest age groups to be admitted into full manhood: the age group that called itself Otakagu, and the one below it which was nicknamed Omumawa.

These two groups never got on well together. They were, like two successive brothers, always quarrelling. In fact it was said that the elder group who, when they came of age, took the name Devourer Like Leopard were so contemptuous of their younger brothers when they came of age two years later that they nicknamed them Omumawa, meaning that the man's cloth they tied between the legs was a feint to cover small boys' penes. It was a good joke, and so overpowered the attempt of the new group to take a more befitting name. For this reason they nursed a grudge against Otakagu, and a meeting of the two was often like the meeting of fire and gunpowder. Whenever they could, therefore, they went by separate ways; as in the case of the white man's new road. All that Mr Wright asked for was two days in the week, and so the two age-groups arranged to work separately on alternate Eke days. On these occasions the white man came over from the paid gang which he had turned into an orderly and fairly skilled force to supervize the free but undisciplined crowd from Umuaro.

Because of his familiarity with the white man's language the carpenter, Moses Unachukwu, although very much older than the two age-groups, had come forward to organize them and to take words out of the white man's mouth for them. At first Mr Wright was inclined to distrust him, as he distrusted all uppity natives but he soon found him very useful and was now even considering giving him some little reward when the road was finished. Meanwhile Unachukwu's reputation in Umuaro rose to unprecedented heights. It was one thing to claim to speak the white man's tongue and quite another to be seen actually doing it. The story spread throughout the six villages. Ezeulu's one regret was that a man of Umunneora should have this prestige. But soon, he thought, his son would earn the same or greater honour.

It was the turn of the Otakagu age group to work on the new road on the day following the Festival of the Pumpkin Leaves. Ezeulu's second son, Obika, and his friend, Ofoedu, belonged to this group. But they had drunk so much palm wine on the day before that when all the other people went to work they were still asleep. Obika who had staggered home almost at cock-crow defied the combined effort of his mother and sister to rouse him.

It had happened on the festival day that as Obika and Ofoedu drank with the three men at the market-place, one of the men had thrown a challenge to them. The conversation had turned on the amount of palm wine a good drinker could take without losing knowledge of himself.

'It all depends on the palm tree and the tapper,' said one of the men.

'Yes,' agreed his friend, Maduka. 'It depends on the tree and the man who taps it.'

'That is not so. It depends on the man who drinks. You may bring any tree in Umuaro and any tapper,' said Ofoedu, 'and I shall still drink my bellyful and go home with clear eyes.'

Obika agreed with his friend. 'It is true that some trees are stronger than others and some tappers are better than others, but a good drinker will defeat them both.'

'Have you heard of the palm tree in my village which they call Okposalebo?'

Obika and Ofoedu said no.

'Anyone who has not heard of Okposalebo and yet claims to be a good drinker deceives himself.'

'What Maduka says is very true,' said one of the others. 'The wine from this tree is never sold in the market, and no one can drink three hornfuls and still know his way home.'

'This Okposalebo is a very old tree. It is called *Disperser of a Kindred* because two brothers would fight like strangers after drinking two hornfuls of its wine.'

'Tell us another story,' Obika said, filling his horn. 'If the tapper adds medicine to his wine that is another matter, but if you are telling us of the fluid as the tree yields it, then I say tell us another story.'

Then Maduka threw the challenge. 'It is not profitable to speak too many words. The palm tree is not in the distant riverain country, but here in Umuaro. Let us go from here to Nwokafo's compound and ask him to give us a gourd from this tree. It is very costly – the gourd may be *ego-nese* – but I shall pay. If you two drink three hornfuls each and still go home let it be my loss. But if not you must give me *ego-neli* whenever you come to your senses again.'

It was as Maduka had said. The two boasters had fallen asleep where they sat, and when night came he left them there and retired to his bed. But he came out twice in the night and found them still snoring. When he woke up finally in the morning, they were gone. He wished he had seen them depart. Perhaps when they heard their betters talking about palm wine in future they would not open their mouths so wide.

Ofoedu did not seem to have fared as badly as Obika. When he woke up and found that the sun was already shining he rushed to Ezeulu's compound to call Obika. But although they shouted his name and shook him he showed no sign of stirring. Eventually Ofoedu poured a gourd of cold water over him and he woke up. The two then set out to join their age-group working on the new road. They were like a pair of Night Masks caught abroad by daylight.

Ezeulu who lay in his *obi* prostrate from the exhaustion of the
festival was wakened by all the commotion in the inner compound.
He asked Nwafo the meaning of all the noise and was told that
they were trying to rouse Obika. He said nothing more, only
gnashed his teeth. The young man's behaviour was like a heavy
load on his father's head. In a few days, Ezeulu said within himself,
Obika's new bride would arrive. She would have come already if
her mother had not fallen sick. When she arrived what a husband
she would find! A man who could not watch his hut at night because
he was dead with palm wine. Where did the manhood of such a
husband lie? A man who could not protect his wife if night
marauders knocked at his door. A man who was roused in the
morning by the women. *Tufia!* spat the old priest. He could not
contain his disgust.

Although Ezeulu did not ask for details he knew without being
told that Ofoedu was behind this latest episode. He had said it over
and over again that this fellow Ofoedu did not contain the smallest
drop of human presence inside his entire body. It was hardly two
years since he sent everybody running to his father's compound
in a false fire alarm for which his father, who was not a rich man,
paid a fine of one goat. Ezeulu had told Obika again and again that
such a person was not a fit friend for anyone who wanted to do
something with his life. But he had not heeded and today there
was as little to choose between them as between rotten palm nuts
and a broken mortar.

When the two friends first set out to join their age group they
walked in silence. Obika felt an emptiness on top as if his head
had been numbed by a whole night's fall of dew. But the walking
was already doing him some good; the feeling was returning that
the head belonged to him.

After one more turning on the narrow, ancient footpath they saw,
a little distance ahead of them, a vast opening which was the
beginning of the new road. It opened like day after a thick night.

'What do you think of that thing Maduka gave us?' asked Ofoedu.
This was the first mention either of them made to the incident of
the previous day. Obika did not reply. He merely produced a sound
which lay half-way between a sigh of relief and a groan.

'It was not naked palm wine,' said Ofoedu. 'They put some potent herbs in it. When I think of it now we were very foolish to have followed such a dangerous man to his own house. Do you remember that he did not drink even one hornful.'

Obika still said nothing.

'I shall not pay the *ego-neli* to him.'

'Were you thinking at any time that you would pay?' Obika looked surprised. 'I regard anything we said yesterday as words spoken in honour of palm wine.'

They were now on the portion of the new road that had been built. It made one feel lost like a grain of maize in an empty goatskin bag. Obika changed his matchet from the left hand to the right and his hoe from right to left. The feeling of openness and exposure made him alert.

As the new road did not point in the direction of a stream or a market Ofoedu and Obika did not encounter many villagers, only a few women now and again carrying heavy loads of firewood.

'What is that I am hearing?' asked Obika. They were now approaching the old, ragged *egbu* tree from which the night spirits called Onyekulum began their journey loaded with song and gossip in the carefree season after the harvest.

'I was just about to ask you. It sounds like a funeral song.'

As they drew nearer to the work site there was no longer any doubt. It was indeed the dirge with which a corpse was taken into the burial forest:

> Look! a python!
> Look! a python!
> Yes, it lies across the way.

The two men recognized it now and also recognized the singers as men of their age group. They burst out laughing together. Someone had given the ancient song a new and irreverent twist and changed it into a half familiar, half strange and hilarious work-song. Ofoedu was certain that he saw the hand of Nweke Ukpaka in it, it was the kind of malicious humour he had.

The approach of Obika and his friend brought about a sudden change among the workers. Their singing stopped and with it the sound of scores of matchets cutting together into tree trunks. Those who bent forward with hoes to level the cleared parts stopped and straightened up, their feet still planted wide apart, covered with red earth.

Nweke Ukpaka raised his voice and shouted: '*Kwo Kwo Kwo Kwo Kwo!*' All the men replied: '*Kwooooh oh!*' and everyone burst out laughing at this imitation of women acknowledging a present.

Mr Wright's irritation mounted dangerously. He clutched the whip in his right hand more firmly and planted the other hand menacingly on his hip. His white helmet made him look even more squat than he was. Moses Unachukwu was talking excitedly to him, but he did not seem to be listening. He stared unwaveringly at the two approaching late-comers and his eyes seemed to Moses to get smaller and smaller. The others wondered what was going to happen. Although the white man always carried a whip he had rarely used it; and when he had done he had appeared to be half joking. But this morning he must have got out of bed from the left side. His face smoked with anger.

Noticing the man's posture Obika put more swagger into his walk. This brought more laughter from the men. He made to pass Mr Wright who, unable to control his anger any more, lashed out violently with his whip. It flashed again and this time caught Obika around the ear, and stung him into fury. He dropped his matchet and hoe and charged. But Moses Unachukwu had thrown himself between the two men. At the same time Mr Wright's two assistants jumped in quickly and held Obika while he gave him half a dozen more lashes on his bare back. He did not struggle at all; he only shivered like the sacrifical ram which must take in silence the blows of funeral dancers before its throat is cut. Ofoedu trembled also, but for once in his life he saw a fight pass before him and could do nothing but look on.

'Are you mad to attack a white man?' screamed Moses Unachukwu in sheer amazement. 'I have heard that not one person in your father's house has a right head.'

'What do you have in mind when you say that?' asked a man from Obika's village who had smelt in Unachukwu's statement the hostility between Umuachala and Umunneora.

The crowd which had hitherto watched in silence now broke hurriedly into the quarrel and before long loud threats were uttered on all sides and at least one person wagged his finger in another's face. It seemed so much easier to deal with an old quarrel than with a new, unprecedented incident.

'Shut up you black monkeys and get down to work!' Mr Wright had a grating voice but one that carried far. Truce was immediately established. He turned to Unachukwu and said: 'Tell them I shall not tolerate any more slackness.'

Unachukwu translated.

'Tell them this bloody work must be finished by June.'

'The white man says that unless you finish this work in time you will know the kind of man he is.'

'No more lateness.'

'Pardin?'

'Pardon what? Can't you understand plain, simple English? I said there will be no more late-coming.'

'Oho. He says everybody must work hard and stop all this shit-eating.'

'I have one question I want the white man to answer.' This was Nweke Ukpaka.

'What's that?'

Unachukwu hesitated and scratched his head. 'Dat man wan axe master queshon.'

'No questions.'

'Yessah.' He turned to Nweke. 'The white man says he did not leave his house this morning to come and answer your questions.'

The crowd grumbled. Wright shouted that if they did not immediately set to work they would be seriously dealt with. There was no need to translate this; it was quite clear.

The matchets began to sound again on tree trunks and those who worked with hoes bent down once more. But as they worked they arranged a meeting.

Nothing came of it. The first disagreement was over the presence of Moses Unachukwu. Many people – largely from Umuachala village – saw no reason why a man of another age-group should sit in on their deliberations. Others pointed out that this was a special meeting to discuss the white man and for that reason it would be foolish to exclude the only kinsman who knew the ways of these white people. At this point Ofoedu stood up and, to everyone's surprise, joined those who wanted Moses to stay.

'But my reason is different,' he added. 'I want him to say before us all what he said before the white man about Obika's family. I want him also to say before us all whether it is true that he incited the white man to whip our comrade. When he has given us these answers he may go away. You ask me why he should go away? I shall tell you. This is a meeting of Otakagu age-group. He belongs to Akakanma. And let me remind you all, but especially those who are murmuring and interrupting me, that he also belongs to the white man's religion. But I do not want to talk about that now. All I say is that Unachukwu should answer the questions I have asked, and after that he may go and take with him all his knowledge of the white man's ways. We have all heard stories of how he came by this knowledge. We have heard that when he left Umuaro he went to cook like a woman in the white man's kitchen and lick his plates . . .'

The rest of Ofoedu's speech was drowned in the tumult that broke out. It was just like Ofoedu, many people were saying, to open his mouth and let out his words alive without giving them as much as a bite with his teeth. Others said he had spoken the truth. Anyhow, it took a very long time to establish peace again. Moses Unachukwu was saying something but no one heard, until the tumult had spent itself. By then his voice had gone hoarse.

'If you ask me to go away I shall do so at once.'

'Do not go!'

'We permit you to stay!'

'But if I go away it will not be due to the barking of that mad dog. If there were any shame left in the world how could that beast of the bush who could not give his father a second burial stand up before you and pass shit through his mouth . . .'

'It is enough!'

'We have not come here to abuse ourselves!'

When the discussion began again someone suggested that they

should go to the elders of Umuaro and tell them that they could no longer work on the white man's road. But as speaker after speaker revealed the implications of such a step it lost all support. Moses told them that the white man would reply by taking all their leaders to prison at Okperi.

'You all know how friendly we are with Okperi. Do you think that any Umuaro man who goes to prison there will come back alive? But that apart, do you forget that this is the moon of planting? Do you want to grow this year's crops in the prison house in a land where your fathers owe a cow? I speak as your elder brother. I have travelled in Olu and I have travelled in Igbo, and I can tell you that there is no escape from the white man. He has come. When Suffering knocks at your door and you say there is no seat left for him, he tells you not to worry because he has brought his own stool. The white man is like that. Before any of you here was old enough to tie a cloth between the legs I saw with my own eyes what the white man did to Abame. Then I knew there was no escape. As daylight chases away darkness so will the white man drive away all our customs. I know that as I say it now passes by your ears, but it will happen. The white man has power which comes from the true God and it burns like fire. This is the God about Whom we preach every eighth day . . .'

Unachukwu's opponents were now shouting that this was a meeting of an age-group, that they had not assembled to join with him in chewing the seed of foolishness which they called their new religion.

'We are talking about the white man's road,' said a voice above the others.

'Yes, we are talking about the white man's road. But when the roof and walls of a house fall in, the ceiling is not left standing. The white man, the new religion, the soldiers, the new road – they are all part of the same thing. The white man has a gun, a matchet, a bow and carries fire in his mouth. He does not fight with one weapon alone.'

Nweke Ukpaka spoke next. 'What a man does not know is greater than he. Those of us who want Unachukwu to go away forget that none of us can say come in the white man's language.

We should listen to his advice. If we go to our elders and tell them that we shall no longer work on the white man's road, what do we expect them to do? Will our fathers take up hoes and matchets and go out to work themselves while we sit at home? I know that many of us want to fight the white man. But only a foolish man can go after a leopard with his bare hands. The white man is like hot soup and we must take him slowly-slowly from the edges of the bowl. Umuaro was here before the white man came from his own land to seek us out. We did not ask him to visit us; he is neither our kinsman nor our in-law. We did not steal his goat or his fowl; we did not take his land or his wife. In no way whatever have we done him wrong. And yet he has come to make trouble for us. All we know is that our *ofo* is held high between us and him. The stranger will not kill his host with his visit; when he goes may he not go with a swollen back. I know that the white man does not wish Umuaro well. That is why we must hold our *ofo* by him and give him no cause to say that we did this or failed to do that. For if we give him cause he will rejoice. Why? Because the very house he has been seeking ways of pulling down will have caught fire of its own will. For this reason we shall go on working on his road; and when we finish we shall ask him if he has more work for us. But in dealing with a man who thinks you a fool it is good sometimes to remind him that you know what he knows but have chosen to appear foolish for the sake of peace. This white man thinks we are foolish; so we shall ask him one question. This was the question I had wanted to ask him this morning but he would not listen. We have a saying that a man may refuse to do what is asked of him but may not refuse to be asked, but it seems the white man does not have that kind of saying where he comes from. Anyhow the question which we shall beg Unachukwu to ask him is why we are not paid for working on his road. I have heard that throughout Olu and Igbo, wherever people do this kind of work the white man pays them. Why should our own be different?'

Ukpaka was a persuasive speaker and after him nobody else rose to speak. And the only decision of the meeting was then taken. The Otakagu age-group asked Unachukwu to find out, at a well-chosen moment when it was safe to approach the white man, why he had not given them any money for working on his road.

'I shall carry your message to him,' said Unachukwu.

'That message is not complete,' said Nwoye Udora. 'It is not enough to ask him why we are not paid. He knows why and we know why. He knows that in Okperi those who do this kind of work are paid. Therefore the question you should ask him is this: Others are paid for this work; why are we not paid? Or is our own different? It is important to ask whether our own is different.'

This was agreed and the meeting broke up.

'Your words were very good,' someone said to Nwoye Udora as they left the market-place. 'Perhaps the white man will tell us whether we killed his father or his mother.'

Ezeulu was not as broken down as his young wife had feared. True he had pains in his feet and thighs and his spittle had a bitter taste. But he had forestalled the worst effects of his exertion by having his body rubbed with a light ointment of camwood as soon as he returned home and by ensuring that a log fire burned beside his low bamboo bed all night. There was no medicine equal to camwood and fire. Very soon the priest would rise as sound as newly fired clay.

If anyone had told Ezeulu about his younger wife's concern he would have laughed. It showed how little of a man his wives knew especially when, like Ugoye, they were no older than the man's first children. If Ugoye had known her husband in his earliest years as priest she might have realized that the exhaustion he felt after the festival had nothing to do with advancing age. Had it been that Ezeulu would not have yielded to it. His daughters made light of the wife's concern because they were wiser, being his daughters. They knew that this was a necessary conclusion to the festival. It was part of the sacrifice. For who could trample the sins and abominations of all Umuaro into the dust and not bleed in the feet? Not even a priest as powerful as Ezeulu could hope to do that.

The story that the white man had whipped Obika spread through the villages while the age group held its meeting under the shade of ogbu trees in the market place. The story was brought home to Ezeulu's compound by Edogo's wife who was returning from the bush with a bundle of firewood on her head. Ezeulu was wakened from sleep by Obika's mother and sister weeping. He threw off the mat with which he had covered himself and sprang to his feet, his mind having run immediately to death. But then he heard Edogo's wife talking, which would not happen if anyone had died. He sat down on the edge of his bed and, raising his voice, called Edogo's wife. She immediately came into the *obi* followed by her husband who had been carving an iroko door for the compound of a titled man when his wife returned.

'What are you saying?' Ezeulu asked Amoge. She repeated the story she had heard.

'Whip?' he asked, unable to understand. 'But what offence did he commit?'

'Those who told the story did not say.'

Ezeulu screwed his face in thought. 'I think he was late in going. But the white man would not whip a grown man who is also my son for that. He would be asked to pay a fine to his age group for being late; he would not be whipped. Or perhaps he hit the white man first . . .'

Edogo was touched by the distress which his father felt but tried to conceal. It ought to have made him jealous of his younger brother but did not.

'I think I shall go to Nkwo where they are meeting,' said Edogo. 'I cannot yet find meaning in this story.' He returned to his hut, took his matchet and made to go out.

His father who was still trying to understand how it could have happened called after him. When he came back into his *obi* Ezeulu advised him not to be rash.

'From what I know of your brother he is likely to have struck the first blow. Especially as he was drunk when he left home.' There was already a change in his tone, and Edogo nearly smiled.

He set out again, wearing only his work cloth – a long, thin strip passed between the legs and secured around the waist, with one end dangling in front and the other behind.

Obika's mother came out of the compound sniffing and drawing the back of her fist across her eyes.

'Where is that one going?' asked Ezeulu. 'I see that those who will fight the white man are lining up.' He laughed as Matefi turned round to hear what he was saying. 'Go back to your hut, woman!' Edogo had now reached the main footpath and turned left.

Ezeulu now sat down on the iroko panel with his back against the wall so that he could see the approaches to his compound. His mind raced up and down in different directions trying vainly to make sense of the whipping story. Now he was thinking about the white man who did it. Ezeulu had seen him and heard his voice when he spoke to the elders of Umuaro about the new road. When the story had first spread that a white man was coming to talk to the elders Ezeulu had thought it would be his friend, Wintabota, the Destroyer of Guns. He had been greatly disappointed when he saw it was another white man. Wintabota was tall and erect and carried himself like a great man. His voice sounded like thunder. This other man was short and thick, as hairy as a monkey. He spoke in a queer way without opening his mouth. Ezeulu thought he must be some kind of manual labourer in the service of Wintabota.

Some people appeared at the junction of the main footpath and the approaches to Ezeulu's compound. He jerked his head forward, but the men passed.

Ezeulu came finally to the conclusion that unless his son was at fault he would go in person to Okperi and report the white man to his master. His thoughts were stopped by the sudden appearance of Obika and Edogo. Behind them came a third whom he soon recognized as Ofoedu. Ezeulu could never get used to this worthless young man who trailed after his son like a vulture after a corpse. He was filled with anger which was so great that it also engulfed his son.

'What was the cause of the whipping?' he asked Edogo, ignoring the other two. Obika's mother and all the others in the compound had now hastened into Ezeulu's *obi*.

'They were late for work.'

'Why were you late?'

'I have not come home to answer anybody's questions,' Obika shouted.

'You may answer or not as you please. But let me tell you that this is only the beginning of what palm wine will bring to you. The death that will kill a man begins as an appetite.'

Obika and Ofoedu walked out.

CHAPTER NINE

Edogo's homestead was built against one of the four sides of his father's compound so that they shared one wall between them. It was a very small homestead with two huts, one for Edogo and the other for his wife, Amoge. It was built deliberately small for, like the compounds of many first sons it was no more than a temporary home where the man waited until he could inherit his father's place.

Of late another small compound had been built on the other side of Ezeulu's for his second son, Obika. But it was not quite as small as Edogo's. It also had two huts, one for Obika and the other for the bride who was soon to come.

As one approached Ezeulu's compound off the main village pathway Edogo's place stood on the left and Obika's on the right.

When Obika walked away with his friend, Edogo returned to the shade of the ogbu tree in front of his compound to resume work on the door he was carving. It was nearly finished and after it he would leave carving for a while and face his farm work. He envied master craftsmen like Agwuegbo whose farms were cultivated for them by their apprentices and customers.

As he carved his mind kept wandering to his wife's hut from where the cry of their only child was reaching him. He was their second child, the first having died after three months. The one that died had brought sickness with him into the world; a ridge ran down the middle of his head. But the second, Amechi, had been different. At his birth he had seemed so full of life. Then at about the sixth month he had changed overnight. He stopped sucking his mother's breast and his skin took the complexion of withering cocoyam leaves. Some people said perhaps Amoge's milk had gone bitter. She was asked to squirt some of it into a bowl to see if it would kill an ant. But the little ant which was dropped into it stayed alive; so the fault was not with the milk.

Edogo's mind was in pain over the child. Some people were already saying that perhaps he was none other than the first one. But Edogo and Amoge never talked about it; the woman especially was afraid. Since utterance had power to change fear into a living truth they dared not speak before they had to.

In her hut Amoge sat on a low stool, her crying child set on the angle of her two feet which she had brought together to touch at the heels. After a while she lifted her feet and child together on to another spot leaving behind on the floor a round patch of watery, green excrement. She looked round the room but did not seem to find what she wanted. Then she called: '*Nwanku! Nwanku! Nwanku!*' A wiry, black dog rushed in from outside and made straight for the excrement which disappeared with four or five noisy flicks of its tongue. Then it sat down with its tail wagging on the floor. Amoge moved her feet and child once again but this time all that was left behind was a tiny green drop. Nwanku did not consider it big enough to justify getting up; it merely stretched its neck and took it up with the corner of the tongue and sat up again to wait. But the child had finished and the dog was soon trying without success to catch a fly between its jaws.

Edogo's thoughts refused to stay on the door he was carving. Once again he put down the hammer and changed the chisel from his left hand to the right. The child had now stopped crying and Edogo's thoughts wandered to the recent exchange of words between his father and brother. The trouble with Ezeulu was that he could never see something and take his eyes away from it. Everybody agreed that Obika's friendship with Ofoedu would not bring about any good, but Obika was no longer a child and if he refused to listen to advice he should be left alone. That was what their father could never learn. He must go on treating his grown children like little boys, and if they ever said no there was a big quarrel. This was why the older his children grew the more he seemed to dislike them. Edogo remembered how much his father had liked him when he was a boy and how with the passage of years he had transferred his affection first to Obika and then to Oduche and Nwafo. Thinking of it now Edogo could not actually remember that their father had ever shown much affection for Oduche. He seemed to have lingered too long on Obika (who of all his sons resembled him most in appearance) and then bypassed Oduche for Nwafo. What would happen if the old man had another son tomorrow? Would Nwafo then begin to lose favour in his eyes? Perhaps. Or was there more to it than that? Was there something in the boy which told their father that at last a successor to the priesthood had come? Some people said Nwafo was in every way an image of Ezeulu's father. Actually Edogo would feel greatly relieved if on the death of their father the diviner's string of beads fell in favour of Nwafo. 'I do not want to be Chief Priest,' he heard himself saying aloud. He looked round instinctively to see if anyone had been near enough to have heard him. 'As for Obika,' he thought, 'things like the priesthood did not come near his mind.' Which left only Oduche and Nwafo. But as Ezeulu had turned Oduche over to the new religion he could no longer be counted. A strange thought seized Edogo now. Could it be that their father had deliberately sent Oduche to the religion of the white man so as to disqualify him for the priesthood of Ulu? He put down the chisel with which he was absent-mindedly straightening the inter-secting lines on the iroko door. That would explain it! The priesthood would then fall on his youngest and favourite son. The reason which Ezeulu gave for his strange decision had never convinced anyone. If as he said he merely wanted one of his sons to be his eye and ear at this new assembly why did he not send Nwafo who was close to his thoughts? No, that was not the reason. The priest wanted to have a hand in the choice of his successor. It was what anyone who knew Ezeulu would expect him to do. But was he not presuming too much? The choice of a priest lay with the deity. Was it likely that he would let the old priest force his hand. Although Edogo and Obika did not seem attracted to the office that would not prevent the deity from choosing either of them or even Oduche, out of spite. Edogo's thinking now became confused. If Ulu should choose him to be Chief Priest what would he do? This thought had never worried him before because he had always taken it for granted that Ulu would not want him. But the way he saw things now there was no certainty about that. Would he be happy if the diviner's beads fell in his favour? He could not say. Perhaps the only sure happiness it would give him was the knowledge that his father's partiality for his younger sons had been frustrated by the deity himself. From Ani-Mmo where dead men went Ezeulu would look up and see the ruin of all his plans.

Edogo was surprised by this depth of ill will for his father and relented somewhat. He remembered what his mother used to say when she was alive, that Ezeulu's only fault was that he expected everyone – his wives, his kinsmen, his children, his friends and even his enemies – to think and act like himself. Anyone who dared to say no to him was an enemy. He forgot the saying of the elders that if a man sought for a companion who acted entirely like himself he would live in solitude.

Ezeulu was sitting at the same spot long after his quarrel with Obika. His back was set against the wall and his gaze on the approaches to his compound. Now and again he seemed to study the household shrine standing against the low threshold wall in front of him. On his left there was a long mud-seat with goatskins spread on it. The eaves on that part of the hut were cut back so that Ezeulu could watch the sky for the new moon. In the daytime light came into the hut mostly from that part. Nwafo squatted on the mud-seat, facing his father. At the other end of the room, on Ezeulu's right, stood his low bamboo bed; beside it a fire of ukwa logs smouldered.

Without changing his fixed gaze Ezeulu began suddenly to talk to Nwafo.

'A man does not speak a lie to his son,' he said. 'Remember that always. To say *My father told me* is to swear the greatest oath. You are only a little boy, but I was no older when my father began to confide in me. Do you hear what I am saying?'

Nwafo said yes.

'You see what has happened to your brother. In a few days his bride will come and he will no longer be called a child. When

414

strangers see him they will no longer ask *Whose son is he?* but *Who is he?* Of his wife they will no longer say *Whose daughter?* but *Whose wife?*. Do you understand me?' Nwafo saw that his face was beginning to shine with sweat. Someone was coming towards the hut and he stopped talking.

'Who is that?' Ezeulu screwed up his eyes in an effort to see. Nwafo jumped down from the mud-seat and came to the centre of the hut to see.

'It is Ogbuefi Akuebue.'

Akuebue was one of the very few men in Umuaro whose words gained entrance into Ezeulu's ear. The two men were in the same age group. As he drew near he raised his voice and asked: 'Is the owner of this house still alive?'

'Who is this man?' asked Ezeulu. 'Did they not say that you died two markets come next Afo?'

'Perhaps you do not know that everyone in your age-group has long died. Or are you waiting for mushrooms to sprout from your head before you know that your time is over?' Akuebue was now inside the hut but he still maintained the posture he had assumed to pass under the low eaves – the right hand supported above the knee and the body bent at the waist. Without rising to his full height he shook hands with the Chief Priest. Then he spread his goatskin on the floor near the mud-seat and sat down.

'How are your people?'

'They are quiet.' This was always how Akuebue answered about his family. It amused Nwafo greatly. He had an image in his mind of this man's wives and children sitting quietly with their hands between their laps.

'And yours?' he asked Ezeulu.

'Nobody has died.'

'Do they say that Obika was whipped by the white man?'

Ezeulu opened both palms to the sky and said nothing.

'What did they say was his offence?'

'My friend, let us talk about other things. There was a time when a happening such as this would have given me a fever; but that time has passed. Nothing is anything to me any more. Go and ask your mother to bring me a kola nut, Nwafo.'

415

'She was saying this morning that her kola nuts were finished.'

'Go and ask Matefi then.'

'Must you worry about kola nuts every time? I am not a stranger.'

'I was not taught that kola nut was the food of strangers,' said Ezeulu. 'And besides do not our people say that he is a fool who treats his brother worse than a stranger? But I know what you are afraid of; they tell me you have lost all your teeth.' As he said this he reached for a lump of white clay in a four-sided wooden bowl shaped like the head of a lizard and rolled it on the floor towards Akuebue who picked it up and drew four upright lines with it on the floor. Then he painted the big toe of his right foot and rolled the chalk back to Ezeulu and he put it away again in the wooden bowl.

Nwafo was soon back with a kola nut in another bowl.

'Show it to Akuebue,' said his father.

'I have seen it,' replied Akuebue.

'Then break it.'

'No. The king's kola nut returns to his hands.'

'If you say so.'

'Indeed I say so.'

Ezeulu took the bowl from Nwafo and set it down between his legs. Then he picked up the kola nut in his right hand and offered a prayer. He jerked the hand forward as he said each sentence, his palm open upwards and the thumb holding down the kola nut on the four fingers.

'Ogbuefi Akuebue, may you live, and all your people. I too will live with all my people. But life alone is not enough. May we have the things with which to live it well. For there is a kind of slow and weary life which is worse than death.'

'You speak of truth.'

'May good confront the man on top and the man below. But let him who is jealous of another's position choke with his envy.'

'So be it.'

'May good come to the land of Igbo and to the country of the riverain folk.'

Then he broke the kola nut by pressing it between his palms and threw all the lobes into the bowl on the floor.

'O o-o o-o o o-o,' he whistled. 'Look what has happened here. The spirits want to eat.'

Akuebue craned his neck to see. 'One, two, three, four, five, six. Indeed they want to eat.'

Ezeulu picked up one lobe and threw it outside. Then he picked up another one and put it into his mouth. Nwafo came forward, took the bowl from the floor and served Akuebue. For a short while neither man spoke, only the sound of kola nut as it was crushed between the teeth broke the silence.

'It is strange the way kola nuts behave,' said Ezeulu after he had swallowed twice. 'I do not remember when I last saw one with six lobes.'

'It is indeed very rare, and you only see it when you are not looking for it. Even five is not common. Some years ago I had to buy four or five basketfuls of kola nuts before I could find one with five lobes for a sacrifice. Nwafo, go to your mother's hut and bring me a big calabash of cold water . . . This type of heat is not empty-handed.'

'I think there is water in the sky,' said Ezeulu. 'It is the heat before rain.' As he said this he rose three-quarters erect and walked a few steps to his bamboo bed and took from it a goat-skin bag. This bag was sewn together with great cunning; it looked as though the goat which lived in it had been pulled out as one might pull out a snail from its shell. It had four short legs and the tail was intact. Ezeulu took the bag to his seat and began to search arm-deep for his bottle of snuff. When he found it he put it down on the floor and began to look for the small ivory spoon. He soon found that also, and he put the bag away beside him. He took up the little white bottle again, held it up to see how much snuff there was left and then tapped it on his knee-cap. He opened the bottle and tipped a little of the content into his left palm.

'Give me a little of that thing to clear my head,' said Akuebue who had just drunk his water.

'Come and get it,' replied Ezeulu. 'You do not expect me to provide the snuff and also the walking around, to give you a wife and find you a mat to sleep on.'

Akuebue rose half-erect with his right hand on the knee and

the left palm opened towards Ezeulu. 'I will not dispute with you,' he said. 'You have the yam and you have the knife.'

Ezeulu transferred two spoonfuls of the snuff from his own palm into Akuebue's and then brought out some more from the bottle for himself.

'It is good snuff,' said Akuebue. One of his nostrils carried brown traces of the powder. He took another small heap from his cupped left hand on to his right thumbnail and guided it to the other nostril, throwing his head back and sniffing three or four times. Then he had traces on both nostrils. Ezeulu used the ivory spoon instead of his thumbnail.

'I do not buy my snuff in the market,' said Ezeulu; 'that is why.'

Edogo came in dangling a calabash of palm wine from a short rope tied round its neck. He saluted Akuebue and his father and set down the calabash.

'I did not know that you had palm wine,' said Ezeulu.

'It has just been sent by the owner of the door I am carving.'

'And why do you bring it in the presence of this my friend who took over the stomach of all his dead relatives?'

'But I have not heard Edogo say it was meant for you.' He turned to Edogo and asked: 'Or did you say so?' Edogo laughed and said it was meant for two of them.

Akuebue brought out a big cow's horn from his bag and hit it thrice on the floor. Then he rubbed its edges with his palm to remove dirt. Ezeulu brought out his horn from the bag beside him and held it for Edogo to fill. When he had served him he took the calabash to Akuebue and also filled his horn. Before they drank Ezeulu and Akuebue tipped a little on to the floor and muttered a barely audible invitation to their fathers.

'My body is full of aches,' said Ezeulu, 'and I do not think that palm wine is good for me yet.'

'I can tell you it is not,' said Akuebue who had gulped down the first horn and screwed up his face as though waiting for a sound inside his head to tell him whether it was good wine or not.

Edogo took his father's horn from him and filled himself a measure. Oduche came in then, saluted his father and Akuebue and sat down with Nwafo on the mud-seat. Since he joined the white man's religion he always wore a loincloth of towelling material instead of the thin strip of cloth between the legs. Edogo filled the horn again and offered him but he did not drink. 'What about you, Nwafo?' asked Edogo. He also said no.

'When is it you are going to Okperi?' Ezeulu asked.

'The day after tomorrow.'

'For how long?'

'They say for two markets.'

Ezeulu seemed to be turning this over in his mind.

'What are you going for?' asked Akuebue.

'They want to test our knowledge of the holy book.'

Akuebue shrugged his shoulders.

'I am not sure that you will go, said Ezeulu. 'But let the days pass and I shall decide.' Nobody said anything in reply. Oduche knew enough about his father not to protest. Akuebue drank another horn of wine and began to gnash his teeth. The voice he had been waiting for had spoken and pronounced the wine good. He knocked the horn on the floor a few times and prayed as he did so.

'May the man who tapped this wine have life to continue his good work. May those of us who drank it also have life. The land of Olu and the land of Igbo.' He rubbed the edges of his horn before putting it away in his bag.

'Drink one horn more,' said Edogo.

Akuebue rubbed his mouth with the back of his hand before replying.

'The only medicine against palm wine is the power to say no.' This statement seemed to bring Ezeulu back to the people around him.

'Before you came in,' he said to Akuebue, 'I was telling that little boy over there that the greatest liar among men still speaks the truth to his own son.'

'It is so,' said Akuebue. 'A man can swear before the most dreaded deity on what his father told him.'

'If a man is not sure of the boundary between his land and his neighbour's,' continued Ezeulu, 'he tells his son: *I think it is here but if there is a dispute do not swear before a deity.*'

'It is even so,' said Akuebue.

'But when a man has spoken the truth and his children prefer to take the lie . . .' His voice had risen with every word towards the dangerous pitch of a curse; then he broke off with a violent shake of the head. When he began again he spoke more quickly. 'That is why a stranger can whip a son of mine and go unscathed, because my son has nailed up his ear against my words. Were it not so that stranger would already have learn what it was to cross Ezeulu; dogs would have licked his eyes. I would have swallowed him whole and brought him up again. I would have shaved his head without wetting the hair.'

'Did Obika strike the first blow then?' asked Akuebue.

'How do I know? All I can say is that he was blind with palm wine when he left here in the morning. And even when he came back a short while ago it had still not cleared from his eyes.'

'But they say he did not strike the first blow,' said Edogo.

'Were you there?' asked his father. 'Or would you swear before a deity on the strength of what a drunken man tells you? If I was sure of my son do you think I would sit here now talking to you while a man who pokes his finger into my eyes goes home to his bed? If I did nothing else I would pronounce a few words on him and he would know the power in my mouth.' The perspiration was forming on his brow.

'What you say is true,' said Akuebue. 'But in my thinking there is still something for us to do once we find out from those who saw it whether Obika struck the first blow or . . .' Ezeulu did not let him finish.

'Why should I go out looking for strangers to tell me what my son did or did not do? I should be telling them.'

'That is true. But let us first chase away the wild cat, afterwards we blame the hen.' Akuebue turned to Edogo. 'Where is Obika himself?'

'It appears that what I said has not entered your ear,' said Ezeulu. 'Where . . .'

Edogo interrupted him. 'He went out with Ofoedu. He went out because our father did not ask him what happened before blaming him.'

This unexpected accusation stung Ezeulu like the black ant. But he held himself together and, to everybody's surprise, leaned back against the wall and shut his eyes. When he opened them again he began to whistle quietly to himself. Akuebue nodded his head four or five times like a man who had uncovered an unexpected truth. Ezeulu moved his head slightly from side to side and up and down to his almost silent whistling.

'This is what I tell my own children,' said Akuebue to Edogo and the two boys. 'I tell them that a man always has more sense than his children.' It was clear he said this to mollify Ezeulu; but at the same time it was clear he spoke truth. 'Those of you who think they are wiser than their father forget that it is from a man's own stock of sense that he gives out to his sons. That is why a boy who tries to wrestle with his father gets blinded by the old man's loin-cloth. Why do I speak like this? It is because I am not a stranger in your father's hut and I am not afraid to speak my mind. I know how often your father has pleaded with Obika to leave his friendship with Ofoedu. Why has Obika not heeded? It is because you all – not only Obika but you all, including that little one there – you think you are wiser than your father. My own children are like that. But there is one thing which you all forget. You forget that a woman who began cooking before another must have more broken utensils. When we old people speak it is not because of the sweetness of words in our mouth; it is because we see something which you do not see. Our fathers made a proverb about it. They said that when we see an old woman stop in her dance to point again and again in the same direction we can be sure that somewhere there something happened long ago which touched the roots of her life. When Obika returns tell him what I say, Edogo. Do you hear me?' Edogo nodded. He was wondering whether it was true that a man never spoke a lie to his sons.

Akuebue wheeled round on his buttocks and faced Ezeulu. 'It is the pride of Umuaro,' he said, 'that we never see one party as right and the other wrong. I have spoken to the children and I shall not be afraid to speak to you. I think you are too hard on Obika. Apart from your high position as Chief Priest you are also blessed with a great compound. But in all great compounds there must be people of all minds – some good, some bad, some fearless and some cowardly; those who bring in wealth and those who scatter it, those who give good advice and those who only speak the words of palm wine. That is why we say that whatever tune you play in the compound of a great man there is always someone to dance to it. I salute you.'

CHAPTER TEN

Although Tony Clarke had already spent nearly six weeks in Okperi most of his luggage, including his crockery, had arrived only a fortnight ago – in fact the day before he went on tour to the bush. That was why he had not been able until now to ask Captain Winterbottom to his house for a meal.

As he waited the arrival of his guest Mr Clarke felt not a little uneasy. One of the problems of living in a place like this with only four other Europeans (three of whom were supposed to be beneath the notice of Political Officers) was that one had to cope with a guest like Winterbottom absolutely alone. Of course this was not their first social encounter; they had in fact had dinner together not very long ago and things did not altogether grind to a stop. But then Clarke had been guest, without any responsibilities. Today he was going to be host and the onus would rest on him to keep the conversation alive, through the long, arduous ritual of alcohol, food, coffee and more alcohol stretching into midnight. If only he could have invited someone like John Wright with whom he had struck up a kind of friendship during his recent tour. But such a thing would have been disastrous.

Clarke had shared the lonely thatch-roofed Rest House outside Umuaro with Wright for one night during his tour. Wright had been living in one half of the Rest House for over two weeks then. The Rest House consisted of two enormous rooms each with a camp-bed and an old mosquito-net, a rough wooden table and chair and a cupboard. Just behind the main building there was a thatched shed used as a kitchen. About thirty yards away another hut stood over a dug latrine and wooden seat. Farther away still in the same direction a third hut in very bad repair housed the servants and porters who were sometimes called 'hammock boys'. The Rest House proper was surrounded by a ragged hedge of a native plant which Clarke had never seen anywhere else.

The entire appearance of the place showed that it had not had a caretaker since the last one vanished into the bush with two camp-beds. The beds were replaced but the key to the main building and the latrine was thereafter kept at headquarters so that whenever a European was going on tour and needed to lodge there the native Chief Clerk in Captain Winterbottom's office had to remember to give the key to his head porter or steward. Once when the Police Officer, Mr Wade, had been going to Umuaro the Chief Clerk had forgotten to do this and had had to walk the six or seven miles at night to deliver it. Fortunately for him Mr Wade had not suffered any personal inconvenience as he had sent his boys one day ahead of himself to clean the place up.

As he walked round the premises of the Rest House Tony Clarke felt that he was hundreds of miles from Government Hill. It was quite impossible to believe that it was only six or seven miles away. Even the sun seemed to set in a different direction. No wonder the natives were said to regard a six mile walk as travelling to a foreign country.

Later that evening he and Wright sat on the veranda of the Rest House to drink Wright's gin. In this remote corner, far from the stiff atmosphere of Winterbottom's Government Hill, Clarke was able to discover that he liked Wright very much. He also discovered to his somewhat delighted amazement that in certain circumstances he could contain as much gin as any Old Coaster.

They had only met for a very brief moment before. But now they talked like old friends. Clarke thought that for all the other man's squat and rough exterior he was a good and honest Englishman. He found it so refreshing to be talking to a man who did not have the besetting sin of smugness, of taking himself too seriously.

'What do you think the Captain would say, Tony, if he were

424

to see his young Political Officer being nice and friendly to a common roadmaker?' His big red face looked almost boyish.

'I don't know and don't much care,' said Clarke, and because the fume of gin was already working on his brain, he added: 'I shall be happy if in all my years in Africa I succeed in building something as good as your road . . .'

'It's good of you to say so.'

'Are we having a celebration to open it?'

'The Captain says no. He says we have already overspent the Vote for it.'

'What does it matter?'

'That's what I want to know. And yet we spend hundreds of pounds building Native Courts all over the division that nobody wants, as far as I can see.'

'I must say though that that is not the Captain's fault.' Clarke was already adopting Wright's half-contemptuous manner of referring to Winterbottom. 'It is the policy of Headquarters which I happen to know the Captain is not altogether in agreement with.'

'Damn the Headquarters.'

'The Captain would approve of that sentiment.'

'Actually, you know, the Captain is not a bad fellow at all. I think that deep down he is quite a decent fellow. One must make allowances for the rough time he's had.'

'In the matter of promotions, you mean?'

'He's been badly treated there too, I'm told,' said Wright. 'Actually I wasn't thinking of that at all. I was thinking of his domestic life. Oh yes. You see, during the war while the poor man was fighting the Germans in the Cameroons some smart fellow walked away with his wife at home.'

'Really? I hadn't heard about that.'

'Yes. I'm told he was very badly shaken by it. I sometimes think it was this personal loss during the war that's made him cling to this ridiculous Captain business.'

'Quite possibly. He's the kind of person, isn't he, who would take the desertion of his wife very badly,' said Clarke.

'Exactly. A man as inflexible as him can't take a thing like that.'

In the course of the evening Clarke was given every detail of

Winterbottom's marital crisis and he felt really sorry for the man. Wright also seemed to have been touched with sympathy by the very act of telling the story. Without any conscious design the two men dropped their contemptuous reference to *the Captain* and called Winterbottom by his name.

'The real trouble with Winterbottom,' said Wright after deep thought, 'is that he is too serious to sleep with native women.' Clarke was startled out of his own thoughts, and for a brief moment he completely forgot about Winterbottom. On more than one occasion during his present tour he had come up in his mind against the question: How widespread was the practice of white men sleeping with native women?

'He doesn't seem to realize that even Governors have been known to keep dusky mistresses.' He licked his lips.

'I don't think it's a question of knowing or not knowing,' said Clarke. 'He is a man of very high principles, something of a missionary. I believe his father was a Church of England clergyman, which is a far cry from my father, for instance, who is a Bank of England clerical.' They both laughed heartily at this. When Clarke recalled this piece of wit in the morning he realized how much alcohol he must have drunk to find such an inferior joke so amusing.

'I think you are right about the missionary business. He should have come out with the CMS or some such people. By the way, he has been going around lately with the woman missionary doctor at Nkisa. Of course we all have our different tastes, but I would not have thought a woman missionary doctor could provide much fun for a man in this Godforsaken place.'

Clarke wanted to ask about native women – whether they were better than white, and many other details – but not even the effect of the gin could bring out the questions. Rather he found himself changing the subject and losing this great opportunity. The thoughts he had had since first seeing fully grown girls going about naked were again forced to sleep. Later he would bite his lips in regret.

'From what I heard of Winterbottom at headquarters,' he said, 'I expected to see some sort of buffoon.'

'I know. He is a stock joke at Enugu, isn't he?'

'Whenever I said I was going to Okperi they said: *What! With Old Tom?* and looked pityingly at me. I wondered what was wrong with Old Tom, but no one would say any more. Then one day a very senior officer said to another to my hearing: *Old Tom is always reminding you that he came out to Nigeria in 1910 but he never mentions that in all that time he has not put in a day's work.* It's simply amazing how much back-biting goes on at Enugu.'

'Well,' said Wright, yawning, 'I cannot say myself that Old Tom is the most hard-working man I've ever met; but then who is? Certainly not that lot at Enugu.'

All this was working on Clarke's mind as he awaited Winterbottom's coming. He felt guilty like one who had been caught backbiting one of his own group with an outsider But then, he told himself in defence, they had said nothing that could be called uncharitable about Winterbottom. All that had happened was that he got to know a few details about the man's life, and felt sorry for him. And that feeling justified the knowledge.

He went into the kitchen for the tenth time that evening to see how Cook was roasting the chicken over a wood fire. It would be terrible if it turned out as tough as the last one Clarke had eaten. Of course all native chicken was tough and very small. But perhaps one shouldn't complain. A fully grown cock cost no more than twopence. Even so one wouldn't mind paying a little more now and again for a good, juicy, English chicken. The look of Cook's face seemed to say that Clarke was coming into the kitchen too frequently.

'How is it coming?'

'Ide try small small,' said Cook, rubbing his smoke-inflamed eyes with his forearm. Clarke looked around vaguely and returned to the veranda of his bungalow. He sat down and looked at his watch again; it was quarter to seven – a full half-hour to go. He began to think up a number of subjects for conversation. His recent tour would have provided enough topics for the evening, but he had just written and submitted a full report on it.

'But this is funny,' he told himself. Why should he feel so nervous because Winterbottom was coming to dinner? Was he afraid of the man? Certainly not! Why all the excitement then? Why should he get so worked up about meeting Winterbottom simply

427

because Wright had told him a few background stories which were in any case common knowledge? From this point Clarke speculated briefly on the nature of knowledge. Did knowledge of one's friends and colleagues impose a handicap on one? Perhaps it did. If so it showed how false was the common assumption that the more facts you could get about others the greater your power over them. Perhaps facts put you at a great disadvantage; perhaps they made you feel sorry and even responsible. Clarke rose to his feet and walked up and down, rather self-consciously. Perhaps this was the real difference between British and French colonial administrations. The French made up their minds about what they wanted to do and did it. The British, on the other hand, never did anything without first sending out a Commission of Inquiry to discover all the facts, which then ham-strung them. He sat down again, glowing with satisfaction.

The dinner was almost entirely satisfactory. There were only two or three uneasy moments throughout the evening; for example, when Captain Winterbottom said at the beginning: 'I have just been reading your report on your tour. One could see that you are settling down nicely to your duties.'

'It was all so exciting,' said Clarke, attempting to minimize his part in the success story. 'It's such a wonderful division. I can imagine how you must feel seeing such a happy district growing up under your direction.' He had stopped himself just in time from saying *your wise direction*. Even so he wondered whether this rather obvious attempt to return compliment for compliment was altogether happy.

'One thing worries me, though', said Winterbottom without any indication that he even heard Clarke's last piece. 'You say in the report that after careful inquiry you were satisfied that there was no truth in all the stories of Wright whipping natives.' Clarke's heart fell. This was the one falsehood in the entire report. In fact he completely forgot to make any inquiries, even if he had known how to set about it. It was only on his return to Okperi that he found a brief, late entry *Wright & natives* scribbled in pencil on the second page of his touring notebook. At first he had worried over it; then he had come to the conclusion that if Wright had in fact been employing unorthodox methods he would have heard of it without making inquiries as such. But since he had heard nothing it was safe to say that the stories were untrue. In any case how did one investigate such a thing? Did one go up to the first native one saw and ask if he had been birched by Wright? Or did one ask Wright? From what Clarke had seen of the man he would not have thought he was that sort.

'My steward is a native of Umuaro,' continued Winterbottom, 'and has just come back after spending two days at home; and he tells me that the whole village was in confusion because a rather important man had been whipped by Wright. But perhaps there's nothing in it.'

Clarke hoped he did not betray his confusion. Anyhow he rallied quickly and said: 'I heard nothing of it on the spot.' The words *on the spot* stung Winterbottom like three wasps. The fellow's cheek! He had been there barely a week and already he was talking as though he owned the district and Winterbottom was the new boy, or some desk-ridden idiot at headquarters. On the spot indeed! But he chose not to press the matter. He was immersed in his plans for appointing two new Paramount Chiefs in the division and throughout dinner he spoke of nothing else. Clarke was surprised that he no longer spoke with strong feeling. As he watched him across the table he seemed too tired and old. But even that soon passed and a hint of enthusiasm returned to his voice.

'I think I told you the story of the fetish priest who impressed me most favourably by speaking the truth in the land case between these people here and Umuaro.'

'Yes, I think you did.' Clarke was nervously watching his guest in difficulty with a piece of chicken. These damned native birds!

'Well, I have now decided to appoint him Paramount Chief for Umuaro. I've gone through the records of the case again and found that the man's title is Eze Ulu. The prefix *eze* in Ibo means king. So the man is a kind of priest-king.'

'That means, I suppose,' said Clarke, 'that the new appointment would not altogether be strange to him.'

'Exactly. Although I must say that I have never found the Ibo man backward in acquiring new airs of authority. Take this libertine we made Chief here. He now calls himself His Highness Obi Ikedi

the First of Okperi. The only title I haven't yet heard him use is
Fidei Defensor.'

Clarke opened his mouth to say that the love of title was a
universal human failing but thought better of it.

'The man was a complete nonentity until we crowned him, and
now he carries on as though he had been nothing else all his life.
It's the same with Court Clerks and even messengers. They all
managed to turn themselves into little tyrants over their own people.
It seems to be a trait in the character of the negro.'

The steward in shining white moved out of the darkness of the
kitchen balancing the rest of the boiled potatoes and cauliflower
on one hand and the chicken on the other. His heavily starched
uniform crackled as he walked over and stood silently on Captain
Winterbottom's right.

'Go over to the other side, Stephen,' said Clarke irritably.
Stephen grinned and moved over.

'No, I won't have another,' said Winterbottom, and turning to
Clarke he added: 'This is very good; one is not usually so lucky
with the first cook he gets.'

'Aloysius is not first rate, but I suppose . . . No, I won't have
any more, Stephen.'

As they ate fresh fruit salad made from pawpaw, banana and
oranges Winterbottom returned to his Paramount Chiefs.

'So as far as Umuaro is concerned I have found their Chief,' he said
with one of his rare smiles, 'and they will live happily ever after. I
am not so optimistic about Abame who are a pretty wild set anyhow.'

'They are the people who murdered Macdonald?' asked Clarke,
half of whose mind was on the salad that had gone a little sour.

'That's right. Actually they're no longer very troublesome –
not to us anyhow; the punitive expedition taught them a pretty
unforgettable lesson. But they are still very uncooperative. In the
whole division they are the least co-operative with their Native
Court. Throughout last year the court handled less than a dozen
cases and not one was brought to it by the natives themselves.'

'That's pretty grim,' said Clarke without being sure whether he
meant it to be ironical or not. But as Winterbottom began to fill
in the details of his plans for the two Native Court Areas Clarke

could not help being impressed by a new aspect of the man's character. Having been overruled in his opposition to Paramount Chiefs he was now sparing no effort to ensure the success of the policy. Clarke's tutor in Morals at Cambridge had been fond of the phrase *crystallization of civilization*. This was it.

Over their after-coffee whisky and soda Captain Winterbottom's opposition reared its head momentarily. But that only confirmed Clarke's new opinion of him.

'What I find so heart-rending,' said Winterbottom, 'is not so much the wrong policies of our Administration as our lack of consistency. Take this question of Paramount Chiefs. When Sir Hugh Macdermot first arrived as Governor he sent his Secretary for Native Affairs to investigate the whole business. The fellow came over here and spent a long time discovering the absurdities of the system which I had pointed out all along. Anyhow, from what he said in private conversation it was clear that he agreed with us that it had been an unqualified disaster. That was in 1919. I remember I had just come back from leave . . .' Some strange emotion entered his voice and Clarke saw a rush of blood to his face. He mastered himself and continued: 'More than two years and we still have heard nothing about the man's report. On the contrary the Lieutenant-Governor now asks us to proceed with the previous policy. Where does anyone stand?'

'It is very frustrating,' said Clarke. 'You know I was thinking the other day about our love of Commissions of Inquiry. That seems to me to be the real difference between us and the French. They know what they want and do it. We set up a commission to discover all the facts, as though facts meant anything. We imagine that the more facts we can obtain about our Africans the easier it will be to rule them. But facts . . .'

'Facts are important,' cut in Winterbottom, 'and Commissions of Inquiry could be useful. The fault of our Administration is that they invariably appoint the wrong people and set aside the advice of those of us who have been here for years.'

Clarke felt impotent anger with the man for not letting him finish, and personal inadequacy for not having made the point as beautifully as he had first made it to himself.

CHAPTER ELEVEN

The first time Ezeulu left his compound after the Pumpkin Festival
was to visit his friend, Akuebue. He found him sitting on the floor
of his *obi* preparing seed-yams which he had hired labourers to plant
for him next morning. He sat with a short, wooden-headed knife
between two heaps of yams. The bigger heap lay to his right on
the bare floor. The smaller pile was in a long basket from which
he took out one yam at a time, looked at it closely, trimmed it with
his knife and put it in the big heap. The refuse lay directly in front
of him, between the heaps – large numbers of brown, circular yam-
skins chipped off the tail of each seed-yam, and grey, premature
tendrils trimmed off the heads.

The two men shook hands and Ezeulu took his rolled goatskin
from under his arm, spread it on the floor and sat down. Akuebue
asked him about his family and for a while continued to work on
his yams.

'They are well,' replied Ezeulu. 'And the people of your
compound?'

'They are quiet.'

'Those are very large and healthy seed-yams. Do they come from
your own barn or from the market?'

'Do you not know that my portion of the Anietiti land . . .? Yes.
They were harvested there.'

'It is a great land,' said Ezeulu, nodding his head a few times.
'Such a land makes lazy people look like master farmers.'

Akuebue smiled. 'You want to draw me out, but you won't.'

He put down the knife and raised his voice to call his son, Obielue, who answered from the inner compound and soon came in, sweating.

'Ezeulu!' he saluted.

'My son.'

He turned to his father to take his message.

'Tell your mother that Ezeulu is greeting her. If she has kola nut let her bring it.' Obielue returned to the inner compound.

'Although I ate no kola nut the last time I went to the house of my friend.' Akuebue said this as though he talked to himself.

Ezeulu laughed. 'What do we say happens to the man who eats and then makes his mouth as if it has never seen food?'

'How should I know?'

'It makes his anus dry up. Did your mother not tell you that?'

Akuebue rose to his feet very slowly because of the pain in his waist.

'Old age is a disease,' he said, struggling to unbend himself with one hand on the hip. When he was three-quarters erect he gave up. 'Whenever I sit for any length of time I have to practise again to walk, like an infant.' He smiled as he toddled to the low entrance wall of his *obi*, took from it a wooden bowl with a lump of chalk in it and offered it to his guest. Ezeulu picked up the chalk and drew five lines with it on the floor – three uprights, a flat one across the top and another below them. Then he painted one of his big toes and dubbed a thin coat of white around his left eye.

Only one of Akuebue's two wives was at home and she soon came into the *obi* to salute Ezeulu and to say that the senior wife had gone to inspect her palm trees for ripe fruit. Obielue returned with a kola nut. He took the wooden bowl from his father, blew into it to remove dust and offered the kola nut in it to Ezeulu.

'Thank you,' said Ezeulu. 'Take it to your father to break.'

'No,' said Akuebue. 'I ask you to break it.'

'That cannot be. We do not bypass a man and enter his compound.'

'I know that,' said Akuebue, 'but you see that my hands are full and I am asking you to perform the office for me.'

'A man cannot be too busy to break the first kola nut of the day in his own house. So put the yam down; it will not run away.'

'But this is not the first kola nut of the day. I have broken several already.'

'That may be so, but you did not break them in my presence. The time a man wakes up is his morning.'

'All right,' said Akuebue. 'I shall break it if you say so.'

'Indeed I say so. We do not apply an ear-pick to the eye.'

Akuebue took the kola nut in his hand and said: 'We shall both live,' and broke it.

Two gunshots had sounded in the neighbourhood since Ezeulu came in. Now a third went off.

'What is happening there?' he asked. 'Are men leaving the forest now to hunt in the compounds?'

'Oh. You have not heard? Ogbuefi Amalu is very sick.'

'True? And it has reached the point of shooting guns?'

'Yes.' Akuebue lowered his voice out of respect for the bad story. 'What day was yesterday?'

'Eke,' replied Ezeulu.

'Yes, it was on the other Eke that it happened. He was returning home from the farmland he had gone to clear when it struck him down. Before he reached home he was trembling with cold in the noonday heat. He could no longer hold his matchet because his fingers were set like crooks.'

'What do they say it is?'

'From what I saw this morning and yesterday I think it is *aru-mmo*.'

'Please do not repeat it.'

'But I am not telling you what Nwokonkwo or Nwokafo told me. This is what I saw with my own eyes.'

Ezeulu began to gnash his teeth.

'I went to see him this morning. His breath seemed to be scraping his sides with a blunt razor.'

'Who have they hired to make medicine for him?' asked Ezeulu.

'A man called Nwodika from Umuofia. I told them this morning that had I been there when they took the decision I would have told them to go straight to Aninta. There is a doctor there who nips off sickness between his thumb and finger.'

'But if it is the sickness of the Spirits, as you say, there is no medicine for it – except camwood and fire.'

'That is so,' said Akuebue, 'but we cannot put our hands between our laps and watch a sick man for twelve days. We must grope about until what must happen does happen. That is why I spoke of this medicine-man from Aninta.'

'I think you speak of Aghadike whom they call Anyanafummo.'

'You know him. That is the very man.'

'I know many people throughout Olu and Igbo. Aghadike is a great doctor and diviner. But even he cannot carry a battle to the compound of the great god.'

'No man can do that.'

The gun sounded again.

'This gun-shooting is no more than a foolish groping about,' said Ezeulu. 'How can we frighten Spirits away with the noise of a gun? If it were so easy any man who had enough money to buy a keg of gunpowder would live and live until mushrooms sprouted from his head. If I am sick and they bring me a medicine-man who knows more about hunting than herbs I shall send him away and look for another.'

The two men sat for a little while in silence. Then Akuebue said:

'From what I saw this morning we may hear something before another dawn.'

Ezeulu moved his head up and down many times. 'It is a story of great sorrow, but we cannot set fire to the world.'

Akuebue who had stopped working on his yams went back to them now with the proverbial excuse that greeting in the cold harmattan is taken from the fireside.

'That is what our people say,' replied Ezeulu. 'And they also say that a man who visits a craftsman at work finds a sullen host.'

The gun sounded yet again. It seemed to make Ezeulu irritable.

'I shall go over and tell the man that if he has no medicine to give to the sick man he should at least spare the gunpowder they will use for his funeral.'

'Perhaps he thinks that gunpowder is as cheap as wood ash,' said Akuebue, and then more seriously: 'If you go there on your way home say nothing that might make them think you wish their kinsman evil. They may say: What is gunpowder to a man's life?'

Ezeulu did not need two looks at the sick man to see that he could not pass the twelve days which the Spirits gave a man stricken with this disease. If, as Akuebue had said, nothing was heard by tomorrow it would be a thing to tell.

The man's trunk was encased in a thick coat of camwood ointment which had caked and cracked in countless places. A big log fire burned beside the bamboo bed on which he lay and a strong whiff of burning herbs was in the air. His breathing was like the splitting of hard wood. He did not recognize Ezeulu who on entering had greeted those in the room with his eyes alone and made straight for the bedside where he stood for a long time looking down on the sick man in silence. After that he went and sat down with the small crowd of relations talking in very low voices.

'What has a man done to merit this?' he asked.

'That is what we all have been asking,' replied one of the men. 'We were not told to expect it. We woke up one morning to find our shinbone deformed.'

The herbalist sat a little apart from the group, and took no part in the conversation. Ezeulu looked around the room and saw how the man had fortified it against the entry of the Spirits. From the roof hung down three long gourds corked with wads of dry banana leaf. A fourth gourd was the big-bellied type which was often used for carrying palm wine. It hung directly over the sick man. On its neck was a string of cowries, and a bunch of parrots' feathers danced inside it with only their upper half showing. It looked as if something boiled about their feet forcing them to gyrate around the mouth of the gourd. Two freshly sacrificed chicks dangled head downwards on either side of it.

The sick man who had been silent except for his breathing began quite suddenly to groan. Everyone stopped talking. The medicine-man, a ring of white chalked dubbed round one eye and a large leather-covered amulet on his left wrist, rose up and went outside. His flint-gun lay at the threshold, its base on the ground and the barrel pointing into the hut. He picked it up and began to load. The gunpowder was contained in a four-cornered bottle which had once carried the white man's hot drink called *Nje-nje*. When he had loaded the gun he went to the back of the house and let it off. All the cocks and hens in the neighbourhood immediately set up an alarm as if they had seen a wild animal.

When he returned to the hut he found the sick man even more restless, saying meaningless things.

'Bring me his *ofo*,' he said.

The sick man's brother took the short wooden staff from the house-shrine held by ropes to a rafter. The medicine-man who was now crouching by the bed took it from him and opening the sick man's right hand put it there.

'Hold it!' he commanded pressing the dry fingers round the staff. 'Grasp it, and say no to them! Do you hear me? Say no!'

The meaning of his command seemed at last to seep through many clogged filters to the sick man's mind and the fingers began to close, like claws, slowly round the staff.

'That's right,' said the medicine-man beginning to remove his own hand and to leave the *ofo* in Amalu's grasp. 'Say no to them!'

But as soon as he took his hand completely away Amalu's fingers jerked open and the *ofo* fell down on the floor. The little crowd in the hut exchanged meaningful glances but no words.

Soon after Ezeulu rose to go. 'Take good care of him,' he said.

'Go well,' replied the others.

When Obika's bride arrived with her people and he looked upon her again it surprised him greatly that he had been able to let her go untouched during her last visit. He knew that few other young men of his age would have shown the same restraint which ancient custom demanded. But what was right was right. Obika began to admire this new image of himself as an upholder of custom – like the lizard who fell down from the high iroko tree he felt entitled to praise himself if nobody else did.

The bride was accompanied by her mother who was just coming out of an illness, many girls of her own age and her mother's women friends. Most of the women carried small headloads of the bride's dowry to which they had all contributed – cooking-pots, wooden bowls, brooms, mortar, pestle, baskets, mats, ladles, pots of palm oil, baskets of coco-yam, smoked fish, fermented cassava, locust beans, heads of salt and pepper. There were also two lengths of cloth, two plates and an iron pot. These last were products of the white man and had been bought at the new trading store at Okperi.

The three compounds of Ezeulu and his sons were already full of relatives and friends before the bride and her people arrived. The twenty or so young maidens attending her were all fully decorated. But the bride stood out among them. It was not only that she was taller than any of them, she was altogether more striking in her looks and carriage. She wore a different coiffure befitting her imminent transition to full womanhood – a plait rather than regular patterns made with a razor.

The girls sang a song called *Ifeoma*. Goodly Thing had come, they said, so let everyone who had good things bring them before her as offering. They made a circle round her and she danced to their song. As she danced her husband-to-be and other members of Ezeulu's family broke through the circle one or two at a time and stuck money on her forehead. She smiled and let the present fall at her feet from where one of the girls picked it up and put it in a bowl.

The bride's name was Okuata. In tallness she took after her father who came of a race of giants. Her face was finely cut and some people already called her Oyilidie because she resembled her husband in comeliness. Her full breasts had a very slight upward curve which would save them from falling and sagging too soon.

Her hair was done in the new *otimili* fashion. There were eight closely woven ridges of hair running in perfect lines from the nape to the front of the head and ending in short upright tufts like a garland of thick bristles worn on the hairline from ear to ear. She wore as many as fifteen strings of *jigida* on her waist. Most of them were blood-coloured but two or three were black, and some of the blood-coloured strings had been made up with a few black discs thrown in. Tomorrow she would tie a loincloth like a full-grown woman and henceforth her body would be concealed from the public gaze. The strings of *jigida* clinked at she danced. Behind they covered all her waist and the upper part of her buttocks. In front they lay string upon string from under her navel to her genitals, covering the greater part and providing a dark shade for the rest. The other girls were dressed in the same way except that most of them wore fewer strings of *jigida*.

The feasting which followed lasted till sunset. There were pots of yam pottage, foo-foo, bitter-leaf soup and *egusi* soup, two boiled legs of goat, two large bowls of cooked *asa* fish taken out whole from the soup and kegs of sweet wine tapped from the raffia palm.

Whenever a particularly impressive item of food was set before the women their song-leader raised the old chant of thanks:

> *Kwo-kwo-kwo-kwo-kwo!*
> Kwo-o-o-oh!
> We are going to eat again as we are wont to do!
> *Who provides?*
> Who is it?
> *Who provides?*
> Who is it?
> *Obika Ezeulu he provides*
> Ayo-o-o-o-o-oh!

But in the end her mother and all the protecting company from her village set out for home again leaving her behind. Okuata felt like an orphan child and tears came down her face. Her mother-in-law took her away into her hut where she would stay until the Sacrifice at the crossroads was performed.

The medicine-man and diviner who had been hired to perform the rite soon arrived and the party set out. In it were Obika, his elder half-brother, his mother and the bride. Ezeulu did not go with them because he rarely left his *obi* after dark. Oduche refused to go so as not to offend the catechist who preached against sacrifices.

They made for the highway leading to Umuezeani, the village where the bride came from. It was now quite dark and there was no moon. The palm-oil lamp which Obika's mother carried gave little light especially as she had to cup one hand round the wick to protect the flame from the wind. Even so it was blown out twice and she had to go into nearby compounds to light it again – first into Anosi's compound and then into the hut of Membolu's widow.

The medicine-man, whose name was Aniegboka, walked silently

in front of the group. He was a small man but when he spoke he raised his voice as one might do in talking over the compound wall to a neighbour who was hard of hearing. Aniegboka was not one of the famous medicine-men in the clan; he was chosen because he was friendly with Ezeulu's compound and besides the sacrifice he was going to perform did not call for exceptional skill. Children in all the neighbourhood knew him and fled on his approach because they said he could turn a person into a dog by slapping him on the buttocks. But they made fun of him when he was not there because one of his eyes was like a bad cowry. According to the story the eye was damaged by the sharpened end of a banana shaft which Aniegboka – then a little boy – was throwing up and catching again in mid-air.

As the group walked in the dark they passed a few people but only recognized them from their voice when they spoke a greeting. The weak light of the oil lamp seemed to deepen the darkness around them making it difficult for them to see others as easily as they themselves were seen.

There was a soft but constant clatter coming from the big skin bag slung on Aniegboka's shoulder. The bride had a bowl of fired clay in one hand and a hen in the other. Now and again the hen squawked the way hens do when their pen is disturbed by an intruder at night. As she walked in the middle of the file Okuata suffered the struggle of happiness and fear in her thoughts. Obika and Edogo who led the way held their matchets. They spoke now and again but Obika's mind was not in what they said. His ear strained to catch the gentlest clinking together of his bride's *jigida*. He could even isolate her footsteps from all the others behind him. He too was anxious. When he took his wife to his hut after the sacrifice, would he find her at home – as the saying was – or would he learn with angry humiliation that another had broken in and gone off with his prize? That could not be. Everyone who knew her witnessed to her good behaviour. Obika had already chosen an enormous goat as a present for his mother-in-law should his wife prove to be a virgin. He did not know exactly what he would do if he found that he could not take it to her after all.

On his left hand Obika held a very small pot of water by the neck. His half-brother had a bunch of tender palm frond cut from the pinnacle of the tree.

Before long they reached the junction of their highway and another leading to the bride's village along which she had come that very day. They walked a short distance on this road and stopped. The medicine-man chose a spot in the middle of the way and asked Obika to dig a hole there.

'Put down the lamp here,' he told Obika's mother. She did so and Obika crouched down and began to dig.

'Make it wider,' said the medicine-man. 'Yes, like that.'

The three men were all in a crouching position; the women knelt on both knees with the trunk erect. The light of the oil lamp burnt with vigour now.

'Do not dig any more,' said the medicine-man. 'It is now deep enough. Bring out all the loose soil.'

While Obika was scooping out the red earth with both hands the medicine-man began to bring out the sacrificial objects from his bag. First he brought out four small yams, then four pieces of white chalk and the flower of the wild lily.

'Give me the *omu*.' Edogo passed the tender palm leaves to him. He tore out four leaflets and put away the rest. Then he turned to Obika's mother.

'Let me have *ego nano*.' She untied a bunch of cowries from a corner of her cloth and gave them to him. He counted them carefully on the ground as a woman would before she bought or sold in the market, in groups of six. There were four groups and he nodded his head.

He rose to his feet and positioned Okuata beside the hole so that she faced the direction of her village, kneeling on both knees. Then he took his position opposite her on the other side of the hole, with the sacrificial objects ranged on his right. The others stood a little back.

He took one of the yams and gave it to Okuata. She waved it round her head and put it inside the hole. The medicine-man put in the other three. Then he gave her one of the pieces of white chalk and she did as for the yam. Then came the palm leaves and the flower of the wild lily and last of all he gave her one group of six cowries which she closed in her palm and did as for the others. After this he pronounced the absolution:

Any evil which you might have seen with your eyes, or spoken with your mouth, or heard with your ears or trodden with your feet; whatever your father might have brought upon you or your mother brought upon you, I cover them all here.

As he spoke the last words he took the bowl of fired clay and placed it face downwards over the objects in the hole. Then he began to put back the loose earth. Twice he eased up the bowl slightly, so that when he finished its curved back showed a little above the surface of the road.

'Where is the water?' he asked.

Obika's mother produced the small pot of water. The bride who had now risen to her feet bent down at the waist and tipping the water into her palm began to wash her face, her hands and arms and her feet and legs up to the knee.

'Do not forget,' said the diviner when she had finished, 'that you are not to pass this way until morning even if the warriors of Abam were to strike this night and you were fleeing for your life.'

'The great god will not let her run for her life, neither today nor tomorrow,' said her mother-in-law.

'We know she will not,' said Aniegboka, 'but we must still do things as they were laid down.' Then turning to Obika he said: 'I have done as you asked me to do. Your wife will bear you nine sons.'

'We thank you,' said Obika and Edogo together.

'This hen will follow me home,' he said as he slung his bag on one shoulder and picked up the hen by the legs tied together with banana rope. He must have noticed how their eyes went again and again to the fowl. 'I alone will eat its flesh. Let none of you pay me a visit in the morning because I shall not share it.' He laughed very loud, like a drunken man. 'Even diviners ought to be rewarded now and again.' He laughed once more. 'Do we not say that the flute player must sometimes stop to wipe his nose?'

'That is what we say,' replied Edogo.

All the way back the medicine-man was full of loud talk. He boasted about the high regard in which, he said, he was held in distant clans. The others listened with one ear and put in a word now and again. The only person who did not open her mouth was Okuata.

When they got to Ilo Agbasioso the diviner parted with them and took a turning to the right. As soon as he was out of earshot Obika asked if it was the custom for the diviner to take the hen home.

'I have heard that some of them do,' said his mother. 'But I have never seen it until today. My own hen was buried with the rest of the sacrifice.'

'I have never heard of it,' said Edogo. 'It seems to me that the man does not get enough custom and is grabbing whatever he sees.'

'Our part was to provide the hen,' said Obika's mother, 'and we have done it.'

'I wanted to put a question to him.'

'No, my son. It is better that you did not. This is not the time to quarrel and dispute.'

Before Obika and his wife, Okuata, retired to their own compound they went first to salute Ezeulu.

'Father, is it the custom for the diviner to take home the hen bought for the sacrifice?' asked Obika.

'No, my son. Did Aniegboka do so?'

'He did. I wanted to speak to him but my mother made a sign to me not to talk.'

'It is not the custom. You must know that there are more people with greedy, long throats in the pursuit of medicine than anywhere else.' He noticed the look of concern on Obika's face. 'Take your wife home and do not allow this to trouble you. If a diviner wants to eat the entrails of sacrifice like a vulture the matter lies between him and his *chi*. You have done your part by providing the animal.'

When they left him Ezeulu felt his heart warm with pleasure as

443

it had not done for many days. Was Obika already a changed person? It was not like him to come to his father and ask questions with so much care on his face. Akuebue had always said that once Obika had a woman to provide for he would change his ways. Perhaps it was going to be so. Another thought came to Ezeulu to confirm it: in the past Obika would have stood over the diviner and made him bury the hen. He smiled.

CHAPTER TWELVE

Although Okuata emerged at dawn feeling awkward and bashful in her unaccustomed loincloth it was a very proud bashfulness. She could go without shame to salute her husband's parents because she had been 'found at home'. Her husband was even now arranging to send the goat and other presents to her mother in Umuezeani for giving him an unspoilt bride. She felt greatly relieved for although she had always known she was a virgin she had had a secret fear which sometimes whispered in her ear and made her start. It was the thought of the moonlight play when Obiora had put his penis between her thighs. True, he had only succeeded in playing at the entrance but she could not be too sure.

She had not slept very much, not as much as her husband; but she had been happy. Sometimes she tried to forget her happiness and to think how she would have felt had things turned out differently. For many years to come she would have walked like one afraid the earth might bite her. Every girl knew of Ogbanje Omenyi whose husband was said to have sent to her parents for a matchet to cut the bush on either side of the highway which she carried between her thighs.

Every child in Ezeulu's compound wanted to go to the stream and draw water that morning because their new wife was going. Even little Obiageli who hated the stream because of the sharp stones on the way was very quick in bringing out her water-pot. For once she cried when her mother told her to stay back and look after Amoge's child.

Obika's younger sister, Ojiugo, rushed up and down with the proprietary air of one who had a special claim on the bride because even the smallest child in a man's compound knew its mother's hut from the others. Ojiugo's mother, Matefi, carried the same air but with studied restraint which made it all the more telling. Needless to say she wanted it to tell on her husband's younger wife and to prove to her that there was greater honour in having a daughter-in-law than in buying ivory anklets and starving your children.

'See that you come back quickly,' she said to her daughter and her son's wife, 'before this spit on the floor dries up.' She spat.

'It is only bathing that could delay us,' said Nwafo. 'If we just draw water now and bathe another time . . .'

'I think you are mad,' said his mother who had so far pretended to ignore her husband's senior wife. 'But let me see you come back from the stream with yesterday's body and we shall see whose madness is greater, yours or mine.' The vehemence with which she said this seemed so much greater than the cause of her annoyance. In fact she was angry with her son not for what he had proposed but for his disloyalty in joining the excited flurry of the other hut.

'What are you still crawling about like a millipede for?' Matefi asked her daughter. 'Will going to the stream be your day's work?'

Oduche wore his loincloth of striped towelling and white singlet which he normally put on only for church or school. This made his mother even more angry than had Nwafo's proposal, but she succeeded in remaining silent.

Soon after the water party left Obiageli came into Ezeulu's hut carrying Amoge's child on her back. The child was clearly too big for her; one of his legs almost trailed the ground.

'These people are mad,' said Ezeulu. 'Who left a sick child in your hands? Take him back to his mother at once.'

'I can carry him,' said Obiageli.

'Who is carrying the other? Take him to his mother, I say.'

'She has gone to the stream,' replied Obiageli bouncing up on her toes in an effort to keep the child from slipping down her back. 'But I can carry him. See.'

'I know you can,' said Ezeulu, 'but he is sick and should not be shaken about. Take him to your mother.'

Obiageli nodded and went into the inner compound, but Ezeulu knew she still carried the child (who had now begun to cry). Obiageli's tiny voice was striving valiantly to drown the crying and sing him to sleep:

> *Tell the mother her child is crying*
> *Tell the mother her child is crying*
> *And then prepare a stew of úzízá*
> *And also a stew of úzìzà*
> *Make a watery pepper-soup*
> *So the little birds who drink it*
> *Will all perish from the hiccup*
> *Mother's goat is in the barn*
> *And the yams will not be safe*
> *Father's goat is in the barn*
> *And the yams will all be eaten*
> *Can you see that deer approaching*
> *Look! he's dipped one foot in water*
> *Snake has struck him!*
> *He withdraws!*
> *Ja – ja. ja kulo kulo!*
> *Traveller Hawk*
> *You're welcome home*
> *Ja – ja. ja kulo kulo!*
> *But where's the length*
> *Of cloth you brought*
> *Ja – ja. ja kulo kulo!*

'Nwafo! . . . Nwafo!' called Ezeulu.

'Nwafo has gone to the stream!' replied his mother from her hut.

'Nwafo has what?' Ezeulu shouted back.

Ugoye decided to go into the *obi* in person and explain that Nwafo had gone on his own account.

'Nobody asked him to go,' she said.

'Nobody asked him to go?' retorted Ezeulu parodying a child's talk. 'Did you say that nobody asked him to go? Do you not know that he sweeps my hut every morning? Or do you expect me to break kola nut or receive people in an uswept hut? Did your father break his morning kola nut over yesterday's wood ash? The abomination all you people commit in this house will lie on your own heads. If Nwafo has become too strong to listen to you why did you not ask Oduche to come and sweep my hut?'

'Oduche went with the rest.'

Ezeulu chose not to speak any more. His wife went away but soon returned with two brooms. She swept the hut with the palm-leaf broom and the immediate frontage of the *obi* with the longer and stronger bundle of *okeakpa*.

Obika came from his hut while she swept the outside and asked: 'Do you sweep the *iru-ezi* nowadays? Where is Nwafo?'

'No one is born with a broom in his hand,' she replied testily and increased the volume of her singing. Because of the length of the broom she held and wielded it like a paddle. Ezeulu smiled to himself. When she had finished she gathered the sweepings into one heap and carried them into the plot of land on the right where she was going to plant coco-yams that season.

Akuebue planned to visit Ezeulu soon after the morning meal, to rejoice with him for his son's new wife. But he had other important things to talk over with him and that was why he chose to go so early – before other visitors in search of palm wine filled the place. What Akuebue wanted to talk about was not new. They had talked about it many times before. But in the past few days Akuebue had begun to hear things which worried him greatly. It was all about Ezeulu's third son, Oduche, whom he had sent to learn the secrets of the white man's magic. Akuebue had doubted the sense in Ezeulu's action from the very first but Ezeulu had persuaded him of its wisdom. But now it was being used by Ezeulu's enemies to harm his name. People were asking: 'If the Chief Priest of Ulu could send his son among people who kill and eat the sacred python and commit other evils what did he expect ordinary men and women to do? The lizard who threw confusion into his mother's funeral rite, did he expect outsiders to carry the burden of honouring his dead?'

And now Ezeulu's first son had joined, albeit surreptitiously, his father's opponents. He had gone to Akuebue on the previous day and asked him to go as Ezeulu's best friend and speak to him without biting the words.

'What is wrong?'

'A man should hold his compound together, not plant dissension among his children.' Whenever Edogo felt deeply he stammered agonizingly. He did so now.

'I am listening.'

Edogo told him that the reason why Ezeulu sent Oduche to the new religion was to leave the way clear for Nwafo to become Chief Priest.

'Who said so?' asked Akuebue. But before Edogo could answer he added: 'You speak about Nwafo and Oduche, what about you and Obika?'

'Obika's mind is not on such things – neither is mine.'

'But Ulu does not ask if a man's mind is on something or not. If he wants you he will get you. Even the one who has gone to the new religion, if Ulu wants him he will take him.'

'That is true,' said Edogo. 'But what worries me is that my father makes Nwafo think he will be chosen. If tomorrow as you say Ulu chooses another person there will be strife in the family. My father will not be there then and it will all rattle around my own head.'

'What you say is very true and I do not blame you for wanting to bale that water before it rises above the ankle.' He thought about it for a while and added: 'But I do not think there will be strife. Nwafo and Oduche come from the same woman. It is fortunate that you and Obika have not set your minds on it.'

'But you know what Obika is,' said Edogo. 'He might wake up tomorrow morning and want it.'

The old man and his friend's son talked for a long time. When Edogo finally rose to go (he had announced his intention to go three or four times before without getting up) Akuebue promised to talk to Ezeulu. He felt pity and a little contempt for the young man. Why could he not open his mouth like a man and say that he wanted to be priest instead of hiding behind Oduche and Obika? That was why Ezeulu never counted him among people. So he had hopes

that the *afa* oracle would call his name when the day came?
'The fellow does not fall where his body might be picked up,'
he thought. 'It does not require an oracle to see that he is not
the man for Chief Priest. A ripe maize can be told by merely
looking at it.'

And yet Akuebue felt sorry for Edogo. He knew how a man's
first son must feel to be pushed back so that the younger ones might
come forward to receive favour. No doubt that was why in the first
days of Umuaro, Ulu chose to give only one son to his Chief Priests,
for seven generations.

On the way to the stream that morning the bride, who had not
seen many white singlets in her life, was inclined to take too much
interest in Oduche and the new religion which provided such
marvels. To curb her enthusiasm jealous Ojiugo whispered into
her ear that devotees of this new cult killed and ate the python.
The bride who, like any other person in Umuaro, had heard of
Oduche's adventure with the python asked anxiously:

'Did he kill it? We were told he only put it in his box.'

Unfortunately Ojiugo was one of those people who could never
whisper, and what she said reached Oduche's ears. He immediately
rushed at Ojiugo and, in the words of Nwafo when he recounted
the incident later, gave her thunder on the face. Whereupon Ojiugo
virtually threw down her pot and attacked Oduche using the metal
bangle on her wrists to give edge to her blows. Oduche replied with
even more fiery slaps and a final, vicious blow with his knee on
Ojiugos belly. This brought great criticism and even abuse on
Oduche from many of the people who had gathered to help separate
them. But Ojiugo clung to her half-brother crying: 'Kill me today.
You must kill me. Do you hear me, Eater of python? You must
kill me.' She bit one of the people trying to hold her back and
scratched another.

'Leave her alone,' said one of the women in exasperation. 'If
she wants to be killed then let her.'

'Don't talk like that. Were you not here when he nearly killed
her with a kick in the belly?'

'Hasn't she hit him enough for it already?' asked a third.

'No, she hasn't,' said the second woman. 'I think he is one of those who become brave when they see a woman.'

The crowd was immediately divided between supporters of Ojiugo and those who thought she had already revenged herself sufficiently. These latter now urged Oduche to hurry away to the stream and not listen any more to Ojiugo's abuse or try to answer back.

'The offspring of a hawk cannot fail to devour chicks,' said Oyilidie, whom Ojiugo had bitten. 'This one resembles her mother in stubbornness.'

'Should she have resembled your mother then?' This came from Ojinika a broad-looking woman who had an old quarrel with Oyilidie. People said that in spite of Ojinika's tough appearance and the speed with which she flew into quarrels her strength was only in her mouth and a child of two could knock her down with its breath.

'Don't open your rotten mouth near me, do you hear?' said Oyilidie. 'Or I shall beat okro seeds out of your mouth. Perhaps you have forgotten . . .'

'Go and eat shit,' shouted Ojinika. The two were already measuring themselves against each other, standing on tiptoe and chests thrust out.

'What is wrong with these two?' asked another woman. 'Give way and let me pass.'

Ojiugo was still sobbing when she reached home. Nwafo and Oduche had returned earlier but Ojiugo's mother had disdained asking them about the others. When she saw Ojiugo coming in she wanted to ask her if they had had to wait for the stream to return from a journey or wake up from sleep. But the words dried in her mouth.

'What is wrong?' she asked instead. Ojiugo increased her snivelling. Her mother helped her put down her water-pot and asked again what was wrong. Before she said anything Ojiugo first went inside their hut, sat down on the floor and wiped her eyes. Then she told her story. Matefi examined her daughter's face and saw what looked like the weal left by Oduche's five fingers. She immediately raised her voice in protest and lamentation so that all the neighbourhood might hear.

Ezeulu walked as unhurriedly as he could into the inner compound and asked what all the noise was about. Matefi wailed louder.

'Shut your mouth,' Ezeulu commanded.

'You tell me to shut my mouth,' screamed Matefi, 'when Oduche takes my daughter to the stream and beats her to death. How can I shut my mouth when they bring back a corpse to me. Go and look at her face; the fellow's five fingers . . .' Her voice had risen till it reverberated in the brain.

'I say shut your mouth! Are you mad?'

Matefi stopped her screaming. She moaned resignedly: 'I have shut my mouth. Why should I not shut my mouth? After all Oduche is Ugoye's son. Yes, Matefi must shut her mouth.'

'Let nobody call my name there!' shouted the other wife as she came out from her hut where she had sat as though all the noise in the compound came from a distant clan. 'I say let nobody mention my name at all.'

'You, shut your mouth,' said Ezeulu, turning to her; 'nobody has called your name.'

'Did you not hear her calling my name?'

'And if she did? . . . Go and jump on her back if you can.'

Ugoye grumbled and returned to her hut.

'Oduche!'

'E-e-h.'

'Come out here!'

Oduche came out from his mother's hut.

'What is all this noise about?' asked Ezeulu.

'Ask Ojiugo and her mother.'

'I am asking you. And don't you tell me to ask another or a dog will lick your eyes this morning. When did you people learn to fling words in my face?' He looked round at them all, his manner changed to that of a crouching leopard. 'Let one of you open his mouth and make *fim* again and I will teach him that a man does not talk when masked spirits speak.' He looked round again, daring anyone to open his mouth. There was silence all round and he turned and went back to his *obi*, anger having smothered his interest in the cause of the affray.

Akuebue's haste in plunging into the subject of Oduche proved to be ill-judged. He was anxious to finish with it before more people arrived, for there could be no doubt that quite soon the three compounds would be filled. Many of the people who came last night would come again, and many more would be coming for the first time because, at this hungry season when most barns were empty of all but seed-yams, no one would miss the chance of biting a morsel and drinking a horn in the house of a wealthy man. Akuebue knew that as soon as the first man arrived he could no longer talk with Ezeulu; so he wasted no time. Had he known how much Ezeulu had just been annoyed perhaps he would have waited for another day.

Ezeulu listened silently to him, holding back with both hands the mounting irritation he felt.

'Have you finished?' he asked when Akuebue ceased talking.

'Yes, I have finished.'

'I salute you.' He was not looking at his guest but vaguely at the threshold. 'I cannot say that I blame you; you have said nothing that a man could be blamed for saying to his friend. I am not blind and I am not deaf either. I know that Umuaro is divided and confused and I know that some people are holding secret meetings to persuade others that I am the cause of the trouble. But why should that remove sleep from my eyes? These things are not new and they will follow where the others have gone. When the rain comes it will be five years since this same man told a secret meeting in his house that if Ulu failed to fight in their blameful war they would unseat him. We are still waiting, Ulu and I, for him to come and unseat us. What annoys me is not that an overblown fool dangling empty testicles should forget himself because wealth entered his house by mistake; no, what annoys me is that the cowardly priest of Idemili should hide behind him and urge him on.'

'It is jealousy,' said Akuebue.

'Jealousy for what? I am not the first Ezeulu in Umuaro, he is

not the first Ezidemili. If his father and his father's father and all
the others before them were not jealous of my fathers why should
he be of me? No, it is not jealousy but foolishness; the kind that
puts its head into the pot. But if it is jealousy, let him go on. The
fly that perches on a mound of dung may strut around as it likes,
it cannot move the mound.'

'Everybody knows these two,' said Akuebue. 'We all know that
if they knew the way to Ani-Mmo they would go to quarrel with
our ancestors for giving the priesthood of Ulu to Umuachala and
not to their own village. I am not troubled about them. What
troubles me is what the whole clan is saying.'

'Who tells the clan what it says? What does the clan know?
Sometimes, Akuebue, you make me laugh. You were here – or
had you not been born then – when the clan chose to go to war
with Okperi over a piece of land which did not belong to us. Did
I not stand up then and tell Umuaro what would happen to them?
And who was right in the end? What I said, did it happen or did
it not?'

Akuebue did not answer.

'Every word happened as I said it would.'

'I do not doubt that,' said Akuebue and, in a sudden access of
impatience and recklessness, added, 'but you forget one thing: that
no man however great can win judgement against a clan. You may
think you did in that land dispute but you are wrong. Umuaro will
always say that you betrayed them before the white man. And they
will say that you are betraying them again today by sending your
son to join in desecrating the land.'

Ezeulu's reply to this showed Akuebue once again that even to
his best friend the priest was unknowable. Even his sons did not
know him. Akuebue was not sure what reply he had expected, but
it was most certainly not the laugh which he got now. It made him
afraid and uneasy like one who encounters a madman laughing on
a solitary path. He was given no time to examine this strange feeling
of fear closely. But he was to have it again in future and it was
only then he saw its meaning.

'Don't make me laugh,' said Ezeulu again. 'So I betrayed
Umuaro to the white man? Let me ask you one question. Who

brought the white man here? Was it Ezeulu? We went to war against Okperi who are our blood brothers over a piece of land which did not belong to us and you blame the white man for stepping in. Have you not heard that when two brothers fight a stranger reaps the harvest? How many white men went in the party that destroyed Abame? Do you know? Five.' He held his right hand up with the five fingers fanned out. 'Five. Now have you ever heard that five people – even if their heads reached the sky – could overrun a whole clan? Impossible. With all their power and magic white men would not have overrun entire Olu and Igbo if we did not help them. Who showed them the way to Abame? They were not born there; how then did they find the way? We showed them and are still showing them. So let nobody come to me now and complain that the white man did this and did that. The man who brings ant-infested faggots into his hut should not grumble when lizards begin to pay him a visit.'

'I cannot dispute any of the things you say. We did many things wrong in the past, but we should not therefore go on doing the same today. We now know what we did wrong, so we can put it right again. We know where this rain began to fall on us . . .'

'I am not so sure,' said Ezeulu. 'But whether you do or not you must not forget one thing. We have shown the white man the way to our house and given him a stool to sit on. If we now want him to go away again we must either wait until he is tired of his visit or we must drive him away. Do you think you can drive him away by blaming Ezeulu? You may try, and the day I hear that you have succeeded I shall come and shake your hand. I have my own way and I shall follow it. I can see things where other men are blind. That is why I am Known and at the same time I am Unknowable. You are my friend and you know whether I am a thief or a murderer or an honest man. But you cannot know the Thing which beats the drum to which Ezeulu dances. I can see tomorrow; that is why I can tell Umuaro; *come out from this because there is death there* or *do this because there is profit in it*. If they listen to me, o-o; if they refuse to listen, o-o. I have passed the stage of dancing to receive presents. You knew my father who was priest before me. You knew my grandfather too, albeit with the eyes of a little child.' Akuebue nodded in agreement.

'Did not my grandfather put a stop to *ichi* in Umuaro? He stood up in all his awe and said: We shall no longer carve our faces as if they were *ozo* doors.'

'He did it,' said Akuebue.

'What was Umuaro's reply to him? They cursed him; they said their men would look like women. They said: *how is a man's endurance to be tested?* Today who asks such a question?'

Akuebue felt that he had already agreed with Ezeulu sufficiently to be able to dissent again. 'What you say cannot be doubted,' he said, 'but if what we are told is true, your grandfather was not alone in that fight. There were said to be more people against *ichi* in Umuaro than . . .'

'Was that how your father told you the story? I heard differently. Anyhow the important thing was that the Chief Priest led them and they followed. But if there is hearsay in that one, what about events in my father's time? You were not an infant when my father set aside the custom which made any child born to a widow a slave unless . . .'

'I am not the man to dispute any of the things you say, Ezeulu. I am your friend and I can talk to you as I like; but that does not mean I forget that one half of you is man and the other half spirit. And what you say about your father and grandfather is very true. But what happened in their time and what is happening today are not the same; they do not even have resemblance. Your father and grandfather did not do what they did to please a stranger . . .'

This stung Ezeulu sharply but again he kept a firm hold on his anger.

'Do not make me laugh,' he said. 'If someone came to you and said that Ezeulu sent his son to a strange religion so as to please another man what would you tell him? I say don't make me laugh. Shall I tell you why I sent my son? Then listen. A disease that has never been seen before cannot be cured with everyday herbs. When we want to make a charm we look for the animal whose blood can match its power; if a chicken cannot do it we look for a goat or a ram; if that is not sufficient we send for a bull. But sometimes even a bull does not suffice, then we must look for a human. Do you think it is the sound of the death-cry gurgling through blood that we want to hear? No, my friend, we do it because we have reached the very end of things and we know that neither a cock nor a goat nor even a bull will do. And our fathers have told us that it may even happen to an unfortunate generation that they are pushed beyond the end of things, and their back is broken and hung over a fire. When this happens they may sacrifice their own blood. This is what our sages meant when they said that a man who has nowhere else to put his hand for support puts it on his own knee. That was why our ancestors when they were pushed beyond the end of things by the warriors of Abam sacrificed not a stranger but one of themselves and made the great medicine which they called Ulu.'

Akuebue cracked his fingers and moved his head up and down. 'So it is a sacrifice,' he muttered to himself. 'So Edogo was right after all, though he had seemed so foolish at the time.' He paused a while then spoke aloud:

'What happens if this boy you are sacrificing turns out to be the one chosen by Ulu when you are looked for and not found?'

'Leave that to the deity. When the time comes of which you speak Ulu will not seek your advice or help. So do not keep awake at night for that.'

'I don't, why should I? My compound is full of its own troubles, so why should I carry yours home; where would I find space to put them? But I must repeat what I said before and if you don't want to listen you can stop your ears. When you spoke against the war with Okperi you were not alone. I too was against it and so were many others. But if you send your son to join strangers in desecrating the land you will be alone. You may go and mark it on that wall to remind you that I said so.'

'Who is to say when the land of Umuaro has been desecrated, you or I?' Ezeulu's mouth was shaped with haughty indifference. 'As for being alone, do you not think that it should be as familiar to me now as are dead bodies to the earth? My friend, don't make me laugh.'

Nwafo, who had come into his father's hut when Akuebue was saying of Ezeulu that he was half-man, half-spirit, did not

457

understand the present dispute between the two men. But he had seen equally dangerous-looking scenes come to nothing before. He was therefore not in the least surprised when his father sent him to get palm oil sprinkled with ground pepper from his mother. When he returned with it Ezeulu had already brought down his round basket. This basket had a close-fitting lid and dangled from the roof directly above the log fire. Dangling with it were Ezeulu's ceremonial raffia skirt, two calabashes and a few heads of last season's maize specially chosen, on account of their good quality, for planting. Basket, maize and raffia skirt were all black with smoke.

Ezeulu opened the round basket and brought out a boiled and smoked leg of goat and cut a big piece for Akuebue and a very small one for himself.

'I think I shall need something to wrap this,' said Akuebue. Ezeulu sent Nwafo to cut a piece of banana leaf which he held above the smouldering log fire till it wilted slightly and lost its brittle freshness; then he passed it to Akuebue who divided the meat into two, wrapped the bigger half in the banana leaf and put it away in his bag. Then he began to eat the other half, dipping it in the peppered palm oil.

Ezeulu gave a little strand from his own piece to Nwafo and threw the remainder into his mouth. For a long time they ate in silence and when they began to talk again it was about less weighty things. Ezeulu broke off a toothpick from the broom lying on the floor near him and leaned back on the wall. From that position he easily commanded the approaches to his compound and the compound of his two sons. He was thus the first to notice the arrival of the Court Messenger and his escort.

When the two strangers reached Ezeulu's threshold the escort clapped his hands and said: 'Are the owners of this house at home?' There was a slight pause before Ezeulu answered: 'Enter and you will see.' The escort bent down at the low eaves and entered first; then the other followed. Ezeulu welcomed them and told them to sit down. The Court Messenger sat on the mud-bed but his escort remained standing. The greetings over he saluted Ezeulu and explained that he was the son of Nwodika in Umunneora.

'I thought I saw your father's face as soon as you came in, said Akuebue.

'Very true,' said Ezeulu. 'Anyone setting eyes on him knows he has seen Nwodika. Your friend seems to have come from far.'

'Yes, we have come from Okperi . . .'

'Do you live in Okperi then?' asked Ezeulu.

'Yes,' replied Akuebue. 'Have you not heard of one of our young men who lives with the white man in Okperi?'

Ezeulu had indeed heard but deliberately feigned ignorance.

'True?' he asked. 'I do not hear many things nowadays. So you have come all the way from Okperi this morning and you are here already? It is good to be strong and young. How are the people of my mother's land? You know my mother came from Okperi.'

'There was nothing but happiness and laughter when we left; what has happened since I cannot say.'

'And who is your companion?'

'He is the Chief Messenger of the great white man, the Destroyer of Guns.'

Ezeulu cracked his fingers and nodded.

'So this is Wintabota's messenger? Is he a man of Okperi?'

'No,' said the escort. 'His clan is Umuru.'

'Was Wintabota well when you left? We have not seen him in these parts for a long time.'

'Even so. This man here is his eye.'

The Chief Messenger did not seem too pleased with the trend of the conversation. In his mind he was angry with this man in the bush who put on airs and pretended to be familiar with the District Officer. His escort sensed this and made desperate efforts to establish his importance.

'Stranger, you are welcome,' said Ezeulu. 'What is your name?'

'He is called Jekopu,' said the escort. 'As I said, nobody sees the Destroyer of Guns without his consent. There is no one in Okperi who does not know the name of Jekopu. The Destroyer of Guns asked me to accompany him on this journey because he is a stranger to these parts.'

'Yes,' said Ezeulu with a meaningful glance in the direction of Akuebue. 'That is as it should be. The white man sends a man from Umuru and the man from Umuru is shown the way by a man of Umuaro.' He laughed 'What did I tell you, Akuebue? Our sages were right when they said that no matter how many spirits plotted a man's death it would come to nothing unless his personal god took a hand in the deliberation.'

The two men looked puzzled. Then Nwodika's son said: 'That is so; but we have not come on a mission of death.'

'No. I did not say so. It is only a manner of speaking. We have a saying that a snake is never as long as the stick to which we liken its length. I know that Wintabota will not send a mission of death to Ezeulu. We are good friends. What I said was that a stranger could not come to Umuaro unless a son of the land showed him the way.'

'That is true,' said the escort. 'We have come . . .'

'My friend,' interrupted the Chief Messenger, 'you have already done what you were sent to do; the rest is for me. So put your tongue into its scabbard.'

'Forgive me. I take my hands off.'

Ezeulu sent Nwafo to bring kola from Matefi. By this time both Obika and Edogo had come in, news having reached them that a messenger of the white man was in their father's hut. When the kola nut came it was shown round and broken.

'Have the people you sent to the market for palm wine returned yet?' asked Ezeulu. Obika said no.

'I knew they would not. A man who means to buy palm wine does not hang about at home until all the wine in the market is sold.' He was still leaning with his back on the wall, holding one leg a little off the ground with hands interlocked on the shin.

The Court Messenger removed his blue fez and planted it on his knee exposing a clean-shaven head shining with sweat. The edge of the cap left a ring round the head. He cleared his throat and spoke, almost for the first time.

'I salute you all.' He brought out a very small book from his breast pocket and opened it in the manner of a white man. 'Which one of you is called Ezeulu?' he asked from the book and then looked up and around the hut. No one spoke; they were all too astonished. Akuebue was the first to recover.

'Look round and count your teeth with your tongue,' he said.

'Sit down, Obika, you must expect foreigners to talk through the nose.'

'You say you are a man of Umuru?' asked Ezeulu. 'Do you have priest and elders there?'

'Do not take my question amiss. The white man has his own way of doing things. Before he does anything to you he will first ask you your name and the answer must come from your own lips.'

'If you have any grain of sense in your belly,' said Obika, 'you will know that you are not in the house of the white man but in Umuaro in the house of the Chief Priest of Ulu.'

'Hold your tongue, Obika. You heard Akuebue say just now that strangers talk through the nose. Do you know whether they have Chief Priests in his land or the land of the white man?'

'Tell that young man to take care how he talks to me. If he has not heard of me he should ask those who have.'

'Go and eat shit.'

'Shut your mouth!' roared Ezeulu. 'This man has come all the way from my mother's land to my house and I forbid anyone to abuse him. Besides he is only a messenger. If we dislike his message our quarrel cannot be with him but with the man who sent him.'

'Very true,' said Akuebue.

'There are no words left,' said the escort.

'You asked me a question,' continued Ezeulu turning again to the messenger. 'I shall now answer you. I am that Ezeulu you spoke of. Are you satisfied?'

'Thank you. We are all men here but when we open our mouths we know the men from the boys. We have spoken many words already; some were words of profit, some were not; some were words of sanity and some words of drunkenness. It is now time to say why I have come, for a toad does not run in the daytime unless something is after it. I have not come all the way from Okperi to stretch my legs. Your own kinsman here has told you how Kaputin Winta-bor-tom has put me in charge of many of his affairs. He is the chief of all the white men in these parts. I have known him for more than ten years and I have yet to see another white man who does not tremble before him. When he sent me here he did not tell me he had a friend in Umuaro.' He smiled in derision.

461

'But if what you say is true we shall know tomorrow when I take you to see him.'

'What are you talking about?' asked Akuebue in alarm.

The Court Messenger continued to smile menacingly. 'Yes,' he said. 'Your friend Wintabota' (he mouthed the name in the ignorant fashion of his hearers) 'has ordered you to appear before him tomorrow morning.'

'Where?' asked Edogo.

'Where else but in his office in Okperi.'

'The fellow is mad,' said Obika.

'No, my friend. If anyone is mad it's you. Anyhow, Ezeulu must prepare at once. Fortunately the new road makes even a cripple hungry for a walk. We set out this morning at the first cock-crow and before we knew where we were we had got here.'

'I said the fellow is mad. Who . . .'

'He is not mad,' said Ezeulu. 'He is a messenger and he must give the message as it was given to him. Let him finish.'

'I have finished,' said the other. 'But I ask whoever owns this young man to advise him for his own good.'

'You are sure you have given all the message?'

'Yes, the white man is not like black men. He does not waste his words.'

'I salute you,' said Ezeulu, 'and I welcome you again: *Nno!*'

'There is one small thing I forgot,' said the Court Messenger. 'There are many people waiting to see the white man and you may have to wait in Okperi for three or four days before your turn comes. But I know that a man like you would not want to spend many days outside his village. If you do me well I shall arrange for you to see him tomorrow. Everything is in my hands; if I say that the white man will see this person, he will see him. Your kinsman will tell you what I eat.' He smiled and put his fez back on the head.

'That is a small matter,' said Ezeulu. 'It will not cause a quarrel. I do not think that what you will put into that small belly of yours will be beyond me. If it is, my kinsmen are there to help.' He paused and seemed to enjoy the messenger's anger at the mention of his small size. 'You must first return, however, and tell your white man that Ezeulu does not leave his hut. If he wants to see me he must come here. Nwodika's son who showed you the way can also show him.'

'Do you know what you are saying, my friend?' asked the messenger in utter disbelief.

'Are you a messenger or not?' asked Ezeulu. 'Go home and give my message to your master.'

'Let us not quarrel about this,' said Akuebue stepping in quickly to save the situation which his spirit told him was fraught with peril. 'If the white man's messenger gives us some time we shall whisper together.'

'What are you whispering for?' asked Ezeulu indignantly. 'I have given my message.'

'Just give us some time,' said Akuebue to the messenger who complied and went outside. 'You may go out with him,' he told the escort.

Ezeulu took no part in the consultation that followed. When the Court Messenger and his companion returned to the hut it was Akuebue who told them that because of the respect he had for the white man Ezeulu had agreed to send his son, Edogo, to bring back whatever message there was for his father. 'In Umuaro it is not our custom to refuse a call, although we may refuse to do what the caller asks. Ezeulu does not want to refuse the white man's call and so he is sending his son.'

'Is that your answer?' asked the Court Messenger.

'It is,' replied Akuebue.

'I will not take it.'

'Then you can go into that bush there and eat shit,' said Obika. 'Do you see where my finger is pointing? That bush.'

'Nobody will eat shit,' said Akuebue, and turning to the messenger he added: 'I have never heard of a messenger choosing the message he will carry. Go and tell the white man what Ezeulu says. Or are you the white man yourself?'

Ezeulu had turned a little away from the others and begun again to pick his teeth with the broomstick.

CHAPTER THIRTEEN

As soon as the messenger and his escort left Ezeulu's hut to return
to Okperi the Chief Priest sent word to the old man who beat
the giant *ikolo* to summon the elders and *ndichie* to an urgent
meeting at sunset. Soon after the *ikolo* began to speak to the six
villages. Everywhere elders and men of title heard the signal
and got ready for the meeting. Perhaps it was the threat of war.
But no one spoke of war any more in these days of the white
man. More likely the deity of Umuaro had revealed through
divination a grievance that must be speedily removed, or else . . .
But whatever it was — a call to prepare for battle or to perform
a communal sacrifice — it was urgent. For the *ikolo* was not
beaten out of season except in a great emergency — when as the
saying was an animal more powerful than *nté* was caught by
nté's trap.

The meeting began as fowls went to roost and continued into
the night. Had it been a day meeting children who had brought
their father's stools would have been playing on the outskirts of
the market-place, waiting for the end of the meeting to carry the
stools home again. But no father took his child to a night meeting.
Those who lived near the market-place carried their stools themselves; the others carried goatskins rolled up under the arm.

Ezeulu and Akuebue were the first to arrive. But they had hardly
sat down before other elders and men of title from all the villages
of Umuaro began to come into the Nkwo. At first each man as
he came in saluted all those who were there before him but as the

crowd increased he only greeted those nearest to him, shaking hands with only three or four.

The meeting took place under the timeless ogbu tree on whose mesh of exposed roots generations of Umuaro elders had sat to take weighty decisions. Before long most of the people expected at the meeting had come and the stream of new arrivals became a mere trickle. Ezeulu held a quick consultation with those sitting nearest to him and they all agreed that the time had come to tell Umuaro why they had been called together. The Chief Priest rose to his feet, adjusted his toga and gave the salutation which was at the same time a call to Umuaro to speak with one voice.

'*Umuaro kwenu!*'

'*Hem!!*'

'*Kwenu!*'

'*Hem!!*'

'*Kwezuenu!*'

'*Hem!!*'

'I thank you all for leaving your different tasks at home to answer my call. Sometimes a man may call and no one answers him. Such a man is like one dreaming a bad dream. I thank you that you have not let me call in vain like one struggling in a bad dream.' Somewhere near him someone was talking into his talk. He looked round and saw that it was Nwaka of Umunneora. Ezeulu stopped talking for a while, and then addressed the man.

'Ogbuefi Nwaka, I salute you,' he said.

Nwaka cleared his throat and stopped whatever it was he had been saying to those near him. Ezeulu continued.

'I was thanking you for what you have done. Our people say that if you thank a man for what he has done he will have strength to do more. But there is one great omission here for which I beg forgiveness. A man does not summon Umuaro and not set before them even a pot of palm wine. But I was taken by surprise and as you know the unexpected beats even the man of valour . . .' Then he told them the story of the Court Messenger's visit to him. 'My kinsmen,' he said in conclusion, 'that was what I woke up this morning and found. Ogbuefi Akuebue was there and saw it with me. I thought about it for a long time and decided that

Umuaro should join with me in seeing and hearing what I have seen and heard; for when a man sees a snake all by himself he may wonder whether it is an ordinary snake or the untouchable python. So I said to myself: *Tomorrow I shall summon Umuaro and tell them.* Then one mind said to me: *Do you know what may happen in the night or at dawn?* That is why, although I have no palm wine to place before you I still thought I should call you together. If we have life there will be time enough for palm wine. Unless the penis dies young it will surely eat bearded meat. When hunting day comes we shall hunt in the backyard of the grass-cutter. I salute you all.'

For a long time no one stood up to reply. Instead there was general talking (which sometimes sounded like murmuring) among the assembled rulers of Umuaro. Ezeulu sat down on his stool and fixed his eye on the ground. He did not even reply when Akuebue told him that he had spoken all the words that needed to be said. At last Nwaka of Umunneora stood up.

'*Umuaro kwenu!*'

'*Hem!!*'

'*Umuaro kwenu!*'

'*Hem!!*'

'*Kwekwanu ozo!*'

'*Hem!!*'

He put right his toga which had nearly come undone from his left shoulder.

'We have all heard what Ezeulu said. They were good words and I want to thank him for calling us together and speaking them to us. Do I speak the mind of Umuaro?'

'Speak on,' replied the men.

'When a father calls his children together he should not worry about placing palm wine before them. Rather it is they who should bring palm wine to him. Again I say thank you to the priest of Ulu. That he thought it necessary to call us and tell us these things shows the high regard in which he holds us, for which we give him our thanks.

'But there is one thing which is not clear to me in this summons. Perhaps it is clear to others; if so someone should explain it to me. Ezeulu has told us that the white ruler has asked him to go to

Okperi. Now it is not clear to me whether it is wrong for a man to ask his friend to visit him. When we have a feast do we not send for our friends in other clans to come and share it with us, and do they not also ask us to their own celebrations? The white man is Ezeulu's friend and has sent for him. What is so strange about that? He did not send for me. He did not send for Udeozo; he did not send for the priest of Idemili; he did not send for the priest of Eru; he did not send for the priest of Udo nor did he ask the priest of Ogwugwu to come and see him. He has asked Ezeulu. Why? Because they are friends. Or does Ezeulu think that their friendship should stop short of entering each other's houses? Does he want the white man to be his friend only by word of mouth? Did not our elders tell us that as soon as we shake hands with a leper he will want an embrace? It seems to me that Ezeulu has shaken hands with a man of white body.' This brought low murmurs of applause and even some laughter. Like many potent things from which people shrink in fear leprosy is nearly always called by its more polite and appeasing name – *white body*. The applause and laughter was mingled with the salutation: *Owner of words* to Nwaka. He waited for the laughter to die down and said: 'If laughter presses you, you can laugh; as for me it does not press me.' Ezeulu sat in the same way as he had sat when he ended his speech.

'What I say is this,' continued Nwaka, 'a man who brings ant-ridden faggots into this hut should expect the visit of lizards. But if Ezeulu is now telling us that he is tired of the white man's friendship our advice to him should be: *You tied the knot, you should also know how to undo it. You passed the shit that is smelling; you should carry it away.* Fortunately the evil charm brought in at the end of a pole is not too difficult to take outside again.

'I have heard one or two voices murmuring that it is against custom for the priest of Ulu to travel far from his hut. I want to ask such people: Is this the first time Ezeulu would be going to Okperi? Who was the white man's witness that year we fought for our land – and lost?' He waited for the general murmuring to die down. 'My words are finished. I salute you all.'

Others spoke. Although none spoke as harshly as Nwaka, only

two came out clearly against his line of thinking. Perhaps there were others who did also, but they did not speak. Most of those who spoke said it would be foolhardy to ignore the call of the white man; had they forgotten what happened to clans which fell out with him? Nwokeke Nnabenyi tried to soften the harsh words even more. He said that six elders should be chosen to go with Ezuelu.

'You may go with him if your feet are hungry for a walk,' shouted Nwaka.

'Ogbuefi Nwaka, please do not speak into my words. You stood up here and spoke to your fill and no one answered you back.' He repeated his suggestion that six elders of Umuaro should go with their Chief Priest to Okperi.

Ezeulu stood up then. The big fire which had been lit some distance away shone in his face. There was complete silence when he spoke. His words did not carry the rage in his chest. As always his anger was not caused by open hostility such as Nwaka showed in his speech but by the sweet words of people like Nnabenyi. They looked to him like rats gnawing away at the sole of a sleeper's foot, biting and then blowing air on the wound to soothe it, and lull the victim back to sleep.

He saluted Umuaro and began to speak almost with gaiety in his voice.

'When I called you together it was not because I am lost or because my eyes have seen my ears. All I wanted was to see the way you would take my story. I have now seen it and I am satisfied. Sometimes when we have given a piece of yam to a child we beg him to give us a little from it, not because we really want to eat it but because we want to test our child. We want to know whether he is the kind of person who will give out or whether he will clutch everything to his chest when he grows up.

'You yourselves know whether Ezeulu is the kind of man to run away because the white man has sent a message to him. If I had stolen a goat or killed his brother or fucked his wife then I might plunge into the bush when I heard his voice. But I have not offended him in any way. Now, as for what I shall do I had set my mind on it before I asked *ikolo* to summon you. But if I had done anything without first speaking to you you might turn round and say: *Why did he not tell us?* Now I have told you and happiness fills my mind. This is not the time for many words. When the time comes to speak we shall all speak until we are tired and perhaps we shall find then that there are orators in Umuaro besides Nwaka. For the present I salute you for answering my call. *Umuaro kwenu!*'

'*Hem!!*'

One of the people who followed Ezeulu home that night and offered to go with him in the morning to Okperi was his younger half-brother, Okeke Onenyi, a famous medicine-man. But Ezeulu refused his offer as he had refused all others, among them his friend, Akuebue's. He had taken the decision to go alone and he was not going to change.

As soon as he had made his offer and it was refused Okeke Onenyi rose to go although the first sporadic drops of a heavy rain had started to fall.

'Won't you wait and watch the face of the sky awhile?' asked Edogo.

'No, my son,' replied Okeke Onenyi and, feigning light-heartedness, added: 'Only those who carry evil medicine on their body should fear the rain.' He walked out into the coming storm. The darkness was lit up at short, irregular intervals by lightning; sometimes it was a strong, steady light, sometimes it flickered before it went out as if the rushing wind shook its flame.

Okeke Onenyi's voice rose powerfully against the wind and thunder as he sang and whistled a song to keep him company in the dark.

Ezeulu had said nothing to persuade him not to go in the rain. But then he rarely had anything to say to him. It was difficult to think of them as brothers. But even if they had been closer together Ezeulu might still have said nothing because his mind was not there in the hut with them. In fact all he had said for a long time was that this rain was the harbinger of a new moon. But no one took his meaning.

Ezeulu and his half-brother were not enemies, but neither were they friends. Ezeulu was known to harbour an ill-will against all medicine-men, most of whom, he said, were greedy charlatans.

True medicine, he said, had died with his father's generation. Practitioners of today were mere dwarfs.

Ezeulu's father had indeed been a great medicine-man and magician. He performed countless marvels but the one that people talked about most was his ability to make himself invisible. There was a time when war was raging between Umuaro and Aninta and no one from the one clan dared set foot in the other. But the Chief Priest passed through Aninta as often as he wished. He always went with his son, Okeke Onenyi, who was then a little boy. He gave the boy a short broom to hold in his left hand and told him not to speak or salute any passer-by but walk close to the right edge of the path. The boy went in front and the Chief Priest followed at a distance behind, always keeping the boy in sight. Any passer-by who approached them suddenly stopped before they reached him and began to peer into the bush on the other side of the path like a hunter who had heard the rustle of game. He would be peering thus until the boy and his father passed behind him and only then would he turn again and continue on his way. Sometimes a passer-by would turn right round on their approach and go back the way he was coming.

Okeke Onenyi learnt many herbs and much *anwansi* or magic from his father. But he never learnt this particular magic whose name was *Oti-anya afu-uzo*.

There were few priests in the history of Umuaro in whose body priesthood met with medicine and magic as they did in the body of the last Ezeulu. When it happened the man's power was boundless.

Okeke Onenyi always said that the cause of the coolness between him and the present Ezeulu, his half-brother, was the latter's resentment at the splitting of the power between them. 'He forgets,' says Okeke Onenyi, 'that the knowledge of herbs and *anwansi* is something inscribed in the lines of a man's palm. He thinks that our father deliberately took it from him and gave to me. Has he heard me complaining that the priesthood went to him?'

As was to be expected this was how people who did not like Ezeulu saw his estrangement from Okeke Onenyi. They were quick to point out that it was Ezeulu's pride and jealousy that made him so disdainful of his brother's renown in medicine. They pointed to the recent Covering-up Sacrifice for Obika's wife when, rather than ask his brother, Ezeulu had sent for a worthless medicine-man who could not even eat three meals a day from his doctoring.

But there were others like Akeubue who knew Ezeulu better who retorted that there was something which Okeke Onenyi did to Ezeulu. It was not very clear what this thing was. All that was known was that it was not a thing which a brother should do to a brother; that it was unforgivable. The trouble was that Ezeulu would never unburden himself even to his friends on this matter. So his defenders had nothing but conjectures to put forward. Some said that Okeke Onenyi had tied up the womb of Ezeulu's first wife after she had borne him only three children.

'But that cannot be,' was the usual reply to this. 'We know all the evil medicine-men in Umuaro and Okeke Onenyi is not among them. He is not the kind of man to inflict a curse on a woman who has done him no harm, least of all his brother's wife.'

'But you forget that Okeke Onenyi has a big grudge against Ezeulu,' the others might say. 'You forget that in their childhood their father led Okeke to think that he was going to succeed to the priesthood and that on the old man's death Okeke all but questioned the decision of the oracle.'

'That may be so,' the other side might say. 'But we know all our medicine-men and we say again that Okeke Onenyi has never yet been accused by anyone of sealing up his wife's womb. Besides, medicine-men who carry on such vile practices, like men who relish human flesh, never prosper with children. But just look at Okeke Onenyi's compound flowing with sons and daughters!'

This final argument was unanswerable especially when it was pointed out that Okeke Onenyi's best friend in Ezeulu's compound was Edogo, the son of the very woman he was said to have afflicted! In fact this relationship between Edogo and his uncle was known to give Ezeulu great dissatisfaction. Perhaps it was out of pique that he had said that the carving done by the one was about as good as the medicine practised by the other.

'Those two?' he once asked, 'a derelict mortar and rotten palm nuts!'

For two or three days now Captain Winterbottom had been feeling unduly tired and run down. The rains did not seem to bring the expected respite. His gums looked paler than ever and his feet felt cold. He would not be due for another bout of fever for yet awhile; but these were the signs all right. Of course he was not afraid as a new boy might be. Fever to an old coaster was no more than an inconvenience; it laid one off for a few days that was all.

Tony Clarke was suitably impressed. 'You should go and see a doctor,' he said, knowing that this was the kind of stuff expected of new boys.

'Doctor? Good Lord! For a fever? No my boy. It's the first time you want to be careful. Poor Macmillan wasn't careful enough in spite of my warning. I've had a fever every single year for ten years and when you've had it so often you stop taking any notice. No, all I need is a change of air for a week and you'll see me back as sound as a bell. The trip to Enugu will do it.'

He was planning a visit to headquarters in two days' time. For obvious reasons he wanted to tidy up the business of a warrant chief for Umuaro before he met the headquarters' chaps. He could not possibly conclude the matter in two days but he wanted to be able to say that he had taken the first steps. He was a great believer in leaving the house in order as he expected to find it on his return. So he wrote copious handing over notes for Tony Clarke. He put down in black and white what he proposed to do on the subject of the paramount chief. 'I have today sent messengers to Umuaro to bring Ezeulu here for a preliminary discussion. Arising out of this discussion I shall fix an appropriate date in the future when the warrant of office will be given to him in the presence of the elders and *ndichie* of his clan.' Captain Winterbottom enjoyed mystifying other Europeans with words from the Ibo language which he claimed to speak fluently.

Having made these detailed arrangements for the benefit of Ezeulu Captain Winterbottom was understandably enraged when the messenger came back with the insulting reply from the self-important fetish priest. He immediately signed a warrant of arrest in his capacity as magistrate for the apprehension of the priest and gave instructions for two policemen to go to Umuaro first thing in the morning and bring the fellow in.

'As soon as he comes,' he told Clarke, 'you are to lock him up in the guardroom. I do not wish to see him until after my return from Enugu. By that time he should have learnt good manners. I won't have my natives thinking they can treat the administration with contempt.'

Perhaps it was Captain Winterbottom's rage and frenzy that brought it on; perhaps his steward was right about its cause. But on that very morning when two policemen set out to arrest Ezeulu in Umuaro Captain Winterbottom suddenly collapsed and went into a delirium. The only intelligible thing he kept saying was: *My feet are cold; put the hot-water bottle there!* His steward heated some water, put it in the rubber bottle and placed it on the man's feet. Winterbottom screamed that it was not hot enough. The steward poured in boiling water but even that was still not hot enough. He kept changing the water every few minutes and still the Captain complained. By the time Tony Clarke (who could not drive a car) found Wade to take the Captain in his old Ford to the hospital six miles away his feet had been badly scalded. But this was not discovered until the following day in the hospital.

Clarke and Wade were amazed and not a little embarrassed to see Dr Mary Savage, the severe and unfeminine missionary doctor in charge of the hospital, collapse into tears and panic as Captain Winterbottom was brought in. She kept calling, 'Tom, Tom', and behaving generally as though her doctoring had deserted her. But her panic lasted only a short time; she was soon mistress of herself and the situation. However, it had lasted long enough to have been noticed by a few native nurses and ward attendants who spread it not only in the hospital but in the small village of Nkisa. Both in the hospital and outside in the village Dr Savage was known as Omesike, One Who Acts With Power, and it was not expected that she would ever cry for a patient, not even when the patient happened to be Captain Winterbottom whom they mischievously called her husband.

Winterbottom's delirium lasted three days and in all that time Dr Savage rarely left his bedside. She even postponed the operations which she performed every Wednesday for which the day was known throughout the village as *Day of the Cutting Open of Bowels*. It was always a sad day and the little daily market which had sprung up outside the gates of the hospital to supply the needs of patients from distant clans attracted fewer market women on Wednesdays than on any other day of the week. It was also noticed that even the sky knew that day of death and mourned in gloom.

Dr Savage checked through her list of operation cases and was satisfied that there was none that could be called very urgent and decided to postpone them till Friday. Captain Winterbottom's condition had improved very slightly and there was a little hope. The next day or two would be decisive and a lot would depend on skilled nursing to help him over the critical threshold. He was in a special ward all by himself and nobody was allowed in there except Dr Savage and her only European Sister.

Captain Winterbottom's steward, John Nwodika, was told to escort the two policemen to Umuaro as he had done for the messenger. But in his mind he had sworn never again to take a representative of 'gorment' to his home clan. His resolve was strengthened in this case when he got to know that the two policemen would be armed with a warrant of arrest and handcuffs for the Chief Priest of Ulu. But since he could not turn round and say to his master: *No, I shall not go*, he agreed to go but made other plans. Consequently when the two policemen came for him before the crow of the first cock they found him shivering from a sudden attack of *iba*. Wrapped up in an old blanket which Captain Winterbottom had given him for the child his wife delivered four months ago John managed with great effort to whisper a few directions to the men. Once they were in Umuaro, he said, any suckling child could show them Ezeulu's house. This turned out to be literally true.

The two men entered Umuaro at the time of the morning meal. Soon they met a man carrying a pot of palm wine and stopped him.

'Where is Ezeulu's house?' asked the leader, Corporal Matthew

Nweke. The man looked suspiciously at the uniformed strangers.

'Ezeulu,' he said after a long time in which he had seemed to search his memory. 'Which Ezeulu?'

'How many Ezeulus do you know?' asked the corporal irritably.

'How many Ezeulus do I know?' repeated the man after him. 'I don't know any Ezeulus.'

'Why did you ask me which Ezeulu if you don't know any?'

'Why did I ask you—'

'Shut up! Bloody fool!' shouted the policeman in English.

'I say I don't know any Ezeulu. I am a stranger here.'

Two other people they stopped spoke in more or less the same fashion. One of them even said that the only Ezeulu he knew was a man of Umuofia, a whole day's journey in the direction of the sunrise.

The two policemen were not in the least surprised. The only way to make people talk was by frightening them. But they had been warned by the European officer against using violence and threats and in particular they were not to use the handcuffs unless the fellow resisted. This was why they had shown so much restraint. But now they were convinced that unless they did something drastic they might wander around Umuaro till sunset without finding Ezeulu's house. So they slapped the next man they saw when he tried to be evasive. To drive the point home they also showed him the handcuffs. This brought the desired result. He asked the men to follow him. He took them to the approaches of the compound they were looking for and pointed at it.

'It is not our custom,' he told the policemen, 'to show our neighbour's creditors the way to his hut. So I cannot enter with you.' This was a reasonable request and the policemen released him. He ran away as fast as he could so that the inmates of the compound might not catch as much as a glimpse of his escaping back.

The policemen marched into the hut and found an old woman chewing her toothless gums. She peered at them in obvious fright and did not seem to understand any of the questions they put to her. She did not even seem to remember her own name.

Fortunately a little boy came in at that moment with a small

piece of potsherd to take burning coals to his mother for making
a fire. It was this boy who took the men around the bend of the
footpath to Ezeulu's compound. As soon as he went out with them
the old woman picked up her stick and hobbled over at an amazing
speed to his mother's hut to report his behaviour. Then she
returned to her hut – much more slowly, curved behind her
straight stick. Her name was Nwanyieke, a childless widow. Soon
after she got back she heard the boy, Obielue, crying.

Meanwhile the policemen arrived at Ezeulu's hut. They were then
no longer in the mood for playing. They spoke sharply, baring all
their weapons at once.

'Which one of you is called Ezeulu?' asked the corporal.

'Which Ezeulu?' asked Edogo.

'Don't ask me which Ezeulu again or I shall slap okro seeds out
of your mouth. I say who is called Ezeulu here?'

'And I say which Ezeulu? Or don't you know who you are
looking for?' The four other men in the hut said nothing. Women
and children thronged the door leading from the hut into the inner
compound. There was fear and anxiety in the faces.

'All right,' said the corporal in English. 'Jus now you go sabby
which Ezeulu. Gi me dat ting.' This last sentence was directed
to his companion who immediately produced the handcuffs from
his pocket.

In the eyes of the villager handcuffs or *iga* were the most deadly
of the white man's weapons. The sight of a fighting man reduced
to impotence and helplessness with an iron lock was the final
humiliation. It was a treatment given only to violent lunatics.

So when the fierce-looking policeman showed his handcuffs and
moved towards Edogo with them Akuebue came forward as the
elder in the house and spoke reasonably. He appealed to the
policemen not to be angry with Edogo. 'He only spoke as a young
man would. As you know, the language of young men is always
pull down and destroy; but an old man speaks of conciliation.' He
told them that Ezeulu and his son had set out for Okperi early in
the morning to answer the white man's call. The policemen looked
at each other. They had indeed met a man with another who looked

like his son. They remembered them because they were the first people they had met going in the opposite direction but also because the man and his son looked very distinguished.

'What does he look like?' asked the corporal.

'He is as tall as an iroko tree and his skin is white like the sun. In his youth he was called *Nwa-anyanwu*.'

'And his son?'

'Like him. No difference.'

The two policemen conferred in the white man's tongue to the great admiration of the villagers.

'Sometine na dat two porson we cross for road,' said the corporal.

'Sometine na dem,' said his companion. 'But we no go return back jus like dat. All dis waka wey we waka come here no fit go for nating.'

The corporal thought about it. The other continued:

'Sometine na lie dem de lie. I no wan make dem put trouble for we head.'

The corporal still thought about it. He was convinced that the men spoke the truth but it was necessary to frighten them a little, if only to coax a sizeable 'kola' out of them. He addressed them in Ibo:

'We think that you may be telling us a lie and so we must make quite sure otherwise the white man will punish us. What we shall do then is to take two of you - handcuffed - to Okperi. If we find Ezeulu there we shall set you free; if not . . .' He completed with a sideways movement of the head which spoke more clearly than words. 'Which two shall we take?'

The others conferred anxiously and Akuebue spoke again begging the representatives of 'gorment' to believe their story. 'What would be the wisdom of deceiving messengers of the white man?' he asked. 'Where shall we run afterwards? If you go back to Okperi and Ezeulu is not there you can come back and take not two but all of us.'

The corporal thought about it and agreed. 'But we cannot come and go for nothing. When a masked spirit visits you you have to appease its footprints with presents. The white man is the masked spirit of today.'

'Very true,' said Akuebue, 'the masked spirit of our day is the white man and his messengers.'

Ezeulu's head wife was asked to prepare yam pottage with chicken for the two men. When it was ready they ate and drank palm wine. Then they rested awhile and prepared to go. Akuebue thanked them for their visit and told them that if they had met the owner of the house at home he would have given them more hospitality. Anyhow would they accept this small 'kola' on his behalf? He placed two live cocks before them and Edogo placed beside the cocks a wooden bowl containing two shillings. The corporal thanked them but at the same time repeated his warning that if it turned out that they had been telling lies about Ezeulu, 'gorment' would make them see their ears with their own eyes.

The sudden collapse of Captain Winterbottom on the very day he sent policemen to arrest the Chief Priest of Umuaro was clearly quite significant. The first man to point the connection was John Nwodika, Second Steward to Captain Winterbottom himself. He said it was just as he feared; the priest had hit him with a potent charm. In spite of everything then, power still resided in its accustomed place.

'Did I not say so?' he asked the other servants after their master had been removed to hospital. 'Was it for nothing I refused to follow the policemen? I told them that the Chief Priest of Umuaro is not a soup you can lick in a hurry.' His voice carried a note of pride. 'Our master thinks that because he is a white man our medicine cannot touch him.' He switched over to English for the benefit of Clarke's steward who came in just then and who did not speak Ibo.

'I use to tellam say blackman juju no be someting wey man fit take play. But when I tellam na so so laugh im de laugh. When he finish laugh he call me John and I say Massa. He say You too talk bush talk. I tellam say O-o, one day go be one day. You no see now?'

The story of Ezeulu's magical powers spread through Government Hill hand in hand with the story of Captain Winterbottom's mysterious collapse. When Mr Clarke returned from hospital his steward asked how the big master was. He shook his head and said: 'He's pretty bad, I'm afraid.'

'Sorry sah,' said the steward, looking very worried. 'Dey say na dat bad juju man for yonda wey . . .'

'Go and get my bath ready, will you?' Clarke was so exhausted that he was in no mood for stewards' chit-chat. So he lost the opportunity of hearing the reason for the Captain's illness which was circulating not just through Government Hill but very soon throughout Okperi. It was only two days later that Wright told him about it.

Other servants on Government Hill were waiting in his kitchen to hear the latest news from his steward. He went to get ready the bath and whispered to them that there was no hope, that Clarke had told him he was afraid.

Later in the evening Clarke and Wade drove to the hospital again. They did not see the patient or the doctor; but Sister Warner told them there was no change. For the first time since it all started Tony Clarke felt anxious. They drove back in silence.

There was a Court Messenger outside his bungalow when he got home.

' 'Deven sah,' said the man.

'Good evening,' replied Clarke.

'De witch-doctor from Umuaro don come.' There was fear in his voice as though he was reporting the arrival of smallpox in the village.

'I beg your pardon.'

The man gave more details and it was only then that Clarke understood he was talking about Ezeulu.

'Lock him up in the guardroom till morning.' Clarke made to enter the bungalow.

'Massa say make I putam for gaddaloom?'

'That's what I said,' shouted Clarke. 'Are you deaf?'

'No be say I deaf sah but . . .'

'Get out!'

The messenger sent people to sweep the guardroom and spread a new mat in it so that it might be taken for a guest-room. Then he went to Ezeulu who had been sitting in the Court-room with Obika since their arrival and spoke nicely to him.

'The big white man is sick but the other one says welcome to you,' he said. 'He says it is dark now and he will see you in the morning.'

Ezeulu said nothing to him. He followed him into the dark guardroom and sat on the mat. Obika also sat down. Ezeulu brought out his snuff-bottle.

'We shall send a lamp to you,' said the messenger.

Soon afterwards John Nwodika came in with his wife who had a small load on her head. She set it down and it proved to be an enormous mound of pounded cassava and a bowl of bitter-leaf soup. John Nwodika made a ball of foo-foo, dipped it in the soup and swallowed to show that there was no poison in it. Ezeulu thanked him and his wife (who turned out to be the daughter of his friend in Umuagu) but refused to eat.

'Food is not my care now,' he said.

'Pray, eat a little – just one ball,' said the son of Nwodika. But the old man would not be persuaded.

'Obika will eat for both of us.'

'A fowl does not eat into the belly of a goat,' said the other, but the old man still refused.

The messenger came in again with a palm-oil lamp and Ezeulu thanked him.

Corporal Matthew Nweke who had gone to Umuaro with another policeman returned to find his wives weeping quietly and a large crowd in his one-room lodging. He was alarmed, his mind going to his little son who had measles. He rushed to the mat where he lay and touched him; he was wide awake.

'What is the matter?' he asked then.

No one spoke. The corporal who was called 'Couple' then turned to one of the policemen in the room and put the question specifically to him. The man cleared his voice and told him that they did not expect to see him and his companion back alive, especially when the man he had gone to arrest arrived on his own. 'Couple' wanted to explain how they had crossed each other but the man did not let him. He pressed on with a full account of all that had happened since morning and ended with the latest news from Nkisa Hospital to the effect that Captain Winterbottom would not see the dawn.

At that point John Nwodika came in.

'But you were not well in the morning?' asked Couple.

'That is what I have come to tell you. The illness was a warning from the Chief Priest. I am happy I listened to it; otherwise we would be telling another story now.' John then told them how the Chief Priest knew all about Winterbottom's sickness before anyone told him about it.

'What did he say?' asked one or two people together.

'He said: *If he is ill he will also be well.* I don't know what he meant, but it seemed to me that there was mockery in his voice.'

At first 'Couple' Matthew Nweke was not too worried. He had a strong personal protection which a great *dibia* in his village made for him during his last leave. But as he heard more and more about Ezeulu his faith in his safety began to weaken. In the end he held a quick consultation with the policeman who had accompanied him to Umuaro and they decided that to be on the safe side they should go and see a local *dibia* straight away. It was past ten o'clock at night when they arrived at the man's house. He was called throughout the village *The Bow that shoots at the Sky*.

As soon as they came in he told them the object of their mission. 'You have done right to come straight to me because you indeed walked into the mouth of a leopard. But there is something bigger than a leopard. That is why I say welcome to you because you have reached the final refuge.' He told them that they must not eat anything which they had taken from Umuaro. They must bring the two cocks and the money for sacrifice which they would carry and deposit on the highway. For what they had already eaten he gave them a preparation to drink and also to mix into their bath water.

CHAPTER FOURTEEN

As he ate the pounded cassava and bitter-leaf soup Obika watched his father with the tail of his eye and caught a certain restlessness in him. He knew it would be useless asking him questions in his present mood. Even at the best of times Ezeulu only spoke when he wanted to and not when people asked him.

He got up and made towards the narrow door, then seemed to change his mind or else to remember something he should have taken with him. He came back to his goatskin bag and searched for his snuff-bottle. When he found it he made towards the door again and this time went outside saying from the doorway that he was going to urinate.

He had resolved that as long as he was in Okperi he would never look for the new moon. But the eye is very greedy and will steal a look at something its owner has no wish to see. So as Ezeulu urinated outside the guardroom his eyes looked for the new moon. But the sky had an unfamiliar face. It was impossible to put one's finger anywhere on it and say that the moon would come out there. A momentary alarm struck Ezeulu but on thinking again he saw no cause for alarm. Why should the sky of Okperi be familiar to him? Every land had its own sky; it was as it should be.

That night Ezeulu saw in a dream a big assembly of Umuaro elders, the same people he had spoken to a few days earlier. But instead of himself it was his grandfather who rose up to speak to them. They refused to listen. They shouted together: *He shall not speak; we will not listen to him.* The Chief Priest raised his voice and pleaded with them to listen but they refused saying that they must bale the water while it was still only ankle-deep. 'Why should we rely on him to tell us the season of the year?' asked Nwaka. 'Is there anybody here who cannot see the moon in his own compound? And anyhow, what is the power of Ulu today? He saved our fathers from the warriors of Abam but he cannot save us from the white man. Let us drive him away as our neighbours of Aninta drove out and burnt Ogba when he left what he was called to do and did other things, when he turned round to kill the people of Aninta instead of their enemies.' Then the people seized the Chief Priest who had changed from Ezeulu's grandfather to himself and began to push him from one group to another. Some spat on his face and called him the priest of a dead god.

Ezeulu woke up with a start as though he had fallen from a great height.

'What is it?' asked Obika in the darkness.

'Nothing. Did I say anything?'

'You were quarrelling with someone and saying you would see who would drive the other away.'

'I think there must be spiders on the rafters.'

He was now sitting up on his mat. What he had just seen was not a dream but a vision. It had all taken place not in the half-light of a dream but in the clarity of the middle day. His grandfather, whom he had known with the eyes of a child, had emerged again very clearly across a whole lifetime in which his image had grown weak and indistinct.

Ezeulu took out his ground tobacco and put a little in each nostril to help his thinking. Now that Obika was asleep again he felt free to consider things by himself. He thought once more of his fruitless, albeit cursory, search for the door of the new moon. So even in his mother's village which he used to visit regularly as a boy and a young man and which next to Umuaro he knew better than any village - even here he was something of a stranger! It gave him a feeling of loss which was both painful and pleasant. He had temporarily lost his status as Chief Priest which was painful; but after eighteen years it was a relief to be without it for a while. Away from Ulu he felt like a child whose stern parent had gone on a journey. But his greatest pleasure came from the thought of his revenge which had suddenly formed in his mind as he had sat listening to Nwaka in the market-place.

These thoughts were a deliberate diversion. At the end of them Ezeulu had steadied himself from his dizzy nightmare. Now he looked at it again more closely and one thing stood out. His quarrel with the white man was insignificant beside the matter he must settle with his own people. For years he had been warning Umuaro not to allow a few jealous men to lead them into the bush. But they had stopped both ears with fingers. They had gone on taking one dangerous step after another and now they had gone too far. They had taken away too much for the owner to notice. Now the fight must take place, for until a man wrestles with one of those who make a path across his homestead the others will not stop. Ezeulu's muscles tingled for the fight. Let the white man detain him not for *one* day but one year so that his deity not seeing him in his place would ask Umuaro questions.

Following Captain Winterbottom's instruction that Ezeulu should be put in his place and taught to be polite to the Administration Mr Clarke refused to see him on the next day as the Head Messenger had promised. In fact he refused to see him for four days.

On the second morning as Clarke and Wade drove again towards the hospital at Nkisa they came upon a sacrifice and would not normally have stopped. But this one struck them by its extraordinary lavishness. Wade pulled up and they went to see. Instead of the usual white chick there were two fully grown cocks. The other objects were normal; young, yellowish palm fronds cut from the summit of a tree, a clay bowl with two lobes of kola nut inside it and a piece of white chalk. But the two white men only saw these objects later. What caught their eye immediately on reaching the sacrifice was the English florin.

'Well I never!' said Wade.

'Now this is very strange, a most extravagant sacrifice. I wonder what it's all about.'

'Perhaps it's for the recovery of the King's Representative,' said

Wade lightly. Then something seemed to strike him and he spoke seriously. 'I don't like the look of it. I don't mind if they use their cowries and manillas but the head of George the Fifth!'

Clarke chuckled but stopped immediately as Wade put his left hand into the bowl and picked out the piece of silver, cleaned it first with leaves and then on his woollen hose and put it into his pocket.

'Good heavens! What do you think you are doing?'

'I won't have the King of England dragged into a disgusting juju,' replied Wade, laughing.

This incident worried Clarke a great deal. He had convinced himself that he admired people like Wade and Wright who seemed to do an important job without taking themselves too seriously, who were always looking for the lighter side of things. But was this lack of feeling - for it certainly showed a monstrous lack of feeling to desecrate someone else's sacrifice - part of the temperament of looking for the lighter side of life? If so would one not finally come down in favour of the seriousness (and its accompanying pomposity) of the Winterbottoms?

Without making any conscious decision Clarke was preparing himself to assume the burden of the Administration in the event of Winterbottom's death. It would fall on him to defend his natives if need be from the thoughtless acts of white people like Wade.

That same morning Ezeulu sent Obika back to Umuaro to tell his family how things stood, and to arrange for his younger wife to come and cook his meals. But their clansman, John Nwodika, would not hear of it.

'It is not necessary,' he said. 'My wife is the daughter of your old friend and she will not allow you to send home for another woman. I know that we cannot give you the kind of food you would eat at home. But if we have two palm kernels to chew we shall give one to you and a cup of water to swallow it with.'

Ezeulu could not refuse the offer when it was put that way. Whatever he might have against Nwodika's son he could not offend the daughter of his friend, Egonwanne, who died three years come next harvest. So he told Obika not to send Ugoye but to arrange for large quantities of yams and other foods to be brought.

Ezeulu had good reasons for disliking the son of Nwodika. He came from the very village in Umuaro which was always poking its finger into Ezeulu's eye; his job was said to comprise licking plates in the white man's kitchen in Okperi which was a great degradation for a son of Umuaro. Worst of all he had brought the white man's insolent messenger to Ezeulu's house. But by the end of his first day in Okperi Ezeulu was beginning to soften towards the man, and to see that even a hostile clansman was a friend in a strange country. For the Okperi of Government Hill was indeed a strange country to Ezeulu. It was not the Okperi he had known as a boy and young man, the village of his mother, Nwanyieke. There must still be parts of that old Okperi left, but Ezeulu could not possibly go out in search of it at this time of his disgrace. Where would he find the eye with which to look at the old sites and old faces? It was fortunate that he felt that way for it saved him the mortification of being told he was a prisoner and could not come and go as he liked.

As he ate his meal that night he heard the voices of children welcoming the new moon. '*Onwa atu-o-o-o! Onwa atu-o-o-o!*' went up on all sides of Government Hill. But Ezeulu's sharp ear picked out a few voices that sang in a curious dialect. Except for the word moon he could not make out what they said. No doubt they were the children of some of these people who spoke a curious kind of Igbo - through the nose.

The first time Ezeulu heard the children's voices his heart flew out. Although he had expected it, when it did come he was not ready. His mind had momentarily forgotten. But he recovered almost at once. Yes, his deity must now be asking: 'Where is he?' and soon Umuaro will have to explain.

There was great anxiety in Ezeulu's compound throughout the first and second days of his absence. Although it was the heart of the planting season nobody went to work. Obika's bride, Okuata, left her lonely hut and moved into her mother-in-law's. Edogo left his own compound and sat in his father's *obi* waiting for news. Neighbours and even passers-by came in and asked: 'Have they returned yet?' After a while the question began to make Edogo angry especially when it came from those whose main interest was gossip.

By the middle of the second day, however, Obika returned. At first no one dared ask any questions; some of the women appeared on the brink of tears. Even at such a serious and anxious moment Obika could not resist the temptation to alarm them further. He had worn a face like a muddied pond as he came up the approaches to the hut; now he slumped down on the floor as though he had run all the way from Okperi. He called for cold water which his sister brought him. When he had drunk and set the calabash down Edogo put the first question to him.

'Where is the person with whom you went?' he asked, skirting the dreaded finality of a name. Not even Obika could dare to joke after that. He allowed a short pause and said: 'He was well when I left him.'

The tightening fear in the faces broke.

'Why did the white man send for him?'

'Where did you leave him?'

'When is he coming home?'

'Which one shall I answer?' Obika tried to recover the earlier tension again but it was too late. 'I haven't got seven mouths. When I left him this morning the white man had not told us anything. We did not even see him because they said he was at the mouth of death.' This piece of news caused a little stir. From the stories told of the white man it had not occurred to them that he could be sick like ordinary people. 'Yes, he is already half dead. But he has a younger brother to whom he had given his message to give to Ezeulu. But this one was so troubled by his brother's sickness that he forgot to see us. So Ezeulu said to me: *Prepare and go home or they will think we have come to harm*. That is why I returned.'

'Who gives him food?' asked Ugoye.

'You remember the son of Nwodika who brought the white man's first messenger here,' Obika replied, though not to Ugoye but the men. 'It turned out that his wife is the daughter of Ezeulu's old friend in Umuagu. She has been cooking for us since yesterday and she says that as long as she is alive Ezeulu will not send home for another woman.'

'Did I hear you well?' asked Akeubue, who had so far said very litte. 'Did you say that the wife of a man of Umunneora is giving food to Ezeulu?'

'Yes.'

'Please do not tell me such a story again. Edogo, get ready now, we are going to Okperi.'

'Ezeulu is not a small child,' said Anosi, their neighbour. 'He cannot be taught those with whom he may eat.'

'Do you hear what I say, Edogo? Get ready now; I am going home to get my things.'

'I do not want to stop you from going,' said Obika, 'but do not talk as if you alone have sense. Ezeulu and I did not simply open our mouths while our eyes were shut. Last night Ezeulu refused food even though Nwodika's son tasted it for us. But by this morning Ezeulu had seen enough of the man's mind to know that he had no ill will.'

Akuebue was not impressed by anything the others said. He knew enough about the men of Umunneora. As for those who said that Ezeulu was not a child, they could not know the bitterness in his mind. Akuebue knew the man better than his children or his wives. He knew that it was not beyond him to die abroad so as to plague his enemies at home. It was possible that the hands of Nwodika's son were clean, but one must make quite sure even at the risk of offending him. Who would swallow phlegm for fear of offending others? How much less swallow poison?

Ezeulu's neighbour, Anosi, whose opinion had gone unheeded earlier on in the discussion and who had kept quiet since then surfaced again with an opposite view.

'I think that Akuebue is right in what he says. Let him go with Edogo to satisfy himself that all is well. But let Ugoye also go with them, taking yams and other things; in that way the visit will not offend anyone.'

'But what is this fear of causing offence?' asked Akuebue impatiently. 'I am not a small boy; I know how to cut without drawing blood. But I shall not be afraid to offend a man of Umunneora if Ezeulu's life hangs on it.'

'True,' agreed Anosi. 'Very true. My father used to say that it is the fear of causing offence that makes men swallow poison. You enter the house of a bad man and he brings out a kola nut. You do not like the way he has brought it out and your mind tells you not to eat it. But you are afraid to offend your host and you swallow *ukwalanta*. I agree with Akuebue.'

Perhaps no one felt Ezeulu's absence as keenly as Nwafo. And now his mother was going too. But this second blow was greatly softened by the thought that Edogo was going as well.

Ezeulu's absence had given Edogo an opportunity to show his resentment against the old man's favourite. As the first son Edogo had taken temporary possession of his father's hut to await his return. Nwafo, who rarely left the hut now, began to feel his half-brother's hostility pushing him out. Although he was only a little boy he had the mind of an adult; he could tell when someone looked at him with a good eye or with a bad. Even if Edogo had said nothing Nwafo would still have known that he was not wanted. But Edogo had told him yesterday to go to his mother's hut and not sit around the *obi* gazing into the eyes of people older than himself. Nwafo went out and cried; for the first time in his life he had been told that he was not welcome in his father's hut.

Throughout today he had kept away until Obika's return when everyone in the compound and even neighbours had come in to hear the news. He took his accustomed position defiantly; but Edogo said nothing to him - he did not even appear to have noticed him.

Nwafo's sister Obiageli cried for a long time after their mother and the others left for Okperi. Oduche's promise to pick her *icheku* and *udala* did not console her. In the end Obika threatened to go and call out the fearsome masked spirit called Ichele. This produced an immediate result. Obiageli sat in one corner of the *obi* sniffing quietly.

As night drew near Nwafo's mind returned to the thought which had been troubling him since yesterday. What would happen to the new moon? He knew his father had been expecting it before he went away. Would it follow him to Okperi or would it wait for his return? If it appeared in Okperi with what metal gong would

Ezeulu receive it? Nwafo looked at the *ogene* which lay by the wall, the stick with which it was beaten showing at its mouth. The best solution was for the new moon to wait for his return tomorrow.

However, as dusk came down Nwafo took his position where his father always sat. He did not wait very long before he saw the young thin moon. It looked very thin and reluctant. Nwafo reached for the *ogene* and made to beat it but fear stopped his hand.

Ezeulu was still hearing in his mind the voice of the children of Government Hill when Nwodika's son and his wife brought him his supper. As usual Nwodika's son took a ball of foo-foo, dipped it in the soup and swallowed. Ezeulu ate with a good appetite. Although he would not eat *egusi* soup out of choice this one was so well prepared that one hardly knew it was *egusi*. The fish in it was either *asa* or something equally good, and it had been smoked half-dry, which was the beauty of that type of fish. The foo-foo had a very good texture, neither too light nor too heavy; no doubt the cassava had been lightened with green bananas.

He was half way though his meal when his son, his wife and his friend arrived. They were shown in by the Head Messenger whose duty it was to look after prisoners detained in the guard-room. At first Ezeulu feared that something bad had happened at home. But when he saw the yams they brought his mind returned again.

'Why did you not wait till morning?'

'We did not know whether you would be setting out for home in the morning,' said Akuebue.

'Home?' Ezeulu laughed. It was the laughter of those who do not cry. 'Who talks of home? I have not seen the white man who sent for me. They say he is in the mouth of death. Perhaps he wants a Chief Priest to be sacrificed at his funeral.'

'The earth of Umuaro forbid!' said Akuebue, and the others joined in.

'Are we at Umuaro now?' asked Ezeulu.

'If the man is sick and he has not left a message for you then you should go home and come again when he is well,' said Edogo, who did not think that this was the place for his father and his friend to engage in their battle of words.

'This is not a journey I want to do twice. No, I shall sit here until I have seen the head and the tail of this matter.'

'Do you know how long he will be sick? You may be here . . .'

'If he is sick till palm fruits ripen at the tip of the frond I shall wait . . . How are the people at home, Ugoye?'

'They were well when we left them.' Her neck looked shorter from carrying the load.

'The children, Obika's wife and all the others?'

'Everybody was well.'

'And what about the people of your household?' he asked Akuebue.

'They were quiet when I left them. There was no sickness only hunger.'

'That is a small matter,' said Nwodika's son. 'Hunger is better than sickness.' As he said this he went outside and blew his nose. He came back rubbing the nose with the back of his hand.

'Nwego, you need not wait to collect the utensils. I shall bring them home. Go and find something for these people to eat.'

His wife took Ugoye's headload and the two women went to prepare another meal.

There was no time to waste and as soon as the women left Akuebue spoke.

'Obika has told us how Nwodika's son and wife have been taking care of you.'

'You have seen with your eyes.' Ezeulu's mouth was full of fish.

'Thank you,' said Akuebue to John Nwodika.

'Thank you,' said Edogo.

'We have done nothing that calls for thanks. What can a poor man and his wife do? We know that Ezeulu has meat and fish in his own house but while he is here we will share the palm kernel we eat with him. A woman cannot place more than the length of her leg on her husband.'

'When Obika told us about it I said to myself that there was nothing like travelling.'

'True,' said Ezeulu. 'The young he-goat said that but for his sojourn in his mother's clan he would not have learnt to stick up his upper lip.' He laughed to himself. 'I should have travelled more often in my mother's country.'

It has certainly taken away your heavy face of yesterday,' said Akuebue. 'When they told me that a man of Umunneora was looking after you I told them it was a lie. How could it be seeing the war we wage at home?'

'That is for the people at home,' said Nwodika's son. 'I do not carry it with me when I travel. Our wise men have said that a traveller to distant places should make no enemies. I stand by it.'

'Very true,' said Akuebue, wondering how best to lead on to the object of his coming. After a short pause he decided to split it open with one blow of his matchet as the people of Nsugbe were said to split their coconut. 'Our journey has two aims. We brought Ugoye to relieve Nwodika's wife of her burden and to thank Nwodika himself and tell him that whatever his kinsmen may be doing at home he is today a brother to Ezeulu and his family.' As he said this Akuebue was already searching arm-deep in his goatskin bag for his little razor and kola nut. The tying of the blood-knot between Edogo and John Nwodika was over in the short silence that followed. Ezeulu and Akuebue watched in silence as the two young men ate a lobe of kola nut smeared with each other's blood.

'How did you come to work for the white man?' asked Akuebue when they resumed ordinary talking. Nwodika's son cleared his throat.

'How did I come to work for the white man? I should say my *chi* planned that it should be so. I did not know anything about the white man at the time; I had not learnt his language or his custom. It will be three years next dry season. My age-mates and I came from Umunneora to Okperi to learn a new dance as we had done for many years in the dry season after the harvest. To my great astonishment I found that my friend called Ekemezie in whose house I always lodged during these visits and who came and lodged with me whenever our village played host to his village, I found that he was no longer among the dancers of Okperi. I searched in vain for him among the crowd that came out to welcome us. Another friend called Ofodile took me to his house instead and it was from him I heard that Ekemezie had gone to work for the white man. I do not know how I felt when I heard that news. It was almost as if I had been told that my friend had died. I tried to find out more from Ofodile about this white man's work, but Ofodile is not the kind of person who can sit down and tell a story to the end. But the next day Ekemezie came to see me and brought me to this *Gorment Heel*. He called me by name and I answered. He said everything was good in its season; dancing in the season of dancing. But, he said, a man of sense does not go hunting little bush rodents when his age-mates are after big game. He told me to leave dancing and join in the race for the white man's money. I was all eyes. Ekemezie called me Nwabueze and I said, yes, it was my name. He said the race for the white man's money would not wait till tomorrow or till we were ready to join; if the rat could not run fast enough it must make way for the tortoise. He said other people from every small clan - some people we used to despise - they were all now in high favour when our own people did not even know that day was broken.'

The three men listened in silence. In his mind Akuebue was flicking his fingers and saying: *I now understand why Ezeulu has taken such a sudden liking for him. Their thoughts are brothers.* But Ezeulu was actually hearing Nwodika's opinion of the white man for the first time and glowing with justification. Only he concealed his satisfaction, for once he had taken a stand on any matter he did not want to appear eager for others' support; it was not his concern but theirs.

'So my brothers,' continued Nwodika's son, 'that was how your brother came to work for the white man. At first he put me to weed his compound, but after one year he called me and said that my handiwork was good and took me to work inside his house. He asked me my name and I told him my name was Nwabueze; but he could not call it so he said he would call me Johnu.' This brought a smile to his face, but it was short-lived. 'I know that some people at home been spreading the story that I cook for the white man. Your brother does not see even the smoke from his fire; I put things in order in his house. You know the white man is not like us; if he puts this plate here he will be angry if you have it there. So I go round every day and see that everything is in its right place.

But I can tell you that I do not aim to die a servant. My eye is on starting a small trade in tobacco as soon as I have collected a little money. People from other places are gathering much wealth in this trade and in the trade for cloth. People from Elumelu, Aninta, Umuofia, Mbaino, they control the great new market. They decide what goes on in it. Is there one Umuaro man among the wealthy people here? Not one. Sometimes I feel shame when others ask me where I come from. We have no share in the market; we have no share in the white man's office; we have no share anywhere. That was why I rejoiced when the white man called me the other day and told me that there was a wise man in my village and that his name was Ezeulu. I told him yes. He asked if he was still alive and I said yes. He said: *Go with the Head Messenger and tell him that I have a few questions I want to ask him about the custom of his people because I know he is a wise man.* I said to myself: *This is our chance to bring our clan in front of the white man.* I did not know that it would turn out like this.' He bent his head forward and looked at the ground in sorrow.

'It is not your fault,' said Akuebue. 'Things are always like that. Our eye sees something; we take a stone and aim at it. But the stone rarely succeeds like the eye in hitting the mark.'

'I blame myself,' said Nwodika's son sadly.

'You are a suspicious one,' said Ezeulu. The others had gone to pass the night at the place of Nwodika's son leaving Akuebue and Ezeulu in the small guardroom.

'I stand for a man dying when his *chi* says so.'

'But this man is not a poisoner although he comes from Umunneora.'

'I don't know,' said Akuebue, shaking his head. 'Every lizard lies on its belly, so we cannot tell which has a bellyache.'

'No. But I tell you Nwodika's son has a straight mind towards me. I can smell a poisoner as clearly as I can a leper.'

Akuebue still shook his head. Ezeulu could just make out the movement in the weak light of the palm-oil lamp.

'Did you not watch him when you brought up the question of the blood-tie?' Ezeulu continued. 'If he had had an evil thought you would have seen it in the middle of his forehead. No, the man is not dangerous. Rather he acts like a man of olden times, when people liked themselves. Today there are too many wise people; and it is not good wisdom they have but the kind that blackens the nose.'

'How does a man get any sleep with all these mosquitoes?' asked Akuebue, waving his fly-whisk wildly around.

'You have not seen them yet; wait till we have blown this lamp out. I was meaning to ask Nwodika's son to get me a bunch of arigbe leaves to try and smoke them out. But your coming took everything off my mind. Last night they almost carved us up.' He too waved his horse tail. 'Did you say your people were all well?' he asked, trying to shift the conversation from himself.

'They were all quiet,' replied Akuebue, yawning with head thrown backwards.

'What was Udenkwo's story? You know you did not have the chance to tell me all of it.'

'That is so,' said Akuebue with revived interest. 'If I told you I was happy with Udenkwo I would be deceiving myself. She is my daughter but I can tell you she takes entirely after her mother. I have told her many times that a woman who carried her head on a rigid neck as if she is carrying a pot of water will never live for long with any husband. I have not heard my in-law's story but from what Udenkwo told me I can say that the cause of the quarrel was very small. My in-law was told to bring a cock to sacrifice. When he got home he pointed at one cock and told the children to catch it and tie it up for him. It turned out to be Udenkwo's cock and she started a quarrel. This is what she told me. I asked her did she want her husband to go to the market for a cock when his wives kept fowls. She said: *Why should it always be my cock; what about the other wife, or did the spirits say they only ate Udenkwo's chicken?* I said to her: *How many times has he taken your cock and how is a man to know which cock belongs to who?* She did not answer. All that she knew was that whenever my in-law wanted a cock for a sacrifice he remembered her.'

'That was all?'

'That was all.'

Ezeulu smiled. 'One would think our in-law made a sacrifice every market.'

'Exactly what I told her. But as I said Udenkwo is like her mother. Her real anger was that my in-law did not put his forehead on the ground to beg her.'

Ezeulu did not speak immediately. He seemed to be reconsidering the matter.

'Every man has his own way of ruling his household,' he said at last. 'What I do myself if I need something like that is to call one of my wives and say to her: *I need such and such a thing for a sacrifice, go and get it for me*. I know I can take it but I ask her to go and bring it herself. I never forget what my father told his friend when I was a boy. He said: *In our custom a man is not expected to go down on his knees and knock his forehead on the ground to his wife to ask her forgiveness or beg a favour. But, a wise man knows that between him and his wife there may arise the need for him to say to her in secret: "I beg you". When such a thing happens nobody else must know it, and that woman if she has any sense will never boast about it or even open her mouth and speak of it. If she does it the earth on which the man brought himself low will destroy her entirely*. That was what my father told his friend who held that a man was never wrong in his own house. I have never forgotten those words of my father's. My wife's cock belongs to me because the owner of a person is also owner of whatever that person has. But there are more ways than one of killing a dog.'

'That is true,' Akuebue admitted. 'But such words should be kept for the ears of my in-law. As for my daughter I do not want her to go on thinking that whenever her husband says yah! to her she must tie her little baby on her back, take the older one by the hand and return to me. My mother did not behave like that. Udenkwo learnt it from her mother, my wife, and she is going to pass it on to her children, for when mother-cow is cropping giant grass her calves watch her mouth.'

It was on his fourth day in Okperi that Ezeulu received a sudden summons to see Mr Clarke. He followed the messenger who brought the order to the corridor of the white man's office. There were many other people there, some of them sitting on a long bench and the rest on the cement floor. The messenger left Ezeulu in the corridor and went into an adjoining room where many people worked at various tables for the white man. Ezeulu saw the messenger through a window as he talked to a man who seemed to be the leader of all these workers. The messenger pointed in his direction and the other man followed with his eye and saw Ezeulu. But he only nodded and continued to write in his big book. When he finished what he was writing he opened a connecting door and disappeared into another room. He did not stay long there; when he came out again he beckoned at Ezeulu, and showed him into the white man's presence. He too was writing, but with his left hand. The first thought that came to Ezeulu on seeing him was to wonder whether any black man could achieve the same mastery over book as to write it with the left hand.

'Your name is Ezeulu?' asked the interpreter after the white man had spoken.

This repeated insult was nearly too much for Ezeulu but he managed to keep calm.

'Did you not hear me? The white man wants to know if your name is Ezeulu.'

'Tell the white man to go and ask his father and his mother their names.'

There followed an exchange between the white man and his interpreter. The white man frowned his face and then smiled and explained something to the interpreter who then told Ezeulu that there was no insult in the question. 'It is the way the white man does his own things.' The white man watched Ezeulu with something like amusement on his face. When the interpreter finished he tightened up his face and began again. He rebuked Ezeulu for showing disrespect for the orders of the government and warned him that if he showed such disrespect again he would be very severely punished.

'Tell him,' said Ezeulu, 'that I am waiting to hear his message.' But this was not interpreted. The white man waved his hand angrily and raised his voice. Ezeulu did not need to be told that the white man said he did not want to be interrupted again. After that he calmed down and spoke about the benefits of the British Administration. Clarke had not wanted to deliver this lecture which he would have called complacent if somebody else had spoken it. But he could not help himself. Confronted with the proud inattention of this fetish priest whom they were about to do a great favour by elevating him above his fellows and who, instead of gratitude, returned scorn, Clarke did not know what else to say. The more he spoke the more he became angry.

In the end thanks to his considerable self-discipline and the breathing space afforded by talking through an interpreter Clarke was able to rally and rescue himself. Then he made the proposal to Ezeulu.

The expression on the priest's face did not change when the news was broken to him. He remained silent. Clarke knew it would take a little time for the proposal to strike him with its full weight.

'Well, are you accepting the offer or not?' Clarke glowed with the I-know-this-will-knock-you-over feeling of a benefactor.

'Tell the white man that Ezeulu will not be anybody's chief, except Ulu.'

'What!' shouted Clarke. 'Is the fellow mad?'

'I tink so sah,' said the interpreter.

'In that case he goes back to prison.' Clarke was now really angry. What cheek! A witch-doctor making a fool of the British Administration in public!

CHAPTER FIFTEEN

Ezeulu's reputation at Government Hill had suffered a sharp decline when the first day passed and the second and the third and still no news came that Captain Winterbottom had died. Now it rose again in a different way with his refusal to be a white man's chief. Such an action had no parallel anywhere in Igboland. It might be thought foolish for a man to spit out a morsel which fortune had placed in his mouth but in certain circumstances such a man compelled respect.

Ezeulu himself was full of satisfaction at the way things had gone. He had settled his little score with the white man and could forget him for the moment. But it was not easy to forget and as he went over the events of the past few days he almost persuaded himself that the white man, Wintobota, had meant well but that his good intentions had been frustrated in action by all the intermediaries like the Head Messenger and this ill-mannered, young white pup. After all, he reminded himself, it was Wintobota who a few years ago proclaimed him a man of truth from all the witnesses of Okperi and Umuaro. It was he also who later advised him to send one of his sons to learn the wisdom of his race. All this would suggest that the white man had goodwill towards Ezeulu. But what was the value of the goodwill which brought him to this shame and indignity? The wife who had seen the emptiness of life had cried: *Let my husband hate me as long as he provides yams for me every afternoon.*

In any case, Ezeulu said to himself, Wintabota must answer for the actions of his messengers. A man might pick his way with the utmost care through a crowded market but find that the hem of his cloth had upset and broken another's wares; in such a case the man, not his cloth, was held to repair the damage.

But in spite of all this Ezeulu's dominant feeling was that more or less he was now even with the white man. He had not yet said the last word to him, but for the moment his real struggle was with his own people and the white man was, without knowing it, his ally. The longer he was kept in Okperi the greater his grievance and his resources for the fight.

At first few people in Umuaro believed the story that Ezeulu had rejected the white man's offer to be a Warrant Chief. How could he refuse the very thing he had been planning and scheming for all these years, his enemies asked? But Akuebue and others undertook to spread the story to every quarter of Umuaro and very soon it was known also in the neighbouring villages.

Nwaka of Umunneora treated the story with contempt. When he could no longer disbelieve it he explained it away.

'The man is as proud as a lunatic,' he said. 'This proves what I have always told people, that he inherited his mother's madness.'

Like every other thing Nwaka said from malice this one had its foundation in truth. Ezeulu's mother, Nwanyieke, had indeed suffered from severe spasmodic attacks of madness. It was said that had her husband not been such a powerful man with herbs she might have raved continuously.

But despite Nwaka and other implacable enemies of Ezeulu the number of people who were beginning to think that he had been used very badly grew every day in Umuaro. More and more people began to visit him at Okperi; on one day alone he received nine visitors, some of whom brought him yams and other presents.

Two weeks after he was first admitted into the Nkisa Mission Hospital Captain Winterbottom had recovered sufficiently for Tony Clarke to be allowed to see him – for five minutes. Dr Savage stood at the door with a pocket watch.

He was incredibly white, almost a smiling corpse.

'How's life with you?' he asked.

Clarke could hardly wait to answer. He rushed in with the story of Ezeulu's refusal to be chief as though he wanted to extract an answer before Winterbottom's mouth was closed for ever.

'Leave him inside until he learns to co-operate with the Administration.'

'I did say you were not to talk,' said Dr Savage, coming quickly between them wearing a false smile. Captain Winterbottom had shut his eyes and was already looking worse. Tony Clarke felt guilty and left immediately but with a big weight taken off his mind. On his way back to Government Hill he thought with admiration of the facility with which Captain Winterbottom even in sickness could hit on the right word. Refusing to co-operate with the Administration.

After Ezeulu's refusal to be chief Clarke had made one more attempt through the Chief Clerk to persuade him to change his mind, and had failed. The situation thus became quite intolerable. Should he keep the man in prison or let him loose? If he let him go the reputation of the Administration would sag to the ground, especially in Umuaro where things were only now beginning to look up after a long period of hostility to the Administration and Christianity. According to what Clarke had read Umuaro had put up more resistence to change than any other clan in the whole province. Their first school was only a year or so old and a tottering Christian mission had been set up after a series of failures. What would be the effect on such a district of the triumphant return of a witch-doctor who had defied the Administration?

But Clarke was not the person to lock a man up without fully satisfying his own conscience that justice had not only been done but appeared to have been done. Now that he had been given the answer his earlier scruples sounded a little silly; but they had been very real. What had worried him was this: if he kept the fellow in jail what would he say was his offence? What would he put down in the log? For making an ass of the Administration? For refusing to be a chief? This apparently small point vexed Clarke like a fly at siesta. He realized it was insignificant but that did not help matters; if anything it made them worse.

He could not just clap an old man (yes, a very old man) into jail without reasonable explanation. All very silly really, he thought, now that Winterbottom had given him the answer. The moral of all this was that if older coasters like Winterbottom were no wiser than younger ones they at least had finesse, and this was not to be dismissed lightly.

Captain Winterbottom had a setback in his recovery and for another fortnight no one was allowed to see him. Among the servants and African staff on Government Hill the rumour spread first that he was insane and then that he was paralysed. Ezeulu's reputation continued to rise with these rumours. Now that the cause of his imprisonment was generally known it was impossible not to have sympathy for him. He had done no harm to the white man and could justifiably hold up his *ofo* against him. In that position whatever Ezeulu did in retaliation was not only justified, it was bound by its merit to have potency. John Nwodika explained that Ezeulu was like a puff-adder which never struck until it had first unlocked its seven deadly fangs one after the other. If while it did this its tormentor did not have the good sense to run for its life it would have only itself to blame. Ezeulu had given enough warning to the white man during the four markets he had been locked in prison. So he could not be blamed if he now hit back by destroying his enemy's sense or killing one side of his body leaving the other side to squirm in half life, which was worse than total death.

Ezeulu had now been held for thirty-two days. The white man had sent emissaries to beg him to change his mind but had not had the face to see him again in person - at least so the story went in Okperi. Then one morning, on the eighth Eke market since his arrest he was suddenly told he was free to go home. To the amazement of the Head Messenger and the Chief Clerk who brought him the message he broke into his rare belly-deep laugh.

'So the white man is tired?'

The two men smiled their agreement.

'I thought he had more fight than that inside him.'

'The white man is like that,' said the Chief Clerk.

'I prefer to deal with a man who throws up a stone and puts his head to receive it not one who shouts for a fight but when it comes he trembles and passes premature shit.'

The two men seemed by the look on their faces to agree with this too.

'Do you know what my enemies at home call me?' Ezeulu asked. At this point John Nwodika came in to express his joy at what had happened.

'Ask him; he will tell you. They call me the friend of the white man. They say Ezeulu brought the white man to Umuaro. Is that not so, Son of Nwodika?'

'It is true,' said the other, looking a little confused from being asked to confirm the end of a story whose beginning he had not heard.

Ezeulu killed a fly that had perched on his shin. It fell down on the floor and he looked at the palm with which he killed it: then he rubbed the palm on the mat to remove the stain and examined it again.

'They say I betrayed them to the white man.' He was still looking at his palm. Then he seemed to ask himself: Why am I telling these things to strangers? and stopped.

'You should not give too much thought to that,' said John Nwodika. 'How many of those who deride you at home can wrestle with the white man as you have done and press his back to the ground?'

Ezeulu laughed. 'You call this wrestling? No, my clansman. We have not wrestled; we have merely studied each other's hand. I shall come again, but before that I want to wrestle with my own people whose hand I know and who know my hand. I am going home to challenge all those who have been poking their fingers into my face to come outside their gate and meet me in combat and whoever throws the other will strip him of his anklet.'

'The challenge of Eneke Ntulukpa to man, bird and beast,' said John Nwodika with childlike excitement.

'You know it?' said Ezeulu happily.

John Nwodika broke into the taunting song with which the bird, Eneke, once challenged the whole world. The two strangers laughed; it was just like Nwodika.

'Whoever puts the other down,' said Ezeulu when the song was ended, 'will strip him of his anklet.'

Ezeulu's sudden release was the first major decision Clarke had taken on his own. It was exactly one week since his visit to Nkisa to obtain a satisfactory definition of the man's offence and in that time he had already developed considerable self-confidence. In letters he had written home to his father and his fiancée after the incident he had made fun of his earlier amateurishness - a certain sign of present self-assurance. No doubt his new confidence had been helped by the letter from the Resident authorizing him to take day to day decisions and to open confidential correspondence not addressed personally to Winterbottom.

The mail runner brought in two letters. One looked formidable with red wax and seal - the type junior Political Officers referred to as *Top Secret: Burn Before Before You Open*. He examined it carefully and saw it was not personal to Winterbottom. He felt like a man who had just been initiated into an important secret society. He put the packet aside for the moment to read the smaller one first. It turned out to be no more than the weekly Reuter's telegram sent as an ordinary letter from the nearest telegraphic office fifty miles away. It carried news that Russian peasants in revolt against the new régime had refused to grow crops. 'Serve them right,' he said, and put it aside; he would take it at the close of day to the notice board in the Regimental Mess. He sat up and took the other packet.

It was a report by the Secretary for Native Affairs on Indirect Rule in Eastern Nigeria. The accompanying note from the Lieutenant Governor said that the report had been discussed fully at the recent meeting of Senior Political Officers at Enugu which Captain Winterbottom had unfortunately been too ill to attend. It went on to say that in spite of the very adverse report attached he had not been given any directive for a change of policy. That was a matter for the Governor. But as a decision might be taken one way or another soon it was clearly inadvisable to extend the appointment of Warrant Chiefs to new areas. It was significant that the Warrant Chief for Okperi was singled out in the report for criticism. The letter concluded by asking Winterbottom to handle the matter with tact so that the Administration did not confuse the minds of the natives or create the impression of indecision or lack of direction as such an impression would do untold harm.

When days later Clarke was able to tell Winterbottom about the Report and the Lieutenant-Governor's letter he showed an amazing lack of interest, no doubt the result of the fever. He only muttered under his breath something like: *Shit on the Lieutenant-Governor!*

CHAPTER SIXTEEN

Although it was now the heart of the wet season Ezeulu and his companion had set out for home in dry, hopeful, morning weather. His companion was John Nwodika, who would not hear of his plan to do the long journey alone. Ezeulu begged him not to trouble himself but it was all in vain.

'It is not a journey which a man of your station can take alone,' he said. 'If you are bent on returning today I must come with you. Otherwise stay till tomorrow when Obika is due to visit.'

'I cannot stay another day,' said Ezeulu. 'I am the tortoise who was trapped in a pit of excrement for two whole markets; but when helpers came to haul him out on the eighth day he cried! Quick, quick: I cannot stand the stench.'

So they set out. Ezeulu wore his shimmering, yellow loincloth underneath and a thick, coarse, white toga over it; this outer cloth was passed under the right armpit and its two ends thrown across the left shoulder. Over the same shoulder he carried his long-strapped goatskin bag. On his right hand he held his *alo* – a long, iron, walking-staff with a sharp, spear-like lower end which every titled man carried on important occasions. On his head was a red *ozo* cap girdled with a leather band from which an eagle feather pointed slightly backwards.

John Nwodika wore a thick brown shirt over khaki trousers.

The weather held until they were about half-way between Okperi and Umuaro. Then the rain seemed to say: *Now is the time; there are no houses on the way where they can seek shelter.*

It took both hands off its support and fell down with immense, smothering abandon.

John Nwodika said: 'Let us shelter under a tree for a while to see if it will diminish.'

'It is dangerous to stand under a tree in a storm like this. Let us go on. We are not salt and we are not carrying evil medicine on our body. At least I am not.'

So they pressed on, the cloth clinging as if terrified to their bodies. Ezeulu's goatskin bag was full of water and he knew his snuff was already ruined. The red cap too never liked water and would be the worse for it. But Ezeulu was not depressed; if anything he felt a certain elation which torrential rain sometimes gave – the heady feeling which sent children naked into the rain singing:

> '*Mili zobe ezobe!*
> *Ka mgbaba ogwogwo!*

But Ezeulu's elation had an edge of bitterness to it. This rain was part of the suffering to which he had been exposed and for which he must exact the fullest redress. The more he suffered now the greater would be the joy of revenge. His mind sought out new grievances to pile upon all the others.

He crooked the first finger of his left hand and drew it across his brow and over his eyes to clear the water that blinded him. The broad, new road was like an agitated, red swamp. Ezeulu's staff no longer hit the earth with a hard thud; its pointed end sank in with a swish up to the length of a finger before it met hard soil. Occasionally the rain subsided suddenly as if to listen. Only then was it possible to see separately the giant trees and the undergrowth with limp, dripping leaves. But such lulls were very short-lived; they were immediately overrun by new waves of thick rain.

Rain was good on the body only if it lasted so long and stopped clean. If it went on longer the body began to run cold. This rain did not know the boundary. It went on and on until Ezeulu's fingers held on to his staff like iron claws.

'This is what you have earned for your trouble,' he said to John Nwodika. His voice was thick and he cleared his throat.

'It is you I am worried about.'

'Me? Why should anyone worry about an old man whose eyes have spent all their sleep? No, my son. The journey in front of me is very small beside what I have put behind. Wherever the flame goes out now I shall put the torch away.'

Another gust of rain came and smothered John Nwodika's reply.

Ezeulu's people were greatly worried when he came in numb and shivering. They made a big fire for him while his wife, Ugoye, quickly prepared cam-wood ointment. But first of all he needed some water to wash his feet which were covered with red mud right up to his *ozo* anklet. Then he took the cam-wood paste from the coconut shell and rubbed his chest while Edogo rubbed his back. Matefi whose turn it was to cook for Ezeulu that night (they had kept count even in his absence) had already started preparing utazi soup. Ezeulu drank it hot and his body began gradually to return to him.

The rain was already spent when Ezeulu got home and soon stopped altogether. The first thing he did after he had drunk his utazi soup was to send Nwafo to tell Akuebue of his return.

Akuebue was grinding his snuff when Nwafo brought him the news. He did not wait to finish his grinding. He transferred the half-ground snuff into a small bottle using a special thin knife-blade. Then he swept the finer particles to the middle of the grinding stone with a feather and transferred them also to the bottle. He used the feather again on the big and the small stones until all the powder had gone into the bottle. He put the two stones away and called one of his wives to tell her where he was going.

'If Osenigwe comes to borrow the stones,' he said as he threw his cloth over his shoulder, 'tell him I have not finished.'

There were already a handful of people in Ezeulu's hut when Akuebue arrived. All the neighbours were there and every passer-by who heard of his return interrupted his errand to greet him. Ezeulu said very little, accepting most of the greeting with his eye and a nod. The time had not come to speak or to act. He must first suffer to the limit because the man to fear in action is the one who first submits to suffer to the limit. That was the terror of the puff-adder; it would suffer every provocation, it would even let its enemy step on its trunk; it must wait and unlock its seven fangs one after the other. Then it would say to its tormentor: *Here I am!*

All efforts to draw Ezeulu into the conversation failed or achieved only limited success. When his visitors spoke about his refusal to be white man's chief he only smiled. It was not that he disliked the people around him or the subject about which they spoke. He enjoyed it all and even wished that Nwodika's son had stayed on to tell them about all the things that had happened; but he had only stopped for a short while and then gone on to his own village to pass the night before returning to Okperi in the morning. He had even refused to wash the mud off his feet.

'I am going out in the rain again,' he had said. 'Washing my feet now would be like cleaning the anus before passing excrement.'

As if he knew what Ezeulu was thinking about at that moment one of his visitors said: 'The white man has met his match in you. But there is one side to this story which I do not understand – the role played by the son of Nwodika in Umunneora. When the matter had cooled down he must answer one or two questions.'

'I stand with you,' said Anosi.

'Nwodika's son has already explained,' said Akuebue, who had been acting as Ezeulu's mouth. 'What he did was done in the belief that he was helping Ezeulu'.

The other man laughed. 'He did? What an innocent man! I suppose he puts his bowl of foo-foo into his nostrils. Tell me another story!'

'Never trust a man of Umunneora. That is what I say.' This was Ezeulu's neighbour, Anosi. 'If a man of Umunneora tells me to stop I will run, and if he tells to me run, I shall stand where I am.'

'This one is different,' said Akuebue. 'Travelling has changed him.'

'Hi-hi-hi-hi,' laughed Ifeme. 'He will only add foreign tricks to the ones his mother taught him. You are talking like a small boy, Akuebue.'

'Do you know why it has rained all afternoon today?' asked Anosi. 'It is because Udendu's daughter is going on *uri*. So the rain-makers of Umunneora chose to spoil their kinsman's feast. They not only hate others, they hate themselves more. Their badness wears a hat.'

'True. It is pregnant and nursing a baby at the same time.'

'Very true. They are my mother's people but all I do is peep fearfully at them.'

Ifeme rose to go. He was a short, stoutly built man who always spoke at the top of his voice as though every conversation was a quarrel.

'I must go, Ezeulu,' he shouted so loud that those in the women's huts heard him. 'We thank the great god and we thank Ulu that no bad story has accompanied your travel. Perhaps you were saying to yourself: *Ifeme has not come to visit me, I wonder whether there is a quarrel between us.* There is no quarrel between Ezeulu and Ifeme. I was thinking all the time that I must visit Ezeulu; my eyes reached you but my feet lagged behind. I kept saying: *Tomorrow I shall go*, but every day gave me a different order. As I said before: *Nno.*'

'It was the same with me,' said Anosi. 'I kept saying: *Tomorrow I shall go, tomorrow I shall go*, like the toad which lost the chance of growing a tail because of *I am coming, I am coming.*'

Ezeulu moved his back from against the wall where it had rested and appeared to be giving all his attention to his grandson, Amechi, who was trying in vain to open the old man's clenched fist. But his mind was still on the conversation around him, and he spoke a word or two when he had to. He looked up momentarily and thanked Ifeme for the visit.

Amechi's restlessness increased and soon turned to crying even though Ezeulu had allowed him to open his fist.

'Nwafo, come and take him to his mother. I think sleep is coming.'

Nwafo came, bent down on both knees and presented his back to Amechi. But instead of climbing on he stopped crying, clenched his little fist and landed a blow in the middle of Nwafo's back. This caused general laughter, and he looked round the company with streaks of recent tears under his eyes.

'All right, you go away, Nwafo; he doesn't like you – you are not a good person. He wants Obiageli.'

And truly Amechi climbed on to Obiageli's back without any trouble.

'You see,' said two or three voices together.

Obiageli raised herself to her feet with difficulty, bent slightly and made a sudden jerk with the waist. This threw the child further up her back and she walked away.

'Softly,' said Ezeulu.

'Don't worry yourself,' said Anosi. 'She knows what to do.'

Obiageli went out in the direction of Edogo's compound singing:

> Tell the mother her child is crying
> Tell the mother her child is crying
> And then prepare a stew of úzízá
> And also a stew of úzìzá
> Make a watery pepper-soup
> So the little birds who drink it
> Will all perish from the hiccup
> Mother's goat is in the barn
> And the yams will not be safe
> Father's goat is in the barn
> And the yams will all be eaten
> Can you see that deer approaching
> Look! he's dipped one foot in water
> Snake has struck him!
> He withdraws!
> Ja - ja . ja kulo kulo!
> Traveller Hawk
> You're welcome home
> Ja - ja . ja kulo kulo!
> But where's the length
> Of cloth you brought
> Ja - ja. ja kulo kulo!

As long as he was in exile it was easy for Ezeulu to think of Umuaro as one hostile entity. But back in his hut he could no longer see the matter as simply as that. All these people who had left what they were doing or where they were going to say welcome to him could not be called enemies. Some of them – like Anosi – might be people of little consequence, ineffectual, perhaps fond of gossip and sometimes given to malice; but they were different from the enemy he had seen in his dream at Okperi.

In the course of the second day he counted fifty-seven visitors excluding the women. Six of them had brought palm wine; his son-in-law, Ibe, and his people had brought two big pots of excellent wine and a cock. Throughout that day Ezeulu's hut had the appearance of a festival. Two or three people had even come from Umunneora, the enemy village. Again, at the end of the day, Ezeulu continued his division of Umuaro into ordinary people who had nothing but goodwill for him and those others whose ambition sought to destroy the central unity of the six villages. From the moment he made this division thoughts of reconciliation began, albeit timidly, to visit him. He knew he could say with justice that if one finger brought oil it messed up the others; but was it right that he should stretch his hand against all these people who had shown so much concern for him during his exile and since his return?

The conflict in his mind was finally resolved for him on the third day from a very unexpected quarter. His last visitor that day had been Ogbuefi Ofoka, one of the worthiest men in Umuaro but not a frequent visitor to Ezeulu's house. Ofoka was well known for speaking his mind. He was not one of those who would praise a man because he had offered him palm wine. Rather than let palm wine blind him Ofaka would throw it away, put his horn back in his goatskin bag and speak his mind.

'I have come to say *Nno* to you and to thank Ulu and thank Chukwu for seeing that you did not stub your foot against a rock,' he said. 'I want to tell you that all Umuaro heaved a sigh of relief the day you set foot in your hut once again. Nobody sent me to deliver this message to you but I think you should know it. Why do I say so? Because I know the frame of mind in which you went away.' He paused and then stretched his neck out towards Ezeulu in some kind of defiance. 'I am one of those who stood behind Nwaka of Umunneora when he said that you should go and speak to the white man.'

Ezeulu's face did not show any change.

'Do you hear me well?' continued Ofoka. 'I am one of those who said that we shall not come between you and the white man. If you like you may ask me never to set foot in your house again when I have spoken. I want you to know if you do not already know it that the elders of Umuaro did not take sides with Nwaka against you. We all know him and the man behind him; we are not deceived. Why then did we agree with him? It was because we were confused. You can say that Ofoka told you so. We are confused. We are like the puppy in the proverb which attempted to answer two calls at once and broke its jaw. First you, Ezeulu, told us five years ago that it was foolish to defy the white man. We did not listen to you. We went out against him and he took our gun from us and broke it across his knee. So we know you were right. But just as we were beginning to learn our lesson you turn round and tell us to go and challenge the same white man. What did you expect us to do?' He paused for Ezeulu to answer but he did not.

'If my enemy speaks the truth I will not say because it is spoken by my enemy I will not listen. What Nwaka said was the truth. He said: *Go and talk to the white man because he knows you.* Was that not the truth? He spoke in malice but he spoke truth. Who else among us could have gone out and wrestled with him as you have done? Once again, *Nno.* If you do not like what I have said you may send me a message not to come to your house again. I am going.'

This summed up all the argument that had been going on in Ezeulu's mind for the past three days. Perhaps if Akuebue had spoken the same words they might not have had equal power. But coming from a man who was neither a friend nor an enemy they caught Ezeulu unprepared and struck home.

Yes, it was right that the Chief Priest should go ahead and confront danger before it reached his people. That was the responsibility of his priesthood. It had been like that from the first day when the six harassed villages got together and said to Ezeulu's ancestor: *You will carry this deity for us.* At first he was afraid. What power had he in his body to carry such potent danger? But his people sang their support behind him and the flute man turned his head. So he went down on both knees and they put the deity on his head. He rose up and was transformed into a spirit. His people kept up their song behind him and he stepped forward on his first and decisive journey, compelling even the four days in the sky to give way to him.

The thought became too intense for Ezeulu and he put it aside to cool. He called his son, Oduche.

'What are you doing?'

'I am weaving a basket.'

'Sit down.'

Oduche sat on the mud-bed and faced his father. After a short pause Ezeulu spoke direct and to the point. He reminded Oduche of the importance of knowing what the white man knew. 'I have sent you to be my eyes there. Do not listen to what people say - people who do not know their right from their left. No man speaks a lie to his son; I have told you that before. If anyone asks you why you should be sent to learn these new things tell him that a man must dance the dance prevalent in his time.' He scratched his head and continued in a relaxed voice. 'When I was in Okperi I saw a young white man who was able to write his book with the left hand. From his actions I could see that he had very little sense. But he had power; he could shout in my face; he could do what he liked. Why? Because he could write with his left hand. That is why I have called you. I want you to learn and master this man's knowledge so much that if you are suddenly woken up from sleep and asked what it is you will reply. You must learn it until you can write it with your left hand. That is all I want to tell you.'

As the excitement over Ezeulu's return died down life in his compound gradually went back to its accustomed ways. The children in particular rejoiced at the end of the half-mourning under which they had lived for more than a whole moon. 'Tell us a story,' said Obiageli to her mother, Ugoye. Actually it was Nwafo who had put her up to it.

'Tell you a story with these unwashed utensils scattered around?'

Nwafo and Obiageli immediately went to work. They moved away the little mortar from grinding pepper and turned it over and put the smaller vessels on the bamboo ledge. Ugoye herself changed the nearly burnt-out taper on the tripod with a new one from the palm-oil-soaked bunch in the potsherd.

Ezeulu had eaten every morsel of the supper Ugoye prepared for him. This should have made any woman very happy. But in a big compound there was always something to spoil one's happiness. For Ugoye it was her husband's senior wife, Matefi.

No matter what Ugoye did Matefi's jealousy never let her rest. If she cooked a modest meal in her own hut Matefi said she was starving her children so that she could buy ivory bracelets; if she killed a cock as she did this evening Matefi said she was seeking favour from her husband. Of course she never said any of these things to Ugoye's face, but all her gossip eventually got back to Ugoye. This evening as Oduche was dressing the chicken in an open fire Matefi had gone up and down clearing her throat.

After the room had been tidied up Nwafo and Obiageli spread a mat and sat by their mother's low stool.

'Which story do you want to hear?'

'Onwuero,' said Obiageli.

'No,' said Nwafo, 'we have heard it too often. Tell us about —'

'All right,' cut in Obiageli. 'Tell us about Eneke Ntulukpa.'

Ugoye searched her memory for a while and found what she looked for.

> Once upon a time there was a man who had two wives. The senior wife had many children but the younger one had only one son. But the senior wife was wicked and envious. One day the man and his family went to work on their farm. This farm was at the boundary between the land of men and the land of spirits . . .

Ugoye, Nwafo and Obiageli sat in a close group near the cooking place. Oduche sat apart near the entrance to the one sleeping-room holding his new book, *Azu Ndu*, to the yellow light of the taper. His lips moved silently as he spelt out and formed the first words of the reader:

> a b a aba
> e g o ego
> i r o iro
> a z u azu
> o m u omu

Meanwhile Ezeulu had pursued again his thoughts on the coming struggle and began to probe with the sensitiveness of a snail's horns the possibility of reconciliation or, if that was too much, of narrowing down the area of conflict. Behind his thinking was, of course, the knowledge that the fight would not begin until the time of harvest, after three moons more. So there was plenty of time. Perhaps it was this knowledge that there was no hurry which gave him confidence to play with alternatives - to dissolve his resolution and at the right time form it again. Why should a man be in a hurry to lick his fingers; was he going to put them away in the rafter? Or perhaps the thoughts of reconciliation were from a true source. But whatever it was, Ezeulu was not to be allowed to remain in two minds much longer.

'Ta! Nwanu!' barked Ulu in his ear, as a spirit would in the ear of an impertinent human child. 'Who told you that this was your own fight?'

Ezeulu trembled and said nothing, his gaze lowered to the floor.

'I say who told you that this was your own fight to arrange the way it suits you? You want to save your friends who brought you palm wine he-he-he-he-he!' Only the insane could sometimes approach the menace and mockery in the laughter of deities - a dry, skeletal laugh. 'Beware you do not come between me and my victim or you may receive blows not meant for you! Do you not know what happens when two elephants fight? Go home and sleep and leave me to settle my quarrel with Idemili, whose envy seeks to destroy me that his python may again come to power. Now you tell me how it concerns you. I say go home and sleep. As for me and Idemili we shall fight to the finish; and whoever throws the other down will strip him of his anklet!'

After that there was no more to be said. Who was Ezeulu to tell his deity how to fight the jealous cult of the sacred python? It was a fight of the gods. He was no more than an arrow in the bow of his god. This thought intoxicated Ezeulu like palm wine. New thoughts tumbled over themselves and past events took on new, exciting significance. Why had Oduche imprisoned a python in his box? It had been blamed on the white man's religion; but was that the true cause? What if the boy was also an arrow in the hand of Ulu?

And what about the white man's religion and even the white man himself? This was close on profanity but Ezeulu was now in a mood

to follow things through. Yes, what about the white man himself?
After all he had once taken sides with Ezeulu and, in a way, had
taken sides with him again lately by exiling him, thus giving him
a weapon with which to fight his enemies.

If Ulu had spotted the white man as an ally from the very
beginning, it would explain many things. It would explain Ezeulu's
decision to send Oduche to learn the ways of the white man. It
was true Ezeulu had given other explanations for his decision but
those were the thoughts that had come into his head at the time.
One half of him was man and the other half *mmo* – the half that
was painted over with white chalk at important religious moments.
And half of the things he ever did were done by this spirit side.

CHAPTER SEVENTEEN

The people of Umuaro had a saying that the noise even of the loudest events must begin to die down by the second market week. It was so with Ezeulu's exile and return. For a while people talked about nothing else; but gradually it became just another story in the life of the six villages, or so they imagined.

Even in Ezeulu's compound the daily rounds established themselves again. Obika's new wife had become pregnant; Ugoye and Matefi carried on like any two jealous wives; Edogo went back to his carving which he had put aside at the height of the planting season; Oduche made more progress in his new faith and in his reading and writing; Obika, after a short break, returned to palm wine in full force. His temporary restraint had been largely due to the knowledge that too much palm wine was harmful to a man going in to his wife - it made him pant on top of her like a lizard fallen from an iroko tree - and reduced him in her esteem. But now that Okuata had become pregnant he no longer went in to her.

Even Ezeulu himself seemed to have put away all his grievance. No hint of it came into his daily offering of kola nut and palm wine to his fathers or into the simple ritual he performed at every new moon. It was also time for his younger wife to be pregnant again having rested for over a year since the death of her last child. So she began to answer his call to sleep some nights in his hut. This did not improve her relations with Matefi who was past child-bearing.

The minor feasts and festivals of the year took place in their proper season. Some of them were observed by all six villages together and some belonged to individual ones. Umuago celebrated their *Mgba Agbogho* or the Wrestling of the Maidens; Umunneora observed their annual feast in honour of Idemili, Owner of the python. Together the six villages held the quiet retreat called *Osu Nwanadi* to placate the resentful spirits of kinsmen killed in war or in other ways made to suffer death in the cause of Umuaro.

The heavy rains stopped as usual for a spell of dry weather without which yams could not produce big tubers despite luxuriant leaves. In short, life went on as though nothing had happened or was even going to happen.

There was one minor feast which Ezeulu's village, Umuachala, celebrated towards the end of the wet season and before the big festival of the year - the New Yam feast. This minor celebration was called *Akwu Nro*. It had little ritual and was no more than a memorial offering by widows to their departed husbands. Every widow in Umuachala prepared foo-foo and palm nut soup on the night of *Akwu Nro* and put it outside her hut. In the morning the bowls were empty because her husband had come up from Ani-Mmo and eaten the food.

This year's *Akwu Nro* was to have an added interest because Obika's age group would present a new ancestral Mask to the village. The coming of a new Mask was always an important occasion especially when as now it was a Mask of high rank. In the last few days there had been a lot of coming and going among members of the Otakagu age group. Those of them who had leading roles to play at the ceremony would naturally be targets of malevolence and envy and must therefore be 'hard-boiled' in protective magic. But even the others had to have some defensive preparation rubbed into shallow cuts on the arm.

All the arrangements were made secretly in keeping with the mystery of ancestral spirits. In recent years new thinking had gone into the need for strengthening the defences around this mystery in Umuaro. It had become clear to the elders that although no woman dared speak openly when she saw a Mask it was not too difficult for her to guess the man behind it. All that was necessary was to look at all the people around the Mask and see who was absent. To overcome this difficulty the elders had recently ruled that whenever a group or a village wished to bring out a Mask they must go outside their group or village for their man. So the Otakagu age group in Umuachala had gone all the way to Umuogwugwu to select the man to wear the mask. The man they chose was called Amumegbu; he was in Umuachala during all the preparations but his presence was kept very secret.

Both Edogo and Obika were intimately concerned with the Mask that was to come. It belonged to Obika's age group, but more than that he had been selected as one of the two people to slaughter rams in its presence. Edogo came into it because he had carved the mask.

It was a little past midday. Obika sat on the floor of his hut, his feet astride the stone on which he sharpened his matchet. Trickles of sweat ran down his face and he held his lower lip with the upper teeth as he worked. He had already used a whole head of salt to give greater edge to the stone; and now and again he squeezed a little lime juice onto the blade. Two emptied fruits lay near the stone with three or four uncut ones. Obika had been working on his new matchet at intervals during the past three days and it was now sharp enough to shave the hair. He rose and went outside to see it well in the light. He held it up before him and by twisting his wrist made it flash like a mirror in the sun. He seemed satisfied, went back into his hut and put it away. Then he passed through to the inner compound and saw his wife turning water from the big pot outside the hut into a bowl. She stood up wearily and spat as she always did nowadays.

'Old woman,' Obika teased her.

'I have said if you know what you did to me you should come and undo it,' she said, smiling.

Not very long after that the first sounds of the coming event were heard in the village. Half a dozen young men ran up and down the different quarters beating their *ogene* and searching for the Mask; for no one knew which of the million ant holes in Umuachala it would come through. They kept up their search for a very long time and the sound of their metal gong and of their feet when they were near kept the whole village on edge. As soon as the sun's heat began to soften the village emptied itself onto the *ilo*.

The *ilo* of Umuachala was among the biggest in Umuaro and the best kept. It was sometimes called Ilo Agbasioso because its length cowed even the best runners. At one of its four corners stood the *okwolo* house from where those initiated into the mystery of ancestral spirits watched the display on the *ilo*. The *okwolo* was a tall, unusual hut having only two side and back walls. Looking at it from the open front one saw tiers of steps running the whole breadth of the hut and rising from the ground almost to the roof. The elders of the village sat on the lowest rungs which had the best view and the others sat on the back and higher rungs. Behind the *okwolo* stood a big udala tree which like all udala trees in Umuaro was sacred to ancestral spirits. Even now many children were playing under it waiting for the occasional fall of a ripe, light-brown fruit – the prize for the fastest runner or the luckiest child nearest whom it fell. The tree was full of the tempting fruit but no one young or old was allowed to pick from the tree. If anyone broke this rule he would be visited by all the Masked spirits in Umuaro and he would have to wipe off their footsteps with heavy fines and sacrifice.

Although Ezeulu and Akuebue were early there were already immense crowds on the *ilo* when they arrived. Everybody in Umuachala seemed to be either there or on his way, and many people came from all the other villages of Umuaro. Women and girls, young men and boys had already formed a big ring on the *ilo*; as more and more people poured in from every quarter the ring became thicker and the noise greater. There were no young men with whips trying to keep the crowd clear of the centre; this would take care of itself as soon as the Mask arrived.

A big stir and commotion developed in one part of the crowd and spread right round. People asked those nearest them what it was and they pointed at something. Thousands of fingers were soon pointed in the same direction. There, in a fairly quiet corner of the *ilo*, sat Otakekpeli. This man was known throughout Umuaro as a wicked medicine-man. More than twice he had had to take kola nut from the palm of a dead man to swear he had no hand in the death. Of course he had survived each oath, which could mean he was innocent. But people did not believe it; they said he had immediately rushed home and drunk powerful, counteracting potions.

From what was known of him and by the way he sat away from other people it was clear he had not come merely to watch a new Mask. An occasion such as this was often used by wicked men to try out the potency of their magic or to match their power against that of others. There were stories of Masks which had come out unprepared and been transfixed to a spot for days or even felled to the ground.

Perhaps the most suspicious thing about Otakekpeli was his posture. He sat like a lame man with legs folded under him. They said it was the fighting posture of a boar when a leopard was about: it dug a shallow hole in the earth, sat with its testicles hidden away in it and waited with standing bristles on its head of iron. As a rule, the leopard would go away, in search of goats and sheep.

The crowd watched Otakekpeli with disapproval; but no one challenged him because it was dangerous to do so but even more because most people in their hearts looked forward to the spectacle of two potent forces grappling with each other. If the Otakagu age-group chose to bring out a new Mask without first boiling themselves hard it was their own fault. In fact most of these encounters produced no visible results at all because the powers were equally matched or the target was stronger than the assailant.

The approach of the Mask caused a massive stampede. The women and children scattered and fled in the opposite direction, screaming with the enjoyment of danger. Soon they were all back again because the Mask had not even come into sight; only the *ogene* and singing of its followers had been heard. The metal gong and voices became louder and louder and the crowd looked around them to be sure that the line of flight was clear.

There was another stampede when the first harbingers of the Mask burst into the *ilo* from the narrow footpath by which it was expected to arrive. These young men wore raffia and their matchets caught the light as they threw them up or clashed them in salute of each other from left to right and then back from right to left. They ran here and there, sometimes one would charge at full speed in one direction. The crowd at that point would scatter and the man would brake all of a sudden and tremble on all toes.

The gong and the voices were now quite near but they were

almost lost in the uproar of the crowd. It was likely that the Mask had stopped for a while or it would have appeared by now. Its attendants kept up their song.

The first spectacle of the day came with the arrival of Obika and a flute man at his heels singing of his exploits. The crowd cheered, especially the women because Obika was the handsomest young man in Umuachala and perhaps in all Umuaro. They called him Ugonachomma.

No sooner was Obika in the *ilo* than he caught sight of Otakekpeli sitting on his haunches. Without second thoughts he made straight for him at full speed then stopped dead. He shouted at the medicine-man to get up and go home. The other merely smiled. The crowd forgot all about the Mask. Okuata had taken a position away from the thickest press because of her pregnancy. Her heart had swollen when the crowd greeted her husband; now she shut her eyes and the ground reeled round her.

Obika was now pointing at Otakekpeli and then pointing at his own chest. He was telling the man that if he wanted to do something useful with his life he should get up. The other man continued to laugh at him. Obika renewed his progress but not with the former speed. He prowled like a leopard, his matchet in his right hand and a leather band of amulets on his left arm. Ezeulu was biting his lips. It would be Obika, he thought, the rash, foolish Obika. Did not all the other young men see Otakekpeli and look away? But his son could never look away. Obika —

Ezeulu stopped in mid-thought. With the flash of lightning Obika had dropped his matchet, rushed forward and in one movement lifted Otakekpeli off the ground and thrown him into the nearby bush in a shower of sand. The crowd burst out in one great high-vaulting cheer as Otakekpeli struggled powerlessly to his feet pointing an impotent finger at Obika who had already turned his back on him. Okuata opened her eyes again and heaved a sigh.

The Mask arrived appropriately on the crest of the excitement. The crowd scattered in real or half-real terror. It approached a few steps at a time, each one accompanied by the sound of bells and rattles on its waist and ankles. Its body was covered in bright new cloths mostly red and yellow. The face held power and terror; each exposed tooth was the size of a big man's thumb, the eyes were large sockets as big as a fist, two gnarled horns pointed upwards and inwards above its head nearly touching at the top. It carried a shield of skin in the left hand and a huge matchet in the right.

'*Ko-ko-ko-ko-ko-ko-oh!*' it sang like cracked metal and its attendant replied with a deep monotone like a groan:

'*Hum-hum-hum.*'

'*Ko-ko-ko-ko-ko-ko-oh.*'

'*Oh-oyoyo-oyoyo-oyoyo-oh: oh-oyoyo-oh. Hum-hum.*'

There was not much of a song in it. But then an Agaba was not a Mask of song and dance. It stood for the power and aggressiveness of youth. It continued its progress and its song, such as it was. As it got near the centre of the *ilo* it changed into the song called *Onye ebuna uzo cho ayi okwu*. It was an appeal to all and sundry not to be the first to provoke the ancestral Mask; and it gave minute details of what would befall anyone who ignored this advice. He would become an outcast, with no fingers and no toes, living all by himself in a solitary hut, a beggar's satchel hanging down his shoulder; in other words, a leper.

Whenever it tried to move too fast or too dangerously two sweating attendants gave a violent tugging at the strong rope round its waist. This was a very necessary, if somewhat hazardous, task. On one occasion the Mask became so enraged by this restraint that it turned on the two men with raised matchet. They instantly dropped the rope and fled for their lives. This time the cry of the scattering crowd carried real terror. But the two men did not leave the Mask free too long. As soon as it gave up chasing them they returned once more to their task.

A very small incident happened now which would not have been remembered had it not been followed by something more serious. One of the young men had thrown up his matchet and failed to catch it in the air. The crowd always on the look-out for such failures sent up a big boo. The man, Obikwelu, picked up his matchet again and tried to cover up by a show of excessive agility; but this only brought more laughter.

Meanwhile the Mask had proceeded to the *okwolo* to salute some of the elders.

'*Ezeulu de-de-de-de-dei*,' it said.

'Our father, my hand is on the ground,' replied the Chief Priest.

'Ezeulu, do you know me?'

'How can a man know you who are beyond human knowledge?'

'Ezeulu, our Mask salutes you,' it sang.

'*Eje-ya-mma-mma-mma-mma-mma-mma-eje-ya-mma!*' sang its followers.

'*Ora-obodo*, Agaba salutes you!'

'*Eje-ya-mma-mma-mma-mma-mma-mma-eje-ya-mma!*'

'Have you heard the song of the Spider?'

'*Eje-ya-mma-mma-mma-mma-mma-mma-eje-ya-mma!*'

It broke off suddenly, turned round and ran straight ahead. The crowd in that direction broke up and scattered.

Although Edogo could have taken one of the back seats in the *okwolo* he chose to stand with the crowd so as to see the Mask from different positions. When he had finished carving the face and head he had been a little disappointed. There was something about the nose which did not please him – a certain fineness which belonged not to an Agaba but to a Maiden Spirit. But the owners of the work had not complained; in fact they had praised it very highly. Edogo knew, however, that he must see the Mask in action to know whether it was good or bad. So he stood with the crowd.

Looking at it now that it had come to life the weakness seemed to disappear. It even seemed to make the rest of the face more fierce. Edogo went from one part of the crowd to another in the hope that someone would make the comparison he wanted to hear, but no one did. Many people praised the new Mask but no one thought of comparing it with the famous Agaba of Umuagu, if only to say that this one was not as good as that. If Edogo had heard anyone say so he might have been happy. He had not after all set out to excel the greatest carver in Umuaro but he had hoped that someone would link their two names. He began to blame himself for not sitting in the *okwolo*. There, among the elders, was a more likely place to hear the kind of conversation he was listening for. But it was too late now.

The climax of the evening came with the slaughtering of the rams.

As a chair was set in the middle of the *ilo* and the Mask sat down there was comparative silence. Two attendants took up positions on either side of the seated Mask and fanned it. The first ram was led forward and the Mask touched the neck with its matchet. Then it was taken a short distance away but still in full view of the presiding spirit. There was now complete silence except for the flute which, in place of its usual thin and delicate tone, produced broad, broken sounds. Obika came forward, threw up his matchet with a twirl so that it revolved and caught the light of the evening on its blade. He did this twice and each time caught it perfectly in mid-air. Then he stepped forward and with one precise blow severed the ram's head. The crowd cheered tumultuously as one of the attendants picked up the head which had rolled in the sand and held it up. The Mask looked on with the same unchanging countenance.

When the noisy excitement went down the second ram was brought forward and the Mask again touched its neck. Obikwelu stepped forward. He was nervous because he had dropped his matchet earlier on. He threw it up thrice and caught it perfectly. He stepped forward, raised it and struck. It was as if he had hit a rock; the ram struggled to escape; the crowd booed and laughed. Obikwelu was very unlucky that day. The ram had moved its head at the last moment and he had struck the horn. The Mask looked on unperturbed. Obikwelu tried again and succeeded but it was too late; the laughter of the crowd drowned the few belated cheers.

CHAPTER EIGHTEEN

After a long period of silent preparation Ezeulu finally revealed that he intended to hit Umuaro at its most vulnerable point – the Feast of the New Yam.

This feast was the end of the old year and the beginning of the new. Before it a man might dig up a few yams around his house to ward off hunger in his family but no one would begin the harvesting of the big farms. And, in any case, no man of title would taste new yam from whatever source before the festival. It reminded the six villages of their coming together in ancient times and of their continuing debt to Ulu who saved them from the ravages of the Abam. At every New Yam Feast the coming together of the villages was re-enacted and every grown man in Umuaro took a good-sized seed-yam to the shrine of Ulu and placed it in the heap from his village after circling it round his head; then he took the lump of chalk lying beside the heap and marked his face. It was from these heaps that the elders knew the number of men in each village. If there was an increase over the previous year a sacrifice of gratitude was made to Ulu; but if the number had declined the reason was sought from diviners and a sacrifice of appeasement was ordered. It was also from these yams that Ezeulu selected thirteen with which to reckon the new year.

If the festival meant no more than this it would still be the most important ceremony in Umuaro. But it was also the day for all the minor deities in the six villages who did not have their own special feasts. On that day each of these gods was brought by its custodian and stood in a line outside the shrine of Ulu so that any man or woman who had received a favour from it could make a small present in return. This was the one public appearance these smaller gods were allowed in the year. They rode into the market place on the heads or shoulders of their custodians, danced round and then stood side by side at the entrance to the shrine of Ulu. Some of them would be very old, nearing the time when their power would be transferred to new carvings and they would be cast aside; and some would have been made only the other day. The very old ones carried face marks like the men who made them, in the days before Ezeulu's grandfather proscribed the custom. At last year's festival only three of these ancients were left. Perhaps this year one or two more would disappear, following the men who made them in their own image and departed long ago.

The festival thus brought gods and men together in one crowd. It was the only assembly in Umuaro in which a man might look to his right and find his neighbour and look to his left and see a god standing there - perhaps Agwu whose mother also gave birth to madness or Ngene, owner of a stream.

Ezeulu had gone out to visit Akuebue when his six assistants came to see him. Matefi told them where he had gone and they decided to wait for him in his *obi*. It was approaching evening when he returned. Although he knew what must have brought them he feigned surprise.

'Is it well?' he asked after the initial salutations.

'It is well.'

As awkward silence followed. Then Nwosisi who represented the village of Umuogwugwu spoke. It was not his custom to waste words.

'You have asked if all is well and we said yes; but a toad does not run in the daytime unless something is after it. There is a little matter which we have decided to bring to you. It is now four days since the new moon appeared in the sky; it is already grown big. And yet you have not called us together to tell us the day of the New Yam Feast —'

'By our reckoning,' Obiesili took up, 'the present moon is the twelfth since the last feast.'

There was silence. Obiesili was always a tactless speaker and no one had asked him to put his mouth into such a delicate matter. Ezeulu cleared his throat and welcomed the people again - to show that he was neither in a hurry nor excited.

'You have done what you should do,' he said. 'If anyone says you have failed in your duty he is telling a lie. A man who asks questions does not lose his way; that is what our fathers taught us. You have done well to come and ask me about this matter which troubles you. But there is something I did not fully understand. You said, Obiesili, just now that according to your reckoning I should have announced the next New Yam Feast at the last new moon.'

'I said so.'

'I see. I thought perhaps I did not hear you well. Since when did you begin to reckon the year for Umuaro?'

'Obiesili did not use his words well,' said Chukwulobe. 'We do not reckon the year for Umuaro; we are not Chief Priest. But we thought that perhaps you have lost count because of your recent absence —'

'What! Are you out of your senses, young man?' Ezeulu shouted. 'There is nothing that a man will not hear these days. Lost count! Did your father tell you that the Chief Priest of Ulu can lose count of the moons? No, my son,' he continued in a surprisingly mild tone, 'no Ezeulu can lose count. Rather it is you who count with your fingers who are likely to make a mistake, to forget which finger you counted at the last moon. But as I said at the beginning you have done well to come and ask. Go back to your villages now and wait for my message. I have never needed to be told the duties of the priesthood.'

If anyone had come into Ezeulu's hut after the men had left he would have been surprised. The old priest's face glowed with happiness and some of his youth and handsomeness returned temporarily from across the years. His lips moved, letting through an occasional faint whisper. But soon the outside world broke in on him. He stopped whispering and listened more carefully. Nwafo and Obiageli were reciting something just outside his *obi*.

'*Eke nekwo onye uka!*' they said over and over again. Ezeulu listened even more carefully. He was not mistaken.

'*Eke nekwo onye uka! Eke nekwo onye uka! Eke nekwo onye uka!*'
'Look it's running away!' cried Obiageli and the two laughed excitedly.
'*Eke nekwo onye uka! Nekwo onye uka! Newko onye uka!*'
'*Nwafo!*' shouted Ezeulu.
'*Nna,*' replied the other fearfully.
'Come here.'
Nwafo came in with a tread that would not have killed an ant. Sweat was running down his head and face. Obiageli had melted away the moment Ezeulu called.
'What were you saying?'
Nwafo said nothing. His eyelids blinked almost audibly.
'Are you deaf? I asked you what you were saying.'
'They said that was how to scare away a python.'
'I did not ask you what anybody said. I asked what you were saying. Or do you want me to get up from here before you answer?'
'We were saying: Python, run! There is a Christian here.'
'And what does it mean?'
'Akwuba told us that a python runs away as soon as it hears that.'
Ezeulu broke into a long, loud laughter. Nwafo's relief beamed all over his grimy face.
'Did it run away when you said it?'
'It ran away *fiam* like an ordinary snake.'

The news of Ezeulu's refusal to call the New Yam Feast spread through Umuaro as rapidly as if it had been beaten out on the *ikolo*. At first people were completely stunned by it; they only began to grasp its full meaning slowly because its like had never happened before.

Two days later ten men of high title came to see him. None of the ten had taken fewer than three titles, and one of them - Ezekwesili Ezukanma - had taken the fourth and highest. Only two other men in the entire six villages had this distinction. One of them was too old to be present and the other was Nwaka of Umunneora. His absence from this delegation showed how desperate they all were to appease Ezeulu.

They came in together, giving the impression that they had already met elsewhere. Before he entered Ezeulu's hut each of them planted his iron staff outside and transferred his red cap on to its head.

Throughout their deliberation no one came within hearing distance of the hut. Anosi who had wanted to take scraps of gossip to Ezeulu and pick up what he could on the crisis came out of his hut carrying snuff in his left hand and then saw all the red-capped *alo* staffs outside his neighbour's hut. He turned away to visit another neighbour.

Ezeulu presented a lump of chalk to his visitors and each of them drew his personal emblem of upright and horizontal lines on the floor. Some painted their big toe and others marked their face. Then he brought them three kola nuts in a wooden bowl. A short formal argument began and ended. Ezeulu took one kola nut, Ezekwesili took the second and Onenyi Nnanyelugo took the third. Each of them offered a short prayer and broke his nut. Nwafo carried the bowl to them in turn and they first put in all the lobes before selecting one. Nwafo carried the bowl round and the rest took a lobe each.

After they had all chewed and swallowed their kola Ezekwesili spoke.

'Ezeulu, the leaders of Umuaro assembled here have asked me to tell you that they are thankful for the kola you gave them. Thank you again and again and may your stock be replenished.'

'Perhaps you can guess why we have come. It is because of certain stories that have reached our ears; and we thought the best thing was to find out what is true and what is not from the only man who can tell us. The story we have heard is that there is a little disagreement about the next New Yam Festival. As I said we do not know if it is true or not, but we do know that there is fear and anxiety in Umuaro which if allowed to spread might spoil something. We cannot wait for that to happen; an adult does not sit and watch while the she-goat suffers the pain of childbirth tied to a post. Leaders of Umuaro, have I spoken according to your wish?'

'You have delivered our message.'

'Ezekwesili,' called Ezeulu.

'*Eei*,' answered the man who had just spoken.

'I welcome you. Your words have entered my ears. Egonwanne.'

'*Eei.*'

'Nnanyelugo.'

'*Eei.*'

Ezeulu called each one by his salutation name.

'I welcome you all. Your mission is a good one and I thank you. But I have not heard that there is a disagreement about the New Yam Feast. My assistants came here two days ago and said it was time to announce the day of the next festival and I told them that it was not their place to remind me.'

Ezekwesili's head was slightly bowed and he was rubbing his hairless dome. Ofoka had taken his snuff-bottle from his pure white goatskin bag and was tipping some of the snuff into his left palm. Nnanyelugo who sat nearest to him rubbed his own palms together to clean them and then presented the left to Ofoka without saying a word. Ofoka turned the snuff from his own hand into Nnanyelugo's and tipped out some more for himself.

'But with you,' continued Ezeulu, 'I need not speak in riddles. You all know what our custom is. I only call a new festival when there is only one yam left for the feast. Today I have three yams and so I know that the time has not come.'

Three or four of the visitors tried to speak at once but the others gave way to Ononyi Nnanyelugo. He saluted everyone by name before he started.

'I think that Ezeulu has spoken well. Everything he has said entered my ears. We all know the custom and no one can say that Ezeulu has offended against it. But the harvest is ripe in the soil and must be gathered now or it will be eaten by the sun and the weevils. At the same time Ezeulu has just told us that he still has three sacred yams to eat from last year. What then do we do? How do you carry a man with a broken waist? We know why the sacred yams are still not finished; it was the work of the white man. But he is not here now to breathe with us the air he has fouled. We cannot go to Okperi and ask him to come and eat the yams that now stand between us and the harvest. Shall we then sit down and watch our harvest ruined and our children and wives die of hunger? No! Although I am not the priest of Ulu I can say that the deity does not want Umuaro to perish. We call him the saver. Therefore you must find a way out, Ezeulu. If I could I would go now and eat the remaining yams. But I am not the priest of Ulu. It is for you, Ezeulu, to save our harvest.'

The others murmured their approval.

'Nnanyelugo.'

'*Eei.*'

'You have spoken well. But what you ask me to do is not done. Those yams are not food and a man does not eat them because he is hungry. You are asking me to eat death.'

'Ezeulu,' said Anichebe Udeozo. 'We know that such a thing has never been done before but never before has the white man taken the Chief Priest away. These are not the times we used to know and we must meet them as they come or be rolled in the dust. I want you to look round this room and tell me what you see. Do you think there is another Umuaro outside this hut now?'

'No, you are Umuaro,' said Ezeulu.

'Yes, we are Umuaro. Therefore listen to what I am going to say. Umuaro is now asking you to go and eat those remaining yams today and name the day of the next harvest. Do you hear me well? I said go and eat those yams today, not tomorrow; and if Ulu says we have commited an abomination let it be on the head of the ten of us here. You will be free because we have set you to it, and the person who sets a child to catch a shrew should also find him water to wash the odour from his hand. We shall find you the water. Umuaro, have I spoken well?'

'You have said everything. We shall take the punishment.'

'Leaders of Umuaro, do not say that I am treating your words with contempt; it is not my wish to do so. But you cannot say: *do what is not done and we shall take the blame.* I am the Chief Priest of Ulu and what I have told you is his will not mine. Do not forget that I too have yam-fields and that my children, my kinsmen and my friends – yourselves among them – have also planted yams. It could not be my wish to ruin all these people. It could not be my wish to make the smallest man in Umuaro suffer. But this is not my doing. The gods sometimes use a whip.'

'Did Ulu tell you what his annoyance was? Is there no sacrifice that would appease him?'

'I will not hide anything from you. Ulu did say that two new moons came and went and there was no one to break kola nut to him and Umuaro kept silent.'

'What did he expect us to say?' asked Ofoka, a little hotly.

'I don't know what he expected you to say, Ofoka. Nnanyelugo asked me a question and I answered.'

'But if Ulu —'

'Let us not quarrel about that, Ofoka. We asked Ezeulu what was Ulu's grievance and he has told us. Our concern now should be how to appease him. Let us ask Ezeulu to go back and tell the deity that we have heard his grievance and we are prepared to make amends. Every offence has its sacrifice, from a few cowries to a cow or a human being. Let us wait for an answer.'

'If you ask me to go back to Ulu I shall do so. But I must warn you that a god who demands the sacrifice of a chick might raise it to a goat if you went to ask a second time.'

'Do not say that I am fond of questions,' said Ofoka. 'But I should like to know on whose side you are, Ezeulu. I think you have just said that you have become the whip with which Ulu flogs Umuaro . . .'

'If you will listen to me, Ofoka, let us not quarrel about that,' said Ezekwesili. 'We have come to the end of our present mission. Our duty now is to watch Ezeulu's mouth for a message from Ulu. We have planted our yams in the farm of Anaba-nti.'

The others agreed and Nnanyelugo deftly steered the conversation to the subject of change. He gave numerous examples of customs that had been altered in the past when they began to work hardship on the people. They all talked at length about these customs which had either died in full bloom or had been stillborn. Nnanyelugo reminded them that even in the matter of taking titles there had been a change. Long, long ago there had been a fifth title in Umuaro – the title of king. But the conditions for its attainment had been so severe that no man had ever taken it, one of the conditions being that the man aspiring to be king must first pay the debts of every man and every woman in Umuaro. Ezeulu said nothing throughout this discussion.

As he promised the leaders of Umuaro Ezeulu returned to the shrine of Ulu in the morning. He entered the bare, outer room and looked round vacantly. Then he placed his back against the door of the inner room which not even his assistants dared enter. The door gave under the pressure of his body and he walked in backwards. He guided himself by running his left hand along one of the side walls. When he got to the end of it he moved a few steps to the right and stood directly in front of the earth mound which represented Ulu. From the rafters right round the room the skulls of all past chief priests looked down on the mound and on their descendant and successor. Even in the hottest day a damp chill always possessed the shrine because of the giant trees outside which put their heads together to cut off the sun, but more especially because of the great, cold, underground river flowing under the earth mound. Even the approaches to the shrine were cold and, all year round, there was always some *ntu-nanya-mili* dropping tears from the top of the ancient trees.

As Ezeulu cast his string of cowries the bell of Oduche's people began to ring; for one brief moment he was distracted by its sad, measured monotone and he thought how strange it was that it should sound so near – much nearer than it did in his compound.

Ezeulu's announcement that his consultation with the deity had produced no result and that the six villages would be locked in the old year for two moons longer spread such alarm as had not been known in Umuaro in living memory.

Meanwhile the rains thinned out. There was one last heavy downpour to usher in a new moon. It brought down the harmattan as well, and each new day made the earth harder so that the eventual task of digging up whatever remained of the harvest grew daily.

Disagreement was not new in Umuaro. The rulers of the clan had often quarrelled about one thing or another. There was a long-drawn-out dispute before face marks were finally abolished and there had been other disagreements of more or less weight before it and since. But none of them had quite filtered down to the ground – to the women and even the children – like the present crisis. It was not remote argument which could end one way or the other and still leave the ground untouched. Even children in their mother's belly took sides in this one.

Yesterday Nwafo had had to wrestle with his friend, Obielue.
It had all started from the moment they went to inspect the bird-
snare they had set with the resin on the rop of two icheku trees.
Obielue's trap held a very small *nza* while Nwafo's was empty.
This had happened before, and Obielue began to boast about his
skill. In exasperation Nwafo called him 'Never-a-dry-season-in-the-
nose'. Now, Obielue did not care for this name because his nose
ran constantly and left the precincts of his nostrils red and sore.
He called Nwafo 'Ant-hill nose'; but it was not nearly as appropriate
as the other and could not be turned into a song as readily. So he
put Ezeulu's name in the song children sang whenever they saw
an Udo ram, one of those fierce animals that belong to the shrine
of Udo and could come and go as they wished. Children enjoyed
teasing them from a good distance The song, which was accompanied by the clapping of hands, implored the ram to remove the
ugly lumps in its scrotum. To which the singers answered (on behalf
of the ram): How does one remove yam tubers? The request and
the response were sung in time with the swinging of the tubers.
In place of *ebunu* Obielue sang *Ezeulu*. Nwafo could not stand this
and gave his friend a blow in the mouth which brought blood to
his front teeth.

Almost overnight Ezeulu had become something of a public
enemy in the eyes of all and, as was to be expected, his entire family
shared in his guilt. His children came up against it on their way
to the stream and his wives suffered hostility in the market. The
other day at the Nkwo Matife had gone to buy a small basket of
prepared cassava from Ojinika, wife of Ndulue. She knew Ojinika
quite well and had bought from her and sold to her countless times.
But on this day Ojinika spoke to her as if she was a stranger from
another clan.

'I shall pay *ego nato*,' said Matefi.

'I have told you the price is *ego nese*.'

'I think *ego nato* suits it well; it's only a tiny basket.' She picked
up the basket to show that it was small. Ojinika seemed to have
forgotten all about her and was engrossed in arranging her okro
in little lots on the mat.

'What do you say?'

536

'Put that basket down at once!' Then she changed her tone and sneered. 'You want to take it for nothing. You wait till the yams are ruined and come and buy a basket of cassava for eighteen cowries.'

Matefi was not the kind of person another woman could tie into her lappa and carry away. She gave Ojinika more than she got – told her the bride-price they paid for her mother. But when she got home she began to think about the hostility that was visibly encircling them all in Ezeulu's compound. Something told her that someone was going to pay a big price for it and she was afraid.

'Go and call me Obika,' she told her daughter, Ojiugo.

She was preparing some coco-yams for thickening soup when Obika came in and sat on the bare floor with his back on the wooden post in the middle of the entrance. He wore a very thin strip of cloth which was passed between the legs and between the buttocks and wound around the waist. He sat down heavily like a tired man. His mother went on with her work of dressing the coco-yams.

'Ojiugo says you called me.'

'Yes.' She went on with what she was doing.

'To watch you prepare coco-yams?'

She went on with her work.

'What is it?'

'I want you to go and talk to your father.'

'About what?'

'About what? About his . . . Are you a stranger in Umuaro? Do you not see the trouble that is coming?'

'What do you expect him to do? To disobey Ulu?'

'I knew you would not listen to me.' She managed to hang all her sorrows and disappointments on those words.

'How can I listen to you when you join outsiders in urging your husband to put his head in a cooking pot?'

'Sometimes I want to agree with those who say the man has caught his mother's madness,' said Ogbuefi Ofoka. 'When he came back from Okperi I went to his house and he talked like a sane man. I reminded him of his saying that a man must dance the dance prevailing in his time and told him that we had come – too late

– to accept its wisdom . But today he would rather see the six villages ruined than eat two yams.'

'I have had the same thought myself,' said Akuebue who was visiting his in-law. 'I know Ezeulu better than most people. He is a proud man and the most stubborn person you know is only his messenger; but he would not falsify the decision of Ulu. If he did it Ulu would not spare him to begin with. So, I don't know.'

'I have not said that Ezeulu is telling a lie with the name of Ulu or that he is not. What we told him was to go and eat the yams and we would take the consequences. But he would not do it. Why? Because the six villages allowed the white man to take him away. That is the reason. He has been trying to see how he could punish Umuaro and how he has the chance. The house he has been planning to pull down has caught fire and saved him the labour.'

'I do not doubt that he has had a grievance for a long time, but I do not think it goes as deep as this. Remember he has his own yam-fields like the rest of us . . .'

'That was what he told us. But, my friend, when a man as proud as this wants to fight he does not care if his own head rolls as well in the conflict. And besides he forgot to mention that whether our harvest is ruined or not we would still take one yam each to Ulu.'

'I don't know.'

'Let me tell you one thing. A priest like Ezeulu leads a god to ruin himself. It has happened before.'

'Oh, perhaps a god like Ulu leads a priest to ruin himself.'

There was one man who saw the mounting crisis in Umuaro as a blessing and an opportunity sent by God. His name was John Jaja Goodcountry, catechist of St Mark's CMS Church, Umuaro. His home was in the Niger Delta which had been in contact with Europe and the world for hundreds of years. Although he had been in Umuaro only a year he could show as much progress in his church and school as many other teachers and pastors would have been proud to record after five or more years. His catechumen class had grown from a mere fourteen to nearly thirty – mostly young men and boys who also went to school. There had been one baptism in St Mark's Church itself and three in the parish church at Okperi. Altogether Mr Goodcountry's young church provided nine

candidates for these occasions. He had not been able to field any
candidates for confirmation, but that was hardly surprising in a
new church amongst some of the most difficult people in the Ibo
country.

The progress of St Mark's came about in a somewhat unusual
way. Mr Goodcountry with his background of the Niger Delta
Pastorate, which could already count native martyrs like Joshua
Hart to its credit, was not prepared to compromise with the heathen
over such things as sacred animals. Within weeks of his sojourn
in Umuaro he was ready for a little war against the royal python
in the same spirit as his own people had fought and conquered the
sacred iguana. Unfortunately he came up against a local stumbling
block in Moses Unachukwu, the most important Christian in
Umuaro.

From the beginning Mr Goodcountry had taken exception to
Unachukwu's know-all airs which the last catechist, Mr Molokwu,
had done nothing to curb. Goodcountry had seen elsewhere how
easy it was for a half-educated and half-converted Christian to
mislead a whole congregation when the pastor or catechist was
weak; so he wanted to establish his leadership from the very
beginning. His intention was not originally to antagonize
Unachukwu more than was necessary for making his point; after
all he was a strong pillar in the church and could not be easily
replaced. But Unachukwu did not give Mr Goodcountry a chance;
he challenged him openly on the question of the python and so
deserved the public rebuke and humiliation he got.

Having made his point Mr Goodcountry was prepared to forget
the whole thing. He had no idea what kind of person he was dealing
with. Unachukwu got a clerk in Okperi to write a petition on behalf
of the priest of Idemili to the Bishop of the Niger. Although it was
called a petition it was more of a threat. It warned the bishop that
unless his followers in Umuaro left the royal python alone they
would regret the day they ever set foot on the soil of the clan. Being
the work of one of the knowedgeable clerks on Government Hill
the petition made allusions to such potent words as law and order
and the King's peace.

The bishop had just had a very serious situation in another part

539

of his diocese on this same matter of the python. A young, energetic ordinand had led his people on a shrine-burning adventure and had killed a python in the process, whereupon the villagers had chased out all the Christians among them and burnt their houses. Things might have got out of hand had the Administration not stepped in with troops for a show of force. After this incident the Lieutenant Governor had written a sharp letter to the bishop to apply the reins on his boys.

For this reason, but also because he did not himself approve of such excess of zeal, the bishop had written a firm letter to Goodcountry. He had also replied to Ezidemili's petition assuring him that the catechist would not interfere with the python but at the same time praying that the day would not be far when the priest and all his people would turn away from the worship of snakes and idols to the true religion.

This letter from the big, white priest far away reinforced the view which had been gaining ground that the best way to deal with the white man was to have a few people like Moses Unachukwu around who knew what the white man knew. As a result many people – some of them very important – began to send their children to school. Even Nwaka sent a son – the one who seemed least likely among his children to become a good farmer.

Mr Goodcountry not knowing the full story of the deviousness of the heathen mind behind the growth of this school and church put it down to his effective evangelization which, in a way, it was – a vindication of his work against his bishop's policy of appeasement. He wrote a report on the amazing success of the Gospel in Umuaro for the *West African Church Magazine*, although, as was the custom in such reports, he allowed the credit to go to the Holy Spirit.

Now Mr Goodcountry saw in the present crisis over the New Yam Feast an opportunity for fruitful intervention. He had planned his church's harvest service for the second Sunday in November the proceeds from which would go into the fund for building a place of worship more worthy of God and of Umuaro. His plan was quite simple. The New Yam Festival was the attempt of the misguided heathen to show gratitude to God, the giver of all good things. This was God's hour to save them from their error which was now threatening to ruin them. They must be told that if they made their thank-offering to God they could harvest their crops without fear of Ulu.

'So we can tell our heathen brethren to bring their one yam to church instead of giving it to Ulu?' asked a new member of Goodcountry's church committee.

'That is what I say. But not just one yam. Let them bring as many as they wish according to the benefits they received this year from Almighty God. And not only yams, any crop whatsoever or livestock or money. Anything.'

The man who had asked the question did not seem satisfied. He kept scratching his head.

'Do you still not understand?'

'I understand but I was thinking how we could tell them to bring more than one yam. You see, our custom, or rather their custom, is to take just one yam to Ulu.'

Moses Unachukwu, who had since returned to full favour with Goodcountry, saved the day. 'If Ulu, who is a false god, can eat one yam the living God who owns the whole world should be entitled to eat more than one.'

So the news spread that anyone who did not want to wait and see all his harvest ruined could take his offering to the god of the Christians who claimed to have power of protection from the anger of Ulu. Such a story at other times might have been treated with laughter. But there was no more laughter left in the people.

CHAPTER NINETEEN

The first serious sufferers from the postponement of the harvest were the family of Ogbuefi Amalu who had died in the rainy season from *aru-mmo*. Amalu was a man of substance and, in normal times, the rites of second burial and funeral feast would have followed two or three days after his death. But it was a bad death which killed a man in the time of famine. Amalu himself knew it and was prepared. Before he died he had called his first son, Aneto, and given him directions for the burial feast.

'I would have said: Do it a day or two after I have been put into the earth. But this is *ugani*; I cannot ask you to arrange my burial feast with your saliva. I must wait until there are yams again.' He spoke with great difficulty, struggling with every breath. Aneto was down on both knees beside the bamboo bed and strained to catch the whispers which were barely audible over the noisy breathing coming from the cavity of the sick man's chest. The many coatings of camwood which had been rubbed on it had caked and cracked like red earth in the dry season. 'But you must not delay it beyond four moons from my death. And do not forget, I want you to slaughter a bull.'

There was a story told of a young man in another clan who was so pestered by trouble that he decided to consult an oracle. The reason, he was told, was that his dead father wanted him to sacrifice a goat to him. The young man said to the oracle: 'Ask my father if he left as much as a fowl for me.' Ogbuefi Amalu was not like that man. Everyone knew he was worth four hundred bulls and

542

that he had not asked his son for more than was justly due.

In anticipation of the New Yam Festival Aneto and his brothers and kinsmen had chosen the day for Amalu's second burial and announced it to all Umuaro and to all their relations and in-laws in the neighbouring clans.

What were they to do now? Should they persist with their plan and give Amalu a poor man's burial feast without yams and risk his ire on their heads or should they put it off beyond the time that Amalu had appointed and again risk his anger? The second choice seemed the better and the less dangerous one. But to be quite sure Aneto went to *afa*, to put the alternatives to his father.

When he got to the oracle he found that there were not two alternatives but one. He dared not ask his father whether he would accept a poor man's funeral; rather he asked whether he could delay the rites until there were yams in Umuaro. Amalu said no. He had already stood too long in the rain and sun and could not bear it one day longer. A poor man might wander outside for years while his kinsmen scraped their meagre resources together; that was his penalty for lack of success in his life. But a great man who had toiled through two titles must be called indoors by those for whom he had toiled and for whom he left his riches.

Aneto called a kindred meeting and told them what his father had said. No one was surprised. 'Who would blame Amalu?' they asked. 'Has he not stood outside long enough?' No, the fault was Ezeulu's. He had seen to it that Amalu's kinsmen would waste their substance in buying yams from neighbouring clans when their own crop lay locked in the soil. Many of these neighbouring people were already growing fat out of Umuaro's misfortune. Every Nkwo market they brought new yams to Umuaro and sold them like anklets of ivory. At first only men without title, women and children ate these foreign yams. But as the famine grew more harsh and stringent someone pointed out that there was nothing in the custom of Umuaro forbidding a man of title from eating new yams grown on foreign earth; and in any case who was there when they were dug out to swear that they were new yams? This made people laugh with one side of their face. But if there was any man of title who took this advice and ate these yams he made sure that no one saw him. What many of them did do was to harvest the yams planted around their homestead to feed their wives and children. From ancient usage it had always been possible for a man to dig up a few homestead yams in times of severe famine. But today it was not just a few yams, and what was more, the homestead area crept farther and farther afield as the days passed.

The plight of Umuaro lay more heavily on Ezeulu and his family than other people knew. In the Chief Priest's compound nobody could think of indulging in the many old and new evasions which allowed others to eat an occasional new yam be it local or foreign. Because they were more prosperous than most families they had a larger stock of old yams. But these had long shrivelled into tasteless fibre. Before cooking they had to be beaten with a heavy pestle to separate the wiry strands. Soon even these were finished.

But the heaviest load was on Ezeulu's mind. He was used to loneliness. As Chief Priest he had often walked alone in front of Umuaro. But without looking back he had always been able to hear their flute and song which shook the earth because it came from a multitude of voices and the stamping of countless feet. There had been moments when the voices were divided as in the land dispute with Okperi. But never until now had he known them to die away altogether. Few people came to his hut now and those who came said nothing. Ezeulu wanted to hear what Umuaro was saying but nobody offered to tell and he would not make anyone think he was curious. So with every passing day Umuaro became more and more an alien silence – the kind of silence which burnt a man's inside like the blue, quiet, razor-edge flame of burning palm-nut shells. Ezeulu writhed in the pain which grew and grew until he wanted to get outside his compound or even into the Nkwo market place and shout at Umuaro.

Because no one came near enough to him to see his anguish – and if they had seen it they would not have understood – they imagined that he sat in his hut gloating over the distress of Umuaro. But although he would not for any reason now see the present trend reversed he carried more punishment and more suffering than all his fellows. What troubled him most – and he alone seemed to be aware of it at present – was that the punishment was not for now alone but for all time. It would afflict Umuaro like an *ogulu-aro* disease which counts a year and returns to its victim. Beneath all anger in his mind lay a deeper compassion for Umuaro, the clan which long, long ago when lizards were in ones and twos chose his ancestor to carry their deity and go before them challenging every obstacle and confronting every danger on their behalf.

Perhaps if the silence in which Ezeulu was trapped had been complete he would have got used to it in time. But it had cracks through which now and again a teasing driblet of news managed to reach him: this had the effect of deepening the silence, like a pebble thrown in a cave.

Today Akuebue threw such a pebble. He was the only man among Ezeulu's friends and kinsmen who still came now and again to see him. But when he came he sat in silence or spoke about unimportant things. Today, however, he could not but touch on a new development in the crisis which troubled him. Perhaps Akuebue was the only man in Umuaro who knew that Ezeulu was not deliberately punishing the six villages. He knew that the Chief Priest was helpless; that a thing greater than *nte* had been caught in *nte*'s trap. So whenever he came to visit Ezeulu he kept clear of the things nearest to their thoughts because they were past talking. But today he could not keep silence over the present move of the Christians to reap the harvest of Umuaro.

'It troubles me,' he said, 'because it looks like the saying of our ancestors that when brothers fight to death a stranger inherits their father's estate.'

'What do you expect me to do?' Ezeulu opened both palms towards his friend. 'If any man in Umuaro forgets himself so far as to join them let him carry on.'

Akuebue shook his head in despair.

As soon as he left Ezeulu called Oduche and asked him if it was true that his people were offering sanctuary to those who wished to escape the vengeance of Ulu. Oduche said he did not understand.

'You do not understand? Are your people saying to Umuaro that if anyone brings his sacrifice to your shrine he will be safe to harvest his yams? Now do you understand?'

'Yes. Our teacher told them so.'

'Your teacher told them so? Did you report it to me?'

'No.'

'Why?'

Silence.

'I said why did you not report it to me?'

For a long time father and son looked steadily at each other in silence. When Ezeulu spoke again his tone was calm and full of grief.

'Do you remember, Oduche, what I told you when I sent you among those people?'

Oduche shifted his eyes to the big toe of his right foot which he placed a little forward.

'Since you have become dumb let me remind you. I called you as a father calls his son and told you to go and be my eye and ear among those people. I did not send Obika or Edogo; I did not send Nwafo, your mother's son. I called you by name and you came here – in this *obi* – and I sent you to see and hear for me. I did not know at that time that I was sending a goat's skull. Go away, go back to your mother's hut. I have no spirit for talking now. When I am ready to talk I shall tell you what I think. Go away and rejoice that your father cannot count on you. I say, go away from here, lizard that ruined his mother's funeral.'

Oduche went out at the brink of tears. Ezeulu felt a slight touch of comfort.

At last another new moon came and he ate the twelfth yam. The next morning he sent word to his assistants to announce that the New Yam Feast would be eaten in twenty-eight days.

Throughout that day the drums beat in Amalu's compound because the funeral feast was tomorrow. The sound reached every village in Umuaro to remind them; not that anyone needed reminding at such a time when men were as hungry as locusts.

In the night Ezeulu dreamt one of those strange dreams which were more than ordinary dreams. When he woke up everything stood out with the detail and clarity of daylight, like the one he had dreamt in Okperi.

He was sitting in his *obi*. From the sound of the voices the mourners seemed to be passing behind his compound, beyond the tall, red walls. This worried him a good deal because there was no path there. Who were these people then who made a path behind his compound? He told himself that he must go out and challenge them because it was said that unless a man wrestled with those who walked behind his compound the path never closed. But he lacked resolution and stood where he was. Meanwhile the voices and the drums and the flutes grew louder. They sang the song with which a man was carried to the bush for burial:

> Look! a python
> Look! a python
> Yes, it lies across the way.

As usual the song came in different waves like gusts of storm following on each other's heels. The mourners in front sang a little ahead of those in the middle near the corpse and these were again ahead of those at the rear. The drums came with this last wave.

Ezeulu raised his voice to summon his family to join him in challenging the trespassers but his compound was deserted. His irresolution turned into alarm. He ran into Matefi's hut but all he saw were the ashes of a long-dead fire. He rushed out and ran into Ugoye's hut calling her and her children but her hut was already falling in and a few blades of green grass had sprouted on the thatch. He was running towards Obika's hut when a new voice behind the compound brought him to a sudden halt. The noise of the burial party had since disappeared in the distance. But beside the sorrow of the solitary voice that now wailed after them they might have been returning with a bride. The sweet agony of the solitary singer settled like dew on the head.

> I was born when lizards were in ones and twos
> A child of Idemili. The difficult teardrops
> Of Sky's first weeping drew my spots. Being
> Sky-born I walked the earth with royal gait
> And mourners saw me coiled across their path.
> But of late
> A strange bell
> Has been ringing a song of desolation:
> > Leave your yams and coco-yams

And come to school.
And I must scuttle away in haste
When children in play or in earnest cry:
    Look! a Christian is on the way.
    Ha ha ha ha ha ha ha ha ha ha ha ha ha . . .

The singer's sudden, demented laughter filled Ezeulu's compound
and he woke up. In spite of the cold harmattan he was sweating.
But he felt an enormous relief to be awake and know that it had
been a dream. The blind alarm and the life-and-death urgency fell
away from it at the threshold of waking. But a vague fear remained
because the voice of the python had ended as the voice of Ezeulu's
mother when she was seized with madness. Nwanyi Okperi, as they
called her in Umuaro, had been a great singer in her youth, making
songs for her village as easily as some people talked. In later life when
her madness came on her these old songs and others she might have
made forced themselves out in eccentric spurts through the cracks
in her mind. Ezeulu in his childhood lived in fear of these moments
when his mother's feet were put in stocks, at the new moon.

The passage of Ogbazulobodo at that moment helped in establishing
Ezeulu in the present. Perhaps it was the effect of the dream, but
in all his life he had never heard a night spirit pass with this fury.
It was like a legion of runners each covered from neck to ankle
with strings of rattling *ekpili*. It came from the direction of the *ilo*
and disappeared towards Nkwo. It must have seen signs of light
in someone's compound for it seemed to stop and cry: *Ewo okuo!
Ewo okuo!* The offender whoever it was must have quickly put out
the light, and the pacified spirit continued its flight and soon
disappeared in the night.

Ezeulu wondered why it had not saluted him when it passed near
his compound. Or perhaps it did before he woke up.

After the dream and the commotion of Ogbazulobodo's passage
he tried in vain to sleep again. Then they began to fire the cannon
in Amalu's place. Ezeulu counted nine claps separated by the
beating of *ekwe*. By that time sleep had completely left his eyes.
He got up and groped for the latch of his carved door and opened
it. Then he took his matchet and his bottle of snuff from the head

of the bed and groped his way to the outer room. There he felt the dry chill of the harmattan. Fortunately the fire had not died from the two big ukwa logs. He stoked it and produced a small flame.

No other person in the village could carry the *ogbazulobodo* as well as Obika. Whenever somebody else tried there was a big difference: either the speed was too slow or the words stuck in his throat. For the power of *ike-agwu-ani*, great though it was, could not change a crawling millipede into an antelope nor a dumb man into an orator. That was why in spite of the great grievance which Amalu's family nursed against Ezeulu and his family Aneto still came to beg Obika to run as *ogbazulobodo* on the night before his father's second burial.

'I do not want to say no to you,' said Obika after Aneto had spoken, 'but this is not something a man can do when his body is not all his. Since yesterday I have been having a little fever.'

'I do not know what it is but everybody you see nowadays sounds like a broken pot,' said Aneto.

'Why not ask Nweke Ukpaka to run for you?'

'I knew about Nweke Ukpaka when I came to you. I even passed by his house.'

Obika considered the matter.

'There are many people who can do it,' said Aneto. 'But he whose name is called again and again by those trying in vain to catch a wild bull has something he alone can do to bulls.'

'True,' said Obika. 'I agree but I am agreeing in cowardice.'

'If I say no,' Obika told himself, 'they will say that Ezeulu and his family have revealed a second time their determination to wreck the burial of their village man who did no harm to them.'

He did not tell his wife that he would be going out that night until he had eaten his evening meal. Obika always went into his wife's hut to eat his meals. His friends teased him about it and said the woman had spoilt his head. Okuata was polishing off the soup in her bowl when Obika spoke. She crooked her first finger once more, wiped the bowl with it, stretched it again and ran it down her tongue.

'Going out with this fever?' she asked. 'Obika have pity on yourself. The funeral is tomorrow. What is there they cannot do without you until the morning?'

'I shall not stay long. Aneto is my age-mate and I must go and see how he is preparing.'

Okuata maintained a sullen silence.

'Bar the door well. Nobody will carry you away. I shall not stay long.'

The *ekwe-ogbazulobodo* sounded *kome kome kokome kome kokome* and continued for a while warning anyone still awake to hurry up to bed and put out every light because light and *ogbazulobodo* were mortal enemies. When it had beaten long enough for all to hear it stopped. Silence and the shrill call of insects seized the night again. Obika and the others who would carry the *ayaka* spirit-chorus sat on the lowest rung of the *okwolo* steps talking and laughing. The man who beat the *ekwe* joined them, leaving his drum in the half-light of the palm-oil torch.

When the *ekwe* began to beat out the second and final warning Obika was still talking with the others as though it did not concern him. The old man, Ozumba, who kept the regalia of the night spirits took a position near the drummer. Then he raised his cracked voice and called *ugoli* four or five times as if to clear the cobweb from it. Then he asked if Obika was there. Obika looked in his direction and saw him vaguely in the weak light. Slowly and deliberately he got up and went to Ozumba, and stood before him. Ozumba bent down and took up a skirt made of a network of rope and heavily studded with rattling *ekpili*. Obika raised both arms above his head so that Ozumba could tie the skirt round his waist without hindrance. When this was done Ozumba waved his arms about like a blind man until they struck the iron staff. He pulled it out of the ground and placed it in Obika's right hand. The *ekwe* continued to beat in the half-light of the palm-oil torch. Obika closed his hand tight on the staff and clenched his teeth. Ozumba allowed him a little time to prepare himself fully. Then very slowly he lifted the *ike-agwu-ani* necklace. The *ekwe* beat faster and faster. Obika held his head forward and Ozumba put the *ike-agwu-ani* round his neck. As he did so he said:

> *Tun-tun gem-gem*
> *Oso mgbada bu nugwu.*
> The speed of the deer
> Is seen on the hill.

As soon as these words left his mouth Ogbazulobodo swung round and cried: *Ewo okuo! Ewo okuo!* The drummer threw down his sticks and hastily blew out the offending light. The spirit planted the staff into the earth and it reverberated. He pulled it out again and vanished like the wind in the direction of Nkwo leaving potent words in the air behind.

'*The fly that struts around on a mound of excrement wastes his time; the mound will always be greater than the fly. The thing that beats the drum for* ngwesi *is inside the ground. Darkness is so great it gives horns to a dog. He who builds a homestead before another can boast more broken pots. It is* ofo *that gives rain-water power to cut dry earth. The man who walks ahead of his fellows spots spirits on the way. Bat said he knew his ugliness and chose to fly by night. When the air is fouled by a man on top of a palm tree the fly is confused. An ill-fated man drinks water and it catches in his teeth . . .*'

He was at once blind and full of sight. He did not see any of the landmarks like trees and huts but his feet knew perfectly where they were going; he did not leave out even one small path from the accustomed route. He knew it without the use of eyes. He only stopped once when he smelt light . . . '*Even while people are still talking about the man Rat bit to death Lizard takes money to have his teeth filed. He who sees an old hag squatting should leave her alone; who knows how she breathes? White Ant chews* igbegulu *because it is lying on the ground; let him climb the palm tree and chew. He who will swallow* udala *seeds must consider the size of his anus. The fly that has no one to advise him follows the corpse into the ground . . .*'

A fire began to rage inside his chest and to push a dry bitterness up his mouth. But he tasted it from a distance or from a mouth within his mouth. He felt like two separate persons, one running above the other.

'. . . *When a handshake passes the elbow it becomes another thing.
The sleep that lasts from one market day to another has become death.
The man who likes the meat of the funeral ram, why does he recover
when sickness visits him? The mighty tree falls and the little birds scatter
in the bush . . . The little bird which hops off the ground and lands
on an ant-hill may not know it but is still on the ground . . . A common
snake which a man sees all alone may become a python in his eyes . . .
The very Thing which kills Mother Rat is always there to make sure
that its younger ones never open their eyes . . . The boy who persists
in asking what happened to his father before he has enough strength
to avenge him is asking for his father's fate . . . The man who belittles
the sickness which Monkey has suffered should ask to see the eyes which
his nurse got from blowing the sick fire . . . When death wants to take
a little dog it prevents it from smelling even excrement . . .*'

The eight men who would sing the *ayaka* chorus were still talking
where Obika left them. Ozumba had come to sit with them to await
his return. They were talking about the big bull which Amalu's
children had bought for his funeral when they heard the voice
already coming back. The *ayaka* men scrambled to their feet and
got ready to break into song as soon as Ogbazulobodo re-entered
the *ilo*. They were all amazed that he was already returning. Had
he left out any of the paths?

'Not Obika,' said Ozumba proudly. 'He is a sharp one. Give
me a sharp boy even though he breaks utensils in his haste.'

This was hardly out of his mouth when Ogbazulobodo raced in
and fell down at the foot of the *okwolo*. Ozumba removed the
necklace from his neck and called his name. But Obika did not
answer. He called him again and touched his chest.

They poured some of the cold water which was always kept handy
over his face and body. The song of the *ayaka* had stopped as
abruptly as it had started. They all stood around unable yet to talk.

The first cock had not crowed. Ezeulu was still in his *obi*. The fire
still glowed on the big logs but the flame had long gone out. Were
those footsteps he was hearing? He listened carefully. Yes, they
were getting louder, and voices too. He felt for his matchet. What
could this be?

'Who?' he called. The footsteps stopped, and the voices. For a moment there was silence, heavy with the presence of the strangers outside in the dark.

'People,' said a voice.

'Who is called people? My gun is loaded, let me warn people.'

'Ezeulu, it is me, Ozumba.'

'Ozumba.'

'Eh.'

'What brings you out at this time?'

'An abomination has overtaken us. Goat has eaten palm leaves from off my head.'

Ezeulu merely cleared his throat and began slowly to stoke the fire. 'Let me build a fire to see your faces.' One of the sticks of firewood was too long and he broke it across his knee. He blew the fire a few times and it broke into a flame.

'Come in and let me hear what you are saying.'

As soon as he saw Obika's body coming in under the low eaves he sprang to his feet and took up his matchet.

'What happened to him? Who did this? I said who?'

Ozumba began to explain but Ezeulu did not hear. The matchet fell from his hand and he slumped down on both knees beside the body. 'My son,' he cried. 'Ulu, were you there when this happened to me?' He hid his face on Obika's chest.

When the first light came nearly every arrangement had been made for the announcement of the death. The village death-drums were leaning against a wall. A bottle of gunpowder had been found and put aside. Ezeulu wandered up and down among the busy people trying to help. At one point he found the long broom they used paddlewise to sweep the compound, took it up and began to sweep. But someone took it from him and led him by the hand back to his hut.

'People will soon be here,' he said weakly, 'and the place is still unswept.'

'Leave it to me. I shall find somebody to do it straight away.'

Obika's death shook Umuaro to the roots; a man like him did not come into the world too often. As for Ezeulu it was as though he had died.

Some people expected Ezidemili to be jubilant. Such people did not know him. He was not that kind of man and besides he knew too well the danger of such exultation. All he was heard to say quietly was: 'This should teach him how far he could dare next time.'

But for Ezeulu there was no next time. Think of a man who, unlike the lesser men, always goes to battle without a shield because he knows that bullets and matchet strokes will glance off his medicine-boiled skin; think of him discovering in the thick of battle that the power has suddenly, without warning, deserted him. What next time can there be? Will he say to the guns and the arrows and the matchets: *Hold! I want to return quickly to my medicine-hut and stir the pot and find out what has gone wrong; perhaps someone in my household – a child, maybe – has unwittingly violated my medicine's taboo?* No.

Ezeulu sank to the ground in utter amazement. It was not simply the blow of Obika's death, great though it was. Men had taken greater blows: that was what made a man a man. For did they not say that a man is like a funeral ram which must take whatever beating comes to it without opening its mouth; that the silent tremor of pain down its body alone must tell of its suffering?

At any other time Ezeulu would have been more than a match to his grief. He would have been equal to any pain not compounded with humiliation. But why, he asked himself again and again, why had Ulu chosen to deal thus with him, to strike him down and then cover him with mud? What was his offence? Had he not divined the god's will and obeyed it? When was it ever heard that a child was scalded by the piece of yam its own mother put in its palm? What man would send his son with a potsherd to bring fire from a neighbour's hut and then unleash rain on him? Who ever sent his son up the palm to gather nuts and then took an axe and felled the tree? But today such a thing had happened before the eyes of all. What could it point to but the collapse and ruin of all things? Then a god, finding himself powerless, might take flight and in one final, backward glance at his abandoned worshippers cry:

> If the rat cannot flee fast enough
> Let him make way for the tortoise!

Perhaps it was the constant, futile throbbing of these thoughts that finally left a crack in Ezeulu's mind. Or perhaps his implacable assailant having stood over him for a little while stepped on him as on an insect and crushed him under the heel in the dust. But this final act of malevolence proved merciful. It allowed Ezeulu, in his last days, to live in the haughty splendour of a demented high priest and spared him knowledge of the final outcome.

Meanwhile Winterbottom, after a recuperative leave in England had returned to his seat and married the doctor. He did not ever hear of Ezeulu again. The only man who might have carried the story to Government Hill was John Nwodika, his steward. But John had since left Winterbottom's service to set up a small trade in tobacco. It looked as though the gods and the powers of event finding Winterbottom handy had used him and left him again in order as they found him.

So in the end only Umuaro and its leaders saw the final outcome. To them the issue was simple. Their god had taken sides with them against his headstrong and ambitious priest and thus upheld the wisdom of their ancestors – that no man however great was greater than his people; that no one ever won judgement against his clan.

If this was so then Ulu had chosen a dangerous time to uphold that truth, for in destroying his priest he had also brought disaster on himself, like the lizard in the fable who ruined his mother's funeral by his own hand. For a deity who chose a moment such as this to chastise his priest or abandon him before his enemies was inciting people to take liberties; and Umuaro was just ripe to do so. The Christian harvest which took place a few days after Obika's death saw more people than even Goodcountry could have dreamed. In his extremity many a man sent his son with a yam or two to offer to the new religion and to bring back the promised immunity. Thereafter any yam harvested in his fields was harvested in the name of the son.

A GLOSSARY OF
IBO WORDS AND PHRASES
(o *indicates* aw *sound as in awful*)

agadi-nwayi	old woman.
agbala	woman: also used of a man who has taken no title.
chi	personal god.
efulefu	worthless man.
egwugwu	a masquerader who impersonates one of the ancestral spirits of the village.
ekwe	a musical instrument: a type of drum made from wood.
eneke-nti-oba	a kind of bird.
eze-agadi-nwayi	the teeth of an old woman.
iba	fever.
ilo	the village green, where assemblies for sports, discussions, etc. take place.
inyanga	showing off: bragging.
isa-ifi	a ceremony: if a wife had been separated from her husband for some time and were then to be re-united with him this ceremony would be held to ascertain that she had not been unfaithful to him during the time of their separation.
iyi-uwa	a special kind of stone which forms the link between an *ogbanje* and the spirit world. Only if the *iyi-uwa* were discovered and destroyed would the child not die.
jigida	a string of waist beads.
kotma	court messenger: the word is not of Ibo origin, but is a corruption of 'court messenger'.
kwenu	a shout of approval and greeting.
ndichie	elders.
nna ayi	our father.
nno	welcome.
nso-ani	a religious offence of a kind abhorred by everyone.
nza	a very small bird.
obi	the large living quarters of the head of the family.
obodo dike	the land of the brave.

ochu	murder or manslaughter.
ogbanje	a changeling: a child who repeatedly dies and returns to its mother to be reborn. It is almost impossible to bring up an *ogbanje* child without it dying, unless its *iyi-uwa* is first found and destroyed.
ogene	a musical instrument; a kind of gong.
oji odu achu-ijiji-o	cow. (i.e.: the one that uses its tail to drive flies away).
osu	outcast; having been dedicated to a god, the *osu* was taboo, and was not allowed to mix with the freeborn in any way.
Oye	the name of one of the four market days.
ozo	the name of one of the titles or ranks.
tufia	a curse or oath.
udu	a musical instrument; a type of drum made from pottery.
uli	a dye used by women for drawing patterns on the skin.
umuada	a family gathering of daughters, for which the female kinsfolk return to their village of origin.
umunna	a wide group of kinsmen: (the masculine form of the word *Umuada*).
Uri	part of the betrothal ceremony when the dowry is paid.

Jamaica Kincaid
Annie John   £2.95

Annie John transports us to a world quite different from our ordinary experience — the Caribbean island of Antigua. But it is also the enchanted landscape of a child on her way to womanhood, as seen through her own adolescent eyes. This is the tale of a girl's gradual discovery that, although she loves this paradise filled with marbles the size of plums, guava fruit free for anyone willing to climb the tree to pick it, rains that last for months, and herbs her grandmother can endow with magical properties, she must leave it, just as she (and all of us) must abandon childhood itself.

'Rarely does a writer move as surely forward as Kincaid does in the plain, sharp, affecting first novel. Poetic without a single intrusive image, emotional without a trace of hysteria, evocative without a bit of self-conscious exotica: a model, in fact, of selective, invisibly artful autobiographical fiction' KIRKUS REVIEWS

edited by Alberto Manguel
Black Water   £3.50
the anthology of fantastic literature

Here in this huge anthology is a kaleidoscope of brilliant writing from the Magi of the imagination. Alberto Manguel has selected seventy-two tales — including possibly the shortest fantastic story in the world — from life on the edge of the twilight zone. Stories from Herman Hesse, Bruno Schultz, Italo Calvino, Vladimir Nabokov, Jorge-Luis Borges, Frank Kafka and many, many more: irresistible masterpieces, many of which are appearing for the first time in the English language.

'Fantastic literature makes use of our everyday world as a facade through which the undefinable appears, hinting at the half-forgotten dreams of our imagination . . . the impossible seeping into the possible, what Wallace Stevens calls ''black water breaking into reality'' '
ALBERTO MANGUEL

All Pan books are available at your local bookshop or newsagent, or can be ordered direct from the publisher. Indicate the number of copies required and fill in the form below.

Send to: **CS Department, Pan Books Ltd., P.O. Box 40, Basingstoke, Hants.   RG21 2YT.**

or phone: 0256 469551 (Ansaphone), quoting title, author and Credit Card number.

Please enclose a remittance* to the value of the cover price plus: 60p for the first book plus 30p per copy for each additional book ordered to a maximum charge of £2.40 to cover postage and packing.

*Payment may be made in sterling by UK personal cheque, postal order, sterling draft or international money order, made payable to Pan Books Ltd.

Alternatively by Barclaycard/Access:

Card No.

Signature:

Applicable only in the UK and Republic of Ireland.

While every effort is made to keep prices low, it is sometimes necessary to increase prices at short notice. Pan Books reserve the right to show on covers and charge new retail prices which may differ from those advertised in the text or elsewhere.

NAME AND ADDRESS IN BLOCK LETTERS PLEASE:

Name—

Address—

3/87